ZERO RI$K

BY
SIMON HAYES

THE RUBRIQS PRESS

First published in Great Britain in by
The Rubriqs Press Limited
The Flag Store
London SE1 2LP
www.rubriqs.com

Copyright © Simon Hayes 2024

Simon Hayes has asserted his right to be identified as the author of this work in accordance with the Copyright, Designs and Patents Act 1988.

All rights reserved. No part of this publication may be reproduced, stored in a retrieval system, or transmitted, in any form, or by any means (electronic, mechanical, photocopying, recording or otherwise) without the prior written permission of the publisher.

This is a work of fiction. Names and characters are the product of the author's imagination and any resemblance to actual persons, living or dead, is entirely coincidental.

A CIP catalogue record for this book is available from the British Library.

ISBN: 978-1-738462407

Typeset using Atomik ePublisher from
Easypress Technologies Ltd, Guildford, Surrey.

Printed and bound by TJ Books Ltd, Padstow, Cornwall.

This book is sold subject to the condition that it shall not, by way of trade or otherwise, be lent, hired out, or otherwise circulated without the publisher's prior consent in any form of binding or cover other than that in which it is published and without a similar condition including this condition being imposed on the subsequent purchaser.

Rather than love, than money, than fame
… give me truth

Walden
Henry David Thoreau

Посвящается Татьяне

13. СКАЗКА
Встарь, во время оно,
В сказочном краю
Пробирался конный
Степью по репью.

Он спешил на сечу,
А в степной пыли
Темный лес навстречу
Вырастал вдали.

Доктор Живаго
Борис Леонидович Пастернак

PROLOGUE

EIGHT YEARS EARLIER
FRIDAY 24 JUNE 2016

HOLLY BRAND WAS TRYING DESPERATELY to hide her nerves. Sweating despite the glacial chill in the conference room, she thanked God she had opted for the sleeveless dress that morning. Her colleagues shuffled their papers and looked at their watches, their faces cold from apprehension, not aircon. No one enjoyed the weekly meeting of FROG—the Financial Risk Operations Group—at National Bank.

No one, that is, except Martin Kellett.

Kellett may have been listed as Chief Risk Officer on the bank's website, but among his subordinates Kellett's title was "the Toad." He was third in importance, behind the Chief Executive Officer and the Chief Financial Officer, at the country's fourth largest bank. Holly had no doubt that in his own mind he was already the world's greatest living financier. This weekly gathering of his court was where the frog king's subjects paid homage to his magnificence and bore witness to his cruelty. For Kellett had a habit of devouring, froglike, the insects beneath him.

Just so long as it's not me, prayed Holly, leaning forward to ease the fabric of her dress from her clammy back. She cursed herself for the hundredth time for not losing some weight and repeated the familiar silent self-admonishment that accompanied such thoughts: more time at the gym and less in front of computer screens. Forget more, some would be a start. And fewer of Joan Morris's cakes.

Holly shot another glance around the table. She was looking for comfort, or support, but she saw only the tops of heads slumped in silent misery. At that very moment, offices across London were buzzing with the morning's bombshell referendum result and news of the prime minister's resignation.

But there was no such excitement here. In the kingdom of the Toad, the governing emotion was fear.

The tension in the room was broken by the entry of a smiling, handsome man in his mid-to-late thirties. Rob Tanner, Kellett's deputy, was as warm as the Toad was cruel. No one knew why he had stayed with the Toad for so long; Holly could only speculate that he was too decent to leave the group to the mercy of their sovereign lord. And perhaps, on Kellett's side, somewhere deep in his psyche, there was an understanding that it was only Tanner's cheery presence that kept the whole damn show on the road – not that you'd have guessed it from the Toad's attitude to his number two. But each put-down seemed merely to fortify Tanner's good nature and further incense the Toad. It was a feedback loop which tightened with every passing week.

Kellett's arrival, almost immediately after Tanner's, killed any hopes of a lasting thaw. Brooding and pugnacious, the Toad entered each room as if it were a boxing ring: fists clenched, glaring silent belligerence at anyone who would meet his eyes. A muscular middleweight in his youth, Kellett's sedentary, over-indulged lifestyle had begun to take its toll in middle age. The years had loosened his physique and padded his girth, and now he had the look of an ageing prize-fighter, carrying too many pounds but still bristling with menace. The silence deepened as he lumbered to the head of the table and took his place.

Today, he appeared to be in an unusually placid mood, each agenda item passing in an aura of benign indifference. Until item eight, that was. Holly's specialist subject.

'Ah, *Miss Brand*,' invited Kellett. 'I believe you have an update on legacy security consolidation?' The syllables tripped off Kellett's tongue with reptilian sibilance.

'Yes, sir,' she replied firmly. She made a point of looking him in the eye. 'I do.'

Holly had never cared for Kellett's nickname. She had always liked toads and frogs – all amphibians, really. They were clever. Adaptable. In her eyes, Kellett was more of a snake; his bulging stare reminded her of Ka, the mesmeric serpent in the *Jungle Book*. She looked away, taking a second to collect her thoughts. A feeling of immense calm settled over her. Holly knew everything there was to know about legacy security consolidation.

'Well, no time like the present.' Foiled in his attempt to intimidate, Kellett switched to saccharine insincerity. 'We mustn't keep these dear people waiting. I'm sure you have such an important contribution to share with us.'

Kellett's favourite-uncle niceties were so theatrically bogus that they would have brought laughter in any other setting. But here they occasioned only an abrupt jolt. Everyone knew what this change of tone meant: today's prey had been identified. Holly knew it too. She took a deep breath and began.

'To recap: bank computer systems have been built over six decades, with each new program bolted on to form a complex patchwork of technologies. We currently spend three-quarters of the bank's IT budget on making sure our legacy systems don't fall apart. That's over two billion pounds every year.' She smiled and looked around the room. 'But effectively all we're doing with that money is sticking plasters upon yesterday's plasters. Imagine you have sixty years of sticking plasters on top of each other. Well, I've discovered that a lot of them are just plain rotten.'

'Very graphic and very droll,' jibed Kellett with undisguised sarcasm, 'but not terribly enlightening.'

'Well, if you'd let me finish, I will try to *enlighten* you,' Holly stabbed back, with unintended vehemence. 'It's really very simple. I believe I've found a vulnerability, a backdoor left open by our outdated security. There might be others, and the next person to find a weakness like this might not have the bank's best interests at heart. We have no choice but to tear off those plasters and introduce a completely new computer system. It'll take time, of course, but we must start planning for it immediately. Otherwise, we'll be leaving the bank vulnerable to cyber-attack.'

Kellett raised his eyebrows and fixed his subordinate with an expression that would snuff out a candle. 'Don't be ridiculous! No bank in history has ever transitioned to a completely new computer system. It's bad enough that you appear to have gone mad, but it's unforgivable that you're wasting my time!'

'Actually,' returned Holly, 'I'm with Einstein on that. Madness is doing the same thing over and over again and expecting something to change.'

Kellett's eyebrows inched even higher. He was not used to being challenged – and certainly not by one of the most junior employees at the bank. 'Miss Brand,' he said, with a sigh. 'I understand your youthful enthusiasm for all things new, but I think our systems have shown themselves to be perfectly resilient for all those sixty years you mention. I see no reason why that should not continue, despite your fanciful talk of Band-Aids and backdoors.'

'Well, perhaps you'd like me to show you otherwise,' offered Holly. She was nervous, of course, but she knew was right, and that certainty gave her strength. The truth was all that mattered, wasn't it? 'It will take just a minute to set up.'

Anticipation, almost gladiatorial, smacked across Kellett's thin lips. 'If you must, my dear.'

Holly looked up from connecting her laptop to the screen in the conference room, but none of her colleagues would meet her gaze. Except for Rob Tanner, whose smile gave her the nudge she needed to start her demonstration.

'As you can see,' she began, 'I have made a straight-forward connection to the internet. From here I will access the dark web.' Holly worked systematically through a series of web pages until she reached what looked like an old-fashioned command prompt screen on a PC with a blinking green C:\.

'And this is where the fun starts.' Holly entered line after line of code. Her colleagues watched in enthralled silence. Occasionally, the computer would freeze, as if thinking, and then another batch of text would present itself. In the quiet, Kellett couldn't help but try to re-establish his primacy. The bullfrog had to croak.

'I'm sure it's very interesting, Miss Brand, for some of our colleagues to see a computer programmer at work. But I really don't see where you're going with this.'

'You will, sir, don't worry,' she said. Then, 'May I assume your National Bank account is in your full name: Martin Andrew Kellett?'

'My bank account? What on earth has this got to do with *my* bank account?'

'You'll see, sir, if I might continue.' Holly took Kellett's response as the cue for her final entry. The text "Martin.Andrew.Kellett" was clearly visible amidst the on-screen jumble.

The display froze again before stuttering on. Then, without warning, the code dissolved into the homepage of Martin Kellett's personal bank account. There was a collective gasp from the room, followed by a panoply of individual exhalations, as Holly's colleagues noticed, in the upper right-hand corner, Kellett's swollen balance.

'Perhaps you'd care to confirm that this is your account, sir?' ventured Holly. Her eyes twinkled with puckish amusement.

In the quiet that followed, those present might have questioned whether time itself had stopped. The king humiliated in his own court! An eternal second elapsed in perfect silence before Kellett exploded, unleashing an avalanche of rage.

'I don't know what stunt you've pulled here, but it's the last thing you will ever do in this company!' His eyes roamed the room: a challenge. He met a wooden wall of blank faces, offering nothing but quiet contempt. He tried to regain control by ratcheting up the threat. 'You're finished in this industry, Brand. You're finished in this city, in fact. Hear me? *Finished*. Now, get out!'

Holly calmly disconnected her laptop and walked to the door: gaze forward, back straight. She had gone too far this time, she realised. Oh Lord, why did she always have to be such a smart-ass? Why hadn't she spoken to Tanner first? Every eye in the room followed her. There was more than one look of admiration as well. Then silence, again, before a bellowed, 'All of you, out!'

Kellett's roar contained a violence that had the remaining members of the Financial Risk Operations Group scrambling for the door with fear, shock and none of Holly's poise.

TANNER HADN'T MOVED as the room cleared out around him. He'd seen Kellett angry many times over the years, and—whilst this level of fury was something else—he knew the trick was always to remain level-headed, to find a way to defuse his rage.

'Well, Martin. I think that was a pretty impressive demonstration.'

As quick as any boxer off his corner-stool, Kellett was on his feet, his

5

index finger at Tanner's throat. Globs of spittle glistened at the corners of his lips, and his eyes bulged with rage.

'Get rid of her, Tanner! And make sure that everyone here today understands that if they mention a single word of what happened, they'll be lining up behind her at the Jobcentre tomorrow morning. Understand?'

'But Holly's brilliant,' countered Tanner. 'We both know she's the best of all the graduates we've hired in the last ten years. By far. Of course, she's impetuous, she's—'

Kellett was in no mood for equanimity. He pressed even closer and jutted his chin with upper-cut precision to within an inch of Tanner's face. Tanner caught the rank tang of sweat, saw up close his boss's pupils burning like coal. But while Kellett's visage was still inflamed, his tone was now icily chill.

'Perhaps you didn't hear me, Rob, so let me make myself absolutely clear. I may not be an expert in securities law, but I do understand enough to know that Miss Brand has just committed a criminal act.' He jabbed that vengeful finger into Tanner's chest. 'If you don't get rid of her, *today*, I will contact the police and the securities regulator myself. I never want to see or hear of her again. Do you understand?'

'Yes, Martin,' was all the reply that Tanner could muster against the onslaught.

'Good. So get on with it!'

DAY ONE

MONDAY 23 DECEMBER 2024

1

ROB TANNER WAS IN HIS ELEMENT. It was a filthy day—sleet and rain and coal dust skies—but that was fine with him. He loved walking the ancient chalk downs of Uffington, whatever the weather. The fresh Oxfordshire air was always rejuvenating, and the chief local attraction—a great white horse, carved into the hillside some 3,000 years ago—posed a tantalising mystery. In such a place, under the watchful, equine eye of prehistory, and with Christmas just days away, not even the English climate could dampen Tanner's spirits.

He smiled as he remembered one of his mother's childhood admonitions: 'There's no such thing as bad weather, Robert, only unsuitable clothing.' His smile broadened as he thought of what was to come. A well-earned pint at the White Horse Inn at Woolstone and then lunch with Judith. By God, he had earned it. Not just by dint of the five miles he had walked, in the teeth of an icy wind, but for another year's hard graft at the bank. Somehow, he'd kept the wheels from falling off, despite Kellett's best efforts.

How the Board had appointed Kellett CEO was beyond him, but appoint him they had. That was three years ago; Kellett's influence—and his hubris—seemed to have grown every day since. And while the Toad's rise had, in turn, led to Tanner's promotion to Chief Operating Officer, the position was a poisoned chalice. It ought to be the most interesting role in the firm, but these days he spent most of his time putting out Kellett's fires.

These thoughts melted away as Tanner approached the pub. The only fires he cared to think about now were the log ones burning inside. The windows were festooned with decorations, and in the deepening winter gloom the fairy lights were like beacons, the gentle hubbub emanating from the door a siren song. Better still, he could see Judith's bright red Mini Cooper in the car park.

He had booked a room, so they didn't have to worry about driving back to London. And now the remains of the day stretched ahead: a vision of languorous pleasure. He'd only been seeing Judith for a couple of months, and he was still consumed by the physical intoxication of this new relationship – even before the invigorating effects of a healthy walk and, hopefully, the altogether more relaxing effects of a decent bottle of St-Émilion. To top it off, his timing was perfect; the first snowflakes began to settle on his Carson Parka just as he was stepping up to the front door. Perhaps the forecasters had got it right, for once, and a white Christmas was on the cards. God truly was in his heaven, and all was justly right with the world. Until the ringing started.

Tanner stared at his phone in disbelief: David Nash, Kellett's successor as Chief Risk Officer. He briefly considered ignoring the call, but he knew he couldn't.

'This had better be good,' answered Tanner. 'This is my first day off in three months, I'm just walking into my favourite pub and, more importantly, there's a strikingly attractive woman waiting for me with a cold beer and a warm smile.'

Nash was suitably apologetic. 'I'm so sorry Rob. You know I'd have done anything not to disturb you.'

'But?'

'But we have a problem here, at the bank. It's unlike anything I've ever seen before.'

Tanner might have made a joke at this point, but there was something unsettling in Nash's tone. The man was clearly rattled.

'Give me the thirty second version, David, so I know how to mollify my date, then let me have the detail.'

'I only need thirty seconds Rob, but I'm afraid it's going to spoil your lunch.'

'Go on.'

'The balance of about a thousand of our current accounts has increased ten-fold over the past twenty-four hours.'

Tanner couldn't help himself. The disappointment in having his perfect day interrupted, and for such a ridiculous reason, was too much to supress.

'Have you been on the sherry, David? Of course people have bigger balances before Christmas! They get paid early, they—'

'No Rob, *listen*.' Nash's voice cut across Tanner's objections. 'Do you seriously think I'd bother you without checking? Without double and treble-checking? Today, of all days? It's not a simple mistake. And it's not something I've ever seen before. These accounts have seen their balances inflated exactly—I repeat *exactly*—tenfold. With no logical explanation: no unanticipated deposits, no early salary payments. Just an adjustment to the balance, seemingly out of thin air.'

'What? That's impossible.' Tanner racked his brain and came up short. 'Shit. Okay. I guess I'll have to come in.' So much for perfect days.

But first: Judith. She was sitting at a corner table, lost—despite the festive din—in a copy of *Vogue*. She didn't look up until he was nearly on top of her. Her smile faded as soon as she took in his expression.

'What's the matter, Rob?'

'I'm sorry, Judith. I've just had a call from the bank. We've got a major problem. Something unprecedented. Possibly a cyber-attack.' The staccato soundbites fell heavily into the space between them.

'So, what are you saying?'

Tanner had known she'd take it badly. Why on earth wouldn't she? But there was a hard edge to the question that warned of more than simple upset.

'Judith, I'm so sorry,' he repeated. 'I'd have done anything not to spoil this day, but I have to go back to London.' He tried to take her hands in his, but she recoiled from his touch, as if stung. 'Judith, *I'm sorry*. What else do you want me to say?' His appeal was sincere, his eyes bright and winsome. 'I'll make it up to you.'

'You'll make it up to me? Really? Care to share when? The man who doesn't care about anything or anyone other than himself and his work!' Her mouth curled into an ugly sneer as she mimicked him. '*Sorry Judith*, I have to work late tonight. *Sorry Judith*, I can't see you this weekend, I have to go to the office. *Sorry Judith*, Christmas is cancelled.'

Tanner reached towards her. 'Please, don't make a scene.'

'Don't make a scene! Don't make a bloody *scene*! You've got to be kidding me, Rob? You think because you're suave, and charming, and have a nice smile, you can always get what you want? You think you can simply schmooze your way through life, and to hell with whoever you hurt along the way?'

'Judith,' he said, stunned by the bitterness of the attack. 'That's not fair.'

She scoffed. 'You know, I felt sorry for you when we met, Rob. I knew you were a loner, but I thought maybe you were lonely too. I thought I could reach you—get you to open up—but you're not a loner, you're just cold. Heartless.' She had found her stride now, resentment giving way to spite, every word honed on a whetstone of malice and primed to cut. 'You're like the Tin Man, except you don't even realise your heart's missing. You may be smart and shiny and rich—maybe you're the twenty-first century version, the Platinum Man—but that's only show. You're just as empty.'

Even in the noisy pub, Judith's outburst had garnered an audience. It was impossible to miss the embarrassed whispers, sideways looks and tittered ridicule. Tanner blocked them out. He'd always been good at blocking things out. He sat back and looked into Judith's face, now taut where it had once been so open.

'You're right, Judith. I could give you reasons—you'd probably call them excuses—but what's the point? I have, so I'm told, "commitment issues." It's who I am. There's no magic solution, no Yellow Brick Road, no rainbow. Just life and the cards we're dealt. I'm sorry I hurt you, I really am, but you know what? Better to find out now that we're not meant to be – that you're not Dorothy.'

He stood and made for the door, fighting the urge to look back over his shoulder. Women… who needed them? And the Tin Man, really? At least he wasn't the cowardly lion or the brainless scarecrow, he supposed. He could still be fixed. All he needed was a can of oil.

2

AN HOUR AGO, the snowfall had seemed an augury of festive magic. Now it presaged only winter chaos. Tanner had paid way over the odds for a taxi to the nearest mainline station, hoping to outrun the elements. Now he was stuck on a slow train back into London.

Tanner was looking out into the snow, watching the whitening countryside beyond the window, when his phone rang again. This time it was his sister whose name flashed on the screen. His heart sank; had Judith called her? The last thing he needed was yet another sisterly sermon about his inability to hold on to a relationship. He knew she meant well, but now was not the time.

'Hi, Liz,' he answered, trying his best to muster some fraternal cheer. 'What's up?'

'Hi, Rob. Sorry to bother you, I know you're with Judith.'

She didn't know! Relief coursed through him, but the remission was fleeting. Her next two words filled him with an altogether heavier dread.

'It's Dad.'

That familiar gambit. It didn't matter how many times he'd heard it, the hammer blow was always the same. It was never good news, and it was never *the* bad news. It was always just another complaint, another criticism… half a lifetime of compound blows.

Tanner steeled himself. 'What is it *this* time?'

Liz tried, unsuccessfully, to stifle a snigger. 'He says he's got too much money in his bank account.'

'Oh Christ!' exclaimed Tanner, more loudly than he'd intended, to the patent displeasure of the elderly lady sitting opposite. He held up a hand in apology before leaning towards the window, cupping the handset. Outside, the first flint flashes of urbanity were appearing among the fields, the outskirts of a satellite town trapped in the capital's unsightly and ever-expanding orbit. 'It's possible that he has.'

'What?'

Tanner's voice was little more than a whisper. 'We've got a few computer issues, Liz. Nothing to worry about. A coding error or something.' The lie came easily, too easily. He hated himself for it, but what else could he say? And why did his father have to bank with National anyway? What the hell was wrong with the other banks? But no, the old bastard had to have an account with National so he could moan every time something went wrong. Another opportunity to blame Rob for everything that was wrong with the world.

'Rob, are you there? Rob?' Liz's voice brought Tanner back into the present. The train had slowed, and a featureless platform hove into view. A robotic woman's voice announced the station. Anyplace, anywhere on the commuter corridor. A moment later, the doors hissed open.

'Sorry, sis. The line dropped for a second.'

'What should I tell him?' pressed Liz. The first strains of impatience pricked beneath her words.

Tanner's heart went out to his sister, stuck between father and son. 'Tell him to ignore what the bank says and to rely on his own reckoning. That'll make him happy.' He warmed his tone for her benefit. 'And Liz, don't worry. He knows exactly how much he has in his account, down to the last penny. We'll sort our computers out and he'll be able to say, "Told you so! I was right! Useless banks!"'

'Really?'

'Seriously, Liz.' Tanner smiled to himself. 'It'll make his Christmas. He'll sit there throughout Christmas dinner, saying, "In my day, banks didn't need computers. In my day, you knew who your bank manager was."' Tanner mimicked one of his father's curmudgeonly rants, his voice rising as he warmed to the subject matter. 'In my day, banks were banks, not bloody coffee shops!'

This outburst brought another, more equivocal, look from the fellow traveller opposite, who seemed to approve of the sentiment if not the delivery. Tanner motioned another apology and turned back to the window. They were on the move again.

'Listen, Liz,' he said. 'I've got to go, but I'll call when I have news. For now, just tell him that all banks are officially useless, mine more than most.' He let out an exasperated sigh. 'Christ, he's worse than Scrooge.'

'Rob, don't.' Liz sounded physically pained. 'He's your father.'

'That's exactly the problem,' Tanner shot back, regretting the words before they were out of his mouth. Silence settled on the line, heavy and pregnant like snow on a bough. He forced the necessary apology and, with a final wish of fraternal affection, he rang off and settled back into his seat.

Suburbia begat inner city beyond the window; civilisation grew ever denser, ever busier, ever brighter – even in the wintry gloom. But try as he might to focus on the computer problem, Tanner could find no enlightenment; his father's stern countenance kept intruding on his thoughts. Whatever the problem, it was Tanner's fault. Not the bank's, *his*. And it wasn't just the bank, it was everything Tanner had ever done. Or, rather, everything Tanner had done since his mother died. Nearly a quarter of a century of fault-finding, disparaging comments, disapproving looks and, worst of all, silence. The cold, unyielding silence of blame.

3

IT WAS DARK when Tanner finally reached National Bank's offices on Cannon Street. While the City of London was blanketed in a sepulchral quiet, the fourth floor of the bank's HQ was ominously bright and busy, a hive of activity. Nearly every desk in the Risk Department was occupied, and a sizeable team was ensconced in the large conference room at its heart. As he entered, Tanner was struck by the reams of computer printouts on the huge central table. And by the sombre expressions of those around it.

'I haven't seen printouts like these since the 1990s,' Tanner joked, but David Nash was in no mood for banter.

'We're manually checking every account where there's a discrepancy,' the risk chief responded, deadpan. 'There's nothing like pen, paper and old-fashioned calculators to ensure we get it right.'

Nash was a pretty dry fish, but he was nothing if not polite. The absence of even the smallest of small talk told Tanner all he needed to know about the seriousness of the situation. He took a seat at the head of the table.

'Let me have everything you know,' he said. 'From the top.'

Nash took a breath and began. 'At 3 p.m. in Bangalore—9.30 a.m. in London—we received a call from D.K. Reddy, the Finance and Risk Manager for our customer service operation in India. It seems that in the previous twenty-four hour period, they'd had over six hundred customers call up to question unexpectedly large credit balances. The first two shifts hadn't reported it—we'll deal with that later—so they didn't appreciate the scale of the problem until this morning. Reddy is a good sort: a tough bastard, but sensible, so he checked this wasn't the usual seasonal credits—early salaries, bonuses, that kind of thing—and realised that there was a pattern of unexplainable adjustments to the accounts. He called Suzanne here, who's in charge of Account Reconciliations.' Nash drew breath and nodded at a rather severe, bespectacled lady of a certain age sitting behind an enormous heap of paper.

Tanner held up a hand to stop the flow. 'And you're sure, despite these balance enlargements, that no money's been withdrawn? That the increases aren't a front for theft elsewhere? A diversion?'

'We're sure,' answered Nash. He itched at his collar, blinking long and hard, like a man who had spent too long staring into blue light.

'Okay,' said Tanner. 'Go on.'

'Once we'd confirmed that there were no rational explanations—timing discrepancies, transfers from related accounts, anything real—we ran a report to see how many accounts across the whole bank were exactly, and I stress *exactly*, ten times larger at the start of business yesterday compared to the previous evening's close. We then ruled out a small number where there was a straightforward explanation – the coincidences. And we were left with a number where there was absolutely no rational justification.'

'How many?' asked Tanner.

'One-thousand-and-one,' replied Suzanne. She spoke impassively, without any hint of irony.

'That sounds like something from a fairy-tale.' Tanner looked back to his risk chief. 'How is this happening, David? Who's got the magic lamp?'

'That's the thing,' said Nash. 'We have absolutely no idea. All we know is that each balance had an extra zero yesterday morning compared to the previous night's close. We've checked and double-checked. No discernible IT glitches. No signs of manual adjustment by someone internally. No evidence of a hack. Nothing. Those accounts just grew overnight.'

Tanner scoffed. 'But that's not possible!'

'Now you see why I called you!' Nash was looking increasingly alarmed, as if stating their problem out loud had made it more real.

'Don't worry David, we'll find the answer.' Tanner tried to dredge greater assurance into his voice. 'Think about it rationally. It can *only* be a computer glitch. And look on the bright side: it's not as if any of the customers have lost money. Worst case, we'll let them all keep it. It's Christmas after all!' Tanner's cheery tone evaporated when he realised what he had to do next. 'And now I have to call the Grinch himself: Kellett.' He began to get up, but then stopped himself. 'Would you mind checking if there's a Tanner on the list, please, Suzanne?'

She rifled easily through the oversized sheets, finding the information at once. 'Yes, there is, as it happens. A Harold Tanner. Aged eighty-one. Address: Ealing, London W7.' Was that a slight crack in her po-face, the hint of a grin? 'Is he a relation, by any chance?'

Tanner's resigned nod was answer enough. One-thousand-and-one affected accounts. And of course, his father had to be the one.

4

MARTIN KELLETT HAD CARVED OUT an extended Christmas break—a long week of indulgence and pleasure—well-earned after another year of ball-busting atop the food chain. And how better to spend such a week than ensconced in his exclusive chalet in Zermatt, in the Swiss Alps? Tanner had always found it amusing—if not downright bizarre—that the unhealthiest man on the planet should keep a second home in one of the best and most demanding ski resorts in the world, but that was the contradiction that was Martin Kellett. The Toad's response to being disturbed, however, was decidedly unequivocal.

'This had better be good, Tanner!' Kellett's voice thundered down the phone. 'I thought I'd made it clear that I wanted to be left alone for a few days.'

'I'm afraid it's not good, Martin, or I wouldn't be calling.'

Kellett's theatrical bluster had never cowed Tanner. And in this instance, Tanner had vowed to play a straight bat and stick to the facts. Kellett might be obnoxious, but he was far from stupid. He would want to hear this.

'Go on then,' sighed the older man.

Tanner explained in calm, precise terms the events of the previous thirty-six hours, his recital interrupted only by Kellett's laboured breathing. Tanner had steeled himself for an explosion, but instead he was met with the tones of a weary schoolmaster dealing with a slow-witted child.

'Rob, are you aware of the principle of Occam's Razor?'

Tanner could picture Kellett paring his nails as he spoke, so disinterested was the voice on the other end of the line.

'Yes, Martin,' he said. 'Of course.'

'Would you care to remind me?' asked Kellett.

Tanner, unseen by his boss, rolled his eyes and played along.

'Occam's Razor states, Martin, that among competing hypothetical explanations, the simplest is likely to be true.'

'Splendid!' exclaimed Kellett with sham delight. 'And in this case, Rob, what is the simplest likely cause?'

'A fault in a computer program,' offered Tanner dutifully. 'Followed by human error. Then crime.'

'Exactly.'

'But Martin, we're sure it's none of those.'

'You're sure?' Kellett acknowledged dispassionately. 'Sure enough that you'd bet your job on it?'

'What?'

Having played the point to perfection, Kellett now pressed home his advantage with casual detachment. 'I asked if you are so sure that there isn't a perfectly reasonable explanation that you'd be prepared to bet your job on it? It's really a very simple question, Rob.'

'Why are you doing this?' asked Tanner, struggling to keep his temper.

'Doing what? You thought it was so important to raise this matter that you called me on my holiday and yet, now that I put you on the spot, you seem to have lost all your conviction.' The Toad sounded almost affronted. 'Presumably you want me to do something? Yes? And yet you don't seem very sure of your ground. Well? Which is it? Do you want me to do something on the basis of your sureness or not?'

So, this was the moment, thought Tanner. That point in time when a whole career boils down to one decision. And on the basis of what? A stack of computer printouts, a brief conversation with the risk team? Little more than the toss of a coin? No, it was more than that. A feeling in the gut, an intuition, a pricking on the back of the neck.

When Tanner replied, there was no equivocation, no doubt, no coin toss. He trusted his gut; in business, he always had.

'Yes, Martin. Something is very wrong, and I want you to get on a plane back to London. *Right now.*'

DAY TWO

CHRISTMAS EVE
TUESDAY 24 DECEMBER 2024

5

TANNER HAD HASTILY CONVENED a meeting of ExCo, the bank's ten-strong executive committee, for 8.30 a.m. in the boardroom. All the firm's functional heads were gathered at the less-than-festive table, together with the leaders of the retail, major commercial and small and mid-size enterprise banking units. David Nash and the Chief Technology Officer, Mike Sorensen, had briefed each of the group on their progress—rather, the lack thereof—in finding the cause of the computer issues which had appeared under the tree. Now they were sitting, on Christmas Eve, in melancholic gloom, looking at hands, papers—anything to avoid eye contact—as they awaited Kellett's entrance.

'Season's greetings!' boomed an unseen but instantly recognisable voice from just outside the room. Kellett's bulk filled the doorframe a second later. He scanned each of the room's occupants in turn before taking his seat in the empty space, the void, at the centre of the room. 'What an unexpected Christmas treat.' He clapped his meaty hands together, and the resultant slap threatened to break the floor-to-ceiling windows. London, with its nine million naughty and nice, sprawled in the distance beyond. 'Shall we have a starter for ten?'

Tanner couldn't help but smile at the Toad's aptly inappropriate opening, but he was the only one who did. The mood in the room needed a lift, and it fell to him—as it so often did—to take up the challenge.

'I'll let each of the team speak in more detail, Martin,' he opened, 'but here's the summary. There have been no further account "adjustments."' He emphasised the word with air quotes. 'Another one hundred and seventy customers have called to report an identical over-statement, but they're just laggards from the original one-thousand-and-one. We've had a local branch manager call—or at least, attempt to call—every one of the affected customers to let them know we'll be reversing the adjustment at the close of business tonight and that we'll be making an ex gratia payment of one hundred pounds to each of them at the same time, as a token of our concern. So far, we've seen very little negative social media coverage, mostly jokes and memes about the bank's newfound Christmas spirit. In fact, Martin, you appear to be the new embodiment of Santa Claus.'

Kellett sighed, before waving for Tanner to continue.

'The bad news is that we still don't know how this happened,' resumed Tanner. 'Or what we need to do to make sure it doesn't happen again. And obviously, we need to figure that out as soon as possible to avoid any more unexpected surprises. The good news is that the press has hardly mentioned it. Presumably the hacks have either gone home for Christmas or can't see how to spin it as the usual bad bank story.'

With that last small piece of cheer, Tanner sat back and waited for Kellett's reaction. The other eight pairs of eyes remained resolutely fixed on the table in front of them – a familiar scene for any passing ghost of meetings past.

'Well, isn't that a relief,' offered Kellett into the silence. The mood around the table brightened at his words. Rather too quickly. 'Yes, isn't it a blessed relief that we've just given away one hundred thousand pounds to our customers because we can't count to ten… or is it a hundred, or a thousand? Perhaps we should use a fucking abacus in the future?'

A wall of bewildered looks incensed Kellett further.

'Christ, if you don't know what a fucking abacus is, what chance do we have with computers? Do we really not have any clue as to what's causing this fuck up?'

The tirade was stopped in its tracks by a knock on the door, the "Do Not Disturb" notice evidently ignored by Christina Ferreira, Kellett's long-suffering PA. The poor woman could not have looked more pained if she had been squinting into the very flames of hell, rather than her boss's blazing face.

'I'm sorry, Martin,' she stammered. She looked downwards, as if inspecting her shoe points. 'There's something I think you need to see.'

'Well, if this doesn't cap it all,' thundered Kellett. 'Can you not fucking read? Even someone of your limited intelligence should be able to understand the words "Do Not Disturb!" No? Well, what the fuck is it?'

'It's your email. I mean… it's all your emails. I…' She gave up her losing battle with words and pointed at Kellett's phone on the table. 'Please could you just look?'

Christina's transparent discomfort had an oddly pacifying effect on Kellett. He raised his eyes to the heavens in mocking invocation and groaned, 'Could this fucking day get any weirder?'

On looking at their mobiles, it became clear to everyone present that indeed it could. Every member of ExCo was copied into an email to Kellett.

TO: MAKCEO2024@NatBank.uk
FROM: Joen van Aken
DATE: Tuesday, 24 December 2024 at 08:30
NUMBERS, NUMBERS, NUMBERS!

Hello, Martin.
  I believe you've been having some number problems.
  Here are a couple more for good measure: 32:23.
  Just remember, as my old friend Yogi Bear said, "It ain't over till it's over!"
  And it certainly won't be 'over' tonight, they say it's going to be minus five.
  So wrap up warm…
  JvA

Although expressed in ten different ways, the response around the table was wholly consistent – complete and utter bafflement.

'Is this some kind of joke?' demanded Kellett. 'This is my confidential email.' He glanced around the table. 'Most of *you* don't even have it. Who the fuck is Joen van Aken, and what the hell is 32:23? And what in God's name has Yogi Bear got to do with anything?'

Tanner stepped in before Kellett had a chance to lose himself in one of his rants. 'Martin, you've heard the update. Nothing's changed, and we're all on the case. Why don't we take a break to look at this email and then re-group?'

'Right, yes, of course,' said Kellett. Tanner, not for the first time, had pacified him, and now he tried to laugh off the intrusion. 'Numbers, eh? Send three and fourpence!' Only Tanner had the slightest idea what he was talking about, but at least Kellett's feeble attempt at humour provided cover for everyone else to slink out of the room.

Tanner watched them go, then turned his gaze back to Kellett. For the first time in their long years together, he saw uncertainty in the Toad's expression. No, that wasn't the word – it was insecurity. A Martin Kellett without the supreme, innate assurance that he knew everything and was therefore unchallengeable. Well, Tanner thought, he was the one who'd said it; could this day get any weirder?

'Let me go and take a look at this, Martin. I'll come and find you as soon as I have some news.' And with that, Tanner was only too pleased to join the exodus and make for the private sanctuary of his office.

6

WHATEVER TANNER HAD EXPECTED, it wasn't this. A simple Google search revealed Joen van Aken, the self-identified author of the email, to be the birth name of the medieval Dutch painter known to the world as Hieronymus Bosch. Tanner was no art aficionado, but the briefest scroll down the artist's Wikipedia page was enough to jog a handful of half-remembered images. And the recollection was distinctly unnerving.

Bosch's most famous work was painted around the end of the fifteenth century: *The Garden of Earthly Delights,* a huge, folding, three-section masterpiece. The leftmost panel showed a surreal depiction of the Garden of Eden, the centrepiece a fantastical panorama of lustful excess, and the last a grotesque portrayal of the future hell which awaits mortal sinners. The final montage was all flames and gore, mutant beings dismembering the naked and damned among a nightmare forest of oversized human organs and intricate torture devices. Tanner could almost hear the screams. If that was a portent for what was to come, then Kellett was right to be worried.

Trying to force from his mind the fantastical and surreal images of sin, torment and horror, Tanner typed 32:23 into the search engine. The numerical palindrome carried no obvious significance, but one click and… of course! A Bible reference – the *Book of Numbers*, no less. Brought up Catholic, but now lapsed to the extent that any other club would have cancelled his membership, Tanner should have known better.

> But if you fail to do this, you will be sinning against the Lord; and you may be sure that your sin will find you out.
> Numbers 32:23

More sin! What the hell was all this about? Tanner hurriedly Googled the final clue – for that's what the third line of the email undoubtedly was.

The top hit was a nine-year-old BBC article, an obituary for the American baseball legend Yogi Berra. The phrase "It ain't over till it's over" was first uttered by the sportsman in 1973, and was one of many daft and tautological expressions known as "Yogi-isms." Allegedly, Berra had even been the inspiration for the cartoon bear. But Tanner had no idea what all this had to do with one-thousand-and-one engorged bank accounts.

And then the enormity of the situation hit him. The specific references weren't important – at least, not for now. Only one thing mattered: they demonstrated *intent*. This was someone's way of claiming responsibility for the account adjustments. The anomalies were no computer glitch, nor could they be explained away by human error, an honest mistake. Instead, this was surely evidence of a pre-meditated attack on the bank – one which demonstrated extraordinary capability and know-how. Unbidden, his father's remonstrative countenance stole into his thoughts. Tanner arched his fingers to his temple, closed his eyes, took a deep breath and, with deep feeling, uttered a single word.

'Shit.'

Five minutes later, having stopped briefly in the men's room to douse his face with cold water, Tanner entered Kellett's office, steeling himself for an outburst. What he certainly didn't expect was silence. Kellett was sitting, chin in hand, in a position of quiet repose. He seemed lost in the huge monitor on his desk. After a long and excruciating moment, Kellett turned the screen to reveal a grotesquely blown-up image of *The Garden of Earthly Delights*.

'Beautiful isn't it? Such an extraordinary work.'

Tanner was astonished. He had expected shock, rage, even fear, but here was Kellett acting for all the world like an expert on the *Antiques Roadshow*. Had he lost his mind?

Kellett continued as if bewitched. 'Amazing to think it was painted more than five hundred years ago. It seems so modern. All our excesses and temptations, the evils of the present as well as the past, in psychedelic technicolour. Just… sublime. And then the retribution waiting at the end of it all.'

'Yes, Martin, I know.'

Kellett held an index finger to his lips for silence. Then he turned to look Tanner straight in the eye.

'It seems, Rob, that someone wants to fuck with us. Or with *me*, to be precise. That really isn't very nice – or very wise.' Kellett's gaze fell back on the screen. 'I imagine the unfortunates in this painted hellscape wish they'd never been born. Well, let me assure you, so will this *Joen van Aken*.' The name was said with such spleen that Tanner was momentarily taken aback. 'Get everyone back in the boardroom. Now!'

Tanner tried to wrench himself away, but his mind frothed with images of the tortured sinners in Bosch's triptych: broken figures skewered by spears, men and women being torn apart by mutant beasts, mouths and bodies contorted in screaming agony – all before the backdrop of a burning city besieged by machines of war. Presiding was a demon in the form of a bird-headed monster, the Prince of Hell, eating whole the corpses of fallen sinners, then excreting them into the depths. Tanner shook himself from this stupor and met the steely glare of his boss.

The old Martin had returned.

7

THE GROUP RECONVENED at 9.30 a.m., but already it felt like a very long day. Without preface or niceties, Kellett launched his offensive. His first target was technology head Mike Sorensen, a laid-back Trekkie from California who looked like he'd lost a surfboard and found, instead, the sheaf of notes he'd carried into the meeting room.

'Mike, what progress have you made in finding the source of these attacks?'

If Sorensen had a transporter at his disposal, he would have teleported himself from the room – to the most distant planet in the galaxy if necessary. But as it was, all he could do was shuffle his papers and raise an eyebrow at his boss. 'Attacks, Martin?'

'Yes, you fool, attacks! Don't get all fucking coy on me. If you haven't worked out that these are deliberate attacks, then you're more stupid than I suspected. Either that, or you're criminally negligent. Show me some progress within the hour or I'll find someone else who will.'

Sorensen, usually the most relaxed man in the room, was too shocked to reply. Not that it mattered; Kellett had already turned his attention to communications supremo Pattie Boyle.

'What's our line for the press, Pattie?'

A hard-bitten veteran of the old Fleet Street—and the old tenements of Glasgow before that—Pattie was more than capable of mixing it with the hardest of bastards. No one other than the bank's Head of Communications would have dared to serve Kellett a look of such open disdain.

'Simple, Martin.' Her harsh Scottish accent was flecked, today, with a cheerful lilt. 'The spin is that one of our marketing executives dreamt up a wonderful idea for a customer promotion: "Open a deposit account with a hundred quid and you get the chance to win a thousand." We'll say that some tit in IT pressed the wrong button, but it's as good as sorted, and you're Father fucking Christmas. What's not to like?'

Kellett chuckled. 'I like it.' Then his eyes narrowed once again as he moved on to Ollie Lawrence, Head of Human Resources. To Lawrence, Kellett simply barked an order: 'I want a list of everyone who's had top-level risk authority at the bank at any point in the past year.'

'Current *and* past employees, Martin?'

'Everyone, obviously!' The Toad had reached his patience threshold. 'The rest of you, make sure every single one of your staff knows not to breathe a word of this, or they'll be answering to me personally. Now go.'

'No, wait,' interjected Tanner. He met his boss's disapproving look without blanching. 'Martin, we have to notify the Board and the regulators about this.'

Kellett's face spread in emoji-worthy astonishment. 'Are you mad, Tanner? It's Christmas Eve! They've already fucked off to the country or wherever it is the great and the good fuck off to for Christmas. Listen: we'll find who did this, and we'll fix it. But in the meantime, you heard Pattie – we've got a small computer glitch. It'll cost us a couple of hundred thousand to put it right. Tops. If we ruin everyone's Christmas by telling them we're incapable of sorting a fucking computer problem, they'll never, ever forgive us.'

'But Martin, don't you get the message?'

'Message? What fucking message?'

'It ain't over till it's over.'

'*What*?'

Tanner tried to contain his growing frustration. 'That's what Joen van Aken's message says, Martin. The email! Don't you see? This may be the beginning of something more serious. We should at least try to establish contact with him – find out what he wants.'

'Oh, for fuck's sake, Tanner. Grow a pair, will you? No money's been stolen, and I'm not starting a dialogue with every nutter who thinks the Old Testament is a blueprint for modern life. All we have to do is get through the rest of the day without any further publicity.' He glanced sideways at Pattie Boyle.

'Dinnae worry Martin,' she responded, playing up every syllable. 'We're going to have a very jolly Christmas lunch for every financial journo still in the City. By 4 p.m. they'll be incapable of standing up, let alone writing copy.'

'Perfect!' pronounced Kellett. His tone softened as he turned back to his deputy. 'Look, Rob, it's Christmas Day tomorrow, and Thursday is Boxing Day. No one's going to be working on Friday. Then it's the weekend. That's five days before anyone even thinks about banks or business, or anything other than their crappy presents and stuffed stomachs. We'll have sorted this mess long before then, and all this nonsense will be nothing but a bad memory. So, enough said.' Kellett smiled, or perhaps he was passing trapped wind. The latter was certainly more common.

But Tanner was not so easily convinced – and nor was he so easily placated.

'Martin,' he said, 'we have a fiduciary duty to tell the Board and the regulators. If we don't fix this—or, God forbid, it gets any worse—they'll string us up. Remember when TSB botched their IT switchover a few years back? They were pilloried on social media and the press slaughtered them. Then the Government got involved. The regulators and Treasury Select Committee called for the CEO's head, and guess what, the chairman delivered it on a plate.' A throat-cutting gesture accentuated the point. 'And you know why? Precisely because they were overly optimistic and complacent. We can't make the same mistake.'

Kellett waited a moment, though it wasn't clear whether he was considering Tanner's appeal or merely taking in the wintry view of St Paul's beyond the window. When he replied, his voice was as cold as the wind buffeting the dome.

'Does anyone else here share Tanner's view?'

Silence enveloped the two antagonists.

Kellett doubled-down on the challenge. 'Or do you all share my own confidence in your ability to resolve this—' he paused for emphasis, '—*short-term* problem?'

No one dared speak. In the streets outside, only a straggle of latecomers and the hardiest of tourists battled through the freezing financial heart of the city. Nobody in the boardroom saw them. Not a single pair of eyes lifted from the table on which all were resolutely locked.

Tanner, for his part, kept his gaze firmly fixed on Kellett, whose smugness at the subjugation of the group could not have been plainer. Tanner experienced a wave of deep revulsion, followed by a sudden, deeper understanding. In a moment of epiphany, he recognised Kellett for what he really, most succinctly, was: a living embodiment of all that was wrong with the financial system.

The enduring lesson of the financial crisis a decade or so earlier was that the weak had failed to stand up to the bullies. Vital questions had remained unasked, bullshit had overwhelmed logic and too many people, cowed by selfishness or fear or both, had failed to do the right thing. Things had only got worse in the intervening years.

Bastards were everywhere, and if you didn't stand up to the bully in your own back yard, how could you expect others to stand up, elsewhere?

For the second time in less than twenty-four hours, Rob was faced with a career-defining decision. The previous evening he'd made a split-second call on instinct; now he made one based squarely on principle.

'I'm sorry, Martin, but you're wrong.'

Heads jerked up in disbelief. That wasn't a phrase anyone had heard before, even though they had all thought it often enough.

Kellett's thin lips were still curled, but now they formed a rictus grin – one with which his eyes were no longer collaborating.

'You're wrong, Martin,' Tanner continued. 'You say no money went missing, but we know full well that someone has broken into our system. We've no idea who or why, or if they'll try again. It's our duty to notify the Board and regulators or—'

'Or? Or *what*?'

Tanner had wanted to make a point, begin a noble fightback, but he'd boxed himself into a corner. He'd been about to say something completely different—even now, he could have prevaricated—but he'd been pushed too far. His bluff had been called; it was time to go all-in.

'Or if you choose to ignore my advice, then I'll have no option other than to resign.'

Tanner knew his fate before Kellett so much as uttered a word. The return of the smug look said it all.

'Well, that's entirely your decision, Rob.' Kellett was almost gracious in his delivery of the *coup de grâce*. His frog eyes bulged with delight as he gestured to the door. 'So don't let us detain you. And, please, feel free to take the rest of the day off. In fact, I insist. It is *Christmas* after all.'

So that was it, after twenty-four years at the bank. What was that movie called? *Gone in 60 Seconds*. Tanner stood to leave, but no, Kellett had a final warning to convey.

'And Rob, I'm sure you won't need me to remind you of the confidentiality clause in your contract. Should you disclose a single word of this, or any other bank matter, to anyone, you will be in breach of that contract, and every penny of remuneration you may be owed—and every single share of bank stock you own—will be forfeited.' Kellett could hold back his emotion no longer. Cold threat gave way to primal fury. 'NOW GET OUT!'

8

TANNER PRACTICALLY STUMBLED back to his office. He was in a daze, and the corridors in which he had spent so much of his life—the views of London which unfolded in every direction, the panorama of steel and glass—suddenly seemed unfamiliar. It wasn't even ten o'clock. This time yesterday, he had been walking along the Ridgeway, thinking only of the pleasant afternoon (and even more gratifying evening) he had hoped to spend with Judith. The packed festive football schedule stretched ahead, and with Kellett away on holiday, Tanner had hoped the bank would loom a little less large in his mind – for a few days, at least. Now he faced the prospect of a lifetime without the job which had lent purpose to his whole adult life. What's more, Kellett's threat to whisk away his financial reward for all that hard work was ringing in his ears.

Tanner was a rare breed of banker, one who had never been the type to obsess over his remuneration. He lived relatively simply for a man who had done so well for himself: he'd never been one for flashy cars and expensive holidays, and he had long paid off the mortgage on what he thought of as his first and only home. In recent years, his greatest personal expenditure had been on gifts and trinkets for the succession of women that had come and—like Judith—all-too-swiftly disappeared.

But that wasn't to say he didn't need the money, because he did. He needed it desperately, not for him but for the Foundation. He cared about the bank; he cared about his reputation; but the Foundation was the thing that mattered above all else. And it all depended on his funding: the slice of salary he contributed every month, the yearly bonuses he gave away, and the donations he raised through his City contacts. The leverage from his position, basically. The position he'd just surrendered without a fight.

He cursed himself for not having cashed in his National Bank stock – or, at least, some of it. Other than the house, all his wealth was tied up in the bloody stuff. Why the hell hadn't he? He knew full well: he'd allowed himself to be seduced by an ugly mixture of greed and pride. He had always believed he could make a difference. From his first day at the bank, he'd wanted to build a financial institution to be proud of. Somewhere deep in his psyche, he guessed he'd wanted to achieve something that might finally impress his old man. And, as he became more senior, he *had* been able to influence the firm's performance. National Bank was widely regarded as best in class – a successful bank, no less! But not a good bank.

How could it be, when he had ignored the cancer at its heart? Kellett was a brilliant businessman, and Tanner had convinced himself that by mitigating his boss's excesses, he was doing the best for everyone. But it was a sham, a self-deceit. Kellett's slip-ups weren't mere foibles, they were wilful wrongdoings. And by cleaning up the mess every time, Tanner had been a willing accomplice every bit as guilty as the Toad.

Tanner shook his head. He was alone now, in the admonishing silence of his office. He stood by his desk, staring at the cast of anonymous characters in the trading room two floors below in the building across the street. Like figures in an absurd diorama, frantically tapping at keyboards and screens. Everyone in the City liked to feel important, Tanner knew – never mind the day, no matter what the markets were doing.

And he was no different, was he? He had accepted the promotions and the plaudits, riding the elevator up, floor after floor, with Kellett. And now, having finally done the right thing, Tanner stood to lose everything he had worked for. More importantly, the Foundation—and everyone it helped—would suffer in tandem with him, their fate tied inexorably to the bank's, to the Toad's. He cursed himself again. Choices and consequences. Hubris and bloody nemesis.

Tanner might have spent the whole day standing there, beating himself up, consumed by angst about the Foundation and grappling with unanswerable questions about the nature of his character. But further introspection was cut short by the unanticipated arrival of Frank Garner, the Head of Security.

'Christ,' said Tanner, looking up at his visitor. 'That was quick, Frank.'

'I'm sorry, Rob, but direct orders from His Majesty.' Garner rolled his eyes. 'I'm to ensure you don't take any items of bank property and escort you from the premises, *toute suite*.'

The last two words in Garner's heavy Geordie accent brought a welcome smile to both their faces. They were both National Bank lifers, but whereas Tanner had been on the fast track from day one, entering the graduate scheme with the shining kudos of a Cambridge economics degree, Frank had risen the hard way. He'd joined at sixteen as a night security guard in his local branch, long-since closed, in the West End of Newcastle, then worked his way up through a succession of tough postings. There was no sign of that toughness now, merely embarrassment. Tanner did his best to cover it.

'It's okay, Frank. As they say, all good things come to an end, and we've had nearly a quarter of a century!'

'But what's this about?' pressed Garner. His brow creased. 'You don't just leave on Christmas Eve with no warning. You're the only one who keeps him straight.'

'I'm sorry Frank, but I really can't say anything, even to you.' Tanner sighed. He opened a drawer in his desk and, seeing it contained only business documents, relics from a soon-to-be former life, closed it again. 'We'll have a bevvy after the dust has settled and put the world to rights. Maybe catch a Toon game at the pub?'

Garner smiled, a warmth at odds with the weather and with Tanner's mood. 'Howay, man! Now you're talking.'

Tanner gathered the effects he knew he had to hand over: work phone, credit card, security pass, keys. After all this time, the only personal item in the room was a wood-burned coaster with a bee motif – something one of the Foundation lads had made for him. He put it in the pocket of his Harris Tweed overcoat and nodded towards the door.

'Shall we?' he asked. He forced a smile he didn't feel and turned his back on his office, on the tableau below.

9

SAFELY DEPOSITED ON THE SNOWY PAVEMENT outside, Tanner faced a novel dilemma. What should he do? For as long as he could remember, every day—virtually every waking hour—of his life had been planned, often months ahead. Meetings, conference calls, investor presentations; you name it, his diary was filled with it. Now, for the first time in years, he had a whole day yawning ahead without a single obligation. There wasn't even a fire he could put out.

Tanner started walking, letting his legs carry him where they might. Soon he was looking up at the dome of St Paul's, its golden ball and cross proud against the murk above. Beside him, a tourist took a photograph on her phone, carefully framing the cathedral so she didn't capture the man with frayed trousers and a matted beard who was talking to himself in the nearby bus shelter. The tourist swiped away the photo and retuned to a navigation app. She put her head down and started walking, eyes fixed on her phone and the route it presented for her, the ancient, double-edged splendour of London relegated to the periphery of her awareness. Just for a moment, Tanner flashed back to Hieronymus Bosch, to the nude figures cavorting in front of fantastical orbs and towers, unaware of their impending doom, all rendered in awful, artful detail.

He supposed he should start telling people the news of his departure before it leaked, but who wanted to be disturbed on Christmas Eve? He knew he really ought to phone Liz, in case she tried to call him, but she would only worry, and she had her hands full with the family – not least his father. Christ, he'd also have to call the old misery about *his* bloody account! Well, that one could wait. Instead, he made for home, Ravenscourt Park, seven miles to the west.

His route took him below ground, into the shallowest bowel of the Underground, the District Line. Bodies pressed all around him—on the escalators, on the platform, in the carriage—but no one looked at him. Not a single fellow-traveller made eye contact. Tanner was no different, focusing instead on the consumer bunting hanging the length of the train: adverts for cryptocurrency trading platforms, fast fashion websites (payments on instalment encouraged) and cosmetic surgeons. It occurred to him, in that moment, that the more people you packed into a place like London, the more impersonal daily life became.

He was strangely grateful when he surfaced, and he made for the certainty of his neighbourhood at a brisk walk, breathing deep the still, cold air of midmorning. He passed a pair of teenagers vaping in a shop doorway, and he almost lost himself in the sickly-sweet, cherry-scented cloud which fogged around them. Tanner started to walk even faster, and by the time the artificial taste was gone from the air, he was almost home. So much had changed in recent years, he thought; even nicotine was yesterday's drug. Would the switch bring new side-effects, he wondered?

One thing that had stayed the same was his home: Tanner had kept the same terraced house for nearly sixteen years. Living on his own, he had plenty of space, and he loved the area. The street had changed, of course, with younger middle-class professionals replacing older working-class owners as they retired and took advantage of staggering, sudden valuations for what had originally been two-up, two-down labourers' cottagers. In recent years, there had been an influx of French and Japanese families, drawn by specialised local schools. West London had been a melting-pot of immigration throughout Tanner's life, and it suited him fine.

Still shell-shocked by the day's events, he did what he did whenever he needed to think: made himself a cup of tea. But even as the bag was steeping, 'What am I going to do?' became 'What *the hell* am I going to do?' He'd only ever been a banker; he had no other skills. He knew some of his concern was irrational—a connate fear of the unknown—and faced it down with a well-practiced, slow-paced mantra. 'Baby steps. Baby steps.' Big ideas could wait for another day.

Tanner sipped at his hot, strong tea and almost immediately felt more like himself. In all the chaos he had almost forgotten it was Christmas Eve, and now he decided to surprise Liz and the family, even if it meant he would have to deal with his father.

This new-found sagacity didn't prevent him checking his personal email; the habit was too ingrained. He justified it to himself with the thought that there wouldn't be anything urgent; in fact, he doubted there would be anything other than festive spam. But messages there were—three of them—from David Nash's personal account. An initial 'Please call' had become 'Rob, PLEASE call asap' and finally, a febrile, 'ROB, PLEASE CONTACT ME URGENTLY. I HAVE TO SPEAK TO YOU.'

Tanner knew he was in a bind. He wanted to help Nash, of course, but Kellett had made it clear that he wasn't to speak to anyone. His entire financial security was at stake, and that meant the Foundation was at stake as well. He knew whistle-blowers were protected by law if they reported certain types of wrongdoing, but was this situation covered? On the other hand, Nash was clearly desperate. There wasn't time to get a lawyer's opinion either way.

Tanner rubbed his temples and stared at the screen. How many of these make-or-break decisions could one man make in twenty-four hours? He emailed back, his words crafted to offer plausible deniability, if the communication ever came to light.

'David. DO NOT contact me from the bank. If you'd like to speak outside the office about non-bank matters, feel free to call my home phone number. And DELETE this message.'

The last sentence was fatuous but would hopefully remind Nash to be circumspect. However, when the phone rang fifteen minutes later, it seemed the warning had been missed. There were no pleasantries. Just, 'It's getting worse, Rob.'

Tanner's heart sank. 'David, you know I'm not allowed to talk to you. I could lose everything.'

'I *know*,' countered Nash. 'Which is why I'm in a phone box half a mile from the office. And I'm not asking you to speak. I just want you to listen.' Taking Tanner's silence as agreement, Nash continued. 'Rob, we're not getting anywhere with the accounts. But that's not why I called. *It's getting worse.*'

It wasn't his pig anymore—not even his farm—but Tanner couldn't help himself. He took a deep breath, 'What's happened?'

'I ran another risk report at 11 a.m. We looked for accounts with the same pattern: tenfold increases with no verifiable cause.'

'And?'

'And this time it wasn't a thousand and one accounts.' Nash paused, as if he was gathering his wits. 'It was one-thousand-*one-hundred*-and-one.'

'Christ.'

'And Rob, it's not stopping. I ran another report half an hour ago.'

'Let me guess. Twelve hundred and one?'

'You've got it.'

'Shit.' Tanner stared into the base of his mug. He sloshed the russet residue of his brew, watching it break against the side like a wave against a sea wall. Again, the images of Bosch's hell sprang unbidden into his mind: the torment of the damned, diabolically skewered in tea-stained brown, under the wistful gaze of a monstrous beast riding on tar-black water. 'What's Kellett doing?'

'Ranting at everyone.'

'Okay, David, here's what we're going to do.' There was a calm certainty as Tanner spoke. 'Call the chairman's PA. Find out where he is right now. Let's pray he's not on a plane or up a mountain. Then get back to me in an hour. In the meantime, I need to make a couple of calls.'

10

TANNER CALLED HIS SISTER FIRST. He had intended to ask about their father, to see if anything had changed with the old man's account, but from the racket in the background, it sounded like his niece and nephew were approaching peak pre-Christmas excitement. Liz was clearly distracted and in no mood to chat, and she was all too willing to accept his promise to call back when things were quieter. He hung up, having gleaned no new information and come up with no new ideas. Undeterred, Tanner dialled the one person in the world he trusted with his life.

Brinsley "Brin" Eliot had been a Rhodes Scholar at Oxford while Rob was at Cambridge. Blessed with every advantage you might possibly crave—birth into a wealthy Massachusetts family that traced its roots to the founding fathers, an undergrad education at Harvard, and the bushy-top golden looks of a young Redford or Pitt—he'd turned up at Tanner's May Ball with the most beautiful girl in the place. Along with every other man in attendance, Tanner had hated him on sight. But when Brin later bumped Tanner's shoulder at the bar, the American, noting Tanner's sidewards look, turned on an electric smile and stretched out a hand.

'Brin Eliot. Short for Brinsley. Or to remind me of my Brahmin forebears… I forget which. Pleased to meet ya.' The good-natured self-mockery and the parody Boston drawl combined to sweep aside any ill will at a stroke.

'Rob Tanner. Short for Robert. Like your relative Mr Kennedy, no doubt.'

'Touché,' conceded Brin. They touched glasses, and both men laughed.

And they hadn't really stopped laughing together in the two decades since. While Tanner had joined National Bank and gradually risen to the top by way of logical, measured steps, Brin had flown ever higher at an astonishing rate, straddling the twin worlds of government and finance in various postings. He had now started down the path of a serious political career – one which might yet match that of fellow Rhodes alumnus Bill Clinton, according to those in the know. Brin had recently walked the race for his home Congressional seat in Massachusetts, his first major victory at the polls. He was to be sworn in next month, and Tanner wouldn't miss the ceremony, or the after-party, for the world.

Of more consequence for the here and now, however, was Brin's nose for finance. In recent years, he had made a fortune for his investment firm—and topped-up his own not-inconsiderable birthright—by betting big on financial technology stocks. Given everything going on at National, he was the obvious man to call. If there was anyone who could proffer the constructive advice and total discretion Tanner sought, it was Brin.

Tanner knew exactly where his friend was, and he prayed he would answer the phone. The Eliot clan's holiday routine never changed – Brin's ageless grandmother made sure of that. Thanksgiving in Palm Beach, Christmas in Vail, Summer vacations on Nantucket. Tanner had been a guest at each over the years. But now the line rang and rang. Tanner feared he was out of luck, until finally there was a click and Brin's smooth voice came through.

'You're lucky I picked up. I was about to go down for breakfast, and phones are strictly banned from the meal table. Grandmother's orders.'

'I remember,' Tanner acknowledged. 'Listen, Brin: I need your advice.'

No chit-chat, no small talk, no pleasantries. This was a first in their long friendship, and Brin took his cue.

'What's the problem, Rob?'

'A cyber-threat. Potentially grim. I need to find the best security expert there is. I mean *the best*, and in a hurry.'

'That bad, huh? Let me think for a minute.'

Tanner could almost feel Brin's intensity radiating through the phone, his brain purring like a well-oiled engine, as he worked through the options.

'I know plenty of experts,' the Bostonian offered at last. 'But there are two that really stick out. At the fund, we used an ex-Pentagon guy at one of the big consultancies. An outstanding professional. He's one. Then recently I came across this lady with her own small firm. Unbelievably knowledgeable, super smart, thinks outside the box… quite wacky, in fact. Made me think of stuff I'd never considered.'

'Both discreet?'

'You think anyone would mess with a future Congressman of the United States?' joked the American, subtly providing the assurance Tanner needed.

'Who's the lady?' asked Tanner instinctively.

'Typical Robert Tanner!' Brin's throaty chuckle warmed the line. 'Always the man for the ladies.'

'It's not that,' said Tanner, shrugging off the banter. 'It's just that something tells me I'm going to need "outside the box."'

'Okay, Rob, I get it. Her name's Ashley Markham. Funny thing is, she kind of appeared out of nowhere. Came up to me at a cyber-tech conference in San Francisco. She's got master's degrees from Stanford *and* MIT, she already works with the likes of Goldman, we know the same people at the Federal Reserve and Treasury… she checks out. Oh, and did I mention already that she's damned pretty?'

'Stop it!' Tanner tried to suppress a laugh, good humour tinged with relief. Brin's expert sounded just what he needed. 'How can I get hold of this Ashley Markham?'

'Leave it to me,' replied Brin. 'I'll call her and let her know how far back you and I go. Should she use this number?'

'For now, Brin, at least.'

'Understood.'

The American's knowing tone conveyed more than words ever could.

11

TANNER TREATED HIMSELF to a second shower, gradually increasing the temperature until he could bear the heat no longer. Then he turned the thermostat all the way down and counted to sixty. A new set of clothes and a fresh pot of tea completed the reinvigoration just in time for a call-back from National Bank's mild-mannered risk chief.

'Rob, it's David. Good news.'

For a second, Tanner's hopes rose, but then Nash added a deflating coda, 'The chairman's still in London.'

Tanner covered his disappointment with a question. 'Okay, but first, where are we with accounts?' He realised he still said "we" like an insider.

'Another one hundred affected at 1 p.m. That's thirteen hundred and one now.'

Tanner glanced at the clock: 13:47. In less than fifteen minutes there would undoubtedly be another hundred alterations. There was no time for prevarication, and with his own hands tied by Kellett, he needed Nash to act on his behalf.

'Right, here's what we're going to do,' began Tanner. 'You're not going to like the first bit, but hear me out. First, you've got to find Kellett and convince him to speak to me. Tell him I'm on the way to the chairman's house right now; tell him I'm contacting the Bank of England; tell him I've been with a lawyer who's confirmed I'm protected as a whistle-blower. Tell him whatever you like, David, whatever it takes, but you have to persuade him to call me.'

Nash breathed heavily into the receiver. 'I don't know, Rob…'

'David, listen to me. If you don't persuade him, then I *will* do all those things.' Tanner reached for the stick. 'I know you've done nothing wrong, but once this goes public…' He trailed off, letting the threat hang for a second before tendering the carrot. 'Here's your chance to do the right thing. It's your choice.'

'I'll try, Rob…'

Tanner understood Nash was terrified of Kellett, but there was no time for irresolution. 'Trying's not good enough, David. You have to *do* it.' Then he added, more encouragingly, 'You *can* do it.'

'Okay, Rob, I will.' The words carried at least a modicum of conviction. Tanner hurriedly thanked Nash and ended the call before it could wane.

No sooner had the conversation ended but his phone rang again.

'Hello, is that Rob?' This time it was a bright female voice on the other end of the line. 'This is Ashley Markham. Brin Eliot asked me to call you.'

'Wow,' said Tanner. 'That was quick.'

'Well, I'm actually on vacation, so for once my day isn't clogged up with meetings and calls.'

Tanner tried to place the accent. Her tone was light, softly spoken, with a small rise in pitch at the end of her sentences. Tanner guessed that was the California influence, although maybe the trait was more generational than geographic. Maybe the world had moved on while he had been looking elsewhere.

'I'm so sorry to disturb your holiday,' said Tanner. He caught his reflection in the hallway mirror and only then realised he was pacing. 'Are you somewhere nice?'

'I'm not sure yet.' Ashley laughed. 'I only arrived this morning, and it feels like I've been stuck in traffic most of the day. Still, at least I'm set for a white Christmas.'

'Really? Where are you?'

'You won't believe this, but I'm actually in London.'

'London?' Tanner couldn't believe his ears – nor, he hoped, his good fortune. 'What on earth are you doing here?'

'I don't have family,' Ashley replied, with no hint of self-pity. 'So I always go away for Christmas. I don't ski, and I get bored lying on beaches, so I do city breaks. This year it's London. I'm at the Lanesborough. Do you know it?'

For the first time that day, Tanner felt the comforting warmth of optimism. 'Of course I know it! What a stroke of luck.'

She laughed again. 'Luck? I haven't done anything—' a hint of tease crept into her voice, '—yet.'

'I know,' allowed Tanner. 'But it must be a positive omen. And we need one.'

'What's the problem?'

'Ashley, I can't go into it right now. Is there any chance we could meet, later this afternoon? I know you're meant to be on holiday, but the issue we have is unusual, to say the least, and pressing. The bank will make it worth your time.'

'Hey, don't mention it,' countered Ashley. 'Like I said, I don't have any plans, and Brin promised me I'd enjoy working with you. You can at least show me what's up, and we'll take it from there. I'd be happy to help, if I can.'

'I can't thank you enough,' said Tanner. 'That's perfect.' He had stopped pacing, and now he stood by the front door, grateful to have caught a break at last. He remembered his manners at the last minute. 'Oh, and by the way,' he added. 'Welcome to London.'

'Thank you, Rob.' There was unmistakeable pleasure in her tone. 'It's nice to be back.'

12

TANNER WATCHED THE CLOCK. Ten minutes, twenty, half an hour. He began to think Nash had failed, that Kellett wasn't going to call. But just as he was steeling himself to follow through with his threat to go directly to the chairman, his personal mobile trilled. The sound had never been more welcome, although the same couldn't be said of Martin Kellett's angry tones.

'Give me one fucking reason why I should speak to you,' opened the Toad, rage incarnate.

'You should *fucking* speak to me,' answered Tanner equably, 'because you can't contain *your* fucking problem.' Silence at the other end of the line told him he had Kellett's attention. 'Listen: if it wasn't Christmas Eve, you'd be trending on social media and the first item on tonight's news. And it's getting worse. If you don't front-up now, you know who's liable, Martin? *You.* Fiduciarily, commercially, maybe even criminally. Me? I'm all right. You ordered me to get out. I'm in the clear. But you, you're the boss. To use one of your favourite phrases… *you're fucked.*'

'So why waste my time talking to you?'

'Because I actually care.' The words came to Tanner without premeditation. 'Because I don't want my twenty plus years at the bank to end like this. And because I want my money.' He paused. That was a gambit Kellett would surely understand. 'So, I'll trade. I'll help you sort this out—I've already got one of the world's best cyber-security experts on standby—and then I'll walk away. I get all my stock, free and clear, and you'll be shot of me for good.'

'What's the catch?' asked Kellett. His voice dripped with suspicion.

'There's no catch,' replied Tanner. 'But we do it my way. We come clean. We call the chairman, the regulators, the Bank of England, the Treasury… everyone. We bring my external expert on board. We put out an honest holding statement to the press. We do the right thing, and we do it now, or I can put down this phone and leave you to it. For good.'

For a moment, Tanner thought he'd overplayed his hand. He waited for the explosion. But for once, there was no insult, no threat. Not even an expletive. Just, 'Okay.' Kellett rarely conceded ground to anyone, and Tanner knew he had to press the advantage.

'First,' he went on, 'we have to convince the chairman that we're on top of this. If we do that, he'll do the heavy lifting with the politicians and regulators – let us focus on fixing the mess. So, call him and ask if we can meet at his house in a couple of hours. Meanwhile, we have to get our story straight and get it out there. We have to admit that we have a problem, and we need to spread the message that we have all our internal resources—and the best external ones—devoted to fixing it.'

'But—'

'No, Martin,' interrupted Tanner. 'No buts. Tell Ollie to send a note to all employees. And ask Pattie to write a script for you to use with the media.'

'*Me?*' Kellett sounded shellshocked now, as if finally comprehending the enormity of the situation.

'Yes, Martin,' said Tanner. '*You*. It's a balancing act; we need to show we're on top of this, from the top down, but not seem like we're panicked. Remember how that TSB CEO failed to take responsibility? He got fired. Do you want that?'

The threat of defenestration forestalled any further questioning.

'While you do that,' Tanner continued, 'I'll tee up the external expert. She's an American – Ashley Markham. We'll get her in with Mike and work everything through, line by line, until it's fixed.'

'Okay.'

'And Martin, one more thing, with all these people… *try to be nice!*'

Tanner rang off before Kellett had chance to respond. He could only imagine the look on the Toad's face: shock-and-awe at Tanner's insubordination paired with the realisation of all he stood to lose. Part of him wished he could see Kellett's reaction first-hand, but his better nature was glad to be well clear of the blast zone.

With Kellett under control—for now—Tanner called each ExCo member in turn to let them know there was, if nothing else, a plan. Everyone seemed genuinely relieved by his re-involvement, but Tanner couldn't see how their faith in him was remotely justified. If they and their teams hadn't the faintest idea how to sort out the mess, he wasn't sure what he could add. At least he seemed to bolster a few spirits, which was something.

And now there was one more thing Tanner needed to do. He dialled the number Ashley had given him. It rang for a long time before she answered.

'Sorry, Rob.' She sounded slightly breathless. 'I was in the shower.'

Brin's description of the American flashed unhelpfully through Tanner's mind. He stammered, 'Ashley,' and regathered his thoughts. 'I'd very much like to take you up on your offer to help. I've got a meeting with our chairman first, but it's not far from your hotel, so I could pick you up afterwards. Probably around six. Would that work?'

'Of course,' said Ashley. The hint of playfulness was back. 'I'm entirely in your hands.'

13

SIR PETER WILFORD LIVED in a beautiful Georgian terraced house—a residence befitting a City grandee—in Paultons Square, Chelsea. Through a combination of good taste, good luck and good financial acumen, he'd bought the property back in the late Seventies for a fraction of its current value. He had lived there ever since.

Tanner took the tube to Gloucester Road and walked the rest of the way, avoiding the main thoroughfares and their attendant clots of last-minute shoppers. The affluent backstreets, on the other hand, were deserted. There was no sign of life in many of the living rooms he passed, but even if the property owners had left town, lights still twinkled merrily from Christmas trees in virtually every window. Tanner was happy to savour the sights and the absence of sounds in this unfamiliar London, enjoying the monochrome stillness that only a heavy blanket of snow can provide.

As he turned the corner into the Square, he saw the bank's black Mercedes S-Class parked outside Sir Peter's home. At the wheel, as always, was Tommy Steele, driver to a succession of the bank's chairmen and CEOs for more than thirty years. Although the main arteries out of London were at a near standstill, Tanner was not remotely surprised to find Tommy already in situ. His ability to duck and dive effortlessly through London's increasingly clogged streets was legendary: eco-protesters might glue themselves to the capital's roads, and politicians dream up ever-more-restrictive traffic management schemes, but Tommy would always get you there on time.

Tommy caught Tanner's look and then, slowly, subtly, let his eyes slide to the passenger side of the vehicle. A warning that the Toad was slumped in the darkness within.

Taking the cue, Tanner walked nonchalantly over. Tommy wound down his window at Tanner's approach.

'Evening, Sixpence,' said Tommy.

'Evening, Thruppence,' responded Tanner.

That familiar greeting had been repeated hundreds of times over the years. Regardless, both men grinned as they delivered their lines, each remembering the occasion of their first encounter.

As a young lad starting out at the bank, Tanner had spent a hectic and happy year as personal assistant to the then-chairman. Accompanying his boss to an external event for the first time, Tanner found Tommy waiting on the pavement outside the bank's main entrance with the rear passenger door open. The chairman, with customary good manners, made introductions.

'Robert Tanner, meet Tommy Steele. And vice versa.'

'Tommy Steele!' blurted Tanner. 'Like the singer?' Faced with an uncomprehending look, Tanner babbled on. 'You know? He sang "*Half-A-Sixpence*."'

'In that case, I suppose you're twice the man I am,' offered Tommy, deadpan. It was Tanner's turn to look baffled.

'A tanner is sixpence,' Tommy explained. 'Half that is thruppence. So we've established our worth, no?'

At which point the chairman dissolved into fits of laughter, and Tanner knew he'd been had. But those were days long past, and now the bank was a very different entity, in very different circumstances.

'When you've quite finished,' growled a petulant voice from the rear of the Mercedes.

'Oh, Martin, I didn't know you were back there.' Tanner afforded Tommy a conspiratorial wink. 'I assumed you were already in with Sir Peter.'

Growl begat bark. 'Get in.'

Tanner slid into the seat next to Kellett. The pair took a moment to study each other.

'I thought we should—how shall I put this—agree our approach,' Kellett opened.

But Tanner was done with mincing words. 'Don't worry Martin. It's in neither of our interests to rock the boat.' He cocked his head towards the chairman's doorway. 'Let's just sort this out and move on, as we agreed.'

Even in the blackness, there was no mistaking Kellett's glower at the reminder of his acquiesence. The leather seats squealed in protest as he shifted his bulk forwards. For a moment, Tanner thought the Toad would renege, but then the door was open and that angry figure was hauling itself onto the street beyond.

14

THE CHAIRMAN GUIDED HIS VISITORS into an understated drawing room. Only a few decorative tells revealed the wealth and taste of the man who lived here. A pair of blue and white Chinese vases stood sentry on the mantelpiece over a welcoming fire, and a pair of equally matched spaniels dozed contently before the grate, lying on a fine, duck egg rug patterned with exotic flowers of every conceivable colour. Neither dog stirred as Sir Peter motioned his guests towards a pair of armchairs, upholstered in classic style.

The room reflected the man. Sir Peter was old-fashioned in the best kind of way; he was courteous, thoughtful and dependable. And used to taking command.

'Sit,' he instructed. 'Now, why don't you run me through from the start. It never hurts to see things in the proper context.' He glanced briefly at Kellett before turning his gaze to Tanner. The chairman had always had his favourites, and he wasted no energy hiding that fact.

Tanner laid out the events to date. Sir Peter interrupted from time to time to clarify details or to ask characteristically insightful questions. He made studious notes on a leather writing case balanced on his knee. Only when he was sure Tanner had finished did he seek to take back control of the meeting.

'So, may I sum up, Rob, just to be sure? You're telling me that fifteen hundred—no, by now it's presumably sixteen hundred—of our accounts are exactly ten times larger than they should be?'

'Sixteen hundred and one,' corrected Kellett, bristling at his third-wheel discomfort.

'Yes, Martin, I haven't forgotten the one,' said Sir Peter, looking pointedly at his Chief Executive. 'So, sixteen hundred accounts have been inflated ten-fold, and this has been done intentionally, either by an outside agent or internal infiltrator. And our problem seems to be getting worse, and more expensive, by the hour. You're absolutely sure it's not a computer error or malfunction, and the combined investigations of our risk and technology teams—teams we justifiably believe are as good as any in the industry—have found not a single clue as to the origin or cause?'

Stereo silence acknowledged the completeness of Sir Peter's summation.

'Gentlemen, I have to say that is the most preposterous thing I have ever heard. It's like the plot of a thriller!' Sir Peter stared into the middle distance for a second before snapping back to the moment. 'But it is what it is. So, what's the plan?'

'Sir Peter,' said Tanner, sensing Kellett was content to let him respond. 'Given your personal connections, we'd like you to call the Bank of England, the Prudential Regulation Authority and the Treasury. It's vital that the authorities believe we're doing everything we can to fix this. We don't want a repeat of the fiascos at TSB, RBS and the like. The executive team is briefing our advisers and stakeholders. Fortunately, the markets are closed for the holidays now, so that's one thing we don't have to worry about.' Tanner looked fixedly at Kellett. 'Martin is going to speak to the major news channels. We have a statement ready to go out. And we'll have a customer helpline up and running within the hour.'

'Excellent!' Sir Peter spoke loudly enough to raise a sleepy eyelid from the nearest of the two spaniels. After a moment, it rolled onto its side and resumed its slumber. The dog's master, however, looked anything but relaxed. 'And what if those sixteen hundred customers try to spend the extra money?'

'Frankly, there's not a lot we can do,' sighed Tanner. 'If we introduce arbitrary spending limits, we risk hitting innocent customers. It's a judgement call, but at the moment, our maximum financial exposure is less than fifteen million, so I'd recommend not spooking people further.'

'More to the point, they're all going to be opening presents, stuffing their faces and watching soaps,' interjected Kellett. 'By the time they wake up on Boxing Day, this will be a distant memory.'

'I hope you're right, Martin.' The narrowing of Sir Peter's eyes suggested he had his doubts. 'But yes, I agree, we don't want to cause unnecessary alarm.' He paused. 'Most importantly, how are we going to stop the *bastard* who's doing this?'

Tanner had never heard the chairman curse, but now he was strangely comforted by his vehemence. If Sir Peter was taking the attack so personally, that practically guaranteed his support. As long as Tanner had an answer for his on-the-money question.

He didn't, but at least he had a plan. 'Obviously we have to start with technology,' he began confidently. 'Mike Sorensen has already engaged the top—'

'The Californian chap?' interrupted Sir Peter. 'The one with the tan and the long hair?'

'Yes, that's Mike,' replied Tanner. He caught Kellett's smirk at the prejudgement and attempted to trump it with a laugh of his own. 'Don't be put off by appearances, Sir Peter. There's no one I'd rather have.'

The chairman didn't return Tanner's smile, and nor did he look convinced by his assurances. 'Last time I spoke to him, he started going on about *Star Wars* or something, I didn't have the foggiest what he was talking about, although I think he was trying to make a point about the American business climate. Something about US enterprise?'

'*Star Trek*, sir,' clarified Tanner reflexively. Noting the chairman's confused look, he added, '*Star Trek*. Not *Star Wars*. Mike is a bit obsessed; it's just his thing. But more importantly, he knows cyber inside out. I should also add that my oldest friend is one of the most knowledgeable tech investors in the world, and he's recommended an American expert who happens to be in London. I'm meeting her once we're done here to get an external perspective.'

'Ah!' Now Sir Peter's smile did return. 'Excellent. And are we? Done?'

Tanner steadied himself. He hadn't had a chance to discuss his final recommendation with Kellett. But there was no option other to press on.

'There is just one more thing, Chairman.' Tanner noticed Kellett twitching in his periphery. 'It's clear this is an external intervention, but as yet, there's no real crime involved. There's no connection between any of the customers affected, so it's unlikely to be fraud in the narrow sense. We don't know what the motive is, but there's significant potential for this to get worse. We need to decide whether to call in the police or one of the other law enforcement agencies.'

Kellett's twitch was turning into a spasm, but Sir Peter had anticipated the reaction. With unruffled smoothness, he said, 'Don't you worry about that, gentlemen. I happen to know the Permanent Secretary responsible for the National Economic Crime Centre. Smart chap… knows all the folk at the NCA, SFO, GCHQ and every other acronym the authorities appear determined to invent. I'll speak to him. *Off the record.*' The last three words were intended as a balm to Kellett.

Tanner rose to his feet. 'Thank you, Sir Peter.'

'No, thank *you*, gentlemen,' returned the chairman. 'I'm glad we have such a joined-up approach.'

There was nothing in the intonation, but Tanner was sure he detected a knowing glint in Sir Peter's eye as he shook his hand. Tanner brushed the thought aside and shifted all attention to his imminent meeting with Ashley Markham.

Beside the fireplace, the dogs slept on.

15

IN THE BACK OF THE BANK'S MERCEDES, there was no hint of the earlier froideur. Kellett's mood had patently been lifted by the constructive tone of the meeting with Sir Peter. He was blissfully and ego-centrically unaware that the chairman's insight into human character was as perceptive as his analysis of balance sheets and income statements. If there had been a subtle message about teamwork, Tanner doubted Kellett had heard it. Still, Tanner took advantage of the thaw to suggest they pick up Ashley on the way back to the bank.

Assent grunted, Kellett returned to his phone, leaving Tanner to enjoy the short journey into the West End in peace. For the most part, Tommy stuck to quiet backstreets, but there was no avoiding a few of the busier throughfares. Tanner's eye was drawn to a bustling, brightly lit Belgravia wine merchants. In the City too, the demand for Champagne was unscathed, despite the recession. The price of fine wines had risen, of course, but not as fast as bonuses, and the thirst of the rich was not easily quenched. And yet Tanner knew that in many of London's more working-class enclaves, Christmas simply wouldn't have the same sparkle. Tanner was certain that the Foundation would be busy over the next few days. He knew, only too well, that the less you have, the harder Christmas is.

The car made a sharp turn, and he looked up, jolted from his thoughts. Tommy had them turning off Hyde Park Corner into the Lanesborough's front drive in the time it would take the average driver on the quietest of summer Sunday mornings. Tanner barely had time to warn Ashley of their impending arrival. He dialled her number, and she picked up almost instantly.

'I'm close to the Lanesborough,' he told her. 'I'll be there very soon.'

'Great,' replied Ashley, real warmth in her voice. 'I'll meet you in the lobby.'

'How will I recognise you?' he asked.

'Oh, don't worry,' she said. 'I've looked you up on the bank's website. I'm sure I'll get the right man!' Again, her words contained a hint of ribbing.

'But then you have an advantage.'

'Which I promise not to take,' Ashley flashed back. 'See you in the lobby.'

Tanner smiled to himself. He was forty-five years old. The bank was under threat, potentially grave. Christmas was probably cancelled. He'd soon be out of the only job he'd ever wanted. He'd just lost another girlfriend. And yet, bizarrely, he felt more energised than he had in months. What was that old adage about travelling and arriving?

His mood lifted further upon entering the Lanesborough. It was like striding into a stately home. The hotel was the epitome of five-star luxury, replete with gastronomic grill room and grandiose library bar. With its marble floors, imposing columns, crystal chandeliers, sumptuous antiques and fine art on every wall, the lobby provided an entrance as rich as its clientele. Tonight, it bustled with sharp looking men and women, talking loudly, dressed to the nines, and frothing with cheer as they clacked across the floors.

Tanner positioned himself beside a magnificent Christmas tree. Festooned in gold, the tree glinted with decorations of musical motifs arranged in perfect harmony. Spellbound, he felt as if he had been transported to the foot of another huge tree. Only last Friday he had watched the Royal Opera House's magical production of *The Nutcracker* – an annual tradition of his. Over the last decade, his companions had changed as regularly as the cast; 2025 would require yet another. And yet he dared to hope the next companion might be his last.

He was soon lost in thought, drowning in the hubbub of the lobby, alone among a multitude. A tap on the shoulder made him start. He turned, only to be arrested by a slim woman, with an intense stare.

'Hello,' she said, the faintest West Coast lilt. 'I hope you're Rob. I'm Ashley.'

Her eyes were the first thing he noticed. They were brown, with the patina of an old copper penny. Her pupils twinkled in the light of the lobby, but a profound intelligence seemed to spark somewhere deeper—and maybe a profound sadness, too—or was he just projecting? Then came the natural, full lips and the shoulder-length hair, the colour of deep walnut. And, finally, he took in her outfit: heels and a contoured suit, straight off the pages of *Vogue*. There was something of Julia Roberts about her, circa *Notting Hill*, and like the character in that film, she was beautiful. No, that wasn't the word; she was *lovely*. Just lovely.

'Ashley?' Tanner almost choked on the name. 'Yes, I'm Rob. It's a pleasure to meet you.'

'The pleasure's all mine.' She smiled and held out her hand. At his touch, her eyes seemed to light up brighter than any Christmas tree.

'I don't mean to be abrupt,' apologised Tanner, 'but we're pressed for time. Our CEO, Martin Kellett, is waiting for us outside. If it's okay with you, we'll ride back to the office together and I'll brief you on what's been going on.'

Ashley smiled, looking at him for a moment longer than necessary. 'As I said, I'm in your hands.'

Tommy was standing ready at the Merc's rear passenger door as they emerged from the twinkling din of the lobby.

'Good evening, Miss Markham. I'm Tommy Steele. Welcome to London.'

'Thank you, Tommy. That's sweet of you.' Ashley slid gracefully into the rear seat beside Kellett. A gentleman might have got out to perform Tommy's task, but Kellett merely stretched out a meaty hand.

'I'd like to say it's nice to meet you,' he said, 'but in the circumstances, you'll appreciate my reluctance, I'm sure.'

'I quite understand, Martin. I may call you Martin?'

Kellett accepted her show of deference with a lime-sucked smile. 'You may.'

'I just hope I'm able to help with this problem you've been having,' offered Ashley.

'I hope so too,' answered Kellett, raising his voice so Tanner, sitting in the front, could hear. 'Rob is staking rather a lot on it.'

'He is?' queried Ashley. She caught Tanner watching her in the rear-view mirror and held his eyes in place with her smile. 'Then let's waste no more time on polite conversation.'

For the second time in ninety minutes, Tanner found himself sketching out the events of the past three days. As he finished, he noted with surprise that Tommy was already pulling up outside the bank's headquarters in the City. A glance at the dashboard showed 18:37.

'We'll convene ExCo in the boardroom at seven-fifteen,' barked Kellett. With remarkable agility, given his unathletic bulk, he was up and out of the car in a second… without so much as a second glance for his companions.

Neither Tanner nor Tommy missed the sotto voce, 'Quite the charmer,' that followed him from the back seat.

16

ASHLEY WAS ONE OF THOSE PEOPLE whose presence sent ripples wherever she went. Her effect on the members of ExCo was immediate, and even those minded to be wary of her were quickly disarmed by her charm. It helped that she appeared not only to have worked out in advance who everyone was, but that she also seemed to know what made most of them tick.

'You did your homework,' whispered Tanner. Everyone was taking their places at the board table, a gentle hum of chatter serving to mask Tanner and Ashley's conversation.

'First impressions are lasting impressions,' she said. 'Better to make good ones.'

Kellett lumbered in, an angry bear roused from his hibernation, and counted heads around the table. He paused, a strange blend of theatricality and menace, as he held a finger in the air. The evident shortfall was explained by the hurried arrival of David Nash behind him. A beaming David Nash. Which was the very last thing Tanner expected.

Nash was quiet—some said meek—at the best of times. The events of the last forty-eight hours had placed him under enormous strain, and now he was late for one of the Toad's crisis meetings. Yet, he compounded this cardinal sin by offering no apology, only a breathless gush of words, skinny arms waving from short sleeves as he spoke.

'Martin, it's unbelievable! It's over. They've... it's gone! Every one!'

'Collect yourself, for God's sake,' demanded Kellett. He narrowed his eyes as he lowered himself into his chair. 'Now, what are you saying?'

'I said it's over!' Nash laughed, borderline hysterical. 'We've been running risk reports every hour, on the hour. Fifteen hundred inflated bank accounts at three o'clock, sixteen at four, seventeen at five, eighteen at six, but then—' Nash looked around the room, taking in the assembled faces, before turning back to Kellett, '—at seven there were none.'

'What?' chorused every voice around the table. A flurry of wild chatter started up, an unintelligible snowstorm of speculation. Remembering his conversation with the chairman, Tanner looked over at Mike. The technology head was the one person who was perfectly still amid the maelstrom, staring silently through the windows. Tanner followed his gaze, briefly catching the red and green lights of a distant plane before they were lost in the overcast sky.

Tanner waited a second or two, and then he silenced the uproar with a raised hand. 'David, I don't want to be disrespectful, but are you *absolutely* sure?'

'Yes, Rob,' answered Nash, his wild eyes flitting momentarily across the room. 'We've run separate reports on previously affected accounts, at random. None has more than a thousand pounds or so. The adjustments have been reversed. It's as if they never happened.'

Tanner shook his head in bewilderment, met Kellett's eyes. 'I don't know what to say.' Similar looks were being shared around the table.

'Well, I fucking do!' snapped Kellett. He turned to the Head of Comms. 'Pattie, kill that press release. Right now. And not a word more to anyone.'

'But, Martin,' Tanner cut in, 'this hasn't gone away. We haven't solved anything. This is a pause, an intermission… not a fix. We don't know when the attacks will start up again, or if we're exposed to something even worse. We need to proceed as we agreed with the chairman.'

'Oh, fuck!' screeched Kellett. He lurched to his feet. 'The chairman. We have to stop him.'

If ever there was a lesson in why you shouldn't try to outrun a bear, it was the astonishing speed with which Kellett was out of his chair and down the hall. Tanner ran after him, leaving Ashley—and the remaining members of ExCo—staring mutely through the open door, straining to hear the exchange receding down the hallway.

'Martin, listen,' implored Tanner. '*Please*. Nothing has changed. We may have a temporary respite, but it could still get worse. We still need to do all the things we agreed with Sir Peter.'

'Don't be ridiculous!' Kellett strode as fast he could, swatting at Tanner's objections like so many flies. 'We'll be the laughing stock of the City. Don't you see? It's a joke! Someone wanted to make us look stupid… and we almost let them.' He stopped suddenly, turned on his heels so he was face-to-face with Tanner. His chest was heaving, his face red. 'No, not *we*. You!' Kellett jabbed a pugnacious finger in Tanner's face. 'Why the fuck did I listen to *you*?'

'But Martin—'

'Don't "but Martin" me.' Kellett glared at his subordinate. The Toad's face was slick with sweat; it was beading above his eyebrows, and great blooms were spreading beneath his armpits. Kellett's suit jacket was still adorning a chair in the boardroom, and Tanner could smell his boss's locker-room tang in the air. But Tanner knew that with most wild animals, you had to make yourself big and stare them down. He stepped forward so that their noses were a mere inch apart.

'I knew you were an arrogant, rude prick, Martin,' he said. 'But I never took you for stupid. And if you think this is going away, you truly are stupid. I don't know how, or why, or by whom we're being played – but I guarantee you, we are being played.'

'In *your* opinion,' countered Kellett dismissively.

'You know I'm right, Martin. You just don't want the public humiliation of admitting it. "The CEO whose bank screwed up." Luckily, Sir Peter will have already called the governor and his other friends.'

Mention of the chairman reminded Kellett why he'd been in such a hurry to get to his office. 'Fuck!' he cried, tearing himself away from Tanner and barrelling down the hall. 'I have to call him.'

Mere seconds later, Kellett's desk phone was broadcasting the chairman's precise, enunciated tenor. The Toad was already updating Sir Peter on this strange turn of events, the sudden reprieve from out of nowhere, when Tanner came bursting into the room.

'Well, I never,' offered Sir Peter. 'What a to-do.' He paused. 'Right, let's think. But first, an update from my side. I'm having a devil of a job getting hold of anyone. I've spoken to the personal assistant to the governor of the Bank of England. Apparently, he's on a flight back from New York, landing in three hours' time. The Chief Executives of the PRA and FCA are similarly incommunicado.' In Sir Peter's lofty vowels, this sounded to Tanner like a place one would really not want to visit. 'I did manage to get hold of my chum the Perm Sec. He said that the GCHQ spy chaps never clock off, but that everyone else would be gone until next Monday – if not the sixth of January! He said that he hoped we could sort it all out, because there'd be precious little support from them. Typical government. Hopeless. Looks like we're pretty much on our own.'

'In which case,' wheedled Kellett, sensing his cue, 'it's only the public relations angle we need concern ourselves with.'

'What? Er, yes. Of course.' Here Sir Peter found himself on unfamiliar footing. 'What are you suggesting, Martin?'

'Well, Chairman, clearly we have to do the right thing.' Kellett looked pointedly at Tanner. 'But to use Rob's phrase from earlier: I'd recommend not spooking people further.'

Tanner leaned forward. 'That was in the context of cashpoint machines, not PR.'

Sir Peter sounded flustered. 'I don't understand, Rob. I thought you'd suggested—that we'd agreed only two hours ago—that we don't want to cause unnecessary alarm, especially at Christmas. Now this problem has gone away, surely there's nothing to alarm them about?'

'But, Sir Peter—' Tanner's retort sounded like a whine.

'No, no, Rob. Enough.' The chairman cut Tanner off, leaving him feeling like the boy who cried wolf once too often. 'There's nothing else to be said or done tonight. Your IT chaps can work out the whys and wherefores and what-comes-afters, but for now, let's just thank our lucky stars and enjoy the festivities. Well done gentlemen. And a very Merry Christmas to you both!'

Kellett's face was pure joy. A put-down for Tanner, hand-delivered by the chairman, was the best present he would get this Christmas. The Toad had turned the tables – not just the cards. He addressed Tanner gleefully, clapping his hands as an unsavoury smile split his overripe face.

'Now, Rob, why don't you take the lovely Miss Markham and get out.' Glee mutated rapidly to spite. 'And don't ever think about coming back.'

17

ONCE AGAIN, TANNER FOUND HIMSELF leaving the National Bank building for the last time. This time was different, though. For one thing, Ashley Markham was leaving with him. And whereas his previous departure had made him feel like a guilty prisoner being taken down from the dock, he now felt a sense of release, as if a long period of incarceration was ending. He'd been ambivalent for too long, working within the system rather than trying to change it. Sure, he had spent the financial rewards on a good cause—and that way he had justified everything to himself—but the spoils from his work at the bank were ill-gotten all the same. There would be no such double standards in the future. Whatever Joen van Aken's purpose, Tanner would use his bizarre intervention to spur a new beginning. Starting with his father. *Tomorrow.*

For now, he had an intelligent and interesting woman at his side, and the mystery of the inflated—and then restored—balances to contemplate. Ideally, over a relaxing dinner with Ashley at his favourite restaurant. She accepted his invitation on the way down to the lobby with no outward signs of surprise. He was lucky, he supposed, that she was on holiday with no firm plans and nobody else to see. And as she said herself, as floor numbers flashed downwards in the lift, 'Somehow, I don't think we've heard the last of this Joen van Aken character.' Something told Tanner she would have her own thoughts about the events of the day.

The bank's glass and chrome atrium had been designed to evoke the airy grandeur of a Victorian railway station. But while stations across the country were filled with countless travellers going away for the holidays, National Bank's reception was deserted, save for one security guard behind the front desk and Tommy Steele waiting by the door. Snow was falling again outside, and Christmas was looking whiter by the minute.

'Sixpence,' was Tommy's ceremonious salute.

Tanner met Ashley's quizzical look with a smile. 'I'll explain later,' he said, before shooting another grin at Tommy. 'Thruppence. What are you doing here?'

'I thought you might need a ride,' explained Tommy. 'You won't find a taxi for love nor money tonight.'

'What about Kellett?'

'Christina called me to say you were leaving. She and I decided that the Merc's engine must be overheating. We're putting it out of service for the night.' He nodded at the Mercedes outside and laughed. 'Must be the weather, or something.'

'Thank you, Tommy,' said Tanner. He smiled at his friend's innate knack for the right place, right time. 'At least my final exit will be a stylish one.'

'Final?' asked Tommy. 'Seriously?'

'Why don't we get in the car, and I'll explain,' answered Tanner, making for the Mercedes. 'But first I have to make two quick calls.'

While Tommy attended ceremoniously to Ashley's comfort, Tanner placed a call to his favourite Italian restaurant, a Knightsbridge institution where he had been a fixture for decades. It said everything about Tanner's impeccable standing as a customer that the long-time manager was able, through sheer force of will, to find a table for two on Christmas Eve.

Then, when they were safely under way, Tanner called Liz. There was no background din this time.

'Peace at last, eh, sis?' he prompted lightly.

Silence suggested his sister was in no mood for banter, so he switched tack. 'I just wanted to let you know that our computer problem seems to have gone away. Can you tell Dad?'

'Can't you tell him yourself?' snapped Liz. 'Why do I always have to be stuck in the middle?'

'Liz, please, not now. I can tell you've had a bellyful.' Tanner thought for a moment, and then he fell back on his usual strategy for dealing with his family: infinite postponement. 'Let's speak in the morning,'

'Speak? So, do I take it you're not coming over? Oh, well don't worry about us! Suit your bloody self… You always do.' And with that, the phone went dead.

If they were aware of Tanner's embarrassment, neither of his companions showed it. Tommy made a show of concentrating on the road, and Ashley appeared engrossed in the festive spectacle at its edge: the last few stragglers escaping, belatedly, from near-deserted offices; the loose legged revellers stumbling from brightly lit pubs. And, seemingly the only one without a shopping bag, the Big Issue seller huddled against the snow flurries in the entrance to Mansion House tube station. Tanner collected his thoughts in the silence.

Only when they were on the Embankment did he speak. Addressing Ashley, but speaking up for Tommy's benefit, he said, 'I've been at the bank for over two decades. In recent years, I thought I was helping by keeping Martin in check, or at least providing some balance to his, let's say, eccentricities.' He caught Tommy's wry look in the mirror. 'I thought I was protecting the bank—and all the people who work there—but I can see now that by not taking a stand, I've been condoning the very behaviour I detest. All this account manipulation nonsense has made me realise that I've become an enabler.'

'I'm sure that's not true,' offered Ashley, her voice gentle.

'I'm afraid it is. Or rather: it was. Sometimes it takes the unexpected to make you realise you've lost your way. It's no good having principles if you bend them to suit yourself.' Tanner leaned towards the driver. 'So, tonight's our last journey, I'm afraid, Thrup. It's time for a fresh start.'

Ashley sensed the perfect opportunity to lighten the mood.

'I'm sorry, but what in heaven's name is a "thruppence?"'

Gloom averted, the rest of the journey was spent in exaggerated retelling of the pair's first meeting, which inevitably melted into a series of other long-remembered anecdotes from their early years at the bank.

Half an hour later, and in humour more appropriate to the season, they were at the restaurant. No sooner had Tommy applied the brakes but a smiling figure in a black jacket and silver waistcoat appeared at the double doors. He made for Ashley, holding an umbrella against snow flurries that were easing to feathery insignificance.

'*Buona sera, signora.* Welcome.' With his spare hand, the head waiter waved his greetings at Tanner – a gesture which flowed effortlessly into the lightest of touches on Ashley's shoulder to steer her away into the warmth of the restaurant, leaving the two old friends on the pavement outside.

Tanner winked at his friend. 'I never have been able to keep hold of a girl.'

Tommy laughed, and a quiet settled on the two men.

'Well,' ventured Tommy eventually, 'it's a shame it's ended like this, but you know what they say? A change is as good as a rest.'

'That they do,' answered Tanner. 'And I've got plenty of that coming.'

'It's the right time, Rob. It's not like the old days. We joke about the funny incidents, the long lunches, the toffs. But they were proper people. They did things because they believed it was right, not to make a few more quid for themselves.'

'There were some scoundrels, too.'

'I know,' conceded Tommy. 'But when we found a wrong 'un, they were shown the door, sharpish. I should have packed it in myself when Kellett became CEO.'

Tanner could only nod in rueful agreement. 'With hindsight,' he said, 'we both should.'

'Well, now we can.'

'What?' Tanner asked. 'You're going to go back to driving a black cab after an S-Class?'

'Don't be daft,' replied Tommy. In the buttery light of the restaurant, his face looked older, lined. 'Not with Uber and all that malarkey.'

'Then what will you do?' asked Tanner.

'Hospitality.' Tommy gave a knowing look. 'You won't believe what people will pay to be chauffeured to Royal Ascot or Henley. Especially—' he tapped his nose twice, '—if they know you can keep shtum.'

Tanner couldn't help but laugh. 'It sounds like you've got it all worked out.'

'I have indeed,' said Tommy. 'I have for a while, to be honest. I was just waiting for the right moment, and your leaving is that. In the nicest possible way, of course.' He smiled. 'Now, go and take care of that lovely lady.'

'You take care too, Tommy. And stay in touch.'

'Will do, Six.'

'Thanks, Thrup.'

The two men gripped hands a final time and turned apart.

18

INSIDE, THE RESTAURANT WAS WARM AND LIVELY. Tides of conversation, punctuated by raucous laughter, rose above the clinking of cutlery, the popping of corks and the muffled clash of pans from the kitchen. Rich sauces jousted with airy soufflés on snow-white tablecloths. A flambé cart circled, a sporadic firework display of piquant flame. And, everywhere, the deep aroma of fine wines and finer perfumes. In short, the place was overflowing with the best kind of Christmas cheer.

Tanner looked around for his companion. Seated at his favourite corner table, Ashley was the centre of fawning attention. The maître d' and a succession of waiters were tripping over each other to see to her comfort. Tanner couldn't help but laugh as he walked over.

'Oh Rob, isn't this place delightful?' cooed Ashley, her eyes brilliant—effervescent, almost—in the glow of the restaurant.

'*You've* certainly made an impression,' said Tanner.

'Well, you did leave me alone for such a *very* long time,' she teased, smiling up at him from her seat.

'I'm sorry,' replied Tanner. A chair was pulled out for him, and he duly sat down. 'I didn't expect to be that long, but it turns out that Tommy, rather appropriately, has come to the end of the road too.'

Ashley smiled again at Tanner's choice of metaphor. 'How so?'

'Let's have a drink first.'

No sooner were the words uttered than Flavio, the maître d', was at his elbow with a bottle of Champagne.

'I didn't realise we had ordered,' queried Tanner, looking from Ashley to Flavio.

'No *signor*, this is on the house,' explained the latter. 'When you bring such a beautiful lady to our restaurant for the first time, and at Christmas, we must celebrate.'

'Thank you, Flavio.' Tanner could only accept that he had been bested by a master charmer.

Flavio filled their gasses with deliberate care and made an equally unhurried withdrawal. Finally, they were alone. They raised and touched glasses; eyes fixed on one other.

'What should we drink to?' asked Tanner.

'To Christmas, obviously.'

'*Merry Christmas*, Ashley. May it bring you everything you wish for.'

'Oh, wouldn't that be nice, Rob? Unlikely, but nice.' Ashley's eyes danced with Champagne ebullience.

They drank, each taking in the other as much as the taste, letting the moment linger, until Ashley broke the spell. 'Shall we get business out of the way first?'

Tanner glanced aside to ensure they wouldn't be overheard, but none of their fellow diners had the slightest interest in anything other than their own festive celebrations.

'Well,' began Tanner. 'As far as Kellett's concerned, everyone at National can pack up and go home for Christmas, as if nothing ever happened.' He scoffed. 'I felt that we, they… that *the bank* should proceed as if the threat hadn't gone away: notify the authorities, make an immediate public statement, set up helplines, re-double our efforts at tracing the attack. In short, do everything humanly possible to be transparent and honest.'

'But?'

'But Kellett outmanoeuvred me. I thought he would do the right thing. Lord, how many times have I used that phrase today?' Tanner sighed, fingers playing absently at the base of his Champagne flute. 'I thought he would put the bank's interests first, but his only care is his own reputation and covering up anything that might damage it. He played the chairman like a fish and used me to do so.'

'So, what you're saying, basically, is that we've learned nothing from past mistakes?' The gaiety faded from Ashley's eyes as she warmed to her subject, lips tautening in solidarity. 'Greedy executives still take unjustifiable risks. Chairmen and non-executive directors are too stupid, frightened or lazy to question them – let alone hold them to account. Regulators are the same. And the big banks know that if anything goes really wrong, the government will bail them out. People thought Lehman was a watershed, then fifteen years later we get Silicon Valley Bank and Credit Suisse. No one culpable ever serves time, and Joe Public foots the bill.' A strident note had entered Ashley's voice. She paused for breath. 'I'm sorry. It's just… this is something I feel strongly about.'

'No, don't apologise,' insisted Tanner. 'You're right.'

'Maybe, but there's a time and a place for diatribes.' The warmth returned to Ashley's features as her gaze fell to the menu. 'Cheer me up. Tell me where I should start with this?'

Tanner grinned. 'You probably won't believe me when I say it really is all good.'

'I'm sure I'd believe *anything* you told me.'

He tried his best to ignore the coquettishly raised eyebrows opposite him. 'Well, I'd particularly recommend the calamari, the truffles, the lobster linguine…' He laughed. 'This is hopeless, it sounds like I'm reeling off the whole menu.'

'I'm surprised. I had you down as someone who knows what he likes.' Ashley regarded him inquisitively. 'And, possibly, likes what he knows?'

'Are you suggesting I'm stuck in my ways?'

'No, not at all. Knowing what you like is a good thing. Just so long as it doesn't stop you from trying new experiences.' She fixed him with another mischievous look, then laughed. 'I'd like to try everything on here, but I don't think a lifetime is long enough.'

'It's always the same story,' said Tanner. 'There's never enough time.'

Ashley raised her glass in toast. 'To time, then. The most precious thing that money can't buy.'

'To time,' responded Tanner. 'And lots of it.' Had he not been distracted at that very moment by a glass being dropped across the room, he might have noticed an almost imperceptible flickering, as if the voltage in Ashley's eyes had momentarily dimmed. By the time he returned his gaze, the brilliance was restored, and the night continued unsullied. With consummate, unobtrusive care, Champagne glasses were refilled, selections of bread offered, and first courses brought.

Conversation, like the wine, flowed easily, but Tanner realised he was finding himself constantly on the back foot. He was used to calling the tune—or at least holding it—in most social situations, but this woman seemed to have him at a permanent disadvantage. He didn't know what to make of her; at turns whimsical, flirtatious and knowing, she was utterly beguiling, and more than once he had to remind himself that they had only just met. What was that old saying? Befuddled, bemused and bewildered. He put it down to the strange and draining events of the past couple of days. Clearly, he needed to regain the initiative.

'Do you mind me asking a little about your background?' he ventured.

'Of course not. I've been looking forward to trading stories. Finding out a little about the real you.'

'The real me?' Tanner gave a self-deprecating shrug. 'What you see is what you get.'

'We'll see about that. Anyway, I'll go first before the Champagne kicks in and loosens my tongue too much.' Ashley paused to check she had Tanner's complete attention, then began her story.

'I'm the archetypal military brat,' she said. 'Dad was always moving: a year here, a couple of years there. If there's a country where the U.S. Army has a presence, I've probably lived there. Europe, Asia, Hawaii, a whole bunch of places in the States you've never heard of. The same house. The same schools. Even the same movie theatres. In a hundred different locations. Just with different smells and different climates.'

'That's why you don't have much of an accent?' asked Tanner.

Ashley laughed. 'I guess. It's funny; people ask me where I'm from and I never know how to answer. Do they mean where was I born? Where did I live the longest? Where do I feel most nostalgic about?'

'And?' probed Tanner.

'Nowhere. When you don't really bother unpacking and leave half your belongings in a box to save time on the next move, it's hard to get attached to a place.'

'What about friends?'

Ashley shrugged. 'This may surprise you, but I'm not normally a sociable sort.' She laughed. 'An upbringing like mine… I mean, isn't that why computers were invented? Still, moving around a lot makes you independent. Not to mention incapable of meaningful relationships.' Tanner thought he caught a fleeting look of sadness, but Ashley continued before it had a chance to take root. 'After school I went back to the States for college in California. Hard to stay in one place, so another move—to Massachusetts—and now New York.'

'Why fintech? Cyber-crime?' asked Tanner.

'It's a multi-billion-dollar problem, and it's skyrocketing, so I figured I'd never be short of work!' Ashley laughed. 'And those itchy feet, I guess. I like working with smart people. Being challenged. I like to think I'm doing something useful.'

'And family?'

'All gone, sadly.' The air of openness evaporated, and her eyes fell to the table. She seemed to take a moment to rebuild her defences, to pull the drawbridge back up. Then, composed again, she raised her glance to Tanner and continued brightly. 'Enough of me, what about you?'

'First, let's allow Flavio to work his magic.' Tanner was all too happy to stall while the waiters approached and, with quiet show, laid the main courses. Wine was ritually presented—a 2016 Valtellina, at Flavio's insistence—tested, and accepted. For a short while, Tanner and Ashley ate in silent pleasure, their table an island of companionable quiet detached from the swelling, swirling conversations of the restaurant. Ashley was first to praise the food, and Tanner happily concurred.

'I told you everything here was good!'

Their eyes met, and then Ashley set down her fork, reaching for her glass. She drank, and Tanner watched the constricting muscles of her delicate neck as she swallowed. She set down her glass and offered him a smile of encouragement.

'Okay. Your turn,' she prompted.

'Well,' Tanner began, dabbing at his lip with the napkin. 'I'm afraid it's going to sound very dull after your account, but there's nothing I can do about that. I was born in West London, suburbia. My father was from a working-class family, and he left school at fifteen to serve an apprenticeship. Luckily for us, being denied a formal education imbued him with a lifelong passion for learning.'

'Us?'

'An older sister, a younger brother.' Tanner tried to keep it light, but he recognised he was straying into dangerous territory. Something of his discomfort crept into his tone.

'Sorry,' said Ashley. Had she sensed his trepidation? 'I interrupted.'

'Don't apologise.' Tanner smiled, setting his cutlery on an empty plate. 'Please do. Anyway, we went to good schools and studied hard. We didn't have a choice. My sister and I went to university. I was lucky, and I got into Cambridge. This was back in the days when they cared as much about whether you could play sport as the number of A grades to your name.'

'You were lucky?' queried Ashley. Her eyes were flecked with mirth. 'Luck got you into Cambridge?'

'No, seriously,' insisted Tanner, although he knew how it sounded. 'It was the age-old story: one fantastic teacher who steered me in the right direction at the right time. Then, lots of fun at university.' He scrutinised his glass and took a draught. 'Too much. I had no idea what I wanted to do, so joined the graduate programme at National Bank, and I'm still there. Or rather, I was!'

'And now?'

'Not the faintest idea.'

'Really?' Ashley was clearly dubious about this unwritten part of the story, but she let it pass. Instead, she asked, with a discomforting intensity, 'So why did you stay so long?'

'If you'd asked me yesterday, I'd have given you a glib response about career progression,' answered Tanner. 'I had a succession of really interesting jobs, I was good at them, so I got promoted. That meant more money, then a bigger job, then another promotion. The golden treadmill.'

'And Kellett?'

'I started working with him before he became Head of Risk. He'd risen quickly during the financial crisis and had a reputation for shaking things up. You have to remember we were sleepier then—a bit old-fashioned—but decent. A couple of our Board members were worried he might be too progressive, too *aggressive*. They wanted a safe pair of hands to keep him in check. They chose mine.'

Ashley's eyebrows lifted. 'And did you?' She was staring at him intently now. '*Keep him in check.*'

Tanner rubbed his chin and looked for the right words. 'Kellett was—is—a genius. In a technical sense. At cutting costs and making money. But as a person, he was a complete nightmare from day one. Rude, overbearing, just a garden variety bully, in fact. I certainly tried to keep him in check. I spoke to the then CEO and CFO, to those directors I mentioned. But it was the aftermath of the crash. Boards were terrified of risk – not just losing money but actually going bust. Kellett was brilliant at ensuring we remained unscathed while all around us were falling apart.'

Tanner looked away. He lacked the strength to keep eye contact and make the next confession. 'And, of course, I was flattered. "Only you can rein him in, Rob. We'd be lost without you, Rob." The usual blandishments and inducements. Ego. Cowardice. Pride. Call it what you will. I justified it by thinking it would be worse for everyone else if I left.'

'So Kellett ascended through the ranks, and you kept getting promoted in his wake.'

'I did,' Tanner admitted. 'Right to the top: COO. The most interesting role in the whole bank. At the heart of everything: strategy, operations, technology, customer engagement. Or, rather, it should have been.'

'What went wrong?'

'I seemed to spend my whole life looking back, clearing up Kellett's messes. Whenever I put forward new customer initiatives, he found a way of side-lining them. If I complained, people said, "Look at the profits! Look at the share price! You're doing a great job, stop worrying!"' Tanner's head dropped. 'So, I did.'

'Okay,' said Ashley, the same even tone. 'Going back to my original question. Why didn't you leave before now?'

'Honestly?' Tanner took a breath before answering, 'I guess I wanted to have my cake and eat it. I enjoyed being seen as Saint Rob, the force for good, even though I'm beginning to realise I was only enabling Kellett's bad behaviour.'

'I'm sure you did what you could,' countered Ashley. But if her tone was more uncertain than the words, Tanner missed it. He was in full-on confessional mood now.

'I said I'd tell all, so let me. Please.' He took another breath. 'There was another reason why I stuck around: I wanted the money.'

'Money? You put up with Kellett for years for *this*?' Ashley's eyes flashed as they swept the room, taking in the quietly expensive outfits of the other diners, the winks of Rolexes at the periphery of sleeves and the sparkle of necks strung with elegant gold.

'Actually, no,' Tanner replied with force. 'I use the money to fund a project I'm involved with. Something good – something really good, in fact. Helping under-privileged youngsters who don't…' He trailed off, waving a hand dismissively. 'It's a long story.'

'So, tell me.'

'Not now. It's…' He hesitated. 'It's a complicated story, and I don't want to put any more of a dampener on this evening than I already have. But it is a good cause, and I'm not in it for myself.'

'Well, aren't you a contradiction, Mister Tanner?' Ashley's dark red lips formed a wry smile. 'And you had the nerve to tell me what I see is what I get.'

Tanner shrugged, and his shoulders suddenly felt light and loose – the way they never normally did after a day at the bank. All those thousands of days. And for what? To help Kellett further his own career. To appease an army of faceless shareholders? His relief at unburdening himself seemed to have taken years off him. He felt younger, and an observer, noticing the mischief in his eyes, the uplift at the corner of his lips, might have said he suddenly looked it, too.

'And you really don't have a plan?' pressed Ashley. Tanner remembered where he was. He met Ashley's eyes and shook his head.

'No,' he insisted. 'But at least I'm out now. Past the point of no return.'

'You're sure?'

'Oh yes. Nothing would make me go back.'

Ashley seemed to like that. She pushed a loose strand of hair back behind her ear and treated Tanner to her warmest smile of the night. 'Well, then,' she proposed. 'Here's to new beginnings.'

'New beginnings,' agreed Tanner, and they touched glasses in mutual compliment.

The rest of the evening was spent in simple appreciation of good food, fine wine and each other's company. Conversation developed like water droplets on a winter window, one topic gathering beautiful momentum before falling away, naturally, to be replaced by another. Tiramisu was shared at Flavio's insistence; aperitifs were brought, and further toasts were made. Until, having been so engrossed in Ashley, Tanner became aware of the maître d' hovering at his shoulder.

'*Scusa*, Signor Tanner, but…'

Tanner looked up and was astonished to see the very last of the diners being helped with their coats in the vestibule. The restaurant, otherwise, was empty. With a profuse apology he settled the bill and, amongst renewed fawning, led Ashley to the exit. It was snowing heavily, but a black cab, unhailed by Tanner, was already waiting for them.

Flavio answered Tanner's look of surprise with a dip of the head before stepping forward and taking Ashley's hand. With reverence, he bowed and kissed it.

'*Bella signora*,' he said. 'It has truly been our pleasure. I hope we will see you again very soon.'

Ashley beamed, cranking her film-star smile up to maximum voltage.

'Thank you, Flavio, that's so sweet. *Buon Natale*.' Then, to his visible delight, she kissed him on both cheeks before getting into the cab.

Tanner got in beside her. He leant forward, towards the driver's partition, to give instructions for the short journey to Hyde Park Corner and the longer one to Hammersmith. Then he settled back in his seat, beside the beautiful enigma who had so captivated him, coaxed him into the open and made him forget, for a night, about the perennial pressures of the bank.

'That really was the nicest Christmas Eve I can remember,' said Ashley. There was a discordant note of melancholy in her voice. When he turned to reply, Tanner saw she was not looking at him but at the festive shopfront beyond the window. Her stare was vacant. Detached.

'Well, it's not midnight yet,' Tanner protested cheerfully. He was desperate to preserve the evening's spell. 'And it's only five minutes to the hotel, so you'll be home before the taxi turns into a pumpkin.'

'I know,' replied Ashley, turning to face him. 'It's just that I hadn't expected this evening to be so nice. When I called you, when I offered to help, even when I agreed to dinner tonight, it was meant to be work – but it hasn't felt anything like it.'

Tanner smiled, meeting her eyes in the low light of the cab. 'Well, that's a good thing, no?'

'Yes, of course.' Ashley reached out and squeezed his hand. She hesitated, apparently in two minds as to whether to say more, then added, 'You know what's funny?'

'What's that?'

'We discussed everything this evening. Our upbringings, our families, our careers – our pasts and our futures. But not relationships. Not love.'

Tanner exhaled. 'Not really my strong suit.'

'Never?'

'Not like you see in the movies or books.'

Ashley laughed. 'Well, now you're being ridiculous.'

'You think. No cupid's arrow? Thunderbolts from the sky? Love at first sight?'

'First sight?' Ashley affected a look of serious contemplation, 'No, not at *first* sight.'

'That's disappointing.'

The driver interrupted their conversation. They were at the Lanesborough already. The bowler-hatted doorman leapt to action, and neither Tanner nor Ashley knew what to say next. For the first time that evening, an uncomfortable silence stretched between them, filling the cab.

It was Ashley who broke it, eyes twinkling in amusement. 'Do you remember our first toast this evening?'

Tanner cast his mind back, 'I wished you a Merry Christmas.'

'No. *Precisely*.' She wagged a finger in admonition.

Tanner smiled. 'I believe I said, "May Christmas bring you everything you wish for."'

'Indeed, you did. And are you a man of your word?'

'I like to think so.'

She leaned forward, as if to kiss him on the cheek. She let the smoothness of her face linger, and Tanner breathed in notes of rose and sandalwood. Then, very slowly, she whispered, 'What I want for Christmas is to turn my phone off for the entire day, eat an unfeasibly large Christmas lunch, take an afternoon stroll to walk it off, make a snowman, spend the evening in front of a fire and the night making love. With you.' She answered his look of pure astonishment with a gleeful, 'Merry Christmas, Rob.' And then she was gone, out into the night, leaving Tanner alone in the back of the taxi.

The journey home passed in a blur.

Tanner had lived his share of extraordinary days, but nothing compared to this. He had resigned, been reinstated, then fired. He had thought the bank to be at serious risk and now, apparently, everything was fine. He had met the most extraordinary, unknowable, beautiful woman: at turns frivolous and serious, expressive and reflective, joyous and melancholic. He was wildly attracted to her and, ridiculously, it seemed that the feeling was reciprocated. And all on Christmas Eve.

It occurred to Robert Tanner, as the taxi pulled up outside his front door, that you really couldn't make it up.

DAY THREE

CHRISTMAS DAY
WEDNESDAY 25 DECEMBER 2024

19

MARTIN KELLETT'S SPIRITS SOARED as high as the majestic peaks surrounding his picture-postcard chalet. He had managed to catch the last flight back to Geneva, and it had been late in the night—or, rather, very early in the morning—when he finally turned the last of the keys to the cabin door. But it was worth every Franc to open the curtains today and see the towering shark-tooth of the Matterhorn. The neighbouring rooftops were thick with snow, but now the skies had cleared, and the town was lit in a cold, pale light.

There was no room for clouds on Kellett's horizon this Christmas morning. He was in his favourite place in the world. A former farmstead with a high-tech interior, his hideaway appeared wholly unchanged to passers-by and prying eyes. Discretion could be bought at a (very high) price in a resort such as this, one frequented by the über-rich.

His housekeeper had laid in breakfast while he slept, and he woke late to a veritable smorgasbord: eggs, bacon and rosti in the warmer, a selection of cheeses and cold cuts, croissants, butter, jams and honey. Juices had been freshly squeezed, and the coffee machine was ready to go.

He had no commitments and no one else to consider; he could do exactly as he wanted. A perfect day of lazy relaxation lay ahead. And what better way to relax than with some female company? Even on Christmas Day—probably with particular pleasure on Christmas Day, given the fee he would charge—Stefan Ziegler, the local procurer, would find one of the distinctly alternative "chalet girls" he managed. Then, suitably relaxed, Kellett would take a sauna. Or perhaps, he thought with a smirk, the relaxation should take place *in* the sauna.

And lastly, dinner at the Schweizer Grand. Here, Kellett was delighted with himself; he had had the foresight to keep his reservation at the best, and most prestigious, table in town.

Kellett contemplated the spread, and the day ahead, with porcine pleasure. Then he thought of his lucky escape with the account manipulation and exhaled to the wooden beams in relief. Thank God they hadn't gone public with a statement about the computer foul-up. He'd have been a fucking laughing stock. Instead, that weakling Tanner had been the fool. Kellett had wanted to get rid of the quisling for years, but his deputy had supporters on the Board, so he'd had to bide his time. But no longer! Now, at last, the idiot had cooked his own Christmas goose.

Had there ever been a better Christmas, Kellett wondered? He snorted with delight and made to fork the first rasher of bacon into his smirking mouth. As he set his jaw in motion, delighting in the salty taste of the bacon, he had to concede that surely no, there hadn't been.

20

TANNER WOKE EARLY, fully refreshed from a deep, dreamless sleep. His first thought was to wonder whether his memory was playing tricks; images of the previous evening came flooding back with such a dreamlike quality that he had to ask himself whether fatigue had misrepresented them. But then a ping on his phone announced a message and, happily, put his memories of last night beyond doubt.

Ashley, 08:00: Happy Christmas, Rob. *Dictum tuum pactum?*

Tanner smiled. The message was a play on the age-old Latin motto adopted by the London Stock Exchange at the turn of the nineteenth century. *My word is my bond.* An unwavering commitment to keeping one's promise. As seemed the norm with Ashley, the choice of words was suggestively playful. He responded with matching brevity.

Rob, 08:05: *Semper.* 1 p.m. at your hotel?

Within seconds, Tanner had his reply: a thumbs up emoji followed immediately by more Latin.

> ✉ **Ashley, 08:06:** *Venies. Videbis. Vinces?*
> *You will come. You will see. Will you conquer?*

With typical wit, Ashley had teased Caesar's famous summation of swift conquest into a question. Tanner had no idea if he'd triumph, but at least he had a plan: he'd make a traditional Christmas dinner at home. He loved cooking, but his work kept him so busy that he rarely had a chance to enjoy being in the kitchen. Ingredients would be no problem; one of the great benefits of living in his neighbourhood was the abundance of food stores of every caste and kind, oblivious to dates in the calendar. Moreover, his house contained a real fireplace, in satisfaction of another of Ashley's six wishes.

It occurred to Tanner that if he got a move on, he could make a quick detour from the shops and drop in to see Liz and the family on the way back, too. He was still smarting from his sister's reproof of the previous evening. Mainly because she was right; he didn't do enough to help her. Money, yes, but effort? *Time?* Oh well, that would all change now he was free of the bank. He'd start with a surprise Christmas Day visit.

It wasn't even ten o'clock when he reached Liz's front step in Chiswick. Armed with flowers, chocolates and Champagne for the adults, and envelopes for the children, he began to feel decidedly Christmassy. Until his father, Harry, answered the door.

'Oh,' said the old man. 'It's you.'

'And a Happy Christmas to you too, Dad.'

Tanner was spared further interaction by the breathless arrival of his niece and nephew, literally falling over one another in their excitement to shout stories of the morning's presents and see if there were any more to be had. Tanner's confirmation of that happy outcome—'But only if you're quiet'—stemmed the noise. Just in time, judging by the coldness on his sister's face, and on her tongue.

'That's a turn up for the books,' huffed Liz, by way of greeting. But Tanner's flowers, gifts and, more importantly, a hug and a whispered apology began to restore her humour. Coffee was brewed, presents were exchanged, and crisp new fifty-pound notes were retrieved by the children from their envelopes, occasioning a further round of shrieks.

'What time are you seeing Judith?' asked Liz once they were settled in the living room.

Tanner was caught off-guard. 'I'm not. We split up.'

The cheer—and sound—drained from the room. Other than a *harrumph* from Harry and a stage-whispered, 'There goes another one.' More stage than whisper.

'Something you want to say, Dad?'

Harry replied with the most innocent shake of his head, as if the very idea was preposterous, and made a pantomime of blowing on his mug of coffee.

'Well, why don't you stay for lunch with us?' asked Liz.

'Sorry, Liz, bank stuff.' Tanner had come with the lie already prepared, wrapped with a bow. But now he clenched his teeth in anger at his father and at himself for resorting, as always, to untruths. So much for a fresh start.

'But it's Christmas Day, Rob!'

'I know, sis, but the account problem's yet to be fully sorted.' What had his mother told him about telling lies, even the smallest fib? They always come back to haunt you. Well, not this time. There would be no Ghost of Christmas Yet to Come to appease. Tanner was out of National Bank, and now he had to get out of here.

He gulped down his coffee while it was still much too hot and made his excuses. Steadfastly ignoring his father's look of disapproval, Tanner exchanged rapid goodbyes with the rest of the family and headed for the door. He couldn't even meet Liz's eyes. There was no avoiding her tongue though.

'Another happy Christmas at the Tanner household,' she fumed. And, to prove that she could do theatrics just as well as their father, she slammed the door behind him.

By the time he was back in the car, Tanner had begun to see the ridiculousness of it all. He permitted himself a wry smile. Next time, he'd stick to Plan A and use the phone. If there *was* a next time. Surely the old bastard couldn't live forever.

21

SEVEN HUNDRED MILES AWAY, the Prime Minister of the United Kingdom was in a frame of mind no less optimistic than the Toad's. There were no majestic peaks to be seen from his study window—only the flatlands of Norfolk—but there was nothing flat about his mood. His eyes twinkled as he took in the view, and he allowed himself a real, genuine smile—not for the cameras, this time—as he stopped to consider the successes of the past year. He was approaching fifty, but he had a distinct boyishness about him that Christmas morning. It was only a shame there wasn't a focus group there to appreciate it.

James Allen had risen to power one summer ago, cashing in on the demise of the previous, unlamented administration. The rank, almost unknown, outsider of an initial field of nearly twenty candidates for the leadership of the party, and thus the premiership, Allen snuck through on the rails, ignored by the other contenders and their supporters until it was too late.

This new premier—a witty and articulate speaker, energetic, handsome—seemed made for television. A charming wife who worked for the NHS and two state-schooled teenage children only helped the image. Few seemed to mind that the state school in question sent as many sixth formers to Oxbridge as many of the best private schools. It had been the same story when Allen was a pupil there.

Naturally, it had been a busy first year in the hot seat. Allen had worked the electorate hard, visiting schools and hospitals, opening factories and making occasional high-profile overseas visits. As global headwinds subsided, the economy began to bounce, and politics moved away from talk of pandemics and the European Union. The party's slide in the polls was finally arrested, and Allen banned his cabinet members from even talking about Brexit, on pain of them being banished to another, more dreaded, 'B word': the backbenches. So yes, it had been a busy year. But it had also been a good year.

Now, as he stared out of the window, Allen thought again how much he loved this landscape. Big skies, poppies in spring, vast fields of ripe corn in summer, ancient churches everywhere you looked (you could see nine of them on a clear day from the top bedroom).

Allen could have spent Christmas at Chequers, but he considered the

PM's country home in Buckinghamshire a dreary, draughty old pile. It was better for the family—and his image—to be at home. It didn't hurt, either, that he had been invited the forty miles north to Sandringham for lunch the following week.

The kids were off playing with their new gadgets, and his in-laws had gone for a walk. The protection squad was warm and snug in the converted barn, with a barrage of equipment monitoring the surrounding area. All was quiet in his study. The peace felt like a reprieve.

That was when Allen's wife, Anna, walked in to find him closing the lid on the red ministerial box on his desktop.

'I thought you promised no work today,' she chided. She had a knack for scolding him without the warmth ever leaving her face. In that moment, Allen reflected, yet again, how lucky he had been to find, and keep, this woman.

'It's not work, actually,' Allen replied. 'I was being completely and utterly self-indulgent and looking at our latest popularity ratings.'

'You vain pig,' said Anna, walking over to his desk. She pushed him and laughed.

'I know, I know. But it seems I—*we*—are rather popular.' Allen beamed and pulled her closer. 'So, in the spirit of red boxes…' He reached sideways into the despatch box and, with dextrous sleight-of-hand, brought out a small red leather jewellery box. 'A little something to say how grateful I am for your support. And how much I love you.'

'Oh, James.' Anna's blue eyes shone with tears even as she bit her lip. 'You silly man.'

'That's not what the electorate thinks,' he beamed, hugging her tightly. A hint of a leer appeared on his features, an expression nobody would have ever chosen for a campaign leaflet. 'Now, open your box.'

22

TANNER PULLED UP TO THE PORTICOED ENTRANCE of the Lanesborough with four minutes to spare. Ashley was already waiting, engrossed in an animated conversation with the two doormen. Almost before the car had come to a stop, one of them had the passenger door open for her. Ashley thanked her chivalrous new acquaintance and, with A-lister elegance, slid into her seat.

Tanner and Ashley regarded one another for a moment. Tanner thought he had remembered Ashley exactly, but he was struck anew by how naturally lovely she was. Today she was wrapped in a coat of deep midnight blue with a collar he assumed had been made in homage to, rather than from, the pelt of a silver fox. She wore the faintest hint of blue-grey eye shadow and the narrowest line of silver above her dark brown lashes. It was hard to tell if there was any cosmetic embellishment of her smooth, fine cheeks or whether standing in the chill had brought a natural blush of colour to them. Her hair was tied in a loose bun, held by two antique floral hair pins, also silver, with delicate rhinestone leaves.

'Ashley,' declared Tanner. 'You look simply beautiful.'

'That's a nice thing to say.'

'Compliments are easy to give when they're true,' answered Tanner. His eyes flitted to the rear-view mirror. 'And I'd like nothing more than to sit here and give you more… but I can't.'

Ashley pursed her lips in mock displeasure.

'We're on a tight schedule,' Tanner explained, flicking on an indicator. 'Every second counts.'

'Are London restaurants that strict on timings?'

'This one is,' replied Tanner, turning to check his mirrors one more time before driving off, hiding the broadest of grins.

Tanner's luck held. Traffic remained light, and they passed the journey in easy conversation, mostly about the character of London: how much it had changed in the years since Ashley had last been here on another vacation. Huge new apartment blocks had sprung up the length of the two royal parks that ran most of the way to Notting Hill, while the cleaners and baristas and cooks who serviced those Babylonian towers had been pushed ever further from the centre. To forestall any dampening of spirits, Tanner made a point of highlighting what *had* endured, including many of his youthful haunts – particularly the pubs where he had celebrated victories for his football team out west. After barely twenty-five minutes of driving, they pulled up at Tanner's terraced house.

Ashley looked from Tanner to the house and back. 'I'm intrigued,' she said. 'This doesn't look like any restaurant I've ever visited.'

Tanner shut off the engine and winked. 'All will be revealed.'

He led her to his front door, opened it, and stood aside. The unmistakeable aroma of roasting assailed them: transient notes of meat, oils, herbs and seasonings, discrete in their wonderful amalgam like a fine wine.

Ashley's eyes sparkled. 'What a wonderful surprise.'

'Let me take your coat,' offered Tanner, reaching out a hand. 'And then I *have* to check the oven!'

It seemed the culinary gods were on Tanner's side; everything was as it should be. He took a bottle of Champagne—a 2008 Pol Roger Cuvée Sir Winston Churchill—from the fridge, opened it with unaffected skill and slowly filled two glasses. An impressed look suggested Ashley had missed neither the vintage nor the practiced ease with which he'd opened it. He passed the first to glass to her and raised his own in obeisance. 'To you.'

'Thank you, Rob,' she replied. 'It's wonderful.' She indicated the wine before spreading her hand towards the beautifully set table. 'Everything's wonderful.'

Ashley stood by the kitchen island, watching Tanner work. He calmly moved saucepans, stirred sauces and checked ovens with the effortlessness of a stage magician. When all was prepared to his satisfaction, he bade her sit. A look of total concentration came over him as he carved the turkey and began to serve. Now the magician became an artist; with huge white China plates as his canvas, Tanner laid slices of meat, a multicolour hue of vegetables, sculpted servings of stuffing and white sauce and, with a final flourish, a delicate ladling of gravy.

'It's too beautiful to eat!' protested Ashley, studying her plate in unfeigned wonderment. 'How on earth did you learn to cook like this?'

'You haven't tasted it yet!' laughed Tanner. '*Bon appetit.*'

Ashley paused and raised her glass, 'To the chef.'

Tanner nodded his acknowledgement and clinked Ashley's glass. He was even more gratified than his face let on. 'Now eat.'

They tasted in silence until Ashley had tried it all.

'Rob, this is *truly* delicious,' she said.

'I'm glad you like it.'

'How *did* you learn to cook so well?'

Tanner thought for a moment. 'I suppose I watched my mother and assimilated. I don't remember being "taught" as such.' He held up his fingers in quotation, then paused in longer reflection. 'I've probably always been like that. I've always enjoyed watching and listening. Analysing. Watching my older sister screw up and making sure not to repeat her mistakes.' They both laughed.

'Observation is an underrated skill,' Tanner continued. 'Experts believe it's one of the fundamental reasons why Leonardo DaVinci was so extraordinary, for example. He didn't have much formal schooling, but he spent hours and hours simply observing. The movement of birds and animals, rivers and trees, everything around him. He never stopped. As he got older, he made detailed investigations of anatomy, theatre props, you name it. It was that curiosity to observe, and learn with his own eyes, right from the start, that set him apart.'

Ashley waited to see if Tanner would continue, but instead he took a long, slow mouthful from his glass, his face lost in thought.

'What you're implying,' she suggested evenly, 'is that looking back five hundred years might help us move forward again. *Interesting*.'

'How so?'

'Well, everyone's so glued to their phones these days, they don't notice anything around them. Who needs to observe and learn when you have Wikipedia? Who needs to read a map when you have Google? Need to work out how to do something? Look on YouTube.' Her voice hit a sharper note. 'Phones, gadgets, computers. They're killing conversation, manners, common sense. Probably, in time, the human race!'

Tanner winced. He saw Ashley, but the words may as well have been his father's. And yet there was truth in it, wasn't there? Take the bank: billions had been spent on new technology, and yet they couldn't even guarantee that customers' accounts had the correct balance. A warning from years before flashed through his mind: an uncomfortable meeting, a dereliction of duty, which he had forgotten until this very moment.

Ashley saw Tanner's expression and tried to back-track. 'Sorry. I'm going off on one again.'

'No, it's me who should be sorry,' insisted Tanner. 'I was miles away.'

'Care to share?'

'I was thinking about the bank's systems,' offered Tanner. 'Whether they're fundamentally fit for purpose. We're so excited about opening new revenue streams from our customers' data that we've forgotten it's all stored in legacy systems held together by sticking plasters. I was contemplating what would happen if someone started ripping off the bandages.' Unease tightened his mouth. 'No, not contemplating… dreading.'

Ashley looked away, seemingly discomfited at the mood change she'd occasioned. She stole a glance at her watch and then flourished it in a theatrical change of subject. 'Heavens, have you seen the time?'

Tanner accepted the diversionary tactic with relief. He didn't want to spend the rest of the day worrying about the bank; he had wasted enough of his life on that already. And he certainly didn't want it to spoil this perfect day.

'No,' he smiled. 'I can honestly say I hadn't given it a thought. Should I?'

'You owe me, remember?' Ashley said. She fixed him with a look of steely intent. 'A walk. You *promised*. And a snowman!' She rose from her chair and walked over to the window, peering out at the snowscape beyond. Then she disappeared down the hallway to where she had left her coat and bag, by the front door. She returned brandishing a small, wrapped package, which she placed on the mantelpiece above the yet unlit fire. 'For later,' she said.

Within a few minutes, they were both wrapped in their coats, ready for the elements. Tanner paused for a solicitous final check at the door. 'All set?'

'Almost.'

Tanner had just started to open the door when Ashley stepped close to him, her eyes fixed on his. Without warning, she reached up and pulled his face downwards. Her lips brushed his—soft waves of exploration at first—then more insistent as they became locked in a gentle, slow kiss. She drew her other hand around Tanner's back and pulled him even closer. They stayed like that for what felt like a long time before Ashley broke off and, with a smile, made for the fresh carpet of unbroken snow beyond Tanner's door.

23

WITH HIS CARNAL APPETITE SATISFIED, at least for now, Kellett showered for the second time since breakfast. He had hours to fill before dinner, his next meal, but first he had to meet his sole external obligation in an otherwise entirely self-indulgent day.

Kellett lowered himself into his desk chair and dialled a US 330 area code – something he tried not to do more than three times a year. The line rang, and he was relieved to meet with his sister's flat tones rather than those of her godly Ohioan husband. Kellett and his sister exchanged perfunctory greetings before the phone was handed to his nephew.

Remarkably, Kellett's sister and her husband had produced a son who appeared to have inherited, in Kellett's opinion, all the best family characteristics – namely, his own. The boy was a spoilt, devious little brat with, as far as Kellett could tell, an ambiguous attitude towards the truth and little consideration for others. But he was smart and unashamedly ambitious, and Kellett was determined to help his nephew escape the rust belt, if only to spite his brother-in-law. This year, Kellett—or rather, Christina—had arranged for the wretch to receive a top-end gaming PC as a Christmas present, and the boy's obvious delight more than justified the expense.

Kellett listened, or at least pretended to, as his nephew gabbled about boot partitions, CPUs and the like. When the torrent finally ceased, Kellett adopted a serious tone.

'Now,' he intoned. 'I'm glad you like it, but remember, your dad won't want you playing computer games all day. You'll still have to put in those long hours on the football field.' Kellett could barely contain his mirth. He knew the boy's father would be listening on the other end.

'But football's *boring*!' whined the youngster.

'Yes, I should rather think it is,' agreed Kellett, happily picturing his brother-in-law's disgust. 'Merry Christmas!'

Mission accomplished, Kellett hung up and returned to his schedule of lazy indulgence. He poked around a couple of singularly private websites, but these held little appeal after his morning exertions. He basked in the glow of his personal brokerage account for a while, and then he logged in to his National Bank email. He doubted he would find anything of note, but it wouldn't hurt to send a few nudges to keep the bastards on their toes.

The first item in his inbox, however, put all such thoughts to flight:

| From | Subject | Date |
| Joen van Aken | Acedia | 25/12/2024; 16:00 |

The hacker was back! Kellett gulped. His body heaved in panic as the situation dawned on him, a colic of consciousness choking his entire being. With breath coming in ragged bursts, he shot to his feet and hurried to the kitchen, where he filled and drained a glass of water. Then another. Eventually, the heaving subsided a little, though it took all his concentration to inhale and exhale with anything like a healthy rhythm. He returned to his desk and stared at the email's subject line. Then he double-clicked into the body.

Kellett was drawn immediately to the image embedded in the email. It was a pizza-slice of a painting, depicting an old man in a medieval setting. He appeared to be sitting in front of a fire, while a dog dozed and a woman—a nun?—offered him something. The text on the image, a single word, was almost impossible to read. Thoroughly confused, Kellett scrolled down the screen. There was a short message.

TO: MAKCEO2024@NatBank.uk
FROM: Joen van Aken
DATE: Wednesday, 25 December 2024 at 16:00
Acedia

Hello again, Martin.

Did you think it was over? Oh dear, how disappointing for you. But then, I am very disappointed in you.

Belphegor's a Prime old devil and he has your number. Or is it the Beast's? Three sixes are never good. And he liked his zeros too: twenty-six of them! Imagine the power of that when you've seen what just one can do!

My friend Daniel certainly understood that 5 and 25 doesn't always imply multiplication.

Maybe watch Homer[3] if you need a little more help to understand how scary maths problems can be when they get mixed up with new technology. And don't even think about Marie Antoinette...

Toodles!

JvA

Kellett let out a primal scream of raw, unbelieving anguish. The nightmare was supposed to be over! Everything was meant to be back to normal!

He forced himself to think. It was gone five in Zermatt, four o'clock in the UK. Tanner was the obvious person—frankly, the only person—he could call. Kellett groaned at his own stupidity; he had let his ego overcome his common sense in forcing his deputy out. Whatever his shortcomings, Tanner had always been an effective problem-solver. More than that, it was Tanner who usually managed to ensure the bank avoided the elephant traps into which their competitors regularly fell.

Would Tanner even take a call now, Kellett wondered? This was unusual for the Toad: he had come over uncharacteristically indecisive. He stared again at the email. What did it all mean, and what on earth was this picture, this strange wedge from the past?

Kellett searched for "*Acedia*" and was provided with the answer at a stroke. The second result was the very image in the email, replete with a Wikipedia link. He clicked through, engrossed. "Sloth (deadly sin) from the Latin *Acedia*." And there was the picture – the all-but-indecipherable Accidia in *The Seven Deadly Sins and the Four Last Things* by Hieronymus Bosch.

Kellett shook his head in bafflement. Bosch again? He clicked on the

80

link, which took him to the page for another painting attributed to the Dutch master. While not as immediately fantastical as *The Garden of Earthly Delights*, closer inspection showed *The Seven Deadly Sins and the Four Last Things* to address many of the same themes. At its centre was a large circle, believed to represent the eye of God, surrounded by a circular montage of the seven sins. In the four corners were smaller roundels, depicting the "last things": Death, Judgement, Heaven and Hell.

The pizza slice in Kellett's inbox was one of the seven representations of sin at its centre: sloth, depicted by a man dozing in front of the fireplace. Meanwhile, a nun appears to him, in a dream, reminding him to say his prayers.

Kellett was still none the wiser. He reread the email. Belphegor? Again, Wikipedia provided the answer: Belphegor, a demon who seduces people with ingenious inventions to bring them riches. The chief demon of the deadly sin of sloth!

The link was obvious, but what did it have to do with him? Unconsciously, Kellett rubbed his chin. People might accuse him of many things, but laziness? The bank was his life; he had few interests beside it. And he worked as hard as anyone to earn profits for the shareholders – and bonuses for himself. Modern society, a world in which apathy was a virtue, may have been full of examples of idleness. But Martin Kellett was not one of them.

Still floundering, he tried to make sense of the remaining clues. 666 was, he knew, the Number of the Beast: the devil's number. And Belphegor's

Prime, it turned out, was a 31-digit palindromic prime number with that diabolical number at its centre: 1000000000000066600000000000001. Other than the allusion to a worrying number of zeros, its meaning was utterly beyond him, but it clearly didn't augur well. Next, he searched for Daniel 5 25.

A Bible quote: the book of Daniel, chapter 5, verse 25.

> And this is the inscription that was written:
>   MENE, MENE, TEKEL, PARSIN.
>
> Daniel 5:25

Kellett pressed Google into service once more. In the famous Old Testament story, these were the ancient Aramaic words that appeared miraculously on the wall during King Belshazzar's Feast. Literally: *Numbered, Numbered, Weighed, Divided.* Daniel interprets them to mean that God has doomed the king and his kingdom, hence modern references to the proverbial writing on the wall.

The rest of the clues could wait. Kellett didn't need to understand the full context: the warning could not have been clearer.

He, Martin Kellett, had been weighed, and he had been found wanting.

24

THERE WAS LITTLE WANTING in Rob Tanner's world. He and Ashley strolled arm-in-arm to the Thames towpath without a care in the world. The sublime symmetry of her face, her laughter and her intoxicating intensity, the way her eyes sparkled like the silver pins in her hair… with each look at her, his heart lifted anew.

They stopped at a small park where two children were building a snowman. The parents were pitching in, rolling a ball of snow amid peals of laughter. Tanner pointed to the convivial scene.

'Time for the next promise?' he asked.

'Do you always keep your promises so flawlessly?'

Tanner laughed, but Ashley fixed him with wide, solemn eyes. 'No, I'm serious,' she said. He was struck again at how quickly her mood could shift, as if there was a deep-seated sadness within her, held in check but never far away.

'More than that,' Ashley continued, turning to look towards central London, lights rising into the sky, twinkling in the distance. 'How do you hold on to your beliefs and values when there's so much out there that's wrong?'

'Out where?'

'Here, there. Everywhere.' Ashley gestured towards the skyscrapers of the City on the horizon, the glass-and-steel behemoths so representative of Tanner's daily life. The future dwarfing London's wood-and-stone past. 'Did you know that life expectancy for the poorest in this city is fourteen years lower than for the richest? I struggle with places like this, Rob. I don't know what any one of us is supposed to do in the face of everything wrong with this world.'

Tanner saw her shiver. Echoes of the Bosch hellscape returned to his mind: that sacked city of sinners, an eternal siege against legions of demons. Thanks to his work with the Foundation, Tanner knew as well as anyone that for many perfectly innocent souls, the struggles of daily life in this city could be hellish enough. He could understand why this subject was so important to Ashley – even if, at the same time, he desperately wanted nothing more than to rekindle the joyful flame they'd shared only a few moments ago. He squeezed her hand and fixed her with a warm, open smile.

'Let's walk and I'll try to answer. Unless you'd rather…' He pointed at the snowman. Ashley declined with a light shake of the head. They walked on.

After a while, Tanner said, 'I think we're all born with a moral compass. North, south, right, wrong. It gets refined over time, by people, or experiences, or beliefs – many different things at different stages. Then we get older and think we can be clever, maybe persuade ourselves that there's no true north or south—that north-east or south-west are close enough—or find some other way to avoid where the needle's pointing. Perhaps a very small number of people are born without a compass, or with a broken one—or, worse, they *get* broken—but for most people, when it comes down to it, you know where the arrow points. The question is whether you have the honesty and courage to follow it.'

'That's a nice way of putting it.' Ashley gave an affectionate tug on Tanner's elbow. The sparkle was back in her eyes. 'But what happens when you have to deal with people who ignore the compass? Who don't care about right and wrong – only their own interests?'

Tanner mulled the question. 'I guess you try to point them in the right direction, and if they won't go that way, you let them go.'

'What if Kellett asks you to go back to the bank?'

'He won't,' laughed Tanner. 'Is that what this is about?'

Ashley stopped and fixed him with a look of searching examination. 'But what if he *did* ask you back?'

Tanner's face clouded for a second before answering. 'No, we're done. Our compasses point in opposite directions.'

'Good,' said Ashley, with unexpected vehemence. 'That man is a pig.'

25

PANIC WAS NOT AN EMOTION with which Kellett was familiar. Ever industrious, Kellett had sailed through school, university and his professional exams with ease. After that, he'd let others do the worrying for him. But right now, this problem was his and his alone. And there was only one way out: he had to call Tanner.

Kellett tried lines of approach in his head, ways to mitigate the humiliation, but it was no good, he'd have to suck it up. For now. He forced a smile onto his face and dialled. The line rang, again and again. Kellett's frustration mounted with each tone.

'Hi, you've reached Rob Tanner,' came his former deputy's voice at last. 'I'm sorry I can't take your call, but please leave a number and I'll call you back.'

'Who the fuck turns their phone off?' raged Kellett. He was beyond worked up, so far gone that it didn't even register that he was speaking to himself. He tried to call again, to the same effect. Then he remembered: he'd insisted Frank Garner confiscate Tanner's work phone, and he didn't have his personal number. Double fuck!

Kellett knew he had to pull himself together. But then his own phone rang. He grabbed it with a grateful expulsion of relief. Please let it be Tanner! But of course, it wasn't – how could it be? The screen showed David Nash.

Kellett's gut tightened in fearful apprehension, a presentiment so strong that it was all he could do to make himself answer.

'What is it?' he demanded, but with none of his customary fire.

'It's started again.' Nash's voice carried no more conviction than his boss's. 'There are more adjustments. *Attacks*,' he corrected weakly.

The word—or Nash's feebleness—sparked Kellett out of his torpor. 'Pull yourself together,' he barked. 'Give me the details.'

'Yes, of course. So, I told Reddy in Bangalore to contact me immediately if anyone called customer services to say their balance had risen unexpectedly. There was nothing all day. Until…' Nash trailed off, his nervous swallow audible down the line. He pulled himself together and continued. 'Until four-thirty. A couple of calls. I suppose people wanted to check their balances before going to the sales tomorrow.'

'Just a couple? What in—'

'Martin, please,' interrupted Nash. 'Just *listen*. We ran a report immediately. We couldn't believe it, so we ran it again.'

'And?'

Nash's voice took on an otherworldly, almost reverential air. 'It's thousands, Martin. *Thousands*.'

'What?' Kellett choked down irritation. 'Thousands of what?'

'Accounts, Martin.'

'David, you need to be more specific. How many? How much? Take a moment, man. Breathe.'

Nash did as he was told. Kellett heard the deep intakes of breath at the other end of the phone. Then the risk chief continued.

'Martin, it's hundreds of thousands of accounts which are affected now, maybe more. We're running a full report, but the scale is enormous – it's going to take time.' For the first time, a touch of normality returned to Nash's voice. 'The weird thing is that it's only affecting accounts with less than a thousand pounds in them.'

'What?' Kellett's eyes bulged. 'I don't understand.'

'It appears that every single account in the bank that had a balance less than one thousand pounds last night is now ten times the size. *Every* account.'

Kellett tried to process the information, but his brain was struggling with the enormity. 'Just to be clear,' he managed, after a moment had elapsed. 'You're saying current accounts, savings accounts, personal, business, everything... they've all, effectively, had a zero added to the balance?'

'As far as we can tell.'

'Oh God,' groaned Kellett. A wave of clarity broke over him. In a way, the certainty was reassuring, somehow better than the fear of the unknown. The worst was happening, and Kellett would be judged by how he responded.

First though, he had to calm Nash.

'David,' instructed Kellett. 'I need you to do two things immediately. So, *listen*. First, we have to stop people accessing internet and mobile banking. Put up a notice saying we're carrying out essential maintenance. No one will be surprised on Christmas Day. Secondly, shut the call centres off. *Now*. Put a recorded message on. "We're closed for Christmas and we'll be back tomorrow," something like that. Got it?'

'Yes, Martin.'

'And text me the minute it's done.'

Kellett rang off. Now he had to track down Pattie Boyle in a hurry. It would only be a matter of time, he knew, before the press got hold of this one.

26

TRISH DIXON WAS THOROUGHLY BORED. She'd dreamed of being a journalist for as long as she could remember, but manning the Financial Desk of *MailOnline* on Christmas Day wasn't exactly what she'd had in mind. Markets were closed, no news had broken all day, and now it was a matter of toughing it out until 8 p.m., when she could go home. She'd trawled the news wires, watched her share of mind-numbingly dumb TikTok videos, even resorted to browsing Amazon. A steady stream of friends had checked in, offering encouragement and the promise of cocktails that evening. She'd shared commiserations, laughs and mince pies with the guys on the sports desk. Still, the clock ticked ever slower. Finally, she resorted to checking her bank balance on her phone.

'What the hell?' She said the words aloud, dumbfounded. Where had that eight-thousand-pound credit come from? Payday wasn't until the twenty-ninth, and she didn't earn anything like that kind of money. And hang on, the banks were supposed to be closed. Why would there be adjustments on a bank holiday?

She dialled National Bank customer service, but when it connected there was only a recorded message: 'We're sorry, but all our offices are now closed for the holidays. We will be open again tomorrow at 9 a.m. Thank you for your call.' Trish wasn't surprised; even Scrooge gave Bob Cratchit Christmas Day off. She navigated back to her account homepage and hit refresh. This time, the screen defaulted to a holding message.

> **National Bank**
> Sorry, internet banking is currently unavailable.
>
> We're carrying out essential maintenance. Please try again later. We apologise for any inconvenience.

Trish's journalistic instincts kicked in. This smacked of an IT cock-up, reminiscent of what she'd seen in the past with other banks. They had all attempted to mask their failings with euphemistic talk of "migrating" and "upgrading" technology platforms. She thought back. Millions of customers had been unable to access their accounts or make transactions. Some, like her, saw their balances increase by substantial amounts – even if only temporarily.

She turned to X and scrolled through mentions for @NatBankUK. Before 4.30 p.m. there were none, then a few began to appear, and then the trickle became a torrent.

> **MankyMac**
> @JoMcN1994
> can't log into my @NatBankUK account 😡😡 telephone banking shut 😡😡 WTF!!!

> **Viv Holden**
> @HoldViv777
> Balance wrong. Customer Services clueless. Now they're closed. What's going on? #SortItOutNatBankUK

> **Ned Walker**
> @NeddyWalker123
> @NatBankUK gave me £5000 for Christmas 🎅 Bet it won't last 😭

And those were the polite ones. Trish sat forward in her chair and covered her ears to shut out the noise from the sports boys, who were now exuberantly throwing around a rubber rugby ball, just a few metres from her desk.

Trish stood and motioned to them to stop. 'Guys, listen. Do any of you bank with National?'

'I do,' answered the grey-beard amongst the football lads. The ball sailed towards him, and he caught it in one hand, eyes flitting back to Trish.

'Do me a favour?' she pleaded. 'Try logging in, will you?'

He lobbed away the ball and started fiddling with his phone. Then, 'Sorry, Trish, the site's down for maintenance.'

Today was as quiet for the sports boys as it was on her own desk, and it didn't take much persuading to send the old hack down to the ATM to check his balance. Then she repeated the exercise across the newsroom. Any colleague with a National Bank account was cajoled, bribed or browbeaten into visiting the cashpoint. Eighteen went; six found themselves—to varying degrees of bemusement and annoyance—in possession of balances significantly higher than expected. Trish realised her hunch had been right.

She quickly checked the websites of all the other national newspapers. No one else had picked up on the story. She couldn't believe it; she had stumbled across a real, old-fashioned scoop! This was why she had trained as a journalist—not to churn out cheap clickbait or spiteful celebrity rubbish—but to break news and uncover the truth. So much was wrong with the world, and she knew the media was complicit in much of it, but here she had a chance to stick it to a bunch of fat-cat bankers, the ultimate 21st century bogeymen. These days, the only entities people hated as much as banks were the energy companies who profited from war and failed to invest any of the proceeds in green technology. Still, banks were right there atop the list of public enemies, and Trish practically ran to the homepage editor in excitement. He was a man of few words, and his, 'Good work, Trish,' on hearing the story was all the praise she needed. 'See if you can get a quote from them,' he added. 'Or even better, no comment.' He winked.

Trish checked the newspaper's database. There was a phone number for National Bank's Head of Communications, a Pattie Boyle. Trish dialled and got a recording asking her to leave a message and number, which she did. Then she got down to writing her story. She hammered at the keyboard; speed was of the essence, not quality. The Pulitzer Prize could wait for another day.

Copy submitted, she waited, nervously glancing every so often in her editor's direction. Ten minutes later, he raised a thumb across the newsroom, and Trish navigated to the paper's homepage. She waited a second, then hit refresh. It was like all her Christmas wishes had been rolled into one.

CHRISTMAS BANK BUNGLE: CHAOS AS NATIONAL BANK CUSTOMERS WRONGLY CREDITED WITH THOUSANDS OF POUNDS... WHILE WEBSITE CRASHES AHEAD OF YEAR'S BIGGEST SHOPPING DAY

* Thousands of account holders erroneously given up to £9,000 credit
* Customers unable to access mobile and online accounts
* Telephone banking service shut down at 5 p.m.

By TRISH DIXON FOR MAILONLINE
PUBLISHED: 18:25 GMT, 25 December 2024

27

FOR THE MOMENT, Kellett's newfound composure held. He even kept it cool, by his standards, when his call to Pattie Boyle was met with a voicemail in her thick Glaswegian accent. Typical, he thought. The stupid cow was probably passed out under a table somewhere.

Pattie was one of life's straight-talkers; that was why Kellett had hired her. His message, therefore, was suitably short and to the point: 'If you still want to be in your fucking job tomorrow, call me.'

Next, he called Christina. After years of working for Kellett, the PA knew better than to turn her phone off, regardless of the day or time. She put up with more than most people knew, but she stuck with Kellett for the money. Every day, her salary took her further away from the estate where she had grown up. And when her phone rang on the evening of Christmas Day, she swallowed her distaste and answered it, as she always did. Predictably, Kellett made no pretence at festive niceties.

'Listen,' he instructed. 'I need you to get me back to London, right now. It doesn't matter how much it costs. Private jet, whatever, just get me back tonight. Second, send someone round to Pattie Boyle's flat. Find whatever rock she's crawled under and tell her to switch her fucking phone on. Lastly, organise an ExCo meeting for 7 a.m. tomorrow. Everyone. No excuses. You, too.'

'Including Rob Tanner?' asked Christina, her voice rich with artificial sweetness.

'What?' Kellett was momentarily flustered. 'Oh, er, no. Leave Tanner to me.'

28

PATTIE BOYLE WAS LAID OUT on her sofa, her breath an irregular cadence of catches, snuffles and the occasional snort. In her dream, she was figure-skating effortlessly on a vast and empty expanse of ice, powdered snow rising finely in her wake. The near silence had been perfect, the only sound the swishing of her blades, but now there was a discordant ringing in the background. She woke with a start – it was the front doorbell. She stumbled to the door of her flat, scratching at her armpit, and pressed the intercom.

'What the feck's going on?'

'Courier.' A man's voice came through the tinny speakers. 'Strict instructions not to leave without delivering a letter.'

'On Christmas Day? You're having a laugh.' Pattie blinked away sleep. Her head was clearing a little from the effects of too much wine and too short a nap. 'What kind of eejit d'ya take me for? Be off with ya.'

'It's from a Christina Ferreira? At National Bank?'

'What?' Pattie blew out her cheeks. 'Hang on, I'm coming down.'

She made her way downstairs, taking in the sounds of festivities eddying from the neighbouring flats. Corny Christmas music was playing in one, and a line of syrupy-thick, TV-movie dialogue came from another, followed by a burst of laughter. When she reached the front door, she peered through the peephole. There was indeed a motorbike outside and a courier, helmet in hand, on the doorstep.

Pattie took the delivery, shut the door and looked at the envelope. Don't die wondering, she told herself. As she opened the envelope, the colour—a ruddy, Shiraz red—drained from her face. Inside was a simple, typed message.

"Pattie. Martin needs to speak to you urgently. But call me first. Christina."

Pattie retraced her steps and turned her phone on. Shite, why had she turned the bloody thing off in the first place? Because she was half-cut and wanted a peaceful snooze, that's why! And because it was sodding Christmas Day! The phone pinged angrily to life and a stream of red notifications lit up the message, phone and email icons.

She started with the voicemails. The first was from Kellett, requesting a call in his own inimitable style. She was still digesting that as the second began. An unfamiliar voice.

'Hello, Pattie. This is Trish Dixon from *MailOnline*. Sorry to disturb you at Christmas, but I'd love a comment on the computer problems you're having at National Bank. My number is—'

Pattie's face twisted in a grim rictus of shock. Why would a hack be calling now, long after all the computer problems had been sorted? The girl must just be following up. A laggard seduced by a non-story. Old news on a quiet day. Then Pattie stopped, remembering Christina's note.

Pattie dialled and started to pace the cramped living room. She let her legs carry her as she waited for Christina to pick up, skirting the mismatched sofa, the tables rimmed with cup-marks, the old armchair whose provenance she would never know. An ashtray brimmed onto the carpet at her feet. Pattie made more money than most people could dream of; that didn't mean she knew what to do with it. After a few rings, Christina answered.

'Hi, Pattie. Merry Christmas.'

'Is it?' asked the comms chief.

'No,' sighed Christina. 'I don't think it is. Kellett's in a complete panic.

He had me organise a private jet to get him back, again, from Zermatt tonight. He's called a meeting of ExCo for seven o'clock tomorrow morning. And he wants to speak to you, pronto.'

Pattie exhaled and flopped herself down onto the sofa. The TV remote leapt from its cushion and landed on the floor. Pattie ignored it, reaching instead for her iPad. 'Okay,' she said. 'Thanks, darlin, I owe you. Anything else?'

'No. Well, yes: good luck!'

The snort that followed was all the rejoinder needed. Pattie hung up. She quickly checked the MailOnline website but there was nothing, thank God, so she called Kellett. The Toad answered on the first ring.

'Where the fuck have you been?' he snapped.

'And a Merry Christmas to you too, Martin,' offered Pattie, simultaneously hitting the X icon. She pinched the bridge of her nose and closed her eyes. When she opened them, she was met with a wall of abuse, glowing in the blue light of her tablet – hundreds, thousands, of X users tagging National Bank, complaining about everything under the sun. Pattie didn't need to ask, but she did anyway. 'What's happening?'

'A fucking disaster, that's what!'

'I'm just looking at X now. It's a total shower.'

'Just now?' Kellett queried tetchily. 'You're just checking *now*? Don't you have people doing that constantly? Why didn't they tell you?'

'Martin, it's Christmas fecking Day. Do you want to bellyache, or do you want to tell me what's going on, so we can make a plan?'

Kellett harrumphed but backed down. 'It's worse than you can imagine, Pattie. The hacker is back; more accounts have been tampered with. It looks like every account with a balance under a thousand pounds has been inflated, tenfold. *Every* account.'

'You're not serious?'

'Current accounts, savings, ISAs, business… the lot.'

'But that must be thousands of accounts?' Pattie didn't know whether to sound awed or terrified. She scrolled absently down the wall of posts; it seemed the barrage of abuse would never end.

'Hundreds of thousands, Pattie, maybe millions. We have over twenty million customer accounts. How many of them have only a few hundred pounds in them? So many we haven't even got a full risk report yet.'

'Dear God.'

'He's not fucking helping.'

'Give me a second to think, Martin.' Pattie dredged the befuddlement from her brain and weighed their options. 'Okay, here's what we do. First, we put up a proper statement on the website. Something anaemic but sincere. "Really sorry to hear that customers are having issues, unfortunately we're experiencing some intermittent problems, we're working as hard and as fast as we can to fix it, blah, blah, blah."'

'Yeah, yeah. What else?'

Pattie ignored the disdain. 'Then you need to speak to the papers. *You*, Martin. Reassure them we're taking it incredibly seriously. Not like that lot a couple of years back. You're personally not going to rest till it's fixed. No one's going to be out-of-pocket, et cetera.'

'Really?' The Toad wasn't so cocksure now.

'Third: you need someone to speak to the politicians, regulators, anyone who'll want your balls in a vice for this. You'll need Sir Peter.'

The mention of the Chairman drew an audible groan from Kellett, but Pattie pressed on. Or, she tried to, at least.

'Fourth…' Pattie trailed off as she tapped a link to a just-published *MailOnline* article, embedded in one of the latest X complaints. 'Oh SHITE!'

'What?'

'Now we're in it,' she said, her voice darker than a Glasgow winter.

'What?!'

'You need to look at *MailOnline*, Martin. I'm afraid we've just become the lead story on the most popular news website in the world.'

29

TANNER HAD CERTAINLY KEPT the first three of his promises to Ashley: he'd turned off his phone, provided a damn good lunch and taken her on a bracing walk. And if they had failed to make a snowman, at least they watched one being built. Now he was preparing to honour the fifth commitment.

The kindling in the wood-burning stove had been pre-laid days ago, with a few dried pinecones for good measure. The application of a single match was enough to send the tinder roaring into life. Once he was sure it was set, Tanner added a couple of larger logs, and now the fire crackled cheerily as the dry wood began to burn. A scented candle gave off complementary aromas of cedar and winter fruit. The Christmas tree was wrapped with small ivory bulbs, and its silver and glass ornaments shone, reflecting the lights and the fire on their smooth surfaces.

Tanner had opened a bottle of dessert wine, and he and Ashley now faced one another, legs drawn comfortably up, glasses in hand, on the sofa. The brooding air of melancholy had dissipated on the walk home, and now they sat, talking easily about nothing at all and quietly enjoying the fire.

Ashley's skin appeared to glow in the warmth of the firelight. Her eyes, so bright in daylight, were almost black without it. Tanner wanted desperately to kiss her again but, just as the gloom in the park had passed, so too, it seemed, had the intimacy of their earlier embrace. What a contradiction, thought Tanner. He had never met anyone like her.

Ashley caught him staring and gave a quizzical smile. 'What?'

Tanner laughed in return. 'I was just having to remind myself that I've only known you for twenty-four hours. That hardly seems possible.'

'How so?'

'Normally, when you meet someone new, there's an element of tiptoeing about, keeping to safe topics of conversation, avoiding difficult stuff. You know, ten tips for first dates.'

'And?'

'It's not like that with you. I feel like we can talk about anything.' Tanner shook his head. 'Sorry, I know that sounds corny.'

'Maybe we met in a previous life?' asked Ashley, a playful expression warming her features.

'Reincarnation? No, I wouldn't be that lucky.'

Ashley returned his laugh with one of her own. 'Lucky! You might not think that if you got to know me better.'

'If?' Tanner left the question hang in the air.

'Well, I am only here on vacation, Rob,' Ashley reminded him. 'I'm supposed to be going back to the States on Friday.'

Tanner couldn't hide his disappointment. Ashley evidently caught it, and she turned up her smile accordingly. A flicker of mischief, a flame of desire, lit her eyes as she added, 'Unless I get a better offer, that is.'

Tanner looked up from the fire just as she was reaching forward, towards him. With surprising strength, she pinned him to the sofa in an embrace every bit as passionate as their first. All too gladly, Tanner gave in to her searching lips, enjoying the sensation as she knotted her hands in the back of his hair. He kissed back, eyes closed, feeling the comforting warmth of the fire as he quenched his desire for her, drinking her in like the wine they shared as afternoon turned to evening on this, the most perfect of days.

30

KELLETT HAD NO CHOICE – he had to phone Sir Peter. He couldn't risk the chairman learning the latest developments from the press; he could only pray it wasn't already too late.

Kellett's finger had been hovering over the green call button when his doorbell rang. Oh fuck, the taxi; he'd completely forgotten. He lumbered to the hall, grabbing a coat and his briefcase, and stepped out into the cold. With the coat slumped over his arm and the case banging against his leg, he locked the front door behind him and forced himself inelegantly into the electric shuttle. Once again, much too soon, he was saying goodbye to his little slice of heaven in Zermatt. Back to the purgatory of London and the hell of *van Aken*. With great reluctance, he called Sir Peter from the taxi.

The inflection in the chairman's urbane voice revealed more than a hint of surprise. 'Martin? Merry Christmas!'

'Yes, Sir Peter,' managed Kellett. 'Merry Christmas to you, too.'

'What the devil's that racket?' The chairman's tone now conveyed distaste, a want of festive cheer. 'Sounds like you're in a fairground!'

'I'm sorry, I'm in a taxi heading to the airport.'

'Well speak up, man. I can scarcely hear you.'

'Okay, give me a minute,' said Kellett. 'I'll see if the driver can pull over.'

Kellett sighed inwardly. He didn't want to relate the whole saga from the back of a shuttle, but what choice did he have? At least Sir Peter wouldn't be able to see—or smell—him sweating. And hopefully the chairman wouldn't have gone anywhere near a computer on Christmas Day. He'd have been too busy playing charades, or whatever it was the upper classes did at Christmas.

But Sir Peter Wilford was nobody's fool, least of all where Martin Kellett was concerned. The Toad had been the CEO when Sir Peter was appointed, and Kellett had given him no reason to make a change. After all, profits were at record levels, and the shareholders were more than happy. But he was aware of Kellett's reputation, and he had always worked on the principle that he'd trust the man as far as he could throw him – which was a very short distance, indeed.

It was to that end that Sir Peter now reached out for his grandson's tablet, which had been left on the coffee table beside his chair, and opened Chrome. Sir Peter wasn't one for social media, but it took no more than a Google search for "National Bank" to see that something was very wrong. A link to the *MailOnline* article at the head of the page was impossible to miss. Kellett's voice came back on the line just as Trish Dixon's exposé loaded.

'We have something of a situation, I'm afraid, Chairman.'

'Go on,' instructed Sir Peter, scanning the article as he waited for Kellett's reply.

'We seem to be having some computer problems, again.'

'Do you take me for a fool, Kellett?!' the chairman thundered. 'I know exactly what's going on. What I don't know is what you're doing to clear up the mess we're in.'

'I'm on my way to the airport right now. I've called a meeting of the Executive Committee for 7 a.m. tomorrow.'

'I didn't ask for an itinerary, Martin.' Sir Peter set the tablet down in disgust. 'I asked what you're doing to sort it out. What about Tanner and his American expert?'

'What about them, Chairman?'

'What have Rob and… Miss Markham, wasn't it? What have they come up with?'

A series of unconnected monosyllables came babbling down the line as Kellett struggled to think of an answer.

'And what do we think our risk liabilities are?'

'Liabilities? I—'

'Martin, correct me if I'm wrong,' interjected the chairman. He was tired of the bluster, weary of Kellett. 'Here's the situation, as I see it. The bank is experiencing the worst computer meltdown in its history. You've achieved nothing in the past twenty-four hours. You've no idea of the risk or potential liabilities. You're on the ski slopes, for Christ's sake! And I take it Tanner's gone AWOL, along with the external computer genius who I was led to believe represents the best chance of solving this mess? Would that be a fair summary?'

The silence at the end of the line was broken only by Kellett's ragged breath. The Toad gulped like a drowning man, fully waylaid by his fight for air.

Oh, Lord, thought Sir Peter. The oaf is going to have a heart attack! He duly softened his tone.

'Martin, let's get a plan in place. I want you to find Rob and Miss Markham. And I want a call back at eight o'clock to assure me that everything that possibly *can* be done is *being* done. Understood?'

'Yes, Chairman.'

At that, the line went dead.

Kellett set down his phone and looked at his watch. He could feel the interior of the shuttle closing in on him, like he was about to be crushed. It took five minutes of intense concentration—the driver checking his rear-view mirror in alarm all the while—but eventually Kellett was able to bring the heaving in his chest under control. Still wheezing, he called Christina.

'Are you alright, Martin?' she asked, although she knew from the sound he was making that he almost certainly wasn't.

'Don't worry about me,' Kellett panted. 'Got to find Tanner. He's not answering his phone. You've got to get a message to him, like you did with Pattie Boyle. Try the American woman too – Markham. She's at the Lanesborough. Just find Tanner and ask him to call me.' He paused. 'Say… *please*.'

The last invocation was so utterly out of character that Christina was momentarily silenced.

'Have you got that?' Kellett puffed.

'Yes, Martin. I've got it. Take care.'

Those last words, uttered entirely subconsciously in reaction to Kellett's obvious distress, were two more that took her by surprise.

31

THE PRIME MINISTER SURVEYED the remnants of his Christmas dinner. There were clean plates and smiles around the table. If any man alive possessed the knowledge of how to keep Christmas well, he reflected, it was Mr James Allen. Well, Mr *and Mrs* James Allen. Full of food and brimming with cheer, he raised a final toast to Anna, then took personal command of dishwashing. Wouldn't the electorate love to see him elbow deep in the sink? It was a shame there was no photographer with them. He finished just in time for the seven o'clock news.

'Good evening,' came the crisp, classic tones of the male newsreader – one who had been spared or overlooked in the BBC's desperate drive for regional accents. 'Hours ahead of one of the busiest shopping days of the year, National Bank appears to have been hit by a massive IT failure. All computer and mobile systems are down at the country's second largest bank. Customer service lines appear to have been switched off, and we're hearing that many of the bank's twenty million customers are reporting incorrect balances.'

The camera panned to another presenter, a woman. 'In other news, tonight: the King has used his Christmas message to...'

But Allen had already switched off – mentally, if not literally. He already knew precisely what the King's Christmas message said. He pulled out his mobile phone and tried to log into his National Bank account. Like millions up and down the country, he received the same error message. He felt an unaccountable frustration rising within him, an anger he often had to fight to keep in check. That was the trouble with life in the public eye: it only took one outburst, one unguarded moment, and you were finished.

But the last thing Allen needed was Boxing Day being ruined for millions of voters. The previous PM had always appeared to be on the back foot whenever a problem cropped up, and Allen was determined to be different. To be *seen to be different*, at least.

He dialled his chief of staff. She picked up on the third ring.

'Merry Christmas, Prime Minister.'

Even when answering the phone to an unexpected Christmas call from her boss, LJ Oladapo exuded confidence and control. She always did. It was part of why Allen liked her so much; she was one of those people who might be thrashing wildly beneath the surface, but from where he was sitting, she always looked like she was waving, not drowning.

'LJ, I really am terribly sorry to disturb you.' Allen forced a note of pained apology – a convincing one, too. He was good at conveying the impression that he cared; he was not one for letting his true apathy show. It explained why the voters liked him so much.

'It's okay, sir,' returned LJ. If she detected any insincerity, she didn't dwell on it. 'You've caught us in that post-dinner lull, arguing about whether to watch *Die Hard* or *Love Actually*. I want *Die Hard*, but Craig likes the soppy stuff.' Allen and LJ both laughed, and Allen gave thanks yet again for his own astute judgement in choosing this woman—the first—for the role. Smart, funny and empathetic – but tough as nails when necessary. And most importantly, always watching his back.

'What's the problem, sir?' she asked.

'Some breaking news. Apparently National Bank's systems have gone down. All of them.'

'Bloody hell. That won't be good for tomorrow's retail therapy.'

'My thoughts exactly.' Allen huffed. 'Anna's meant to be taking the kids to Norwich, and they're all with National, so it's not only voters at large who'll be unhappy.'

'I'll call my opposite number at the Treasury, sir. See what's going on.'

'Thanks, LJ. Banks really are useless nowadays. It's about time we did something to shake them up!' For a second, Allen sounded put out, but then, with his usual courtesy, the prime minister added, 'I am grateful, LJ. Merry Christmas.'

32

THE CHAIRMAN TRIED TANNER AGAIN, but his phone simply rang and rang. Sir Peter castigated himself for not listening to his Chief

Operating Officer the previous evening. He'd been taken in yesterday by Kellett's blithe reassurances on the phone – a stupid mistake when he couldn't see the bugger's face. Tanner had wanted to take every possible action in the face of the threat, do all the right things, and the Toad had scuppered him. With Sir Peter's help. Now they'd wasted twenty-four hours and all because he'd been too eager to believe that the moment of danger had miraculously passed. He had mistaken a Trojan horse for a Christmas gift.

The chairman caught his own reflection in the black glass of his phone. An old mug stared back, a stuffy relic left behind by the march of technology and society. He shot himself a reproachful look. He was damned if he didn't have a feeling in his water about this one. He thought for a moment, then dialled David Nash's office number. The risk chief answered immediately, just as one of the chairman's spaniels came lumbering into the room. Sir Peter set to scratching behind his faithful dog's ears as he spoke.

'Good evening, David. It's the chairman here.' Sir Peter knew Nash to be a sound man—nothing like the oddball Sorensen—but he also knew the strain he'd be under, both from the attacks and from Kellett. The chairman moved to put Nash at ease, ladling out an extra spoonful of honey.

'I know you're having a frightful time of it, but I wanted to tell you I'm very grateful for your efforts,' he opened. 'I also wanted to offer you a bit of moral support. And the practical kind, of course, if there's anything I can do?'

'That's kind, Chairman.' Nash sounded tired. 'It's been a hell of an afternoon.'

'Yes, Martin has given me the background. He told me what a good job you're doing.'

'Oh, really?'

'Yes of course. We can't do without you.' Sir Peter worried he'd laid the last on a bit thick, but there was an eager yearning to Nash's thanks that showed it had worked. The dog nuzzled at his palm as Sir Peter continued.

'David, here's the thing. Martin is stuck in a car, and I have to speak to the Bank of England and HM Treasury. So, give me the latest, will you?'

'Of course, Chairman. We don't have the full risk analysis yet, but, as you know, it's looking like every account with less than a thousand pounds is affected.'

Sir Peter almost dropped the phone. He most certainly did not know that! Kellett hadn't told him the extent of the problem, the lying toad. Oh, there would be repercussions for this! He steadied himself, then asked the dread question, 'How much are we looking at, David? Round numbers?'

Nash paused, as if girding himself for battle. 'If I had to guess,' he continued, 'I'd say it's about a quarter of our current accounts, fewer of the others. If we take a midpoint of five hundred pounds as the base, that would be about six million accounts, times five thousand pounds. So, we're looking at notional values in the range of twenty-seven billion.'

'Twenty-seven *billion*!' Sir Peter was incredulous. 'But David, that's half our market capitalisation!' He felt his blood run cold, but he knew he mustn't rattle Nash any further. He dredged a guffaw from somewhere. 'Good job we're going to sort it out!'

Nash laughed nervously in return.

'Is Rob, there, by any chance?' the chairman asked.

'Rob?'

'Yes, Rob Tanner.'

'But he's… he and Martin, they…'

Sir Peter adopted the tone that any of his children would have recognised from being "caught in the act," as their father invariably termed it. In those moments, Sir Peter had always become part father-confessor, part supportive parent. And no small part angel of impending doom if the truth—and it had better be the whole truth—were not told PDQ.

'David, I'm sure I don't need to remind you, but I am the chairman of this bank. Martin and Rob are members of *my* board. No one else's. So, I'll ask you once, and I want a straightforward, honest answer. Martin and Rob *what*?'

'Martin fired him, Chairman,' replied a bewildered Nash.

'Oh, dear God,' was all Sir Peter could muster.

33

LJ DID AS SHE HAD PROMISED and called her opposite number at the Treasury, Paul Benham. She'd always found Paul to be pretty dry.

Certainly not dim—you didn't get to work at the Treasury unless you had a brain the size of the national debt—nor even dull. Just dry. Difficult to engage in anything other than statistics and position papers. The only time he got animated was when departmental budget cuts were on the agenda. Fair to say, then, that he was not exactly the life and soul of the festive season.

'Happy Christmas, Paul,' offered LJ. 'Sorry to disturb you.'

Benham scoffed on the other end of the line. 'I suppose you're calling about National Bank?'

'How d'ya guess?'

There was no reciprocal banter; Benham simply launched into the facts. 'Based on social media reports, it looks like it all started between four and five o'clock. Presumably, they were doing a system upgrade and cocked it up, like TSB a few years back.'

'Oh, Lord,' said LJ. 'That went on for days.'

'Weeks, in some cases,' corrected Benham. 'And they were tiny compared to National Bank.'

LJ thought for a moment. This situation, as so many situations did, brought her grandmother to mind. LJ could practically hear her stern, admonishing tones, talking about the importance of having your own house in order, of never owing anything to anyone. LJ's grandmother had been a formidable woman, pulling herself up by her own bootstraps after LJ's grandfather disappeared. She wouldn't approve of this bank tomfoolery, the greed of lending and owing money you didn't have – money which wasn't really there. LJ took a deep breath and shook off the memory, falling as she did so into Benham's staccato rhythm.

'What can we do at our end?' she asked. 'The PM and his family are customers.'

'Not a lot, is the honest answer,' replied Benham. 'I've already been on to the regulators and asked them to find out what's going on. If they're not happy with the answer, they can send a team in. But at the end of the day, it's the bank's software. So, it's up to National's management to sort it.'

'What are they like?'

'The chairman's a safe pair of hands. Used to be one of us – a treasury mandarin. CEO's a nasty piece of work, but he's done an exceptional job, until now. The COO's very capable, too. The City likes the management team. Just goes to show.'

'Show what?'

'That any bank can drop the ball. No matter how big or "well run" they are.' LJ could hear the inverted commas in Benham's tone.

'So, who do you bank with, Paul?' asked LJ. She wasn't winding him up; she was genuinely interested.

'All of them.'

'Sorry?'

'I spread my money between them all.' A rare laugh came down the other end of the line, the dry chuckle of a serial cynic.

'Why?' asked LJ.

'Because they can't all go bust.'

34

TANNER FELT LIKE A DROWNING MAN returned to shore. After the first kiss on the sofa, Ashley had pressed herself on him with such increasing intensity that he found himself almost gasping for breath between each embrace. Not that he was complaining.

Ashley straddled him still, arms wrapped around his neck, kissing him with such unbridled hunger, such animal desire, that Tanner couldn't see past his thirst for her. Any of his normal thoughts—any concerns about the speed with which this fling had developed—were lost to the moment, swamped by passion. And then, like a storm that had blown itself out, Ashley suddenly stopped, leaving him with a last, lingering kiss of exquisite softness before she sighed happily and lay her head on his chest. He said nothing, but he wrapped an arm around her and held her tightly. Gradually, their breathing subsided to stillness. Neither wanted to break the spell, but it was Ashley who eventually spoke. Her words were so soft he barely heard them.

'Thank you for a lovely day, Rob.'

'It's not over yet, I hope.'

'No, we're only getting started. But I just want you to know it's been…' She paused, looking for the right word. 'Perfect.' Then the gaiety was back, and she was looking up at him with eager eyes. 'Now, there was something you never told me about. I want to hear about this Foundation of yours.'

Tanner was about to reply when the motion-sensitive outside light snapped on. A second later, he heard the gate being opened. Then the doorbell rang.

'Who the devil is that?' he said.

Tanner eased himself to his feet. He shrugged Ashley a look of mystification as she pulled herself up, gracefully tucking her legs beneath her. Tanner's puzzlement turned to astonishment upon opening the door and finding Christina Ferreira standing on the outdoor mat.

The PA answered his look with a grimace of regret.

'Sorry Rob. Might I come in for a moment?'

'Christina? Of course.'

Christina followed Tanner into the sitting room. She took one look at Ashley, perched on the sofa, then turned back to Tanner. Her expression was a puzzle; she seemed both apologetic and curious – and maybe something else.

'Oh,' she said. 'I'm sorry, Rob; I didn't know you had company. You know I wouldn't have disturbed you unless it was serious.'

'It's okay,' Tanner replied. He introduced the two women. They greeted one other with guarded smiles and watchful eyes. In Christina's case, an eyebrow may have been subtly cocked, as well. Tanner pointed towards an armchair. 'Let me take your coat. Can I offer you a drink?'

'No. Thank you. I won't be long.' Christina took the proffered chair without taking off her coat. Tanner sat opposite her.

'It's Martin,' explained Christina, eyes fixed on Tanner. 'Something terrible has happened.' Seeing the shock on his face, she hurriedly added, 'No, I don't mean that. Well, not yet anyway.' Quickly, she summarised the latest developments. 'He told me to find you.' She turned towards Ashley. 'And Ms Markham.'

Tanner turned instinctively towards Ashley, who met his glance with a blank look. He looked back to Christina, who was staring intently at the fire, seemingly mesmerised by the lick of the flames.

'What does he want?' Tanner asked.

'He asked if you'd call him,' Christina answered, eyes flitting back to Tanner's. '*Please.*'

Tanner sat back in surprise. 'He actually said—?'

'Yes, Rob. Those were his exact words.'

Tanner raised one hand to his temple and let out a deep breath. After a few seconds he asked, 'Anything else I should know?'

'No, that was the last I heard. He's on his way back from Zermatt now.'

Silence fell. Tanner closed his eyes and continued to massage up and down his forehead, lost in thought. Ashley and Christina eyed each other but said nothing. The silence was broken by a loud pop from the fire.

Tanner looked up. 'Sorry,' he said. 'I need a moment to think.' It was a monumental understatement; he needed far more than that. He had assured Ashley that his and Kellett's attitudes were utterly irreconcilable, that there would be no going back. He'd given his word, and he desperately wanted to get out and start afresh. Yet all he could hear in his head was his father telling him he'd failed to look after those in his care. Again.

'What are you going to do?' asked Christina.

'I'm not sure, yet.' Tanner stole a glance at Ashley. Her face betrayed little emotion, but those dark eyes were fixed intently on him. Fire glowed in her pupils. 'There's a lot to consider. But you can tell him I have the message. You've done all you can. As always.'

In the years of working as Kellett's PA, Christina had learned to recognise when she was being fobbed off. No matter how courteous the delivery.

'Rob,' she pressed. 'No one knows better than me what Martin's like, but surely this isn't about him? It's about the bank.' She made a final plea. 'What about all the good people who'll lose out? The customers, the shareholders? Your colleagues?'

Tanner raised his hands in submission. 'I've got the message.'

Christina stood and forced down her obvious disappointment. 'Thanks Rob,' she said, and then she turned to Ashley. 'And I'm sorry again for spoiling your evening.'

Ashley rose, reached out a hand, and reciprocated sweetly, but without warmth, 'Hey, you do what you have to do.'

The front door was opened, cheek-kisses were exchanged, and Christina was gone, back into the cold night from which she had come.

35

THE FEELING IN SIR PETER'S WATERS had developed into a chill creeping up his spine. The more he thought about his conversation with David Nash, the more he realised how little Kellett had told him. The chairman had instructed Kellett to call him back at 8 p.m., but he was damned if he was going to wait a minute longer. He rang Kellett's number and heard the overseas ringtone, followed by a nervous, 'Chairman?'

'Martin, I'm going to come straight to the point,' said Sir Peter. 'So shut up and listen.'

Kellett had never heard Sir Peter like this. He did as he was told.

'I am well aware that the scale of the problem is far greater than you led me to believe,' continued Sir Peter. 'I am also now aware that you have fired Rob Tanner, who is a member of *my* board. I'm expecting calls any minute from the governor's people and from the Treasury. Thank the Lord, they haven't already called, or I'd have been leading them up a very dangerous garden path. I've spent forty-five years building my reputation and, thanks to you, I could have destroyed it in minutes. But Martin, that's not going to happen, because you're going to come clean about everything that's happened from the start of this fiasco, and then we're going to fix it. And by we, I mean the Board, of which Rob Tanner is still a member.'

'Yes, Chairman,' replied Kellett. His voice was barely a whisper.

'I haven't finished, yet.' Sir Peter fought to contain his anger. 'If you leave out a single thing that I later find to be relevant, I'll have you not only drummed out of the City but investigated by each and every authority I have sway with, from my friend the home secretary all the way down. Therefore, I want you to reflect very carefully before you speak. I don't want excuses, or justifications or flannel. Just facts. Do I make myself clear?'

Kellett's voice was tremulous and his breathing ragged, but gradually both settled as he unburdened himself of the details: the ExCo discussion about Joen van Aken's first email; Tanner's determination that the bank be transparent and his resignation when Kellett disagreed; Tanner's reinstatement and firing; the latest JvA email and its image from The Seven Deadly Sins; the diabolical references and the writing on the wall. It all tumbled out in an extraordinary monologue, followed by a stunned silence.

Infuriated by his own lack of comprehension, Sir Peter spat his rage at Kellett. 'And you didn't think it necessary to tell me any of this before?'

'No, Chairman.'

'Then I'm afraid, Martin, that your career with the bank will be finished as soon as we're out of this mess. The only question is whether you can salvage anything of your reputation before you go.'

36

PATTIE BOYLE, TOO, was feeling decidedly uncomfortable. She knew the bank needed to get out a positive message to stem the tide of shite that was flooding social media. But that was easy to say and much harder to do.

Firstly, there was the fact that she, along with all the other comms chiefs from the big banks, had been called in to see the regulator that very autumn for a talking to. They had been cautioned in no uncertain terms that they were to be "proactive, open and transparent" and, on pain of death, "not allow anything misleading to be said." They'd been reminded that being "overly optimistic and complacent" in dealing with the public and the media no longer just meant fines for the banks, but P45s and appearances before Parliamentary Select Committees—or worse—for the individuals concerned.

Secondly, Pattie had always drummed into her team that any comms had to be SMART: Specific, Measurable, Achievable, Realistic and Timely. Whereas the boat she was now trying to navigate up shite creek had no smart features: not only was it missing a paddle, it had more holes than hull. She had no idea how many accounts were affected, or how severely, and not a clue how, when or by whom the problem would eventually be sorted.

The first thing she'd done was post a personal message from Kellett on X. Pattie was putting words into her boss's mouth, but she didn't have a choice. Neither did Kellett; Pattie had only set up his account twenty minutes ago.

> I want to offer a personal apology to all our customers for the temporary problems we're experiencing with our systems. I understand how frustrating this is and assure you we're doing everything to fix them.
>
> **Martin Kellett**
> @NatBankUKMartin

Next, she called Trish Dixon at *MailOnline*. There was no point hiding away or making excuses – sometimes you had to take responsibility and be ballsy, show a bit of contrition. More importantly, the lass at the paper had sounded young, so Pattie might be able to roll her a little. In the nicest possible way, of course.

'Bloody computer system update,' explained Pattie. She launched into her spiel before Trish even had time to pick up a notepad. 'One machine not talking to another machine because one thought it was Christmas lunch, the other Christmas dinner.' Pattie laughed heartily. 'Obviously, we're getting it sorted ASA-fucking-P. But I want to stress that no customers have suffered a loss because of this, and in the unlikely event that anyone's incurred expenses, we'll obviously look to reimburse them.'

Trish interrupted. 'But what about reports of customers seeing inflated balances on their accounts?'

'See what I mean?' laughed Pattie. 'No one's *lost* money.'

Trish made to jump on the comment, but it was all part of Pattie's patter. 'Trish, I'm pulling your leg. There's a serious message I'd like you to reflect in your article, which was very quick off the mark, I have to say. Obviously, we expect to have this sorted in a hurry, but it wouldn't hurt to remind people not to spend what they know isn't theirs. I'd add the usual guff about being more alert to potentially fraudulent activity on their accounts and what steps they should take, blah blah, but that's not the case here.' Well, that part was technically true. Probably.

Trish tried a further series of questions, all of which Pattie batted back, politician-style, with a finesse that would have impressed even James Allen.

The playbook here wasn't necessarily "the truth, the whole truth and nothing but the truth," but at least Pattie didn't say anything deliberately misleading. Eventually, Trish wrapped up her inquisition.

Pattie put the phone down and took a decent swig of Teeling's. What would her old dad say, her drinking Irish whiskey? She savoured the notes of the malt and the triumphant aftertaste of her conversation with the Dixon girl. Pattie had put Kellett firmly in the frame, and the *Mail* would have to take out that line about no one at the bank being available for comment – meaning she'd covered her own backside to boot. She took another sip of whiskey and felt the warmth rising inside her. That was a hell of a win-win if ever there was one.

37

ASHLEY HAD RESUMED HER POSITION on the sofa as soon as Christina left, legs tucked beneath her and one arm resting on the cushion. The smile was still there, but where Ashley's eyes had previously been filled with longing and warmth, they now regarded Tanner with cool enquiry.

'What are you going to do?' she asked.

Tanner shuffled beside her on the sofa. He put a hand on her knee and met her gaze.

'I'm torn,' he replied. 'I really am. I meant it when I said earlier that I'm through with Kellett. But I've spent all my working life at the bank. I can't pretend I don't care about it. For friends, for customers—selfishly, I suppose, for my reputation—I don't think I have any option but to call him. At least to find out what's going on.'

The corners of Ashley's mouth rose in sympathy, but a sadness settled in her eyes. She had a look of nostalgia, almost. Tanner couldn't shake that impression even as he recognised how ridiculous it was, given the vanishingly short time they had spent together.

'I understand,' she said. She laid her hand on top of his. 'And I know I'm the one being selfish. I shouldn't be putting myself before all those people. The bank's bigger than my little Christmas wish.'

'I'm sorry. You know it's the *last* thing…'

'It's okay. Do what you have to do.'

Tanner gave Ashley's leg a gentle squeeze, and she smiled sadly in response. With a sigh of resignation, he stood and went into the kitchen, where he had left his phone. No sooner had he turned it on than it was ringing. He answered.

'Thank God.' The relief in Sir Peter's usually unruffled tone was obvious. 'I'd almost given up hope of reaching you!' The chairman collected himself before he continued. 'Listen, Rob, I need to start with an apology for not backing you and your judgement. And I don't just mean yesterday but over the past couple of years. I've always known in my heart that Kellett is a wrong 'un, and that you've been the one keeping us on the side of the angels, but I was too cowardly to do anything about it. All too happy, you might say, to bask in reflected glory.'

Tanner fell headfirst into the ensuing silence. He didn't know how to respond, but thankfully, he didn't have to. After a short pause, Sir Peter continued.

'It's too easy to do nothing when everything looks fine on the surface,' he went on. 'I fell into the trap of my own pride. But I should have taken the hints that you—and plenty of others—were giving me. They say fish rots from the head down, and we've all known for a while that our headman is rotten. All I can say is that I'm sorry and I hope it's not too late to do something about it.'

Tanner was taken aback by the chairman's outpouring. He paced to the sink, where the washed-up evidence of a dinner for two was drying in the rack, and said, 'We all could have done more.'

'Possibly, but I'm the chairman and I should have shown leadership.' Then, as if merely saying the words aloud had cauterised a wound, Sir Peter's tone brightened. 'Anyway, what's done is done, so now we've got to fix the mess. Rob, I need you'.

'Of course, Chairman,' replied Tanner, without thinking. Sir Peter's bluntness was disarming. 'What do you need?'

'Not what – who. I want you to take over as CEO of National Bank. With immediate effect.'

Now Tanner really was stunned. 'But what about Martin?'

'We'll say he's taking a "temporary leave of absence" on medical advice, or something similar. The City will assume it's stress. Everyone will understand.

We'll get this fixed, and he can retire gracefully to a quieter life in the Alps, which is more than he deserves. What do you say Rob? Will you help me?'

The personal appeal played to all Tanner's deepest emotions: guilt, loyalty, the desire to do the right thing and, less altruistically, to prove people wrong. Sir Peter had him hooked.

'Don't worry, Chairman, I'm on it. I'll get a progress report and call you back.'

Tanner had been completely engrossed in the conversation, and it was only when he rang off and looked towards the sitting room that he remembered Ashley. He needed her, now, in a professional as well as personal capacity. But something was wrong. She was no longer sitting on the sofa but standing at the front door, re-shod in her winter boots and fastening her coat.

'Ashley! What's going on?'

She fixed him with a rueful smile. 'It's time to go.'

'But—'

'No buts, Rob. Like I said, you do what you have to do.' Her eyes shone again; could that faint glimmer really be a tear held barely in check? 'It was the loveliest, loveliest day, but all good things come to an end. It's just a bit sooner than I'd hoped.' She tried to force a smile. 'Seems you can take the boy out of the bank, but you can't take the bank out of the boy.'

Before Tanner could respond, Ashley stepped forward, took his chin in one hand and gently pulled his face down to hers. She fixed her lips to his in the slowest, softest kiss he had ever experienced.

Then, in a voice that was little more than a murmur, she added, 'Meat Loaf was wrong; five out of six ain't bad.' She turned and opened the door. And then she was gone, and Tanner—as usual—was alone.

38

SIR PETER WILFORD WAS A DECISIVE MAN BY NATURE. Confident in the knowledge that Rob Tanner would be taking control in London, he called Martin Kellett.

'Where are you, Martin?'

'I'm at the airport, Chairman.'

'Well, you can turn around and go back to your chalet,' Sir Peter instructed brusquely. 'You're no longer needed.' Short became sharp as his disdain for the man at the other end of the line took root. 'No, that's not quite it. Not required. Your services are no longer *required*, Martin. Understand? As of now, you're taking a "leave of absence" for personal reasons, which, to spare your reputation, we'll say is temporary. But I can assure you it won't be.'

'But, Chairman, you can't!'

'Really, Martin? I think you'll find that I can. I can fire you for cause right now, with loss of all your salary, accrued bonuses and stock. Would you rather we went that route?' Neither Sir Peter's tone nor his analysis brooked any argument. 'Enjoy your time in Switzerland, Martin. Oh, and lastly, you are not to disclose any information concerning the bank at any time – now or in the future. Or you will lose every penny of that financial interest. Once you've sent me a copy of the latest email from our attacker, you are expressly forbidden to contact any member of staff unless specifically requested by either me or Rob Tanner.'

'Tanner?' Kellett couldn't keep the surprise from his voice.

'Yes, Martin. Robert Tanner. Our new CEO.' He paused to allow the words to sink in. Then, with an exquisitely enunciated, '*Auf Wiedersehen,*' he hung up.

39

TANNER BREWED A POT OF STRONG COFFEE and made a series of calls to the members of the Executive Committee. His committee. In less than a day, they had gone from colleagues to ex-colleagues. Now they were not only colleagues again but subordinates. Ordinarily, a new boss might expect an element of discontent—or worse—from former equals on whom a peer had been foisted without warning and whose own hopes of advancement had been dampened in the process. But not here. The collective relief at Tanner's ascendancy and the Toad's demise was palpable, and Tanner was genuinely touched by the warmth of his colleagues' reaction.

Less welcome, and distinctly worrying, was the lack of progress. Neither David Nash's risk team nor Mike Sorensen's technology group had made any material discoveries as to the means or methods behind the security breach and account adjustments. In all previous cyber-attacks Tanner was aware of, there was some clue or trail to follow. Here, they'd found literally nothing.

Pattie Boyle had, at least, spoken to the financial journalists leading on the story. But the tide of social media complaints was building relentlessly as news of the problems spread and customers began to think about how all this might affect their Boxing Day shopping expeditions.

Faced with any intractable problem, Tanner resorted to basic principles: who, what, where, how, when and why? If he didn't want to be the CEO with the shortest tenure in City history, he'd have to work methodically through each of those until inspiration struck.

He started with the second email from Joen van Aken. Ten minutes poring over the references rekindled vague memories of Sunday School but left him none the wiser about their relevance to the current predicament. He decided to bite the bullet and call Kellett. After the day's events it was impossible to guess if the Toad would even pick up, but he did answer… and with unexpected politeness.

'Hello, Rob. Congratulations on your appointment. I tried to call, you know.'

'Thank you, Martin. My phone was off.' Tanner changed tack quickly; he had to banish Ashley from his mind, for now. Work came first. 'I just wondered if the new email meant anything to you?'

'What, that nonsense about deadly sins, laziness and demons?' asked Kellett. 'Biblical claptrap about being weighed and found wanting? Oh, it's all very meaningful stuff.' Sarcasm dripped down the line.

'But do you have any idea at all who might be responsible?'

The Toad's touchpaper was lit. 'No, Rob. At the moment, I don't have the faintest idea as to the identity of the fucker who has taken away my job, my reputation and pretty much everything I live for.' Kellett's voice turned to a rasp, the veneer of composure and reason stripped away. 'But I can tell you one thing. When I do find out who it is, I'll give them a punishment worthy of Hieronymus fucking Bosch himself. Now, is there anything else I can help you with?'

Images of medieval torment flashed again through Tanner's mind. He had the sense he would be haunted by those visions for a long time yet. He cut them and the call short. 'No, Martin, I don't believe there is.'

'Right. Well, in that case, fuck off!'

40

TANNER WAS TEMPTED TO CALL ASHLEY, but he knew she wouldn't pick up. How had he been such a fool? Getting involved personally in the first place, mixing business with pleasure, had been plain stupid, but he'd been so drawn to that extraordinary woman. Then, having somehow managed to attract her, he'd managed to blow it in five minutes. All he knew, as he paced his living room like a caged animal, was that he wanted her desperately and needed her urgently.

For the moment, Tanner recognised he had to bide his time and let Ashley cool off. But time was something he didn't have. The Boxing Day sales loomed hugely in his mind; National Bank would find itself in one hell of a black hole if customers started spending their inflated balances. In less than twelve hours, the shutters would come up and the card machines would blink into life, and yet the bank's brightest minds had achieved precisely nothing in the previous thirty. Tanner grabbed his laptop from the side table and positioned himself on the sofa, the same spot where, until so recently, Ashley had been sitting. Was the cushion still warm from her body, or was he imagining it? He pushed the thought away and called Sir Peter.

'Any news, Rob?' asked the chairman. There was a hopeful note to his tone.

'I'm afraid not, Chairman.'

'You can drop the "Chairman" and "Sir Peter" stuff, Rob. We're in this together now, sink or swim.'

'Yes, Peter,' replied Tanner haltingly. He opened his laptop, woke up the screen. 'It's the craziest thing. Nobody can find any evidence of the incursion. There's no trace of an attack. It's as if the whole architecture of the bank's systems has been changed at a stroke.'

'Who do you have leading on this?'

'Sorensen, of course.'

Sir Peter sighed. 'And you're sure you trust him?'

'Of course.' Tanner answered in a heartbeat. 'He's as smart as they come.'

'Then why hasn't he found anything?' queried Sir Peter. He paused a moment, as if thinking. 'Hold on a minute – you said the architecture of our systems has been changed. Maybe that means we need to find a different architect.'

'I don't follow,' responded Tanner. Sir Peter's words echoed in his mind. He could trust Mike, couldn't he? Idly, almost without thinking, he opened a new tab, typed the name "Hieronymus Bosch." He hit search.

'Maybe it's time to go back to basics,' offered the chairman, cutting short Tanner's thoughts.

'We're trying, but the problem is that the architecture—the foundations, the bricks, so to speak—were laid forty, fifty, even sixty years ago and have been built on relentlessly since.'

'Then you'll need an architect as ancient as me,' Sir Peter suggested, with a laugh.

'Not necessarily,' said Tanner. The house was dead quiet in the second's pause that followed. 'But you have given me an idea, although it doesn't solve our immediate problem.' Tanner's voice took on a sombre tone. 'Short of a miracle, we're not going to find a solution in the next few hours. Our customers are going to be hitting the shops first thing tomorrow and, to be blunt, probably a quarter of them have seriously overstated balances.'

On the other end of the line, Sir Peter inhaled deeply. 'Then we have a straightforward choice, don't we? We either block their accounts or we don't. Which is it to be?'

Tanner weighed the options. 'If we block accounts, particularly with no guarantee as to when the problem will be resolved, there will be a shi… firestorm to end all storms. The bank's reputation—*our* reputations—will be tarnished for an awfully long time, probably permanently.'

'We can't have that,' huffed the chairman. 'Bloody Kellett! But if we let customers spend willy-nilly?' The very idea sounded positively distasteful.

'At least it's only smaller accounts that are compromised.'

'Twenty-seven billion pounds' worth! That's not a small number in my book.'

'I can't argue with that,' agreed Tanner. He had zoomed into Bosch's *Garden* while he was talking, and now his face was washed in red and orange shades, fire and blood. 'But, bear in mind that for all the adjustments, no actual transactions have gone through yet. It's a bank holiday. So, in terms of what funds customers can legitimately spend, they need only look at their closing balances last night. Yes, they could spend more than they ought to, but if we go out with an honest message, I don't believe many will overspend *deliberately*.'

'You're being very trusting.' The chairman paused to consider Tanner's suggestion. 'I'm not sure if that's very wise, very naïve, or very, very foolish.'

'Peter, I think there's a chance we can turn this in our favour. Be candid with people. Say to our customers: "Look, we're under attack, but we trust you."' Again, the fire, and the unheard screams, choking in burning throats. Tanner zoomed out, taking in the whole painting: the pink-hued scenes of Earthly indulgence and the innocence of man's genesis. 'People have lost trust in banks over the last decade. Perhaps this might help gain a little back.'

'So, you're effectively betting the bank on people's good nature?'

'I hadn't thought of it like that, but yes, I'm prepared to make that bet.'

'All right, fine. I'm with you. What else do we need to do?'

Tanner spent ten minutes running through a comprehensive action plan of practicalities, involving communications with customers, regulators, advisers, funders and every other stakeholder that might conceivably be affected. He was happy to enjoy a moment's silence at the end of it as Sir Peter digested the raft of detail.

Eventually, Sir Peter responded. 'It strikes me you've left one thing out.'

'Left till last, Peter, but not forgotten,' corrected Tanner. '*Government*. If we're going to be open and honest about this, then we need support at the highest level. And frankly, given the scale of the problem, we may need more than verbal support. But first, we need to be seen as the good guys, not a target for political point-scoring.'

'Who do you want me to call?'

'I think we should go straight to the top.'

'Allen?'

'We haven't had a more popular PM for twenty years. If he's on our side, people will take it seriously. We'll gain credibility… and some breathing space.'

'Yes, but if you don't fix it quickly, the politicians will wash their hands of you.'

'They will anyway!' Tanner forced a laugh.

'Okay, Rob. I'll get through to his chief of staff. In the meantime, find that bloody architect.'

41

TANNER TOOK ONE LAST LOOK at the Bosch painting. It had taken Sir Peter's mention of architects for Tanner to properly notice the psychedelic constructions in the painting's background: strange, monumental things, spheres and spires elegantly fused, hued in blue and pink. But more importantly, whilst he didn't know any ageing software architects, Sir Peter's advice had given him an idea – something he should have done years ago. He opened a new tab and spent five fruitless minutes searching online for a half-forgotten name, now suddenly in the forefront of his mind after so many years. Then he picked up the phone to Tommy Steele.

'Evening, Thruppence,' said Tanner. 'And a very Merry Christmas.'

'And to you, Six. Or should I say *Boss*?'

Tanner laughed. 'I wouldn't worry about that, but I need your help. I need to find someone.'

'Woah.' Tommy was momentarily taken aback. 'I didn't expect that.' There was a pause as the request sunk in. Then, 'Problem?'

'Not as such,' replied Tanner. 'Well, no more than we already have. I just think there's someone who might be able to help us.'

'Who?'

'Holly Brand. We hired her as a tech graduate ten years ago. Probably the best we ever had. Then she fell out with Kellett over a warning which, at this moment, looks very prophetic indeed.' Tanner paused a second. 'Ringing any bells?'

'Oh, yes. I remember. Talk of the office, it was. She made a fool out of him in front of a roomful of people, right? Not a good career move. What happened to her?'

'That's the thing,' answered Tanner. 'I've no idea. I've just had a quick look in all the obvious online places, but there's no sign of her. Kellett warned her off in a very heavy-handed way. Threatened her with the regulators, the police, you name it, if she didn't leave the industry. Maybe she did something completely different or went somewhere else. She could be married, teaching yoga, dead? Who knows? But I'm sitting here wishing we had her on our team right now.' A little of the merriment came back into Tanner's voice. 'I thought with your *connections,* you might know someone who—'

'Knows someone?' The euphemism brought a familiar chuckle.

'Exactly.'

'Let me make a couple of calls,' offered Tommy. 'It should be doable unless she's gone off the grid and *really* doesn't want to be found.'

'Well, once she left the bank, Kellett would have completely forgotten about her, so I'm guessing she probably just moved on. There may even be one or two people here who are still in touch with her, but I don't want to distract anyone.'

'Gotcha,' said Tommy. 'I don't suppose you have any more information? The more you have, the easier it'll be to get things going.'

'No, I don't. But I'll get Ollie Lawrence to call you with whatever HR have on file. Off the record, of course. And, on the record—' Tanner waited a beat, '—thanks Thrup.'

'You're welcome, Six. It's good to have you back. You were gone so long, I was almost starting to miss you.'

42

ALL IT TOOK WAS A CALL TO AN OLD SCHOOL CHUM and Sir Peter had a number for the prime minister's chief of staff and an assurance that she would happily take his call in fifteen minutes. He had seen LJ Oladapo interviewed a number of times on television, and his friend's description of her tallied with his own impression: smart, straightforward and decent. He had asked for advice as to how he should deal with her. The reply—'Just be open and honest; she has the most accurate bullshitometer I've ever encountered'—was such an un-Etonian thing to say that further discussion was rendered unnecessary.

At the allotted time, 9.30 p.m., and on the second ring, Sir Peter's call was answered.

'Hello, this is LJ.'

'Good evening, LJ,' said Sir Peter. 'And a belated Merry Christmas. And my particular apologies for disturbing you during it.'

LJ noted the familiar patrician politeness and smiled inwardly. As chief of staff to a Conservative PM, she met regularly with lords, grandees and other exemplars of the "old school." And it seemed that no matter which educational establishment they'd attended, their manners had all been finished to the same, silver-spoon sheen. The great irony, she supposed, was that her grandmother, who had grown up dust poor, would have approved more than anyone of these aristocrats and their excessive courtesy. LJ's grandmother had always been a stickler for politeness, and when she heard it for the first time, she had been tickled by the accuracy of the old English aphorism: manners cost nothing. LJ wasn't certain that was strictly true, and she recalled her grandmother's fussy politeness as sometimes skirting into scraping deference. That was one habit, a legacy of her own upbringing, that LJ was still trying to unlearn.

'Don't worry, Sir Peter,' she replied now, trying to picture the face of the former mandarin on the other end of the line. 'I know you wouldn't be calling unless it was important. And I know you're a friend of the party.'

'Thank you, LJ. Now, I'll come straight to the point. I'm going to give you the truth and nothing but the truth. Unexpurgated. The only other person aware of the entire picture I'm about to give you is our new CEO, Rob Tanner.' Without waiting for a response, the National Bank chairman divulged everything. LJ listened, intent. She started taking notes, but then she stopped and just focused on digesting Sir Peter's words. It was a lot to take in.

When he had finished, LJ spent a few seconds forming her thoughts. Her first was that perhaps this Sir Peter wasn't quite as typical as she had suspected. And she rarely missed the mark on these sorts of things.

In fact, Leah Jolaade Oladapo was a woman who collected life lessons, wrapping herself in the wisdom she accrued – much of it at a high price. An only child, raised as much by her grandmother as her mother, LJ had spent her entire childhood doing everything possible not to stand out. Which was ridiculous, given that she was usually and effortlessly the best at anything she attempted: studies, sport, art. Only when she'd won a place at Oxford did she finally begin to believe what a succession of schoolteachers had assured her since infancy: she really was smarter and more capable than most of her contemporaries. The new-found confidence had allowed her finally to be herself. Leah Jolaade became LJ, she stopped trying to look or be like anyone else, and most importantly, she gave up worrying about fitting in. People could take her as they found her. But she'd never lost the habit of thinking deliberately before she spoke, a holdout from her less-assured days which had served her well ever since.

'Three questions,' she said. 'If I may, Sir Peter.'

'Of course.'

'Firstly, what's the motive, in your opinion? Secondly, what's the *real* financial risk here? And thirdly, and please be candid, how can the PM help most effectively?'

Sir Peter was used to dealing with government insiders, even if few were as effortlessly incisive as LJ, so he wasted no time on caveats or context.

'On motive,' he answered, 'neither Rob nor I, nor anyone else I think, has the faintest idea. There's no sign of any fraudulent activity. No money has been withdrawn. So, at the moment, it's not a financial crime in the narrow sense of the term. Obviously, if it's not fixed by the time the markets open again on Friday there are potentially significant ramifications, but we're two days away from that.'

'So, for now, it's a primarily a question of reputational damage?'

'Absolutely. To the bank. And its *management*.' Sir Peter's emphasis on the last word conveyed acute personal discomfort.

'But there obviously *is* financial risk? Even if that's further down the line.'

The question drew a whale-like blow from the older man. 'If every customer whose balance has been tampered with spent every penny of that extra money tomorrow, we'd be short getting on for thirty billion. Now, I really don't think that's likely, but it does lead me on to your third question.'

'How so?'

'LJ, no one is more aware than me of the low esteem in which banks and bankers are held. But your party has, in the past, seen through some of that bluster, and more negative headlines won't help either of us. With hindsight, I should have moved Martin Kellett on sooner, but everyone in the City thinks he's a genius and there hadn't been the slightest inkling of anything truly untoward until now. However, that's the past. What matters now is that Rob Tanner is a good banker *and* a good man.'

'Understood,' acknowledged LJ. She knew what everyone said about bankers, but she wasn't the type to copy and paste her judgements from others. That was the kind of attitude that had done her family so much harm, the source of the discrimination faced by her mother and grandmother in the days when it meant even more than it did today to be a single Black woman in Britain, a Nigerian immigrant. 'So, how might the PM help?'

'We want to send a message that we're doing everything possible to sort out this mess,' said Sir Peter. 'We're not hiding anything, we'll accept any advice or help offered, and afterwards, we'll take any medicine we're given. If the PM stood up and said he's behind us because we're doing the right thing—and reminded customers of their personal responsibility to do the same—it would be enormously helpful.'

'And you're sure that Tanner's the right man for the job? You do know that the PM and his family bank with National?'

Sir Peter played the straight bat he'd learnt in his years at the Treasury. 'LJ, one thing I do know is that there's no one I would rather have running our bank than Rob Tanner. I trust him with my reputation, which is to say, I trust him with my life.'

'Fine,' concluded LJ. 'Then let's see what we can come up with.'

43

THE WORLD STOPPED AT THE LIMOSUINE'S WINDOWS. Kellett was utterly oblivious to the soaring peaks, the snow-covered trees, the pretty Alpine towns and villages. Martians might have landed on the road from Brig to Zermatt and he wouldn't have noticed. All he could see was his own reflection in the glass.

Kellett had never considered himself a weak man. He had idiosyncrasies, predilections, but nothing more than that. Nothing of which anyone had ever taken advantage. Until now. He seethed at his own stupidity. Why hadn't he shifted the blame sooner onto Nash, or that geek Sorensen? Sacrificed one of them to show he was taking action? Or, better, Tanner. Fucking Tanner. That would have served a better purpose. Two birds with one stone.

Instead, he had sat in mute surrender whilst that prissy fogey Peter

Wilford emasculated him with a few clipped sentences. The old buffer had been happy to sit in reflected glory while the share price was rising, as National Bank grew and grew until it was the second largest in the country. Then, at the first sign of trouble, he had simply thrown out Kellett like yesterday's newspaper.

It was only the conversation with Tanner that had rekindled Kellett's inner spark. Well, he thought, let them believe Martin Kellett has slunk off like an old cur ready to be put out of his misery. Now, while their attention was elsewhere, it was time for the real Martin to stand up.

He started with a call to Stefan Ziegler, his Swiss procurer.

'Ah, Martin!' Ziegler answered. 'I wasn't expecting to hear from you so soon. Surely you don't have the energy for another liaison? You are a lion!'

Kellett flinched at the unctuousness oozing down the phone, but he forced himself to conviviality.

'No, Stefan, you have excelled yourself already on that front. You are a prince among...' He struggled for a word: Pimps? Ponces? Parasites? 'Professionals.'

'You are too kind, Martin. But then, how may I assist you?'

'Stefan, I need a service.' Kellett smiled as he imagined the lurid images and their accompanying price tags flashing through Ziegler's mind. His reflection leered back at him. 'And no, not *that* kind of service.'

'Then what?'

'Stefan, listen. I'm not stupid. To do what you do, where you do it, with your clientele, you must have some pretty good connections.'

'Martin!' Ziegler feigned innocence. 'I don't know what you mean!'

'Stefan!' snapped Kellett. 'I said listen. It's nothing illegal, and nothing compared to the other stuff that you probably get up to. But I need to find someone. Quickly. Quietly. Surreptitiously. You understand?'

'Yes, Martin, I understand.' A brief pause suggested the procurer's mental cash register was already totting an unexpected fee. 'Maybe I can help you *surreptitiously*. I think we would say *sub rosa*.'

'Exactly, Stefan.' Kellett sat back in his seat; he was nearly back at his chalet, after all that ridiculous to-ing and fro-ing with the airport. '*Sub rosa*. Off-the-record. With no trail to me.'

'Yes, I think it is possible I might know someone.' Ziegler's voice had regained its habitual charm and confidence. 'But if you want it done surreptitiously and quickly, I fear it won't be cheap.'

'Is it ever?' Kellett let the query sit for a second. 'All is as I said, Stefan: you are a prince. I'll call you back in an hour with some details.'

Thieves, he realised as he hung up. That was it: a prince among thieves. And on the subject of thieves… what about the fools who had stolen his job?

Tanner had been wrong in his earlier assumption: Kellett had certainly not forgotten about Holly Brand – or indeed, about anyone else who had ever crossed him over the years. As soon as Kellett had turned the taxi around and regained a little composure after his defenestration, he had given rather more rational thought to the question of who might be responsible for his current predicament. He had dredged up a list of sinners deserving of retribution for past slights, both real and imagined. One incident, however, stuck particularly prominently in his throat – before today, the moment of his greatest humiliation. If word of that unfortunate episode had reached the chairman, consciously or not, it had probably influenced Sir Peter's decision to fire him.

Technology had brought his downfall, so Kellett would dish out some ice-cold revenge on the young woman who had shown him up in that arena all those years ago. An eye for an eye. What hurt most was that the bitch had clearly been right with her sticking plaster nonsense all along, and now she was going to pay for it.

Biblical? Oh, he'd give them fucking biblical.

44

IT TOOK TANNER LESS THAN FORTY MINUTES to drive the eerily silent streets from Hammersmith to the Bank's head office in the City. He probably shouldn't have taken the wheel, but if the day's events weren't sobering enough, the almost deserted thoroughfares seemed to offer their own kind of quiet assent. By coincidence, he arrived at the front entrance just as Pattie Boyle was stepping out of a taxi. He waited while she paid off the driver and was rewarded with a hug that tightened his ribs. Then came a whiff of alcohol that neither perfume nor mints could conceal. But any concern that Pattie was a bit worse for wear was immediately assuaged as she launched into action.

'That's enough standing around, you wee layabout. We've got Downing Street's press secretary to speak to.'

'We have?'

'Aye. The chairman spoke to a pal. The pal put him onto the PM's chief of staff. She spoke to the PM. Who spoke to his press secretary, Zack Hardy. Degrees of separation, they call it.' Pattie laughed. 'I call it the bloody old boys' network. Anyway, I've drafted a press release for us to put out. Now they're coming up with a form of words to show the PM's support.'

Tanner was astonished.

'What's that look for?' asked Pattie. 'Did you think I was some useless auld drunk on the whiskey?'

'Never, Pattie, but I didn't realise you'd been given a Superwoman costume for Christmas.'

'Aye. Sir Peter's giving them to everyone this year.' She smiled, and then tugged his arm to show she harboured no animus. 'Come on, we've got work to do.'

Five minutes later, they were in Tanner's office. The first editions of the next day's newspapers were fanned out on his desk, faintly warm from the printers. As expected for a traditionally slow news day, every publication led with the National Bank story. But rather than being vitriolic, there was an almost weary tone to the articles: here was yet another bank blunder to add to the ever-growing list.

Tanner nodded his approval to Pattie. 'I'd say we got away lightly. Shame it's only the first round.'

'Aye, the calm before the storm.' Pattie tried to laugh, but it was forced and came out as a sigh. 'Once they knew no one had lost any money and that everyone can still merrily hit the shops tomorrow, the spleen went out of it. Speaking of round two, here's the press release I'm suggesting.'

She handed him an A4 sheet bearing the National Bank logo. The release carried a personal message from the chairman, aimed squarely at customers. It read: "We have decided, in good faith, not to restrict our customers' usage of their accounts at this important time of year. They have trusted us for over 200 years, and we place our trust equally in them." It was blatant PR, but nicely done.

Tanner was impressed. His comms director might be old-school, but she was damn good. 'It's great, Pattie. Well done. No hostages to fortune, just facts… and a nice sentiment.'

'No more nasty bankers, eh?'

'Exactly.' Tanner leaned back in bis chair, rubbing his eyes. Through the window behind him, the City rose, its buildings like so many jagged spines. Closed for the holidays, the towers were like ghostly spectres in the Christmas night. The National Bank building was the only one with all the lights on. 'So, what's next?'

As if by magic, Pattie's phone rang. She switched it to speakerphone and placed it between them, atop the jumble of newspapers—loud headlines, op-eds about a refugee "invasion" alongside celebrity sex sidebars—on Tanner's desk. From the caller's tone, it was clear there would be no chit-chat.

'Hi, Pattie, it's Luke at Number Ten. Thanks for the press release. The minute it goes out, I'll call the key political correspondents and tell them the PM's been fully briefed and is one hundred percent supportive. Then, tomorrow morning, the PM will do a live link for *BBC Breakfast*.'

'You're kidding?' asked Pattie. It seemed she had outdone herself.

'I told you the PM is supportive. All his family bank with National. They have for generations. He takes this as a personal attack.'

Tanner and Pattie looked at each other in amazement, but the relief was short-lived. Tanner's mood clouded over the second Pattie hung up. Having the prime minister in their corner would make things a lot easier, Tanner knew, but the whole thing reeked of opportunism. It was classic James Allen, Mister Popularity. The man would never miss a chance to get in front of a camera and reinforce his image as a man of the people. Any excuse to go on about how his wife was off shopping like everyone else.

Tanner knew he should have been grateful—and he was—but he couldn't help wondering who was helping who here. And as he asked that question, he couldn't help hearing an answer in Ashley's voice. Tanner rose to his feet and walked to the window. He looked down at the city below, empty but for a single black cab, yellow-lit, in a canvas of white. Pure driven snow, he smiled to himself – the perfect cover for a grubby soul.

45

PATTIE'S PRESS RELEASE WOULD BE OUT ANY MINUTE. And the scheduled interviews would start soon after. Given the enormity of the news—that the nation's second largest bank had been laid low by a major cyber-attack—Tanner doubted there would be any let-up until late into the night. These were the last quiet moments he would have for a while, and he desperately wanted to use them to speak to Ashley. He had to try to explain, to apologise. It had been such a perfect day with her and then suddenly, like a mirage, gone.

Tanner didn't have the words, but he hoped they would come once he heard her voice. He shut his office door and sat at his desk, which was still cluttered with newspapers. He dialled her number and waited, watching the blinking of red beacons atop skyscrapers in the near distance and the navigation lights of a plane tracking high above them. Christmas colours in their wintry sky. The call went to voicemail.

'Ashley, it's Rob.' Deflated, Tanner searched for the right balance of regret and optimism. 'I'm so sorry the day ended the way it did. It was… it was the nicest day I can remember. I'd really like to speak to you. No, I'd really like to see you again. There's a lot to explain. Anyway, I just wanted to say I'm sorry. Bye'.

Tanner's voice ebbed as surely as his spirits as he hung up.

He leant forward, closed his eyes and massaged his forehead. What a mess. Losing Ashley was a personal blow, but right now, losing one of the world's leading cyber experts was a setback of far greater significance. He took a deep breath and turned to look at St Paul's. The cathedral was luminously resolute, as it was every night. But there was no inspiration beyond the glass, only the first flakes of renewed snowfall.

Tanner's introspection was interrupted by a knock at the door. Christina Ferreira. She grinned at the surprise on Tanner's face.

'What? she enquired, blithely. 'I am the CEO's PA, you know. And if he's working, then I should be too.'

'Christina? But how did you even know I had been promoted?'

The PA tapped the side of her nose. 'Ways and means, Rob. Ways and means.'

'You mean Tommy Steele?' Now a smile spread over Tanner's features as well. The expression transformed him, revealing the handsome, unburdened boy so rarely seen in recent years. He shook his head and laughed, then fixed her with a serious look. 'Thank you, Christina. I can't tell you how much I appreciate this.'

'Don't mention it, Rob. I'm on your side. Now, tell me how I can help.'

Tanner gave a rapid summary of the current state of events, leaving out only Ashley's abrupt departure. But Christina was too astute to miss the omission. She forced an innocence into her voice. 'And Ms. Markham?'

'She went back to her hotel.'

'I see.' Christina had been biting the inside of her lip, but now she affected a smile. 'Well, if I were you, I'd give her a while. It's been a long day for all of us.'

'And it's about to get longer.'

At that, Pattie poked her head around the door, which had been left open in Christina's wake.

'Sorry to interrupt,' she said. 'We're ready for you now.'

Tanner rose from his chair and focused on his head of comms. 'Any last words of advice?' he asked.

Pattie barked a laugh. 'Remember what Gareth Southgate said about Sven? "We needed Churchill, but we got Iain Duncan-Smith?" Make sure you're bloody Churchill.'

Tanner smiled. 'Blood, toil, tears and sweat it is then.'

As he made for the door, he chanced a final glance at the dome of St Paul's, resolute and proud amidst the renewed winter barrage. The famous photograph of the cathedral taken at the height of the Blitz—Christmas 1940—flashed into Tanner's mind. How he needed some of the fortitude it symbolised, this very different Christmas Night. He too had a war to fight, a very modern war. And that meant Ashley would have to wait.

DAY FOUR

BOXING DAY
THURSDAY 26 DECEMBER 2024

46

CHRISTMAS WAS OVER BY THE TIME Tanner was finished with the journalists. Or, more accurately: it was over by the time the journalists were finished with him. His words were already being hammered into the second and third editions of the nationals as he left the office and headed, at last, for home. All he could do was hope they had got the message: that he was determined to protect customers' interests, that the Government was fully behind him, and that he personally would not rest until the situation was resolved.

He finally crawled into bed, mind racing, at 1.30 a.m. He worried that his brain was too active for rest; he feared he would spend the night staring up at his ceiling, or worse, dwelling on the Bosch painting that so seemed to haunt him. But he needn't have worried. It felt like he had only just closed his eyes when his alarm went off, four hours later.

That morning, Tanner followed the routine he had stuck to his whole adult life, starting with a bleary cup of tea in the kitchen. He fixed himself a good breakfast: scrambled eggs on toast made with the best eggs—the yolks a bright and sunny orange—and butter from a stall in Berwick Street. He washed breakfast down with a smoothie and, of course, coffee. Tanner was particular about his coffee, regularly changing beans in search of the perfect mix (today it was Blue Mountain and Nicaraguan).

This was, more or less, how all his days started. The only difference was that today, as he cooked, he made a point of watching the morning news. National Bank was the lead story on every channel. The key soundbites had been lifted verbatim from the script Tanner and Patty had fed the media. So far, so good. He checked his phone: nothing from Ashley.

He shaved, showered and dressed, choosing a tailored, single-breasted dark blue suit and white shirt, with his favourite gold horseshoe cufflinks for luck. To these he added a mid-blue tie with a ball-juggling sea lion motif, Hermès animal ties being another unbreakable habit. It was his first day as CEO, and he was determined to look the part. Nor had the thought escaped him that he, too, might be on television by the end of the day.

47

NIKKI CHEUNG HAD TAKEN THE CALL at ten-thirty the previous evening. It had been the perfect late Christmas present: the gift of an interesting commission. Less than eight hours later, she was back at her desk, chipping away at this new project. Boxing Day was a bloated and redundant holiday as far as Nikki was concerned, and there was nothing else she'd rather be doing. Now, as she watched and waited for her computer to spit out its results, the memory of the previous night's conversation brought a smile.

'Nikki, I'm really sorry for disturbing you so late, and on Christmas Day, but it's rather urgent. My name's Tommy Steele.'

Nikki had been intrigued from the off. Although the name Tommy hadn't rung any bells, Nikki's father, a detective inspector of the Metropolitan Police, had talked over the years about various members of a Steele clan with whom he'd sparred. As far as crime families go, the Steeles had been at the Arthur Daley rather than the Reggie Kray end of the villainy spectrum. They had robbed only the Inland Revenue, but they had done so on a scale that had seriously ruffled her father's feathers and kept many of his colleagues up at night. Fair to say, then, that Nikki had heard many tales of the nefarious Steeles over the years, but there had been no mention of a Tommy. And she would have remembered if there had been. She didn't forget names, or places, or anything, really.

Such tales of criminality were part of the Cheung family's fabric. Nikki's grandfather had been a police officer back in Hong Kong, and her father had transferred from the colony to London after the '97 handover. She'd grown up with their respective tales of felonies, misdemeanours and much worse at the dinner table; stories from the most sordid nooks of Hong Kong and the dirtiest crannies of London. Sex and drug trafficking, gangland murders, she'd heard it all—too many times—and the Steeles were no triad. So, she had taken Tommy's call with an open mind.

'Please don't worry about the time,' she said. 'I get used to it in my line of business. But may I ask who gave you my number?'

The question drew a short, easy laugh. 'You won't believe this, but it was an acquaintance of your father's.'

Nikki's breath caught in her throat. Her father had died years ago, and yet she seemed forever destined to stumble across bittersweet traces of him wherever she went.

'Sorry,' answered Nikki, looking for the right words with a detective's determination. 'I don't really follow. Dad has been dead for a long time. Who do you mean? Which acquaintance?'

Tommy, picking up on Nikki's discomfort, softened his tone. 'I'm talking about someone he sent to prison. Years ago.'

Briefly lost for words, Nikki took a moment to digest this information.

'Well,' she offered at last. She smiled wryly. Her father had always been thorough; that barely narrowed it down. 'That's a first.'

'And yes,' ventured Tommy. 'Before you ask, my name is Tommy Steele, as in *Steele*. If he was still with us, I'm sure your father and I would know plenty of the same faces. But don't worry, I've never been involved with that side of my family's… activities. The thing is, I need a private investigator in a hurry. It's something completely above board, but I need someone I can trust completely.'

'Hang on,' replied Nikki. 'I'm just having a hard time following this. Are you saying it was a Steele, someone my father locked up, who suggested you talk to me?'

'A cousin, yes. He always said your father was the best—and the straightest—copper he ever encountered. He and your father used to talk; you see, they came to know each other pretty well. Must have been all those interviews, long nights in the cells. Typical everyday social interaction!' A wry laugh echoed on the line. 'Anyway, he said your old man raised you right, and that he always used to go around saying you were just like him… only smarter and tougher. I believe my cousin followed your career with some interest after that. His precise words were: "If she's available, you won't find better. It's lucky for us she didn't go into the force."' Tommy gave a stage cough. 'Not that anyone's doing anything dodgy anymore, obviously.'

'What a recommendation!' Nikki laughed, shrugging off the strangeness of the encounter. She was too grateful for these breadcrumbs of history, leftover memories of her parents, to care about anything else. 'Known and trusted by all the best retired criminals,' she affirmed happily. 'How can I help?'

Tommy explained National Bank's current situation, leaving nothing out.

'So where do I come in?' asked Nikki. 'I'm a freelance, licensed investigator. I'm no cyber expert.'

'We have to try everything we can think of to beat this attack,' answered Tommy. 'That means we have to try both the conventional and the *unconventional*. We had a genius young computer expert in the bank eight, nine years ago, name of Holly Brand, but Martin Kellett, the old boss, fired her. Rob Tanner, the new boss, wants to find her. If she can suggest one thing that no one else has come up with, it's a step forward. So, we'd like to contact her. But Rob did a quick search, and nothing came up. We don't have the resources or the know-how to go looking for her.'

'No leads at all?' asked Nikki.

'I'm afraid not. Just her CV, with her last known address, from nearly a decade ago, and a social security number.'

'Telephone number?'

'Dead. I tried.'

Nikki paused, looking for the right words. 'Tommy, however I say this it's going to sound rude, so I'll just say it. How can I be sure this is legit, given your family connections?'

'It's okay, Nikki. I understand. When I joined National, thirty years ago, I was checked out, and I've never had a record. Remember Nikki, you can choose your friends; you can't choose your family. And here's the thing with mine: one side of the family are honest law-abiding citizens, and the other half are…' He paused for effect.

'…taxi drivers.'

The database search finally spilled out its answer, jolting Nikki back to the moment, back to Boxing Day. She shook off her gentle smile at the memory of the strange call from Tommy Steele—and the cascading memories of her father the conversation had evoked—and looked up at her computer screen. Nothing new. She sat back and tapped the desk. She didn't know whether to be perturbed or not. Tommy had said this Holly Brand was a computer genius, so it wouldn't be wholly surprising if she'd decided to cover her tracks after Kellett had threatened her. And it had been far easier to go off the grid then than it was now, given the last decade's explosion in data collection and digitalisation.

Easier, but not easy. Nikki understood and feared the long arm of the surveillance state more than most – the power of digital scrutiny armed with AI. She hadn't been back to Hong Kong since the pandemic, but she still had relatives and acquaintances there who now felt the ever more powerful grip of those oppressive tentacles first-hand. That experience lent Nikki the conviction that Holly Brand, despite all her computer knowledge, would surely show up somewhere. Nikki had access to more databases – conventional and *unconventional*, to use Tommy's phrase – than anyone she knew outside the force. It was only a matter of time until something substantive came up, wasn't it?

Nikki had already been able to find addresses, financial records and credit checks—even travel details—for Holly Brand. They were there alright, all the usual traces we leave in the digital ether as we go about our lives. But then, like footsteps on a beach after the tide comes in, Holly's tracks stopped in August 2016. Nikki could find nothing after that. Not a single print, nor even a thread; there was no evidence of Holly's person having snagged anywhere online. Nikki tried searching chatrooms and forums on the dark web for any signs of a disgruntled ex-employee seeking revenge. She checked for new issuances in similar names. She wracked her brain and used every resource she possessed. Nothing.

There had been times in Nikki's career when she'd struggled to find an actual human being, the physical manifestation of a missing person, but she'd never completely and utterly failed to find a single electronic tag belonging to a live target. The desk-tapping started again.

'Interesting,' she exhaled. 'Very interesting.'

It was murky in her home office; the blinds were open, but the street beyond was dark and dead, still with that post-Christmas lethargy born of overeating and under-exercising. Nikki was glad she hadn't overdone it yesterday. Something told her she'd need all her wits about her for this one.

48

TANNER DROVE CAREFULLY along the deserted Westway. Gritting lorries had been out overnight, and twin snakes of salt and pepper tarmac stretched ahead in an otherwise whitewashed horizon. Sunrise wasn't until after eight this time of year, and even then, Tanner doubted much light would penetrate the heavy clouds above. He hoped the gloom was not an omen for the day.

Tanner enjoyed driving, and his despondency lifted as the car purred beneath him. Freed from the snarling congestion of the working week, the road was his private highway. It was still too early for even the keenest of bargain hunters to be heading for the sales, and anyone else in their right mind would still be tucked up warm and cosy in bed. At that, a brief thought of Ashley penetrated Tanner's concentration.

He forced his mind back to the present, to the plan of action for the day. Over the years, the Bank had regularly conducted emergency planning and disaster recovery exercises, but no one had ever considered the possibility of an attack on this scale. Joen van Aken was right: they had been lazy. And now it was down to him to sort it out.

What was the virtue that defeated sloth? Diligence? Effort? Industriousness? Well, from today, there would be no more industrious bank in the world. They would engage honestly and candidly with the best experts in every relevant field. They would take any and every action necessary, no matter the embarrassment or personal cost.

For the third time in as many days, Tanner's thoughts went back to that FROG meeting of nearly a decade ago. It had gone down in internal folklore: the time a graduate trainee had shown up the Toad on his home turf. It was like Brentford beating Manchester City at the Etihad. Holly Brand had become a legend, and she had paid the price with her job.

Of course, Tanner had tried to follow up with Holly after the event, but it was already too late by the time he got round to it. She had moved on. And soon enough, so did he. With the passing of the years, he forgot all about her – and he forgot about her warning. Her all-too-prescient warning of what might happen to a bank that kept relying on sticking plasters for security.

But Tanner dared to hope that maybe it wasn't too late. Maybe, even now, he could find a way to reward Holly for being right. And maybe he could salve his burning conscience with the same stroke.

49

YOU DIDN'T RUN THE PREMIER ESCORT SERVICE in a place like Zermatt without the assistance of a carefully chosen and generously rewarded cadre of connivers. And Stefan Ziegler was a master schmoozer, responsible for lubricating some of the greasiest palms in Switzerland. Everywhere he went, he weaved around himself a tangled web of favours; he traded rumours, he traded contacts. And all that industrious trade made him a powerful man, wealthy with knowledge and kompromat. Blind eyes were turned at his instigation, and the burden of bureaucracy always seemed a touch lighter in his presence. In return, he looked after his nest of collaborators, comprised of the most crooked officials and the wealthiest patrons. Those most useful to him, in other words.

Martin Kellett was good to Ziegler – he always had been. So, when Kellett had asked for the procurer's assistance in finding a missing person, Ziegler had been all too happy to help. As it happened, he knew just the man – a 'security professional' in Geneva whom he had engaged once or twice before. What's more, he was the sort of professional who had a reputation for getting results without asking the wrong kind of questions.

A private eye to Switzerland's rich and famous, Gérard Dumont was, indeed, "just the man." But at the same time, he was cut from a very different cloth to Ziegler, Kellett and those in their milieu.

The only son of a Swiss banker and a well-bred but headstrong English mother, Gérard had been brought up in a sumptuous house on the shores of Lake Geneva with the expectation that he would follow his father—as five preceding generations of first-born sons had done—into the family business. But life got in the way, as it so often does. To his father's immense disappointment, Gérard followed a different path, prompted by a successful spell in military intelligence as part of his national service. He took to investigations and analysis, and after leaving the military, he did well for himself as a freelancer. He cultivated a glean of exclusivity and propriety about his work by marketing himself to Swiss high society. His father had never approved, of course; it was that same high society which Gérard himself had been fated to join – not serve.

That same, disappointed father died just a week before Christmas. The funeral was still fresh, like so many clods of earth, as Gérard found himself at his father's old desk, answering a call from Stefan Ziegler, that awful spider in Zermatt with whom he'd had to liaise from time to time. It seemed Ziegler had another job for him: a missing woman, to be sought with utmost discretion.

This time, Gérard seriously considered turning down Ziegler's unexpected commission. There would be money in the job, of course, but nothing that could motivate him – particularly given his forthcoming inheritance. What did swing him, however, was that he had nothing else to do beside the morbid tedium of sorting his father's affairs, with that black hole of a week, the void of the festive period—Betwixtmas, some English newspapers were calling it—stretching ahead of him.

And Ziegler's proposal did sound interesting; it wasn't every day that young professionals became unmoored in time and space. From the sound of it, this girl, Holly Brand, had done a very good job of disappearing. So, Gérard said yes and asked Ziegler to send through everything he had. He didn't know why anyone would want to find this woman, and he didn't know who had retained Ziegler – who his real client was. But what he did know was that he needed a distraction from the grief which compounded itself with every desk drawer that yawned open, every sheaf of papers he had to file or throw away. And here one had presented itself.

50

A FRESH STACK OF NEWSPAPERS sat on Tanner's desk. The old ones, yesterday's news—made obsolete by Tanner and Pattie's late-night briefing—had been swept into the wastepaper basket. Tanner saw the National Bank building looming surreally on more than one front page. Another showed a mock-up of the National Bank website, an account with an infinite balance whose zeros kept on going and going, over and beyond the edge of the frame.

Pattie—eyes bleary, voice hoarse, mind sharp—started the morning by giving Tanner a thorough update on the social media reaction, a live temperature check of the bank's public image. Nobody was saying anything complimentary, but the tone had softened, for now. Clearly, there were serious questions to be asked about the bank's security systems, but there was also a sense that the gravitas of the situation spoke to deeper, darker forces at play than simple human incompetence. News of the prime minister's personal concern—and rumours that he was going to throw the government's weight squarely behind the bank—had at least checked the vitriol and agitation. Likewise, the bank's statement about trusting its customers to do the right thing.

As soon as she finished her update, Pattie glanced at her watch. She lurched for the TV remote with all the grace of a walrus slipping from an ice flow. The BBC credits were coming to an end, revealing the familiar *Breakfast* co-presenters in not-so-familiar festive jumpers. They took it in turns to summarise the night's news and tee up the next half-hour's features. Then the picture on the screen changed to show a female BBC Norfolk presenter under the white portico of an elegant Georgian farmhouse. The front door was open, and through it a perfectly framed shot revealed a large Christmas tree, aglow in warm light. In the gloomy, snow-flecked dawn, the entrance spoke of warmth, happiness and welcome.

Right on cue, a jumper-clad James Allen appeared. He took a moment to thank the broadcaster, then turned to speak directly to camera. There was no smile, only a look of profound concern, as the PM launched into a slickly-rehearsed speech assuring customers—'including my family'—that everything possible was being done to rectify the problems at National Bank. His face became almost severe as he delivered the final line, promising the perpetrators of the attack that they would feel 'the full weight of the law,' that oldest of political clichés. Then, in an instant, the severity melted like snow under a hairdryer. With boyish charm, Allen re-thanked the presenter, took a moment to wish viewers a merry Christmas and was gone. The camera panned out, giving a final glimpse of festive allure, and cut back to the studio.

'Fuck, but the bastard's good,' exhaled Pattie. Her tone was awed, almost reverential, despite herself. 'That creep is wasted as a politician. He should be in Hollywood.' She waited a few moments, as if in grudging hope of an encore, and then turned the TV off.

51

TANNER SPENT THE NEXT THIRTY MINUTES drawing up a list of the advisors he needed to call after the ExCo meeting. All the major professional services firms now had cyber-security units, and he knew that the bank's auditors and management consultants had already provided forensic support to Mike Sorensen's technology group. Now, Tanner would ask them for a significant increase in manpower, Christmas or no Christmas. Similarly, the Bank's IT systems experts and equipment providers would be tapped for extra resource. No expense would be spared in rectifying the failure. His failure.

With hindsight, it was painfully obvious that he should have taken a deeper personal interest in the bank's cyber security, but he'd always been happy to delegate to whoever was head of the technology group. Worse, Tanner had been personally involved in recruiting Mike Sorensen from one of the major US financial firms two years previously, believing a fresh perspective from Silicon Valley would keep the bank current. The Californian's quirks—the *Star Trek* and the beach look—had somehow provided an added gloss of modernity, rather than being a cause for concern.

Mike might be only the latest in a long succession of custodians, but at the end of the day, some responsibility for this crisis had lie with the CTO. It was fine to be Sir Peter's architect—or the builder or maintenance man—but you had to be the security guard too. Logic dictated that if anyone should have seen this coming, it was the American. Surely, he'd heard the story about Holly Brand? The brightest graduate in the tech cohort had pointed out a fatal flaw in the bank's infrastructure nearly a decade ago: there had been a backdoor, and it had been propped open all this time. How had Sorensen missed it? Why hadn't he or any of his predecessors acted on, or at least investigated, Holly's warning? How could he have been so negligent? Had nobody else been able to find this backdoor? Surely Mike couldn't have…? No, the idea was ridiculous.

For the umpteenth time, Tanner castigated himself for his own stupidity. Sorensen had done no more, no less, than Tanner himself. And it was Kellett who had dropped Holly Brand and her findings into the trash can. She'd been cancelled long before the term became fashionable, and he, Tanner, had accepted it along with everyone else.

His train of thought was derailed by a knock on the door. He looked up to see Christina, coffee in hand.

'Morning! I thought you might need this.' Christina smiled and set the cup on his desk. She was close enough that Tanner could smell her perfume. He wasn't sure he had ever been this close to her before. He looked at her, really looked at her, and realised how much she had changed in the last twenty-four hours. It was as if she had drawn energy and vitality from the crisis, like she was feeding off the bank's misfortune.

The cool, almost stern reserve that had been her stock-in-trade from her earliest days with Kellett had disappeared. The tautness in her face had melted away, and her shoulders were a touch straighter. She was wearing, for the first time Tanner could remember, something other than black or grey: namely a tailored Air Force blue dress. And today, subtly but surely, there was make-up where he swore none had been before.

'Good morning to you, Christina,' he said. It was an effort to keep the surprise from his voice.

'Chrissie, Rob, *Chrissie*.' She locked eyes with his. 'It's time for a fresh start. For all of us, I think.'

Tanner held her gaze. 'Yes, it is. There's a lot we need to do very differently from now on.'

Chrissie smiled once more and made to go.

'Honestly,' Tanner went on, speaking to her back. 'I mean it, *Chrissie*. Thank you.' He paused as she turned to face him again. 'And I don't just mean for the coffee. I know it can't have been easy working for Martin.'

'Thank you,' replied Chrissie. 'I know I shouldn't say it, what with everything that's going on, but today's the first day I've looked forward to going to work in a long, long time.'

Tanner gave a quiet nod of understanding. He had worked with Kellett for long enough to understand at least some of what he had put her through. Then, all other thoughts pushed aside, Tanner picked up the coffee and gave Chrissie a smile of maximum encouragement.

'Right. Let's get to ExCo and sort this out.'

52

NIKKI FORCED HERSELF TO WAIT UNTIL EIGHT-THIRTY. Then, unable to curb her curiosity any longer, she began to call in favours. She knew that working the phones at the crack of dawn on Boxing Day wasn't likely to win her many friends. But, she reasoned, it was nearly half an hour since daybreak, so there was no excuse to still be lying in bed. More importantly, those on the receiving end of her calls all owed her something.

'Only do favours for people who appreciate it enough to return them,' had been one of Nikki's father's favourite admonitions, followed by a finger-wagged coda: 'And don't call them in unless you *really* have to.'

It had taken Nikki half an hour's deliberation and a cup of tea to decide whether a simple missing-person case passed her father's test. Her head told her it didn't, *obviously*, but something else just kept nagging at her. Part of it was that she and Holly were the same age, their births just three weeks apart: Nikki's on 27th November and Holly's on 16th December, 1991. And Holly was an orphan, too.

Nikki tried, as a rule, to keep emotion out of her job, it was hard enough without adding the human dimension, but as she sat in the pre-dawn gloom she kept returning to a single thought. What if it were her, and something awful had happened, and nobody cared? So, she went over the known facts one more time.

An only child, Holly Brand had spent her early life in Farnborough in Hampshire, where her father had been an engineer. After his death in 1997, she moved with her mother, a teacher, to Harrogate in Yorkshire, where her mother had been born. Her mother died while Holly was at university in London, studying computer science at Imperial College. Then, graduation in 2014 and her first job at National Bank. She was twenty-four, and on the rise, when she was fired by Martin Kellett, at which point she effectively dropped off the radar.

People like Holly—smart, university-educated professionals—didn't just disappear overnight, not without a trace nor a good reason. Losing her second parent might have unmoored her somehow, but there were years between her mother's death and Holly's disappearance. And Nikki knew well enough what that loss was like; it happens to almost everyone, eventually, and life somehow goes on. It's not reason enough to disappear, no matter how much it hurts.

The sun had barely risen when Nikki got her first call back and her first let-down: the first contact she had tapped up for a lead had reached the same cul-de-sac as her. Then came another call, and another blank. And then another. And, after breakfast, yet another.

Nobody in any sphere, using any means, could find any recent trace of Holly Brand in any system. It was as if she had existed to a certain point, then simply un-existed. Here one minute, then completely and absolutely gone.

By now, it was clear to Nikki that either Holly was a genius who really didn't want to be found, or someone had gone to great lengths to hide her. Or Nikki realised with a jolt, she was already dead, gone before life had really started. But there was no record of any death certificate, she reminded herself. Holly was probably still alive, and Nikki still had options.

Of course, there would probably be a friend or two from university, and peers from Holly's school in Harrogate, but you couldn't exactly Facebook a stranger at 9 a.m. on Boxing Day without knowing a little more background. So, with the usual avenues of enquiry exhausted—and none of her professional contacts having had any luck either—Nikki supposed she would have to get out there and look for Holly Brand herself… the old-fashioned way.

53

THE MEMBERS OF EXCO WERE ALREADY GATHERED around the table as Tanner entered the boardroom. Despite the gravity of the situation, the atmosphere was still less tense than a typical meeting in the Kellett era.

Tanner sat at the head of the table and pointedly made eye contact with each of his subordinates. Outside, the sun was doing battle with winter clouds, and a weak but clean light trickled into the glass-walled boardroom.

'Okay,' Tanner began, forcing calm into his voice. 'Let's go around the table.'

David Nash started with an update on the latest risk analysis. The scenarios he presented increased sequentially in severity even as they declined rapidly in probability. His almost-worst-case-but-very-unlikely projections all saw the bank lose eye-watering sums of money. The doomsday scenario, vanishingly improbable but not impossible, was insolvency. A chill settled over the assembly at the mention of that word, anathema to bankers the world over.

Ingrid Kovacs, the bank's finance director, spoke next. She confirmed that the bank's own lenders were standing by with emergency loan facilities to demonstrate creditworthiness, even in the unlikely event of those upper limits being reached. The Bank of England and Prudential Regulation Authority were content that the bank had enough capital and loan facilities in place to meet its globally recognised requirements. This news was better received than Nash's dire projections.

Human resources director Ollie Lawrence gave an assurance that all staff members had been contacted directly by their line managers. Many had volunteered to come to work even before the internal announcement that anyone working over the holiday period would be given two extra days off in lieu.

Pattie was next, with an update on the comms front. The mood of press and the public was still fairly forgiving, she judged, and the PM's interview had been a great help.

Tanner's eyes moved slowly around the table. He assessed each colleague in turn, mentally taking the temperature of the situation.

'What I'm hearing,' he said, 'is that we're just about keeping our head above water. And that we're still likely to come through this in decent shape, provided we fix the problem soon. Which brings us to Mike. No pressure, then.'

Tanner turned to the Chief Technology Officer and, upon seeing his face, immediately came to regret his joke. The man had clearly been ravaged by the past couple of days.

Mike Sorensen was in his early forties, but until two days ago, most people would have placed him a solid five years younger. With a mop of fair hair, a year-round tan and a predilection for T-shirts and chinos, he maintained a surf-dude image befitting his native San Francisco. But now the staring, hollow eyes, sunken cheeks and jailhouse pallor suggested a man released from years of sunless incarceration in San Quentin. Even his hair seemed greyer somehow. Lifeless.

Tanner desperately wanted to ease the burden on his friend's shoulders. Out of all his senior colleagues, Sorensen was the one with whom Tanner would most happily share an after-work drink. Smart, interesting and funny, he usually radiated warmth and energy. Now it seemed as if every drop of vitality had been drained from him. Tanner gave him a smile of real affection.

'Mike, give us the latest, and then let's talk about what we can all do to help you.' Tanner's obvious sincerity sparked a little life into Sorensen's grim demeanour.

'Sure, Rob. Thanks.' Sorensen sucked a breath through clenched teeth. 'We're no closer to finding the actual cause or source, I'm afraid. We've been looking for an incursion, or series of incursions, and for manipulation of data, but every single road is a dead-end. It's almost impossible to imagine how anyone could have got in from the outside and left no trace whatsoever of how they did it.'

Tanner let the words sit. Then came the epiphany. He cursed himself for not having seen it sooner.

'So, you're saying this isn't an attack from outside the Bank? You're saying one of our own employees is almost certainly behind this?'

Sorensen flinched like Tanner had just primed a grenade, right there in the boardroom.

'I, um… I was just getting to that part. We've called in a team of independent consultants, and that's the conclusion they've all come up with. Now, bear in mind that we can't prove anything, at this stage. It's just our latest working theory.'

Tanner swore under his breath. He had just been made captain and already he was dealing with that most dangerous of situations: a mutiny. Sir Peter's distrust of Sorensen flashed in his mind like a semaphore.

'Let me get this straight,' said Tanner. 'There are no breaches in our firewall?'

Sorensen shook his head. 'No.'

'There's not a single sign of external tampering with data or programs?'

'No.' Then, for added emphasis, 'Not one.'

'Then surely it can only be—' Tanner searched unsuccessfully for a better phrase. 'An inside job.'

Tanner looked around the boardroom once more, meeting a wall of drawn faces. He found himself thinking suddenly in terms of suspects, grievances, and motives. And not the motives of malicious strangers – but of his friends and colleagues. It was no longer clear to him who he could trust.

'Are you okay, Mike?' Tanner asked. 'You don't look yourself.' Sorensen had a queasy expression, not unlike the look the American usually developed when talking to someone who confused *Star Wars* and *Star Trek*. Only this was worse.

'I'm okay,' the Californian replied. 'I don't want it to be true that the culprit is—or was—here at the Bank, but I just can't see what other explanation would hold water.' Sorensen looked around the room, as if running the same mental calculations as Tanner. 'I didn't want to say anything until the consultants were done with their assessments and it was beyond reasonable doubt. I'd have brought it to you sooner, otherwise.'

'It's fine, Mike.'

At this, David Nash cast a glance towards Sorensen.

'Is it fine?' asked Nash. 'Can we really say everything is okay when there's a chance the attacker is in this very room, sitting at this table?'

'Aye,' interjected Pattie. Her face flared to life with fiery indignation. 'If it's the case that one of us is behind this, isn't there an obvious suspect? You don't need fucking Poirot to tell you whose fingerprints are all over the dodgy tech.' She turned to Sorensen. 'I'm sorry, laddie, but you can see how this looks.'

'I know,' agreed Sorensen. He scratched at his scalp, ruffling his hair. 'I know how it looks. But you guys have to believe me; I was blindsided on this, just like you!' Sorensen looked to Tanner, an almost pleading expression on his face.

'Enough!' said Tanner, raising his palms for calm. He gave Pattie and Nash a firm look. 'Now's not the time for pointing fingers.' He turned to Sorensen and flashed what he hoped was a supportive smile. 'Mike. What can *we* do to help?'

The show of support worked. A little colour returned to the tech chief's face before he responded, pointedly looking from Nash to Pattie. 'We're bolstering external protection as a precaution, but our advisers confirm our defences are as good as any they're aware of. So, we have to find what's causing the system to override that from the inside. We'll need every member of the team, internal and external, to focus on identifying the person, or persons, responsible.'

'But how many of our people would have the ability or the access to sabotage us to this extent, Mike?' Tanner shook his head in barely registered disbelief. He didn't notice Pattie glaring across the table once again at the embattled CTO, her stare all the answer anyone would need. The sun moved behind a cloud, and the temperature in the boardroom dropped by another degree or two.

'Not many,' said Sorensen. 'That's why we need forensic investigators. Now we know to look for an attack from the inside, we might be able to find a clue somewhere.' Giving voice to the unthinkable seemed to have lanced the boil of despair and self-pity. A glint of renewed determination shone in his eyes.

It was Tanner who now needed an injection of optimism. It seemed there was nothing more to say – not until they uncovered a clue as to the traitor. As he dismissed the committee, Tanner made a point of looking into the eyes of every colleague, knowing that the attacker—who he still knew only as Joen van Aken—might have been in that very room all along.

54

TANNER RETURNED TO HIS OFFICE and sat heavily at his desk. He'd known in his gut that divining the perpetrator's motive would be the key to understanding the attacks. That JvA had personalised the emails to Kellett suggested a direct connection, and now they could say beyond reasonable doubt that it was an inside job. But which of his senior colleagues—and it had to be someone senior—would, let alone *could*, do something like this? Who was the real Joen van Aken?

Chrissie had noticed the grim look on Tanner's face as he passed. She gave him a minute before putting her head round the door.

'Coffee?' she asked.

Tanner sighed and forced a smile. 'Thanks, Chrissie. That would be good.'

Her eyes and voice united in kindly concern. 'We all have faith in you. I hope you know that.'

'Thanks, Chrissie. But let's start with that coffee.'

Chrissie turned, and Tanner watched her departing form. He was struck again by the strength of her inner conviction. Then he turned his attention to his computer screen. He didn't need to look beyond the first email.

TO: Robert.Tanner1@NatBank.uk
FROM: Joen van Aken
DATE: Thursday, 26 December 2024 at 10:00
Invidia

Hello, Rob.

Congratulations on your appointment. There were two dogs, and now there's only one. Martin won't be happy.

Did you Shop him? Or were you his Pet? Whatever happened between you Boys, your Behaviour will definitely have him on track 10. If not the B-side!

And don't look to Ben and Jack for inspiration. Their '04 movie is definitely doggie do.

I see that nice prime minister is helping you now. "Non est potestas Super Terram quae Comparetur ei. Job 41:24" (although that reference is wrong!).

But is Mr Allen the right sort of Leviathan? Maybe have a look at Hobbes's first part, because you definitely don't want to find yourself in the last, let alone following Aquinas or Binfeld's friends into the Hellmouth.

Anyway, let's hope the pair of you can agree to sort things out. Everyone's going to be counting on you...

Laters!

JvA

Tanner scanned the missive, then he reread it carefully, line by line, trying to make sense of every word. Having dealt with JvA's previous emails, he knew there would be subtext galore; the difference was that this latest message had been addressed directly to him. He knew also that the wedge of painting would be another of Hieronymus Bosch's seven deadly sins, just as before. Tanner returned to Wikipedia for a description.

"Envy (*invidia*): A couple standing in their doorway cast envious looks at a rich man with a hawk on his wrist and a servant to carry his heavy load for him, while their daughter flirts with a man standing outside her window, with her eye on the well-filled purse at his waist. The dogs illustrate the Flemish saying, "Two dogs and only one bone, no agreement." Was that behind the canine reference to him and Kellett?

Now the second paragraph caught Tanner's eye. He began typing but didn't get far before the answer to his query appeared: *Behaviour* (Pet Shop Boys album). Tanner followed the link to the last track. "*Jealousy!*" Released as a single in May 1991, with "*Losing My Mind*" as the B-side. Was Tanner beginning to lose his, or was it JvA who had a screw loose?

Envy, a further search told him, is when you want what someone else has, but jealousy is when you're worried someone's trying to take what you have. The implication of that couldn't be clearer, but so far JvA had been adding to accounts – not taking away. So far!

A repeat of the exercise with "Ben+Jack+04+movie" brought up a Ben Stiller and Jack Black comedy from that year, *Envy*, of which Tanner was completely unaware. The plot centred on a get-rich-quick scheme involving the invention of a spray that disintegrates dog faeces.

Tanner moved on to the Latin quote, expecting to see the translation of a straightforward Bible reference. Instead, the search engine threw up multiple links to *Leviathan*, a 1651 treatise by the political philosopher Thomas Hobbes. The quote—attributed to Job 41:24, but 41:33 in modern bibles—was on the original géometrique frontispiece and translates to: "There is no power on earth to be compared to him."

Delving further into one of the links, Tanner read that *Leviathan* was a four-part discourse on the nature of government. One of the earliest and most influential examples of social contract theory, no less. Part I was an account of human nature; the final part discusses the "Kingdom of Darkness" – in this case, the darkness of ignorance.

For a moment, Tanner was reminded of William Beveridge, the architect of the welfare state who had identified the "five giants" whose presence blocked the reconstruction of post-war Britain. Ignorance was one of Beveridge's giants, along with want, squalor, idleness and disease. Tanner remembered studying Beveridge at university, and his own voluntary work with the Foundation had been a further, first-hand education in the persistence and intransigence of the evils that hampered British society. How many more great ills would Beveridge identify if he were around today? Would he recoil from the Britain which had been made in his image – the same way that Joen van Aken seemed to be recoiling from the modern world, clinging to medieval allusions to a forgotten morality as a salve for our sins?

Tanner's head began to spin. Surely it was all gobbledygook?

Without realising what he was doing, he began following more links. He couldn't stop himself, and he practically disappeared down a rabbit hole of tangential information. Leviathan was a biblical sea-serpent, but also a prince of hell. Like the man-eating prince in Bosch's *Garden of Earthly Delights,* Tanner wondered? Another click took him to a page about the classification of demons, specifically the work of a German bishop, Peter Binsfeld, who, in 1589, published a list of the principal ones, based on the seven deadly sins:

Lucifer: Pride
Mammon: Greed
Asmodeus: Lust
Leviathan: Envy
Beelzebub: Gluttony
Satan: Wrath
Belphegor: Sloth

Belphegor and Leviathan again! More connections. Tanner took a deep breath and closed his eyes to compose himself. He bookmarked the page on Bosch's *Seven Deadly Sins*, certain that he would be back, and blew out his cheeks. How could you cram so much meaning into such a short email? He reread the final paragraph. "Everyone's going to be counting on you." On "the pair of you."

In true JvA style, the references to the prime minister were at once unambiguous and vague. Was he the man of incomparable power? Tanner hadn't the faintest idea, but he knew by now that JvA didn't waste words. He pressed the intercom to his PA's desk.

'Chrissie, forget the coffee. I need to speak to the prime minister's chief of staff. Urgently. Sir Peter has the number.'

55

CHRISSIE'S KNOCK CAME SOON AFTER. Tanner's new PA entered his office, an enigmatic smile painted across her face. She had an expression like the *Mona Lisa* brought to life: wary, perhaps, and yet faintly amused.

'LJ Oladapo's just on a call to the prime minister,' she began matter-of-factly, as if calls to Downing Street were an everyday occurrence in their world. 'She's going to call back as soon as she can. Meanwhile, there's someone here to see you.'

Chrissie moved to the side to let Tanner's visitor into his office. He couldn't help blurting out her name when he saw her; the intelligence burning in those eyes, the notes of mischief at the corners of her lips.

'Ashley!'

'I'll get that coffee,' Chrissie said. What was that look? Did she know something he didn't? Or was she… jealous? Envious, even? Either way, she shut the door on her way out, leaving Tanner and Ashley alone in the office.

Tanner stood, trying to find the right words. Ashley, seeing his discomfort, held her ground. In the end, both blurted out, 'I'm so sorry' at the same time. And then they laughed, a hairline crack in the ice which had frozen between them.

Tanner stepped around his desk, unsure of his next move. But then

Ashley gave him a smile of such undiluted pleasure that he instinctively grasped both her hands in his and squeezed them for all his worth.

'Ashley, I'm so sorry, I was such a fool. I should have made more of an effort to explain. I shouldn't have answered the phone when the bank came calling again. I should—' he ran momentarily out of words. 'I don't know what I should have done. But I do know that I shouldn't have let you leave last night.'

'And I shouldn't have left.' She fixed him again with that smile of hers and squeezed his hands in return. 'It was childish, and selfish, and I'm sorry. I just didn't want the day to end.'

At that moment, Chrissie returned with a tray of coffee, which she laid carefully in the centre of the small table by the window. The pavements below, not that anyone was looking, were showing the first signs of life. Hardy tourists, wrapped in scarves and coats, headed for St Paul's, The Tower of London or the West End sales. London buses were back, like Bob Cratchit, after their annual day of rest, and rather more punctual.

'Do you need anything for the call with LJ?' Chrissie asked.

Tanner appreciated the cue, the subtle offer of an escape route, and gave her a smile of appreciation.

'No thanks, Chrissie. It will be the perfect opportunity to bring Ashley up to speed.' He gestured for Ashley to sit and offered her coffee before he launched into a rapid summary of the latest developments.

'Yesterday was the best day I can remember,' he added. 'And I would really like to continue what we started. But I also need your help here, at the bank. I've been put in a position I didn't want, but now I have to see it through.' Tanner took a deep breath. 'Is there any chance that I can enlist the help of Miss Markham, the cyber expert, without damaging the relationship with Ashley, the woman who made my Christmas?'

Ashley hid her smile for a moment behind her coffee cup. Much too hot, the coffee burned her lips, her fingertips. 'You don't ask for much, do you?' she said.

'Not usually.'

Ashley studied him intently. She set her cup back down, the clink of the saucer loud in the quiet of the office. 'And in the longer term? Are you staying at National?'

'For the moment.' The lines at Tanner's mouth tightened. 'I can't look beyond each day.'

'Okay, Rob,' she replied. Her smile dimmed by a lumen or two, just enough for him to notice. 'Then we'll take it day by day and see how we go. But for today, it's *Ms* Markham. Not Ashley. Do we have a deal?' She extended her hand to seal the bargain.

'Deal,' agreed Tanner. It was an effort not to notice the softness of her skin, the prick of electricity as they touched for the first time since the previous night.

56

TANNER AND ASHLEY had just begun to talk strategy when the intercom buzzed. Chrissie had LJ Oladapo on the line.

'Hi, LJ,' answered Tanner. 'Thanks for calling back. I'm here with Ashley Markham, the US cyber expert who's helping us. Can I put you on speaker?'

'Of course.' LJ's confident tones were like a balm. 'What's up?'

'Two things. Firstly, I have an update: our tech guys are convinced that the attack couldn't have succeeded without some kind of internal involvement.'

'Internal?' The surprise in LJ's voice was unmistakeable.

'Yes, so we're obviously running every possible check to see where that trail leads.'

'Okay… and secondly?'

Tanner inhaled. 'Another email from JvA—*Joen van Aken*—and this time he mentions the prime minister specifically.'

'What?'

'Let me read it to you.'

When Tanner had finished, LJ said she needed a second or two to think. A second turned into half a minute, but just as Tanner was about to ask if she was still there, LJ's voice came back down the line. Her words carried the same surety, but the tone was a note lower and a beat slower, leaving no room for doubt that she was used to having her instructions followed to the letter.

'Here's what's going to happen. First, send me the correspondence. Second, I'm sending over someone from the National Cyber Security Centre to act as liaison. They're to be treated as having the PM's full personal authority. Third, I want a list of all members of staff who have had access to your systems.'

'But—' Tanner checked himself. Privacy considerations were the least of his worries. 'Yes, of course.'

'Start with the past twelve months. Get me those names in a hurry. Then go back three years. Then five.'

'Okay.' Tanner looked over at Ashley. She smiled, a look of encouragement to fill the silence.

Then, her voice brighter, as if struck by a moment of inspiration, LJ asked, 'Have you replied to this *JvA*? Did Kellett?'

'No,' said Tanner. 'I called you as soon as I received the new email, given the reference to the prime minister. And Kellett just thought JvA was a nutcase. Should I reply?'

LJ laughed. 'I can see why a conversation with a biblical, sin-obsessed nutter with a grudge against the financial system wouldn't be your first thought. But every piece of information is a data point. I think we might as well ask JvA what he wants.'

Tanner, seemingly for the hundredth time over the past few days, was struck by his own stupidity. Why hadn't he replied straight away? It was so obvious. He had to stop being reactive and take the fight to the enemy.

'Okay,' concluded LJ. 'That's all we can do right now. Thanks, Rob. You too, Ashley. Just make sure you fix this. *Fast.*'

The line went dead before either could answer, and Tanner and Ashley were left staring at each other, one man and one woman in the eye of a hurricane that could bring down a bank.

57

TRISH DIXON GLANCED AT THE ARRAY OF CLOCKS on the newsroom wall. She had done well with her National Bank scoop, she had enjoyed her fifteen minutes of fame, but now she was back to the dull day-to-day of the financial desk. What was that old saying? Tomorrow's fish and chip wrapper.

Thoroughly bored, she typed @NatBankUK into the X search bar. There were plenty of comments about the PM's support for the bank, despite its lethargic response to the attacks, but nothing appeared to have got in the way of the traditional Boxing Day retail therapy. On balance, the tone was pretty neutral.

Trish got up, grabbed a coffee from the machine and was back at her desk five minutes later. It didn't seem possible that time could move so slowly.

Her eye caught the still open X feed. And for a second, she was unable to take in what she was seeing. Whereas minutes ago there had been a slow stream of tame posts, there was now a sudden torrent of disbelief, anger and abuse. In the moments it took her to read the first few posts, a deluge of further comments had been posted. Within seconds, there were forty new results. Trish refreshed the page and began to read.

---

yardsy
@GlennTheYardman
@HSBC Trying to shop. Bank balance is wrong. No customer service. Are you @NatBankUK? Sort it!

Jill Knight
@ChillyJillyNights
@LloydsBank WTF? You're as bad as @NatBankUK. Why can't I access my account? 😡

KrishPatel
@LordKrishna7381
@Barclays Same shit as @NatBankUK. No service. NOTHING. Can't you fking fix it????

Christy S.
@InterstellarSellar
@NatWest Can't login 😭 Keep getting error messages. Is this to do with @NatBankUK?

Dan Hyde
@5MTHyde
@santanderuk hi. Is your OTP service down? I'm trying to pay someone @NatBankUK and can't get a code?

Every post was a complaint. And not just from National customers – there were references to all the banks. It was as if the whole banking system had tanked.

Trish stood on her chair and shouted for attention. The newsroom—usually a cacophonous place of clacking keys, expletive-laden instructions and frantic phone calls—fell quiet.

'Everyone, please stop what you're doing. I know this sounds weird, but will you all try to log into your bank accounts? Like, *now*?'

Her audience knew Trish had broken the National Bank story the previous afternoon. So, it was mostly with fascination—and no small measure of concern—that dozens of her colleagues reached for their phones.

Then came pandemonium.

58

LJ HAD JUST FINISHED READING JvA's latest email when her phone rang. It was Paul Benham from the Treasury. His greeting was sombre, even for him, and foreboding hollowed her stomach as he began to speak.

'I told you last night that the banks can't all go to pot,' he said. 'Well, it appears I was wrong: they can. And have. Now all the major banks are reporting widespread issues with manipulation of customer accounts – the same as National. We're talking millions of accounts.'

LJ sighed and leaned back in her desk chair, JvA's latest email open on the screen in front of her. Merry Christmas indeed.

'Tell me everything,' she instructed calmly, instinctively matching the Treasury man's economy with words.

'My entire team has been working in relays since you and I spoke last night,' said Benham. 'We've been checking Bank of England returns, money flows, inter-market prices, anything that's an indicator of unusual activity. At the same time, we've been in personal contact with the risk teams at all the major institutions on the hour, every hour. We've been following social media. And we've asked GCHQ and the security services to notify us of anything suspicious, no matter how small.'

'That's thorough.'

Benham continued, seemingly oblivious to the compliment. 'Until 10 a.m., there was nothing new at all. Lots of chatter around National Bank but, in essence, no change in the situation.'

'Then?'

'Then the heads of risk at all the other banks called, all within two minutes of one another. Data from the regulators began to spike. And within five minutes, a trickle of posts on social media became a tsunami.'

LJ rubbed at her eyes. It already seemed a very long time ago that she and Craig had been sat on the sofa with a box of chocolates between them, arguing about what film to watch. 'So, what have we got?'

'The same as National Bank. Every account with less than a thousand pounds has been adjusted. No, inflated, that's the word. It appears there isn't a single bank account in the UK now with less than a thousand pounds in it. And if you had nine hundred and ninety-nine pounds in your account yesterday, you've now got an extra zero. You're only a tenner short of ten grand.'

'How is that possible?' asked LJ. JvA's latest email swam before her, the words melting into one another, a cryptic soup of threat and menace.

'It isn't,' Benham replied, before hurriedly correcting himself. 'Well, it *shouldn't* be, on any known principle.'

LJ's mind turned immediately to damage limitation. 'Who knows the extent of this?'

'It's hard to say, I'm afraid. Internally, we report solely to the Permanent Secretary here at Treasury. Externally, we've notified the governor and deputy governors at the Bank of England, and that's it. But the risk teams at the various banks are bound to have compared notes. Despite our very clear instruction not to, I hasten to add.'

'Fuck!' Expletives from LJ were rare as snow at Christmas, but she couldn't prevent this one. 'Then the world and his wife already know.'

'I'm afraid that's probably the case.'

'Should we be? Afraid? You said this wasn't possible.'

'It's a Black Swan event.' Benham was musing aloud, his tone grounded in the Senior Common Room. 'Hugely consequential events that people never considered possible, but in fact, are easily explainable. But only in retrospect.'

'I know what a Black Swan is, thank you, Paul. Like Nine-Eleven.' Silence fell over the call, each lost in thought. LJ broke it with the all-important question. 'How much time do we have?'

'Some, LJ, but not a lot.' Benhams's uncharacteristic imprecision was only momentary. 'The London Stock Exchange is closed, but Boxing Day's not a public holiday in the US, so their markets will be opening in three hours' time. All the major UK banks have New York listings, so it's theoretically possible to trade their stock there, but the Americans have circuit-breaks to curb panic-selling. We can get through today relatively unscathed. Tomorrow in London's another matter; it's a normal trading day. So, to answer your question literally, twenty hours.'

LJ sighed again. 'Anything else I should be thinking about?' she asked.

'*Motive*,' said Benham. LJ found herself nodding along as he spoke. 'No money has been taken. It's not a crime in the sense of theft or fraud. Well, at least not yet. I can't get my head round it.'

Glancing at her computer screen, LJ was struck again by the Hieronymus Bosch pizza slice: the covetous couple, the green-eyed girl seduced by silver, two dogs fighting over a bone. Envy was everywhere, not least in the so-called corridors of power that she trod, and even at the best of times, it was difficult to know who wanted to help you and who wanted to screw you over and take everything you had. JvA certainly had a point.

LJ thanked Benham, making sure he would keep her in the loop, and hung up. She closed her eyes to shut out the image and gather her thoughts. Then she reached for her phone, thinking already about how to tell the prime minister that the National Bank contagion had spread.

59

TANNER CALLED MIKE SORENSEN and gave him the good news: Ashley was back and keen to help. In a little over a minute, the Californian was at Tanner's door, slightly breathless, having clearly run up the three stories from the technology floor. With something of his boyish energy visibly restored, he launched into a torrent of technical jargon while simultaneously beckoning for Ashley to follow him. Ashley went without demur, shrugging Tanner a smiling, wordless goodbye as she went.

That freed up Tanner to compose a reply to JvA. What on earth did you say to a biblical cyber-nutter with the power to break a bank? He'd barely started drafting when there was a pounding on his office door. It was his favourite force of nature: Pattie Boyle.

'You need to see something, Rob.' Pattie's unfeasibly plucked eyebrows arched towards the wall-mounted television, usually reserved for rolling financial news, as she reached for the remote.

The screen snapped on to BBC News. A reporter was doing a piece to camera. An enormous queue snaked behind him – men and women lined up, looking impatient, as if they were waiting to get into an Apple store on launch day. The ticker at the bottom of the screen read: "BREAKING NEWS: Cyber crisis worsens as customers of all major banks report problems with accounts."

Tanner's immediate reaction was entirely subconscious. Relief flooded through him. This latest news meant the attacks weren't just a National Bank problem. It wasn't *his* fault. Well, at least not all his fault. Then, with sickening clarity, he realised what he was looking at, and with that conscious realisation came shame at his own selfishness.

All those people were queuing for a cash machine. They weren't eager punters; they were desperate workers trying to withdraw tangible, hard cash before all their computer money vanished into the ether. Tanner recognised the danger immediately. These people were inadvertently building a nest of kindling, and Joen van Aken held the match. For the first time in generations, the country faced a real-life run on the banks.

But Pattie's brain was running a few seconds slower. 'At least it's not just us,' she said.

'Christ, Pattie!' Tanner leapt to his feet, venting the anger he now felt towards himself. 'This is as far from good news as it's possible to get. The financial system could cope with us having to sort out an IT mess. It could probably even survive a bank as big as us failing. But if all the banks are useless, we're all screwed. This could be financial Armageddon.'

Pattie had long thought Tanner the most imperturbable man she'd ever met. Even in the most difficult situations, when put under the utmost stress (usually by Martin Kellett), Tanner was invariably the calmest man in the room. But there was only one word for the look now on Tanner's face. It was dread. Classic B-movie, Hammer Horror dread.

60

JAMES ALLEN HEARD THE SPECIFIC TRILL of the ringtone dedicated to his Chief of Staff. With his family away shopping in Norwich, he had hoped to be left in peace for the morning – for just *one* morning. If LJ was calling, he doubted it would be good news.

'Hello, LJ,' he answered. 'I was just thinking of a poem we were made to learn at school: "I heard the bells on Christmas Day, their old, familiar carols play. And wild and sweet, the words repeat. Of peace on earth, good-will to men!"' He sighed. 'You're not calling with goodwill I take it?'

'No, Prime Minister.' LJ passed over her boss's recitation. 'It's the cyber-attacks. They've spread to the other big banks.'

'What?' Allen practically spat his coffee all over the red box on which his cup rested. 'All of them?' he asked.

'Yes, Prime Minister. Every small account at every major bank has been inflated so it now contains at least a thousand pounds. Accounts that previously had hundreds now have an extra zero. All of them.'

'Christ!' Allen looked to the window; Norfolk flat in the gloom beyond the glass. He took a deep breath. 'But no… what's the word I'm looking for?' he asked. 'Withdrawals? Theft? Blackmail?'

'No, Prime Minister. Nothing.'

Silence reigned as LJ waited for Allen take it all in. Each knew the other's style and idiosyncrasies, how to get the best out of one another. A partnership of social opposites anchored in conservative values: the Prime Minister's with the big 'C' of his personal, true-blue heroes, LJ's the small-c sort, influenced by her grandmother.

'So, let me get this straight,' said Allen. 'People with smaller balances are seeing notional alterations to their accounts, but nothing's actually happening to the money. It's like an accounting adjustment?'

'Yes, Prime Minister… until people start withdrawing that money, which they're already doing. And now there's the small matter that the country's largest banks might be *notionally* bust. They keep large cash reserves, of course, but only a portion of the total deposits. Artificially inflate the deposits, and the whole system of fractional reserve banking goes out the window.'

'Right!' Allen's voice deepened a tone, the surest of signs that his thoughts had already turned to action. 'We need to get on the front foot. We'll call an emergency COBRA meeting later this afternoon. Who should attend?'

'The chancellor, obviously,' replied LJ, having anticipated the question. 'The governor of the Bank of England or whichever of the deputy governors he delegates. The head of NCSC to co-ordinate with the security and intelligence services. The head of the police Financial Crime Unit. And, of course, the cabinet secretary. You'll want Jonathan to chair it?'

Allen thought for a moment. 'No. I'll lead, but with you as my nominated deputy.'

'Me, sir? It's usually the cab sec.' There was genuine surprise in LJ's voice.

Allen noted LJ's discomfort. The cabinet secretary was a safe pair of hands, but Allen's instinct told him they'd need more than that. And LJ was naturally attuned to digital, cyber and new technology in a way that Morse could never be.

'I know, LJ,' said Allen. 'But I've got a feeling this is going to require creativity and some shiny, new ways of thinking – not to mention getting a load of very different people to work together. Cyber-tech is a young person's game. None of that points, with due respect, to Jonathan.'

'If you're sure, Prime Minister. He's not going to be pleased.'

'Yes, I'm sure.' Allen's reply was definitive. 'Let's say 4 p.m. at the Cabinet Office. That should give you time to organise everyone.'

'Yes, Prime Minister.'

'Oh, and have someone from National Bank on standby to attend. They've had longest to look at this so far. Let's hope they'll have something useful to add.'

'Of course. Anything else, sir?'

'No, that covers it for now. Will you brief the press secretary? Have Zack come to Downing Street at three and we'll discuss how we handle the press before we go into COBRA.' Allen picked up his sheaf of papers—climate forecasts, trend reports, Foreign Office briefings—and straightened them against the desk. He would be in the car, on the way back to London, in minutes. 'Well done, LJ. By the way, do you know that Longfellow poem about Christmas I quoted?'

'I'm afraid not, Prime Minister.'

'It gets a lot worse before it gets better. But don't worry, it does end well.'

Allen couldn't help playing to an audience, if only one. He launched into party-conference baritone. '"The wrong shall fail, the right prevail, with peace on earth, good-will to men." See you later, LJ.'

And with that final invocation, the line went dead.

61

TANNER REREAD THE EMAIL. It was pathetic. *He* was pathetic. But as LJ had said, what could you say to a man like Joen van Aken? Tanner decided that brevity was best. As his wisest friend, Brin, had always said: 'Be brief, be bright, be gone.' It was with this maxim in mind that Tanner had composed his reply.

> TO: Joen van Aken
> FROM: Robert Tanner
> DATE: Thursday, 26 December 2024 at 10:37
> RE: Invidia
>
> Dear JvA,
> You have me at a disadvantage. You know my name, but I don't know yours, so JvA will have to do.
> Thank you for your congratulations, although I suspect they're not wholly sincere. I'd rather not have received the promotion, to be honest – particularly in the circumstances.
> Much as I can appreciate the artistic and literary references of your emails, I'm afraid I'm missing the point of them. Sloth? Envy? If that's an accusation against me, or other senior managers in the bank, I'll happily take responsibility; I don't see how it's fair to hurt millions of innocent customers as a consequence.
> What is it you want from us?
> RT

In the end, Tanner reasoned, he could write and re-write his message a thousand times, and it would make no more sense. It was probably a waste of time anyway, so he bcc'd LJ, pressed send, and was done with it.

62

THE LAST KNOWN RESIDENCE on Holly Brand's personnel file was an address in SW9. Tommy Steele had sent over the file when he engaged Nikki's services, and despite all her online searches—and all the favours she had called in—there was nothing more for her to go on. She considered driving but reasoned that it would be far less hassle, given the weather, to take the tube to Stockwell and walk. Wrapped up in her new Max Mara down jacket—a fully-deserved Christmas present to herself (not least since she wouldn't be getting one from her ex)—and Highlander faux fur long boots, she was intrigued enough by the case of her missing twin that the prospect of more snow mattered not a jot.

Nikki was fit; she ate well and exercised daily, so she was not remotely bothered by the prospect of some old-fashioned legwork. Plus, her best friend had cooked a Christmas dinner to feed a small army the previous day. They had eaten together, just the two of them. Christmas could be a lonely time of year – a time when losses seem to be amplified, absences felt more keenly. The food had been a distraction. With the gym closed, a good walk was just what she needed to work off its lingering after-effects, regardless of the weather.

Holly's last address turned out to be on a quiet, tree-lined street stretching down to the heart of Brixton. Most of the houses were three-storey Victorian terraces, some converted into flats but many still intact as single properties. Holly's old house was opposite a modern school building. In the snow-expectant gloom, it was easy to see which properties showed signs of life and which were empty. As everywhere in the capital, too many were dark, their absentee owners having departed to second homes elsewhere or never having arrived in the first place. The unbridled blight of property for investment not inhabitation. Luckily, light shone from all three floors of Holly's former address and in both the adjacent premises.

Nikki pulled a photograph from her pocket. She doubted Holly's decade-old picture would be much help, however. It showed an oval-faced girl, young for her years, with a bad, dark bob. Nikki smiled at the memory of her own hairstyle disasters at the same age. Since then, she'd tried shaggy, spiky and pixie looks—you name it, so long as it was short—before settling on a peroxide blonde cut that accentuated both her features and her femininity.

She caught a warped reflection of that same blonde cut, atop an inquisitive face, on the silvered intercom panel. She rang the buzzer for the top-floor flat, and a man answered. 'Hello?'

'Hi,' said Nikki. 'I'm really sorry to bother you. My name's Nikki Cheung. I'm a licensed private investigator. Do you have a minute?'

'What is it?' came the man's voice, distorted by the tinny speaker.

'I'm looking for someone who lived here eight years ago,' said Nikki, trying for her sweetest, friendliest tone.

'Sorry, I only moved here in September. I can't help you.'

Nikki repeated the process with the neighbours, but nobody had been in the building for anywhere near long enough to be of help. Nobody had heard of a Holly Brand, and why would they have? Tenants moved all the time; the London rental market saw to that. Nikki was on the verge of giving up, but then Holly's old front door opened. It was the young woman from the ground floor – one of the people she had already spoken to and who supposedly knew nothing.

'We've had a thought,' the woman said. 'Try Mrs Morris, three doors down.' She lowered her voice. 'The rather shabby one. She's lived here forever.'

'Thank you,' replied Nikki. 'That's really helpful.'

A moment later, Nikki was standing outside the dilapidated front door. She knocked. Sounds of movement came from inside, and the drone of television chatter grew quieter. Nikki heard muffled footsteps, then a fumbling at the lock. At last, the door jammed open on a chain to reveal a sharp, quizzical face under tightly curled white hair.

'Yes?' enquired the old woman.

'Mrs Morris?' asked Nikki.

'Joan Morris, yes, that's me.'

'Hello, Mrs Morris,' offered Nikki. 'I'm a licensed private investigator. I'm looking for a missing woman who lived on this street eight years ago. Name of Holly Brand.'

'Holly?' asked Mrs Morris. 'She's not in any trouble, is she?'

'No, not at all. Quite the opposite, I hope.' Nikki flashed a comforting smile through the gap. 'Actually, I'm trying to find her to reassure myself that she's okay.'

'A private investigator, you say?' Mrs Morris fixed Nikki with a still-doubtful look, then laughed. 'We don't get many of those round here! Jehovah's Witnesses, yes. Scallywags selling stolen dishcloths. Even a few charity collectors. But not private detectives.'

Nikki took the cue. 'Mrs Morris, here's my licence, and—' she fumbled in her bag, '—here's some ID. And here's a photo of Holly.'

Mrs Morris gave a peremptory glance at Nikki's credentials, then a long, hard look at the image.

'Oh yes,' she beamed. 'That's our Holly.'

Doubt dispelled; Mrs Morris took the door off the latch. 'Come on, dear, you'll catch your death out there. Come in and let's have a nice cup of tea.' She pointed to the first door on the left, which opened on to a small sitting room. 'You go in and make yourself comfortable.'

Nikki took off her coat and made her way into the sitting room. There was a sofa, off to one side, and a television with an armchair squarely opposite it, replete with a deep indentation in the seat. Beside the armchair, on a small coffee table, rested a newspaper, a book, and a pair of spectacles. A radiator worked away in the corner but didn't appear to be giving off much heat. In was warmer in the room than outside on the street, but not sufficiently to stop Nikki pulling her coat back up over her shoulders.

Nikki listened to the sounds of tea being made in the kitchen before the old lady returned, slowly but steadily bearing a tray of tea and biscuits.

'I'm sorry, dear. I'm not as sprightly as I used to be.'

Nikki waited while Mrs Morris settled herself in the armchair. The old woman carefully poured and handed her a cup of tea.

'Now, what can I tell you about Holly? You say she's gone missing?'

'It's like she's dropped off the edge of the earth,' answered Nikki, accepting the tea with a smile. 'I'm looking for anything that might help me find her – information, mostly. What was she like? Were there any friends you might remember? A boyfriend? Anything at all.'

'Well, I can tell you that she didn't have any friends.'

The statement was so blunt, so absolute, that Nikki was taken aback. 'What? None at all?'

'No,' said Mrs Morris. 'That's what she was doing spending time with an old crone like me. My Ronald died ten years ago, just before Holly moved in down the road. I was all alone, and so was she. Neither of us had any family, nor any friends. My friends have all died, you see, and she never made any, from what I could tell. We got chatting when we bumped into each other one day, and we just hit it off.' Mrs Morris reached for the photo, studying the face in the crude bob.

'Such a nice girl. So smart. Attractive, too, not that she ever bothered about looks. She liked her sweet treats you see… comfort eating, they'd call it now. And I suppose I indulged it. I made us too many cakes.' A sad smile clouded the old woman's face. 'She lived for that job at the bank, but then they fired her. Fired her for doing her job too well! I think it broke her heart because she was never the same after that.'

The recollection seemed to drain the life from Mrs Morris, so Nikki waited before gently prompting, 'What happened?'

'She just walked in one morning and said, "Sorry Joanie, but I have to go. Too many bad memories. Other than you, of course!" "Go where?" I asked, but she just shrugged. I said, "Well, at least send me a postcard," but she replied, "Sorry Joanie, can't do that where I'm going." I didn't really think what she meant at the time. I was too shocked. I didn't think she'd never come back! And now she's gone missing, you say?'

The old lady's reserve cracked. Moisture welled at the corner of her eyes. She tried to dab it away with a handkerchief, hurriedly pulled from the inside of her cuff, but it was no good; the flow of tears could not be stemmed. Nikki rushed to put an arm around her, and only when Mr's Morris's hankie had been safely returned to its hiding place—and Nikki was sure the pain had subsided—did she release her grip and retake her seat.

'Can I do anything, Joan?' she asked.

'Just find out what happened to her dearie.' The old woman reached for her teacup with a shaking hand. 'I don't know that I could take another loss.'

63

TANNER WAS SOMWHERE DEEP INSIDE TEN DOWNING STREET. LJ had summoned him to the residence with just a few hours' notice, and now he sat in an anteroom with the air of a consultant's waiting room – albeit an extremely expensive one if the furniture was anything to go by. Given the intricacy of its detail, the small, double, chair-back settee on which he was perched was probably Chippendale. It was certainly as old as the ancient portraits of Britain's former leaders in the entrance hallway. The only other piece in the room, a slim grandfather (or was it a grandmother?) clock, was scarcely less modern.

Tanner's eyes kept returning to it. He'd arrived half an hour early for the four o'clock meeting, expecting laborious security checks, but had been whisked through so quickly he'd hardly had time to take in the famous surroundings. The hour had long since chimed, and he was still waiting.

Three days ago, he'd have said his life was pretty normal. In some ways it was dull, even. Sure, he had a ridiculously well-paid job which ought to have been interesting enough, but just like millions of others, he spent too much time, on any given day, on the mundane and the urgent, rather than the important. Now he was here, at the epicentre of government, tasked with helping the prime minister handle a catastrophe of unimaginable scale.

Or was it unthinkable? He'd spent the afternoon trying to answer that very question. Should the bank—should he—have seen this coming? Surely the lesson of the past few years was that our understanding of the possible was inherently flawed. There had been plenty of novels and movies over the years predicting pandemics, and yet the state of preparedness for a real one had been lamentable. Likewise, there had been stories about hacks and financial collapse, but no one had extrapolated those into a real-world cyber-disaster.

Tanner recognised if there was one lesson to be taken from previous crises, it was this: however bad you think it can get, assume it will get worse – and act fast. But what if there was no solution, no cyber-vaccine, for a week, or a month… or ever? What if every number in every bank account ceased to have any meaning? How would any of us survive such a collapse, and how would we rebuild a new world in its wake?

Unaccountably, Harry's face came to mind. Oh Christ, thought Tanner. He'd have to call his father later. Whatever else you might say about the old sod, he'd always worked hard and paid his way; he didn't rely on hand-outs from anyone. But what if he couldn't get his pension? What if he couldn't get any cash out next time he needed some shopping? If money was stripped of all meaning—if the banks failed and the government collapsed—it would be like going back in time to the centuries of subsistence farming and bartering. There would be mass unrest, certainly; global supply chains would break, and shortages and starvation would loom.

What was the saying? At any time, our fragile society is never more than nine missed meals away from anarchy. If the financial system collapsed, and supermarkets were cleared out, there was no limit to what otherwise moral people might do to protect themselves and their families. Public services would fail; the lights would go out, and the sick would be left to die.

In many ways, Tanner realised with a start, it would be like a return to the Middle Ages. To the days of none other than Hieronymus Bosch.

64

GÉRARD DUMONT LOOKED UP AND DOWN THE STREET. Getting to London had been painless enough, but crossing the city was an ordeal. There had been delays on the tube, as usual, and the roads were snarled beyond all sense. What they said was true: nobody in this country could handle a little snow. Perhaps he shouldn't have been surprised, but the taxi ride to south-west London seemed to have taken longer than the flight from Geneva.

Gérard was no stranger to the capital. Nowhere else in the world could be so awash with dirty money whilst at the same time maintaining such an impeccable aura of high-class respectability. As a result, Gérard's work often drew him into the megacity's labyrinthine crosshatch of shady greys. London was a magnet for the super-rich, or at least for their assets, and many a tangled investigation, particularly those concerning fraud or money laundering, had been unravelled here.

He had a suite at Claridge's to look forward to tonight, and he fully intended to dine out at Stefan Ziegler's expense. He certainly knew all the best spots; not only had his work brought him here but he had lived in the city for four years as a university student. But it no more felt like home than Geneva, Zurich or any of the other cities in which he'd lived over the years. He was, he supposed, a very modern man of the world:

cosmopolitan, multicultural and rootless, the sum product of twenty-five years of wandering.

Gérard had always been a clever, inquisitive boy, but that precocious child had soon grown into a querulous young adolescent. Having inherited his father's name and his mother's rebellious streak, he had found himself both constrained and bored by the narrow boundaries of his parents' natural habitat – in both a social and geographic sense. They sent him away to England for boarding school, but in Gérard's mind, this was simply the swapping of one cage for another.

His natural intelligence saw him scrape through his exams, but with nothing like the grades of which he was capable. Then, after the last of his A Levels, high on vodka and dope, Gérard stole a master's car. He was barely a mile from the school when he swerved to avoid an oncoming tractor and rolled the car into a ditch. With charm and financial compensation befitting his calling, his father had been able to prevent the matter escalating, but it was clear a change was needed.

One of his father's friends, Félix Berger, a member of another of the great Swiss banking families, owned and ran a luxury safari lodge in the Selous game reserve in southern Tanzania. Gérard's father offered his wayward son the chance to spend a year working with Félix, rather than going back to school to re-take his exams. Gérard had jumped at the opportunity, but he regretted it at the first meeting with his prospective boss.

A grizzled, brown bear of a man and a former soldier, Félix met Gérard at the steps of the light aircraft on the bush airstrip. He had a hard grip and a harder look. The environment was dusty and dry, and the air seemed to vibrate with raw heat.

'I hear you're smart,' opened Félix. 'Very smart, in fact. I'm told you're charming. Very charming. They say you're good with languages. Very good with languages. But it seems you're also lazy. Very, *very* lazy.'

'But—'

'Let me finish, then you can speak.' Félix softened his glare a little. 'One thing I've learned in life is to make my own judgements on people. So, Gérard Dumont, you get a fresh start with me. But only one.' Now his voice morphed into a drill-sergeant's bark. 'One fuck up, and you're back in

England. You do what I say, when I say it – simple as that. Or do you want to get back on that plane right now?' He pointed to the still-open door.

'No!' exclaimed Gérard.

'No, what?' shouted Félix.

'No, sir!' Gérard was even louder.

Félix met his ward's gaze for two seconds, three. There was perfect silence on the runway. Then Félix leant back and roared with laughter. His body shook, and he rolled forward, slapping his knees. Fat tears rolled down his ruddy cheeks. Gérard looked on, dumbfounded.

Eventually, the older man managed to gather himself. 'Sorry, lad. I couldn't resist.' He draped a protective paw around the youngster's shoulder and, for the first time, fixed him with the kind smile that Gérard would grow to love. 'Seriously, though: don't waste this opportunity.' He gestured at the wide-open landscape all around them. 'Treat this land, these people and these animals with respect. And I promise you the time of your life.'

And Félix had been true to his word. Gérard was made to rise ever earlier, work ever longer and do ever more menial jobs, dealing with the most difficult clients… anything that Félix could think of to try to break the youngster's spirit. Because he knew it wouldn't happen. The difficult adolescent became an impressive young man. Gérard was thriving, and he was enjoying himself immensely.

Near the end of the prescribed year, Félix had called him into his office. Two bottles of beer were open on his desk. He handed one to Gérard.

'To you, lad. Well done. I couldn't be prouder of you if you were my son.'

Gérard's eyes watered. He tried to gulp a response, 'I—'

'No, lad. Listen for a minute. We need to discuss what you're going to do with your life.'

Gérard shrugged the question off easily. 'I want to stay here. Obviously.'

Félix sighed and shook his head. 'You can't stay here. You've got the world to see.'

'But this is the world!'

'Gérard, listen. I've seen plenty of the world and yes, for me, this is the only place that matters. But you can't decide that for yourself until you've seen the rest of it.' Félix held up a hand to prevent further interruption, then slowed his voice. 'You are all those things they told me. Smart. Charming. Good with languages. And—' he let suspense hang for a second, '—the polar opposite of lazy.'

That was when Félix had lain out his plan. Gérard was to return to school and re-take his exams. If he did well, he could spend next summer in the Selous. Then university, with the same annual incentive for success. At the time, this had seemed such a ridiculously distant horizon that Gérard could only focus on the promise of a return the following summer. It was an outcome he desired so completely that no other carrot was needed. He promised Félix that he would apply himself to the best of his abilities, regardless of any temptations to return to his old ways. And he was better than his word. He achieved straight As in his exams. He was a model of good behaviour. Well, most of the time.

School led duly to university. Consumed by his love of the Selous, Gérard attained a first-class degree in International Relations and African Studies from SOAS University of London and learned Swahili. And every year, literally the day after his final exam, he headed for Tanzania. The one place that had ever felt like home. But it had only felt that way for a while, and that was a long time ago. His game reserve days were far behind him; the only quarry he tracked now was human.

And it seemed he would need all his stalking skills with this one. Gérard had been given an old address for Holly Brand, but there was nothing more recent to be found online. His research had uncovered a trail, surely enough, a young woman's life pieced together from fragments of data left in the ether – like so many fossilised footprints. But the trail stopped abruptly more than eight years ago, when Miss Brand seemed to have disappeared from the face of the earth.

It was known, in certain circles, that Gérard was the man for these sorts of odd jobs. He was dogged, smart and discreet, and those were cardinal virtues in his line of work. Which, he reminded himself, was how a bereaved Swiss investigator had come to find himself in London on the wrong side of Christmas, walking unfamiliar streets because it hurt less to be working than it did to be sitting at his father's desk, shuffling what-ifs like playing cards.

Dusk gathered early at this time of year, and the lights were on at the ground floor of the address he had been given. He rang the buzzer, and a man appeared at the front window. The Swiss flashed him his most reassuring smile, and shortly after, there came the sound of a security chain being fastened. The door opened, just a crack. Gérard supposed he would have to work on that smile.

'Yes?'

'I'm really sorry to bother you,' began Gérard. 'But I'm hoping to track down someone who used to live here.'

'You're kidding?'

A woman in her late twenties, who had evidently been listening in, came to the doorway, awkwardly trying to see through the narrow opening. She pushed her way past the man – her husband, Gérard supposed.

'I spoke to your colleague already,' she said.

'Pardon?' asked Gérard.

'The other private investigator. I spoke to her this morning.'

The husband laughed. 'You wait for ages for a private investigator and then two come along at once.'

'I told her go and see Mrs Morris,' the woman offered. Seeing Gérard's puzzlement, she continued. 'That's the old lady, three doors down. She's lived here forever. No one else will know. I told all this to the other woman.'

'Yes, of course,' said Gérard. It was snowing more heavily again, and the afternoon was fading fast. He had to get to the bottom of what was happening here – preferably without making a fool of himself in the process. 'Thank you. And I'm sorry about the confusion. I'm from the Paris office, and we've obviously got our wires crossed, what with Christmas and everything. I don't suppose my colleague left her details?'

The woman was so pleased with herself that she positively ran into her flat. She returned half a minute later, brandishing a card. 'Here.'

Gérard studied it, committing the mobile number to memory. He mentally repeated each digit as he passed it back.

'Oh, of course,' he beamed. 'Nikki! I'll call her, and I'll make sure you're not bothered again. Thank you so much. Merry Christmas.'

Gérard turned his back on the door and punched the number into his phone. He saved 'Nikki' as a new contact, and then he headed back into the gathering darkness.

65

COBRA MEETINGS WERE FIRST CONVENED in the 1970s as a mechanism for co-ordinating ministerial-level responses to national or regional crises, or events involving British nationals abroad. Whilst the name conjures images of a fast-striking snake, the acronym merely stands for Cabinet Office Briefing Room A – one of the rooms at 70 Whitehall where meetings are often held. Whenever there's a major emergency, here's where you'll find the key players.

James Allen tapped his knuckles on the meeting room table to commence proceedings of this latest COBRA gathering. LJ sat, appropriately, at his right hand. Around the table were Hugh Westwood, the Chancellor of the Exchequer; Anthony Fleming, the governor of the Bank of England; Saeed Akhtar, the head of the National Cyber Security Centre; and Sally Bickford, head of the police Financial Crime Unit. The participants were rounded out by a grumpy-looking Jonathan Morse, the cabinet secretary. After greeting them all, Allen began.

'You certainly don't need me to tell you that this attack represents the gravest of threats to our economy. But I would like to stress two things.' He paused for effect. 'Firstly, this is an unconventional attack on our nation, a very modern form of assault. So, I want our response to be innovative and forward-looking. Secondly, if there is one lesson to be taken from the response to the pandemic, it is that we must consider actively—*proactively*—the worst possible outcomes, regardless of whether we presently think they're likely. And then we must move damn fast to ensure they don't happen.' He waited for his words to sink in before continuing.

'I would like each of you to give a summary of where we currently stand from your individual perspectives. Then I would like you to finish with two very specific comments. Firstly, what you think we should be doing *differently*. And then… I'd like you to think the unthinkable. The *absolute* worst-case scenario.'

The temperature drained from the room, as Allen had intended. 'Now, to start, I've asked Rob Tanner, acting Chief Executive of National Bank, to brief us on what they've been doing. They've been fighting this since Christmas Eve, so they have the longest perspective. LJ, would you be so kind?'

While LJ went to fetch Tanner, an extra chair and another glass was placed at the head of the table. And before anyone had time to notice that this was not the first heavily choreographed move of the meeting, Allen's guest of honour was already stepping through the doorway. The prime minister stood and offered Tanner a hand.

'Thank you for coming, Rob. Please, take a seat.' Once the introductions had been made, and having himself filled Tanner's glass with water, Allen continued. 'Now, Rob, perhaps you'd be so good as to give us the full picture.'

'Of course, Prime Minister.' Tanner took a deep breath and began. He was nervous—his mouth was dry and his palms were slick—but he had learned over the years how to hide it. His manner was naturally authoritative, with an easy, calm flow. When he knew his subject matter—and he generally made a point to know it—Tanner exuded confidence yet stopped short of self-importance or arrogance. While he delivered his run-down of everything that had happened so far at National Bank, he held the room's full attention.

'So, not to over-simplify, Rob,' said Allen, once Tanner had finished. 'What you're saying is that this couldn't have been achieved without significant activity by someone at the bank? An inside job, so to speak.'

'Yes, Prime Minister.'

'And you're sure of that?'

'I'm not sure I can be certain of anything to do with banks or computer systems anymore, but that's our internal conclusion. It's also the unanimous view of the independent experts working with us.'

'But then there's a bigger problem.' Allen looked around the table. 'If that's the case at National, then there must have also been, what? Half-a-dozen simultaneous inside jobs at all the other banks?'

'That would be the logical conclusion,' replied Tanner.

'Which suggests collusion and co-ordination on a massive scale.' The prime minster looked, for a moment, to the ceiling. 'Rob, I've asked everyone here to finish their contribution with two things. Firstly, what could we be doing differently? And secondly, what's the absolute worst-case scenario you can imagine?'

Tanner thought for a moment. 'To your first question,' he answered, 'we should create an operations centre, a war-room, across all the banks. That way, we can look at this as one single problem, not seven, without regard to individual interests.'

Nods were shared around the table. Allen took in the unanimity and responded. 'Excellent. And Rob, I'd like you to lead that. With my full authority.'

Tanner was unable to suppress his surprise. He thought his mouth had been dry before, but this was something else. 'Of course, Prime Minister.'

'And worst case?'

Tanner reached for his glass, took a sip of water. He felt the keenness of all those eyes on him, including those looking down from the gold-framed portraits on the wall.

'Worst case is completely catastrophic,' he said. 'If we can't turn back the changes wrought by the attackers, or if they worsen, then customers' bank accounts will just become catalogues of very large but ultimately meaningless numbers. Notionally, any one of us might be as wealthy as the largest FTSE100 company. Or as indebted as the largest country.'

Allen let the words sink in before responding. 'Thank you, Rob. We're counting on you.' The prime minister made to stand up, intending to show his guest to the door, but something in Tanner's body language gave him pause. 'Is there something else?'

Tanner felt like a child again. He was back in the earliest days of school, wanting to venture an answer, but fearing he'd be laughed at.

'One thing, sir. Might I ask the governor to make an urgent request of his overseas counterparts?' Tanner asked, swallowing his anxiety. 'Especially the US Treasury?'

Allen indicated that Tanner should continue.

'Governor.' Tanner turned to face Anthony Fleming, a man whose visage appeared often on the financial news channels he spent his life watching. 'Would you send a request to all US banks, even the smallest ones, asking specifically for any instances of *internal* system manipulation – especially if the means was through older rather than newer technology? No matter how long ago.'

Tanner received a curt nod of assent from the governor, and now Allen did make it to his feet. He shook Tanner's hand with surprising force and led him to the open doors.

66

LJ ESCORTED TANNER BACK to the anteroom with its prize antiques.

'You have the prime minister's full confidence and authority,' she stated. 'And you have a head-start: use it.' She issued instructions as effortlessly and elegantly as she had moved through the maze of corridors connecting Downing Street with the Cabinet Office. 'If any of the other bank CEOs try to be difficult, just tell them to call me.'

LJ's words were like a balm for Tanner's unusually tender confidence. As the implication settled over him, Tanner felt both energised and reassured in equal measure. Here was another extraordinary woman who had appeared in his life from nowhere. Like Ashley, LJ was a gift of a human being, the likes of whom he would probably never meet again.

They said their goodbyes in the anteroom, where Tanner gripped LJ's hand and thanked her with total sincerity. She made to disappear once more into the labyrinth, her mind already back in the briefing room where Allen was still holding court, but she stopped in the doorway. She looked back over her shoulder and caught Tanner's eye.

'I'll call you later to check in,' she said. 'Good luck.'

'You too,' replied Tanner, although as he sat, and tried to gather his thoughts, he wasn't quite sure what he had meant by it. And although LJ had reassured him, he still had his doubts. Of course, he wanted to do his bit, to contribute. But he had never wanted the limelight. He'd always been happy to take personal responsibility, to be accountable for his actions, but he'd never wanted ultimate responsibility. Ultimate liability.

How could he have been so naïve? He should have known this day would come—*had been coming*—with every rung he climbed on the career ladder. And now it wasn't the weight of National Bank on his shoulders, it was the entire bloody financial system. Nothing to worry about, then, just the small matter of the nation's economy, the five centuries of economic and technological progress since the days of Hieronymus Bosch. Tanner saw his father's face in his mind again, an expression with all the warmth of a death mask, doubting and dismissive. But the image gave him strength.

'I'll show you,' Tanner muttered under his breath. 'I can do it. I will do it!'

Tommy was waiting nearby to take him back to the bank's offices. Once settled, Tanner used the car's speakerphone to make a number of calls, heedless that Tommy could hear every word. First, he briefed Chrissie on the COBRA committee and asked her to arrange a meeting for 9 a.m. the following morning with the CEOs and the Chief Technology Officers of the other six major banks.

Next, he called Mike Sorensen. Sorensen and Ashley had been working through various what-if scenarios, but while they'd thrown up several new ideas, none of them had resulted in a significant development.

'Is she with you now?' Tanner asked.

'No, she's just left,' Sorensen informed him. 'We agreed some new tests to run, which will take a couple of hours, at least, so she's gone back to her hotel to freshen up and get something to eat.'

'Thanks, Mike,' said Tanner. 'You need to do that too. Take a break, but obviously call me if there's any news. Otherwise, I'll be in at the crack of dawn tomorrow.'

'Thanks, Rob.'

'There's one more thing,' offered Tanner. 'Just before you go. I just want you to know that I trust you.'

'Thanks, buddy.' Sorensen's voice was infused with warmth, the glow of a California sunrise. 'That means a lot.'

Finally, Tanner called Ashley. She picked up on the first ring.

'Hey, how you doing?' she said. 'I hear you've moved up to the big leagues already!' The familiar tease was back in her voice, but for once, Tanner didn't fully appreciate the banter.

'Why does that make me think of an old Jimmy Cliff song?' he asked. '"The harder they come, the harder they fall."'

Ashley picked up on his mood immediately. 'No. That's the wrong song of his, Rob. You mean, "You can get it if you really want."'

Tanner laughed, despite himself. 'Is there anything you don't have an answer for?'

'Oh yes.' She drew out both words and let them linger. Then, less seriously, 'But not music! So, what goes?'

Tanner took the phone off speaker. Tommy tried to catch his eye in the rear-view mirror, but Tanner made a point of not seeing. Instead, he watched the city beyond the glass—charity muggers on a street corner, trying to find marks in the passing tide of shoppers—as he told Ashley what had happened.

'All of which means I have to corral the other bank CEOs to put their egos aside, work together, and take instructions from a rival who's been in role for less than twenty-four hours!'

'No probs then.' Ashley's easy laugh was back. 'What else?'

'Oh, and I have to come up with a plan for how we're going to save the world.' He glanced at the clock on the dashboard. 'In the next fourteen hours. So, I'm afraid…' He stopped, embarrassed.

Ashley took his meaning immediately. 'Hey, we agreed that today is a "Ms Markham" day. So, let me get back to helping Mike, and we'll start a new day tomorrow. Okay?'

'Okay.'

'Take care, Rob.'

'You too, Ms Markham.'

67

GÉRARD HURRIED BACK TO CLARIDGE'S. The weather was worsening rapidly, and he wanted to check out this Nikki Cheung as quickly as possible. A quick search from the warmth and comfort of his suite revealed a single-page website, and he soon confirmed her listing as an accredited member, since 2018, of the Association of British Investigators. A couple of the databases to which he had immediate access showed she had been at a North London address for three years. He also noted that she was the same age as Holly Brand, the target of their mutual interest. He wondered briefly if that fact was pertinent, but he quickly dismissed it – probably a coincidence, he reasoned, like so many things in this game. So why would this rival investigator also be on the hunt for Holly? And on whose behalf? It wasn't as if she worked for one of the major corporate investigators, like Kroll.

For a few moments, Gérard sat motionless, gazing at the falling snow beyond his window. He eased his neck from side to side, unleashing the tightness in his shoulders. As he took in the beautiful Art Deco furnishings and newly lit fire, he realised he had barely thought about his father all day. Going back to work really had been good for him – even a case as strange as this one: a missing woman sought not only by whoever Ziegler was working for but also by a rival PI.

The rival investigator! Unbidden, a bear's voice in his head spoke to him, 'Two heads are better than one, boy – even one as big as yours!'

Gérard smiled and found the mobile number he had saved in his phone earlier. He stood and walked to the fire before pressing the call button. He felt the heat on his calves, intense and deeply relaxing, as the phone rang. Two rings, three. Then a woman's voice.

'Hello? This is Nikki Cheung speaking.'

'Hello, Nikki,' said Gérard, trying to emulate the hospitable warmth of the fire. 'My name is Gérard Dumont. I used to work for Swiss Federal Intelligence, and I spent some time on secondment with your own services here in London. I'm freelance now, like yourself. I'm calling about a missing person.'

'Really?' The light female voice at the other was polite but reserved. 'May I ask how you got my number?'

'I got it from a helpful lady in Dalyell Road, less than two hours ago.'

'What?' At a stroke, Ms Cheung sounded altogether less composed.

'It seems we're looking for the same person: Holly Brand. I thought it might be worthwhile to "compare notes."'

Nikki hesitated. 'I don't think—'

'Nikki, you don't have to tell me anything,' offered Gérard. As he had intended, he had caught her off guard. 'But I would be willing, unilaterally, to share the little I know, and perhaps we'll take it from there?'

'Well, I—'

'I'm staying at Claridge's. At least come and join me for supper. Then decide.' Gérard's low, mellifluous voice oozed Gallic charm. 'No obligation. Think of it as a good deed – saving me from a lonely dinner at Christmas. Nothing more.'

He could almost hear Nikki's indecision. But then, as if something had settled suddenly into place, she spoke. 'Give me a couple of hours. Seven-thirty?'

'Perfect,' said Gérard. The fire crackled, as if laughing, at his feet. 'I look forward to it.'

68

THE COBRA MEETING CONTINUED WITHOUT TANNER. After a break for refreshment, Allen called the meeting back to order. He turned to the governor of the Bank of England. 'Anthony, perhaps you'd lead us off?'

Anthony Fleming's voice had always reminded Allen of the shipping forecast. And now the governor stated in clipped tones that he had spoken to his counterparts in the major G7 countries and a few others besides. All had offered moral support but, frankly, little else. British banks were as cyber-proof as any in the world, so the responses appeared to consist more of relief at their own escape—and no little fear that they might be next—than constructive ideas.

'What else could we be doing, Anthony?'

'Two things, Prime Minister. Firstly, we need to make contingency plans for keeping the markets closed tomorrow. And possibly beyond.'

'Can we do that?' asked Allen.

'It's obviously not ideal, but they've closed for technical or natural reasons before and survived. It's Friday tomorrow, so I doubt many people will be working in the City. Most will be off next week as well.'

'Fine,' acknowledged the premier. 'You said two things?'

Fleming looked nervously from side to side. 'My second is rather more drastic, I'm afraid. We're going to have to come up with a completely new way to pay for things.'

'Sorry?' Allen gave a thin smile, an expression like a teacher fielding a nonsense answer from a problem pupil. 'I don't understand.'

'Well, Prime Minister, it's like this.' Fleming looked down at the table, then he flashed his eyes back to Allen. 'If our money becomes worthless, as it just well might, how will we pay at all for goods and services?'

A shocked silence fell over the room. The unthinkable had not only been thought; it had been said aloud.

'I'm hoping that's also your worst-case scenario?' offered Allen weakly.

'Yes, Prime Minister.'

Allen gave the merest nod of acceptance, then, with greater resolution, dipped his forehead to the governor's neighbour, Hugh Westwood.

The chancellor cleared his throat and launched into a concise summary of the Treasury's response to date. Neither his own, nor his department's, international counterparts had been any more helpful than the Bank of England's. In short, there had been no progress. Westwood concluded the monologue, without prompt, by turning his attention to Allen's first question. 'As to what we should do? I think we have no option but to declare tomorrow an extraordinary bank holiday. Anthony's comments about the markets are equally true of the banking system.'

'Fine,' agreed Allen. 'And what's the worst case, Hugh, as you see it?'

'I really don't think I could suggest anything worse than the governor already has, Prime Minister.' Westwood looked at Fleming and then back at Allen. 'Frankly, we'd effectively find ourselves rolling back the clock by hundreds of years if that came to pass.'

Allen let the room digest this apocalyptic utterance, then turned to the head of the country's top cyber defence body, the NCSC. He was beginning to regret his appeal for total candour, his invitation for worst-case thinking.

'Anything from GCHQ or the security services, Saeed?'

'Nothing yet, Prime Minister.' Saeed Akhtar had not long been in the role, and Allen thought of him as rather a closed book. He might be a genius, or he might be a total fool, for all anyone knew. He certainly did not waste words.

'We've followed the email trails from this Joen van Aken, but they're routed through so many dead-drops and foreign jurisdictions that the origin is untraceable,' Akhtar continued. 'We've not detected any unusual patterns of activity elsewhere, but we're obviously in constant touch with our counterparts across the globe.'

'And thinking the unorthodox?' asked Allen.

'My first thought is to cross to the other side. Use the dark web. Incentivise the bad guys to help, not hurt us.'

'We put a bounty on the attackers' heads?'

'Exactly.'

'And worst case?'

'If they can do this to banks, with the money those companies spend on cyber-security, what could the attackers do elsewhere? I'm thinking utilities, the health service, the military…' Akhtar trailed off. There was no need to heap more misery onto the pile.

Sally Bickford, the financial crime specialist, was up next, taking command of a room whose mood was increasingly despondent. She ran through an overview of measures taken by the police in response to other, major incidents of financial crime, but in the circumstances, they were wholly inadequate.

'We're shaking the tree with all known financial criminals of any substance and asking Europol and Interpol and other nations to do the same,' she added. 'Even our usually less helpful friends to the East. Given the situation, even some of our usual sparring partners might be worried enough to help.'

'Do we think that could be where the threat originates?' asked Allen.

'I'm sorry, Prime Minister, but as yet there's nothing to indicate the location, identity or motive of the attackers.' Bickford spoke quickly, with a schoolmarm voice that brooked no dissent. 'Our psychologists have taken a first pass at the emails. At face value, they might suggest a lone sociopath, but the scope and scale of the attacks obviously point to a group with extraordinary reach and resources.'

'What else?' Allen prompted.

'We need to prepare for serious public order disturbances,' offered Bickford.

'I hope that's the worst case?'

'The worst case is that they happen sooner rather than later, Prime Minister.'

'Christ!' Allen grimaced as the exclamation reverberated around the room. He felt as if he was under personal siege; misery only seemed to beget more misery. He closed his eyes, aware he was being watched, and waited as the spasm of rage receded.

The cabinet secretary didn't need to use his formidable IQ to read the mood of the room. 'I think we've heard enough to keep us going, Prime Minister, but I would add one thing.'

'Please,' interjected LJ. She could see Allen needed a moment, and she was happy to speak on his behalf.

'The police can focus on—how shall I put it?—the criminal side of things,' said Morse. 'On dealing with trouble. But we should also draw up contingency plans for preventing problems with basic goods and services. Food, health, that kind of thing.'

Allen opened his eyes. He looked knowingly at the huge portrait which hung across from him. His most famous predecessor, staring him down, almost. Then he turned his gaze back to the cabinet secretary.

'You're absolutely right,' agreed Allen, 'And so was Churchill—' he indicated the portrait '—with Beaverbrook.' Something of the usual verve came back into the Prime Minister's voice. 'So, you've got yourself a job, Jonathan. Minister of Supply. Well done!' Morse nodded in acknowledgement of the compliment.

Allen, meanwhile, surveyed the gloomy expressions around the committee table. He recognised he had to lift the mood somehow; despondency didn't get anything done – only hope could serve as an engine, a motive power.

'Come on everyone,' he said. 'This is the whole point of COBRA. Disaster management, emergency planning, war-gaming doomsday scenarios. As my dear old mother says, "Hope for the best and prepare for the worst."'

Allen stood, indicating that the meeting was over. Everyone else—the collection of ministers and experts who constituted his inner circle, his war council—did the same. Allen looked once more around the room, trying to find his election day smile. Everyone knew they would be back here again, and soon. As Allen pressed palms, thanking everyone for their contributions, the mood remained sober. Only LJ was willing to meet his eye.

69

GÉRARD SPENT NINETY MINUTES CALLING IN FAVOURS. This involved speaking to acquaintances in police forces and security services across Europe and in the US. But, for all his efforts, he had no new information. For the moment, all he had to go on were the sparse details he had been given by Stefan Ziegler that morning.

He dressed for dinner and, with one eye on the clock, reread his notes. He had already committed all the relevant details to memory but hoped that a further perusal would stimulate an idea or spark much-needed inspiration. He studied Holly's photo intently. A rather—what was the English word?—*chubby* girl stared back, a slightly surprised look on her face. Probably taken in a passport photo-booth, Gérard reasoned. In her early twenties then, she'd be thirty-three now. The unflattering bob cut would probably have changed, but to what?

He retraced the path Holly had taken through life: school in Yorkshire, then a first-class degree from Imperial. Just one job: IT at National Bank. Then nothing. No social media profile or trace for eight years. No evidence of overseas travel. He considered the possibilities. Which was she: dead, or buried deep undercover?

When Gérard asked, Ziegler had told him that the client, on whose behalf he was acting, was a distant relative of Holly's. This client had supposedly lost touch with the girl but, full of remorse and the joys of Christmas, had now decided to track her down. Gérard had made and underlined a note: *No close family*.

Having looked back over the facts, Gérard shook his head. Was he really expected to believe that it had taken a distant relative a full decade to try to find a missing twenty-four-year-old? And that this elusive relative had come looking for the computer specialist just as National Bank, her one former employer, was hit by the largest cyber-attack in history? And by pure coincidence, after all those years, another freelance investigator just happened to be looking for her this very same day? Gérard had seen the news; he wasn't born yesterday. None of this passed his smell test, which was why he found himself so intrigued. He wondered if Ms Cheung might be able to shed some light on this murky situation.

The thought of Nikki prompted another look at his watch – a Patek Philippe brought for him by his father as a graduation present, many years ago. It had taken a long, long time before small things had stopped reminding Gérard of Félix, after he died, and he realised the same would now be true of his father. A simple glance at a watch and Gérard was transported fifteen years back.

That summer after graduation, he recalled, had been a particularly special time. He had spent it—as he spent all his summers, then—in the Selous with Félix, whose lodge had never been more popular. Accolades rained down as surely as April monsoons, and demand far outweighed their capacity. After four years' dedicated, ever-intensifying study, Gérard was more appreciative than ever of the land. His improving Swahili, meanwhile, made him increasingly comfortable with its people, and they with him. And with every summer of joyous industry, his bond with Félix deepened and matured, like the fine Bordeaux they always shared on their last night together. Guests to the lodge often assumed they were father and son, and as far as Gérard was concerned, they may as well have been.

Far too soon, the time came for Gérard to return to Switzerland for his military service. As was their custom, on the final evening, he and Félix sat down to a formal dinner in the lodge's private dining room.

Félix poured the Champagne. 'We need to celebrate your graduation. You—no, we—have come a long way together since that scrawny lad stepped onto the airstrip for the first time.' They smiled at each other in remembrance, the moment hanging like a happy thread between them. Then Félix continued, 'Which is why I've changed my will.'

A look of concern spread over Gérard's face, but Félix waved it away with a laugh. 'No, there's nothing like that. I just wanted you to know that when I finally get eaten by one of those lions out there—' he tilted his head towards the open veranda, '—which I sincerely hope won't be for another thirty years… well, when it happens, this will all be yours.' He raised his hands to encompass everything around them. 'I can't think of anyone I'd rather entrust it to.'

Gérard could only stare blankly in disbelief. 'I don't know what to say,' he eventually managed.

'Then we won't say another word!' Félix banged the table as heartily as if he'd been draining steins in a bierkeller. 'We'll just get thoroughly, disgustingly drunk!' And they did.

At the end of the dinner, deep in drink, Félix enveloped the younger man in a crushing bear hug, from which there was no escape. Félix's words tumbled out.

'You've got an early start in the morning, and I don't like goodbyes, so I'll say *au revoir* now. You coming here was the best thing that's happened to me and this place. I love you, lad.' Then Félix gave Gérard one last rib-straining squeeze and stumbled off to his bungalow.

Gérard had flown with the dawn to Addis Ababa, watching the natural world wake beneath him. Then on to Nairobi and an overnight connection to Zurich, arriving with another sunrise over a very different landscape. In those pre-iTech times, a journey like that would leave you blissfully cut off from the world. The flights allowed Gérard to lose himself in memories of the Selous and dream of the things that he and Félix would do there in the future.

At Zurich, he walked out of arrivals, scanning for his father's driver. Instead, he was surprised to see his parents, both there in person. As he got closer, he saw the grim look on his father's face and the tear lines ruining his mother's perfect make-up. 'It's Félix—' was all she could manage before dissolving into sobs and embracing her son.

Later, Gérard learned the full story. Félix had driven out of the lodge late in the afternoon, intent on finding a pack of wild dogs he had been monitoring through the generations, ever since his arrival in Africa. Perhaps still hungover from the night before, or simply driving too fast in the excitement of the chase, Félix had turned his Land Rover on the edge of a dried river gully. He was thrown out and crushed as the vehicle rolled on top of him. It wasn't until well after dark that a search party found him, by which time it was too late.

Gérard was initially distraught, but the thought of Félix saying, 'Come on lad, where's your backbone?' sprung him into cold, focused action. He returned immediately to the Selous, oversaw the arrangements for Félix's funeral and burial, and then buried himself in the practicalities. His military service was postponed for three months on compassionate grounds – more easily than it might ordinarily have been, owing to the family's myriad connections. But as time went on, the hole in Gérard's heart grew rather than mended; the lodge, and everything around it, was a constant reminder of what had been lost. So, he promoted the capable assistant manager, brought in a new number-two, and returned 'temporarily' to Switzerland.

And never went back.

When his national service started, Gérard was seconded to military intelligence. There he found his *métier*; he possessed the perfect mix of hard and soft skills, from an appreciation for the rigours of research to an aptitude for communication and teamwork. He was asked to stay on after his nominal conscription period ended and was only too happy to do so, willingly losing himself in the work. He justified this to himself with the thought that he was doing what Félix had wanted him to, seeing different aspects of the world. In time, he was sent overseas to work with international partners in Washington and London, and once he was asked to lead a co-ordination taskforce with cantonal forces. It was an education, but nothing like the education he had received in the Selous.

The fire crackled, and Gérard returned to the present. He had been doing so well today, but just looking at his watch had been enough to provoke a cascade of memories. Long buried but, clearly, forever there. It was sad enough to lose one father; to lose two, in one lifetime, felt like an impossible tragedy.

He knew he had to pull himself together. He had to be strong: for himself, for his departed father and for Félix. Strangely enough, he also felt a sudden and unaccountable need to be strong for Holly. Who knew where the girl was, and if, perhaps, she needed help?

It was nearly seven o'clock; eight in Switzerland. He rang Ziegler's number, but it went through to voicemail. Gérard left a short message and followed up with a text. He liked to have things in writing; nobody could claim to have missed anything that way.

> ✉ **Gérard, 18:55:** In London on your challenge. Essential I speak to your client.

He was surprised to receive a reply almost immediately.

> ✉ **Ziegler, 18:59:** Don't think that's possible today. Client travelling.

> ✉ **Gérard, 18:56:** Understood. Will try again tomorrow.

Gérard understood, alright. He understood only too well… when he was being fed a line.

He looked again at the timepiece, feeling the warmth of not one but two fathers' pride, and wondered what his dinner companion would make of all this. The exquisite watch-face told him he'd very soon find out.

70

ARC LAMPS GLARED, illuminating a lectern at the steps of 10 Downing Street. James Allen stood in the familiar spot from which so many of his predecessors had addressed the nation. A light dusting of snow began to fall as he started to speak.

'We do not yet know,' he said, 'if the coordinated attacks on this country's banks are the work of terrorists or criminals, of rogue nations or rogue individuals. Frankly, that is irrelevant right now. What matters is that London is the world's financial capital, for centuries a centre of innovation and enterprise. Our banks operate at the heart of our economy, and of our peoples' lives. An assault on our financial system is an assault on the very fabric of our society. And as such, we will do everything necessary to restore order to our banking system and bring the perpetrators of this outrage to justice, wherever they reside. They are being confronted and they will be defeated.

'It does not appear that anyone has yet suffered any financial loss as a result of these attacks, but I feel huge sympathy for the worry and distress caused to millions of innocent Britons at what should be the happiest time of the year. I urge those affected—and, indeed, all bank customers—to ignore the manipulations and to behave normally.

'In the short term, we are doing everything possible to thwart these attacks. We have created a task force to coordinate the banks' responses, and we are acting as one united body. To assist their efforts, I am declaring that tomorrow, Friday, will be an extraordinary bank holiday. This will undoubtedly cause inconvenience, but it is a necessary intervention.

'The digital revolution has provided us with many benefits. However, this latest development is a sobering reminder that we also face novel and unwelcome dangers. As the pace of technological change increases, so does the capability of our adversaries to do us harm. As a matter of urgency, I have therefore asked the home secretary to lead a wide-ranging review of the broader threats we face in the cyber age, and how we may best counter them, so that we do not again face events such as today's.

'COBRA will meet again tomorrow, and rest assured, I will update you as soon as there is any further news.

'Thank you.'

Ignoring the shouted questions and oblivious to the storm of flashbulbs, Allen turned on his heels. As he disappeared into the welcoming light and warmth of Number Ten, he couldn't help wondering, despite himself, what Winston would have made of that performance. The truth was that James Allen feared his own darkest hour was yet to come.

71

NIKKI FOUGHT HER WAY UP THE HILL to Highgate tube station. She wouldn't have called it a blizzard, exactly, but both the snow and the wind were picking up, and the forecast showed little sign of a reprieve. However, the cold air did have the benefit of clearing her head.

She had been completely thrown by Gérard's call. What had started out as an unusual job was getting odder by the hour. And what made it even stranger was the backdrop to the case; the hunt for this missing ex-National Bank employee seemed all the more urgent given the day's news and the bank's status as cyber-attack Ground Zero. Even as she walked, she caught glimpses of TV screens in living rooms and shop windows, replaying the prime minister's emergency address and his attempt to reassure an increasingly worried public that the government was on top of things. Social media was awash with speculation, and the front pages of discarded freesheets in the station entrance reflected the nation's—and particularly the capital's—worry.

Nikki had her own concerns; her account hadn't been tampered with, but her savings would go up in smoke if her bank collapsed. She wasn't poor by any stretch, but she wasn't so rich—as five minutes' research had revealed Gérard Dumont to be—that her work was a hobby rather than a means of paying her mortgage. She wasn't yet at the point where she would consider joining the ever-lengthening queues at the cashpoints, but she feared that time wasn't far off. For now, though, work had to come first. Something told her there was much more to this case than she had first realised.

Speaking to another investigator was contrary to all of Nikki's natural instincts, but it was the very strangeness of the situation which made her give in to Gérard's suggestion that they meet. Besides, she reasoned that she could get the measure of the man before giving anything away. And it didn't hurt that his was the kind of voice she wanted to trust.

Tonight, she was wearing a simple, black, knee-length merino wool dress and matching high leather boots. It was a simple and elegant look, complementing her short, platinum hair. She felt eyes on her in the elevator, on the platform, on the escalators; all the places where heads were usually kept well down. Nikki's looks—and, more than that, the aura of mischievous magnetism she radiated—tended to attract attention. She only hoped she could win over Gérard so easily; it certainly never hurt to make a good impression.

The tubes were still running, despite the weather, and she arrived at Claridge's ten minutes before the scheduled meeting time. The maître d' showed her to a quiet corner table, where a sandy-haired, rather chiselled man rose to greet her. Standing at six feet and change, and with a slim, almost athletic build, Gérard Dumont turned out to be a man of high cheekbones and pale blue eyes, which now appraised her carefully and coolly. The effect was disconcerting, almost intimidating. Then he smiled, and his whole demeanour changed. An impish warmth flushed his upper cheeks. He looked like a friend-in-waiting.

'You must be Nikki,' he began. His voice, that thick accent, evoked high fashion, something from a designer perfume advert. He stretched out his hand and shook hers with careful firmness. 'Thank you for joining me.'

Nikki looked round the dining room, a glittering sanctum of silver and white. A striking glass sculpture hung chandelier-like from the ceiling. Art Deco mirrors lined the walls, and light seemed to dance from every surface.

'I can think of worse places to meet for dinner,' she answered.

Gérard laughed, and in the second of quiet that followed, Nikki realised that his blue eyes weren't cold at all – they were sad. With easy charm, Gérard properly introduced himself and offered a glass of Champagne. The sadness in his expression disappeared as he poured.

'Thank you,' said Nikki. 'And thank you for inviting me.'

'Not at all.' Gérard raised his glass. 'I am glad you came.'

Nikki met his eyes across the table. She had come with the intention of sizing him up, but now she was here, with the taste of Champagne on her tongue, she couldn't force so much as an adversarial expression. And after the ubiquitous excesses of Christmas, she was delighted to follow his recommendation of grilled Dover sole and creamed spinach, the embodiment of class and restraint. The man was of good stock – Nikki knew that much. That would normally have counted against him, in her eyes, but not right this moment.

'Now, I know there's no such thing as a free lunch,' Nikki acknowledged, once their orders had been taken. 'So, let's talk about Holly Brand. What's your interest?'

Gérard shrugged, smiled. 'At this precise moment, pure selfish curiosity.'

Whatever answer Nikki had expected, this certainly wasn't it. 'I don't understand,' she replied.

'Then let me explain.'

Gérard fixed her eyes and surprised her—and possibly himself—by telling the full, unexpurgated story: his father's death, the confusion and uncertainty he had felt in those empty days of bereavement, and then the call from Ziegler which had rescued him from himself. He explained his contempt for the high-class crook—the head and handwashing required after any contact—but how the happy coincidence of a distracting project and a change of scenery seemed like a sign from the universe.

'And then I found out two things,' continued Gérard. 'Firstly, this is no straightforward task, and secondly, this notional client for whom I'm working is almost certainly a sham. I like challenges, but I don't like being taken for a fool. So now I have two puzzles to solve: where is Holly Brand, and why was I retained to find her? I'd like some answers.' He paused for emphasis. 'To satisfy my own curiosity.'

'You're no longer working for your "client," then?'

Gérard made an equivocal gesture. 'I wouldn't necessarily say that. But I would say I'm working for myself, first and foremost. Whatever happens with Ziegler, and whoever he's working for, depends on what happens next. It might even depend on what *we* agree.' Gérard indicated with his index finger that the "we" comprised him and Nikki.

'We?'

'Yes, *we*. But first…' Gérard trailed off at the arrival of the waiter with their Dover sole. Nikki swallowed her confusion along with her Champagne. 'First,' Gérard instructed, 'we should eat.'

The sole was sublime. As they ate, they commented on the food and served one another the occasional question about their lives, their personal histories. Nothing too intrusive, though each was eager to size up the other. Conversation flowed as easily as the wine, which the waiter re-filled unobtrusively whenever their glasses dipped too low.

Gérard volunteered his background first: from his privileged but lonely childhood to a first career in Swiss intelligence—via an extended gap year, as he called it, in Tanzania—to his work, now, as an investigator for the upper echelons, a mind for hire. The way he told it, you'd think that everything had just fallen in his lap, but Nikki detected deep reserves of willpower, a steeliness completely in keeping with his looks. He was handsome, she thought, in both his brooding and smiling guises.

Nikki reciprocated, describing first her childhood as an expatriate policeman's daughter in London. She told Gérard how she empathised with him, having a father who wanted his child to follow in the family footsteps, and for a moment her resolve seemed to waver. But only momentarily. Emboldened by the Champagne, she moved the conversation on to her decision to study fine art at Edinburgh University.

'I wanted to do something creative,' she explained, realising too late that the words were crashing out before she could stop them. 'Policing was the family business—in London and back in Hong Kong—and I wanted to do something different. I thought I was sick of my father's stories from the Met, and I used to roll my eyes every time we went back to Hong Kong and had to sit through the same thing from my grandfather and uncles. My mother used to worry herself sick about it – she lived in fear of gangsters turning up at the flat, looking for retribution. Anyway, I was consumed with a kind of teenage rebellion, I guess you'd call it. I thought I knew better, and so I decided I'd do something as far removed from policing and detection as you could get. Hence fine art. Then I spent a year "finding myself" in India.'

'And did you… find yourself?' asked Gérard, eyes sparkling with mirth.

'Yes.' Nikki laughed, despite the sting behind her eyes. 'I realised I was just the same as my dad after all.'

Gérard held her gaze, saying nothing, offering her the opportunity to continue, but not pushing her to do so unless she wanted to. She found that she did.

'It wasn't long before I was due to come back from India,' she went on. 'By then I'd realised the errors of my ways. I didn't really care about art at all. All I could think about was being a detective, which branch of the force I'd go into. I was desperate to get back to London and get started. That was when the phone call came through from my mother. My father had had a heart attack. He simply went to bed one night and never woke up. All those years worrying about gangsters, flinching whenever a door slammed, and he died peacefully in his sleep. At fifty-one! I rushed back to London, but of course it was too late.' She took a breath, then restarted. 'He never said it, but I knew my dad was disappointed I never showed much interest in following him into his work. He was quite progressive that way – it was my mum who thought the force was no place for a woman. But dad always said I would have been great at it, better than he ever was. And I never got to tell him he had been right all along.'

A silence settled over their table, and for a moment it felt to Nikki as if both of them—she and the stranger to whom she had just poured out her heart—were enclosed in their own private snow globe. The noises of the restaurant had become that much duller, as if they were muffled, and her focus stopped at the periphery of her vision. Why did she feel that she could speak so openly with a man she had just met? Was it his candour about his own loss? Had it dislodged something in her? Maybe she was lonelier than she cared to admit, and Christmas had finally got to her. Whatever it was, her dinner companion clearly had a knack for getting people to open up, a skill of no little import for an investigator.

He had good timing, too. Instead of responding to her, an unseen signal from the Swiss brought table service. Plates were collected, desserts rejected and coffees accepted in smooth, short order and they were left alone again.

Grateful for the intermission, Nikki returned to the reason for their dinner tonight. 'If I didn't know better, I would think you were offering me some kind of deal.'

'Maybe you know me well already, because that's exactly what I'm doing.' Gérard winked. 'What I'm offering is my assistance, my intelligence, my contacts, my *resources*...' He cast his eye around the opulent dining room. 'I want to solve this riddle.'

'And then what happens when—if—we find Holly Brand?'

'We both get paid. Or maybe *I* won't… I'm certainly not sharing anything with Ziegler's client until I get to the bottom of what he wants with this girl.'

'Do you always require such openness from your clients?'

'Nikki, my clients don't normally give me reason to suspect I am being lied to. Or worse, taken for a fool.'

At this, the coffees arrived, and Gérard received them with a smile. He thanked the waiter and returned his gaze to Nikki.

It was the "Neekie" that swung it. Nikki had grown up hating the name Nicola. Nikki was the best she could do, but she still bridled at it. But now, for the first time in her life, Gérard had made it sound desirable. He made her sound sexy.

'I normally like to work alone,' she declared. A voice in her head told her that she had been alone for years – not out of choice but out of circumstance. And look where that had got her.

Gérard's smile dimmed ever so slightly. 'I have always worked alone, too. But this is different.'

'I'd have to check with my client,' returned Nikki.

'Naturally.'

'But in this case,' she added, meeting his deep, blue eyes, 'I think I can make an exception.'

72

TANNER COULDN'T PUT OFF THE CALL any longer. He wasn't sure which he dreaded more: having to explain the latest banking developments to his father or having to apologise again to his sister. In the event, it was his sister's husband who answered. Liz had retired to her bath, and Harry had returned home.

'Harry said guests, like fish, begin to smell after three days,' laughed Tanner's brother-in-law. 'So, he was taking himself off before he went off.'

Liz's husband did not sound remotely disappointed at this turn of events. But if Tanner's reckoning with Liz could be delayed, there was no postponing the conversation with their parent. Tanner rang his father's home number, and the call was soon answered.

'Hello, Dad,' Tanner said. He spoke gingerly, picking at words the way one might pick at the Christmas leftovers. 'It's Rob.'

'I can hear that.'

Forget pleasantries, then. Why, just once, could the old man not start a conversation with something constructive? A simple hello would have been more than enough. Tanner forced down his resentment.

'I thought you might like an update?' he pressed on. 'I just got back from Downing Street. The prime minister has asked me to sit on the COBRA committee.'

'I saw his speech.'

The coldness was impressive, even by Harry's standards. The pointed brush-off stung Tanner to sarcasm.

'You don't want to hear what the PM and his top advisers were discussing?' he asked.

'Why would I want to hear what a bunch of politicians have to say? They're all useless. The bigger the group, the more useless they are. What do they want, anyway?'

'Who?'

'The attackers!' Harry wheezed on the other end of the line. 'The bad guys! Villains always want something. What is it?'

'They haven't said. We don't even know who they are. They call themselves Joen van Aken. It's a pseudonym. The name of a medieval painter.'

'A pseudonym,' mimicked Harry contemptuously. 'And you're telling me this Joan's done all this without saying what she wants?'

'It's *Joen*. Not she. It's—' Tanner pulled himself up again and tried for calm. 'There are no demands – just rants about the seven deadly sins. Sloth yesterday. Envy today. And obscure warnings about consequences.'

Harry let out an earthy chuckle. 'Well, in that case, I'm on her side.'

'Joen's not a *she*! I told you!'

'On *his* side then,' shot back Harry, petulantly. 'And can you blame him? Everyone's lazy nowadays, wanting what the other bugger's got without having to work for it, wanting to stick their nose in the trough. Like your new politician friends. I'm not surprised this Joen bloke's had enough. I know I have. Anyway, what are you doing about it? Your bank got us into this mess, after all. You're the boss.'

Tanner was exhausted, and he couldn't be bothered to fight any longer. Instead, he wearily offered up a question of his own.

'Do you ever say anything nice, or positive, or supportive, Dad?'

'Yes. When I go to visit your mum or your brother.'

Tanner was too astonished at the words to respond with any of his own. Seconds elapsed in perfect silence before his wits returned enough for him to end the call. He swore into the handset: dead, like the relationship between the two men. And the family they had both lost.

73

AFTER THE OASIS OF LIGHT, WARMTH AND HAPPINESS that was Claridge's dining room, the wintry fastness of Brook Street gave Nikki an abrupt shock.

What in heaven's name was she doing? She prided herself on being the most principled of operators in an industry full of rogues and charlatans, but here she was compromising those very principles. She had crossed a line, already, by agreeing to meet with Gérard. And then she had let herself get sucked in by his smooth charm like a teenager on a first date. Or had she been addled by the Champagne?

But then she considered the facts of the matter. Gérard clearly *was* connected. And smart. And rich. Most importantly of all, he seemed trustworthy. And she had to admit that the thought of working *with* someone, rather than on her own, was exciting.

The underground was beginning to buckle under the wintry conditions, and the journey, which had taken forty-five minutes one way, took well over an hour in reverse. Not that it mattered. It gave Nikki time to think, to check and cross-check her decision before she called Tommy Steele. She dialled her client from the hallway of her flat before she had even taken off her boots.

'Let me get this straight,' said Tommy, after Nikki had filled him in. 'This guy, Gérard—who you don't know from Adam—has offered to help just because he's *intrigued*?'

'When you put it like that, I give you it does sound far-fetched, but when you meet him, he's… *different*. Frankly, he doesn't need me, with his connections and money. And why would he tell me all the stuff about his dodgy client? What's there to lose?'

The line went quiet as Tommy weighed her words. Nikki paced the welcome mat as she waited.

'And you trust him not to do the dirty on us?' asked Tommy. 'You don't think it's a set-up?'

'He says he won't do anything until he knows who is posing as his client. He thinks they've lied to him already, and he's convinced something suspicious is going on. He'd rather work with us. I suspect he'd like to stick it to his client, actually.'

'Well, he's not the only one!'

Nikki stopped pacing. 'What do you mean?'

Tommy laughed, the sound strangely bitter coming from a man who was usually so warm and open. 'It's just that I'm pretty sure I know who his client is.'

'How?' Nikki's tone was incredulous.

'Well, I can only think of one person who's currently in Switzerland—Zermatt, to be precise—with the money and connections to retain a high-end private investigator at a moment's notice, and who would also have a sudden interest in a forgotten National Bank techie.'

'Who?' asked Nikki.

'Martin Kellett,' replied Tommy. 'Until two days ago, our CEO. Or as we prefer to call him: the Toad.'

DAY FIVE

FRIDAY 27 DECEMBER 2024

74

ROB TANNER WAS TRAPPED in an art gallery from hell. Perhaps an art gallery *in* hell. The walls on all four sides were bleeding, and graphic depictions of suffering, torment and punishment screamed at him from gilt frames in vivid, surreal colour. A severed human ear loomed hugely before him, and off to the side was a grotesquely inflated set of bagpipes, evocative of an organ—a heart, maybe—and coloured in a sick, fleshy pink. A bipedal, anthropomorphic bird led a naked slave in its wake, while rats the size of crocodiles gorged themselves on a man's corpse. Everywhere he looked, human figures, shameful in their nudity, crawled over one another in their desperation to flee the torture. But there was no door, no escape, and the only sound was the frantic tolling of a distant bell.

Tanner woke with a start. Only the bell was real; it was his mobile phone. He glanced at the screen: 01:32 – Mike Sorensen. Christ, he'd only been asleep for an hour or so. He sat up, fighting to shake the drowsiness from his brain.

'Mike, what is it?'

'It's just plain weird, Rob,' said Sorensen. He made no allowance for the time, and Tanner guessed he was yet to sleep. 'Half an hour ago, we were hit by a completely different kind of cyber-attack. Or rather, *attacks*, plural. Thousands of separate money transfer requests using the credentials of our most senior people—you, me, the chairman, all the ExCo—asking us to transfer tens of millions to various accounts at the other six major banks.'

'What? That's ridiculous!' If Tanner hadn't been fully awake before, he was now. 'The other major banks here in the UK? Not to some dodgy banks in the Cayman Islands or the Philippines?'

'No, Rob. To our counterparts at the six major banks here in London.'

'Our systems caught them?'

'Yes. But the sophistication of the attacks is unlike anything I've seen before.'

Tanner tried to engage his brain, shake off the hellscape of his dream. 'But what's the point, if the transfer's so easily traceable?'

'They're playing with us, Rob.' Sorensen's tone was desperate. 'The resources we used to counter the attacks stretched us to the limit. Presumably, the other banks are the same. You almost have to admire the genius of whoever is behind this. It's a like a game of cat and mouse, with one mighty cool cat.'

'Okay.' Tanner exhaled heavily. 'I'm coming in.'

'No, Rob, don't.' The Californian's tone brooked no argument. 'I just called because you told me to keep you in the loop. But you should try to get a few hours' sleep. We'll need you at your best tomorrow.'

Tanner rechecked the alarm on his phone and turned out the lights. Remarkably, he was out again as soon as his head hit the pillow. He slept—this time in a mercifully dreamless void—until his alarm went off at 5.30 a.m.

Tanner followed the same tea and TV routine as always. The prime minister's statement was the lead item on the morning news, but there was no mention of further attacks. He checked his phone for voicemails and was relieved to see there were none, and then he opened his mail app. His gaze fell immediately to the third message.

> TO: Robert Tanner
> FROM: Joen van Aken
> DATE: Friday, 27 December 2024 at 06:00
> RE: Invidia
>
> Hello, Rob.
>   You say you don't know my name, but what's in a name? Anyway, I've rather gotten used to Joen. "A gift from God," apparently!
>   You ask if it's "fair" to hurt millions of "innocent" customers. Come on, Rob – it's not just bankers who are lazy and greedy.

Technological advances should be making people smarter and more thoughtful. Society should be fairer and more civilised, but the opposite is happening. Who needs knowledge when we have technology? That's the mantra of our times. The original JvA had it right.

Sometimes you have to take a step back to move forward, accept short-term pain for long-term gain. But you can't cure a sick patient unless they accept they're ill.

Humanity is sick, Rob, but people are too lazy and greedy to recognise the symptoms, let alone treat the cause. So think of me as a diagnostician.

Did you know that the number of objects an average person can hold in working memory is seven? That's why it's such a magical number: seven days of the week, colours of the rainbow, ages of man, notes on a musical scale. Seas, continents, wonders, you name it. Snow White didn't have six dwarves, or eight, did she?

Well, let's see if seven really is a lucky number. For everyone.

JvA

Tanner ran to his first-floor study and opened the email on his computer. There was no mistaking the artist, nor the tenor, of the embedded painting. Heaven and hell were depicted on the left- and right-hand panels, but the subject matter of the large middle section was less immediately obvious. Google had the answers.

"The *Haywain Triptych* is a panel painting by Hieronymus Bosch, now in the Museo del Prado, Madrid." Tanner skimmed the Wikipedia entry and soon understood the relevance. "A large wagon of hay surrounded by a multitude of fools engaged in a variety of sins… is drawn by infernal beings to Hell."

The proverbial—or was it the original?—going to hell in a handcart.

JvA's meaning could not be clearer. The world was tumbling into the abyss, thanks in no small part to advances in technology and the trends of ignorance and hubris these advances had accelerated. But why attack the financial system in response?

Tanner forwarded the email to LJ, with a brief note detailing the hacking attempts overnight. Then he rushed to shave, shower and dress. Breakfast would have to wait. By 6:20 a.m., he was driving towards the City, alone in a world of white. London was devoid of cars and, it seemed, of life.

75

TANNER TOOK A MOMENT to appreciate the view outside his office window; the familiar horizon beautiful and strangely still in its unfamiliar winter garb. The snow would last longer than the peace, he guessed. The trill of his mobile proved him correct within seconds.

'Morning, LJ.'

'Thanks for the email.' There was no pretence at pleasantries from the chief of staff, none of the previous evening's warmth. 'Let me make sure I've got this right. You're dealing with a nutter with the most advanced technological capabilities your bank has ever encountered. They could have stolen as much money as they wanted to at any other time, but they're doing this now, at Christmas – the one time of year when they can't actually transfer any money. Then they play games with our systems in a parody of "conventional" cyber-crime. It's so far-fetched, it's literally unbelievable. It's like we're dealing with a Bond villain.'

'What, Blofeld with his cat?'

'Got a better idea?'

Tanner bit back the retort he'd been set to offer. The question deserved more than verbal serve and volley.

'No,' he answered at last. 'I haven't. But I do know one thing about Bond villains, LJ. They always wanted something, something big. All the gold in Fort Knox, nuclear weapons, global domination… that sort of thing. I understand JvA's gripe, in a theoretical sense, but the bit I *don't* get is what he might actually want. What's the "ask" going to be?'

'You don't think it's financial?'

From the corner of his eye, Tanner caught a glimpse of the image in JvA's latest email. 'Not from what I've seen so far.'

And the thing was, Tanner *could* see where JvA was coming from – at least partly. How many people would really take in the beauty of London this morning? And how many, instead, would be glued to their phones, posting vile comments about people they had never met or gambling money they didn't have on the afternoon's football? Was that progress?

'So where does that leave us?' asked LJ.

'In need of the Kipling test,' replied Tanner with the conviction of habit. 'What, why, when, how, where and who? It doesn't answer your question, but it does clarify how we should get there. Roles and responsibilities.'

'Go on.'

'The latest JvA email suggests grand, big-picture motives. Let's say that's the who, why and what. Whilst they're intriguing, they're no longer about National Bank or, maybe, any other bank. So, they're above my pay grade. But the how, when and where—the logistics of the tech problem—that's my group's focus. *My* responsibility. I'll leave the first three to those higher up the food chain. Like you. Okay?'

Tanner was relieved to hear a light chuckle at the other end of the line. 'Understood. Let me know how the meeting with the other CEOs goes.'

The line dropped, leaving Tanner to his thoughts. What he'd said was entirely logical. So why did he have the uncomfortable feeling that he was missing something obvious? Why did he get the sense that he, too, was guilty of the same ignorance JvA had been rallying against? The latest email reminded him again of Beveridge and his account, now eighty years old, of the "giant evils" rotting Britain from within. The idleness, ignorance, disease, want and squalor which the post-war welfare state was meant to eradicate. How much had changed since then, really?

The "giant" evils were an everyday enemy at the Foundation, Tanner's endless endeavour to ease the pain of destitution still felt by so many in this grand, wealthy metropolis. For every Michelin-starred restaurant there was still a foodbank. For every millionaire, a beggar. Did JvA see themselves as a modern-day Beveridge? Not a psychopath with a grudge, but a social reformer with a taste for the psychedelic?

Whatever he'd missed or failed to understand, Tanner did know one thing. JvA had been very clear that sometimes you had to take a step back to move forward, accepting short-term pain for long-term gain. He had no idea what the gain might be, but he knew the pain would be excruciating if the banking system was shut down for any length of time. Excruciating, and possibly fatal.

76

NIKKI AWOKE WITH AN UNEXPECTED FEELING OF EXCITEMENT; the sadness of the previous night having been buried beneath restorative sleep. She felt a little tingle of anticipation, in fact, at the knowledge she would be spending the day—and maybe the weekend—with the suave Swiss stranger. She was just so used to working alone.

The sensation was still there as she knocked on the door of Gérard's suite, having woken up early to make the journey across London. There had been a late-night phone call before bed, Nikki sharing what Tommy had told her and confirming he was willing to bring Gérard onboard. She and Gérard had also established they were both morning people, and she accepted his suggestion that they meet first thing for breakfast in his suite. She had no doubts as to his propriety, and the benefits of privacy were obvious. They probably did a mean breakfast at Claridge's, too.

Nikki arrived wearing a midnight blue, long-sleeved sweater dress and her favourite knee-length boots. The dress again showed off her fine, smooth neck, and she dabbed an extra drop of precious Portrait of a Lady on each earlobe in the lift. She was gratified to see the look on Gérard's face as he opened the door, his senses combining in appreciation.

Gérard regained his composure just in time to usher her in. She sat at the table for two, an island of professionalism amid the opulence of the suite, and made a point of ordering before they got down to business. Gérard seemed not to know what to make of her, and he was strangely apologetic when they came to discuss the investigation.

'You're sure your client was okay with me being involved?' he asked.

'The circumstances are unusual enough that I think he'd welcome anyone who might be able to help,' answered Nikki. 'So long as you commit to working with me and don't share anything with *your* client first.'

'I don't like being lied to so brazenly,' said Gérard. 'So, you can believe me when I say I don't want anything to do with this Toad of yours.'

Nikki beamed. 'We're a team, then. We'll crack it together.'

Doubt clouded the Swiss's face. 'I'm sorry Nikki, because here I feel like a charlatan. The truth is I've come up with nothing so far.' Gérard's English was perfect, but only a native French-speaker could say "char-la-ton" as he did.

'Well, that's good, in a way,' offered Nikki. 'Because neither have I. Although I do have an idea of where we can start.'

'Go on.'

'I have a record of all the graduates who joined the tech group at National Bank in Holly's year and on two years either side. And I've made a list of everyone I could find at her school—or with similar degrees to her at Imperial—who are roughly the same age. It's a long shot, but maybe we can track down someone who knew her?'

'That's smart. There's no alternative to grunt work now. Hopefully two pairs of hands will double our chances.'

'Or, at least, they'll halve the time.'

Gérard laughed. 'Indeed. We'll eat first, shall we? And then we can get started.'

77

LJ HAD A KNACK FOR READING PEOPLE and their motives. She'd spent most of her working life in the civil service, navigating the choppy waters of Whitehall and Westminster, learning how to look beyond face value for the real meaning of words and deeds. Manipulation, obfuscation and deception were the stock-in-trade of mandarins and politicians alike, and LJ considered herself more attuned than most. But JvA had her stumped.

She texted James Allen with a brief update, but she barely had time to grab a coffee and croissant from the Downing Street service kitchen when there came a knock at her office door. Without waiting for a response, the man himself walked in.

'Prime Minister!' LJ stood hurriedly, surprised at both the unannounced visit and the sight of the PM in a casual jumper and chinos. He carried a steaming coffee in one hand and a sheaf of papers in the other.

'No, sit, sit,' Allen gestured, making himself comfortable in the chair opposite hers. 'I've been upstairs, thinking about this bank nonsense. I've been wracking my brains for an hour, and I haven't the foggiest.'

LJ smiled at his use of words, wholly appropriate for the gloom which had settled outside. 'I've just been having exactly the same conversation with Rob Tanner.'

'And?'

'We ran it through what he calls his Kipling test: what, why, when, how, where and who?'

Allen smiled. 'Ah, the poem! "*Six Honest Serving Men.*" Not very inclusive perhaps, but quite useful for problem-solving. Let's give it a go… brainstorm the likeliest perpetrators. Like speed chess. You say the first one that comes to mind, then I'll do the same. Rapid fire. Okay?'

LJ nodded her agreement. 'Okay.'

'You write them down, then we'll go back through the list for means and motive. I'll start.' As she reached for her notepad, LJ was struck, as always by Allen's winning combination of charm, drive and enthusiasm. She wondered if there was anyone else in the world who knew how much of a paper tiger he was, if he himself appreciated how much only got done because of LJ's unglamorous diligence behind the scenes, away from the flashbulbs and microphones.

'The Russians or the Chinese,' Allen ventured, kickstarting the first round. 'Or some other rogue state.'

'Terrorists,' she shot back.

'Organised crime.'

'Popular movements and pressure groups. Eco warriors and the like.'

'An overseas banking competitor.'

LJ paused for a moment. 'Bond villain.'

Allen almost spat out his coffee, but recovered to offer, 'Disgruntled employees?'

'Political opponents,' countered LJ, under the cover of raised eyebrows.
Allen thought for a moment. 'That's me done. Any more from you?'
LJ shook her head.
Allen rubbed his chin. 'Not a very long list, is it?'
'No, sir.'
'Okay, let's rank them for means and motive. The Russians or Chinese?'
'They've been devoting extraordinary resources to cyber warfare for a long time, but why target just the UK? And why when the banks and markets are shut?'
'A test run?' Allen suggested.
'What would be the point?' LJ picked at the croissant on her desk, wiping flakes of pastry from her fingers with a napkin. 'And surely the security services would have picked up something through their networks?'
'You'd think,' Allen agreed. 'Terrorists?'
'Again, I'd question the timing. And whether anyone in those networks would have the sophistication to do this.'
'They managed nine-eleven.'
'Yes, but this is a whole new level of complexity, sir. They'd have needed sleepers in the banks for years.'
'Good point, LJ. Write that down, please.' He pointed at the notepad. LJ found it often helped to put her thoughts into words, and the pages of her pad were duly filled with lists, policy recommendations, briefing notes. 'I can see the motive,' Allen continued. 'A simple act of war, but again, why just the UK?'
'Logistics maybe? The City's a small geographic area. Easy to co-ordinate. But surely the intelligence services would have heard whispers, no?'
'You'd certainly hope so.' Allen took another sip of his coffee. Beyond the windows, the fog was thickening into a real pea-souper – or whatever the modern version might be. Allen didn't pass comment, but he noticed it all the same. Like the Great Smog of December '52. It all added to the week's Churchillian aura, he supposed. 'Who's next?'
'Organised crime. But, if they've got this capability, surely they'd have just stripped the funds and disappeared before everything shut for Christmas?'
'I agree. The timing seems to point away from crime *per se*.'
LJ glanced at her list. 'Popular movements, then? Eco warriors,

anti-capitalists, or maybe anti-globalists. But I can't see how they pass the sophistication test. There's no way they could plot and execute this without leaving a trail. And what would they gain?'

'Leverage?' Allen suggested.

'For what?'

'That's the sixty-four-thousand-dollar question.' Again, Allen gestured, with a smile, at her pad. 'Next?'

'An overseas competitor.' LJ touched her fingers to her forehead in contemplation. 'It's a stretch for me. You destroy the UK banking system, sure, but you also cripple a G7 economy. You'd have customers here. What's the upside?'

'Agreed. I seem to remember your Bond villain was next.' Allen shot her an amused look.

'It fits the "lone nutter" scenario but fails pretty much all of our other tests – prior warning from the security services, sophistication, capability, reach.'

Allen nodded. 'Next?'

'Disgruntled employees.' LJ shook her head. 'But I can't see how there would be enough of them with the requisite seniority and experience, who just happen to have fallen off the grid *and* kept their activities hidden.'

Again, Allen nodded in agreement. 'Which, I believe, leaves political opponents.' He grinned. 'And I think we know they couldn't organise their way out of a paper bag. Let alone do it in secret!' He fixed his eyes on hers. 'So, what have we got?'

'I think we need to follow the sleeper angle,' LJ began. 'We keep coming back to this. In most of these scenarios, you have to assume that there have been multiple antagonists working secretly within the banks. And for an extended period of time.'

'Exactly. So, we'll need to have personnel records re-examined and cross-referenced.'

'Yes, and all recent communications checked. Look for connections. I'll make sure GCHQ are on it.'

Allen nodded, then asked, again, 'So, what's the leverage? What do they want?'

LJ shrugged. 'Tanner asked but got that vague response about society being sick and needing to take its medicine. I know we never—' she coughed theatrically into her hand '—negotiate with terrorists, but that's very different to knowing what JvA's demands might be. What do we lose by asking the direct question?'

'Okay, let's both reflect how best to do that.' Allen took another sip of coffee. 'And what about the idea that this is some kind of warning shot? The gradual build-up with National Bank? The diversionary attacks overnight?'

'We're being played,' LJ replied firmly. Even from where she was sitting, sharing a life-raft adrift in a sea of unknowns, she was sure of that much. 'Banks and markets may be closed, and the weekend gives us some breathing space, but we can't lose sight of the fact that the situation's worsening. If there's an escalation today, then those worst-case scenarios we discussed last night become tomorrow's actualities. We should accelerate preparations accordingly.'

Allen's face took on a cold intensity. 'You're right, LJ. One hundred per cent.' Then it warmed a fraction. 'Is there anything else we're missing?'

'One more thing, sir. Paul Benham at Treasury got me thinking about Black Swan events, the kind of things which seem impossible at the time but which can be explained away with hindsight. I guess I'm just wondering what it is we're all assuming about these attacks that's just plain *wrong*?'

'I thought Wednesday's goose was the last bird I'd have to deal with this Christmas, but you raise a good point.' Allen sucked in his cheeks, then stood. 'I'll think it all over, and we can touch base in a bit. Thanks again, LJ. I'll be in the flat.'

78

TANNER HAD ASKED Chrissie to print the biographies of the six CEOs and CTOs who would shortly be arriving at the National Bank offices. He'd met all the CEOs at one time or another but only a couple of the technology heads. Without needing to be asked, Chrissie brought a selection of croissants and a fresh pot of coffee along with the biographies.

'I don't imagine you had time for breakfast this morning,' she said.

'Security told me you were in just after seven, and I know you were on the phone to Mike at one-thirty.'

Tanner marvelled again at Chrissie's total, understated command of her domain and wondered once more why she had suffered Kellett for so long. In contrast to the subtle blue of yesterday, today she was wearing a figure-hugging dress of deep crimson. Her hair, again, sat loosely but luxuriantly on her shoulders.

'Is there anything that goes on round here you don't know about?' Tanner enquired with a grin.

'Other than who's causing this mess, not a lot!' Then serious, she asked, 'What else do you need? Will Ms Markham be joining you?'

'Yes,' replied Tanner. He made a point of ignoring Chrissie's exaggerated formality, shorthand for what he presumed was distrust. 'Could you ask Mike and Ashley to come up as soon as they're ready?'

'I'd already suggested they be here at quarter to nine, just in case.' Tanner didn't miss the look—a strange, almost told-you-so expression—she tried to hide by glancing at her watch. A very fine watch that he had never seen her wear before. 'So, you've got five minutes to wolf down those croissants.'

At 8.45 a.m. exactly, there was a knock on the door and Ashley appeared.

'May I come in?' she said.

'Of course,' replied Tanner. He stood, looking behind her. 'Is Mike with you?'

Ashley smiled as she glanced over her shoulder. 'He's just finishing up downstairs. He'll only be a minute.'

At the realisation that they were alone, Tanner allowed himself to drink Ashley in. Today she was wearing a simple black shirtdress with contrasting white collar and cuffs, cut just above the knee. Her only jewellery was a pair of small pearl earrings on thin gold chains, which complemented the delicacy of her ears.

Wearing little or no make-up, the minimalism of her style simply drew attention to how naturally beautiful she was. Her hair was tied in a loose bun, through which ran, almost unnoticeable, two small wooden hairsticks the exact same shade of walnut.

'You look stunning,' said Tanner. Regret surged at the missed opportunity of the other night. He felt a rush of blood, a need to be close to her.

'Mike is going to be on his way soon, remember,' Ashley countered. But while her voice was stern, her smile was anything but.

Tanner put his hands up in mock surrender. 'How are you doing?' he asked.

'I'm a bit tired.' Ashley walked over, closing the physical distance between her and Tanner. 'Mike and I were here late. And then early.'

'Lucky man,' offered Tanner.

'You said it.'

Their eyes met, and Tanner could almost feel her breath on his skin. 'Do you trust him?' he said.

'Mike? Of course. I know this happened on his watch, but he's clearly a good man.' Ashley cocked an eyebrow. 'Don't you?'

'I trust him completely.' Tanner smiled. 'I just wanted to check we were on the same page. As usual, it seems we are.'

Ashley returned Tanner's smile, and for a moment he was content just to be near her, sharing the same air and the same light. Then he remembered all that was at stake.

'Any progress?' he asked.

'Not really. We're looking for an answer, but we don't even know what language the question is written in.'

Tanner took her hand in his and squeezed it gently. 'We'll crack it. Codes, riddles, puzzles, they always get solved. It's just a matter of time.'

Her eyes locked once more on his. 'But how long do you have?'

In three days, virtually to the minute, the nation's banks were due to open their doors for business. They'd achieved precious little in the previous four. But before Tanner could answer, there was a knock on the open door. Ashley withdrew her hand just as Mike Sorensen appeared. Something of the jailhouse pallor had faded, despite his incarceration in the bank's offices for most, if not all, of the night.

Sorensen smiled and flashed his eyebrows at Tanner and Ashley. 'I hope I'm not interrupting anything?'

'No,' answered Tanner. 'Not at all, Mike.'

Sorensen laughed and stepped into the office, closing the door behind him. 'In that case,' he said, 'let's get to work.'

79

TANNER BROUGHT THE MEETING OF CEOs AND CTOs TO ORDER. Glancing around the table, he sensed a mix of resentment and apprehension and little goodwill – festive or otherwise. So be it. He was not there to massage egos, but at the same time, Tanner knew it would be counterproductive to antagonise his opposite numbers.

'The prime minister has asked me to co-ordinate our response,' Tanner began. 'But that's simply because National's been fighting this longest. If we work together and harness the expertise around the table, we'll get this beaten faster. Then we can all go back to knocking six bells out of each other.' He grinned, and at least some of the others followed suit.

'Some of you may know Mike Sorensen,' he indicated to his left, 'but probably not Ashley Markham.' He focused his gaze on her, drawing strength from her smile of acknowledgement. 'Ashley is one of the leading cyber experts in the US, and it was fortunate, at least for us, that she happened to be in London for Christmas.' This, or more likely Ashley's presence, took a little more of the chill from the air. 'Now, I'll let Mike give the National perspective.'

Sorensen chronicled the events to date in a concise but comprehensive briefing that provided enough technical detail to inform the CTOs without overwhelming the CEOs. He answered questions with charm and admitted to errors with humility. Tanner then invited each of the other banks to make their contributions.

Some had the grace to admit that their own institutions were far less advanced in their responses than Sorensen's team, as was to be expected. But others had to have their moment in the spotlight, holding forth about systems and capabilities and technologies in a level of detail that did nothing but waste time none of them had.

Thoroughly dispirited, Tanner caught Ashley's eye as the last speaker was droning to an overdue close. She surreptitiously pointed to herself, and Tanner took the hint.

'Thank you,' he said, resisting the urge to roll his eyes. 'That was most helpful. Now before we move on, I wonder if Ashley would like to add anything?'

Ashley acknowledged the question with a quick smile. 'Thanks, Rob. As

I see it, and to state the obvious, we're dealing with something entirely new here. Something beyond not just our knowledge, but our comprehension.' She paused to make eye contact with a couple of the more self-regarding attendees. 'But let's not lose sight of the fact that these aren't seven different attacks, it's one attack in seven different places.' Ashley met a dozen blank looks. Still, she pressed on.

'Imagine you're the lord of a medieval castle. You're impregnable to bows and arrows. You've learned how to deal with battering rams, siege towers, any method known to medieval man. Then, the next day, a new enemy turns up and hits you with gunpowder or cannons. Game over.' Now she had their attention.

'What I'm saying is there's no point in trying to fight the attack alone while your neighbour does the same. You're all, individually, finished. You really *have* to pool resources to work out how to deal with the new reality. That means you all need to send your best people here to work with Mike. One effort. When they find the answer, you can apply it to all your systems. Spreading the effort is like looking at seven symptoms, not one cure. And, if you're worried about competitive advantage—' Ashley deliberately focused on the most pompous pair, '—don't be. What's the risk? Your people get to see inside National, not vice versa.'

There was silence around the table, then a couple of nods and, before long, unanimous consent. At the break-up of the meeting, Tanner worked the room, shaking hands with all and thanking them for their cooperation. He left Sorensen talking logistics with his fellow CTOs and returned to his office. Ashley, having slipped out ahead of him, was already there. She was sitting in his office chair, legs crossed, looking out the window. A wall of fog, punctured here and there by the City's skyscrapers: the Gherkin, the Cheese Grater. Over the river loomed the Shard.

'Well,' offered Tanner brightly, closing the door behind him. 'You saved the day.'

Ashley smiled and uncrossed her legs. Tanner forced himself to focus on her face.

'Sometimes you need a female touch with these middle-aged sorts,' she said. 'I'm sorry though, Rob; I knew they would jump at the chance to work inside National, but I should have asked.'

'It's irrelevant,' replied Tanner, his enthusiasm undimmed. 'Without your intervention, we'd still be going around in circles. Now we've got the pick of the industry's talent under our direct control. So, Ms Markham, let's work out how best to use it.'

80

WITH THEIR COVER STORY AGREED, and with breakfast eaten, Nikki and Gérard launched into the task at hand. Nikki had compiled a huge dossier of names, and it would take a long time to contact them all. The plan was to pose as recruiters so nobody would find their messages suspicious, and there would be no reason for anyone to lie to them.

They started their inquiries via social media. Other than Gérard's occasional requests for fresh coffee and the quiet ticking of a clock on the mantelpiece, they worked in companionable silence. Gérard's suite served as the ideal office: warm, comfortable and private.

Nikki had started by messaging a raft of Holly's former National Bank colleagues, and just after eleven she got her first reply. She soon had her mark, a young man, on the phone, and after a minute of easy banter, she cut to the chase.

'You see, Holly came recommended to us, but we just can't track her down. Our client needs good people right away, so it's a great opportunity for her. Consultancy rates, blah blah, you know.'

'Right,' said the young man, uncertainty lingering in his tone.

'And there would be a finder's fee in it for anyone who provided any useful information.'

The voice at the other end perked up. 'Well, Holly was damn good. She should never have… *left*. But no one ever heard another word from her after that. A few of us tried to stay in touch, but nope, nothing.'

'And she never said where she was going? Where she *might* go?'

'No, she always played her cards close to her chest. She was very private. Very smart, like *ridiculously* smart, but shy. Almost a bit…' he paused, searching for the right word. 'Intense.'

Over the next three hours, Nikki and Gérard each got two more leads, but all with the same outcome. Then Gérard got hold of one of Holly's former course-mates at Imperial, who finally added something new, small though it was.

'She mentioned once that she wanted to do a master's in the US.'

'But no school, or location?' prompted Gérard.

'No, sorry.'

And that was all they had to show for a morning's work when they finally broke for lunch.

81

'FUCK!' Tanner couldn't help the expletive. He'd been discussing with Ashley how best to utilise the new technology task force while keeping a weather eye on his inbox. On the stroke of eleven, a new mail dropped.

'What?' Ashley's eyes widened in concern.

'Come and see.'

Ashley walked around the desk and read over his shoulder.

> **TO:** Robert Tanner
> **FROM:** Joen van Aken
> **DATE:** Friday, 27 December 2024 at 11:00
> Gula
>
> Hello, Rob.
> They say time Flies when you're having fun. Having a Baal? Living like a Lord? Hopefully not one of Mr Golding's.
> Remember, though, you can have too much of a good thing,

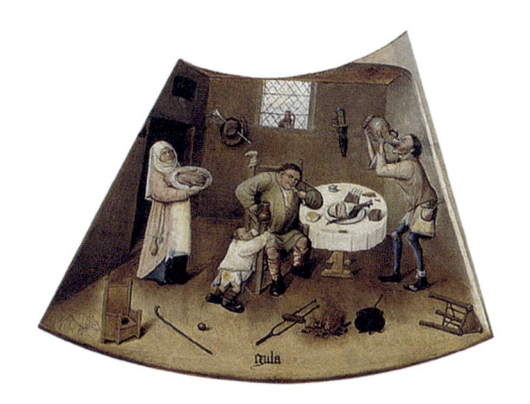

as the old proverb says. 23:20. It's just like in the song Big Time. Everything just gets bigger: eyes, mouths, bellies and... now what was it?

You don't want to end up like Mr Creosote. Not even Ninkarrak could save him. All that Gloop! No, unlike the four greedy losers, you'll need to find Octavian's golden ticket. Perhaps Hassein's grandfather will show you the Way?

Freddie says "Nothing really matters," but this really matters to me. I hope it will to your new friend too.

JvA

Before either could speak, Tanner's internal phone rang. He hit the speaker button so Ashley could hear too.

'Rob, it's Mike.'

'Don't tell me,' said Tanner. 'Things just got worse.'

'How'd you know?' asked a surprised Sorensen.

'Another email from JvA just landed in my inbox.' Tanner exhaled noisily. 'So, what's he done?'

'Another zero.'

'What?'

'Every account has been inflated tenfold,' clarified the technology chief. '*Every* account.'

'Fuck!' Tanner closed his eyed and buried his face in his hands, working the tips of his fingers hard into his forehead, searching for temporary relief. He took a deep breath and looked up to find Ashley staring directly at him. Her expression, usually so vibrant, was entirely blank, that beautiful canvas scraped clean of light and life. Tanner imagined his own face bore the imprint of JvA's email every bit as clearly.

'Rob?' Sorensen's tinny enquiry broke the silence.

'Yes, sorry Mike, we're here. Ashley's with me. Are you sure about this?' The question came out more like a plea.

'Sorry, Rob. No doubt.'

'In that case,' said Tanner, 'I need to call Downing Street.'

'And I'm coming straight down, Mike,' added Ashley, excusing herself to Tanner by pointing a finger towards the floor. 'I'll be right there.'

Tanner thanked Sorensen and rang off. As Ashley's back disappeared through the door, Tanner found himself wishing, improbably, that he was back in his dream world. Nightmares always end when you open your eyes. This, it seemed, would not.

82

LJ PICKED UP TANNER'S CALL on the second ring. Again, there was no preamble.

'How did it go?' she asked.

'The CEO meeting went well, actually, but that's not why I'm calling.'

'Oh.' The utterance carried no surprise, only weary resignation.

'Another zero. On all accounts. Every account in the bank, and I assume the country, now has at least ten thousand pounds in it. And another email from JvA. I've sent it to you. Same style as before – another of the sins. Gluttony, this time, and a whole bunch of obscure references I haven't looked up yet.'

There was no immediate reply, simply a slow exhalation. Then a short, sharp instruction. 'I'm calling an emergency COBRA meeting for five o'clock. Do what you can but be here then.' The line dropped.

After LJ, Tanner's next call was to Sir Peter Wilford. Tanner had been giving the chairman regular updates, for which Sir Peter had expressed his customary gratitude – his politeness out of all proportion to the usefulness of Tanner's calls. The grandee had remained unfailingly positive and supportive thus far, but Tanner knew there must be a limit to the older man's reserves of stoicism.

Tanner could imagine Sir Peter, in his smart drawing room, desperately trying to think of an encouraging response to this latest bulletin. Instead, a gloomy voice replied, 'You realise we're notionally bankrupt, Rob? No doubt about it now.'

'Yes, Chairman. But then so is every bank in the country – and possibly the Bank of England for good measure.' Tanner could have sworn there was a suppressed laugh at the other end of the line.

'Have you got anywhere with my architect chappie?'

With everything else going on, Tanner had completely forgotten Sir

Peter's suggestion of hiring an "ancient" software programmer to reverse engineer the attack.

'Not yet, Chairman,' he admitted, 'but we have all seven banks' resources to deploy now.' Thoroughly embarrassed, he moved swiftly to end the call. After hanging up, and more than a day late, he ran downstairs and put the chairman's suggestion to Sorensen and Ashley.

'What about coming at the problem from the other end?' was how he framed it. 'Rather than looking at the most modern solutions, how about the most ancient?'

Ashley looked at him quizzically. 'I'm not with you?'

'Me neither,' added Sorensen.

Tanner continued. 'There's a fundamental flaw in our systems somewhere. We're trying to fight it with all the most up-to-date knowledge of the twenty-first century. But what if we went back to the 1950s and asked a programmer, "How do we build this flaw into the system from day one, from the first piece of code?"'

Ashley's eyes narrowed in apparent surprise. 'But that's like saying, "Let's solve a problem with sending humans to Mars by using technology from Apollo 11."'

'What do we have to lose?'

Ashley shrugged. Sorensen looked no more convinced than his compatriot, but he acquiesced.

'You're the boss, Rob,' he said.

Tanner sighed and made for the door. Didn't he just know it.

83

TANNER SPENT THE NEXT FEW HOURS walking the floors of the National Bank HQ, offering moral support, but little else. Tea and sympathy, his mother would have called it. The CEO of a major UK bank, and what was he actually equipped to do? He couldn't write code, design apps, or create algorithms – the minutiae of a modern business. He was a dinosaur.

On the way back to his office he caught a brief glimpse of Ashley in a meeting room, but he didn't feel he could disturb her. And when Tommy Steele popped up to put his head around the door, it was only to tell him that Nikki Cheung had found no news of Holly Brand, other than a vague mention of her plans to study in the United States. Tanner called the other CEOs, but none had anything new to offer. What on earth would he say at the COBRA meeting?

Then, just after two-thirty, the intercom buzzed.

'I've got Charlie Griffiths from the Bank of England surveillance team on the line,' said Chrissie.

'Thanks, Chrissie, put him through.'

'*Her.*'

Tanner cursed his clumsiness and waited for the connection.

'Mr Tanner?' came the voice, unmistakably that of a woman.

'Hi, Charlie,' answered Tanner. 'And please, call me Rob. How can I help?'

'Actually, I hope it's we who might be able to help.' The confident, cut-glass voice on the other end of the line might have been lifted straight from the BBC of his childhood.

'Oh?' he replied.

'You requested we ask our foreign counterparts for previous occurrences of unusual IT activity. I've no idea if they'll be of any significance, but we've had a couple of responses from the US. We're happy to follow up at this end, but I thought you'd like to know.'

'Thank you.' Tanner looked to the window. Was the fog lifting, or was he just getting used to it? 'That's kind, but I'd quite like something practical to do. I'll follow up with them myself.'

'If you're sure?' Charlie hesitated. She might have been surprised at his willingness to get his hands dirty with such a task. Or perhaps she doubted his ability to do so.

'Yes, please. If you'd email me their details, I'll get straight on it.' Tanner tried to inject authority into his voice.

Five minutes later, he had a very different accent on the line. It was the soothing Texan drawl of Chad Klotz, chief executive of the First Star Credit Union of Austin, the state capital.

'I hear you're having a few issues over there?' Klotz said. His tone made these "issues" sounded reassuringly insignificant.

'Good morning, Chad,' replied Tanner. 'We are, indeed, which is why I appreciate your help. A contact at the Bank of England put me on to

215

you. I wonder if you'd just describe the problems that you had with your systems. Why you thought it was worth mentioning to the Fed?'

'Well,' began Klotz. He scoffed. 'It was the darndest thing. In fifty years, we'd never had a problem with our systems, then these errors started appearing in customer balances when we did the overnight reconciliations. Always a round number difference. Eight became eighty, that kind of thing. No logic or pattern. And only with small accounts.' He laughed. 'Although as a Texan, I shouldn't really admit we have those!'

Tanner forced a laugh. Klotz's problem sounded astonishingly similar to his own. 'How did you pick it up? And fix it?'

'Pure luck, Rob. I don't mind admitting it. We had a young intern working for us. Studying at the University's school of information science and working here part-time to help pay her fees. She picked it up. Hell! Danged if she wasn't a Brit like you. Well, *Irish,* I should say… You still there, Rob?'

Tanner was, but his mind was racing in a thousand directions. He took a moment before replying, 'Yes, Chad. So, what was the cause?'

'You won't believe it, Rob. It was the simplest thing. A problem with a few lines of code in the oldest part of the systems. Something we'd caused with a software update. One of those patches they talk about had failed. Well, that *patch* threw some kind of monkey wrench into the works.'

'And this intern picked it up?'

'Yes. It was pure luck. They'd been looking at just that type of coding in her college class, so she just took a long shot!'

Tanner's brain kicked up a gear. 'I don't suppose you remember when it was, Chad?'

Klotz laughed. 'I'll never forget. Thanksgiving—Black Friday—twenty-sixteen. The Longhorns were playing the Horned Frogs at the Memorial Stadium. I'd just arrived there when I got a call from Bryony saying the problem was fixed. Let me tell you, I've never enjoyed a pre-game beer so much in my life!'

'Bryony?'

'Bryony Sears. The intern.'

'And is she still with you?' Tanner asked, intensity sharp now in his voice. He jotted the name on the pad in front of him…

'No, she's long gone, Rob, I'm afraid. She was just here for one semester. I wish we could have kept her, but we're just too small. I imagine she'll have gone to one of the big banks or tech companies. She was smart. Real smart! From the University of Texas, same as me. They don't take just anyone there, you know!'

'Would you have any personal details for her on file, Chad?'

'I doubt it. Probably not from eight years ago.'

'It's important, Chad.' There was a harder edge to Tanner's voice now. The cloak of affability thrown off.

'Let me see,' answered Klotz, brusquely. 'I'll get back to you.'

Tanner realised his mistake, a beat too late. 'I'm sorry, Chad. I didn't mean to be short. This is really helpful. Thank you. Thank you very much.'

But the line had already gone dead.

84

THE SECOND AMERICAN RESPONSE was from the Dutchess Savings Bank in Poughkeepsie, New York. This time, Tanner did his homework before dialling the area code. A quick review of the bank's website revealed that it had been founded in 1872 and was one of the dwindling number of mutual savings banks in the country, serving the local mid-state community with small loans and mortgages. Again, a welcoming voice answered, and after a brief explanation, Tanner was put straight through to his opposite number at Dutchess, a Jack Horan.

Of course, all Tanner wanted to do was ask about the historic security breach which had been flagged to the Bank of England. But he bit his tongue, saving his questions until he'd spent two minutes discussing the weather in the Hudson Valley and Jack's family arrangements for the holidays.

'It was a strange one,' began Jack, finally getting to the meat of it. 'One day everything was fine, then we started getting complaints from customers that their balance was wrong. What was so odd was that the balances were larger than they ought to be – inflated, you might say. Our customers choose us because they trust us more than the big banks—no offence!—so something like that's a disaster.'

'When was this, Jack?' The transatlantic echoes of what was going on at National were starting to concern Tanner. It was as if he was being haunted by the Ghost of Breaches Past.

'Two thousand seventeen,' said the American. 'July. It turned out to be a simple glitch in our source code. A problem with some ancient thing everyone had forgotten about. None of our IT consultants had ever seen anything like it; I'll tell you that much.'

'How did you fix it?'

'One of our people was going to a night school class and they'd been looking at early coding. It was pure guesswork on their part, and a hell of a stroke of luck on ours…'

'I don't suppose that employee is still with you, by any chance?' asked Tanner.

'No, Rob. She was only here on a maternity cover.'

Tanner sat upright. 'She?'

'Yes. Rhoda Kane.'

Tanner's hope dimmed, but he kept the disappointment from his voice. The coincidences were stacking up like presents beneath the tree.

'Thanks, Jack,' offered Tanner, having taken a second to collect his thoughts. 'You've been a huge help. Silly question, but what was she like, Rhoda?'

Jack took a breath. 'I didn't speak to her much. She kept herself to herself. Very quiet. But confident when she explained about IT.'

'Age? Background? Looks?'

'Oh, mid-twenties. East coast probably. No accent that I remember. Maybe a little… overweight, you might say? Awful haircut. I do remember that.'

'Would you be able to send me any details you have on file, Jack? As I say, you've been an *enormous* help. I can't thank you enough.'

'Sure. I'll have my PA send them straight away. Now you drop in and see me if you're ever in the Hudson Valley, okay?'

'Will do, Jack. And let me know if ever you find yourself in London.'

Tanner hung up. In the ensuing quiet, he reflected on his two calls. Two isolated incidents at opposite ends of the country, eight months apart. The same problem, solved by temporary female employees in their mid-twenties. One Irish, one American. It wasn't just odd, he reasoned, it was utterly bizarre.

He stood, letting his legs carry him across the carpeted floor until he was at the window. The fog had lifted but the sun shone only timidly, a thin, watery light. Looking into the day's gloom, the main thing Tanner saw was his own reflection, the image of a man who so far had achieved nothing.

His thoughts were interrupted by a knock on the door. Chrissie entered, brandishing a handful of papers. The letterheads showed they were from First Star Credit, Texas.

'The personnel record and CV of Bryony Sears?' Chrissie flicked through the pages, lingering on the cover page. 'From October twenty-sixteen?' She handed them over with a quizzical look.

Tanner turned from the window and accepted them sheepishly. 'Probably a waste of time.'

'Rob, you don't waste time. What is it?'

'You know how I asked the Bank of England to appeal to its foreign counterparts?' Tanner said. 'I had them looking for any other incidences of account balance manipulations.'

'I remember.'

'Well, we got two responses. From Austin, Texas, and Poughkeepsie, New York. Similar problems way back in twenty-sixteen and seventeen, eight months and nearly two thousand miles apart. But the same cause: historic coding issues.'

Chrissie's expression remained unchanged. A faint proto-smile, slightly narrowed eyes. 'That's not so strange, is it?'

'Maybe not on their own.' Tanner drummed his fingers atop the wad of paper. 'But in both cases, the problem was found—and the solution suggested—by a temporary female employee. Different names but both women in their mid-twenties. Meanwhile, we've not heard a peep out of Holly Brand ever since she left, other than a friend saying she had talked about going to the States.'

'So, you're wondering if it's more than a coincidence?'

'It's barmy, I know. But whenever I hear the word coincidence, I think of *Goldfinger*.' In response to Chrissie's look of complete bewilderment, he laughed. 'It's a quote. From the film: "Once is happenstance, twice is coincidence…"'

Chrissie raised her eyebrows. 'And three?'

'"Three times is enemy action."'

85

TANNER SOON HAD NIKKI CHEUNG on the other end of the line. With her was the Swiss investigator Tommy had told him about – the one who had almost certainly been set on the same trail by Martin Kellett but who appeared, for now, to have defected to their side. Tanner was wary, but this was clearly no ordinary case, and he was grateful for all the help he could get.

'It's like Holly Brand lost her job and then evaporated,' Nikki said. She sounded full of energy, like a dog with a bone. 'We've tracked down a few old friends and colleagues, but there's been no contact in eight years. It's the most complete disappearance I—we—have ever encountered. She'd have to have extraordinary technical skills. Not to mention the unbelievable emotional strength you'd need to just vanish and never look back.' She paused. 'Either that—'

'Or?'

There was a pause, just a beat, on the other end of the line before Nikki responded. 'Or she's long dead. And for some reason, it's never come to light.'

Tanner had an image of that last meeting with Kellett and Holly. Another case where he should have stood up for what was right. He asked quietly, 'Any gut feel at all?'

Nikki weighed the question for what must have been the twentieth time that day before replying.

'She told the one person she seemed closest to, a sweet little old lady from down the road, that she couldn't send her a postcard "from where she was going." If that wasn't an allusion to suicide, then Holly's one tough cookie, Rob. Hard as nails. So, I'll turn it back on you, if I may? Is that how you'd have described her?'

Tanner tried to picture Holly objectively, but his memory was too coloured by that final confrontation. 'No. No, it isn't.'

It was Gérard who relieved the resulting silence, his voice coming thickly down the phone. 'Mr Tanner, you said there was something you wanted to discuss?'

'Yes.' Tanner cleared his throat. 'It's strange. Or maybe I'm just so desperate for any new piece of information that I'm clutching at straws. Let me explain.'

He walked them through his conversations with the American bankers, realising as he spoke quite how ridiculous his idea of a connection must sound; the banks' problems had been similar and had been solved by young women – but that wasn't proof of anything. By the end his tone was openly apologetic. 'And that's it. Bryony Sears in Austin and Rhoda Kane in New York. There's probably nothing to it, but I've got nothing else.'

'Neither have we,' said Nikki. 'So, what have we got to lose? Send through whatever you have, and we'll check it out.'

86

GÉRARD TOOK RHODA KANE; Nikki began searching for Bryony Sears.

Gérard sat at a writing table in front of one of the suite's double windows, while Nikki was happy to ensconce herself, feet up, on one of the large sofas in front of the fire. The only sound, to begin with, was the tapping of keyboards, both engrossed in their respective databases. Every now and then, they broke their concentration to share a look of companionship… or possibly something warmer.

But before long, the looks began to change. A tightening in Gérard's face, a biting of Nikki's lip. Gérard made a couple of calls, in French and German, which she assumed were to former colleagues in the security services. The room went quiet, and Gérard sat, immobile, staring out of the window, seemingly lost in thought. Nikki was about to speak when she realised that he still had his phone to one ear and was evidently waiting, very patiently, for a response. Eventually it was received, and with a predictably charming expression of gratitude, Gérard ended the call and turned to Nikki. His blue eyes, evocative of an icy mountain spring, locked with hers. When he smiled, there was an immediate thaw.

'It seems, dear Nikki, that our Rhoda Kane is nowhere to be found. We have another vanishing lady.'

'Vanishing *ladies*,' Nikki countered, with emphasis. 'Plural.'

He cocked an eyebrow at her. 'You first.'

Nikki reeled off information from her notepad. 'Bryony Sears. No social media profile or internet history at all. No travel logs. No one of that name showing up with anything like that age or employment profile in the US or Ireland. I've emailed a couple of contacts who can access the immigration and employment details to confirm it, but I'm guessing there won't be much. You?'

'Rhoda Kane. No profile. No history. Not a thing. I just got a friend to run her through federal systems; that's why I was holding. But nothing.'

'How can there be no record of either of them?' Nikki shook her head in disbelief. 'They were working at banks! Sure, Bryony was a student intern from overseas, but Rhoda was a full-time employee. There must be a social security number?'

'Not necessarily.' Gérard glanced down to his laptop and back. 'Remember, she was working as maternity cover, Nikki. She probably got the job through a temp agency. Maybe she fobbed them off somehow? A fake driver's licence, who knows? If the agency was in a rush to fill a position, and grab a fee, they might cut corners.'

The two investigators stared at each other, searching for inspiration, neither wanting to admit failure. Then a smile broke over Nikki's face.

'What?'

'You said a driver's licence, photo ID. If they were working, they were being paid. If they were being paid, they had to have bank accounts. They'd need photo ID to open those accounts. Surely one of the banks has a record, or the employment agency does?' She jumped from the sofa, a bundle of unspent energy. 'Come on, Gérard, what do we know about these women?'

Gérard's forehead creased in thought. He was feeling increasingly vindicated in having turned his back on Ziegler and his client and thrown his lot in with Nikki. She was sweet and smart and conscientious – a quality alien to Ziegler and his ilk. Plus, Nikki knew how it felt to lose a father – and more. She would understand his compulsion to bury himself in this investigation. He thought for a moment about the women they sought.

'They were in their mid-twenties,' he offered. 'Technology students.'

'Exactly!' Nikki smiled, a look of contagious enthusiasm. 'Bryony Sears claimed she was studying at the School of Information at UT Austin. Her boss was an alumnus, so it would be too big a risk to lie about that. That gives us a time and place, no?' She ploughed on, each word coming faster than the last. 'We just need to find which of the New York universities Rhoda was at. If she's as smart as it appears, it has to be one of the top three or four.'

'What are you proposing?'

'Legwork!'

Gérard smiled, raised his eyebrows. 'You're serious?'

'Why not? We're getting nowhere here.' Nikki looked conspicuously at her watch. 'We can still make the last flight to New York. Then tomorrow, you cover New York and I'll take the first flight down to Austin. I'll bet I can be there by late morning.'

Gérard's expression changed to one of concern. 'You won't have time to get home first.'

'What, you've never heard of airport shopping?'

'And what about your passport?'

Nikki had already begun packing her laptop into a smart leather attaché case. She stopped, delving further into its recesses, and pulled out a matching leather passport holder, which she waved breezily in his direction. He could only laugh, holding his hands in the air in a gesture of acquiescence. New York it was.

With Gérard's credit card they secured two seats on the day's last flight out of Heathrow. Naturally, the hotel concierge had a car at Monsieur Dumont's immediate disposal. He assured them that they'd be at the airport within the hour. All that remained was to run everything by Nikki's client – now Gérard's, also.

'At least we're doing something,' Tanner acknowledged, once the investigators had filled him in on their plan to chase the spectres of Rhoda in New York and Bryony in Texas.

'Exactly,' said Nikki. 'One more thing: we need account details for the two women, from the banks. They're not on the personnel files they sent through, but the banks must have them somewhere. If they used a staffing agency, try them.'

'Anything else?'

Nikki looked at Gérard, who leaned closer to the handset.

'Rob, two things, if possible. First, we desperately need photos of the two women. It's a real long shot, but we should at least ask if there's anyone still at the banks who might have a photo. Maybe a work social event, who knows? It's unlikely, so long ago, but if we don't ask… Secondly, if the CEOs have any personal contacts at the tech colleges, then that would be really helpful. Chad's an alumnus of the Texas school. Maybe he can tap his network? Or members of their banks' IT departments could? *Anything* that gives us a personal connection would help.'

'Okay,' agreed Tanner. 'I'll see what I can dig up.'

87

THE CLOCK WAS TICKING DOWN to the next COBRA meeting. Tanner hardly relished another expedition into that nest of snakes, but he knew that duty was not something you could pick up and put down at your choosing. He put in calls to Texas and New York, and then realised there was another important American he was forgetting. He cursed his own stupidity at not having thought of it sooner, for if there was one person he could turn to in complete confidence, it was Brin Eliot.

Tanner checked his watch – 4:15 p.m. in the UK, but seven hours earlier in Vail. He imagined his friend tearing down a ski run, that boyish grin plastered on his face, desperate to stay ahead of the younger generation. Which was why Tanner was so surprised when the phone rang only twice before the familiar voice answered.

'Hey buddy, everything okay?'

'Sadly, no,' sighed Tanner. 'I'm afraid we're not really getting anywhere.'

'Is Ashley not helping?' asked Brin.

'No, she's great, although I've hardly seen her. She's been cosseted with our tech guys. No breakthroughs so far, but I think she's been good for their morale.'

'And yours, I hope?' Brin let slip a chuckle.

Tanner resolutely avoided the question with one of his own. 'I thought you'd be on the slopes?'

'Nope, sadly. I'm already back in Boston.'

'Really? Won't your grandmother disown you?'

Brin laughed. 'Taking political office is one of only two acceptable excuses for being absent.'

'Death being the other?' queried Tanner.

'You got it, pal!' Brin laughed again, before turning switch-flip serious. 'How can I help?'

This briefest of conversations summed up the rhythm of Tanner and Eliot's quarter-century of friendship: high jollity flowing effortlessly into deep concern, all built on absolute trust. It was in this spirit that Tanner told his old friend everything—from his conversations with the prime minister to the coincidences in Texas and New York—and their possible connection to his missing computer expert, on whom he had somehow placed ludicrous hope of solving this mess.

'Why not just bring it up at COBRA?' asked Brin. 'Let the security services deal with it?'

'I thought about that, Brin, but look at it objectively. We're talking about a twenty-four-year-old girl, more than eight years ago. Maybe she disappeared for a perfectly good reason. Should I bring the weight of the state down on her for that?'

'It's a tough call, but your intuition's usually good, my friend.'

'What bothers me,' continued Tanner, 'is that these are just two reports we've had back in the first couple of hours from small-town CEOs who've probably got nothing better to do. There could be a thousand like them by the end of the day. I'm meant to be fixing the machines, not seeing ghosts in them, and part of me thinks I can't afford to blow my credibility on a wild goose chase – not so soon. Twice is only coincidence, remember…' Tanner trailed off. If it were anyone else on the other end of the line, he would be embarrassed at the sloppiness of his thoughts, his almost childish urge to talk it through out loud. But it wasn't anyone else on the other end of the line; it was Brin. The American understood everything.

'Okay,' Brin replied. 'I get it. Let me see what I can do. Off-the-record.'

'Thanks, Buddy. I owe you.'

Brin was right. Tanner's instincts were generally sound. But what were they telling him here? Nothing. They were as scrambled as one of Bosch's bloody paintings.

88

LJ APPEARED IN THE DOWNING STREET ANTEROOM brandishing a close-typed sheet of paper.

'Official Secrets Act,' she said. 'Say a word about anything and we send you to our equivalent of Guantanamo Bay. Welcome to the committee.'

Tanner looked into LJ's eyes for a flicker of humour but saw only inscrutability. The sphinx in human form. He signed on the dotted line without reading a word and followed her to the committee room, where the usual COBRA suspects, all the way up to the prime minister, were waiting for him. As soon as Tanner was seated, the PM began.

'So, Rob, from what you've told us, we're no nearer a solution. But at least you now have the best brains from every major bank working under one roof. And while the ante has been upped, so to speak, in numerical terms, there's been no change in the fundamental situation. No theft, ransom demands, anything like that?'

'No, Prime Minister,' Tanner replied. 'Although there is the small legal question of whether we're trading while insolvent.'

Allen turned to LJ. 'We'll need the attorney general to look at that.' Then back to Tanner. 'I see from these emails that our friend Joen has some very eclectic tastes. We're up to gluttony now, are we? And after I announced that anti-obesity drive at conference as well!' The attempt at humour fell flat. He moved swiftly on. 'Anyway, what can you tell us about this *JvA*, Saeed?'

The Head of NCSC answered in a crisp monologue.

'The team at GCHQ have analysed language patterns, search histories, internet traffic. Numerologists, psychologists – everything we can think of. But frankly, and I believe Sally's team agrees, the messages are meaningless gobbledygook. As you say, the latest one is focused on the third deadly sin, *Gula*, the Latin for gluttony. The Bible quote is, as you've no doubt realised, from Proverbs: "Be not among winebibbers; among riotous eaters of flesh. For the drunkard and the glutton shall come to poverty: and drowsiness shall clothe a man with rags."

'*Big Time* is a 1986 pop song by Peter Gabriel. The unstated line of the chorus refers to bank accounts getting bigger… Interesting video, by the way. Baal meant lord in the ancient Semitic languages and was taken into the Bible as Ba'al Zəbûb, or Beelzebub, which can be translated literally as "lord of the flies." Hence the reference to the novel by William Golding.'

Allen interrupted. 'The one with the public schoolboys on the desert island?'

'Yes, Prime Minister,' replied Akhtar, before adding, totally deadpan, 'It's an allegorical tale about the immorality of undeserved power.'

Allen bit back a reply. Tanner thought he saw the PM's face twitch, but Allen said nothing, merely indicated with his hand that Akhtar should continue.

'A golden ticket is usually taken to mean a reliable opportunity for great financial or personal success. Most people know it from Roald Dahl, *Willy Wonka*, and all that. Augustus Gloop is one of the other four ticketholders: the fat boy who wants to win the lifetime supply of chocolate but ends up being sucked into a machine and spat out thinner. Another morality tale.

'Octavian became the Emperor Augustus. Mr Creosote is the *Monty Python* character who explodes from eating too much. Ninkarrak was a Babylonian goddess of healing, who later became known as Gula. Hassein is a character in *Beelzebub's Tales to His Grandson*, by the Greek-Armenian mystic George Gurdjieff, who believed it is possible to reach a higher state of human potential through self-development known as the Fourth Way.'

'Not the third way?' asked Allen with a wry smile.

'No, Prime Minister. That's already been tried. And—'

'Even I know that Freddie Mercury sings, "Nothing really matters" in "*Bohemian Rhapsody*,"' interrupted Allen. 'Unbelievable, all that from those few paragraphs! And you're sure it's just a smokescreen? A game? No hidden meanings beyond the obvious?'

'Yes, Prime Minister.'

Allen shook his head in disbelief. Tanner thought, up close, that the premier looked so much older than he did on television. It was the make-up, he supposed, and the lighting. Or maybe just the stress of the past few days, the sickly dawning realisation that this was an existential threat disguised as a financial crisis, a loaded game where the stakes were all of civilisation.

'And nothing else from the security services?' asked Allen.

'Not yet, Prime Minister.'

'Hmmm.' Allen appeared to consider saying more, but instead turned his attention to Anthony Fleming. 'Governor?'

'Our foreign counterparts are being wholly supportive,' said Fleming, in neat, old-school BBC tones. 'They need us to fix this as much as we do. Same with the IMF. We were lucky that today's Friday, so we've only had to close our Stock Exchange for one extra day, but Wall Street's down another five percent already; global bank stocks much more. Everything will bounce when we fix the problem, but it will get bloody first.' The grim look on his face suggested it might become very bloody indeed.

Allen shifted his gaze to the chancellor. 'Anything you want to add, Hugh?'

'Not a lot, Prime Minister. We've got fingers in lots of holes, but if we're still in this mess on Monday morning it will be hard to stop the dyke from bursting.'

The premier, in an increasingly desperate search for a positive note, moved on to Sally Bickford. The tightness at her mouth wasn't encouraging. Nor were her words.

'There's no new intel on criminal or terrorist groups, I'm afraid. We've looked at the suggestion of "sleepers" within the banks. We've run the names of all technology employees through our databases and cross-referenced all consultants, secondees, temps—anyone with access to the bank IT systems—for the past three years. We've begun interviewing line managers individually to see if that throws anything up.' She shook her head wearily. 'But there are no links or patterns yet.'

'Anything else?'

'Yes, sir, the first minor public order problems. Mostly people fighting to get to cash machines. Some are turning back to hard currency out of fear that the banks will collapse, and others are trying to make withdrawals before their balances return to normal.'

Allen considered this for a moment. 'Isn't there a limit?'

'Yes, sir. Two hundred pounds. But some will try to max out on every card they've got, and the limits all reset at midnight. Hence the problems at machines.'

Allen sighed. Tanner saw, again, his own anxiety mirrored in the prime minister's face. Had those grey hairs always been there, he wondered? Had those eye bags been so prominent at yesterday's meeting?

'I don't need to tell you all that we're twenty-four hours nearer to the worst-case scenario,' Allen concluded. 'I'd like to reconvene with clear action points for that eventuality first thing tomorrow, please.' Then, more quietly, 'And let's just pray for some good news overnight.'

89

THE OTHER MEMBERS of the COBRA committee had gone, leaving just the prime minister and LJ in the Cabinet Room.

'It's the public order aspect I'm most worried about,' Allen said, once the door had been closed. 'We've been saved so far by the fact that it's Christmas and, if truth be told, by the weather. No one's going anywhere or doing anything unless they have to. We've got the weekend in our favour, but people will start going back to work on Monday. Or *will they*, with all this going on? Lord, this is a mess.'

LJ said nothing. She knew when her boss just needed her to listen. Allen looked around the room, searching for inspiration from the portraits of his predecessors on the walls. He took a deep breath and continued.

'Let's assume the worst. We'll have to reconvene Parliament. I'll call the leader of the opposition and the other important players after COBRA tomorrow morning. This is too important for them to politicise, at least till afterwards.' A wry smile crossed his lips. 'Then a call with the G7 leaders, or whoever they delegate, to ensure maximum international cooperation. And lastly, we've got to engage with JvA; we can't afford not to.'

'I agree. But how do you think we should go about that?'

The premier shook his head wearily. 'We don't have much choice, do we? All we have is his email, or we make a public address. If we do that, it risks further panic, and frankly, I think the whole country could go up in smoke if we pitch it wrong. The last thing this situation needs is a spark; we're a bloody powder keg already, even if most people don't realise it yet.'

'And if JvA goes public with the contact?'

Allen shrugged. 'It's irrelevant in the grand scheme of things. We either fix this, or Britain will end up on its knees and I'll be remembered as the worst PM in history.' He grimaced, a sinister expression in the late light of the day. 'So, I think a short, sharp email is called for. "Dear JvA. What do you want? Love James."'

LJ laughed. 'That should work.'

'Well, maybe drop the "Love James." But do send the email.'

90

THE NATIONAL BANK OFFICES WERE ALMOST DESERTED. As he made his final rounds to make sure, Tanner kept catching his reflection in the dark glass of empty meeting rooms. Not his face – his father's. With every passing year, the likeness was more apparent: less youthful and more austere. Each time he went to the barber now, Tanner was shocked by the spectre that stared back.

There had been a shock on the way back to the offices, as well – one of those cashpoint melees he had been warned about in Downing Street. A throng of people, thick and broiling with energy like the crowds outside a football stadium, was clustered around an ATM – one of a dwindling number which evidently still had cash to dispense. The scene had not yet descended into violence, but there was a touchpaper atmosphere as men shouldered one another out of the way, most with phones to their ears. The blue light of an approaching police car lent a disaster-movie edge to the proceedings. Tanner had always enjoyed the genre. Until now.

He had intended to go home earlier, but like the captain on a sinking ship, he felt unable to leave until all those under his command were safely away first. So, he'd spent the rest of the evening at his desk. He read and reread JvA's emails, hoping for inspiration, striving to glean an insight the government's finest minds had missed, and he scoured the Bosch paintings over and over again in search of meaning. But it was ridiculous. All he was doing was stumbling in darkness as sure as the night beyond his window. And filling his mind with ever-greater horrors.

At 10:30 p.m., Tanner decided enough was enough. No one was going to come up with anything new by pushing on later into the night. He gave the order to abandon ship – for now. They would start afresh early in the morning.

At his firm suggestion, bordering on instruction, Chrissie agreed reluctantly to clock off. Mike Sorensen and his team, too, were persuaded to switch their screens off, for a few hours at least. Even Ashley had welcomed the chance to get some sleep. Tanner was disappointed, despite himself, that he couldn't bid her goodnight in person, but he knew he'd need a sharp Ms Markham on the morrow.

Confident that he'd at least tried to his duty, he began to put on his coat. Then he sat back down again. Perhaps it was the doppelgänger reflections that reminded him, but he realised he had promised to call his sister and had completely forgotten, what with everything going on. He called her before the temptation to defer could build.

'I just wanted to give you a quick update, sis, so you don't worry. And I wanted to apologise again. I'm sorry, Liz.'

Perhaps the additional twenty-four hours had cooled his sister's anger, or maybe it was his show of contrition. More likely, thought Tanner, it was their father's early departure. Either way, his sister launched into the small talk that was their staple fare as if nothing untoward had ever happened. Only when every other possible topic had been exhausted did Harry come up.

'Was he worried about his bank account?' asked Tanner.

His sister's laughter filled the line. 'You're kidding? He was positively gleeful.'

'Gleeful? Dad?' Tanner scoffed. His reserves of humour had long been drained. 'We are talking about our father, Liz?'

'Well, maybe if you made more of an effort,' she shot back. Then, hurriedly, she stopped herself and tried to backpedal. 'Sorry, that wasn't fair.'

'No,' said Tanner. 'It's okay.' But the barb had already hit home. He could feel the familiar guilt heaping atop worry. He knew there was more than a grain of truth in what his sister had said—that she had a right to be aggrieved by his abandonment of his family—a cowardice born of loss.

'Anyway,' offered Liz, evidently eager to move the conversation on. 'You should have heard him. "Banks? Who needs them? I've got cash in my wallet and the freezer's full of fruit and vegetables from my allotment. What difference will the bank's cock-up make to me?" He positively skipped off; he was so excited about the impending collapse.' Her tone changed abruptly. 'But what about the rest of us? The news is talking about food shortages if this goes on for long and if suppliers can't be paid. Should we be worried?'

The simplest of questions, and yet Tanner didn't have an answer. He resorted to cliché. 'We're doing everything possible, sis. All the banks are in the same boat.' Then deflection. 'I take it *your* freezer's full?'

A heavy, nasal snort answered him. 'Full? We've got enough food to last till New Year. New Year next year!'

She was still laughing as Tanner took his leave.

New Year. Four days' time. They'd have everything sorted before then, wouldn't they? They had to. *He* had to. But there was something else he had to do first. Something he should have done a long time ago.

Tanner had worked with various executive coaches over the years. In his experience, their usefulness was inversely proportionate to the jargon and motivational mantras they spouted. But one quote had stuck with him: "A journey of a thousand miles begins with a single step." If he didn't start now, he never would.

Tanner dialled his father's number, matching his breaths to the rhythm of the ring tone. Eventually the receiver was picked up.

'Hello, Dad,' said Tanner. 'It's Rob.'

'I know,' came his father's voice.

'Well, I'd like you to know a couple more things.'

On the other end of the line: nothing. Ambivalence? Resentment? Anger? It didn't matter. Tanner spoke into the silence, choosing his words with particular care.

'I heard what you said about responsibility.'

There was a hint of noise at the other end of the line, a muffled 'huh' or grunt. Tanner ignored it.

'I wish we weren't in this mess, Dad. I wish I'd listened to you more. I wish we'd talked about things. I wish I'd told you a few things.'

Tanner's words were deliberately ambiguous. If the old man chose to think he was talking about the bank—and only about the bank—so be it.

'But when this is over, I'd like to put that right. It's easy to regret things we've done, but I don't ever again want to regret things I didn't do.'

He caught the faintest of sounds in the earpiece, perhaps more snuffle than snort this time, but still no reply came. Well, he'd tried. With a final, softer, 'Goodnight, Dad,' he hung up and collected his coat. It was time to go home.

Across the city, the lights were going out on this third day of Christmas. People were heading for bed, succumbing to the inexplicable tiredness that descends on holidays – the strain of doing nothing, the stress of dealing with extended family. Some, however, found themselves unable to sleep. Many bedrooms, in fact, were washed in the blue light of phone screens that night as live news websites and social media feeds were refreshed, chatter about the cyber- attacks intensifying. The long-reads were already appearing, conjecture about the total collapse of the banking system.

What did that mean for savings? For mortgages? What would happen to society if nobody owned a thing? Would people come together to build a new system from scratch, or would the desperate turn on each other in a city of empty shelves, overflowing bins and kitchen-knife confrontations at ATMs? If the canon of post-apocalyptic disaster movies was anything to go by, there would be far graver concerns than sloth, envy and gluttony.

Everyone, then, had their fears. And Tanner, as he left his office and made for the lifts, had more than most.

DAY SIX

SATURDAY 28 DECEMBER 2024

91

THE FIFTEEN-MINUTE NEWS CYCLE was now dominated entirely by the cyber crisis. Frostbitten reporters delivered their spiels before a snowy Bank of England; cameras cut to queues at the last of the functioning cash machines; montages of high-tech computer wizardry were overlaid with dystopian conjecture. Interviews were aired with major retailers wary of shortages; studio guests speculated about motives. Debts would vanish, said some. Savings would disappear, cautioned others.

LJ was sitting, feet-up, on the sofa in her Pimlico flat. She had the news on, but her TV was muted. The clock in the corner of the screen showed almost 1 a.m. She had done as Allen had suggested and sent a short email to JvA:

> We're keen to understand your precise requirements.
> I am available 24/7 for open dialogue.
> Leah Oladapo. Chief of Staff, Downing Street.

Now all she could do was wait for a response. She envied Craig, asleep in the bedroom. He had told her not to stay up too late, but with a weary resignation that suggested he expected exactly the opposite.

In any normal conflict, LJ knew, both sides would always strive to maintain side-channels and back doors. Despite public appearances, even the bitterest of foes were never more than a red telephone line away. But this? This was bonkers – an invisible enemy with no obvious motive. LJ was embarrassed at the lack of sophistication in her approach, but what choice did she have?

She had spent the rest of the evening going over the developing contingency plans from the COBRA members. Yet again, she was struck by how quickly a modern superpower could be reduced to impotence by the very technology on which its ostensible superiority was founded – a nation strangled by its own complex web of debt and credit. Derivatives and cryptocurrencies conjured from the machine, not balanced in leatherbound ledgers. It couldn't have happened in her grandmother's day. Whatever had happened to 'Neither a borrower nor a lender be?'

LJ finished the latest paper on emergency food supply and looked at the next item on her to-do list. A Bank of England paper on hyperinflation. The latest warnings evoked awful echoes of the spiralling inflation which had taken hold in Germany's Weimar Republic in the early 1920s. The price of a loaf of bread rose from one mark to 100 billion marks in four years. Zimbabwe, in recent times, had seen similar currency destruction. Could the same happen in the UK? She tried to concentrate, but unbidden images forced themselves into her head: decadent Berlin cabaret clubs; the roaring twenties; the great depression; the Nazis. She realised she needed to finish for the night, calm down and sleep.

She went to the kitchen to make a cup of peppermint tea. Immediately, there was a ping from the sitting room. She left the bag stewing and rushed to her laptop. And there it was:

TO: Leah Oladapo
FROM: Joen van Aken
DATE: Saturday, 28 December 2024 at 01:00
RE: Dialogue

Hello, LJ.
  Thank you for reaching out.
  Dialogue is such an interesting word. From the Greek, διά+λόγος. "Through + words." And I only need one:
  Truth.
  From a wonderful Old English word *triewð* meaning faithfulness, probably dating back to the Sanskrit *dāruṇa* for hard.

Rather appropriate, no? You should have faith in people and tell them the truth. Even when it's hard. Or we'll end up like poor François Lemoyne in 1737.

Not that words alone are enough. I think we've had enough of those from politicians and bankers and their ilk. As a woman in politics, I'm sure you'll know Emmeline's Suffragette motto!

The prime minister likes his television appearances, but if he's not careful, he'll find himself on ITV at 9pm. And then he might find that Frank and Celeste were right after all!

J.

LJ's focus was back – with interest. On the face of it, the first three paragraphs were self-explanatory. She began working through the other references.

A search for "François Lemoyne, 1737" brought up an image of the picture in the email: *Time Saving Truth from Falsehood and Envy,* along with a commentary.

"The naked figure of Truth is held aloft by her father, Time, who with his scythe subdues Falsehood, in her fine clothes and play-acting mask, while the baleful figure of Envy looks on. The subject may have held a personal significance for the artist; he committed suicide the day after completing it." LJ grimaced. Not a good omen.

She didn't need to look up Emmeline Pankhurst. After years of campaigning for universal suffrage, Pankhurst had founded the group whose uncompromising protests eventually won women the vote with the unambiguous motto, "Deeds, not words."

Next, she searched the TV listings. There it was, 9 p.m. on ITV: *Who Wants to Be a Millionaire?* Her search for Frank and Celeste, the final clue, made her smile despite herself. She'd grown up with Sinatra in her grandmother's house and Celeste Holm, it turned out, was the partner who sings, "I don't" in the duet with the same title as the TV show.

LJ reread the email in this context. Its meaning was clearer now: the bank balance increases were just the start. JvA was threatening to make every account holder in the country a millionaire unless, what? Unless people started telling the truth? Unless he saw actions, not words, on the seven deadly sins? And in a hurry.

She reached for her phone and called James Allen.

After four rings and a slight pause, a sleepy-sounding prime minister asked, 'What's up LJ?'

'A response from JvA, sir.'

'Run me through it,' Allen said, his tone quiet.

LJ read the email to Allen verbatim and then gave her interpretation of the text.

He weighed the evidence. 'So, the attacks are going to escalate?'

'I would say so, Prime Minister.'

'And to stop them, we're going to have to atone for sloth, envy, gluttony and… remind me what the others are? I'm still half-asleep.'

'Greed, lust, pride and wrath.'

'Sorry, LJ, but have you seen the state of the country we inherited? How the hell are we supposed to do that overnight?'

'I could always ask!' LJ ribbed. She regretted her meagre attempt at humour immediately, but Allen jumped in before she could apologise for being facetious.

'You're right. That's exactly the thing to do.' There was nothing sluggish about him now. 'We have COBRA at nine, so come here first. Say eight? Get Zack to come in too. We'll have some breakfast in the flat and go through the newspapers.' Allen's charm, it seemed, had returned. 'Well done!'

92

VIRGIN FLIGHT 25 LANDED AT JFK on the stroke of midnight – 5 a.m. in the UK. As soon as Gérard was settled in his seat, he had taken off his watch and wound it back. Then he sat looking at it, lost in thought.

'Penny?' prompted Nikki, watching his eyes.

'Sorry?'

'I said "penny." A penny for your thoughts?'

A bashful smile half-lit Gérard's face – a look Nikki had not seen before.

He waved his wrist gently, drawing her attention to the watch. 'I was thinking of my father, which got me thinking about time.' Then he clenched his fist. 'The tighter you grasp it, the faster it runs through your fingers.'

Nikki smiled, a sad expression. 'I know all about that.'

The best connection to Austin on Saturday morning was at 7.30 a.m., so Nikki opted to stay at an airport hotel. Going into the city would be pointless; she'd have to leave almost as soon as she arrived. Gérard asked if she wanted him to accompany her, but she refused as graciously as he had offered.

'You've got more ground to cover, so you need to be in the city,' she said. 'Thank you, though.' She squeezed his arm gently to show that she meant it.

This time there was no awkwardness to their farewell. Gérard tilted his head towards her and said quietly, 'We make a good team, don't you think?'

Just over an hour later, they were in their respective hotels, where an email was waiting from Rob Tanner. Nikki was in a drab room at one of the global chains, but at least the bed was good and clean. Gérard was in a suite at the Iroquois. There were more expensive, more famous hotels in Manhattan, but he always stayed at the Iroquois, a boutique hotel in the heart of Midtown. He had always loved the streets of New York and, weather permitting, thought nothing of walking a dozen, or even twenty, blocks in one go. From the Iroquois, that radius covered pretty much anywhere he might want to go.

Tanner's email confirmed Gérard's prediction that a staffing agency supplied Rhoda Kane for maternity cover in Poughkeepsie. The agency, however, had no record of her bank details, nor any photo ID. The Austin credit union, meanwhile, did have payroll information for Bryony Sears, but she banked with one of the major nationals rather than a regional or local entity where Chad might have been able to twist an arm for a quick response. Tanner added cryptically that he was trying to get hold of the information they needed through "other channels."

Better news was that Tanner had a list of contacts at their target universities, either on the teaching staff or in the admissions departments. The American CEOs had given him a few names, and Tanner implied he had another source who might have helped.

Neither Nikki nor Gérard had any idea about Brin, Tanner's personal connection at the heart of American politics. But it didn't matter to them where the names came from. All that mattered was that they had leads to chase – anything that might bring them closer to the mystery that was eating away at them…

Who *were* Bryony and Rhoda, and where was Holly?

93

TANNER WOKE WITH A DEEP SENSE OF FOREBODING and the nagging feeling that there was something more he, personally, should have picked up on. The feeling that something awful was about to happen – something even worse than everything that had already come to pass. What he wouldn't give for his usual Saturday routine: a thorough workout to justify a couple of lunchtime beers and a burger, and then two blissful hours forgetting about everything other than the Bees and their ongoing Premier League campaign. Sadly, not today.

On the practical side, there was plenty to keep him busy and distract from the pervading pessimism. There were updates from LJ, regarding contact with JvA, and from Sorensen, who had summoned a cohort of old-school software architects for a meeting later that morning.

With the TV news rolling mutely in the background and tea steeping in its mug, Tanner made to call Ashley. She picked up immediately.

'Hello, Rob. It's lucky you caught me; I was just heading for the shower.'

Tanner remembered a similar conversation the first day he'd met her. Christmas Eve, three and a half days ago, although it felt like much longer. He tried to focus.

'I was really just checking in to make sure you're okay,' he offered. 'It's not exactly the Christmas vacation you had planned, is it?' His question sounded more like an apology.

'What's that old phrase?' she said. 'The best laid schemes…' They both laughed.

'I have to go to Downing Street for a COBRA meeting,' Tanner went on, 'but then I'll come and find you later.'

'Ah, the big cheeses. Very appropriate for mice an' men.'

'Absolutely. But can I bounce an idea off you before I go? It's quite mad.'

'Nothing's mad anymore, Rob.'

Tanner explained quickly his growing interest in finding Holly Brand. Then he told of the curious similarities between the problems at First Star and Dutchess and the shared characteristics of the women who had solved them. He worried he was joining dots which didn't exist, but Ashley listened patiently, without interruption. Tanner finished speaking, and she stayed silent for a few seconds, the only sound her soft, regular breathing.

'So,' she concluded, 'if I get this right, you're asking me if I think these problems are all linked? And you're wondering if your missing intern either has something to do with it or might represent the solution? And this all ties into those other missing women, somehow?'

'I did say it was mad,' confessed Tanner. 'But I'm wondering now whether one person was behind all these incidents. What if Holly Brand is Rhoda Kane is Bryony Sears? And what if the same woman, whichever one of them is real, is linked to the attack on National Bank. Is that even possible?'

'Rob, who knows what's possible? We live in the age of nanotechnology, quantum computing, AI. Remember Moore's Law: computing power has doubled every two years for half a century; another generation and computers will have as much processing power as human brains… maybe more: the pace of change is unbelievable. Just look at ChatGPT!' Ashley paused for a moment. 'But to answer your question, I don't think you'd find a single person out there who thinks these attacks could be the work of one person.'

'Then it's a wild goose chase? I shouldn't raise it with COBRA?'

Ashley hesitated. 'Rob, I can't answer that.' Then added gently, 'Just trust your judgement.'

She was right, like Brin yesterday. No one else could tell Tanner what to do. But just speaking to her had lifted his spirits. And his confidence. Tanner thanked Ashley for her advice. Then he let her get back to her shower and forced his thoughts to the meeting ahead.

94

ALLEN, LJ AND ZACK HARDY SAT in the kitchen of the prime minister's flat at the top of Eleven Downing Street. The day's newspapers were spread on the countertop in front of them. The headlines were grim, but frankly, they could—and perhaps should—have been even worse. The papers appeared to still be labouring under the assumption that the crisis was fundamentally just another computer problem – one to which a solution would eventually be found. They always were. No one had actually lost any money, as yet, and that seemed to temper the press response. The full implications of a collapse of the banking system—and the collapse of society which would inevitably follow—were, so far, lost on many.

Allen sighed and set down the last paper. 'We've been lucky so far. The snow's keeping people indoors, and they can't transfer money that isn't theirs because it's the weekend now. But our luck's not going to last. I mean, what's the point at which temptation becomes too much? Someone who's used to having a hundred pounds a week to spend, or maybe two, suddenly has ten thousand in their account. They know it's not theirs, but if they see others misbehaving, if the dam breaks, so to speak.' He sighed again and turned to his press secretary. 'What's the mood among the newspaper editors, Zack?'

'To be honest, Prime Minister, they don't know which way to jump. They've been toeing the line about not fanning the flames of panic. But if LJ's right about the latest JvA email, that there will be further escalations…' He left the sentence unfinished; there was no need to spell out the likely repercussions.

'So, the sixty-four-thousand-dollar question is—' Allen stopped and closed his eyes. 'Lord, I must never, ever, use that bloody phrase again. The *question* is whether we should give the press any hint of our knowing who the perpetrator is? Or that we're having discussions with them? LJ?'

'You know I'm not one for procrastinating, Prime Minister, but I think we should see if JvA comes back with any concrete demands.'

Allen nodded his resigned agreement. 'Fair enough. Nothing from the security services on the emails?'

'I'm afraid not. They're routed through multiple servers in a wide range of countries: Latvia and Lithuania, Madagascar, Hungary and Romania – you name it. Any country, it seems, with fast internet.'

'And language patterns, content, anything?'

'It's a mix of British and American sources for definitions, references, pretty much everything. No clear pattern. But then, that's the internet. Obviously, the artwork's European.'

'Revenge for us leaving?' grimaced Allen, although it was impossible to tell whether he was joking or not. 'In that case, I suppose all we can do is wait and see what our COBRA friends have for us.'

95

FROM THE EXPRESSIONS ON THE FACES around the COBRA table, the answer was likely to be not a lot. Allen steadied himself, reaching for the still, firm voice of reason he kept always on standby for media interviews.

'The moral of the pandemic,' he began, 'was that a public quickly loses trust in a government which merely hopes for the best – rather than being decisive and proactive. Even the appearance of indecision is fatal. So, here's how I'd like us to proceed.' He paused a second for emphasis. 'At the end of your updates, I want to know what we you would have us do today. *This morning.* How can we respond decisively and proactively to this threat?

Allen looked around the table. 'Now, Rob, I know it's unfair to always pick on you first, but perhaps you'd give us some thoughts on the practical aspects. Could we bar access to accounts? Can we return to back-up data from before Christmas? What do you suggest?'

Tanner took a deep breath and a moment to compose himself.

'Banks have suffered their share of IT outages in the past,' he replied. 'We've seen customers barred from their accounts by accident, payments missed, people out of pocket. In every case, the system has eventually caught up. Erroneous data is erased, and restitution is made.'

'But?'

'But,' acknowledged Tanner ruefully, 'for one thing, the scale here is enormous, and secondly—and much more importantly—we don't have control over our systems. We don't know how JvA's doing it, but he's controlling our systems from the *inside*. We're effectively locked out of our own bank; he has the keys and the upper hand.'

'We can't just turn everything off?' Allen asked. 'Go back to day zero, so to speak. Christmas Eve?'

'On all that I've ever thought possible, I'd have said yes, of course we can, but now? I'm not sure. And if we did, JvA would surely just override the reset.'

Allen tapped his fingers quietly on the table, considering the answer, then asked, 'You've already limited cash withdrawals?'

'Yes, Prime Minister. One hundred pounds per day.'

The chancellor motioned to speak. Allen waved him on.

'Thank you, Prime Minister.' Westwood spoke slowly and precisely, everyone's idea of a rather pedantic schoolmaster. 'It's obviously prudent to limit cash withdrawals or bank transfers, but I'm afraid there's a rather bigger problem.' He waited to ensure that he was the undisputed centre of attention. 'Shopping.'

'*Shopping*?'

'Yes, Prime Minister. Napoleon labelled Britain a nation of shopkeepers, but it would be far more accurate to describe us as a nation of *shoppers*. For many of whom, the temptation to spend inflated balances will prove far too strong. The retailers will be swamped with orders for goods and services, with no idea who really has the money to pay for them.'

'Then we'll have to introduce spending limits,' replied Allen.

'At what level, Prime Minister?' wheedled Westwood.

LJ jumped in, looking at Tanner for assistance. 'Can we try putting in place a spending limit linked to the previous balance. Like an overdraft limit, but in reverse?'

'We'll certainly try,' replied Tanner.

Allen shifted his gaze to the governor. 'Anthony, what news from the financial markets?'

'The Dow Jones closed nearly two thousand points down,' Fleming replied evenly. 'Circuit-breakers prevented meaningful New York trading in UK shares, but indications were that UK bank shares would have traded down by roughly twenty five percent. Other major UK companies by nearer fifteen. UK government bonds were down by ten. The pound...'

Eventually the dismal litany came to an end. Allen tried not to sound as despondent as he felt.

'What's your take on it all, Anthony?' he asked.

'I'd make three observations,' ventured Fleming. 'Firstly, the markets are suggesting they expect the problem to be fixed quickly, but that banks, and to a lesser extent other companies, will bear heavy short-term liabilities as a result, hence the share price falls. Secondly, the markets are seeing this as a very *British* problem—hence the falls in our government debt—but there's remarkably little concern about international contagion. Thirdly, I'd say that on the surface of it, this is a very logical reaction from the markets.'

'But?' asked Allen. He couldn't keep the weariness from his voice. There was always a but, these days.

'But,' the governor confirmed dryly, 'whilst the market response is entirely understandable, it is—not to put too fine a point on it—at the same time, completely and utterly nonsensical.'

Allen, mentally, found himself reliving the major crises that had unstuck his predecessors. Untangling the EU's regulatory web, the pandemic, financial crashes and bailouts. He had thought his tenure would be different, but now events were getting out of hand, and it looked more likely that he'd end up as a footnote—a reference on a Wikipedia page or a tricky pub quiz question, twenty years from now—than a statesman to rival Maggie or Churchill. Allen didn't do it on purpose, but he found himself taking out his frustration on the governor.

'You're losing me, Anthony,' he whined. He was angry with himself, more than anything.

Fleming's expression didn't change. 'Prime Minister, if—and hopefully when—the problem is fixed, there will be little long-term damage to those companies. Their shares will rebound. On that basis, anyone selling at these prices is mad. Pension funds or other entities crystallising losses will be decimated. Remember what happened with Trussonomics? Sterling plunged and then recovered just as quickly after the demise of that project's authors. However, until stability is restored you might as well call red or black at the casino. It's certainly not an orderly market.'

'So, what are you suggesting?'

'Prime Minister, I *strongly* recommend that we keep the London market closed and encourage our foreign counterparts to restrict trading in UK assets.'

Chancellor Hugh Westwood stepped in again. 'But won't that inflame the situation? Increase people's fears?'

Fleming turned to the chancellor. 'Hugh, I admit it's only the *lesser* of two evils, but hear me out. Very few people are actually working in the City over the holidays. Many aren't back to their offices until Monday week, the sixth of January. If the markets stay open, the banks and brokers will demand all their people rush in at the crack of dawn on Monday to "do something." Algorithmic trading will kick in. There will be pandemonium. "Doing something" will exacerbate the situation, whereas if we shut up shop, I suspect it will be the same as in previous closures. People will accept it's a technical problem, stay at home and forget about it.'

'What do you need from us then, Anthony?' asked Allen.

'Prime Minister, I will speak personally to the heads of the major financial institutions to ensure they see things our way. But as so many of them are foreign owned, it would be most helpful if they received the same message from their own governments, particularly our friends in the US. If Hugh would be so kind as to speak to the Secretary of the Treasury, that would be *most* helpful.'

'Of course,' the chancellor beamed; his ego suitably massaged. 'I'll call as soon as Washington's awake.'

'Anything else, Anthony?' queried the prime minister.

'No, I think that's all we can reasonably do, sir.'

Despite his earlier irritation, Allen couldn't help but marvel at the governor's calm, unflustered delivery. The premier had always held the governor in esteem, and now he gave silent thanks that this unflappable man should be at the helm of the Bank in this time of such grave peril. He asked a final question.

'Realistically, how long can we keep markets shut, do you think?'

Fleming paused for a moment, eyes narrowing in thought. 'It's a public holiday next Wednesday for New Year's Day, as it is virtually everywhere else in the world, too. Getting to then is tricky, but not impossible. After that it *has* to be business as usual. So, four days. Or—'

'Or we're out of business,' Allen said. He allowed himself a deep breath before returning to the chancellor. 'Anything more you'd like to add, Hugh?'

'Just one practical issue, Prime Minister. Before we get to January first, we have the small matter of December thirty-first – the year end for the majority of major companies. We'll have to roll over tax deadlines until this is all resolved. Give dispensations. That sort of thing. More work and less money for the Treasury, but I don't see an alternative.'

'Fine,' exhaled Allen. 'Who's next?'

The cabinet secretary, Jonathan Morse, caught the prime minister's eye.

'On the basis of what we're hearing, I think we have to assume we'll have significant public order problems to deal with,' he said. 'Criminal elements, social protesters, even ordinary people getting desperate. I think we have to cancel all leave for members of the police and armed forces. Have them on immediate readiness.'

'But won't that cause more panic?' asked Allen.

'Again, we're damned if we do, damned if we don't, I'm afraid.'

Allen thought for a moment. 'Let's think of the psychology here. It's the weekend. The vast majority of people are still in a festive mood and will stay that way until New Year's Day. I know the bank account numbers—the implications—are mind-bogglingly scary if you stop and think about them, but surely the majority of people will just ignore them as nonsense for the moment?' He looked around the table for support but found only equivocation. Allen couldn't afford to prevaricate; there wasn't time. Churchill came back to him: "I never worry about action, but only about inaction." He trusted his own judgement and acted.

'Get the commanders to prepare the plans. Have them on standby. But let's hold off putting them into action for twenty-four hours. If we've reached the point where we have to do that, I'll need to make an address on television.'

LJ raised a finger, seeking permission to interrupt, which Allen granted with a dip of the head.

'Remember we have parliament coming back tomorrow, Prime Minister. We'll need a statement ready by late morning.'

'Of course, LJ, how could I forget? Let's just hope, given the gravity of the situation, that we can persuade our friends on the other side of the chamber not to be too hysterical.' Allen and LJ shared a dubious look before the prime minister turned to Saeed Akhtar for the security service's contribution.

The head of the NCSC had plenty of data but no progress to report. Neither traditional nor dark-side contacts had provided a single lead. Shoulders slumped around the table. Except for one. Tanner began to raise a hand, again feeling so much like a child back in the classroom.

'Yes, Rob?' offered Allen.

'Prime Minister, it may be nothing, a waste of time.' So much for gut instinct – his stomach was in knots. But he'd started, so he had to continue. 'There's something I'd like to raise with the security services though.' He looked purposefully at Akhtar and Bickford. 'A possible lead.'

Tanner walked them through the Brand-Sears-Kane story. His head told him it was ridiculous to be sitting in this grand room, presenting the prime minister and his most senior advisers with a hotchpotch of speculative scraps, but his heart made him plough on. When Tanner had finished, Allen set his eyes on Akhtar.

'So, Saeed, the suggestion is that this is all caused, or at least driven, by a lone wolf. A missing woman with extraordinary computer skills. A *Deus*—or rather *Dea—ex Machina*. So, simple question, is that possible?'

Akhtar looked momentarily uncomfortable, then regained his composure, answering firmly. 'No, Prime Minister. It isn't.'

'So, we're looking at coincidence? A red herring?'

'I'd say so. A sophisticated hacker might have the ability to break into a few accounts at minor institutions such as those mentioned… but something on this scale? No. And, with respect, Prime Minister, these cases happened eight years ago and five thousand miles away. There's no suggestion of anything similar in the UK. Ever.'

'Fine,' replied Allen. 'But let's have the Americans check out these names and let's have MI5 and Six look for this missing Holly Brand anyway. It sounds like a long shot, but we can't afford to leave any stones unturned.' He swivelled to face Sally Bickford. 'The police too. Check all the names.'

'Of course,' agreed the policewoman, before completing the set of COBRA contributions with yet another gloomy soliloquy which added nothing new.

Allen was a realist. He hadn't hoped for much and had expected less. But even those minimal expectations had proved overly optimistic. He cast his gaze, once again, towards the huge portrait of Churchill opposite. For once, the great man failed him. No stirring words of encouragement came.

He checked his watch and began to stand. 'Let's regroup here at the end of the day. Hopefully, by then, you'll all have some progress to report.'

96

MARTIN KELLETT NO LONGER HAD A MAJESTIC VIEW of the Matterhorn from his bedroom window. He had exchanged Zermatt for London the previous evening, but if the glimpse of the capital was dull, the small house—tucked away in one of the quiet mews off Harley Street—suited him perfectly. Most of the nearby properties had been converted into medical practices, so there was little noise and, more importantly, a lot of discretion. What's more, the Toad now found himself in easy striking distance of the centre of town. Well, he would have been, if Tommy Steele was still on call.

The disloyalty of his driver was just one of the things gnawing at Kellett that day. He was irate that he had been fired for an IT fuck-up which turned out, based on what had happened with all the other banks, to have nothing to do with National. And meanwhile, Ziegler's investigator had reportedly come up with the square root of fuck-all in his search for Holly Brand. Kellett realised that what he needed was a distraction.

He resolved to arrange some company for that afternoon and a damn good dinner for that evening. And he would start yanking a few chains in the meantime. After a call to his lawyer, re-expressing his desire to squeeze every last drop of severance pay from National Bank, he dialled the number of Christina Ferreira.

'Hello, Christina,' he oozed.

'Martin? Mr Kellett?' Chrissie's surprise was evident in her tone.

'I hope you haven't forgotten,' her old boss said.

'Forgotten what?'

'Why, that I'm still CEO of course.' He laughed jauntily into the phone. 'I'm only on temporary leave, you know.'

'Oh, yes,' she stammered. 'Of course, Martin.'

'Good. I wouldn't want you to forget that.' His voice was calm, even solicitous. He waited, imagining Christina's heart pounding, but beginning to settle. Then he added, 'Or the other thing!' and hung up before his shocked underling had a chance to respond.

97

TANNER, BACK FROM DOWNING STREET, walked in to find his PA staring into space, her face as bleak as any he'd just left at COBRA.

'You okay?' he asked. 'You look upset.'

Chrissie forced a smile. 'No, I'm fine.'

In Tanner's experience, the word "fine" in this context invariably meant anything but. 'Is there anything I can do?' he pressed.

'No. Thanks, Rob.' She seemed about to add something else but just looked down at her hands. The lines seemed suddenly tighter around her mouth.

It was clear that Chrissie wanted to be left alone, so Tanner went off in search of Sorensen and Nash. He had tracked them down, and they were discussing how best to implement spending limits, when the call came. He'd been expecting it – dreading it. He had been unable to stop his eyes wandering to the digital wall clock as it ticked towards 11:00, but his heart sank all the same at Chrissie's words.

'Another one.'

The despondency in her tone seemed wholly appropriate.

Tanner ran the three flights of stairs to his office, where the new email was ripening in his inbox.

> TO: Robert Tanner; Leah Oladapo
> FROM: Joen van Aken
> DATE: Saturday, 28 December 2024 at 11:00
> Avaricia

Hello, you two.

I'm sure you have lots to do, but I fear time is not on your side. I wonder if you will be able to goe the distance? HIStory suggests not:

Cursed Mammon be, when he with treasures
To restless action spurs our fate!
Cursed when for soft, indulgent leisures,
He lays for us the pillows straight.

Still, at least you're working together: two servants; one master. Or have I got that the wrong way round? My friend Matthew is better with values: 6:19-24. No risk of his treasure being stolen or his heart broken.

And I regret to tell you that I disagree very strongly with my other friend Gordon the lizard about what is and isn't good. Lucius Annaeus is more my cup of tea.

J.

He had just reached the sign-off when his internal line rang. Sorensen and Nash were on speakerphone in the conference room where he had, until a moment ago, been strategising with them.

'Another zero?' asked Tanner.

'I'm afraid so,' replied Nash. 'But there's a twist this time, Rob. We don't have that many, but every account at the bank with deposits over one hundred million has just had a zero removed. It's now a two-way process.'

Tanner thought he'd been prepared for everything, but JvA's capacity to surprise had floored him again. He mumbled his thanks into the handset and swiftly found LJ's number. But as the PM's chief of staff duly pointed out: the latest development didn't really change anything. If they didn't find a solution, it mattered not whether bank balances were millions or minus figures.

'JvA is just showing the strength of his hand, Rob. Laying another ace on the table,' was LJ's succinct summary. 'He's encouraging us to fold.'

Tanner was increasingly uncertain that JvA really was a *he*. But now wasn't the time to press the point. And besides, LJ had already gone.

98

THE EXPERTS MAY HAVE INSISTED that JvA's emails were gibberish, but Tanner couldn't resist decoding this latest missive. The nonsense was addictive.

He hit the bookmarked link to the Bosch painting. Greed (*avaricia*): "A crooked judge pretends to listen sympathetically to the case presented by one party to a lawsuit while slyly accepting a bribe from the other party." He did an image search for "greed" and was drawn to a painting of a desperate young woman clutching at the knee of a giant figure: a statue of a man holding out a bag of gold. *The Worship of Mammon*, by Evelyn De Morgan, 1909. Another demon. And Mammon, in Hebrew, meant money.

Tanner read again the first full paragraph. "Time is not on your side" was straightforward enough, but no less worrying for that. Then the bizarre "goe the distance? HIStory suggests not." He copied and pasted it into Google and was rewarded with articles about Newton's Law of Gravity, geometry, geography and a John Donne poem: "*Song: Sweetest love, I do not goe.*" It might have been a medieval spelling, Tanner guessed, given JvA's fascination with the period.

The next paragraph read like a stanza of poetry. Another cut and paste brought the answer: Goethe's *Faust*. Tanner cursed first his stupidity—"goe the," Goethe—then his lack of knowledge. Like most English students, he had heard of *Faust* and knew that Goethe's epic version of the legend was a seminal piece of European literature. He had never read a word of it, however. Now he learned that the legend is loosely based on the life of a medieval alchemist and black magician named Johann Georg Faust, who sells his soul to the devil in exchange for knowledge and power. The story had been told and retold countless times over the past five hundred years in every medium.

Tanner looked again at "HIStory." It was bound to be a play on words. History, his story. A byte of information long buried in his brain sparked the memory of a Michael Jackson album. Google confirmed the suspicion: *HIStory: Past, Present and Future, Book I*. Whilst the singer himself was unlikely to be relevant, the implication was clear, the moral of his—and Faust's—story was to be taken at face value.

Tanner therefore had a strong inkling of what was coming when he typed "Matthew 6:21" into the search engine. He'd heard the quotation from St. Matthew's gospel numerous times:

> Do not store up for yourselves treasures on earth, where moths and vermin destroy, and where thieves break in and steal.
>
> Matthew 6:19

He scanned through the following verses, familiar words from the church pews of childhood: "But store up for yourselves treasures in heaven, where moths and vermin do not destroy, and where thieves do not break in and steal." Exhortations to have faith in your heart, not avarice. With the final admonition:

> No one can serve two masters; for either he will hate the one and love the other, or else he will be loyal to the one and despise the other. You cannot serve God and mammon.
>
> Matthew 6:24

The significance of the two masters—or one—was beyond him; was it a reference to the prime minister? Tanner moved on to JvA's final paragraph. The "lizard," he realised, was probably Gordon Gekko, Michael Douglas's slick-haired, braces-wearing financier in the movie *Wall Street*. His most famous line? "Greed is good." Tanner followed the top search link and smiled at the image of the ultimate symbol of late Eighties financial excess. But he was surprised to read the actual quote from the movie: "Greed, for lack of a better word, is good." Yet another misquote that had entered popular consciousness—and a convenient misunderstanding—given how society viewed bankers, financiers and everyone else who worked in the industry. His industry.

Tanner knew the post-2008 crash narrative by heart. He'd read the book, he'd seen the movie, he wore the t-shirt—the hair shirt—every day. Bankers: they crashed the economy and then paid themselves bonuses for it. And the bill, of course, always ended up with the taxpayer. It was a view without nuance, but he couldn't deny that there was truth in it. And he didn't blame the "losers" in the grand game of market Monopoly for despising the winners – especially since many of Tanner's peers *had* cheated along the way.

As for "Lucius Annaeus," Tanner typed the name into his browser and was directed to the Wikipedia page for Seneca. Seneca the Younger, fully Lucius Annaeus Seneca, was a Roman Stoic philosopher, statesman, and a whole lot more besides. Angry with himself for wasting time, Tanner skim-read the entry, committing the key points to memory. Seneca, he learned, was a prolific writer on ethics, one of his musings being that "The highest wealth is the absence of greed." A tutor and advisor to Nero, he had been forced to take his own life for alleged complicity in a conspiracy to assassinate the mad Emperor. His stoic and calm suicide was the subject of numerous paintings; Tanner vaguely remembered seeing one in a museum in Paris. Or was it Madrid?

He shook his head in disbelief. How on earth could you cram so much meaning into such a short email? Barely more than a hundred words. Surely the welter of literary and artistic references had to be relevant? Or were the COBRA bods right? Was JvA really a nutter with too much time, one hell of a grudge and a predilection for stringing everyone along?

Either way, all that was LJ's responsibility. For all the clever allusions, there was only one message that mattered: time was not on their side. Neither Faust nor Seneca's stories had ended well. Nor had Belshazzar's or Augustus Gloop's before them. Tanner did not want his own name added to the list.

99

LJ AND PRESS SECRETARY ZACK HARDY sat with the Prime Minister in the kitchen of his flat. They had just finished reading a third draft of his proposed statement to Parliament the next day. Allen had the look of a man with an acutely aggravating toothache.

'I'm sorry Zack,' he said. 'The balance just isn't right. The first draft was too bland, the second was positively apocalyptic… now this is neither one thing nor the other. LJ, what do you think?'

'Let's go back to basics,' she answered, looking from Allen to Hardy. 'What are we trying to achieve here? We want to reassure people, yes? But we also want to scare the living daylights out of them.'

'Do we?' asked Allen. 'I think the people will want to be reassured.'

'With respect, sir, we do have to reassure them that everything's being done to solve the problem, that we have all the big picture bases covered: co-operation with other governments, safeguarding of essential services and infrastructure, and that sort of thing. But at the same time, we must absolutely drum home the message about personal responsibility: that anyone who thinks they can spend money they didn't have on Tuesday can expect to feel the full weight of the law. So, we need a two-part, good-cop-bad-cop speech: don't worry about the lights going out, but don't you dare step out of line if they do. That's why I'd keep in the parts about police and army leave being cancelled, for example.'

'So, the message is: this is an accounting crisis – don't turn it into a socio-economic crisis by behaving badly?' Allen blew out his cheeks. 'You don't think that risks stoking anxiety? Panic, even?'

'I really don't see that we have an alternative, Prime Minister. Certainly not tomorrow. You need to look strong in the Commons.'

For a moment, Allen looked set on challenging his dentist's course of treatment. Instead, he accepted the medicine, spent a minute giving Hardy his new marching orders and dispatched the press secretary to prepare draft four.

'Well, LJ, what's next?'

If his chief of staff heard him, there was no reply. Head firmly down, she appeared to be doodling number after number on her ever-present pad.

'LJ,' pressed Allen. '*LJ?*'

She gave a start, her face masked in concern. 'Sorry, sir. I was thinking about what you said at COBRA about mind-boggling numbers. JvA's reference to *Who Wants To Be A Millionaire*. I started to do the maths.'

Allen's eyes narrowed. 'Meaning?'

'If a zero gets added each day, it's not a question of being a *millionaire*. By New Year's Day—four days from now—everyone in this country will be a *billionaire*.'

'Christ!'

'I think we've all ignored just how big the elephant in the room might be,' she went on. 'And how quickly it could grow.'

'Well,' replied Allen. He felt sick, like he had eaten one bowl too many of Christmas pudding. 'We can't ignore it anymore.'

100

TANNER HAD JUST TAKEN A CALL from Downing Street. He was *invited*—the assistant really used that word—to another COBRA meeting at 4 p.m. Which left less than an hour before he needed to leave the office – even considering Tommy's driving. He had barely replaced the receiver when his phone rang again. Brin's name flashed up. Neither had ever disappointed the other in over twenty-five years, and Tanner prayed that trend would hold.

'I had the two names run through our databases,' said Brin, after the usual pleasantries. 'There's nothing at all on Rhoda Kane. It might have been a pseudonym or an alias, but whatever it was, she never had any official documentation.'

Tanner knew better than to interrupt when Brin was centre stage and enjoying it. He waited, expectant, for the pay-off.

'But we *have* got a hit on Bryony Sears.'

'You have?' Tanner clenched his fist. 'Who is she?'

'Well, on the face of it: she's Bryony Sears. We have a student visa issued August sixth, twenty-sixteen, in Dublin and a Texas driver's licence issued to an Irish national of that same name later that month. However, there's no record of that person entering the country at that time. Or any other.'

'So, she didn't use Bryony Sears's passport to enter the US. There's no biometric data?'

'No.' Brin, as so often, was a step ahead. 'Nor is there any immigration record for a Holly Brand. As far as our boys at the border are concerned, neither has ever visited the US.'

'And yet we have Bryony in Texas in September twenty-sixteen.'

'Exactly.'

Tanner let out a long breath. 'Then we're no better off, surely?'

Brin laughed off Tanner's despondency. 'Come on Rob, of course you are. There's clear evidence that this isn't normal, law-abiding behaviour. Your security services will have to follow it up. And here's the kicker: we have *two* photo IDs. They're in your inbox now.'

Tanner fumbled with his phone, first putting Brin on speaker and then opening the email from his friend. Copies of the photos on the two official documents stared back at him. A rosy-cheeked young woman with thick, square glasses and very dark hair, cut in an unflattering chopped wedge. Had Tanner seen that face before? Was she really the young woman he had abandoned to Kellett all those years ago? It was difficult to say with any certainty, and there was no immediate jolt of recognition, as Tanner had hoped there might be.

'Well?' quizzed Brin. 'Is it Holly?'

Tanner dithered, looking from one image to the next. The two shots of Bryony Sears were almost identical.

'She's the right sort of age,' offered Tanner, without conviction. 'The hair's shorter and darker, and Holly didn't wear glasses. But it's certainly not impossible. Part of me thinks the face looks similar.' He sucked air through his teeth. 'But that may be wishful thinking. It's been eight and a half years, Brin.'

Brin's confident voice came back on the line. 'You want my advice?'

'Always.'

'Keep following that gut of yours, Rob. Whatever happens.'

'Thanks Brin, I appreciate it. Everything.'

Tanner forwarded the images, without details of their source, to Nikki and Gérard. The former would still be in the air, en route to Austin, so he called the Swiss, but the call rang straight to voicemail. He kept his message short.

'Check your mail.'

101

TANNER FOUND MIKE SORENSEN in David Nash's office, pointing to the risk chief's screen. There was an energy in the air, a febrile, live-wire sort of buzz about the place.

'Anything new?' asked Tanner. It was a question he had recycled so many times over the past couple of days, and each repetition must have felt like another lash of the whip. But now, for the first time, Sorensen didn't turn away or lower his eyes. If anything, he looked pleased at the inquiry.

'It's your ancient architects. They're… *interesting*.'

The word seemed to convey a much deeper meaning in Sorensen's Californian drawl. With everything else going on, Tanner had completely forgotten that the chairman had asked him to chase this particular wild goose. But as Sorensen elaborated, he was glad he had.

'We turned the problem round and asked them what they would have done if they'd wanted to build this kind of capability into software from day one, back in the Fifties or Sixties. Mass account manipulation without leaving any trace. Of course, they said it couldn't be done. Because it can't. So, I said, "Go away and try. What have you got to lose?"' Sorensen's face scrunched in amusement. 'Seriously, a bunch of seniors being paid big consultancy fees to play computer games. What's not to like?'

'And?'

'Well, of course they didn't come up with anything at first. But eventually, they managed to make a couple of lines of code "disappear." I mean in a computing sense, not in reality. In layman's terms, it's like when you delete stuff on your computer but it's still somewhere on the hard drive. An expert could find it and restore it. That's why we always say the only safe way to destroy information on a computer is to take a sledgehammer to it.'

'Like on those TV police shows,' Nash interjected. 'Where the forensic people salvage information from the suspect's laptop.'

'Exactly!' Sorensen beamed his acknowledgement. 'Just a hundred times more complicated and in an ancient language: *Code*.'

Tanner felt a charge of excitement, a small spark of light where there had only been gloom.

'So, they managed to exert an influence on the out-of-date code,' he said. 'What next?'

'It means we're a step closer to figuring out what the heck has been going on here,' replied Sorensen. 'We've got everyone who understands this stuff focused on it. Ashley's co-ordinating the effort.'

The mention of Ashley's name sent another frisson through Tanner's system. For a second, he dared to dream that the tide had turned. Together they would save the day… and then? He shook the thought from his mind and turned his attention back to the present.

'In that case, I'll leave you to it. I've got to get to Number Ten. Well done!'

This flicker of progress was at least something, and Tanner took particular pleasure in calling Sir Peter with the news. The older man was amused rather than self-satisfied.

'Perhaps there's life in us old dogs yet, then?' he chortled.

Tanner hoped that the news might lift Chrissie's mood too, but she was still steeped in gloom, offering only monosyllabic replies and nods or shakes of the head in response to his few requests. Not even the mention of Tommy could lift the pall.

Knowing when he was beaten, Tanner retreated into the silent safety of preparing his notes for the COBRA meeting until it was time to find his friend and driver.

102

FORTIFIED BY A COFFEE AND A DANISH from his favourite Fifth Avenue deli, Gérard began his investigation in earnest. He decided that 8:30 a.m. was a reasonable time to start making calls, and despite the early hour, Gérard's natural charm made the enquiries easy… easy but fruitless. By 10 a.m. he had spoken to admissions and teaching staff at most of the top New York schools. Rhoda Kane had no record; nobody remembered her.

In search of inspiration, he closed his laptop and let his mind wander. Immediately, his subconscious formed an image of Nikki, high above Arkansas or Tennessee, on her way to Texas to meet Chad Klotz's contacts. He knew he mustn't let her down; already he felt such a kinship with this woman – even though she was a stranger, really. Perhaps he recognised himself in her. Perhaps it was her own first-hand experiences of loss, the complex reaction of emotions catalysed by the death of a disappointed parent. And then again, perhaps it was just her smile, her unrelenting enthusiasm. Gérard chased her from his mind, ordered fresh coffee and returned to the task.

By the time his coffee arrived, Gérard had finished pleasant but unproductive calls with the last few names on the list. He was about to redial one of the contacts he'd been unable to reach earlier when his own phone rang. An unfamiliar area code showed on the screen.

'This is Tom Gristwood,' came a gravel voice, an old man. 'You left a message for me this morning. Sorry, but I'm up in Vermont—*White Christmas* country—and had my cell switched off.' Gérard hurriedly searched through his notes. Tom Gristwood: long-tenured professor at Cornell, the Ivy League school with a computer department founded all the way back in the Sixties.

'Hell, I was intrigued,' continued Gristwood. 'I don't often get calls from private investigators.' He laughed, a deep chuckle. 'You said it was about Rhoda Kane?'

Gérard's heart leapt. 'You remember her?'

'Hell, you couldn't forget Rhoda. I've had plenty of bright students over the years, but she was *extraordinary*. I like to think our Ph.D. programme bears comparison with anyone's, and I can't think of any student I'd rather have supervised for a doctorate in the last twenty years. Such a shame.' Regret filled his voice. 'The one that got away.'

'I don't think I understand,' said Gérard. He looked down at his notes. 'You're saying she *wasn't* a student? Do you mind explaining?'

'Sorry.' Gristwood made a noise like he was blowing air from his nose. 'I guess I got over-excited, thinking about her. Your call was a bolt out of nowhere. Let me start at the beginning.' His tone steadied, and now it was much easier to imagine this grizzled old professor standing before of a class of students, lecture board at his back.

'Rhoda applied for a part-time position as a lab technician in the department. There were better qualified candidates, at least on paper, so she didn't get interviewed. When she got the rejection, she replied to say that she was finding it desperately hard to get experience and would be prepared to help out for free if the opportunity arose. It just so happened that I was finishing an important paper and was really up against it, so her offer got passed on to me. I interviewed her and couldn't believe my luck.'

Gérard was taking frantic notes. The New York soundtrack, the incessant background noise of sirens and horns, no longer registered; his ears were on the prize. 'How so?'

'Well, her interests were the same as mine: fundamental programming. I needed someone to double-check information, references, sources, that sort of thing. Deep detail. And she just understood stuff, instinctively. Got there quicker, better, smarter than any assistant I'd ever had.'

'But she just worked with you part-time?'

'Originally,' answered Gristwood. 'We'd agreed ten hours a week. Unpaid. But she worked two or three times that, probably more in the first month. I suggested hiring her as a temporary employee, but she didn't want that.'

'Really? She wanted to work for free?'

'Not exactly.' Gristwood's voice crackled with humour at the memory. 'She proposed a different arrangement. She'd work full time for me during the day if she could use the department's resources in the evening.'

'That's all?' asked Gérard.

'Not quite. She also asked for two hours a week of personal tutoring from me.'

'Which you agreed to?'

'Hell yes! She was saving me fifteen, twenty hours a week, probably more. And I wanted to persuade her to do a Ph.D. at the school.'

'But she wouldn't?'

'No.' The note of sadness was back in the professor's voice. 'She said she hadn't decided where she wanted to live, what she wanted to do with her life. All the big picture stuff.'

'So, what happened?' Gérard's pen paused above his notepad, anticipating the breakthrough he had been longing for.

'I finished the paper,' said Gristwood. 'And she left, pretty much the next day. I tried to call her when the paper was published—I wanted to send her a copy—but both her cell phone and email were dead.'

'After you'd worked so closely together?'

Gristwood took a moment to reflect. 'You know, I actually wasn't that surprised. I guess you had to meet her to understand. There was something different about Rhoda. I wish I could think of the right word. It was like she was searching.'

'Searching? For what?'

'Damned if I know!' Gristwood's throaty chuckle boomed down the line again. 'I guess I've always expected to open the business section of the paper one day and see her leading some new multi-billion-dollar unicorn.'

'You think she would have gone into business, then, after you parted ways?'

'Maybe.' Gristwood sounded less sure. 'Or the CIA.'

'Seriously?'

'It would explain why she disappeared.'

Gérard wasn't sure if he was having his leg pulled. He didn't want to get side-tracked, so he changed the subject. 'What did she look like?'

'Medium height. She wasn't one to waste time worrying about how she looked. I remember thinking it looked like she did her own haircuts. Awful of me, I know. She had these deep brown eyes, though, like her hair.'

'Thanks, Tom.' Gérard's mind was already swimming, but there was something more he needed to know. 'Last question: what was her main area of interest? Your specialty, you said?'

'Not something you'd find interesting I'm afraid, Gérard. I'm the last of the dinosaurs.' He gave a regretful sigh. 'Early computing. Particularly its relationship to the latest technology. Think of the Gutenberg press *vis-à-vis* digital media.'

But Gérard was already thinking of something altogether different.

103

WITHOUT PREAMBLE, THE PRIME MINISTER TOOK HIS SEAT at the centre of the COBRA table and began. Sally Bickford had been replaced by the deputy commissioner of the Metropolitan Police, Sir Richard Lindsell. Whilst titular second-in-command of the country's foremost service, Lindsell carried broad national responsibility for Counter Terrorism and, more importantly, real clout within the force.

'Thank you for coming at short notice, everyone,' said Allen. 'We'll come to your reports, but first I'd like to focus on a point I think we've all been missing. Let's call it the elephant in the room: the maths.'

He ran through the earlier exchange with LJ, feeling the full weight of seven stares as he delivered the punchline. 'As of now, there are fewer than three thousand billionaires in the world. If we stay on the current trajectory, we'll start the New Year with another seventy-odd million of them in this country alone. In aggregate pounds sterling, that's a total of seventy, followed by fifteen zeros. *Quadrillions*, is the technical term, apparently. Whereas our entire national GDP is currently three *trillion*... which is a mere twelve zeros.' He paused to take in the grim looks around the table. Everyone had been doing the maths, scribbling the zeros. But saying the words out loud seemed to imbue the digits with greater power.

'We talked last night,' he continued, 'about worst case assumptions. But we were hopelessly optimistic. So, I need you to tell me what you'd have me do *now* if we assume those quadrillions come to pass. Or worse. Call it the Belphegor's Prime test. Please just answer that one question, without hesitation, deviation or repetition. Imagine you're on *Just A Minute*.'

Allen turned to the governor. 'Anthony, what would you have us do?'

'I think there are two practical issues, Prime Minister. Firstly, your assumption about zeros clearly renders UK stock and bond prices meaningless.'

Allen absorbed the jab, but he knew the hook was coming. He nodded for the governor to continue.

'My second, rather more important point, concerns the pound, which, under your assumption, will also be meaningless. If our currency is irrelevant by the end of the week, then London's position as a global financial centre is destroyed forever. Overseas money flows will just go elsewhere. Half a million people who work in financial services will be redundant overnight. In *both* senses of the word. We weathered Brexit and the pandemic, but this would be something else, a catastrophe on an entirely different scale.'

Allen waited, then tossed the obvious question into the silence. 'So, what do we *do* Anthony?'

'We have to go cap in hand to the Americans,' he answered, as if it was the most obvious thing in the world. 'The EU certainly won't help after all the Brexit shenanigans. We'll have to beg the president for a modern version of the Marshall Plan, like how the Americans rebuilt Europe after the war. Only this would have far bigger ramifications.'

'How much bigger?'

'We'd need a new currency, and that would almost certainly end up being the dollar. We'd have to bank with the Americans, too. Essentially, we'll be a poor—*a very poor*—vassal state. A fifty-first state. With central control of the economy for months, possibly years.'

'Anything else?' Allen asked weakly.

'No, I think that's enough for now, Prime Minister. Except for the one obvious caveat…' A grimace, or was it mischief, tightened the corners of Fleming's mouth. 'It does of course assume that what's happened here won't happen there too.'

The premier let both comment and look pass, without either of his own.

'Right, who's next?' Without waiting for an answer, Allen turned to the governor's neighbour. 'Saeed? If we can't stop the zeros today, what would the security services suggest I do.'

'To that very specific question, Prime Minister,' replied the head of NCSC, 'I'm afraid you're not going to like this, but there really is only one logical answer. We need unfettered access to all communications traffic. Telephones, internet, everything. That's the only way we can hope to prevent widespread discontent evolving into mass criminal unrest.'

Allen almost choked. While he did not especially revere principles, James Allen did revere popularity – and he knew exactly how such an intrusion would be received.

'You're talking about turning us into a police state, Saeed!' he said. 'It would be like the Stasi in East Germany. *Communism*! You can't be serious?'

'Prime Minister, *with respect*, you asked what I would do if we were in a situation where, as the governor has suggested, the nation is facing destruction of an entire way of life and the imposition of central control, *very much* along communist lines.'

'Lord almighty!' Allen blew noisily, but then regained a measure of calm. 'Okay, Saeed, I see the logic, but that's not a path I can take us down. For one thing, the Americans would never buy it.'

He ignored the archly raised eyebrow from Akhtar and took a deep breath.

'There's nothing on those names Rob suggested, I take it?'

The cyber head answered with a shake of the head. 'They're fake identities from eight years ago, Prime Minister, with no recorded usage since. Nor is there any further record of a *Holly Brand*. Probably part of a visa scam to get into the United States after Ms Brand was fired from National.

Identity theft: we see it every day.' Akhtar's tone was positively dismissive. 'She is of no relevance here.'

'But it has to be relevant!' sputtered Tanner, unable to stop himself. 'What happened in America is so similar to what happened here! These women—or this *woman,* as it may turn out to be—could be connected to all this.' Oblivious to convention or manner, he was only now making his first contribution to the meeting.

But Allen wasn't used to having his authority usurped – let alone by the outsider whose myopia had caused the whole bloody problem. Allen shot Tanner a look usually reserved only for the leader of the opposition. It was time, he thought, to put Tanner in his place.

'Rob, with respect—' and clearly, there was little of that now '—I think the security services know what they're doing. So do our cyber experts. Whereas I believe your sole job is to sort out your errant technology. And on that front, do you have anything for us?'

Tanner accepted the reproof with all the grace he could muster, which wasn't much. Fighting to keep his tone even, he briefly summarised the small signs of progress within the technology group at the bank. If he had hoped these small green shoots of optimism might raise his stock, he was mistaken. Disappointment spread around the table as he provided his wider update. Banks were struggling, increasingly failing, to keep cash machines open. No sooner were they filled than they were emptied, with customers hedging their bets by stocking up on hard currency in case the electronic version ceased to function. A run was entirely possible, and such an eventuality had only been forestalled by good Christmas spirit and bad weather. Worst of all, he had no silver bullet answer to the prime minister's diabolical question: "What do I do *now*?"

By the end of Tanner's update, no one would meet his eye. Allen certainly had no further words. He simply waved for the next contribution.

'Sir Richard, welcome! The police view, please.'

Lindsell shot a glance toward the security services, then answered. 'I'm afraid it's along the same lines as Saeed, Prime Minister. Emergency powers to prohibit demonstrations, disperse gatherings, detain suspects and property. Essentially, anything we—' he swept his arms around the table to indicate that the "we" embraced them all, '—consider to be in the public interest.'

'The death of civil liberty?' Allen stared, aghast. 'You're talking about turning one of the world's greatest democracies into a totalitarian regime… overnight. I might as well be President Xi.' Silence, once again, filled the room. It came like a fog, and it settled for as long as it took Allen to gather his wits.

'Again, I see the logic, Richard, but I cannot authorise those measures. I can't stand up in Parliament tomorrow and deny it if I've already done exactly that.' He looked knowingly at Akhtar and then back at Lindsell. 'For now, we proceed as we were. But if there are stratagems or *training exercises* you wish to prepare, I'll leave that to your discretion. And there's no need to minute that, LJ.' He looked dispiritedly around the table. 'Anything else?'

None of the others had any good news to offset Tanner's tale of woe. Retailers were reporting dramatically increased online demand. Although consumers were constrained by the new spending limits on their accounts, it was clear that many people were attempting to make purchases beyond their normal means. Credit card usage had risen significantly. As a result, many shops were beginning to limit purchases.

More worryingly, there were widespread reports of basic foods being hoarded. Panic buying, once again, had set in: shelves were being emptied of fresh items such as bread and milk, and the outsize predilection for toilet rolls was back. Incidences of public order disturbances were continuing, primarily arguments at empty cash machines or petty thefts, but also vandalism and drunkenness. Lastly, a cohort of anti-capitalism activists calling themselves *Zero Use* had called a rally for noon on Monday in Trafalgar Square.

None of the matters in question were desperate in isolation, but taken as a whole, the picture was seriously alarming. Allen looked at Jonathan Morse, two grim faces mirrored in anxiety.

'We need every police officer we have patrolling the streets,' declared Allen. 'Round the clock. A show of force. All other non-essential duties to be cancelled.'

Morse nodded. 'Yes, Prime Minister.'

'And what about the army?'

'They're on standby, confined to barracks, Prime Minister. All leave is cancelled and we're bringing everyone we can spare back to the UK.'

'Well done, Jonathan.' Allen's words were sculpted to encourage, but nothing it seemed could lift the gloom on the cabinet secretary's face, or in the room.

For the second time that day, the premier called on the spirit of the great man immortalised on canvas before him. And, this time, Winston obeyed the summons. The words came easily.

'Eighty-four years ago, my most famous predecessor faced the destruction of our great nation and refused to be beaten,' Allen declaimed. Every eye looked to him.

'I doubt there have been any greater threats to our democracy in the years since. And his words then are just as true now. Without victory there is no survival.' His voice cracked as he brought the meeting to a close. 'We *must* survive; our way of life must survive. So, for all our sakes, find me a victory, ladies and gentlemen. And find me one fast.'

104

TANNER CALLED TOMMY STEELE. Two minutes later, the bank's black limousine was pulling up opposite the Cenotaph to collect him. The warm interior was welcome, as was the familiar smile on Tommy's face. Whereas his own mood summed up the weather: cold, dark and deteriorating.

'That good, eh?' Tommy enquired into the rear-view mirror.

'Don't ask,' sighed Tanner. 'Any news?'

'Lots of speculation on the radio about pretty much everything because no one knows anything. Talking-head academics theorising about new forms of currency. Doom-and-gloom merchants asking how long shops and suppliers will keep taking orders. One berk pontificating about who wins and loses if we return to a barter economy. That sort of thing. The usual for a Christmas Saturday night.' A broad grin crossed Tommy's face.

Tanner couldn't help but return the smile. 'That's all right then, eh?'

Still laughing, Tommy set the Mercedes on its way up Whitehall. Wherever the original palace had been, the designation was no longer unique. The whole area was cloaked in fresh snow. The vista made Tanner think of Ashley and their Christmas Day walk by the river.

He had hardly seen her in the three days since. There had been a couple of briefings, but it was impossible to detach her from the rest of the group. He'd caught an occasional glimpse of her in meetings with greying consultants, but each time she had been deep in conversation and Tanner didn't dare interrupt. He'd tried her mobile the previous evening, but the call had gone unanswered. He assumed she had still been engrossed in the investigations into early coding. He rang again, now, expecting the same outcome, but she picked up almost straight away, electric humour already crackling in her voice.

'Is that the doyen of Downing Street?' she asked.

'More like the wally of Westminster,' Tanner replied, forcing good humour through gritted teeth. 'Can you speak?'

'Yes, it's a good time. I've just finished with our senior architects. They're fascinating.'

Tanner heard what she was saying, but he was caught in her spell; nervous words tumbled out before his brain could stop them.

'I was just calling because I wondered if you'd like to grab a bite to eat later,' he suggested, fully expecting a refusal. Still, he wanted to offer Ms Markham a small reminder of a more personal bond; he wanted Ashley back. She didn't respond at first, and he thought he had said the wrong thing. But then she gave a breathy laugh and surprised him.

'Why not? We do have to eat at some point. But I don't want anything formal. Maybe just a take-out?'

'Your place or mine?' Tanner countered, entering into the spirit.

'Take-out at the Lanesborough? *You cannot be serious!*'

The impersonation of McEnroe's New York brogue was note-perfect, and Tanner was still laughing as he replied.

'What do you fancy? Actually, never mind, we can decide later. Would you like me to pick you up?'

Tanner knew as soon as the words were out of his mouth that he'd gifted her another opportunity to yank his chain, but for once she spurned the opening.

'No, thank you, Rob. There are a couple of things I still have to do. Give me a couple of hours, maybe a little more, and then I'll come over? I'll call when I'm on my way.'

'Of course.'

'Maybe we should have meat loaf,' she offered, laughing as she hung up.

Tanner's smile lingered, an echo of the conversation, as he turned to the window. He looked out past himself, at the London streets beyond, and thought of Ashley. His smile only faltered when they hit traffic and a red double-decker crawled past in the bus lane. Emblazoned on the side of the bus was an advert—for what, Tanner barely understood—with an airbrushed woman posing beside a nonsense slogan. The woman was young—eighteen or nineteen, Tanner assumed—and she was wearing the bare minimum that advertising standards deemed appropriate.

He might just as well have been looking at one of Bosch's paintings; the artist's women were no less scantily clad. If that wasn't a manifestation of the rot eating society from within—the modern seven deadly sins—Tanner didn't know what was. Lust was unquestionably near the top of the twenty-first century list. Forget the hard stuff, the sexual trafficking and porn, sexploitation was mainstream now: from overtly sexual music videos on every social media platform to the beach-body nonsense on the Tube and magazine covers; everywhere you looked there was something sexual. Preying on our animal nature, on ego and insecurity, and—as the bus illustrated—deliberately targeted at the young. A generation prematurely sexualised for commercial gain. Tanner was the least prudish man he knew; perhaps that's why he hadn't realised until now how pervasive it now was.

Anger flared within him and, with it, the first flicker of a different flame. A flash of thought, too fast and too hot to extinguish. What if Joen van Aken was right? He couldn't allow himself to go there. With difficulty, he forced his mind to the mundanity of banking, to the COBRA meeting in which he had been practically laughed out of the room.

Saeed Akhtar was convinced that the leads Nikki and Gérard had been chasing were nonsense; Rhoda and Bryony, he insisted, were irrelevant. But if that was the case, then what should they make of Holly Brand's disappearance? Was she really just a lone, disgruntled ex-employee who had magicked her way into the US, never to be seen again? And the other two women… were they just illusions, fantasies? Something told Tanner there was more to it than that. The question went round and round in his brain. His head told him Akhtar was right, but his heart, or rather his gut, still wanted to bet the other way.

Finally, Tanner took notice of what he was looking at through the window: his own front door. And then he realised, thoroughly embarrassed, that Tommy had turned the engine off.

'Why didn't you tell me we had arrived?' asked Tanner.

'You were a million miles away,' said Tommy. 'It didn't seem like there was any rush to bring you back. I thought you might suddenly shout "Eureka!" if I left you alone.'

'I think Archimedes found his answer in the bath,' replied Tanner with a smiling shake of the head. 'Not in the back of a Merc.'

'Oh well, you've probably just got time for one before Miss Markham arrives,' shot back Tommy, deadpan.

'Good advice as always,' Tanner laughed. 'Any more you'd care to offer?'

'Yes, there is, actually.' Steele turned back to face him. 'Forget all about banks and money for a few hours. Try to relax. The rest will take care of itself.'

Tanner thanked Tommy for the sound advice and got out of the car. He had barely taken two steps towards his front door when he heard the whine of the driver's window being lowered. Tommy leaned out.

'Oh, and no curries!'

105

NIKKI'S PLANE LANDED TEN MINUTES LATE. There had been a delay getting out of New York, and it was past eleven by the time she disembarked in Austin. She hailed a cab, asking for the university's main campus downtown. On the way, she called Gérard.

'Howdy pardner,' he answered – a bright, if goofily Francophone, attempt at a Texas accent.

'Howdy to you too,' replied Nikki, with a laugh. 'Any progress?'

'Have you seen your email?'

'I saw the images from Tanner. It's good to have something, at last.'

'And there's more, besides. I didn't email, as I knew you'd call.'

Gérard repeated the details of his call with Tom Gristwood. Nikki listened attentively, making notes, hearing the change in his tone as he reached his conclusion.

'It suddenly came to me,' he explained. 'We've been chasing needles in haystacks. What we need are magnets.'

Nikki's pen paused between her fingers. 'I'm not with you.'

'I called Tom back and asked him who are the other experts in his field. If Rhoda targeted Tom Gristwood, then there must be a chance she went after other specialists, no?'

'Sure.'

'He gave me ten names. Three on the West Coast, as you'd expect, a couple more here in New York and New Jersey, two in Boston, and one each in Pittsburgh and Atlanta. He had numbers for most of them and told me to drop his name if it helped. How about that?' Gérard was rightly pleased with himself, and Nikki was quick to recognise it.

'You're *gooooood*,' she acknowledged stagily, although the flattery only lasted a moment as she consulted her notes. 'Hang on. You said ten. That's only nine.'

'Dear Nikki,' he replied with a sigh of resignation. 'Is there no sneaking anything past you?'

'There certainly isn't.' Nikki glanced out the window and met with her first proper view of street-level Austin, the looming skyscrapers of downtown. 'So, who's number ten?'

'Professor Joel Vasquez… at University of Texas, where I presume you are already headed. I'm texting his number. Mention Tom's name.'

Nikki shook her head in astonishment. 'Gérard?'

'Yes?'

'You're better than good!' Before he could reply, she realised her cab was pulling into the sidewalk. 'Hey,' she rushed. 'It looks like I've arrived. I'll call you as soon as I have news.'

Twenty-five minutes later, Nikki was sitting in Professor Vasquez's office in the School of Information, a few blocks south of the main campus. She'd already given him a brief outline of the search on the phone, and now she filled in the gaps. Vasquez listened intently; his eyes fixed on hers.

'As you can imagine,' Nikki concluded, 'we're desperate to find this person – these persons. We've only got scraps of information, so anything you can tell me is a bonus.'

Vasquez continued to stare at—or rather, through—her for a while longer.

'Interesting,' he said at last. 'I always wondered about Bryony Sears. Something out of place. *Incongruous*.' He noticed the puzzled look on Nikki's face then added, 'Sorry. I should give you the background, shouldn't I? She enrolled at the last minute – Master of Science in Identity Management and Security. The course was full, but we had a drop-out. Bryony was self-funded and had the right credentials, so she got the place. It wouldn't normally happen, but she offered to pay the full tuition fee upfront. As you can imagine, admissions were happy to rush her application through. Straightaway, it was clear that she was the best student in the class. Everything seemed effortless to her.'

'You taught her?'

'No; I was writing a paper the first two semesters, so other colleagues were covering my part of the first-year programme. However, I needed research support, and she volunteered. I checked her out with those colleagues. They said she was the best I'd get.'

'So, Bryony helped you?'

The question ignited a warm smile. 'To a remarkable degree. She worked the whole Christmas holiday and all though the second semester. I don't know how she found the time, with her coursework and everything. She must have been spending thirty, forty hours a week on my stuff. And she was still top of the class!'

Nikki paused, savouring the similarities between Bryony's and Rhoda's stories. With every scrap of information they unearthed, she became more convinced it was just the one woman they were looking for, after all.

'You used the word incongruous,' she said. 'Why?'

'Well, the fact that she seemed to know almost as much as me – for a start. Not that she wanted to let on.' Vasquez laughed, but then he turned switch-flick serious. 'And then the manner of her leaving, obviously.'

'She didn't finish the course?'

'No. Bryony came to see me not long after I'd finished the paper. She said there'd been an unexpected bereavement at home, and she had no alternative but to go back to Ireland. I managed to arrange a deferral of her second year, but she never returned.'

'What else?' asked Nikki, leaning forwards in anticipation.

'A heap of small, random things,' answered Vasquez in a throwaway voice. 'She didn't make any effort to socialise with other students or do the networking stuff they do to get jobs. She wore glasses, but if there was any magnification in them you could have fooled me. Oh, and her accent. When she concentrated, it was like the Irishness dropped away. As I say, just little things that I'm probably seeing with hindsight.'

Nikki pulled her phone out of her bag and showed Vasquez the ID photo of Bryony Sears. 'That a good likeness?'

Vasquez nodded but continued to regard the image. Then, at last, he shook his head, exhaling breathy disbelief.

'That's Bryony. Funny thing is, she could have been pretty. Please don't get me wrong, I don't mean to sound judgemental or sexist, but it was like she wanted to hide behind *that* image.' He pointed at the picture, then shook off the introspection and glanced at his watch. Nikki took the hint.

'Thanks, Joel, you've been so helpful. Just one last question. What was the subject of your paper?'

'It has a very grand academic title, Nikki, with lots of technical words to demonstrate my astonishing erudition.' Vasquez grinned. 'But in layman's terms it would be something like: The incidence of coding flaws in security software.'

A raised eyebrow obviated the need for further explanation.

106

LJ HAD PROMISED THE PRIME MINISTER an hourly update. She had no victory to report, but there were no new disasters either. She expected to find him watching the six o'clock news, but instead she found him staring out of his study window, lost in thought. London, and the nation, lay beyond. Normally, Allen was an expert at reading the public's mood, but who knows what might appear in the minds of otherwise rational individuals in a crisis? LJ cleared her throat discreetly and waited for a response.

After what seemed like an eternity, Allen spoke, his gaze fixed into the distance. His voice had a gentle, shadowy air.

'Is this how it begins, LJ?'

'Sir?'

'The end. Is this the beginning of the end?'

LJ had never seen this side to the prime minister. She remembered in that moment the admonishment her grandmother had given her whenever she had complained of her own inadequacies, allowed despondency to set in. You had to *act*, was the matriarch's lesson. Wallowing, defeatism, self-pity… they got you nowhere.

'No, Prime Minister, it isn't the end,' replied LJ firmly. She didn't know whether to pity Allen or be disgusted by him. 'So perhaps you'd stop looking out of the window and we can organise ourselves for tomorrow.'

Allen meekly did as he was told. In no time, the premier's usual verve was back, and they had a plan. They would hold a cabinet meeting at eight o'clock the following morning, and before that—this very evening, to be precise—Allen would make calls to the most supportive members of the collective. The lucky few would be flattered at their selection for personal briefing by the PM; they would also be gently reminded where their loyalties lay, in the unlikely event of any dissent. Zack Hardy was summoned to draft a statement for Allen to make immediately following the meeting, and then LJ was able to retreat to the sanctuary of her office, where, for the first time since taking possession of it, she shut the door.

The chief of staff sat at her desk and closed her eyes. A vision came back to her: she was in church with her mother and her grandmother, three generations resplendent in bright colours. It was Christmas, but it was hot, stuffy, in the church. She was just a girl. Her grandmother, beside her, kept nudging her to make sure she was awake.

LJ snapped back to the moment, startled by the strength and suddenness of her recollection. That was the last time she had felt so tired. And she was shocked to realise that, for the first time ever, she hadn't been to church this Christmas. She'd hardly spent a minute with Craig, either. Was it all worth it? A ping on her computer cut her thoughts short.

TO: Leah Oladapo
FROM: Joen van Aken
DATE: Saturday, 28 December 2024 at 18:30
DIRECTIONS

Hello, LJ.

You asked for a route map.

For once, I'll keep this very simple. No allusions, illusions or elusion.

I want the Prime Minister to set up a Truth Commission. A permanent, independent Truth Commission. Like the Royal Commissions we used to have, although I'm not fussed about royalty myself.

It will start by commissioning reports on my seven little friends: the modern-day deadly sins. It will provide people with the truth, not party-political dogma. It will make recommendations.

And here's the fun part: every year it will report to the people on whether the government of the day is meeting its commitments. None of this knockabout Prime Minister's Questions nonsense. Just cold, hard facts and independent review. To which the Prime Minister will be accountable.

We used to be proud of our democracy, "The Mother of Parliaments." Now we're a laughing stock. It's time to change.

Isn't that simple?

So, that's the big picture. I'll be back soon with some large-scale maps showing more detail. Interesting oxymoron don't you think?

J.

LJ was literally stunned. When she'd asked what JvA wanted, she hadn't given much thought to the likely reply. This, however, wouldn't have been in any number of guesses.

The chief of staff's mind reeled, unable to process the words in front of her. She reread them. At face value, JvA's message was very simple. LJ thought of her conversation with Allen about likely perpetrators and their motives as she unplugged her laptop and picked it up. They had discussed foreign states, criminals, terrorists, megalomaniacs, pressure groups and political opponents.

But which was this? Was this the work of a "political opponent?" Or was it just common sense, a citizen pushed to drastic extremes in their attempt to force some decency and honesty back into government? How did you wage war against an opponent like that? LJ could see no clear or easy answers as, laptop in hand, she made as quickly as she could for Allen's office.

107

GÉRARD CALLED THE OTHER NINE NAMES suggested by Tom Gristwood. With the time difference in his favour, he managed to speak with the three senior contacts on the West Coast. He also tried Cornell, Harvard and Princeton. The academics he spoke to were, in turn, intrigued, mystified or sceptical about his story, but none of them could think of anything remotely like Tom's experience with Rhoda. No students or assistants with peculiar backgrounds, no extreme intellect or strange behaviour. Not even so much as a dodgy haircut.

Which just left Carnegie Mellon in Pittsburgh, the Georgia Institute of Technology in Atlanta, and Columbia University, seventy blocks uptown from where he was sitting. His gut told him the last of these was unlikely. If Holly, Bryony and Rhoda really were the same person, he'd be prepared to bet she'd move around rather than risk multiple connections in the same city – even one as big as New York. And he couldn't chase the three outstanding professors yet. They had his message, and it had been enough to make all the others return his call. All he could do was wait for Tanner to get in touch after the latest COBRA meeting.

Gérard doodled the names Holly Brand, Bryony Sears and Rhoda Kane on his notepad, but he could see no connection. Doubt began to creep into his mind again. As if on cue, his phone rang. The name on screen gave him new heart.

'Nikki!' Gérard smiled to himself, glowing with the thought of a new lead and a fresh conversation with his partner.

'I don't normally get that warm a welcome,' laughed Nikki.

'Well, I've got nothing from the six people I've reached. I was hoping you might have something?'

'No new leads, but I do have confirmation that Bryony's area of interest is exactly what we're looking for,' said Nikki. 'And there's too much weirdness for it to be coincidence. Bryony and Holly are the same person, Gérard, I just know it.'

'Okay. I believe that. Rhoda, too. So, what do we do?'

'I'm not sure. I just ran out of the meeting and flagged down a cab. I'm heading back to the airport now. There won't be any more clues here in Austin; she's covered her tracks too well. Let me think, and I'll call you back.'

'But it was worth you going?' Gérard felt a rush of guilt at sending Nikki halfway across America while he'd spent the day between the deli and his hotel suite.

'Oh yes! You only had to see his face to *know*.'

Gérard had barely said goodbye and put down his phone before it was ringing again. A call from London, this time.

'Rob,' answered Gérard, still buoyed from his talk with Nikki. 'How did you get on at COBRA?'

'It was a car crash,' offered Tanner. 'No, worse, whatever that is…' The words fought against a noisy backdrop of wind.

Gérard didn't reply immediately. He knew from his own temperament that sometimes you just had to get things out, let the fireworks explode, then move on.

'Well, Rob,' he said, 'you'll be pleased to know your intuition has proved correct. Holly Brand, Bryony Sears, Rhoda Kane. Too many similarities to be coincidence – we can say that with certainty now. And we're learning a lot more about Holly's proficiency. We've got three more leads to follow up.'

There was a pause, and when Tanner's voice came back online, there was more of his usual urbane equanimity, less of the despondency. The line was quieter; he'd found physical shelter too, by the sound of it.

'It's a shame you weren't at the COBRA meeting, Gérard, they might have listened to you. The head of the National Cyber Security Centre basically told the PM that I'm an idiot for thinking this could be the work of one person. MI5 and MI6 checked Holly out, but they think it's—quote, unquote—a red herring.'

'A red herring?'

'Sorry, Gérard. An irrelevance. A coincidence. The saying was something to do with fox hunting, originally – a kind of distraction that prolongs the hunt.'

'Ah! Of course, I remember now,' Gérard laughed. 'In French we say *brouiller les pistes*, "cover the tracks." Very appropriate in the mountains where I ski.'

'What do we do now then?' Tanner asked.

'We keep up the legwork, as Nikki calls it. Making the calls. Checking the leads. Eventually, we'll find a pattern, or a clue, that gets us closer to the present-day incarnation of Holly Brand. Perhaps the security services will find the fox, not the herring. Or she made a mistake somewhere along the way.'

'You think she's capable of making mistakes?'

'Not really,' Gérard acknowledged. 'But I'm an analyst at heart, Rob. The more trails we find, no matter how well covered, the more chance of that single piece of evidence, however insignificant, that unlocks the puzzle.'

108

LJ WATCHED IN SILENCE as Allen studied JvA's latest email. She'd never known anyone able to master a brief as quickly—and comprehensively—as the prime minister, but there was no rushing this evening. The premier ran his tongue over his teeth, an expression on his face that said he was weighing each word in turn. Finally, he sat back, content with his appraisal, and held up three fingers – a rhetorical habit from the campaign trail.

'One,' he started, 'Do we take JvA's proposal at face value? Two, if we do, what practical steps do we need to take now? And three, when do we go public?' He barely paused before answering the first. 'We have to assume that it's genuine, no? So, on that basis, we have a simple decision. Do we agree to the terms?'

'In my opinion,' LJ answered, 'we don't have any alternative. The tech experts are sure the problem is buried somewhere deep in the original code. Maybe they'll solve it in an hour, or a day, or two days… but maybe they won't. We've been lucky so far.'

Allen raised his eyebrows. 'I don't feel very lucky.'

'Maybe not, but we are. Everyone on holiday, the weather… you name it, it could be worse. But our luck won't last – and certainly not beyond the weekend.' LJ couldn't hide the desperation in her voice, in her face. 'This country is spiralling out of control, Prime Minister. It's just a matter of how quickly we crash.'

'Say we go along with it. JvA's going to want a public commitment.' Allen shifted uncomfortably in his chair. 'Which means we'll have to admit the contact. And the terms of our surrender.'

'But is that so bad?' countered LJ. 'It's blackmail, but is the outcome so awful?'

'The outcome? Not awful?' Allen's face registered genuine surprise. 'You're not serious, LJ?'

'What are we agreeing to do?' she asked. 'To look afresh at a number of major issues and to add some independent oversight. Surely that's all.'

'But it's someone else's agenda, someone else's oversight. Politicians—governments—will be powerless.'

'Sir, with respect, they'll be more *accountable*.'

'You're talking like you agree with him?' Allen's eyes narrowed, and his body seemed to tense. 'With JvA?'

LJ could sense the danger. 'I'm just trying to provide some perspective,' she replied, meeting her boss's eyes.

Neither spoke for a moment, and the prime minister's next words made clear that all discussion was over.

'For now, this new email stays between us. We're sticking with the original plan. I'll brief the key cabinet members tonight, but I'll make it absolutely clear we're still gathering information. I'm certainly not going into Parliament tomorrow admitting I'm in negotiations with…' He searched for the right word, then spat it out. '*Terrorists*! Understood?'

'Yes, Prime Minister,' kow-towed LJ obediently. 'Anything else, sir.'

'Yes,' said Allen, 'there is.' He shook his head, although it wasn't clear whether he was displeased with LJ, with JvA, or with the world at large. 'Get back on to Tanner and all those other idiots. Tell them to bloody well get this sorted before our "luck" runs out.'

109

ASHLEY HAD TALKED ABOUT GETTING TAKE-OUT, but Tanner realised he had everything he needed for one of his favourite simple recipes: pesto pasta with grilled chicken. All he'd have to do when Ashley arrived would be to cook the pasta and prepare it in front of her. He'd even have time for a bath. Archimedes would be proud.

But then his phone rang again. What had Kellett said at the start of all this madness? "Could this fucking day get any weirder?" Apparently, it could. Tanner answered tentatively.

'Dad?' He said it as a question.

Harry's voice came down the line. 'I was thinking about what you said.' Then silence. The old man had probably hung up, Tanner guessed. But when he checked the screen, he saw the connection was still live. He waited. And waited. And he was eventually rewarded with another statement. Neither amiable nor, for once, dismissive. Just blessedly neutral.

'Well,' Harry went on. 'They say a problem shared…'

'You really want to hear?' asked Tanner, unable to keep the surprise from his voice.

'I asked, didn't I?'

Tanner bit his tongue. 'It's a long story.'

'I've nothing else to do.'

What was there to lose, Tanner thought? He launched into a detailed recounting of the chain of events, starting with the trip to the White Horse with Judith.

'I never did like the look of her!' Harry interjected.

Tanner had promised himself not to rise to the inevitable bait that would be thrown his way. He laughed it off and forced himself do the same to a couple more jabs… to surprising effect. The barbs became less frequent, and by the end, their conversation resembled a remarkably normal exchange between family members.

Having considered all the evidence, Harry pronounced his verdict. 'Well, that's a bugger's muddle.'

Tanner winced at the phrase; one he hadn't heard since his childhood. He couldn't deny, however, that it did rather sum up the absolute mess in which they now found themselves.

'Yes, Dad. It is.'

The line went quiet again. When it eventually came, his father's response, and its tone, was surprisingly measured.

'Funny way to go about it, but I do see their point.'

'What do you mean?'

'Well, it's obvious, isn't it? Too many lazy buggers wanting handouts. Too many rich people always wanting more and not paying their taxes. Too many gluttons stuffing their faces and then telling you it's unfair to call them fat. It's enough to rile any sensible person. This Joan van Whatever sounds like she's hit the nail on the head.'

'*Joen*, Dad. The painter. It's a man's name.'

'*He*, then.' The familiar exasperation had crept back into his father's voice. 'What would you do, Dad?' Tanner asked.

'Me?' Harry laughed, a short, bitter outburst. 'You've got to look to the top, haven't you? All this stuff in the emails, the sins, they start with whoever's in charge. So, I'd tell that new friend of yours, the prime minister, to stop nannying everyone. Stop spinning plates. Promising the world for a few more votes. Tell people the truth, even if it's bloody uncomfortable. Starting with the NHS.'

Tanner couldn't recall the last time the old boy had been so animated – or so civil. He wondered for a moment whether his father was unwell. Although he needn't have worried; Harry hadn't quite finished, after all.

'Don't suppose you can tell Mister Allen that though, can you?' he said. 'So, you'd better fix those bloody computers.'

They shared a laugh. But if that was an unexpected experience, his father's final words were unprecedented. 'Good night, son. Oh… and good luck.'

110

NIKKI WAS ON HER WAY BACK TO NEW YORK. It was her third flight in less than twenty-four hours, but at least she was airborne and in business class again, thanks to Gérard.

After her meeting with Professor Vasquez, there was no point in staying in Austin. Nor was there any way of guessing where Bryony/Rhoda's trail led next; it could be anywhere in the US – or even further afield. The logical next step, Nikki reasoned, was to head back to New York or London. She and Gérard could split their resources, one staying in the US and one returning to the UK, or they could stay together and work the trail as a team.

Nikki realised with a jolt that she really wanted it to be the second option. She had always enjoyed working on her own—it was, she reminded herself, the way she had always operated—but this was altogether different. She wanted to see Gérard, for one thing. She liked his commanding presence, the keen decisiveness which governed his life, the calm he exuded. It felt like the world was that little bit less stressful, less disordered, when she was with him. And the advantages of working as a team were becoming clearer by the day.

She had checked there was seat availability when she was in the cab to the airport, but when she went to pay for her flight, the woman behind the ticket desk looked at her like she was stupid.

'I'm very sorry ma'am,' the agent advised, offering a plastered-on smile. 'But we can't process UK-issued cards at the moment.'

'What?' said Nikki, hands and voice raising in stereo exasperation. 'Because of the bank situation? What am I supposed to do?'

'Do you have a US or other international credit card, ma'am?'

Nikki was about to reply, rather less politely than might have been necessary, when her phone rang. Gérard's name flashed on the screen. She stepped away from the desk, miming an insincere apology at the intransigent agent.

'Nikki, I'm so sorry,' Gérard began. 'I was on the phone to Rob, and then the professor from Columbia called.' The velvet Francophone tone was like a soothing balm.

'Any success?'

'I'm afraid not. We're down to our last two chances. Carnegie Mellon and Georgia Tech. What are you doing?'

'I'm stuck in Texas, it seems.' Nikki explained the problem with her UK credit card.

'Yes, it's getting worse, Nikki. Overseas banks and credit card companies are only allowing minimal spends, *if any*. UK card holders are pariahs, I'm afraid.'

'Shit. I knew it was bad, but this is ridiculous.' She looked around her, and the mania of the airport—everyone else around her going somewhere, all that nervous energy—seemed like an insult. 'What am I supposed to do?'

'Don't despair, Nikki.' Gérard's smile, a hint of self-satisfaction, was evident in his voice. 'I think you'll find that whilst there are some things UK money can't buy, the Swiss Franc is always acceptable. Put me on to the agent.'

Five minutes later, and Nikki was on her way, business-class ticket in hand. The whole experience had been profoundly unsettling, however. It didn't take a genius to appreciate the magnitude of the UK's financial meltdown, but somehow it took the refusal of a $200 plane ticket to drive the message home.

Nikki knew she was fortunate; there had been other options for her. But what about everyone else who found themselves stranded or unable to pay their bills? It was only as that thought occurred to her that she truly appreciated how much she valued her partnership with Gérard. After all, only the lucky ones had a Swiss Prince Charming on hand to save the day.

111

ASHLEY ARRIVED JUST AFTER EIGHT-THIRTY. Tanner greeted her with a chaste kiss on the cheek and took her coat. She was surprised to see the table set with a white tablecloth, flickering candles, and an Italian *tricolore* of cherry tomatoes, fresh basil and cream pasta waiting to be mixed.

'I thought we were doing take-out?' she suggested. Her smile was a welcome sight after the day Tanner had endured.

'Plans change, Ashley.' Before her look of surprise could turn into a question, Tanner gestured towards a waiting bottle in an ice bucket. 'But first, Champagne.'

Seated in front of the fire, with a glass of Champagne in her delicate hand, it seemed that Ashley's brown eyes, her whole face, sparkled with playfulness. But then she adopted a more serious expression, setting Tanner immediately on edge.

'I have a request,' she declared.

'Ask away.'

'Can we catch up on all the business stuff first, with a glass or two of Champagne, then just forget all about it and be two people simply having a relaxed dinner together? And then…' She let her words hang.

Tanner caught a reflection of the fire crackling in Ashley's eyes. Her effortless switch from high spirits to deep pathos caught him entirely off guard and the best he could manage was a stuttered, 'Of course.' Then a rather more composed, 'Ms Markham first, and Ashley later.'

'Exactly. If the events of the last few days have taught us anything, it's that we have so little control over our lives. Let's just take back control, even if it's only for a few hours.' She was smiling again as she held out a hand. 'Deal?'

Tanner leant forward to shake. But at their first touch, she pulled him forward with that same surprising strength that had astonished him on Christmas Day. She locked her mouth on his, knotting her fingers in the back of his hair. The softness of her mouth and force of her embrace were an extraordinary combination. Tanner found himself transported to a place where rational considerations were impossible. But then, just as suddenly, she let him go and sat back, wagging an admonishing finger for effect.

'Business first.'

They spent nearly an hour, back and forth, discussing the events of the past couple of days. The tone of the discussion was relaxed but entirely professional. Had he not experienced it first-hand, Tanner would not have believed it possible that this woman sitting at the other end of the sofa was capable of such flights of extraordinary passion, let alone with him. Somehow, he managed to keep his mind fixed on the issues they were discussing, rather than on Ashley herself.

It wasn't easy.

Tonight, she had on a deep scarlet dress, and he longed to run his fingers over the contours of smooth wool, to feel the warmth of her body beneath. She was wearing leather boots the colour of her eyes, the outline of which suggested they ended somewhere around the knee. Her hair was pinned lightly above the ear but fell loosely on her shoulders. And as for jewellery, all she wore were two small pendant earrings, reflecting ruby and gold in the firelight.

The names Holly Brand, Bryony Sears and Rhoda Kane had come up as they talked, but Ashley suggested they save discussion of the phantom women until all the other practicalities had been covered off. Now, Ashley returned to the subject.

'So, to be clear, despite the government's scepticism, you think all this carnage is the work of one young woman?' The look she fixed him with might have defined the word incredulous. 'That this Holly Brand, ex-graduate extraordinaire, was involved somehow, using different names, in account manipulation at two regional banks at opposite ends of the US? That she was able to cross international boundaries at will. That she's Joen van Aken as well?'

'I know, I know.' Tanner held his hands up in mock surrender. 'But my gut tells me I'm right. And besides…'

'Yes?'

'It fits a historical archetype: the solitary genius, the gifted loner on a mission to change the world.' Tanner was determined not to be put off by Ashley's cocked eyebrow. 'Einstein discovered the theory of relativity on his own. I don't remember Newton needing a bunch of others to catch apples falling from trees. Guttenberg. Galileo. DaVinci. Unbelievable *individuals*.'

'All men!'

'Marie Curie, then. The first person to win two Nobel Prizes.'

'You're talking pretty esteemed company, Rob.' Ashley smiled, and then her expression became unreadable. 'You think Holly Brand is up there with those savants?' Her tone was sceptical, and Tanner had to dig deeper into his reserves of faith to not concede the point.

'Yes and no,' he offered. 'We're talking about computer code, not astrophysics or the structure of the universe.'

'Then what's her motive? And why all the weird emails? If she's so smart, why waste time on those?'

Tanner shook his head. 'The emails I don't get. The government spooks assure me they're nonsense—gobbledygook—and they certainly read that way.'

'But you *do* get the motive?'

The hint of a smile crossed Tanner's face as he accepted his inconsistency. 'Bizarrely, yes. I may not understand the words, but I do get the desire to make the world a better place.'

'Well, it's a pretty hardcore way to go about it.' Ashley still looked unconvinced. 'Destroying the financial system to achieve a "fairer" society. Didn't the communists try that?'

'I know, but...' Tanner looked sideways. Then, with a movement of his head, he directed Ashley's gaze to the Christmas tree shining in the corner of the room. 'Take Christmas. What's it for, now?' He counted on his fingers. 'Greed, gluttony, envy, sloth, that's four for a start. I'm not remotely religious, but I somehow doubt they were the gifts baby Jesus wanted from the three wise men.'

'No. I agree.'

'And the rest of the year, throw in lust, pride and wrath.'

'I don't know.' A teasing smile appeared now on Ashley's lips. 'One of those sounds okay.'

Tanner blushed and hoped the low light would conceal it. 'You know what I mean, Ashley. We're well into the twenty-first century, and we're still plagued by the same problems that bothered mankind two thousand years ago. The world would be a better place for more kindness, patience, humility, diligence, wouldn't it? More virtues, less evil.'

'What about chastity?'

'I'll plead St Augustine's defence to that one.'

'What? "Lord, make me chaste, but not yet?" You hypocrite!'

They laughed together for a moment, and then the merriment dropped away. Ashley spoke quietly, delicately.

'It almost sounds like you want her to succeed, Rob.'

'No, of course not.' Tanner shook his head. 'The consequences of what she's doing, the pound becoming worthless at the flick of a switch… it's too horrific to contemplate. So many ordinary people would suffer. If the emergency services collapsed, thousands would die. The lights would go out; the government would have to declare martial law. Not to mention the effect of people's life savings coming down faster than the Christmas decorations. So, no – I don't want her scheme to succeed. But I would like the world to be a fairer place.'

'Says the CEO of a bank!' Although she'd meant it in jest, Ashley's comment had come out tinged with scorn. The pain showed in an involuntary tightening of Tanner's jawline. She apologised immediately.

'You know I think the world of you, Rob. So please don't take a bad joke to heart. Just kiss me. And then make me supper. I'm starving.'

He took her head in his hands and kissed her softly, then with increasing passion, until, finally, his breath failed him. Then once more, very gently, on her forehead, as she subsided into his arms with a sigh.

112

THE CANDLES BURNED DOWN as Tanner and Ashley ate. She was full of praise for his cooking and, at his instigation, full of stories about her time in California: a superficial place of fads and diets, she said – often at the same time. She capped off dinner—a night of good food in good company—with a toast.

'To you, Rob. May take-outs always taste so good!'

They soon found themselves back on the sofa, in front of the fire. A picture of quiet contentment. Tanner looked up to see Ashley staring intently at him and smiled.

'What is it?' he asked.

Ashley shrugged. 'I said no more business, but—'

'But what?'

She fidgeted slightly, glancing briefly at her fingertips.

'I don't know quite how to put this without sounding too direct.'

'Shoot,' said Tanner. 'I won't bite. What is it?'

'Okay, here goes. In for a penny, as you and Tommy might say…' She laughed and looked into his eyes. 'There's something about you I just don't get. I understand why you're a banker. I kind of understand why you stayed at National. What I don't understand is why you didn't want to be the boss, the number one.'

'I told you over dinner the other day. I felt I had to stay to protect people from Kellett and—'

'No, before that. Before he was appointed. You could have made a play for the top job. You had—you *have*—all the attributes.'

'I was always better as a number two,' he replied flatly. The fire crackled, and to Tanner the noise sounded like a laugh, like he was being mocked. 'I could do more that way.'

Ashley challenged him with a look one-part alluring and three-parts sceptical. 'I don't believe you.'

'Ashley, not now.'

'Why not now?' she pressed. Was that a defensive edge to her voice, or did Tanner merely imagine it? The latter, he realised; he was probably projecting his own defensiveness back onto her.

'It's…' he struggled for words and landed on, 'complicated.'

'Oh, come on,' Ashley laughed. 'You're smart. You've done the hard yards. People like you, they like working for you. You've got good values. What's so *complicated*?'

She had said all this with warmth, with a lightness of touch, but there was nothing light-hearted in response. Nothing at all, in fact. The expression merely drained from Tanner's face; his lips set close.

Ashley nudged herself ever so slightly closer. 'I'm sorry, Rob, I didn't mean… Is it something to do with this Foundation of yours?'

Tanner attempted a smile, but then he had to turn his face away, struggling to maintain his composure. He had indeed received a text message earlier that afternoon, from the operations manager at the Foundation. They were worried about how long they would still be able to function if the bank attacks continued. They needed to buy supplies, particularly food, and the card linked to the Foundation's bank account was being declined everywhere. The volunteers had started using cash—their own money—to make sure the kids had enough to eat and everything else they needed when the schools started up in the new year. But it wasn't sustainable. The staff wanted to know when things would get back to normal and what Tanner thought they should do if they didn't. Tanner had barely had time to worry about it, with everything else going on. Nor did he have time to worry about it now, with Ashley's voice snapping Tanner back to the present.

'What is it, Rob? Why do I keep saying the wrong thing? Am I making you unhappy?'

'It's not you,' answered Tanner. 'And you don't make me unhappy – quite the opposite.' He sighed. 'But there's stuff in the past that's best left in the past.'

'Rob, I *know* you,' Ashley persisted. 'You've had an exemplary career. Everyone makes mistakes, but there's nothing you could have done in the past that should have stopped you from going all the way to the top. I could name fifty bankers who have done terrible things and still made CEO. What could you have done that was so shocking?'

'I let my little brother die.'

The six simple words had been uttered so quietly, so matter-of-factly, that they were barely audible.

'*What?*' Ashley's eyes widened, and her mouth dropped open in shock.

'You asked why I never wanted to be the person in charge, didn't you?' said Tanner. 'The one with ultimate responsibility, the one to blame?'

'Yes, but I don't understand, Rob,' Ashley floundered. 'Talk to me.'

Tanner leaned forward and gripped his elbows in their opposite palms. His face said he was there but not there.

'You really want to hear?' he asked. 'It's not a pretty story.'

Ashley leant forward, laid a hand tenderly on his forearm and gave the faintest squeeze before gently asking, 'When did you last talk about this, Rob?'

Tanner looked to the ceiling as he spoke. 'Thirty years ago, give or take.'

'Then surely now would be a good time?'

For a while he yielded no response but continued to sit, lost in some faraway place. Then he sat up straight and stared directly at her. At least part of him had returned, although his eyes suggested he saw little of the present. He took a deep breath then began to speak in a quiet monotone.

'I was ten years old. My brother, Matthew—Matt—was nine. We were inseparable. Our sister, Liz, was—is—four years older, so she was off being a teenager. But Matt and I were like twins. Same school, same hobbies, same bedroom. If you wanted to find one of us, you could call the other's name and we'd both appear.' A sad smile passed over Tanner's face.

'We both loved football. Sorry, soccer. Every day after school, we'd rush through any homework so that we could go out and play. We were so lucky. We had an enormous park only five minutes' walk from our house. Every day we'd meet friends there, maybe eight, ten, even fifteen of them, pick sides and play. Really competitive games. A dozen little kids playing on full size pitches, as if it was the cup final.'

If Ashley did begin to imagine the man opposite her as a tousle-haired little boy, she said nothing to interrupt his flow.

'You won't believe it, but it was the fourth of July. Nineteen-ninety. A Wednesday evening. There was a huge gang of us. The World Cup was taking place in Italy, and England had qualified for the semi-final. Against Germany: our oldest rivals. The excitement – you can't imagine! Anyway, the game was due to start at 8 p.m., and my mother had told us to be home by seven-thirty "*at the latest.*" But of course, we all got carried away pretending to be Gazza or John Barnes or Gary Lineker. He'd scored two penalties in the quarter-final, so of course we had to have a penalty shoot-out of our own to finish our game, and we lost track of time. A passer-by shouted, "Aren't you going to watch the game?" and we realised we were late. We gathered our things and ran like hell. It was only a five-minute walk home, but of course we ran.'

Tanner's eyes rose to the ceiling again. He cleared his throat, tried to compose himself.

'There was a main road between the park and our house. Our parents had drummed into us to always—"*I mean always*"—use the pedestrian crossing with traffic lights to cross it. But it was the biggest game for twenty years; the country was at a standstill. Everyone was glued to their TV sets. Which is where we needed to be.' Tanner paused. 'We ran. But rather than use the crossing, I decided to be clever, cut corners and run straight across the road. There was no traffic, after all. I was a year older, a year faster, probably fifteen, maybe twenty metres ahead. Matt shouted, "Rob, the crossing!" but I just glanced at the road and shouted back, "It's clear. RUN!" Tanner steadied himself, wiped his eyes and took two enormous draughts of air.

'Matt must have stumbled, or maybe he hesitated for a moment. I was already across the main road and running down our street, only fifty metres from home, when there was an enormous screech and a bang.' Tanner's head dropped into his hands, the first sobs breaking through. Ashley moved to get up, but he put a hand up to stop her. 'Let me finish,' he managed.

A minute or more passed, marked only by the sound of Tanner forcing his breath under control. His voice, when it came, was broken, ragged.

'A driver rushing home to watch the game, like us. Matt ran straight in front of him. Maybe the car was going slightly too fast, but to be honest, the driver didn't have a chance. Neither of them did. An ambulance came and took Matt to hospital, but he was already dead.' Tanner's voice trailed off. 'I never saw him.'

This time he let Ashley wrap her arms around him. 'Rob,' she said. 'I'm so sorry. I don't know what to say.'

'Don't say anything.' Tanner hugged her tightly. And when he at last broke from the embrace, he took her hands in his and finished what he had to say.

'And *that's* why I never, ever wanted to be in charge. Of anything. I'd always hear my father shouting at me the day after the funeral—"You were responsible for Matt"—before breaking down in tears. It was the last time he ever spoke his name. People always remember that game for Gazza's tears; I always think of my father's. It was the only time in his life I ever saw him cry.'

'But—'

'How did my parents deal with it? They didn't. They never talked about him in front of Liz and me. My dad retreated into himself, my mum into her faith. But it wasn't enough. She just got sadder and sadder. She died when I was twenty-one. When mum was alive, she used to take us to the cemetery, but dad never came. And yet, my brother's grave was tended immaculately every week. It still is.'

'And how did *you* deal with it?' ventured Ashley.

'Me? I put the memories in a box. And I put the box on a shelf. In a cupboard. In a room. In a house. And locked each of them in turn, somewhere deep in my mind.' He gave her a self-deprecating smile. 'It's probably why people think I have what they call "relationship issues."'

There was a moment of quiet, scored only by the soft popping of the fire and the guttering of the candle on the coffee table.

Eventually Ashley asked, 'Do you?'

'No,' said Tanner. 'I just hadn't met the right person.' His face brightened. 'Until now.'

But in contrast to Tanner's gentle smile, a shadow fell across Ashley's face. Tanner might not have seen it, and if he did, maybe it didn't register. In truth, he was lost in his own grief, oblivious to the sadness of the world beyond his own, internal boundaries. He certainly didn't notice the melancholy which had pooled in Ashley's eyes, flickering in the erratic spasms of light from the candle.

When Ashley spoke, she said the words so quietly that Tanner didn't even hear them. 'But you don't even know me,' she said.

The candle flame flickered wildly, throwing its thrashing light over the walls until, drowning in its own wax, it died. A frayed pillar of smoke began to rise from the wick. Ashley stirred and made to move the candle away. Tanner said nothing.

113

JAMES ALLEN KNEW ONE THING FOR SURE: he deserved a drink. He'd spent an hour and a half briefing the most senior members of the cabinet about the day's events and his forthcoming statement to Parliament. At the same time, he had been forced to remind them where their loyalties lay – or, at least, where they ought to.

Allen had deliberately left the chancellor of the Duchy of Lancaster and the defence and education secretaries off his call list. He trusted these serial leakers as far as he could throw them – which, in two of their cases, was a very short distance indeed. And as for those cabinet members he had spoken to, he had made it absolutely and unambiguously clear that they were to say nothing of the conversation to anyone, upon pain of immediate reshuffle:

a fate far worse than death, given the number of colleagues desperate to step into their shoes under Allen's popular leadership. Or should that be hitherto popular leadership, he wondered?

Each of Allen's cabinet colleagues had sworn to support him, and so that evening he felt he had earned the right to put his feet up in front of the TV with a gin and tonic. His timing was perfect; BBC news snapped on with an immediate bulletin.

'Tonight, at ten: a breakthrough at last in the efforts to resolve the cyber-attacks that have crippled the UK's banking system.' A breakthrough? Allen almost spat out his drink. He felt his heart beating in his ears as he forced himself to sit still and listen to the newsreader.

'In the last few minutes, the BBC has learned from a reliable source in government that the perpetrators of the attacks have now come forward. They are currently engaged in discussions with members of the prime minister's most senior staff and appear to have issued a series of demands in return for reversing the attacks. The precise nature of the demands is not clear, but they are not believed to involve financial extortion. Over to our political editor at Westminster.'

The camera cut, and the next shot showed a woman outside the Houses of Parliament. She was wrapped up all in black and had on her face an expression of smug self-satisfaction, a news-hungry leer Allen had come to associate with journalists of all stripes, but which seemed to be particularly common among political reporters.

'Yes, *dramatic* news in the last few minutes. We're yet to hear any confirmation from Number Ten, but I can confirm that the prime minister's aides are in regular contact with the group behind the cyber-attacks. This does not appear to be a cyber-crime in the conventional sense; no ransom is being demanded, nor does there appear to any other financial motive. Bizarrely, I am told that their demands are merely for political and social reform. Although the discussions have been categorised to me as a useful "exchange of information," James Allen will now be open to the accusation of negotiating directly with terrorists. That's something no British prime minister before him has ever done.'

Allen reached for his phone. LJ answered before the first ring had even sounded.

'Are you watching the news?' he asked.

'Yes.' LJ's voice was unreadable.

'Can you believe one of the bastards leaked this? Don't they understand the predicament we're in?' Allen heaved a deep sigh of exasperation. 'How do we respond?'

'Actually, sir, I don't think the report needs to be a negative. The fact that we now know who's behind the attacks takes away the bogeyman aspect, which is a good thing. People hate uncertainty. It's no longer who and why and what – just what *precisely* do they want? And the fact that it's not some huge financial heist will surely be seen as a positive.'

'But the suggestion that I'm in negotiations with terrorists?' Allen couldn't believe the words coming out of his own mouth.

'Sir, prime ministers have used backdoor channels to talk with our enemies since the beginning of time,' said LJ. 'We'll just get Zack to brief along those lines.'

'That sounds like an awful lot of spin.'

'Well, frankly, sir, it doesn't really matter.' LJ's response sounded blunter than she'd intended, and she hurriedly qualified it. Allen wondered if she was annoyed to have been disturbed at home, again. He knew his wife thought along the same lines whenever he had to work late, which was practically all the time.

'What I mean, Prime Minister,' continued LJ, 'is that we have very little time, anyway. Thirty-six hours at best. We either do a deal with—or catch—JvA, or we find a solution. If we don't, managing the press will be the least of our worries.'

Allen considered her words. 'You're right. Let's get through cabinet and Parliament, then we'll work out how to do this deal with JvA, if that's what it takes.' Allen reached for his gin and took a fortifying sip. 'Oh, and one more thing,' he went on, affecting nonchalance.

'Sir?'

'Find out which bastard leaked this. If we're still here on Wednesday, there's going to be a New Year reshuffle.'

DAY SEVEN

SUNDAY 29 DECEMBER 2024

114

ASHLEY AGREED TO STAY THE NIGHT, as she and Tanner had both known she would. And almost as soon as she alluded to staying, they were both upstairs: tangled in the bedsheets, entangled in each other. It was exquisite, the best Tanner had ever known. Exquisite and exhausting.

While Ashley was in the bathroom, Tanner took the opportunity to go downstairs for two glasses of water. He was still out of breath, his earlier sadness banished, for now, by the immediacy of her presence and the sensuousness of her touch. They had already gone one round, and there were clearly more in store. They had been so hungry for each other, hands frantic at clasps and buttons and then softer, more tender, against bare skin. Even when he was inside of her it felt like it wasn't enough; he wanted more of her, and he suspected his desire would never fully be satiated. Just stepping over her rumpled dress on the bedroom carpet, her underwear in a knot beside it, had sent a thrill through him. They were not finished. He never wanted them to be.

Tanner opened the fridge door, and light flooded the kitchen. His eyes fell upon his mobile phone, which had been left on a counter, forgotten in their hurry to get upstairs and get undressed. A voice in his head told him not to look, but he couldn't help himself.

There were no messages or voicemails, no urgent emails. It was purely out of habit that Tanner pressed the icon for the BBC News app. There appeared on his screen a stock image of James Allen outside Downing Street with the headline: "PM's senior aides 'in discussions' with cyber-terrorists." He was about to click on it when he heard Ashley's voice calling from the top of the stairs.

'Are you leaving me again?' she keened, in a lament so pitiful that it could only be bogus.

The news could wait, Tanner reasoned. There was nothing he could do, or LJ would have called. He had the most beautiful woman in the world warming his bed, and he'd lost her once before by putting work first. He wouldn't make that mistake again.

He returned to his bedroom to find Ashley sitting up against the pillows, the duvet pulled just high enough that he couldn't see anything, just low enough that he could imagine it.

'I thought you'd run away,' she said, eyes widening in mock-terror.

'Never,' he said. 'You're stuck with me.'

'Well, in that case, you're forgiven,' she laughed. Then the humour drained from her face. 'Although you still have work to do.'

'Work?' asked Tanner.

Ashley dropped the duvet and fixed him with a pouted stare. 'Yes, Rob. A girl can't do it all, you know.'

115

GÉRARD LOOKED AT HIS WATCH. That same cascade of memories, of loss, came over him. With each passing minute, his father—and Félix—got further away. Nikki, meanwhile, was getting closer. And yet he still felt remorse at yet more time having slipped through his fingers.

It was nearly 8 p.m.; Nikki's flight was due in at JFK any moment now. But that made it 1 a.m. in London – another day already. Gérard considered their options. Was there any point in staying in the US? What if Holly had gone to ground with no more aliases? What if she'd moved back to Europe? Or Australia? Or who knows where?

Gérard had run the three pseudonyms, if that's what they were, past every contact he had in the security and police services. He had called in every favour he was owed. But no one had come up with anything new, and he found himself now at the proverbial dead-end. Or maybe Holly actually was dead, and all they had were red herrings. A dead herring, even? He remembered one of Félix's favourite lines: "I don't do ifs and buts and maybes. I just do." He tried to concentrate. What would Félix *do* now?

The investigator was spared further introspection by the ringing of his phone. The screen showed a 404 area-code. Atlanta – the professor at Georgia Tech he had been trying to reach all day.

'Gérard? This is Charles Mackinlay. You left me an intriguing message earlier today. I'm sorry it's taken so long to return it, but I've only just got back from New Orleans.'

The Swiss had expected a southern accent, but Mackinlay's was curiously neutral, with a number of different inflections.

'I'm really grateful, Charles.'

'My friends all call me Mac,' replied the professor. 'Reminds me of home.'

'Home?'

'Glasgow. Scotland! But that was a long time ago; I'm a proper southern boy now. But anyway, you called asking about a research assistant. I'm assuming you mean Lily Stamp?'

'Lily Stamp?' The name—another alias?—was a shock to Gérard's brain. For a second, currents ran in a hundred different directions. His subconscious knew that he'd been given the missing key, but the deeper truth of it didn't quite register straight away. He forced himself to listen to Mac's explanation.

'She was the best research assistant I ever had. Appeared out of nowhere, said she was looking for a job while she decided whether to do a master's degree. I was working on a paper for one of the FinTech conferences. She offered to do the grunt-work. You know, checking references, citations, making sure I hadn't missed anything. Said she'd done similar work back in New Zealand.'

'New Zealand?'

'Yes, she was a Kiwi. She was here on a tourist visa, scoping out university courses in the States, so she didn't want to be paid. She didn't want to break immigration rules, tangle with the law. I said I'd give her a week's trial.' The professor paused, the memory calling forth a chuckle. 'Gérard, you wouldn't believe it. My productivity must have gone up 100 per cent that first week. Damn, seemed almost like she knew stuff before I'd even asked her to find it. Of course, I said I'd keep her on. I offered to try to get her paid. But—'

'But I'm guessing she said, "No thank you, Mac, I'd rather barter my time for a little of yours… and your college computers."' Gérard had heard enough variations of that same story to know how it ended.

'Uh-huh,' confirmed Mac warily. 'So, *I'm* guessing this isn't the first time she's done something like that?'

'No,' said Gérard. 'Far from it, in fact. Can I ask when she was with you?'

'Late fall twenty-seventeen. October, November, maybe? Now would you care to let me in on the joke?'

Gérard told the professor the essentials of the Holly Brand story, keeping nothing back.

'So you see,' he said, 'we have this Brand/Sears/Kane/Stamp mystery.' Then it struck him. 'Oh *merde*! That's it!'

'What's it?'

'The names!' exclaimed Gérard. 'I'm such a fool.'

To an incredulous laugh from the professor on the other end of the line, Gérard garbled his hurried thanks and a promise to call back later with an explanation and hung up. It couldn't wait; he had to tell the others.

116

ASHLEY WAITED UNTIL SHE WAS SURE that Rob was asleep. He ought to be, she thought, she had certainly done her best to tire him out.

Watching him sleeping, she was reminded of Tanner's confession, how his life had changed during Italia 90, that iconic World Cup. She was no soccer fanatic, but she knew that particular tournament was at the heart of English football folklore: from Gazza's heroics to the BBC's coverage, which had introduced the world to the tones of Luciano Pavarotti. She looked on as Tanner's strong chest rose and fell, rose and fell, and thought of the tenor's most vaunted aria: "*Nessun Dorma*," or, in English: None Shall Sleep. So much for that, she thought.

She gave it another five minutes. Another ten. Then, slowly and with infinite care, she slid out of bed and gathered her things from the floor. She looked tenderly down at Tanner's still form: a handsome face, lost in sleep to a rare tranquillity. He didn't stir as she tiptoed down the stairs.

She dressed hurriedly in the kitchen and used an app to request a taxi. Tanner's phone was still on the counter. The screen came to life as Ashley picked it up, and she saw three notifications:

✉️ **MESSAGE Gérard Dumont, 01:38**: Please call immediately. Must speak urgently. Repeat, URGENT

📞 **PHONE Gérard Dumont** Missed call (3)

✳️ **VOICEMAIL Gérard Dumont**

A sad smile flickered across her face, and she let out a sigh. She waited for her taxi in the darkened sitting room, listening for sounds from upstairs, but none came. Her gaze never left the Christmas tree, shining brightly against the night.

Before long, she heard a car pulling up outside. She took a last look around the room and moved to the foot of the stairs for a final check. Still no noise came, so she reached into her handbag and pulled out an envelope, which she now placed carefully, almost reverentially, on the mantelpiece above the dwindling embers of the night's fire. Next to her still unopened present, which she had left on Christmas Day, and which had neither been noticed nor disturbed since.

At the front door she paused for a moment. Then, on the way out, she slammed it shut as firmly as she could manage, a combination of noise and force that reverberated through the sleeping street. She was surprised it didn't set dogs barking.

The driver wound down his window as she approached. His face was impassive, his features forgettable.

'Miss Brand?' he asked.

'Yes,' she said, opening the rear door. She allowed herself a smile of quiet satisfaction. 'That's me.'

117

GÉRARD CALLED NIKKI'S NUMBER, desperately hoping that her flight had landed on time. It must have because she answered on the second ring.

'We've got it, Nikki, we've got it!' Gérard's excitement was almost more than he could contain. He wished Nikki was already beside him so he could celebrate with her, but she was still at the airport, and he was in his hotel suite, where he could speak freely.

'Got what?' Nikki asked.

'The link, Nikki!' Gérard laughed, a little hysterically. 'It's *markings*.'

'Woah, slow down,' said Nikki. 'You've lost me.'

She heard Gérard blow out a blast of air, then he came back on the line, slightly calmer.

'Sorry, Nikki, I literally just got off the phone with the professor in Georgia. I haven't had the chance to process it yet.'

'So, process with me.'

'Okay. His story's almost identical. It sounds like Holly went there straight after her time with Gristwood. You don't need to know the detail for the moment, just the name. Lily Stamp. Lily *Stamp*. Stamp! Get it?' The euphoria was back. 'Brand, Sears, Kane, Stamp. If you brand or sear something you leave a mark. The mark of Cain. Stamp a passport.' Words tumbled out in a rush, then stopped, as if Gérard had run out of breath and talked himself out.

Nikki spoke deliberately into the silence. 'It's more than that, Gérard. Holly, Lily… they're tree and plant names. Are you at your computer?'

'Yes, hang on. I know what you're getting at.' There was quiet as he typed into the search bar, then an exclamation. 'A bryony is a wild climbing vine with green flowers!' Nikki heard him hammering his keyboard again. 'And Rhoda: "a female given name, originating in both Greek and Latin. Its primary meaning is rose."'

'How did we miss that?' There was pain in Nikki's voice.

'Oh, come on, Nikki, stop! We've found a link. We've done it!' Gérard was ebullient again. He laughed. 'It's quite festive, in a way. We went looking for Holly, and now we've found not only the ivy but a whole arboretum! We'll pass the information to the authorities. They can scan their databases for every variation of markings, plants, trees, flowers. You name it. Their algorithms will track down other aliases in seconds.'

'We don't need to.' Nikki's tone sounded too flat, given the enormity of the discovery. She seemed sombre, even. Her sudden reticence took Gérard by surprise.

'*What?*' he asked, bewilderment strangling the vowel into a screech.

Nikki let the moment hang, taking in the enormity of what she was about to say. She began to speak, then changed her mind, figuring that another few seconds would make no difference.

'I'm thinking of other names which fit the pattern,' she began.

'And?'

'You know the name of Rob Tanner's independent cyber-security consultant?'

'Ashley?'

'Ashley *Mark*ham.' Nikki stressed the first syllable of the surname. 'Tanner mentioned her in passing, and I never made the connection. Ash – as in tree. Markham – as in mark 'em. Shit! I'm so stupid.'

Gérard felt the truth dawning on him: sunlight after winter gloom. Unwrapping this mystery brought a kind of feverish excitement, like a child opening a Christmas present. He hadn't enjoyed his work this much since he was back in the Selous, and it hurt him—physically, almost—to imagine Nikki beating herself up because they had been blindsided. But all was not lost – far from it. This was a breakthrough, not a defeat.

'Stop it, Nikki,' he demanded. 'None of us saw it. And now we can do something about it.'

'But she's been right under our nose this whole time! What are we going to do?'

Gérard thought for a moment then answered decisively. 'I'm going to call Tanner and you're going to find us a flight back to London. Don't worry about the cost, just get us out of New York tonight.'

'You're sure?'

'A hundred per cent. There's no point in staying here if Markham's in London. The authorities can hunt down other aliases, search where she's been, but we've got to find her now, and my guess is it won't be easy.'

'But we have her name.' Nikki was disbelieving. 'We know what she looks like.'

'And you don't think she can change again?'

Nikki was about to protest, then realised the truth of the Swiss's comment. Four aliases, four nationalities, half a dozen locations. At least.

'You're right,' she agreed. 'So, get your clever backside out to the airport. I'll be here waiting for you. And text me your credit card details so I can get us those tickets!'

118

TANNER AWOKE WITH A START. He certainly hadn't meant to fall asleep, but the evening's concoction of intoxications, both physical and emotional, had lured him into a deep slumber. Momentarily disoriented, memories of the night flooded back: soft, warm skin, the wet heat of animal passion. But Ashley was no longer in the bed beside him. He called out her name, softly at first, thinking she must be in the bathroom. Then he went to the top of the stairs and tried again. No response broke the stillness of the night. His watch read 2:25 a.m.

Tanner grabbed his dressing gown and went downstairs, but there was no sign of Ashley in the kitchen nor the living room. Nor was there any sign of her coat, bag, or any other possessions. He was standing in the middle of the living room, trying desperately to make sense of her disappearance, when he noticed an envelope propped up on the mantelpiece with his name written in large letters.

He almost lunged for it. When he tore the flap open, he found a sheaf of papers, folded double, and a postcard-sized print depicting a surreal representation of a man and woman kissing one another through what appeared to be veils or shrouds. The man wore a black suit and tie, the woman a dress the same shade as Ashley had worn that evening. Both the scene and its shadowed, sombre colours spoke immediately of sadness and secrecy.

Tanner took the papers out and set them down on the mantel. Then he turned the print and read the few short words written in an elegant cursive script.

"I'm sorry, Rob. Sorry beyond any words. But at least not all lust is bad. Holly Brand x"

Tanner felt the blow in the pit of his stomach. He glanced up and caught his reflection in the mirror. A rigid mask, the face of an idiot, stared back at him. He squinted to read the title of the painting, written in small print at the foot of the card. *The Lovers II*, by René Magritte (1928).

It was difficult to comprehend the enormity of Ashley's deception, and his stupidity—or, more accurately, cupidity—in being blindsided. Ashley Markham was Holly Brand? He had suspected the other women, the mysterious Bryony and Rhoda, were aliases of Holly – but Ashley! Surely it wasn't possible? Had he been betrayed by her beauty, by the way she had made him feel comfortable sharing his most intimate thoughts? And how could that confident, sophisticated woman be the chubby ingénue of eight years ago? It should have been impossible, and yet he recognised, deep inside himself, the absolute truth of this revelation – even as he wished he was mistaken, that he was dreaming.

In a state of shock, Tanner set down the print and turned to the papers. He unfolded them to see his own name at the top of the first sheet. It was a letter, he realised – a missive in Ashley's smart, curled script, handwritten on lined paper. The message was long, spanning multiple sides. He almost fell back onto the sofa as he started to read, battling to absorb the words.

> *Dearest Rob,*
>
> *I really am sorry for deceiving you, which is why I decided to write this letter – something more substantial, and yet more ephemeral, to accompany Monsieur Magritte. It's old fashioned, I know, to write by hand in our world of texts and emails, but that's not necessarily a bad thing. The past has much to commend it, in fact – particularly from where I'm standing.*
>
> *Here's another thing: emails leave a trace. The great advantage of a letter is that it can be tossed on the fire, and nobody will ever know about it. Perhaps that is what you will do after you have read this letter – but promise me this: that you will read it first. Every word. Please. I owe you some answers, and here I will do my best to give*

you them all. Perhaps there may even be some catharsis in it for me, too, although I fear I am already beyond redemption, even in my own eyes.

There is so much to tell you, and it's not obvious where to start. So, I'll just follow the song and start at the very beginning. But there is one thing I must say before I say anything else, and it is this: I had forgotten what it was like to feel affection; personal warmth. A hint—the possibility—of something deeper, even? You gave that back to me. Whatever happens, I'll be forever grateful for that.

The life story I told you over dinner, on Christmas Eve, was the life story of Ashley Markham. But she is no more real than the money in our bank accounts, than a character from a film or a novel. So, you can disregard what I told you. My real life story is that of Holly Brand, and you need to understand her story before you can understand why I deceived you and what I am trying to achieve now. So just listen, dearest Rob. Hold on to your questions and read to the end before you send this paper hurtling into the hearth. Here goes.

I was always an introverted child. My father died when I was nine, and that only pushed me further along the spectrum, deeper into my secret world of puzzles, codes and ciphers. To make it worse, my mother moved us from Hampshire—where at least I had a couple of friends—back to her hometown in Yorkshire. I was the geeky southern kid who got one hundred percent in maths and physics tests but couldn't name the boys in Westlife. When my classmates watched Titanic, they drooled over Leonardo DiCaprio; I wanted to understand the science behind the bulwarks failing. You can probably see where this story is going.

I'd already built my first computer by the time we did GCSEs. Nothing else mattered. Schoolwork was a breeze, the other girls left me alone—I was too weird to bully—and I guess I'd already figured out that disappearing was the easiest way to avoid trouble. I sat in my room all hours of the day and night on my computers, with only code and chocolate bars for company.

I went to Imperial to read computer science. I swapped school for university and my bedroom in Harrogate for a bedsit in Gloucester

Road. Life barely changed. All I cared about was computing. I was obsessed.

You might say I collected obsessions, and another was the riddle of the pyramids. How they were built, the secret passageways and hidden tombs, how clever the ancients were… these things gripped me. It was this fixation which sparked the idea that the way to go forward in computer design was to go back to the start. Everyone today just builds on yesterday's latest developments in sequential, incremental steps. I had the idea to start again from scratch and build something completely new.

And I was like Alan Turing in The Imitation Game, convinced I was the only person in the world who could see the way forward. I ignored everyone but my tutor. I spent hours on end playing with code, barely sleeping, living on junk food. Then, just before finals, my mother died, and suddenly I was not only alone but an orphan.

In a way, her death was a blessing. She had cancer, and it had gone on for a long time. I think it started the day my dad died; she just didn't want to live without him. I knew she was unwell and kept making plans to visit her, but she always put me off with those awful words: 'I'm fine.' She didn't want to take me away from my studies, and then it was too late. She was gone. And I really was alone.

My mother's death was also the reality check I needed. It made me realise I had been slowly going mad. Naturally, I was swamped with PhD offers, but any more studying, at that time, would only have pushed me further into myself. So, I went looking for a job instead. And I found one: at National Bank. But there was a whole summer before it started.

Here you must realise something, dearest Rob. In the previous decade I hadn't been to the movies once; I had barely read a book on anything other than computing. I hadn't bought a CD or a dress, had never been to a club or a gym. In short, I had been so consumed by my studies that I didn't do anything normal for ten years. I gave myself three months to catch up on that lost decade. I had to be back in London for the start of the graduate programme in September 2014, but until then I was free. I had literally no idea where to start, *so I bought a Eurail pass and took a train to Paris. After that, I'd see where fate took me.*

I was liberated, and I followed the call of freedom all the way to the Louvre. I went to the Musée, and it was as if my eyes were opened for the first time. Maybe it was the pyramid's energy, but I loved the art. We'd never had art books at home—everything was about science—so it was a revelation to see all the exhibits. Especially so close. I was captivated. And it gave me my answer for the summer: I would conduct a grand tour of Europe's great museums and galleries. Florence, Rome, The Hague, Madrid – I saw it all. But nothing left quite so great a mark as the Prado, where I was introduced to Mr Hieronymus Bosch.

I stayed a week and went every day, basking in the hypnotic genius of his work – the almost psychedelic prescience of it. Then, suddenly, summer was over, and I had to return to London. And it was wonderful. In art, I had a new interest—a passion—which, in time, also opened my eyes to music and movies. I bathed in culture, drinking in years of missed bestsellers and box-office hits. I loved the job at National, and I was able to leave the bedsit and rent my own flat in Brixton. I couldn't believe my luck.

Of course, nothing good in this world can last. And my luck ran out during that FROG meeting. The wonders of legacy security consolidation and sticking plasters... I'm sure you recall well enough. You might say I was lacking in EQ—emotional intelligence—and you'd be right. I know I should have spoken to you first, warned you what I was planning to do, but I was a creature of logic, and to me, everything was so simple. I knew we could improve the bank's technology, ergo I made a point of proving it. I never expected Kellett would come down on me so hard, but more than that, I never thought you'd let him, Rob. But what is life if not a succession of disappointments?

I guess this is the point where you'll be shaking your head and wondering how on earth I found out about National's security problem in the first place? Well, you have to remember I was on the inside, gamekeeper playing at poacher, with unlimited resources.

And how does any discovery get made? Einstein? Edison? Tesla? You build your ideas day after day after day, but then at a precise moment in time—in one specific second, on one actual da—the theory just comes together. Practice, judgement, luck. In my case, of course, I wasn't so lucky, given that I was thrown out of the building a week later.

Anyway, I had been playing with the bank's code every chance I got. Early mornings, late nights, weekends… imagining I was re-writing it from scratch. I'd set up a bunch of dummy accounts to practice on, and one day, they just disappeared. That was when I knew I'd found a way to make code "disappear." To hide it.

I won't bore you, dearest Rob, but I'm sure you want to know. It's all to do with the math: binary numbers versus digital numbers. It's complicated, but it's also the intent. Imagine one of your beloved football matches: if you see eleven players on the pitch all in the same kit, you quite reasonably assume that there's only one team out there. It never crosses your mind that there might be an invisible team, running rings with an invisible ball. So why would it cross your mind to build bank code—any code—with invisible commands and data built in from scratch? Only when the ball starts hitting the back of the visible team's net do you realise what is happening.

What I didn't bargain for was the sheer incandescence of Kellett's fury and your inability to stop him. I was a twenty-four-year-old kid with no clue about office politics, remember. I thought you'd fix it, and so I waited for the phone to ring. One day, two days. Then, on the third day when you didn't call, I guessed that you were obviously on his side. That you were like him, after all. I now know you so much better, and of course, I realise that isn't true. Back then, I tended to see things in binary: black or white, zero or one. People were either part of the problem or part of the solution, for or against me. I lived in a world in which there were no shades of grey.

Regardless, I took Kellett at his word about killing my career in London. That meant there was only one place to go: the US. The home of tech, with the best schools, and banks big and small for experiments and test runs. A nation of transient populations, huge enough that I could lose myself. My mantra became: research, refine, relocate, repeat. And with those words ringing in my ears, I set off on a lonely but fruitful journey – of discovery and revenge. I had a plan to bring down National Bank, to show everyone how wrong they had been to drum me out. To ignore my sticking plasters. It sounds childish, now, but that's how I was thinking at the time. You don't have a monopoly on regret, dear Rob.

My targets, back then, were threefold. I was furious with National Bank, I was furious with Kellett, and although it pains me to say it, I was furious with you. But then I started reading about the financial crisis, how no one was ever really held to account despite all the pain and suffering they caused to so many millions of people. I became fixated by the bailouts and tax breaks. The crypto-scams and pyramid schemes: the Madoffs and SBFs. The Epsteins. That was when I realised it was the whole system that needed to be overhauled, not just one or two bad eggs. The money keeps flowing into the finance guys' troughs, and they keep using it to buy off the politicians. Obama did little to stem it, and he was supposedly one of the good guys. Then Trump. Need I say more? As for the UK? One former PM was a lobbyist for a dodgy financier, and his chancellor went to work for an investment bank. And let's not even mention their successors' dodgy loans and tax avoidance. Plus ça change. I decided I'd shake things up a little, bring truth back into the equation. I stuck to the original plan—hitting National—but now I had a bigger picture in mind. Bigger ambitions.

I learned everything I needed to learn, growing my skills with every job, every course. Because you are intelligent, and because you trusted that gut of yours, dearest Rob, I'm sure you'll soon uncover my trail across America – the empty shells of women, the discarded aliases I was forced to leave behind. But it wasn't too long before I knew everything I needed to know, and that's when I set my plan in motion. I wanted to change the world, you see. And I knew just how to do it: a coordinated series of attacks, paralysing the banks over the Christmas break, when nobody can be badly hurt. I'm sorry about the inconvenience—to your customers and to you personally,

Rob—but it was all in service of something worthwhile. The plan was that I would start jerking National's chain, and then I would come to the politicians with my demands, and of course they would have to accept—they couldn't afford to dither for a single day— and then the revolution would already be over, a bloodless shift to a new, better way of doing things. The world would be a better place, I would have had a chance to test my skills against the best, and the nightmare would be over long before New Year. But what's that saying, Rob? Even the best laid plans…

Everything changed when I met you, mere days ago. You were just so… nice. You kept mentioning that Foundation of yours, but you were too modest to divulge how important it was, how many kids you help. And then you made me that amazing Christmas Dinner, and everything was so perfect. You told me you'd quit the bank for good, that you were done with Kellett. Your compasses pointed in opposite directions. It was such a nice line. You were the first person I'd believed in for a decade. The first person I'd allowed myself to get close to. And then Sir Peter called, and it was like that day of the FROG committee all over again.

I tried to refocus on the accounts, the issues, the plan. I assumed—still—that the prime minister would negotiate, and fast. Why would you let things escalate day after day when you could just have a discussion? Once I'd added a couple of zeros, I expected there would be contact: proper dialogue, negotiation, something. But I hadn't bargained for Allen's ego. Clearly, it will take a few more zeros—and a few more days of disruption—to bring him to the table. So that's what I'll do. That's still the plan, despite everything.

The problem, dearest Rob, is that my demand for a truth commission (surely, you've heard about that already, at COBRA?) strikes at the only thing that seems to matter for Allen: power. And ultimately, the price of power is truth. Sadly, it's a price fewer and fewer of our leaders seem willing to pay. As for this particular leader, Mr Allen: I don't yet know, but he will have to come around, or this story will have a very unfortunate ending.

Here is where you must believe me, Rob, even if you disregard everything else. I don't want anyone innocent to suffer. But I have to try to make the world a better place, and I am committed to the path I am treading. I naively assumed Allen would have thrown in the towel by now, but clearly, he wants to try and fight my incursions. He's using you as a weapon in that battle, I know, so I may as well tell you now: he won't win. You won't win. My attacks are too sophisticated. That's not ego speaking, it's just a fact.

I've probably rambled on too much, but you make me feel free, you make me want to open up, so I'll blame you for that. If nothing else, I hope that you understand me better now.

So, where does that leave you, dear Rob? Probably back where we started, at that FROG meeting. Choices and consequences. Just as it was once up to you to convince the Toad to do the right thing, now it's up to you to convince Allen that this is a battle he will never win. That it's a battle he shouldn't even fight. To embrace the truth, not fight it. The truth always outs. Just as the sun always rises.

And as it rises today, please remember I really am sorry for hurting you. Nothing else. Thank you for everything good this second time around.

I'd love to think there might be a third time lucky for us, but somehow I doubt that's likely. But just in case there's the tiniest chance, I will say adios and not goodbye.

I signed the print as Holly, but that's no more my name than Ashley Markham. Instead, I will sign off this letter as the true me, Joen. As a girl, I always loved the story of Joan of Arc, the fair maid fighting the good fight surrounded by duplicitous men. Then, later on, I had a neighbour of the same name who was uncommonly kind and generous. And, you know the origins of Mr Bosch. So, Joen of Aachen just seems right.

Adios, then. And with no more duplicity. Just love.

"Joen."

Tanner read the letter word for word, twice over. Then he set down the pages, disbelief coursing through him. It was impossible, he thought. All of it was so mad, so wild, so out-there that he was inclined to assume none of it was real. He knew how much Ashley liked to tease, how quickly her moods shifted. Was this a bizarre prank, a joke at his expense? He supposed he would call her, and she would laugh, a bright tinkle of a giggle, and say, 'Ha! Fooled you!'

But this brief glimmer of optimism died as soon as Tanner got up, found his phone and saw the screen full of messages from Gérard. He didn't bother with the voicemail but called the Swiss, who answered immediately.

'I know,' Tanner said, his voice little more than a whisper.

'Sorry, Rob, I didn't hear you?'

'I *know* Gérard,' Tanner pressed on, his tone as empty as his heart. 'Holly, Rhoda, whoever. It's Ashley.'

The line went quiet for a moment as the investigator took in the news. Took it in… but didn't understand. 'But we only just worked it out ourselves, Rob! I was calling to tell you. What happened? Did your security services find her?'

'No, she told me.'

'What?' asked Gérard, disbelief in his tone.

'She was here, Gérard. We made love.' There was no change in his stilted delivery.

'Get a grip, Rob! I need you to focus. Tell me what happened!'

Tanner haltingly, but then with increasing fluidity, began to describe how he and Ashley had met, how they had been attracted to each other, seemingly mutually, from the start. Only now did Tanner realise how expertly he had been suckered; how desperate he had been to believe that his lightning-fast relationship with Ashley had been something real. How he had been played, even if she had fallen for him towards the end. It was plain to see.

'Nikki and I are coming back overnight,' Gérard informed him. 'We'll be there in the morning to help you. But right now, you need to call the authorities. I know it's going to be tough. But you must get them on her trail immediately.'

Tanner realised the delicate tightrope the Swiss was trying to negotiate. 'It's okay, Gérard, there's nothing anyone can say that will make me feel more foolish than I do right now,' he answered. 'What is it they say?

There's no fool like an old fool in love.' He sighed. 'Forgive me, Gérard. Self-pity's an ugly thing, and it's the last thing you need to hear after all you've done. I should be thanking you. It's extraordinary what you and Nikki have achieved.'

'No, Rob, we should have spotted the connection sooner.'

'Connection? Christ, I haven't even asked how you found out.'

'It's the names,' said Gérard. 'Her names. Trees and plants: Holly, Lily, Ashley. Followed by markings: Brand, Stamp, Markham.'

Tanner groaned. 'So bloody obvious. Like hiding in plain sight. Still, she's out in the open now, whatever name she uses. I'll make a call to the prime minister's people, then it'll be out of our hands. With luck, it'll be wrapped up before you even land. Safe journey, Gérard.'

119

THE CALL ENDED just as Gérard's taxi was emerging from the Midtown Tunnel. It surprised the Swiss every time: one minute you were in the middle of Manhattan, then suddenly you were rattling along the Long Island Expressway, high above the industrial sprawl of Queen's. The landscape here changed quickly, the same way people do.

Until now, Gérard hadn't stopped for long enough to reflect properly on how he had got tangled up in this chase – and whose side he was on. But there could be no going back to Ziegler now. He and Nikki worked too well together, and he had uncovered within himself a conscience that wouldn't tolerate the kind of no-questions-asked work he had been tangled up in for so long. He thought it was funny, in a way, that he should have this revelation while he was tracking the elusive Holly Brand, a woman who shed identities like a snake sheds its skin. A fresh start of his own was exactly what he needed – *sans* a completely new identity, of course.

Gérard spent a minute just looking out of the taxi window. New York presented an untroubled and domineering visage, the towers of Manhattan rising in an almost Babylonian defiance of man's subordination to any higher power – or to nature itself.

Thus far, America was untouched by the banking crisis which was unfurling across the Atlantic. But would the attacks, like a contagion, spread across the ocean – another downside of our interconnected world? Would this capital of greed and inequality—panhandlers with bombed-out eyes begging at the base of skyscrapers—become the next target in Joen van Aken's moral crusade?

Gérard didn't know, in truth. He gave a last look over his shoulder at the lights and sights of the city, fast receding in the wintry gloom, and set his mind to happier considerations: his reunion with Nikki, now just minutes away.

120

TANNER HAD BEEN ABOUT TO DIAL LJ when something made him change his mind and dial another number instead. He expected the phone to be off, but instead it rang once, twice, three times. Despite the events of the previous week, Tanner had always thought himself a good judge of character, and now he tried to picture Ashley's expression as she looked down at the phone ringing in her hand. Was she wondering whether to answer or just laughing at his expense? Yet another twitch upon the thread? Before it could ring a fourth time, his call was picked up. Ashley's voice answered. But only in voicemail form. 'Hi, this is Ashley. Please leave a message after the tone.'

Tanner had given no thought to what he would say, but the words came easily as he spoke into the mute receiver.

'Hi Ashley, it's me. I'm sorry, too. Sorry that you're hurting so much, I mean. I know what it's like to carry pain inside for a long time, and I'd do anything to help you. I hope you know that now, even if you didn't when you wrote that letter.' He paused. 'You know, I think I fell in love with you the very first moment I saw you. None of this changes that. And remember, there's nothing that can't be undone.' His voice trailed off. 'Just so you know.'

Tanner swallowed the lump that had formed in his throat, took a deep breath, and called LJ. Again, the sound of ringing, but then a sleepy voice came on the line.

'Rob? What time is it?'

'Sorry, LJ, it's nearly ten to three.'

Hope sparked animation. 'A breakthrough?' asked LJ.

'Yes,' replied Tanner, but in a tone at odds with his answer. 'We know who's behind this.'

'What? How?'

Tanner steeled himself for the humiliation of answering the question. 'It's Ashley Markham.'

'What?'

'You know my theory about the women in America, about them all being linked to Holly Brand's disappearance? Well, now I know for sure. Holly Brand became Bryony Sears in Austin, Texas in September 2016; then Rhoda Kane in Poughkeepsie, New York; we've got a Lily Stamp in Atlanta, Georgia; and God knows who else until she ended up as Ashley Markham. Always moving, probably finding ways to stay off the grid until she became Ashley, leaving no biometric data. Her names all fit the pattern; she's been playing a game all along. And now she's got a new name: Joen van Aken.'

'You're sure she's behind all this? You found an actual link to Markham?'

Tanner took a breath. The wave of embarrassment broke over him. 'No, LJ, she… told me.'

'She told you?' asked LJ, her tone a chimera of disbelief and awe. 'And you never suspected?'

'Not once. And I know, LJ, *I know*. You don't need to ask. How could I not see? Do you think my brain's doing anything but ask that question?' Tanner counted mentally to three, driving the exasperation out. 'All I can say is that if you'd met Holly in twenty-sixteen and Ashley eight years later, you'd see no connection. I'd stake my life on it.'

'Okay, Rob'. LJ's dismissive tone indicated that there was nothing to be gained from further interrogation – not that she believed him. 'I'm afraid the police and security services will want to interview you.'

'Of course. I've got nothing to hide.'

'Where do you think she's headed?'

'She was staying at the Lanesborough. My guess is she left here just before 2.30, so if she's heading back, she must be nearly there. Her phone was still on when I tried just now.'

'Let me get on to the police and security services.' LJ was back on familiar ground, issuing instructions. 'Stay by the phone, Rob. Don't move. Don't go to sleep.'

Tanner doubted she even heard his protestation that he wasn't planning to before the line was cut. And then he was left in the dark and the quiet, with only regrets for company.

It was a cold night, and it seemed only natural to rekindle the fire. But as the logs started to take, the kindling gently aglow, licks of flame rising from among the ashes, Tanner was struck by a strange and unaccountable conviction. He picked up the letter from where he had left it on the coffee table – beside the Magritte print – and carried the pages over to the fire. It felt right, proper, that he should ball up the sheets and toss them into the growing flames. The paper caught almost immediately – and, with it, the logs beneath blazed into life. Tanner watched as the letter, page by crumpled page, curled a black fist. He was so captivated by the glow of the fire, so consumed by Ashley's betrayal, that he forgot all about the wrapped gift perched still on his mantel. It was as if the small box, his Christmas present from Ashley, was looking down at the sad scene taking place at the hearth, flames flickering as hot as the tears running down Tanner's face.

121

LJ's FIRST CALL was to the PM's back-up security detail. There was always an emergency response vehicle within a minute of Downing Street, which itself is only a mile and a half from the Lanesborough. Luckily, LJ knew the duty officer well. It took less than that minute to get a car diverted to the hotel, with instructions to detain Ashley Markham. They would be there in four more minutes, LJ was assured.

As LJ ended her next call, which had been to Sir Richard Lindsell of the Met, a bleary-eyed Craig sat up in bed.

'What's going on?' he asked, taking in the sight of LJ pacing at the foot of the bed, lit by the glow of her phone.

'I need a favour, hon,' answered LJ. She glanced at her watch, hopping on one leg to get into her trousers.

'What is it?'

'Will you drive me to Downing Street? We've got a major breakthrough, at last. Please? I'll owe you – big time.'

Craig rolled his eyes and shook his head, but he got out of bed all the same, reaching as he did so for the previous night's clothes. LJ, meanwhile, took a call from the officer coordinating what was turning into the storming of the Lanesborough.

'Markham hasn't spoken to anyone at reception since the night staff took over,' said the officer. 'And no one's seen her or anyone of her description. I've sent someone up to her room with a passkey, and we'll have two other unmarked backup units in place within five minutes. If she's not back yet, we don't want to scare her off.'

'Great job. I've got to call the PM, so call me on my spare as soon as you have news. I'm texting you the number.'

'Of course.'

LJ gave thanks, yet again, for the cool efficiency of the PM's security detail and uttered a silent prayer that Markham would head back to the hotel. If she did, they'd have her. LJ doubled down on divine intercession. 'And please let this be the day the whole mess is sorted.'

Five minutes later, she was in the car with Craig, heading to Westminster. She'd hurriedly explained the night's developments to him, receiving the expected raised eyebrows at the connection between Markham and Tanner. Astute as ever, even at 3 a.m., he'd asked the all-important question.

'But this suggests that the whole mess is caused by one person. I thought the GCHQ boffins said that was impossible?'

LJ shrugged. 'Maybe's she's part of an elaborate conspiracy? Or maybe the boffins were wrong?' She blew out her frustration, 'Bloody black swans.'

Conspiracy or not, Markham wasn't in her hotel suite. While there were clothes, toiletries and other day-to-day articles in the room, there were no computers, phones, passports or anything else of importance.

LJ woke the prime minister with a call to relay everything that was going on. The part about the previous evening's romantic assignation got the expected response.

'You *are* kidding me?'

'No, sir.' LJ played the straightest of bats.

'Come on, LJ,' Allen was incredulous. 'You're expecting me to believe that Tanner's been in *very* close proximity to this woman, and yet he didn't have an inkling of awareness that he already knew her? That they had worked together and, what's more, that she was the very missing woman he has been so bloody obsessed with?'

'She was twenty-four back then, sir, and thirty-three now. People change.'

'We need to check him out, LJ. I don't buy it.'

'Of course, sir,' replied LJ. 'But I can't see what motive he could possibly have?'

'Sex!' Allen spat with disdain. 'It's what trips up most middle-aged men. I thought you'd know that by now, LJ, you've worked with enough of them.'

LJ was tempted by the dangling bait but said nothing.

'Where are you now?' asked Allen.

'On my way in, sir. I'll be there in half-an-hour.'

'Okay. Come up to the flat. We'll have a cuppa.' Allen snorted, though whether in laughter or disbelief was hard to judge. 'Or is it too late for a drink?'

122

IF THERE HAD BEEN A LONGER NIGHT in Tanner's life, he couldn't remember it. There were numerous people he wanted to call, but he couldn't see what good it would do to wake any of them in the middle of the night. So, he simply sat in the warming glow of the fire, trying to make sense of the past week's events. He realised now how clever Ashley had been, ingratiating herself with Brin to get her in with National Bank, with him. How on earth had she known about his connection to the American? How much planning must her scheme have taken?

And yet, for all her cleverness she'd been ridiculously naïve, assuming Allen would come to the negotiating table the moment she turned the thumbscrews. Tanner, too, hoped the PM would negotiate, but he feared Ashley had miscalculated in assuming Allen would bend before he found her and undid her damage. Now it was already too late for her to back down. It was like the Kellett episode all over again; Ashley's binary way of thinking had blinded her to the flaws of others, the pride which interfered so often with morality.

Because there *was* a morality to what Ashley was doing; Tanner could see that. He even sympathised with her to some extent. But he feared she had made another miscalculation in not realising how much—and how many—ordinary people would be hurt by her actions. The collapse of the banking system would bring about medieval consequences; would she really be willing to unleash that on the world? There was no hint of a bluff in her letter, Tanner knew. The missive had long burned to ash, its sentiment vivid and yet intact only in his memory.

Tanner looked at the time. Three-fifteen in the morning, but only 10.15 p.m. on the US east coast. Tanner thought of Brin and his shiny political career, the embarrassment his association with Ashley might one day cause. Instinctively, Tanner reached for his phone. The Official Secrets Act didn't apply here, surely? Out of an abundance of caution, he set down his phone and went upstairs. There he found the old phone with a pay-as-you-go SIM which he kept in the back of a drawer: the relic of a previous upgrade which he had held on to all this time in case he broke or lost his newer mobile. The old handset had lain topped-up but unused for years. Tanner was grateful for it now.

Brin answered immediately. He was wary of the unrecognised number, but as soon as Tanner explained it was him, the usual conviviality returned.

Tanner cut short his friend's greeting. 'Brin, just listen. I have to be quick, really quick. We've found Holly Brand. She's the one behind all this.' He spoke slowly. 'Ashley Markham is Holly Brand, Brin. I'm not joking. *Ashley Markham is Holly Brand.* She used you to get to me – to the bank.'

'You're kidding,' replied the Bostonian inevitably.

'Sadly not, Brin. I just had to let you know, so you can cover your Brahmin butt. Now I've got to go.'

'I'm so sorry, Rob,' the American sounded shellshocked. But Tanner was already cutting the line and looking for a paper clip. He powered the phone down, opened the back of its case, took out the SIM card and put it, along with the phone, at the back of a drawer in the kitchen.

Five minutes later, Tanner heard the sound of a car pulling up outside the house, followed swiftly by footsteps on the path and the porch light coming on. Tanner answered the door to two police officers—an older man and a younger woman—discreetly brandishing warrant cards.

The man offered a hand. 'Inspector Cartwright,' he announced, before tilting his head towards his companion, 'and this is Sergeant Reagan. From the Financial Crime Unit. May we come in?'

Tanner offered tea, which both officers accepted with courtesy but no warmth, and then spent nearly two hours in the living room, going over every contact he'd had with Ashley Markham. It was not a friendly chat but a cold interrogation: bad cop, bad cop. No detail, however personal, was spared. The fire crackled away as they spoke. It had all but died by the time the officers were finished with him.

At the end, when he finally seemed satisfied with Tanner's testimony, Cartwright asked for his mobile phone. The inspector opened the laptop he'd brought with him, tapped commands into the keyboard, took a cable from his pocket and plugged the phone in. All three sat in silence whilst its contents were uploaded. Once complete, Cartwright repeated the steps in reverse and stood to leave.

Tanner held out his hand for the handset but was met by a polite shake of the head.

'I'm sorry, sir,' the officer said. 'We'll need to hold on to this for a little while. We'll also need your computers, iPads… all those things.'

'But I need to call my chairman, my CTO, my secretary,' Tanner protested. 'I'm still supposed to be working.'

The two police officers shared a look of amused condescension, perfected by officious bureaucrats the world over.

Maintaining the rictus smile, Reagan answered, 'Don't worry about that sir, we'll take care of it. And please don't attempt to contact anyone else until we've cleared it. Anyone. *Understood?*'

The last word was clearly not intended as a question.

Tanner gathered the requested electronics—barring, of course, that old phone which suddenly seemed very handy—and let out the officers. He was stunned by the encounter. In ten hours, he'd gone from a member of the prime minister's COBRA committee to criminal suspect.

Like an automaton, he shaved, showered, dressed and fed himself, then sat, his eyes fixed but unseeing, in front of the television. Gradually, the mist fell away, and with a second cup of coffee, he began to make plans. He took the old phone from its drawer in the kitchen, taking strength from the knowledge that he'd warned Brin. The policemen hadn't specifically asked him if he had a second phone. The way Tanner saw it, it was their mistake, not his. And he had the feeling that if he didn't look out for himself, there would be nobody looking out for him.

123

LJ WAS SURPRISED to arrive at the Downing Street flat and find Allen offering not just tea but an apology.

'I shouldn't have bitten your head off earlier,' he said. 'I just can't believe the security "experts" dismissed the idea of a lone wolf so readily, and now it's looking like one woman may well be at the heart of all this, after all. You and I even talked about black swans, thinking the unthinkable. But it seems that's beyond our tech boffins.'

LJ sipped her tea, waiting for the PM to finish letting off steam.

'And as for Tanner…' He shook his head, looking darkly at the night beyond the windows. The snow flurries had started up again, thick confetti tossed on wild winds.

How many of their fellow citizens were awake right now, she wondered, consumed by worries about the banking crisis? Allen would be fine, even if he lost his job and all he owned; there was always the golden parachute for ex-prime ministers—book deals and the speaking circuit—but what about the single mother whose savings were about to be wiped out? What about the elderly widower who could no longer top up his prepayment meter? What about the children who would be inheriting an impoverished Britain, a declining market vassal state with nothing to laud but its imperial history? These were the people Joen van Aken threatened, and Rob Tanner, in his stupidity, had let the best lead they had—maybe even JvA herself—get out from under him. Literally.

'With respect, sir,' LJ answered, 'if it wasn't for Tanner, we'd have nothing. This was all underway long before he met Markham. I don't see that her physical presence has changed much at this point. She certainly doesn't appear to have obstructed the tech people at the banks. And frankly, if she is the one behind all this then she's so far ahead of them that she doesn't need to.'

'I know, LJ. No point crying over spilt milk and all that. She won't get far now, anyway. No news, I take it?'

LJ shook her head. 'Not yet, but the deputy commissioner is giving us the police sit rep at four-thirty.' They both looked at their watches. Just over half an hour.

'What else?'

'GCHQ are scanning for every variant of tree, plant and flower name known to man.' LJ couldn't help but laugh. 'In case Ashley Markham, whatever her real name is, has been through even more iterations than we realise.'

'What's funny?' asked Allen, lifted by her amusement.

'I found a website with a list of flower-themed names. There were 118 – Acacia to Zinnia.'

'There must be fewer surnames though? Marks and markings.'

'You'd be surprised. Fleck, Stain, Welt, Weal... Blot!'

'Stop it, LJ. I loved those Tom Sharpe books.' Now it was Allen who was laughing.

The night's tension was lifted at a stroke. Allen and LJ spent the next twenty-five minutes in constructive partnership, running through the latest draft of the PM's speech for Parliament, due at noon – although they hoped circumstances would overtake the need for it. The phone rang at 4.30 a.m. exactly.

'Good morning, Deputy Commissioner,' answered Allen. 'Now, what have you got for us?'

The faintest of clearings of the deputy commissioner's throat did not augur well, as his first words confirmed.

'I'm afraid I haven't got a lot, Prime Minister.'

Allen kept his tone light. 'It's early I know, Richard, in every sense. So, what *do* we have?'

'Well, Prime Minister,' said Lindsell, 'we have a timeline of sorts. Markham took a cab from Tanner's house at two twenty-three. The booking was in the name of Holly Brand. The ride sharing account was only opened last night, with a prepaid credit card which appears not to have been used before. Undoubtedly a burner.'

'A burner?'

'Sorry, Prime Minister. I mean a card that you can buy in many high street shops for cash, then top up or throw away. Not tied to a bank account.'

'No registration required?'

'Not necessarily.'

'Then?'

'Then she was dropped off at the Dorchester Hotel on Park Lane at two fifty-one. The driver remembers her going into the hotel, but there's no registration there under the name Brand, or Markham, or anything similar, and she didn't go to reception. We've got people there now checking the CCTV. We've done a sweep of the external camera footage, but nobody matching her description seems to have left.'

LJ spoke up. 'The Dorchester has a rear entrance; what about that?'

'It's a small street and there's only one camera there, ma'am. The lighting isn't great and, with all the snow, the footage is pretty poor.'

'What about her mobile phone?' asked Allen.

'Switched off at two forty-nine, sir. We've got a triangulation near Hyde Park Corner as the final location. Nothing since.'

LJ could sense that Allen was getting ready to blow, so she changed tack. 'What about her previous movements? Her entry into the UK?'

There was no change in Lindsell's wooden delivery. 'We know that she checked into the Lanesborough on Christmas Eve, but there's no record of her clearing immigration under any of the pseudonyms we know, or any obvious variants.'

'Facial recognition?' asked LJ.

'We've only been able to check the major airports so far, but nothing, I'm afraid.'

'How about calls? Who did she call while she was here?'

'Only Rob Tanner and Mike Sorensen at National Bank. Mobiles and landlines.'

Allen was drumming his fingers on the table with increasing tempo, decidedly unimpressed. 'So, what you're saying is that we know Markham was somewhere in the middle of the busiest hotel district in London at 3 a.m. And that's it?'

'For the moment, Prime Minister.'

Allen sucked his teeth, then sat back. He swallowed an acid comment.

LJ pressed the mute button. 'Let's give him a couple of hours,' she suggested. 'Hold a COBRA meeting at seven, before cabinet at eight.'

'Good idea,' Allen agreed. Then he unmuted the phone and leaned towards the handset, affability personified. 'Thank you, Richard. As I said, it's early, and I know you're doing all you can. We'll hold a COBRA meeting at seven. I'd be grateful if you'd join us. Let's see what you can come up with by then.'

Audibly relieved to have escaped a dressing down, the deputy commissioner was still mumbling his agreement as Allen hung up. Neither the PM nor LJ said anything, but they spoke volumes with the nervous look they shared.

'Surely she can't escape from this?' asked Allen, after a while. 'Can she?'

LJ's hands clenched involuntarily into fists. 'Escape? Probably not. But does she need to?'

'Meaning?'

'Think about it, sir. How far is it from the Lanesborough to the Dorchester? Not even a ten-minute walk. In between, there are a dozen hotels that she could be in. And that's just walking distance. She could go to ground anywhere in London. She's been preparing this for eight, nine years.'

'I know, LJ, but someone must have seen her. Someone will spot her.'

'Who will they spot?' asked LJ, shrugging her shoulders in emphasis. 'The beautiful brunette or the chubby girl with the bob? Or someone else entirely? In a city the size of London.'

'*No*,' asserted Allen firmly. His eyes narrowed, and a predatory, exit-poll expression came over his face. 'We'll find her. She can't stay holed up forever.'

'She doesn't need forever, sir.' LJ sighed. 'We don't *have* forever. If Markham adds another zero today, everyone in the country's a millionaire. By Wednesday that million's a billion. The banking system will be worthless. Sterling too. It's only a question of time before the whole edifice collapses and with it…'

Allen cut her short. He was in no mood for hypotheses. 'Then it's very simple. We *have* to find her. And fast.'

124

BACK IN HER OFFICE, LJ surveyed the morning's newspapers. The shades of the headlines varied according to each paper's political leanings and what specifics had been leaked to their editors.

> 'CYBER-TERRORISTS' DEMAND A FAIRER SOCIETY
> MONEY TALKS: ALLEN AIDES 'NEGOTIATING' WITH BANK HACKERS TO END CRISIS
> ALLEN GOES ALL IN AS PM STARTS 'TALKING TO TERRORISTS'
> ZERO USE FOR OUR UNTRUSTWORTHY POLITICIANS, SAY CYBER-TERRORISTS
> NEGOTIATIONS COULD SPELL END OF BANKING CRISIS

Some were even going a step further, suggesting that JvA might prove to be a modern-day Robin Hood, stealing from the rich to give to the poor. There was, however, a strange underlying assumption that the emergency was no longer critical, given that the perpetrators were known and their demands so seemingly insignificant. In the general relief at this outturn, Allen's willingness to engage was broadly seen as pragmatism rather than capitulation.

LJ closed her eyes for a moment, trying to think through the ramifications of the previous night's leak. But she was just so weary. She poured a second cup of coffee, pushed the papers aside and let her mind run with what she knew. Catching Markham still had to be the priority, but the crisis had laid bare an interesting truth: people don't really care about white-collar crime so long as it doesn't affect them. This meant Allen, in theory, could do a deal without the public turning on him. As long as their bank accounts were normalised, the average punter wouldn't care who or where Markham was. It wasn't like there was a serial killer on the loose.

In fact, LJ realised with a start, they'd be better off not searching for Markham at all. Instead, Allen and Markham ought to conduct a quiet, low-key negotiation, well away from the excitement and disruption of the public eye. The trouble was that Allen would never accept that; his pride had been stung, and now he wanted Markham's head. But LJ didn't think like that. And LJ was the one with the direct line of communication.

In a moment of total clarity, she opened her email and began to type.

> TO: Joen van Aken
> FROM: Leah Oladapo
> DATE: Sunday, 29 December 2024 at 06:26
> RE: DIRECTIONS
>
> Ashley,
> Trust me, I'm doing my best to follow them.
> So, Peter Gabriel. Track 3.
> LJ

Allen himself had said to hope for the best and prepare for the worst. Now, everyone was happily assuming that they'd catch Markham and that would be that – a nice, neat conclusion. But LJ knew someone had to keep a dialogue going, just in case. So before heading for the Cabinet Office, she hit send on an email the prime minister had never authorised, knowing that this decision could come at the price of her job. Markham, she knew, would get the musical reference immediately: "Don't Give Up."

125

JAMES ALLEN LOOKED AROUND THE TABLE, hoping this would be the last he would see of this particular COBRA ensemble. If he survived, there would undoubtedly be other emergencies, but surely nothing like this. Sir Winston stared balefully down from within the gold frame of his portrait. Allen imagined him thinking the same. Dunkirk, the Battle of Britain, D-Day... at what point did the great man finally believe he was through the worst?

'I know you've all been all been briefed,' Allen began. 'You will therefore understand why Rob Tanner is no longer a member of the committee. And, given the night's news, I don't think we need another banker to replace him.' He let the equivocal phrasing sit a moment, then turned

323

to the deputy commissioner of police. 'Perhaps you'd like to start us off, Sir Richard?'

'Thank you, Prime Minister,' said Lindsell. 'As you know, Ashley Markham was taken by taxi to the Dorchester Hotel, arriving just before 3 a.m. It appears she had taken a suite there in the name of Nawr Wasima – Arabic names, translating to "white flower" and "blot" or "stain." The policeman intercepted Allen's look of disbelief and pressed on.

'The suite was prepaid yesterday for a week's stay. The caller claimed to be from the embassy of the UAE, booking on behalf of a senior member of the royal family, and the suite was expensive, so the key was handed over with, shall we say, *discretion*, when it came to registration details. In any event, CCTV shows Markham entering the suite at five to three.' He paused. 'We have footage of someone leaving shortly afterwards wearing a burqa. It's impossible to tell who it is.'

Allen stilled the surge of noise around the table with a raise of his hand and indicated that the policeman should continue.

'We believe this person, presumably Markham, then took a taxi to the Hilton London Metropole on Edgware Road. The driver of one of the taxis shown on the forecourt CCTV remembers taking a lady fitting the description there at that time, but after that the trail goes cold. For the moment.'

'What's your guess?' asked Allen.

'Sir, it's one of London's largest hotels. There's no guarantee she even checked in. Women wearing burqas are not an unfamiliar sight in that area, so there will be any number on the security footage, with little in the way of distinguishing features. The taxi driver believes she had a large bag, but she could have switched clothes – changed identity completely – in one of the washrooms then dumped the bag, rather than going to a hotel room. Obviously, we're checking every possibility.'

'But that was, what, four hours ago?' pressed Allen. 'She could be anywhere in London now. Further afield, even.'

'I'm afraid so, sir, unless she's made a mistake.' Lindsell didn't sound hopeful that she had.

LJ caught Allen's eye, and he waved for her to speak.

'As I understand it, Sir Richard, she spent most of her time in London at

National Bank, in the heart of the City, only returning to the Lanesborough in the evenings,' said LJ. 'Surely, she'd have needed a room or a property near there to access her technology? To send her messages?'

'Logically, yes,' the policeman replied, nodding his agreement. 'But that's still a mile and a half radius from Baker Street in the north to Waterloo south of the river. Seven square miles. Again, we're working the data through facial recognition to see if there's anything.'

'What about immigration?' asked Allen. 'How did she enter the country?'

'We still don't know, I'm afraid.' Lindsell made a show of looking at his notes. 'The Americans have been very helpful with her mobile phone records. Before arriving in the UK, Markham last used her phone in New York on the evening of Thursday the nineteenth. Then it appears to have been turned off completely—I imagine she took out the SIM card—before she began using it again in London on Christmas Eve.'

'Which means we have nearly a week unaccounted for.'

'Yes, sir, but the Americans are running every name variation possible through their databases.' Lindsell tried to inject a more positive note. 'Facial recognition. Previous travel records. Financial statements. She would have to be extraordinarily accomplished to avoid leaving *any* footprint.'

Allen gave him a withering look before turning to Saeed Akhtar. Clearly, she *was* extraordinarily accomplished, which was precisely how they had found themselves in such a mess. The prime minister had to resist the temptation to ask if the head of NCSC still believed it impossible that the crisis could all be the work of one woman.

'What have you got from GCHQ?' he asked instead.

Akhtar pursed his lips. 'We're putting her mobile phone records though our systems,' he said. 'We're trying to find similar patterns to other phones she may have or to see if they coincide with spikes from other persons of interest. The same with her known locations. We're running keyword searches in our transmission record data to see if we get any hits that match relevant names, places, phrases.'

'Persons of interest?' Allen queried. 'You're still not convinced she's acting alone?'

'If she is, sir, then she's single-handedly achieved the greatest computer breakthrough in half a century,' offered Akhtar. 'The odds would obviously be against that, but I'm not a gambling man, Prime Minister, just an analyst. We'll keep scouring the data till we find the links – they'll give us the answer.'

'And what about Tanner?'

'He's clean, sir. It appears he's an innocent dupe. There is no evidence of any contact with Markham until a week ago, and the introduction to her was made through a newly elected US congressman, Brinsley Eliot.'

Allen raised a quizzical eyebrow.

'A close friend from Oxford with an unblemished background in financial services,' went on Akhtar. 'He's been thoroughly vetted by US security to the highest level. Markham clearly fooled a lot of people.'

'Understood. Speaking of the Americans?'

'The CIA, FBI, Homeland Security and their secret service will be doing the same things as us, sir. And specifically, they'll be looking at the gaps in her timeline. We know Lily Stamp was in Atlanta at the back end of 2017. Then Ashley Markham turns up at Stanford in August 2018, so there may be another alias or two in between. Between us, we'll get the break we need.'

The prime minister raised his eyebrows. 'You sound confident, Saeed!'

'I am, sir. It's not a question of if we'll find something. But the *when* is a different matter.'

'You may not be a gambler, Saeed, but *I* do need to play the odds. So could you guess at how long?'

Akhtar shifted in his seat. 'Given we have eight years of data to process, we're talking about a number of hours – possibly a lot of hours. If you forced me to, I'd bet late today. At worst, tomorrow.'

Allen nodded as he considered the prediction. Then he fixed his gaze on Anthony Fleming.

'Governor, can we ride out the storm for another day? Two?'

The governor adjusted the set of his spectacles, a neat—if old—trick to focus his listeners' attention.

'Prime Minister,' he began, 'if you're asking me as a banker or financial economist, then the answer is yes. We've only just started Sunday, so the markets here are closed for another twenty-four hours anyway. With the overnight news, we could reasonably keep them shut through New Year's Day – Wednesday. But that's because, to all intents and purposes, the economy is in lockdown. It's almost impossible to conduct any transaction for more than a couple of hundred pounds. Foreign banks and card companies are limiting credit to British travellers. Cash machines are being emptied as quickly as we can fill them. *If* we can fill them. Ditto the shelves in supermarkets.'

Fleming let his words sink in. Then he continued.

'There will be a hit to GDP and tax revenues, and some of the banks may need yet more bailouts, but no worse than the financial crisis or Covid. It's all model-able and manageable.' Fleming's style, like his words, was reassuring and calm. 'But—' he cast his eyes around the table to ensure his message was being heard, '—if you're asking me as a social economist, which I was, a *long* time ago, I'd say we are undoubtedly at tipping point. This is no longer about banking or economics, it's about belief and confidence. Real life. You know as well as I do that we're on the precipice of widespread looting. One major flashpoint, and the genie will be out of the bottle.'

Allen looked grimly towards the cabinet secretary. 'What's the word from around the country, Jonathan?'

'At the moment, the heavy police presence on the streets is working.'

'And what about this march tomorrow? *Zero Use,* or whatever they're called?'

'From social media and our intel—' Morse nodded appreciation towards Akhtar and Lindsell, '—it looks like a rag-bag of anarchists and antis: anti-establishment, anti-capitalist, anti-global; the usual.'

'Numbers?'

'A few hundred. Maybe a thousand. We could do with the snow to start falling again. Keep them indoors.'

'So, hopefully there won't be enough people marching to create Anthony's flashpoint?'

'Hopefully not,' agreed Morse, although the twitch in his shoulders was more equivocal.

Finally, the prime minister turned to his chancellor, hoping to disarm the prickly veteran with flattery.

'Hugh, I'd appreciate the benefit of your thoughts,' Allen said.

'Prime Minister, I'd add just one thing.' Westwood waited, milking his moment in the spotlight. 'Shouldn't we be going public with Markham's details? Surely the chances of finding her rise immeasurably if people are on the look-out for her?'

Allen's eye fell on the deputy commissioner. 'Sir Richard?'

'The chancellor's undoubtedly correct, sir.'

'Anyone disagree?' asked Allen.

Heads were shaken and no one spoke—as Allen had expected—but then LJ broke the unanimity. 'Actually, sir, yes, I do.'

'Really? Why?' Allen was genuinely taken aback, but he was damned if he was going to ignore the input of his most gifted aide, the woman who seemed to have an innate knack for choosing the right path.

'Because it risks her doing something sudden,' said LJ. 'Something rash, sir.'

Allen was disappointed. A bad call from LJ was rare, but even she must have her off days, he supposed. He fixed her with a smile which she, and everyone else, knew was usually reserved for the party's more dim-witted backbenchers.

'I think we're well beyond that, LJ.'

'Are we?' Now it was LJ's turn to be surprised. 'What if she stops negotiating?'

'Lord, no, LJ,' replied Allen in bug-eyed astonishment. He laughed – a cruel sound. 'It's not a negotiation anymore! It stopped being a negotiation as soon as we found out who JvA really is. If it's not Markham—*Brand*—who's behind all this, then it's someone she's working with, or something she's part of. We've got a trail; it's a fox hunt now! We have the scent; we've loosened the bloodhounds! Now we've just got to flush her out.' The prime minister's face lit with his morning-after-the-general-election smile. 'She'll lead us to whoever is responsible, or we'll work out for sure that she's acting alone. And then we'll lock her up for life and take her technology. It'll put us at the forefront of global computing for a generation. So, forget about negotiations! Tally Ho, I say!'

Buoyed by his own rhetoric, the PM rose to his feet and, with a nod of thanks, strutted from the room. The other participants followed, if with less vigour. LJ was left sitting in mute bewilderment, stewing in doubts as her mind filled again with images from the work of Hieronymus Bosch, the medieval fate that awaited them all if Markham ratcheted up the threat. Allen was wrong; this could get worse. And when it did, the torture of the present would seem like nothing compared to the torment which lay in wait, the agony of the future.

126

IT HADN'T BEEN DIFFICULT FOR ASHLEY to switch identities and locations. As the police suspected, she had indeed taken a taxi from the Dorchester to the Metropole. She had been wearing a hoodie, track pants and plain black trainers under her burqa, so the first change was effortless. Further transformations were waiting in the holdall the taxi driver had vaguely remembered.

At the Metropole, she headed straight to the men's room on the lower ground floor, not expecting to find anyone there at three-fifteen in the morning but ready to act out a tableau of misunderstanding if she did. She had already cut the length from her hair and flattened her breasts with tight bandaging at the Dorchester; it was thus a young man, in a baseball cap with a rucksack on his back, who appeared to exit the toilet only a couple of minutes later.

A five-minute walk took the backpacker to the busy St Mary's Hospital in Paddington, where he changed into a new jacket and hat and, withdrawing a smaller bag from within, dumped the backpack and the first two costume changes into one of the huge refuse bins outside A&E. A cab booked in a one-time name from a burner phone, with a driver who spent the entire twenty-minute journey engrossed in a phone call, dropped the traveller at the Tavistock Hotel near Russell Square. Here, an inverse of the first bathroom break effected the corresponding gender switch, with the jacket reversed and a blonde wig donned alongside a skirt and a scarf.

Four minutes later, this unrecognisable young lady was safely ensconced in one of the cheapest rooms at the vast Royal National Hotel across the road. Ashley had paid in full for a week's stay the previous day and had left two further changes of clothes there. She changed again and left the last transformation laid out and ready for the final leg of her journey.

Now came the hardest part. Ashley had to become an old man, relying on stealth, not speed. Again, she wrapped the bandage tightly around her upper body – so tightly that it made her hunch forward, which is exactly what she wanted. Then she put on a heavy woollen jacket and tie, on top of which she added a three-quarter length trench coat and, finally, a cashmere scarf and a long overcoat, also in black. She wore men's brogues, which she now covered with heavy-duty rubber non-slip overshoes. The *pièce de résistance* was a wide-brimmed fedora in the same dark shade.

Bent down by bulk rather than weight, Ashley posted a "Do Not Disturb" notice on the door and left. With the room prepaid for another six days, she doubted it would be touched for a couple of days at least – not that it mattered if anyone entered and found a few discarded items of unexceptional clothing with the tags removed.

Unfurling a sturdy black umbrella, she took her leave of another hotel and, never once looking up, began a slow, shambling trudge southward. She had traced and retraced the route numerous times, identifying roads with few or no surveillance cameras. The most that any of them might capture was a laboured, shuffling, probably elderly figure, bent against the swirling wind and snow flurries.

Thus disguised, Ashley traversed the back streets of Bloomsbury, skirting the British Museum and Tottenham Court Road. Crossing that main drag, she used the shadows of the construction works around the new Elizabeth Line station to hide her passage into the warren of side-streets at the north end of Soho. Here she found the spot she had pinpointed for the next identity switch. There were many rough sleepers in the area, even in these freezing temperatures, and two or three were normally to be found under the scaffolding on the face of a major restoration project just off Wardour Street. Taking care not to disturb any of the sleepers, Ashley huddled down against the cold brickwork and forced herself to wait.

The chill seeped through her, despite the layers, but Ashley stayed unmoving, counting down the longest of hours. But it was only sixty minutes, she realised with a mixture of relief and shame, as time's steady passing drove the reality of homelessness—the cold and the discomfort and the mounting urge towards despair—deeper into her. This was why she had attacked the banks, after all – to force the prime minister to fix his broken society, laden with sin and want, and take the first steps towards a new era of equity and openness. Grand dreams, she knew, but the alternative, apathy, offered no hope at all. And Ashley was a woman used to thinking in absolutes: one or zero, right or wrong. The thoughts churned inside her like the snow flurries swirling around her hideaway, but better that than to think of Tanner and the pain her letter must have caused him. At the stroke of six, she rose stiffly, took off the overcoat and laid it gently on one of the prone figures nearby – one for whom this lifestyle was no choice, no interlude, but an unchanging necessity. The umbrella and hat were similarly donated.

Draping a discarded piece of cardboard over her head and shoulders, Ashley clomped slowly down a block, just another itinerant trying to survive the night, and repeated the same exercise with another sleeping group under different scaffolding. Without the overcoat it was almost unbearably cold, but she knew the end was now in sight. The sounds of the waking city—few as they were on a Christmas Sunday morning—gave her renewed energy. Her good fortune held; none of her companions stirred.

At seven, Ashley stood and discarded the final props: the overshoes and tie. Then she took a black felt newsboy cap from one pocket and a mini umbrella from the other and headed, under new cover, to Dean Street.

It was a mere 180 metres to her destination; she had counted the steps numerous times. She had memorised every security camera too—there were five, each easily avoidable—but none near the entrance to a tall Georgian construction near the corner of Richmond Buildings.

Situated between a health store and a café, the building's entrance had once been a fine eighteenth century portico. A wash of dirty brown paint had since given it a stolid and forgettable aspect. No lights shone from within, as Ashley had expected. The external intercom panel indicated that the first and second floors were occupied by entertainment agencies, but it was the weekend and, in any event, the offices were closed for the Christmas break – a condition of their lease. She pressed the first two buttons on the intercom to be sure. Silence. The third button was for a generic-sounding service company which existed only on paper. The label had been allowed to fade to indecipherability – a description befitting also the building's ownership trail. Ashley had acquired it five years previously, using a web of offshore companies that no one would ever find, let alone unscramble.

Hundreds of customers entered the neighbouring properties every day. Thousands of people passed it. The two agencies, in the very heart of cosmopolitan London, had been deliberately chosen for their very different and very diverse range of clients. No individual who entered that particular front door would ever stand out in the throng, let alone be remembered. And Ashley had only visited twice in all the time she had owned it – once to check the building works had been concluded to her precise specifications, and once to check that all was well with the property, five days ago. On both occasions she had adopted very different disguises.

She unlocked the front door and let herself in. Finally, she allowed herself to relax a little, taking off the cap and running her hands through her newly shortened hair before heading up to the third floor. The stairs led to a shabby corridor with a door lit by a single low-wattage bulb. Ashley opened three security locks in turn and then tapped a code into a keypad, itself hidden under a locked and peeling cover.

The offices beyond the security door had the neglected feel of any down-at-heel sales or marketing agency: cheap desks and chairs, plastic plants and the walls plastered with fading posters offering inspirational quotes at odds with the surroundings. Beneath a fine coating of dust were a few items that looked personal but had, in fact, been acquired in junk shops solely to convey that impression.

Ashley didn't stop in the offices but headed straight for the kitchenette, which was neatly fitted in a corner alcove. The space was just large enough for a small, double-fronted base unit and fridge under a chipped but clean counter, on which sat ready a kettle, cafetiere and mugs. Matching wall-mounted cupboards above housed a microwave, utensils and a selection of non-perishable groceries.

Ashley pulled open the larger of the floor unit's doors and removed the trash can. Then she knelt under the counter-top and found a recessed space behind the top drawer. Here she keyed in a seven-digit code, and a panel at the rear of the unit sprang open. She pushed the rubbish bin into the space, then reverse-crawled after it, pulling the kitchen unit door behind her, before returning the bin to its normal place and ensuring the security panel was tightly shut. The space behind the false kitchen wall was big enough to accommodate a drop-down ladder from the floor above but narrow enough not to make anyone in the kitchen question the proportions. Not that anyone was ever there anyway.

Climbing up to the top floor, Ashley permitted herself a smile of self-congratulation. She was sure her security precautions were way over the top, but she preferred the odds of too much rather than too little effort.

If the police latched on to her trail, and even if they picked up on any of the characters she had played, where would it get them? They would find snatches of CCTV footage of various young men and women with hidden faces. Would any of those point to an old man shuffling into the West End? No, Ashley reasoned, she was safe. There was nothing to link her to this property on Dean Street, and she had enough provisions to see her through a week, if necessary. Although she didn't expect to be there for more than a couple of days, at the very most.

She emerged into a well-formed apartment – a self-contained unit nobody would ever suspect to find. She took a long, scalding shower in the bathroom, luxuriating in the heat and taking inordinate pleasure from the simple aromas of shampoo and bodywash. When, finally, she felt that she had washed the night's adventures from her skin and hair, she stepped out and wrapped herself in a heavy, towel dressing-gown. As she did, Ashley caught her shorn reflection in the mirror, the sharp coiffure bringing back memories of other changes, other times. She stood for a long time scrutinising the novel strangeness of her appearance, wondering where this new incarnation would lead.

Pushing all deeper thoughts aside, she dressed in the intentionally sexless sports clothing she had stored in the wardrobe and made herself a hearty breakfast. Then she turned on the television and caught up with the night's developments—or lack thereof—in the news. Suddenly, she felt tired. Very, very tired. She would need all her wits in the coming hours, so she set an alarm for 10:30 a.m., closed the floor-to-ceiling blinds and buried herself under a duvet on the flat's deep sofa. She was asleep in seconds.

127

THE DEFENCE SECRETARY stared down James Allen across the cabinet table. A former contender for the party leadership, the secretary of state was a thoroughly dull man, and he owed his position to longevity and assiduous pork-barrelling rather than talent. He could, however, always be relied upon to represent the views of "traditional Tories," if such creatures still existed.

'Prime Minister,' he began, defaulting to his laborious—and in his eyes, statesmanlike—style. 'Are we to understand that these reports of negotiation with terrorists are correct?'

Allen fixed him with a deliberate smile. 'Henry, you of all people should know that we don't do that! Of course, there are times when we have to adopt unconventional strategies, find different ways of skinning cats, so to speak, but negotiate with terrorists? No, never. And the night's events would have rendered such discussions meaningless anyway.'

Cut off at his knees, the defence secretary slumped into speechlessness. The other troublemakers decided that discretion was definitely better than valorous dismemberment, and that, pretty much, was that – the one episode of cabinet unpleasantness over before it had even started. Allen wished his government colleagues a Happy New Year and cautioned them not to engage with the media pack gathered outside Number Ten in anticipation of his statement.

LJ sat through the performance in silent dread. Allen had ignored her completely at the end of the COBRA meeting, clearly taking her questioning for disloyalty or stupidity – or both. He had punished her further by freezing her out of his subsequent collaboration with Zack Hardy over the press statement.

Hardy now reappeared in the doorway brandishing a fresh copy of the speech. Allen beckoned him over, catching LJ's eye in the process. She had no idea what the speech said, and part of her didn't want to find out.

'Is there anything else, you need, sir?' she asked.

'No, I know you've lots to do,' said Allen, with a wave of dismissal. 'We'll speak later.'

LJ stood to leave, trying to hide the hurt, that toxic brew of concern and confusion. But she needn't have bothered. Allen was already engrossed in the text, lost in himself.

128

HIS UNSANCTIONED SOUBRIQUET MAY HAVE BEEN THE TOAD, but as Martin Kellett lumbered from one end of his flat to the other, he bore far more resemblance to a caged bear. The only people who would return his calls were the ones expecting money. That slimy pimp Ziegler, for example, still hadn't been able to make contact with the itinerant investigator he had retained. He would come to regret that failure, in time.

The problem was that Kellett only cared for two things in life: work and carnal cravings – in that order. They were his drugs, and five days away from the office was colder turkey than any post-Christmas leftover. What in heaven's name did other people do without the pure adrenalin fix of power, he wondered? They turned on the TV, he supposed, and reached for the control.

As his screen flicked to life, it showed an enormous Christmas tree and an empty podium outside the unmistakeable front door of Number Ten. A caption at the foot of the screen read: "Prime Minister to speak following COBRA and Cabinet Meetings." The camera panned back and forth over a melee of reporters, photographers, and broadcasters, and then Allen appeared, marching purposefully to the lectern, its silver lion and unicorn crest bright in the artificial light.

The briefest of introductions in the PM's normal, easy manner gave way to a much more sombre tone.

'I know that these attacks have affected every single person in our country,' he began. 'You may not be able to transfer money or withdraw cash, and you may have seen empty shelves in parts of your local supermarket. These attacks have impacted us all, and yet I know that they will have a disproportionate effect on the elderly and the disadvantaged. I want those people to be in no doubt that we will prioritise their care over the coming days.

'I am fully aware of the increasing incidence of looting and theft, vandalism and other public order offences. I know these are difficult times but let me be absolutely clear: those are criminal acts, pure and simple, and there is no excuse for criminality. We are a law-abiding nation, and mine is a law-enforcing government. These criminals, for that is what they are, will feel the full force of the law and will pay the heaviest price for their actions. If you are in any doubt as to this government's capacity to respond to lawlessness, do not be. *You have been warned*.

'As always, I wish to pay particular tribute to our police. All police leave has been cancelled around the country, every force is at maximum strength and every active member is engaged in your protection. There will be more officers on the beat tonight than there have been for a generation. Their commitment, their determination and their bravery, is an inspiration to us all.

'Now, turning to developments. We have made significant progress in identifying those responsible for the cyber-attacks. We do not yet know the full extent of the group, but the net is closing on the ringleaders. In particular, on one key individual. And that is where I ask for your help.

'The prime suspect is believed to be in London. She is a woman, using the name Ashley Markham. She may previously have used the name Holly Brand and other pseudonyms, including Bryony Sears, Rhoda Kane and Lily Stamp. It is vital that we apprehend this person at the earliest opportunity, and I would urge anyone with knowledge of her, or her movements, to call their local police or the special number provided.'

Kellett stared at the screen. He was frozen, a grotesque sculpture of shocked disbelief… but only for a beat.

'YES!' he roared, rising to his feet, fists pumping until he began to cough – an ugly wrack born of a surplus of excitement and a want of exercise. He slumped back into his seat and waited for his breathing to ease, unable to keep the smirk from his face.

'Oh, Sir Peter,' he wheezed, a sickly smile plastered to his sweating face. 'Have I got you by the balls, or what?'

129

SIR PETER WILFORD WAS STILL WAITING for his regular morning update from Rob Tanner. The new CEO normally called at eight o'clock on the dot, but this morning there had been nothing. Sir Peter was not often kept waiting, and he didn't like it. Tanner's phone went to voicemail when the chairman tried to reach him. Sir Peter didn't know what to make of it, and he didn't like that either.

A bigger and altogether more unwelcome surprise was the appearance on his doorstep, ten minutes later, of two officers from the Financial Crime Unit. These officers didn't usually pay house calls to addresses as grand as Paultons Square, and the pair, correct in their suspicion that Sir Peter would know the commissioner—if not the home secretary—were uncommonly discreet in their approach. When they were positioned in the sitting room, with coffees gracefully accepted, they informed the chairman of the night's events.

'So, you had no reason to doubt Miss Markham, Sir Peter?' asked Cartwright, the male officer.

'None at all, Inspector,' answered the chairman, his voice betraying his shock. 'Although of course, I never met her. I relied on Tanner.'

'And would you have any doubts about Tanner, sir?'

Sir Peter met the officer's eyes. 'None, Inspector. I trusted him with my bank, and I'd trust him with my life.'

Point duly taken, the pair of officers took their statement from the older man. They made a point of thanking him, although their expressions spoke of half an hour wasted.

'You're very welcome, Inspector, Sergeant.' Sir Peter made sure to treat the junior with equal courtesy. 'But now I have a question for you.' His bearing suggested that he too had spent a lifetime asking questions and expecting unequivocal answers.

'Of course, sir,' replied the senior officer. 'If I can.'

'When do you think Tanner will be back?'

'I'm afraid I don't know, sir.'

The chairman folded his arms. 'Can I speak to him?'

'Not until he's thoroughly cleared, I'm afraid. Orders from above, sir.'

'But I've got no CEO!' Sir Peter was about to say more, but stopped himself, remembering his own days in the services. No point shouting at the Lieutenant if the General had given the order. 'Sorry, Inspector, I know you're doing your job. Let me show you both to the door.'

Unfortunately for Sir Peter, the police visit was merely a warm-up act.

He was thoroughly disquieted by the prime minister's address to the nation, which he had missed while he was being interviewed. Now the news channels were showing replays, summarising Allen's main points. The finger of blame had officially been pointed at Ashley Markham. But behind Markham stood the ghost of Tanner. And behind the CEO stood the chairman. He knew nothing good could possibly come from his implication in this wretched mess, as the visit from the police had already proven. And with Tanner out of action, he had no idea how the bank's staff could be expected to handle the chaos.

Sir Peter was only roused from these dark ruminations by the unmistakeable trill of his mobile phone. It took him a second to find it; it was on the coffee table, beside a cup of tea which had long gone cold. "Martin – CEO" was the name which flashed on the screen. Sir Peter was caught entirely off guard. Still disconcerted by the police visit, his subconscious guided by three years' habit, he took the call.

'Good morning, Chairman. How *are* you?' Kellett asked with the solicitousness of an old, dear friend. 'Probably not feeling *tip top* after the prime minister's revelations, eh?'

'Martin, I don't think this is appropriate.' The chairman knew he should have hung up then and there, but to do so would have been frightfully impolite, and his good breeding forbade it.

'Don't worry,' offered Kellett. 'I'll be brief. Now, on the subject of press statements, I'm sure you won't have forgotten your own press release on Christmas Day? You said I was taking a temporary leave of absence due to illness and that you would make no further comment until I was fully recovered. Well, Chairman, you'll be delighted to know I feel much better after watching the prime minister's speech and having my judgement so thoroughly vindicated. I believe I am, in your very own words, *fully recovered*. And what a stroke of luck that is, given I'm the only person at this bank with the ability to smell a rat.'

The chairman was stunned into sickened silence.

'I mean, really, Chairman,' Kellett continued. 'Appointing Rob Tanner as CEO because I refused to accept Ashley Markham – the same Ashley Markham who was behind the crisis I was trying to fix… that was terribly poor judgement on your part.'

Sir Peter was in danger of boiling over. 'You did no such thing!'

'Really, Chairman? That's *exactly* as I remember it. I fired Holly Brand eight years ago because I was concerned as to her probity. It's on the record. Tanner wanted to bring her back—without any background checks, I might add—and you supported him. I resigned on principle at your folly.'

'That's an outrageous lie!' Sir Peter frothed. 'Outrageous!'

'You think so, Chairman? Well, it sounds entirely believable to me. As I'm sure it will to the financial journalists, brokers and bankers with whom I speak *every* day.' He paused to let his words sink in. 'And what will that do for your impeccable reputation, Sir Peter?'

'How dare you? How very dare you?!'

'Dare? *Dare?*' Now, what's that motto of your army chums?' Kellett asked with rhetorical whimsy. 'Oh, yes, I remember: *Who Dares Wins*. That's the one. And whilst you may have won our previous battle, Chairman, I believe I've won our little war. So, as soon as I end this call I'm heading into my office—the CEO's office—at the bank. And I suggest you keep your head down. *Old chap*.'

Kellett's final words, spat with a lifetime's affected resentment at the City and its ruling class, left Sir Peter too wounded to reply, which mattered not a jot to Kellett.

'Oh, I do feel so very well today,' he oozed. '*Toodle pip*.'

130

CHRISSIE HAD FOUND TANNER'S OFFICE EMPTY when she arrived for work that morning. She assumed he was with Mike Sorensen or David Nash. But when half an hour passed with no sign of her boss, she began calling the other PAs. No one had seen him, and on closer inspection, there was no sign of his having been in the office at all.

The sun had not been up for long, and yet this was not the first strange thing that had happened that day. Chrissie had woken up to a text from her mother saying she couldn't get hold of pasta, bread, flour, or toilet roll at any of her nearest supermarkets. She had evidently been out foraging long before her weekly eight o'clock Sunday mass, but these essentials had vanished almost overnight. Now she wondered if Chrissie might find something for her in a supermarket near her office.

That was one unsettling thing. Then came the news about Ashley Markham—the prime suspect, now, in the bank attacks—and proof that Chrissie had been right to be wary about her, the too-good-to-be-true American dream-girl who had so captured Tanner's attention. The final thing was the fight she had witnessed at an ATM just around the corner from the National Bank building; two men were throwing punches as a small knot of silent bystanders watched, some filming on their phones. Chrissie had simply put her head down, crossed the road, and walked double-time to the office. So, it was fair to say that she had already had her fill of weirdness that morning, and Tanner going AWOL was just another question mark against what was already turning into another strange day.

While Tanner's no-show was unusual, it was not immediately concerning. For all she knew, he had been whisked off to Downing Street again. What was concerning was the call she received soon after settling down at her desk with a fresh coffee. It was Frank Garner, the head of security, calling on her internal line.

'Hi Frank,' she said. 'You're in early.'

Chrissie and Frank had known each other for fifteen years. In all that time, no matter how important the call, there had always been a bit of banter, a shared joke, the very smallest sign of humanity, before they got down to business. Always. Until today.

'Trouble, Chrissie.' Frank's flat, Geordie vowels served only to accentuate the words.

'What?' Chrissie stiffened involuntarily in her chair. 'Another attack?'

'Much worse. It's Rob.'

'Rob? Is he okay?'

'Physically yes, don't worry, Chrissie, he's fine. Sorry. My clumsy mouth. But we've got a security situation. A bad one. I need your help.'

Chrissie was flooded with relief. She doubted that she could have voiced a coherent response in any event, so she sat quietly, letting her heart rate subside, as Garner slowly but surely explained the reason for his call. How he had been woken before dawn by a visit from the Financial Crime Unit. Their account of events overnight and their prolonged questioning about Tanner, Markham and 'security failures' at the bank. Then, finally, the bombshell that Rob was now "on leave and *absolutely not* to be contacted."

The words were enough to shake Chrissie angrily back into life. 'They can't seriously think Rob was involved? He's the only one who could actually get us out of this mess!'

'No, pet, of course not. But they're obviously worried about his…

relationship with Ashley Markham. Whether it compromises him. You can see their point.'

Chrissie was about to say exactly what she thought of their point, but she knew she'd only be taking her frustration out on one of the few people in the bank she cared for. Instead, she reached for her notepad.

'What do you need, Frankie?'

Garner launched into the long list of demands from the police: interviews with all ExCo members and access to secure data rooms, Tanner's office, HR files… you name it. They shared the tasks between them, and Chrissie spent over an hour fulfilling her half of them, all the time keeping one eye on the corridor and half expecting a contingent of police or security personnel to arrive at any moment.

She had just finished, and was carefully double-checking her list, when an entirely unexpected voice shattered her concentration.

'Christina! Well! Don't you look different.'

Chrissie looked up to see the great bulk of Martin Kellett waddling towards her. His wide mouth, bug eyes and heavy, dark glasses were normally set in a sneer of brooding disdain, but not today. Today there was a demonic glow to him, his face an open-lipped leer of manic happiness.

'Martin?' Chrissie's query was a plaintive yelp.

'Surprise, surprise.' Kellett beamed. His visage made him look like the gurning host of a nightmare talk-show.

'But? What…'

'What am I doing here? Are you not pleased to see me? I've been ill, you know.' His face fell in feigned anguish before resuming its nasty smirk. 'But now I'm quite restored. Thank you for asking.'

Kellett lumbered over to Chrissie's desk, staring her down as if she were a recalcitrant dog, a lesser creature he had been burdened with training. He pressed his face ever closer to hers, daring her to defy him. When he was sure she was fully cowed, he grabbed her wrist with a combination of reptilian speed and brute force. She squirmed, but to no avail. His grip was tight.

'Now, Christina, here's the situation,' he said, voice low with menace. 'Tanner's not coming back this time. With a bit of luck, that pompous prig Wilford will be forced to retire, too. So, I'm in charge again, and it's just like the last seven days never happened. *Capisce*? Oh, and I'm sure I don't have to remind you of our little *arrangement*, which remains unchanged.'

Christina was ashen, on the verge of tears.

'Martin, please,' she pleaded. 'You're hurting me!'

Kellett let go and stood back so he could look her full in the face.

'Don't worry, Christina, I have even less desire to see you ever again than you me. So yes, you can fuck off for good as soon as this mess is sorted. The sooner the better, as far as I'm concerned. But until then, you'll do what I tell you. Exactly what I tell you. Or your little secret won't be secret anymore.' Kellett's leer returned. 'I'm sure there's a song in there somewhere. Oh yes! I remember: "*Calamity Jane*." How appropriate.'

131

GÉRARD HAD ALWAYS HATED the overnight flight from New York to London. By the time you'd taken off and had drinks and dinner, you had a measly three-and-a-half hours before you were being woken up again for breakfast. Tonight there was no point in trying to sleep – not through the relentless stream of sensory intrusions. Even cosseted in first class—equipped with eye masks and earplugs—the smells of meals being served, the brightness of the cabin lights and the hum of fellow travellers' conversation would prevent all but the heaviest of sleepers from reaching oblivion. And in any case, both Gérard and Nikki were ravenous. Both for dinner (neither having eaten that evening) and for the details of the other's day.

The two investigators shared their stories, first with congratulatory glasses of Champagne and then with surprisingly good food and a couple of glasses of wine. The alcohol softened the edges of the cabin, dulled the noise and the lights, and the adrenalin rush of their adventure gradually waned. They finished their glasses and said goodnight, but sleep was still a distant prospect. Instead, they lay back and rested their eyes, each listening for sounds of the other. As the wan pre-dawn light began to seep into the cabin, Nikki leaned over the lowered partition between their seats.

'Are you asleep, Gérard?' she whispered.

The Swiss didn't move, so she began to ease herself back into her seat.

The moment she was settled, his Francophone tone drifted across the divide, barely audible.

'I make it a rule never to sleep with colleagues, Nikki.'

Nikki sat forward again. Gérard was prone on his side, the black eye-mask accentuating the stern lines of his mouth in repose. For a second, she wondered if she had imagined the whole thing, but then he slowly lifted the corner of the mask and fixed her with one eye.

'But then, rules were made to be broken. And I've certainly never had a colleague like you.'

Before she could respond, he let the mask fall back into place and resumed his previous stillness. But neither the shade nor the murky interior could hide his smile. Buoyed by the exchange, Nikki fell back into her bed and, finally, into sleep, waking only when the captain announced their imminent descent.

Gérard was wide awake, reading, his bed transformed back into a seat and with all evidence of bedclothes long-since removed. Nikki tried to drag herself out of the fog of jetlag.

'You should have woken me,' Nikki chided him, struggling to shake herself into life.

'You obviously needed the rest.'

'I can sleep tonight,' she said. Just then, Gérard's words came washing back over her; for a moment she thought she had dreamt his invitation – if that's what it was. Either way, it was more than Nikki could fathom, this early in the morning and with so few hours of sleep in the tank. She smiled at Gérard.

'What's the plan until then, *colleague*?'

The Swiss shrugged. 'Our job's done, Nikki. We proved Rob's theory. We found the links. Now it's up to the authorities to find Markham. She's probably already in custody. There's nothing else we can do.'

'So, we're not working together anymore?' Nikki tried to keep the sadness from her tone.

'Well, I guess technically we still are, until we sign off with Rob and close out the assignment properly. You need to get paid.'

'And what about *your* client in Zermatt?'

'Well, he certainly won't be reimbursing me!' laughed Gérard. 'I haven't replied to his messages in days; he probably thinks I've gone the same way as Holly Brand and disappeared. But I don't care. This commission was never about the money.'

Their conversation was brought to an abrupt halt by final pre-landing checks, and then they were descending swiftly through dark grey clouds towards a snow-flurried Gatwick. They were first off the plane, through a near-deserted immigration hall and past customs officers wholly indifferent to their small pieces of hand luggage. By instinct, both reached for their phones as they passed into the arrivals lobby.

'Nothing from Tanner?' Gérard asked. He gave Nikki an inquisitive look. She answered by motioning for him to look at the screen behind him. He turned to see a TV news feed of James Allen speaking in Downing Street, inset with a photo of Ashley Markham. The ticker read: "PM launches appeals to find cyber-terror suspect."

'Let's call him,' suggested Nikki.

She dialled Tanner's number, but the call went straight to voicemail. She left a brief message then looked to the Swiss for guidance. He looked up from his phone and pointed towards the rail station.

'There's an express train in eight minutes, arriving at Victoria at ten forty-five. Let's take it and use the time to make that plan of yours.'

Ten minutes into the rail journey, they were fully up to speed with the overnight developments. There was still nothing, though, from Tanner. Nikki tried Chrissie instead. She had expected cheerfulness or at least mannered professionalism, but instead the PA was formal, distant even. She sounded like she was speaking with her hand over the mouthpiece.

'Sorry Chrissie, I didn't really get any of that,' said Nikki, straining her voice over the sounds of the multilingual announcement reminding passengers to keep their bags close and report any suspicious behaviour.

The line went dead. Nikki stared at her phone in utter bemusement, but then a text came through.

✉ **Christina Ferreira, 10:39:** Try home: 69 Colgrain Street W6

'Well?' asked Gérard.

Nikki shook her head. 'I really haven't the faintest idea, but at least I know where we're off to next.'

132

SECRETS. Or rather; one enormous, life-defining secret. Chrissie sat at her desk, too stunned to move, unable to believe this latest twist of fate. Kellett's departure and Tanner taking over had been the greatest of Christmas presents. For the first time in as long as she could remember, Chrissie had allowed herself to dream of a normal life: a good job, working for a boss she liked and trusted, with no fear of abuse or retribution. Now those hopes were dashed. For the thousandth time, her mind went back to the events of half a lifetime ago. Spring 2008.

It had all been going so well. Chrissie had left her uninspiring sixth form college a-year-and-a-half previously with appropriately mediocre A Levels and no desire to prolong student life. She'd reasoned that a three-month secretarial course would serve her better than three years' media studies at one of Tony Blair's rehabilitated polytechnics. Sure enough, she landed an entry-level job at National Bank the week after achieving the top mark in her diploma. She still remembered her father's smile—slightly bemused, undeniably proud—when she showed him the certificate.

Having emigrated from Naples in the late Sixties, her father had worked day and night to set up his own café. The business flourished into the quintessential neighbourhood Italian restaurant, thanks to Chrissie's mother's cooking and the sheer determination of her father. Now it was as popular as any trattoria in the West End. The only cause for sadness, in her father's eyes, was that Chrissie would not be joining them in the family business.

Chrissie's first job at National was as secretary for the deputy head of risk accounting, a certain Gavin Airlie. A prematurely aged nine-to-five bean-counter, Airlie was the last of a dying breed of old-fashioned bankers who still enjoyed the occasional boozy lunch and afternoon off for golf. Barring Airlie's occasional attacks of wandering hand syndrome after some of the more liquid lunches (and easily enough rebutted by a girl like Chrissie from the dodgy end of Streatham), Chrissie's first fifteen months at the bank could not have been an easier introduction to the City.

Then came the news the following spring that Airlie was "taking early retirement." In reality, he was being pushed out in favour of the rising star in the bank's risk department. Martin Kellett had joined three years previously from the firm's auditors, where he had been one of the youngest partners. He had already established a reputation for having a sharp mind and sharper elbows; he was quick to spot problems and quicker still to castigate the colleagues who had caused them. He had the ear of the head of department, who recognised Kellett's talent and mistakenly believed he could reign in the younger man's consuming ambition.

Chrissie's first one-to-one with Kellett had been short and—a rehearsal for things to come—to the point. She'd seen him often at a distance around the office, a short, stocky figure, whose face seemed permanently set in one of two expressions: sullen on the bad days and pugnacious on the better ones. But as he sidled up to her desk, she grasped for the first time the brooding intensity within him. The more animated he got, the more his chest puffed out and the more his lips and eyes bulged – like Bob Hoskins in *The Long Good Friday*.

'You're going to be working for me now,' he declared, an opening gambit without warmth or ornament.

'Am I?' she asked.

'Yes, and it's going to be very different.' Kellett checked over his shoulder to ensure no one was listening. 'No more of these clock-watching jobsworths. We're going to run this place properly. Kick out the dead wood. Bring it into the twenty-first century.' His eyes shone with evangelical intensity. 'Good people, the best systems, *hard work*!'

Chrissie was a confident girl. She had been earning pocket money in her parents' restaurant since she could walk, and she had spent her teenage years batting away the knuckle draggers drawn to her Mediterranean complexion, her faraway eyes and her nascent beauty. She laughed now, and her face lit up, a tantalising glimpse of the woman she would become.

'What's in it for me?' she asked, full of the bravado of youth.

But Kellett's response was anything but light-hearted, anything but playful. He glared at her and lowered his voice to a growl.

'Do you realise how fucking lucky you are?' The childish smile disappeared from Chrissie's face. Kellett pressed on, not dropping his gaze for a second, like a conspirator sharing a secret. 'I'm going to be head of this department within a year. I'll probably have to run it for a couple of years to get it sorted, then I'm going to get some experience of front-line banking. After that, I figure I'll be a shoo-in for Head of Risk. After that? Who knows? So, the question, *Christina*—' he paused to let the name sink in '—because I'm afraid Chrissie sounds like the name of a Barbie doll, not my PA—the question is whether you've got the gumption and the work ethic to come along for the ride. You'll get a raise, and I guarantee you'll always be the best paid PA at your level. But you'll bloody well earn it.' He fixed her with the tight-lipped smile that she would later regard as the scariest of his expressions. 'So, You in or out?'

'In,' Chrissie said. It was an easy decision.

Chrissie—or Christina, if Kellett was in earshot—spent the "handover period" before Airlie's departure working harder than she'd ever worked in her life, rarely getting home before her parents had locked up the restaurant. Kellett attacked his new role with relish, knocking down the whole department so he could rebuild it in his image. There was no sensitivity towards his outgoing predecessor; all Kellett cared about was results. Those who weren't with him were against him. And those who were against him were out.

After four weeks, Chrissie was exhausted, and yet she was more stimulated than ever. She hadn't been out once in all that time, and so the occasion of Airlie's leaving drinks at a pub in the City was a welcome chance to let her hair down on a Friday night. Airlie had put a credit card behind the bar, like the old-fashioned gent he was, and he encouraged his team to make the most of it. 'It's on expenses and you're going to need it, working for *him*,' had been his final exhortation, raising a disapproving eyebrow towards Kellett.

The team had done just that. Tired, exhilarated, and having hardly eaten, Christina had soon felt a buzz. She tried to pace herself, but there was always someone urging her to have just one more drink. One of the girls in finance had suggested they go to a club on the Embankment where she was meeting her boyfriend and a bunch of his mates.

'Oh, come on, Chrissie,' she chivvied, her voice registering as something distant and indistinct. 'It's only ten-thirty, you've got to let your hair down sometime. You're only young once!'

She was right. Chrissie was nineteen, for heaven's sake. She'd spent her teenage years under strict curfew from her parents. Staying out late, particularly where boys were concerned, was not only discouraged, but forbidden.

'Okay,' she replied. 'But only a couple. I'm knackered.'

'You'll soon wake up when you get an eyeful of his best mate. He's gorgeous!'

And he was. Adam was his name, and it didn't hurt that he was caricature charming to boot. He focused his attention solely on Chrissie from the start, and she was beguiled, moving in time to the techno beat, happily accepting the cocktails he assured her were 'ninety percent juice.' Much later, as they'd begun to grind rhythmically together on the dance floor, an alarm had sounded in her brain, clear enough even to bring lucidity through the befuddlement. It was past midnight.

'I have to go! I'm dead if I don't go now. Seriously dead!'

Adam had seemed genuinely concerned, dutifully retrieving her coat and offering to find her a cab before escorting her into the chill March night, past a line of people waiting to enter the heaving club. Chrissie was swaying. A biting wind was lashing off the Thames, and it hit her like a punch after all the booze. She leaned into Adam's body, warm and solid. He held her tighter and pointed towards a passageway running behind the club.

'Come on, short-cut.'

Chrissie let herself be led down the alley, glad of the support. She was suddenly very light-headed; floating, not walking. Adam stopped halfway down the alley and pulled her close, pushing his face into hers and kissing her hungrily before she even realised what was happening. She wanted to respond, the sexual desire was overwhelming, but something inside also warned her not to. He didn't allow time for the doubt to grow, pushing his tongue deep into her mouth, and she gave into the moment, feeling his hand running between her legs. Oh God, she was drunk. She had no idea what she was doing. She tried to pull away, but he was kissing her more insistently, more intensely. She felt him pulling at her knickers. When she struggled, Adam only pinned her closer to the wall, whispering over and over, 'Come on Chrissie, you know you want to.' She did, but she also didn't – not here, not like this. But she couldn't stop him; it happened so quickly. Then, almost as quickly, it was over, and he was zipping up his flies, his face set in a smirk of satisfaction.

He stepped back, and Chrissie lurched forward. She took a couple of staggering paces then doubled over and vomited, splashing the paving stones and Adam's shoes. He jumped back out of the way, but it was too late; his shoes were ruined.

Chrissie, bent double, heaved for breath. Adam watched her from a distance.

'Get me a cab,' she pleaded.

'Get one yourself! Look at my shoes.' And at that, Adam turned and strutted into the night, leaving Chrissie without a backward glance.

She managed to find a taxi by herself, and the next thing she knew she was awake in her bed with the bilious after-tang of vomit in her mouth. A violent going over with her toothbrush and a scalding shower began to wash away the physical traces of the previous night but could do nothing for the deep bitterness in her soul. She had only the vaguest recollection of the elderly cabbie, a man who could have been her grandfather, and of getting into the flat and assuring her mother that she was alright. The rest, the pieces she could recall—her stupidity, mostly—she just wanted to forget.

Chrissie threw out every item of clothing she'd worn that night and returned to work on Monday as if nothing had happened. She threw herself into the work, finding there the distraction she desperately sought. It was only when she missed her period that she experienced the first deep echo of unease. Except it wasn't just unease – the next morning it was unmistakeable nausea. In a state of panic, Chrissie forced herself onto the Thameslink train to the City, walked ten minutes in the wrong direction to a chemist where there was no chance of meeting any colleagues, and purchased two pregnancy test kits.

The walk up Ludgate Hill on the most beautiful of spring days might as well have been a walk to the gallows. The feeling of impending doom was overwhelming, and it was a relief to reach the National Bank building, to put herself out of her misery. Chrissie took the test in a ladies' room in the basement. As she waited, she prayed to Santa Maria and every other heavenly being she'd ever heard her father mention. But they weren't listening. The line was unmistakeably pink.

She got through that day one minute at a time, one foot in front of the other. She let Kellett's barbs and criticisms wash over her. She retraced her route home to Streatham and somehow managed not to break down when her sister asked her if she'd had a good day. Then she repeated the test the next morning. With the same result.

She tried to switch off, to put every single active thought out of her brain, to become an automaton. But today, of all days, was the day that Kellett's career at National hit its first road bump. It started with the bank's CEO getting a dressing-down from the chairman at the monthly board meeting for being too slow to upgrade the bank's risk reports. The CEO duly bollocked the Head of Risk, and the shit trickled down until it reached Kellett, who duly took it out on his PA.

'What the fuck are you looking at?' he asked her. He was just out of a meeting, and his face was puce.

'Sorry, Martin,' replied Chrissie. Lost in her own misery, she blinked away first surprise and then tears. 'I don't know.'

'Don't know what? And what's that look for? What are you, a fucking baby?'

Chrissie's shoulders heaved, and she began to sob. And sob. And sob. Even Kellett was embarrassed at the reaction his outburst had caused. Eager to deflect the sour looks, he reached for Chrissie's arm and half-led-half-dragged her into his office. Shutting the door, he sat her in a chair opposite hers and tried to adopt an emollient tone. Which wasn't in his usual repertoire.

'It's not your fault, Christina,' he said, groping for what sounded like the right words. 'It really isn't.'

'Yes, it is. It's all my fault!' Her whole body hurt; the tears wouldn't stop coming.

'Of course it's not.' Kellett was so far out of his comfort zone he was struggling for things to say. He didn't even know for sure what she was talking about; he assumed she was upset about work, but he was becoming less certain by the second. 'Why don't you go home early. Start afresh tomorrow, eh?'

'That's the last place I can go,' she answered, between sobs.

By now, even Kellett had the gumption to realise he was dealing with something bigger than a tardy risk report. He passed Chrissie a clean handkerchief, told her to stay put and went in search of tea. That's what they always did on television shows when there was a crisis, he reasoned.

Five minutes later, this wholly unexpected act of compassion had worked its magic. Chrissie's sobs began to subside, she managed to sip the hot, sugared tea and found herself looking directly into Kellett's large amphibian eyes. In that moment, he actually seemed human. His words were, for once, unaffectedly kind.

'I think you'd better tell me what's going on, don't you?'

'I can't,' she replied. 'I can't tell anyone.'

Kellett fixed her with a knowing, conspiratorial look.

'Christina,' he said. 'If there's one thing you should have worked out about me by now, it's that I don't care a toss about what anybody else does or says. I've got no time for chit chat and even less interest in gossip. If you've got a problem, we'll sort it, and it will stay between us. You're a bloody good PA. You make my life easier, and I want to keep it that way. It's in my own best interest.'

It was Kellett's appeal to his own blatant, transparent self-interest that won Chrissie over. She forced down a deep breath.

'I'm pregnant,' she confessed. 'And I can't tell my parents. If I do, my dad will kill me. Then he'll kill the bloke who did it – if I don't first.'

Kellett thought for a moment, letting this news sink in. Then he went on, with an unaccustomed lightness of touch, 'I'll help if you like. We'll add him to my hit-list. But first, tell me what happened. Whatever it is, don't worry. I'll sort it.'

And he did. Two days later he arranged for Chrissie to be taken by taxi to a clinic near Regent's Park. Another pre-arranged taxi took her home.

It was an awful day, but in time, the whole horrific experience began to recede into the depths of Chrissie's hidden memory. In the office too, it was as if it had never happened. Kellett never once mentioned or even alluded to the subject; he treated her as he always had. Which was to say he worked her hard, very hard. He was frequently rude and, not infrequently, bloody difficult, but she knew how to handle him better than anyone else. And he was true to his word: she was the best paid PA in the department.

As predicted, he swiftly supplanted his boss as Head of Risk Accounting. And almost exactly three years later, he earned another promotion to a front-line role running regional banking in the Midlands and North of England. But as he delivered the news (which was not news to Christina) in his office, Kellett did not look like a man who had just won a victory. Anger seethed from him.

'I've been promoted,' he announced, forcing the words through clenched teeth.

Chrissie fixed him with a smile of pure saccharine. A friend, another PA from higher up the National Bank food chain, had forewarned her that morning. She had been expecting this, and her congratulations were as ersatz as her surprise.

'What are you smiling for?' Kellett snapped. 'It's in Birmingham. Why the fuck would I want to go to Birmingham?'

Chrissie's response, this time, was genuine.

'But it's a promotion to a commercial role, Martin. It's what you wanted, isn't it? The next part of the master plan?'

Kellett exhaled before continuing in the vein of a contemptuous teacher explaining the most rudimentary of lessons to a dim-witted child.

'Yes, I wanted something *like* this—something more front-line—but this means being stuck in Birmingham, full-time. Possibly for a couple of years, eighteen months at least.'

'Oh,' said Chrissie.

'Oh, indeed, Christina.' Kellett's face brightened. 'But there is some good news. You're coming too!'

'What?' Chrissie was not ready to leave the only home she'd ever known. 'I can't move! Not now!'

'No such word as *can't*, Christina.'

'But my family?'

'They'll understand. And anyway, it's only for a couple of years.'

Chrissie sat up, strengthening her backbone in every sense. 'I'm sorry, Martin. I don't want to leave London, either. There are plenty of PAs in Birmingham.'

'But I don't want a new PA,' returned Kellett with childlike candour.

'And *I* don't want to go to Birmingham.' Chrissie made to get up, but Kellett's outstretched arm prevented her.

'There will be another pay rise.'

'I don't care about money. I'm not going.'

Kellett appeared lost in contemplation for a moment, weighing up a decision. He looked like a man standing on the brink of something, facing a choice to forever commit one way or the other. Then his face hardened.

'Oh well,' he said. 'Choices and consequences. I ask for your help, and you say no, the one time I really need you. A bit different to your little *predicament* three years ago. You didn't say no then, did you?'

It took Chrissie a moment to realise what Kellett was referring to. There was no strength, only misery, as she asked, 'How dare you?'

'Me? All I did was help you, Christina. I helped you when you couldn't turn to your precious family who you now refuse to leave. Still, I'm sure they'll understand, don't you think?'

'What do you mean?'

'Well, when you explain how you didn't want to work anymore for the nasty man who paid for your *abortion*.' The last word carried with it an almost physical heft.

'Why on earth would I tell them that?'

'Perhaps *you* wouldn't.' Kellett shrugged. 'But someone else might.'

Chrissie was in Kellett's face now, hurt, anger and natural fearlessness driving her forward. 'Are you threatening me?'

'As I said, Christina, choices and consequences. So let me know by the end of the week whether you're still on board.' He threw a dismissive hand at her. 'Now, get out.'

Chrissie should have walked out of Kellett's office and gone to HR. She should have resigned. She should at least have talked to someone. But it was a different world back then, and she had been caught completely off guard. Instead, she went home and weighed up her options. To sell her soul to the devil or to risk that very demon ruining the love she held most dear. The decision was easier than she expected; she had only to imagine her parents' faces if Kellett ever made good his threat.

The next morning, she forwent her usual makeup, tied her hair in a severe bun and put on a black dress that usually only came out for funerals. Then she walked boldly into Kellett's office and stated her terms.

'I want a twenty per cent pay rise.'

'Ten,' countered Kellett. His manner was disinterested, and he made a show of being engrossed in the working papers on his desk.

'Twenty.'

'Alright, fine.'

'And I want you to support a mortgage application so I can buy a flat.'

'Okay.' Still he didn't raise a glance in her direction.

'And lastly, if you ever mention that word again, I *will* kill you.'

At this, Kellett did look up, taking in for the first time Chrissie's changed appearance. He nodded in appreciation.

'Very different. Very *severe*. Care to explain?'

Chrissie made no effort to hide the contempt she felt. 'I figured if you were such a shit that you'd do that to me, Martin, then there's absolutely nothing that you won't do to reach the top. So, the sooner you get to the top, the sooner I do too, and the more money I make. Think of it like *Indecent Proposal* without the sex.'

Kellett's eyes narrowed, whether in incredulity or ignorance Chrissie neither knew nor cared. Instead, she turned and walked out, taking her usual position outside his office, oblivious to the whispered comments and gestures in her direction from colleagues dumbfounded at her new appearance.

And that is how she had endured the last fourteen years. Christina Ferreira, the stoical, stern and rather sorry guardian of the monster's lair. A monster who became successively Head of Wholesale Banking, Head of Risk, Chief Financial Officer and, finally, CEO.

And then, blessedly, for four wonderful days, he was gone. But now he was back. And with his return, out came the old Chrissie—the old *Christina*, to be precise—and back came the torrent of memories that she had only just managed to hold in check for the past few years.

133

ASHLEY WOKE, ENTIRELY REFRESHED, a minute before her alarm. She made herself a pot of coffee and let her mind wander. Her hidden apartment was what estate agents—if they ever found it—would call 'minimalist chic'; anyone looking for the hub of a major cyber-network would not have given the apartment a second look, even if they had been able to see through the perennially slatted blinds.

She was calm as she stood behind the windows and looked out over the rooftops. A few sported satellite dishes of different sizes and construction, but none were as large as the one outside Ashley's window. Hers was entirely hidden from the neighbours' view by a screen painted with a bright collage of vegetation. In summer it might have been mistaken for one of next door's sunshades; for now, it sat indiscernible under a fresh covering of snow.

She allowed herself another smile at the vagaries of British weather—the weather Gods appeared to be firmly on her side—then turned her attention to the earnest seeming LJ Oladapo and her brazenly duplicitous boss, James Allen.

Holly Brand had never been a political person; in fact, she had been positively apolitical growing up. By all accounts, her parents had been left-wing activists in their student days, but then she came along, and then came the death of her father (Fire Brand, they had once called him). His passing drained all life out of Holly's mother. By the time Holly was old enough to show any interest in worldly matters, it was no small achievement to engage her mother in the barest minutiae of life, let alone matters of state.

But the last few years, moving to the US, had changed her. She had been fascinated by the Washington cesspit, enthralled and repulsed in equal measure by the razzmatazz and the chicanery, the triumph of politicking over policies. She had promised herself that she would never again be manipulated by personalities and PR but would focus on understanding the issues – something few others, and certainly not the politicians, appeared to have any interest in. It was all style over substance. Spin at an ever-faster rate. Her limits had been exceeded by recent events.

Holly Brand had never been political, no, but neither had she considered herself a hard-hearted person. Everything in her letter to Tanner had been true; she had started off simply wanting to get her own back on Martin Kellett for the way he had drummed her out of the City, poisoning her name not only at National but also among the firm's rivals. After the breakthrough, the Toad had seemed a ridiculously easy target. But then she'd gradually seen an opportunity to do something for the greater good. To kill two birds with one stone. Hence the zero bank account stratagem, a means of focusing attention.

She'd assumed the government would want to engage with her in a hurry, given the stakes (and the opportunities). Instead, she had been shocked to discover that even when threatened existentially, the establishment stuck to its old, broken way of doing things, dusting off that well-worn playbook of denial, delay and disaster recovery. Allen, it had to be said, had really pissed her off. He was meant to have caved at the first sign of serious trouble, to have acquiesced to her eminently reasonable demands. Then she would have made this whole thing go away. That had always been the plan, but Allen's stubbornness, his politically expedient inclination towards myopia, was so entrenched that now he needed saving from himself. Ashley wondered if LJ, or even Tanner, would be able to guide him to a sensible resolution or if she'd have to turn the pressure up a final, painful notch. It was certainly going to be an interesting, and probably very long, day.

For once, she made herself a second pot of coffee. Something told her she'd need it.

134

LJ WATCHED THE CLOCK ON HER PC. She was living, if you could call it that, in two contradictory half-worlds. In the first, she was forever wishing that time would stand still, so that nothing new and awful could happen. In the second, the antithetical twin of the first, she prayed for time to speed up in hope of a breakthrough or, otherwise, an end to this nightmare.

She couldn't believe that it was already more than two hours since the end of the cabinet meeting. There was still no news about Markham, Brand, whoever she was. The PM had already called twice for updates, agitation held barely in check, and she doubted it would be long before anger replaced angst. In the hope of forestalling that moment, LJ had asked the law enforcement agencies for a formal update at 11.15 a.m.

But first there was the matter of the witching hour. Ashley Markham might be on the run, but eleven o'clock was the time at which the emails and zeros always arrived, and LJ doubted today would be any different. Which sin would it be today, she wondered? Lust, pride, or wrath? LJ spent the penultimate minute of the old hour re-familiarising herself with Bosch's pizza-slice images of medieval sin, then she closed her eyes and began counting. On the count of sixty, she had the answer: Wrath.

TO: Robert Tanner; Leah Oladapo
FROM: Joen van Aken
DATE: Sunday, 29 December 2024 at 11:00
Ira

Hello again.

I'll keep it short today as you must be busy – although it doesn't look like you're making much progress with those infernal bank computers.

Mr Steinbeck was remarkably prescient about bankers way back before WWII. Always making excuses:

We're sorry. It's not us. It's the monster... Men made it, but they can't control it.

It all sounds a bit like Skynet to me. I love those movies, especially T2. Machines trampling all over things. But not to the tune of Julia WH's Hymn of Revelation! All those battles, but she knew what really had to go marching on. Hallelujah!

That's another good song, by the way. Can you believe Lenny released it the same year as the first of the cyborg saga. How about that for dystopian coincidence? Another prophetic writer and another Julia! Spooky!

If you've been counting, you'll know we still have a couple of sins yet to cover so, rest assured, like Arnie...

I'll be back.

J.

LJ hurriedly ran through the references. The only Steinbeck she knew was the American author, John, and a quick search duly confirmed the first quote was from a passage referring to banks foreclosing on tenant farmers in his 1939 masterpiece *The Grapes of Wrath*. LJ certainly didn't need to Google Skynet—she'd seen the *Terminator* films numerous times—but she needed the internet's help with Julia WH. Not for the first time, the answer brought an involuntary smile. The second line of *The Battle Hymn of the Republic*, written in 1861 by Julia Ward Howe, referenced the Book of Revelation, chapter 14 with its doom-laden talk of angels throwing the vines of the earth into "the great winepress of the wrath of God."

The patriotic song and its first line—"Mine eyes have seen the glory of the coming of the Lord"—were famous the world over. LJ remembered Martin Luther King had quoted it at least once. And she remembered the stirring final line: "His truth is marching on." The fact that the tune was that of *John Brown's Body* was hardly encouraging.

The chief of staff didn't need to decipher any more, the inference was clear: there would be a reckoning; rightness, justice and truth would prevail. And JvA—Markham—wasn't finished. But what had she done to the bank accounts today?

LJ started to dial Tanner's number before she realised her mistake. He was no longer at National, and she didn't know for sure whether she could trust him. So, she wasted two precious minutes while the CEO's PA was found who, in turn, tracked down Sorensen, the CTO. It turned out that yesterday's conjuring trick had been repeated: another zero had been added to the 'smaller' accounts and another taken from the 'bigger' ones.

'I use the terms relatively, of course,' cautioned Sorensen.

'Mike, by my maths, every account in the bank—and presumably the country—now has between one and ten million pounds in it,' said LJ.

'Correct,' confirmed Sorensen. 'To all intents and purposes, everyone's in the same boat. There is no longer any great distinction between rich and poor. Tomorrow, I take it, there will be no distinction at all.'

There was no time for LJ to consider the implications of the call before her desk phone rang. It was the deputy commissioner of the Met, Sir

Richard Lindsell, who had been given the task of co-ordinating the police and security services' search for Markham. He was calling with his scheduled update. A taciturn, old-style policeman who believed actions spoke louder than words, Lindsell's sentences were brief at the best of times. Today clearly wasn't one of those.

'Sorry, LJ,' he began. 'No news.'

'Nothing at all?'

'I can give you some flannel about CCTV, phone patterns, every bit of technology we've got. But the bottom line is she's disappeared.'

'There's nothing from the public appeal?'

'The usual nutters. Nothing constructive.'

LJ closed her eyes for a second. The policeman's world-weary tone was beginning to grate.

'So,' LJ said, 'what *would* you like me to tell the PM?'

'You and I both know that we'll find her – and quickly. It's a data processing game nowadays, and we have every possible resource on it. If Allen needs someone to shout at, he can shout at me.'

LJ was embarrassed, her anger eclipsed for the moment by Lindsell's matter-of-fact dignity. Her usual composure had deserted her, and she felt for the moment like a surly teenager. She recalled how her grandmother had chastised her for talking back, once upon a time. Talk about wrath, she thought, as she blustered an apology.

Lindsell dismissed it easily. 'Don't give it a second thought, LJ. I'll call when there's news.'

Not if, "*when.*" LJ stared at the silent handset, wondering where Lindsell got his confidence. She didn't know, and she certainly didn't share it.

135

IT WAS SNOWING HEAVILY AGAIN when the train pulled into Victoria Station. The rail network was straining against the weather, and it took Nikki and Gérard another hour to reach Ravenscourt Park. Not that it mattered; they had done their job well, and they warmed themselves in the satisfaction of that knowledge.

Prompted by the wintry vista beyond the windows—white carpeted fields and trees whose boughs strained under the weight of snow—they spent the journey talking about skiing. Gérard had been given his first pair of skis as soon as he could walk, whereas Nikki had tried and failed to learn twice and seemed in no hurry to make a third attempt, despite the Swiss's animated exhortations.

'But Nikki, it's the most exhilarating thing you can do!' he exclaimed, clearly incredulous at his companion's indifference.

'Really? she shot back, with raised eyebrow. 'Perhaps you should stay in more.'

'What?'

'We usually tell someone who spends too much time doing dull things to get out more. Maybe you should do the opposite?'

Gérard laughed. He tried to think of the right word in English to describe his companion. Sharp? No – that fit her mind, but it had the wrong connotations. Precise? Her hair, make-up, clothes, jewellery, everything, was always in the right place, but that wasn't really it, either. Controlled? Perhaps too controlled, he wondered? They arrived at the address Chrissie had sent them before he had time to work it out.

'What if Rob's not there?' he asked.

'Then you can buy me lunch. Stop worrying.'

Their route had taken them through deserted, whitening backstreets. It was only noon, but it was as gloomy as dusk. Tanner's house was easy to find; lights were shining on the first and second floors. Nikki strode to the front door and gave two loud raps of the brass knocker.

Tanner, meanwhile, having been roused by the knocks, looked through the spyhole and saw an elfin blonde woman framed against a taller, slightly older man. More police, he guessed – or, worse, journalists. He opened the door a crack and guardedly asked the strangers their business.

Nikki had somehow forgotten that she and Tanner had never actually met. She flashed him the sort of smile usually reserved for long-lost relatives.

'Nikki. Nikki Cheung.' She angled her head towards her partner. 'And this is Gérard. We've just flown in from New York.'

'Of course!' Tanner replied, throwing wide the door and waving them in from the cold. 'I'm so sorry, I was mentally preparing myself for people I didn't want to let in.' He breathed a sigh of relief. 'I'm so glad it's you two.'

And clearly, he was. He took their coats and bags, showed them where they could freshen up and then settled them in front of the fire with a pot of fresh coffee. Warmed by this comprehensive welcome, Nikki asked the obvious question.

'What did you mean when you said about people you didn't want to let in?'

Tanner made a wry face then launched into a detailed account of his visit from the police early that morning. He had been blamed, practically single-handedly, for a national crisis which was still worsening by the day. Everyone in the country was notionally now a millionaire, which meant everyone was, in practice, broke. Ashley was still at large, and Tanner's own removal from office and connection to the fugitive had been leaked to the media. Presumably from Downing Street.

'So let me get this straight,' said Gérard. 'You're the person who hired Nikki and suggested we look for Holly in the first place, but now not only are you no longer CEO, you're also not even allowed to talk about what's going on?'

'That's about the size of it.' Tanner smiled, and ten years fell off him at a stroke. 'Thank you both, anyway, for your hard work.' He paused, as an unwelcome thought hit him. 'Although I'm not sure how or when you'll be paid. I'm no longer CEO. I'd pay you myself, but I'm frozen out of my account for now, like everyone else. Not that the money will be worth anything anyway, the way we're going.'

'We're not here for the fee!' answered Gérard. He shared a look with Nikki. Tanner caught it and laughed. He stood and walked to the kitchen, returning moments later brandishing an ancient mobile phone in one hand and SIM card in the other. He indicated the front door, no longer the besieged CEO but a grinning boy.

'Come on,' he said. 'We're going to the pub!' Nikki and Gérard's eyes met once again, but this time their expressions were a shared semaphore of bemusement.

Tanner gave the investigators the explanations they had been hoping for as they trudged the short distance to the Thatcher's Arms. Tanner wasn't a naturally suspicious person, but he had to assume he was under surveillance. Whether that stretched to his house being bugged, Lord only knew, but why risk it?

'I've had this old phone lying around for ages,' he explained, waving the handset. 'I must have forgotten to mention it to our friends this morning. The wonder of pay-as-you-go SIMs!' The grin returned. 'I suspect it'll come in handy over the next few days.'

'Haven't we already done all we can?' asked Nikki. 'Surely the authorities will pick Ashley up now?'

'Ashley's had years to organise all this. She's made some kind of computing breakthrough that no one—*literally* no one—thought possible. She's circumvented all border and security checks. She's able to travel incognito and seemingly leave no footprint on land or in cyber-space. And, most importantly, she must have planned for the eventuality that we'd find her real identity. Maybe she even wanted us to.' Tanner let the statement sink in for a moment, then continued. 'So, the way I see it, we have two options. Firstly, I can try to make her change her mind.' Tanner ignored the pair of incredulous looks offered him. 'And secondly, you two can do what you've already done once… and find another link to her. My instinct tells me to try both. Fast.' He flashed them a *Just William* smile in token of his earnestness.

The pub was just ahead. There was no let-up in the heavy snowfall, and a warm and cosy light glowed from within. In that context, it wasn't a difficult decision to follow Tanner inside and discuss the next steps over a drink and some lunch.

136

TANNER SET HIS PINT ON THE LOW TABLE. The investigators, sinking into a shared sofa, faced him.

'Let's focus on the little we do know,' Tanner began. 'We don't know when Ashley entered this country, but we know that she was here by Christmas Eve. The Americans can place her in New York by her cell phone records on Thursday the nineteenth. So that's the five-day window during which she came to the UK.'

'And there's no clue as to how or where?' asked Nikki.

'None,' replied Tanner, with an emphatic shake of the head. 'No facial recognition at the airports, no suspiciously flowery airline manifests… nothing.'

'She must have entered by a less-policed route,' offered Gérard. 'Probably a ferry port.' He had been thinking out loud, but his words commanded attention.

'Go on,' prompted Tanner.

Gérard explained his rationale, counting the reasons on three fingers in turn.

'First, the security is less rigorous. Second, she could hide in plain sight. She might hitch-hike with a cab driver or get a last-minute, walk-on passenger ticket for a freight ferry, or even drive a car over. No one's really focused on the individuals; they're focused on the freight and the vehicles. And third, the European ports are no distance from at least three of the world's busiest airports: Amsterdam Schiphol, Paris Charles de Gaulle and Frankfurt – all as busy as Heathrow. So, what else do we know?'

Nikki tapped at the glass of her G&T while Tanner leant forward, flexing his fingers in a pyramid of focus. Gérard spoke into the silence, answering his own question.

'We know that she chose to call herself Joen van Aken.'

Nikki gave a dismissive shrug. 'But surely that's just because of the painting? It's a branding thing, almost.'

'Is it?' asked the Swiss. 'Have we questioned that? Perhaps she's always been Joen. Maybe it's fundamentally important for some reason.'

"*The true me.*" Tanner's face clouded for a moment, then he explained the cryptic reference. 'That's what she said Joen was.'

Gérard reached for his laptop, which had been stowed safely in his carry-on bag. While he waited for it to power up, he fixed each of them with a look that suggested they'd do well to listen. His demeanour changed to that of a teacher; he clearly relished this chance to educate his students.

'Okay, so let's assume, for now, that the name is significant,' he said. 'What do we know about the real Joen van Aken? He was born about 1450 in Den Bosch in the Netherlands, south-east of Amsterdam and Rotterdam. That's why he called himself Hieronymus Bosch later in life. Hieronymus is just the Latin for Joen or Jeroen. But—' and here Gérard held up two fingers, '—his birth name was *van Aken*, suggesting his ancestors came from Aachen, or Aix-la-Chapelle, further south, in what's now Germany, near the French and Belgian borders. These are both big cities, with good infrastructure.'

Gérard tapped a few commands, and then he turned the screen towards his two companions. It showed a map of the low countries, the coastal region of north-western Europe consisting of Belgium, the Netherlands and Luxembourg. He took a pen from his pocket and used it as a pointer.

'Here's Aachen.' He held the pen at the bottom-right-hand corner of the map. 'Here's Den Bosch'. The pen fell on a spot halfway between Aachen and Amsterdam. 'And here's Brussels.' Gérard indicated the Belgian capital. The three cities made a perfect triangle, a point he continued to emphasise with a deliberate movement of his wrist until he got a response.

'So?' asked Tanner.

A smile played across the Swiss's face. 'If you wanted to choose a location with a choice of low-security entry points to the UK, where would be better?'

Gérard stabbed the pen at the top of the screen. 'Amsterdam: You can fly from there into Norwich or Southend. I doubt they have the same security as Heathrow.' Then he moved in a southerly arc down the North Sea coast, tapping points on the screen as he went. 'The Hook of Holland: Ferries to Harwich. Zeebrugge: Ferries to Hull. Calais: Hundreds of sailings to Dover every week.' He brought the pen to rest over Brussels. 'And from here: Eurostar, if you need a quick getaway.'

Nikki had been mentally analysing each location as her partner listed them.

'Do you remember that news story about Harwich?' she asked. 'Those poor migrants found dead in a refrigerated trailer a few years back? There was a lot of talk about lax security. People smugglers use the same routes Gérard mentioned for exactly that reason.'

The table went quiet again, each lost in their own thoughts. Had the mention of people smuggling made them think anew about the sins of modern society? The greed of slavers on the other side of the world sending living chattel to the UK, and those here preying on their desperation? The envy of those begrudging them lawful entry? The lust of those taking advantage of the women pressed into slavery? Or the sloth of those happy to pay minimum wage for someone else to do their chores, or deliver food to appease their gluttony?

While Nikki and Gérard sipped their drinks, Tanner took a deep draught of his own. He fixed Gérard with a look of serious, searching intensity.

'So, which is it, *mon ami*? Aachen or Den Bosch? I can't explain why yet—I'm still missing something—but my gut tells me you're right. What have we got to lose?'

'Hang on, Rob!' The Swiss tried to backtrack. 'I come up with a mad-cap hypothesis over a couple of beers and now you want me to narrow it down to a single location?'

'No, of course not!' conceded Tanner, his tone placatory. 'But luckily, you don't need to. There are two of you.'

Nikki didn't seem to hear. She was engrossed in her phone screen, her face a picture of earnest intent. The two men sat watching her for the best part of a minute, not wanting to break her concentration, before she looked up.

'We have to go.'

'Go where?' Gérard asked, taken aback at her peremptory tone.

'St Pancras. There's a Eurostar to Brussels at six.' Nikki was already standing, reaching for her coat, as she continued. 'If we leave now, we can grab a change of clothes on the way. As Rob says, from there we'll split up again. I'll take Den Bosch. It's Holland, so they'll all speak perfect English. You take Aachen, we'll need your French and German there. Come on.'

The command, because that's what it was, was given without warmth or, apparently, consideration for anyone else's views.

'Brussels? Just like that? You're mad.' Gérard turned back to Tanner. 'You're both mad.'

But then Nikki fixed him with one of her smiles. 'I'm only following your intuition, so take it as a compliment! Rob believes in you. And so do I.' She tugged his sleeve. 'Come on *pardner*. We've a train to catch.'

137

TANNER HAD DONE THE EASY PART. He'd convinced the two investigators to follow Gérard's logic and his own instinct and head for Europe. Now there was the small matter of making contact with Ashley and persuading her to change tack. He walked the short distance home, searching for inspiration in the boot prints which ran in wild trails through the snow. Then he looked up. He stopped still. Someone was on his doorstep. It was Harry.

The old man was clearly in a bad way. Tanner supposed he must have been numb from the cold, for one thing, but as he hurried closer, he realised Harry's problems were greater than that. It was his face: a great bruise bloomed over one cheek, up and around the eye, and his nose was crusted with dried blood. Harry's trousers were filthy, wet and muddied, and although his hands were curled up into fists at his side, it wasn't enough to stop them shaking.

'Dad?' Tanner dashed the final few meters, gripping his father at the shoulders. 'What the hell happened?'

Harry regarded Tanner with glassy eyes, as if it took him a moment to realise where he was, what was happening. Before he could even answer, Tanner had the door open and was ushering the older man inside. He steered Harry into the living room without so much as closing the front door behind him. Only when his father was positioned in a chair by the fire, shaking with the cold and perhaps with something else, did Tanner go back and shut the door. He made a point of locking it, and then he returned to his bruised and shellshocked father.

'What happened to you, Dad?'

Harry looked from the fire and met Tanner's stare. For the first time since Tanner had found him on the doorstep, awareness registered in Harry's eyes.

'I had a bit of a fall,' he said.

'A bit?' asked Tanner. He dropped to one knee beside the chair, taking his father's hands in his own. Harry's hands were frozen cold, and only now did Tanner see how muddy they were, how webbed with thin scratches. One of his wrists was bloodied, and great bruises blossomed here too, stark against pale skin.

'Dad,' said Tanner. 'You look awful.'

'Well, I don't feel too chipper,' admitted Harry. 'So, I can't say I'm surprised.'

'I'll call an ambulance,' offered Tanner, but Harry almost jumped to his feet with indignation.

'No need for that,' he insisted. 'Don't! Anyway, I saw on the news that most hospitals are overflowing. There won't be room for a daft old codger like me. All I need is a cup of tea and a chance to warm up.'

Tanner took the hint. He put the kettle on and dashed upstairs in search of plasters and antiseptic cream. Soon a tea, heavily laced with cognac, was steaming in Harry's hands, which were already starting to look much steadier. Not long after, he had some colour back, revitalised by the hot drink and the roaring fire. As Tanner tended to the worst of the cuts and scrapes, Harry recounted his story.

'I saw your face on the news this morning,' he explained. 'Imagine my shock. I thought I had better come over to see if you were okay. The buses were running, but I made the mistake of walking past a cashpoint on the way here.' Harry shook his head and then winced as Tanner dabbed at one of the nastier scrapes.

'There were a few unsavoury sorts about,' continued Harry. 'Young men who think they can smell an opportunity amid all this bank nonsense. You know the type. Anyway, one of them came up to me and asked me if I needed "help" with my bank card. I tried to walk away but he wouldn't let me. He was in my face, giving me lip. I wasn't worried, I just thought he was trying to act the big man in front of his mates. But then he started trying to put his hands into my inside pocket. I tried to push him away, but I slipped and fell over. Luckily, a police car came round the corner at just the right time, and they all scarpered. Some passing Samaritans helped me up. They wanted to call an ambulance, but I said the same thing I said to you: hospital's the last place you'd want to go right now. I thanked them and came here. I didn't realise you'd be out. I assumed you'd be under house arrest, something like that.'

Tanner could feel the tears welling in his eyes. He disguised them by busying himself with the work of disinfecting his father's cuts. Harry's old-man skin was thin and bruised easily, and his arms and face were a patchwork of scrapes and blotches. The older man flinched as the disinfectant bit, but he didn't complain, allowing his son to tend to him. Tanner waited until he had finished before he met his father's eyes.

'I'm so sorry, Dad.'

'You're okay,' said Harry. 'It wasn't your fault that some little yob wanted to have a go at me. I'll be fine. I feel better already, actually. A few days and I'll be good as new.'

Tanner packed away his first-aid things and stood up, as if to appraise his father.

'Does Liz know about this?' he asked.

Harry shook his head. 'I was just down the road when it happened, so I came straight here. Like I said, I didn't bargain that you'd be out. Where were you anyway? The police station?'

Tanner couldn't bear to admit he'd been at the pub.

'It was just a work thing,' he answered. 'Everything has gone a bit mad at the bank. You don't need me to tell you that.'

'No,' agreed Harry. He set his empty mug on the table. 'Any chance of another?' he asked. There was a flicker of a smile now, the old campaigner returning to himself with the comforting heat of the drink and the liquor. Tanner had soon made more tea, suitably laced as before. He sat on the sofa, regarding his father, and sipped at the scalding tea. Relief washed over him that his father seemed okay, that the wounds were mostly superficial, and that Harry hadn't frozen to death before he had found him. Then he asked the question he had been waiting to ask.

'You said you were coming here to see me? Were you really?'

Harry nodded. 'I was. For all the good it did me. No wonder I stayed away for so long.'

There was a beat, and then the older man's expression softened. He started to laugh. Tanner worried for a moment that his father was suffering from shock, but then he too saw the funny side. Both men were soon laughing, warmed by the fire and the drink and perhaps by some newly kindled embers of familial love.

'I heard on the news about your… *situation*,' Harry offered. Well, that was another first, thought Tanner: Harry trying to be diplomatic. More than that, in fact.

'I was worried about you,' Harry continued. 'They said whilst you weren't under suspicion—whatever that means—you were no longer on COBRA and Kellett was back as CEO.'

'You're kidding?' Tanner's mouth gaped in ugly astonishment; this was news to him. But then, was it really so surprising? What had Ashley said at their first dinner, something about learning nothing from past mistakes? And Kellett was like a cockroach; he could survive any apocalypse, sustained by his own ambition and greed and nothing else besides.

'So, son,' said Harry. 'We've wasted enough time fussing over me. What I want to know now is what are you going to do about all this mess with the banks?'

Son. Just the single word brought a lump to Tanner's throat. He swallowed it down and shrugged. 'I'm not sure I've got much more than an outside chance of doing anything.'

Maybe it was the cognac, or maybe he'd taken a blow to the head after all, but Harry clearly wasn't in his usual pessimistic mood. 'Course you have. You're smart,' he said. 'You've got good genes.' He paused a beat. 'On your mum's side, obviously.'

Mum. Was there no end to the day's wonders? They'd not had a civil conversation about her in twenty years. Tanner took a deep breath. In for a penny, he told Harry about the night's events in full detail. Then about his decision to follow Gérard's logic for a European connection. And lastly, the need to engage Ashley and persuade her to backtrack.

Harry sat in silence, staring into his mug. Then he looked up, met Tanner's stare once more. Bruised tissue swelled like beet rot on the older man's face, but there was no shortage of vitality in his eyes. And intelligence too.

'It strikes me you're all missing a few things.'

Typical Dad. Say it as it is. But Tanner had resolved that whatever his father said today, he'd let it pass. What mattered was that he was okay. Tanner would text Liz in a moment and get her to pick Harry up, if she could. Someone needed to watch over him to make sure he wasn't concussed, and Tanner couldn't guarantee that the police wouldn't come back for further questioning.

'Go on,' he replied, aware that this unexpected rapprochement with his father might not last. 'I'm listening.'

'Well, first things first,' began Harry. 'Deal with the obvious. If *your Joen* says she's all het up about the seven deadly sins, then that's what she wants fixed. Take gluttony. It's not some medieval nonsense, it's a real modern-day problem. Do you know how much obesity costs the NHS?'

'No, Dad.'

'Neither do I. But I'd bet it's more than we spend on the police and the fire service combined. But does anyone actually do anything about it? No, of course they don't.' Harry let out an exhalation. 'You said you want to get this woman on side. I've always found with women that if you want them on your side, you'd better bloody well understand what they want.' He gave a throaty cackle. 'Then get it for them. Whatever it takes.'

There was no arguing with Harry's logic. Where it led was more of a problem.

'You said a few things,' said Tanner. 'What's next?'

'The emails,' answered Harry. 'From what you said, everyone thinks they're gobbledygook. But why would a super-smart woman bother with all that nonsense if it was irrelevant? Unless she's a nutter, of course.' Harry stared straight at his son. 'So, is she? If you ask me, *that's* the only question that matters.'

'No,' replied Tanner. He thought back to the letter he had burned. 'I think she's hurt, misguided, all sorts of things, but no, in your sense, she's not crazy.'

'Then there must be a clue in the emails.' Harry seemed certain of himself. If anything, he seemed more well—more with-it—now, after his fall, than he had for years. 'Otherwise, she'd just send a list of demands. And it tells you something else, too.'

'It does?'

'If there's a clue, then there's an acceptance—maybe a desire—that this will all come to an end. She wants these riddles to be solved. It's the reason why she's done it at Christmas, if you ask me. Minimum disruption – not that you'd think it could get much worse out there, but I know it can. Unless she's a complete nutter, it suggests that she's after a negotiation, not a war.'

'So, I'm right to want to get her on side?'

'Obviously! Which leads to my last question.' Again, Harry fixed his gaze on his son. Again, Tanner was warmed by the life in his father's eyes. 'Have you thought what you would do if you found her?'

'I'd contact the…' started Tanner. He trailed off.

Harry gave Tanner a look straight out of his childhood. Point made, his father tried to stand, but it took him two attempts to get out of the deep armchair. He waved away an offer of assistance, reaching towards the mantelpiece to steady himself. Here he caught sight of the Magritte postcard – the two lovers, still propped against the small, gift-wrapped package. The gift had slipped Tanner's mind completely, and even now he didn't even notice it; he was so preoccupied with his father, reaching out to steady him.

'She certainly likes her art.' Harry adjusted his spectacles, better to study the print. 'And I prefer this to the medieval stuff, that's for sure. All that hell and damnation nonsense. That's what your mum was brought up with, you know. Priests and nuns telling her she'd go to hell unless she did everything they told her.' He gave an exasperated shake of the head before repeating himself. 'Nonsense!'

'Sit back down, Dad,' suggested Tanner.

His father returned a withering look.

'I've got to get home,' he said. 'I have things to do. And the buses are still running as normal. Did I say that already?'

'Sit down,' insisted Tanner. '*Please.*'

Perhaps it was the gentleness of his son's request, or maybe it was the combination of warmth from the brandy within and the fire without, but for once, Harry did as he was told and allowed himself to be steered back into the chair.

Tanner pressed home the advantage. 'I'm going to call Liz. I'll get her to pick you up.'

'No, no. She's done enough.'

'Stop it,' said Tanner. He looked firmly at his father. 'Let us help you. God knows you've done enough for us.'

'I haven't done anything yet,' replied Harry. 'That's the trouble at my age. Can't bloody *do* anything.' Then a thought struck him. 'Actually, I can. Get me those emails. I need a puzzle. Make a change from the crossword and bloody sudoku.'

'I haven't got them, Dad.'

'Well get that PA of yours to email them to me then!' Harry's face creased in amusement. 'What? Just because I'm a senior citizen I can't use email or an iPad? Or a smart phone? Though what's so smart about staring at a bloody phone all day is beyond me...' He gave a muffled harrumph at the very idea before adding, 'Get a pen, and you can write down my email address while we wait for your sister to pick me up.'

Tanner shook his head, stunned by this turn of events. On a day packed with unpleasant surprises, Harold Arthur Tanner turning out to have an iPad and an email had to be the best, and strangest, shock of them all.

138

IT DIDN'T HAPPEN OFTEN, but James Allen knew he had miscalculated. And badly. The mistake had been in briefing the leaders of the main political parties—his rivals—immediately after the morning press statement. He had been under the impression that he had their agreement to refrain from political point-scoring in the emergency Parliamentary session that lunchtime.

Indeed, the Leader of the Opposition had assured him, with heartfelt sincerity, 'This is a time for national unity, Prime Minister.' And then proceeded to lambast him in the House of Commons. 'Staggering ineptitude... woefully unprepared... wilfully uncaring... an apathetic administration.' These were just a few of the soundbites that would be leading the evening news bulletins.

Allen had had no news to offer the House about the hunt for Markham and, despite LJ's urgings, had remained steadfast in his refusal to mention her specific demand: the establishment of a truth commission. As a result, he'd appeared cluelessly vague and inexplicably ignorant of the attacker's motives. A veritable rabbit caught in a pair of headlights – headlights which he himself had switched on and stumbled towards. The Labour leader had finished with a wonderfully theatrical piece of grandstanding.

'At this time of crisis, we are bereft of leadership.' He pointed to Allen, his voice rising steadily. 'A prime minister with no competence, insensitive to its consequence, and in whom we have no CONFIDENCE!' The opposition benches roared their support.

For the first time as Prime Minister, Allen had slunk from the chamber in ignominy. He returned to Downing Street in festering silence and summoned LJ to his office. He didn't ask her to sit, as he usually did, but left her standing in front of his desk. The disappointing pupil called to account by a disgruntled headmaster. He fixed her with a look of cold fury.

'That was the most embarrassing moment of my entire bloody life.'

'Yes, Prime Minister.'

'And you know what's worse?'

'No, Prime Minister.'

'The opposition are absolutely right. We *have* been pathetic. We assumed the security services or the police would find JvA. We assumed the banks would fix the problem. We assumed everything, in fact, despite my clear forewarnings.' A nasty, holier-than-thou smugness filled the PM's face. 'And what have we got?'

Again, he waited for LJ to speak, exacting some small measure of revenge for the mauling he had been subjected to at the dispatch box.

'Not much, Prime Minister,' came her response.

'Not much? That's an understatement! We have an ultimatum, which it appears we have no choice but to accept, and other than that we have the square root of fuck all!'

The prime minister wasn't given to swearing, but if LJ thought this was a one-off, she was mistaken. Allen launched into a finger-jabbing, expletive-filled rant, levelling blame at everyone he could think of. No one (other than James Allen) was spared. Not even LJ.

When he was finished, the hardness in his expression fell away into something much less attractive: self-pity.

'I've always thought you had my back, LJ,' he said. 'But I have to say, I'm more than a little disappointed.'

'Yes, Prime Minister,' she acknowledged. 'I'm sorry.'

Allen dismissed the apology, and the meeting, with an airy wave of his hand and buried his head in a stack of papers on his desk. He didn't bother to look up as LJ made her exit, and even if he had, the premier would not have been able to see the look on his chief of staff's face: an expression that suggested that no matter how let down he felt by her, it could be nothing compared to how let down she felt by him.

139

TANNER TRIED TO ORGANISE HIS THOUGHTS. With Harry safely back at Liz's house, he was able to turn his mind back to Ashley. But what could you say to a master cyber-terrorist who also happened to be the only woman you'd ever loved at first sight? He tried drafting and then re-drafting an email, but really, he wanted to speak to her, to see her. In the end, he settled for an instant message. He'd heard his messaging app of choice was encrypted, but he had no idea if that was true, or to what extent. What did it matter, anyway?

> ✉ **Rob, 16:04**: Hi Ashley (because that's still the only way I can think of you, at least for now). I don't care about the past, but I would like to talk about the future. Rob x

It sounded ridiculous – not least because of the kiss. But what the hell, he decided. Life is ridiculous. Then he added a second message.

> ✉ **Rob, 16:09**: The authorities don't know I have this number. Yet. And just so you know it's me – nothing in my life will ever be as bad as Italia 90 x

Tanner felt like an idiot as he sent the message into the ether. His father would be okay, and he had done all he could to reach out to Ashley. Now all he could do was wait. He cast a glance towards the Magritte, the two shrouded lovers locked in a kiss. What he wouldn't give for another passionate embrace with her. Then his eye caught the small box she'd left on the mantelpiece on Christmas Day. In all the chaos and confusion since, he had completely forgotten the gift.

At last, he unwrapped the paper—carefully peeling back the layers—to find a small, polished box of deeply-aged, dark wood. The inside slid out, like a matchbox, revealing a carving of a strange animal figure. No, on closer inspection it was two entwined figures: a snake and a toad. A tiny slip of paper provided confirmation: "Masanao *netsuke*. 18th century. *Sansukumi-ken*. Snake and toad."

Tanner cursed himself for not opening the gift before now. How could he have been so stupid? But then he stopped, mulled it over. Would he have made the connection between an antique carving and Kellett, who he presumed was symbolised by the toad? Would it have revealed to him that Ashley Markham and Holly Brand were the same person? Would he…he stopped himself. Coulda, woulda, shoulda wasn't going to help.

Tanner reached for his phone and Googled the words on the paper. That a *netsuke* was a miniature Japanese sculpture and Masanao the sculptor wasn't surprising. But *Sansukumi-ken* was. It was an ancient Asian game of hand gestures—a precursor to rock, paper, scissors—with the "toad" represented by the thumb, the "centipede" by the little finger and the "snake" by the index finger. The snake defeats the toad by crushing and eating it. Another item from Ashley's bazaar of the bizarre.

Tanner had been instructed in the clearest terms by Officers Cartwright and Reagan not to contact anyone at National Bank, but Ashley's gift spoke to a higher command: do the right thing. Kill the Toad and everyone like him. Tanner couldn't just wait and do nothing. If nothing else, he would contact Chrissie and make sure she got word to the team that he'd not given up. And he would get her to send the batch of JvA emails to Harry, some reading material to occupy him while he was convalescing. But should he risk using his secret phone?

As if by magic, the handset pinged an answer, but it wasn't anyone from the bank. It couldn't be. Only three people had this number: Nikki, Gérard, and now Ashley. He glanced at the screen—number withheld—took a deep breath and opened the link.

✉ **16:21:** Where's my fourth wish. In a box? Jx

For once, Tanner needed no help to decode one of Ashley's messages. He counted off the items from her original Christmas Eve wish-list: no phones, lunch, a walk and—number four—make a snowman. On that Christmas Day stroll, which now felt so distant, they had stopped to watch those children building one, and Ashley had accepted that as fulfilment of his promise. That *had* to be the where. Memories of their walk flashed through Tanner's mind. He was beset by a splash of colour, an iconic streak of red on the periphery of his recollection. Something told Tanner he'd find an old-fashioned phone box in the park. He grabbed his coat and rushed for the door.

He was at the park in less than ten minutes. That same snowman still stood, basking in a radius of light… the light of a red callbox shining bright against the winter gloom! Tanner offered a silent invocation that he had interpreted Ashley's message correctly and that the damn box worked. The deep burr of a long-forgotten ringing announced that it was his wish, now, which had been granted.

140

ROBERT TANNER ANSWERED THE RINGING PHONE WITH HIS NAME.

'Well, that's a relief.' The familiar mellifluous voice, only ever a word away from laughter. 'And this is Ashley Markham. The mysterious Ashley Markham, apparently. Although I'd rather you called me Joen.' She pronounced it in two distinct syllables, like Owen.

She continued: 'Rob, listen. I'd bet the bank my end of this call can't be traced, but you're almost certainly under surveillance. Let's assume we have two minutes. First, write this down. Exactly. *Every* word I'm about to say. Ready?'

Tanner hurriedly cast off his gloves, reached into his pocket and pulled out the small pocket notebook he'd brought in hope of this moment. 'Ready.'

'Nothing before my sins. Gary's goals. Meat Loaf's pair. Winston's year. And Flavio's. René's too. Got that?'

Tanner cradled the receiver with his shoulder, scribbling furiously.

'I've got it,' he confirmed, although he was clueless as to what it was that he had got.

'Okay. You said you wanted to talk?'

'Joen,' said Tanner. He had prepared no spiel; he let the words come crashing out of him. 'I meant it, forget the past. I read your letter, and I get what you're trying to do. The future. Gluttony – obesity. Greed – inequality. Wrath – violent crime. Lust – sexual exploitation. Maybe not those exactly, but the major ills facing society.' Words tumbled out in a jumble of half-formed thoughts. 'Giving all our personal data to Big Tech. Artificial intelligence. The surveillance state. All these crucial things we've done nothing about. That we're blasé about. That the politicians won't have an honest debate about. I get it! Maybe not your methods, but your point? Yes, I get it.'

'And you worked this all out by yourself.'

If he was being mocked, Tanner couldn't tell; there had never been a conversation between them when he hadn't been teased by her to some degree. It was part of her make-up.

'Actually, I got some help from my dad.'

'I thought you two didn't talk?'

'We do now. Thanks to you.'

The line went momentarily quiet before Joen came back; her tone heavier. 'We're out of time.'

'No, wait!' blurted Tanner. 'Let me work with you. I'll persuade LJ, Allen, whoever. And if they won't listen, we'll get the message out some other way. I don't know how, exactly, but I want to be part of the solution.'

There was another beat, a brief pause. Evidently, Joen was thinking. 'And why should I trust you?' she asked.

'Because I love you,' declared Tanner. 'I have from the first moment I saw you.'

'What? Ten years ago?'

Tanner let the mockery ride. There was nothing else he could say. And then Joen's soft voice was in his ear again, barely above a whisper.

'I'd better go. But thank you, Rob. No one's ever said that to me before.'

The line went dead.

Well, he'd tried. Tanner set the phone back in its cradle and began the walk home. A slow, sad trudge after the earlier scrambling rush. He'd learnt nothing; it had been a waste of time, and his despondency lent a hard edge to the cold city around him. The snowman in the park appeared sad and misshapen, and the snow around it was streaked with mud, the treads of children's boots. The impurity of the vista was almost spiritually disturbing.

Tanner thrust his hands into his pockets for warmth. There was his notebook, the sum total of Joen's words – her cryptic message. Tanner had been so blindsided by their conversation that he had practically forgotten! What had she given him? It could be anything. He set his mind to work.

Nothing before my sins. Gary's goals. Meat Loaf's pair. Winston's year. And Flavio's. René's too.

Nothing—zero? naught?—before my sins? No, he realised – *her* sins! Hieronymus Bosch – the seven deadly ones. So, a seven. Nought before seven. Zero seven. Of course! It was a phone number; all mobile numbers start zero seven.

Gary's goals? Well, the only Gary they'd ever discussed was Lineker. The two penalties against Cameroon in the 1990 World Cup quarter final. No England fan of a certain age would ever forget them. Two!

Meat Loaf. What was it Ashley—no, Joen—had said? Tanner cast his mind back. When Sir Peter had disturbed them on Christmas Day, she'd riffed on the Meat Loaf song "*Two Out of Three Ain't Bad.*" What had she said? Five out of six? That was the pair, he realised: five and six!

Winston. Well, the only Winston Tanner knew was Churchill. Of course! The Pol Roger Cuvée Winston Churchill they had shared on Christmas Day. What was the vintage? 2008.

That left Flavio and René.

The way Joen had said it—"Winston's year. And Flavio's"—made it sound like she was talking about a vintage of Flavio's as well. What were they drinking that night at the restaurant? Tanner wracked his brain, then landed on the solution: the maître d' had suggested a 2016 vintage of Valtellina. But 2008 and 2016 were too many digits for a phone number, so the wine clues had to be *the* 08 and *the* 16. If that was right, he had 07256 0816, which left René too.

René had to refer to the Magritte painting on the card that Joen had left him: *The Lovers*. Except that wasn't the full title. He'd never forget finding the card on the mantelpiece, or anything about it. The work was titled *The Lovers II*, using roman numerals for the secondary designation. So did that mean 2 or 02, or 11?

Tanner thought it through again. Joen had been specific, using words with precision; she wouldn't waste so much as an apostrophe. So why had she said, "René's too?" Another moment of clarity dawned. It's not "René's too," you idiot, it's "*René's two!*" Magritte's own particular way of writing the numeral: 11.

Tanner had a number. That meant the call hadn't been a waste of time; there was still hope. His spring came back, and the shambling trudge became an animated glide as he made for his house, where he could sit in privacy and work through the next steps on this never-ending scavenger hunt. The fate of the country hinged on him finding a solution, and with Downing Street searching for accomplices (or, failing that, scapegoats), perhaps his freedom depended on it too.

As if he needed a reminder of the moment's importance, he had barely reached his front door before he caught the ringing of his landline within. Tanner feared it would be Liz, but it was the duty manager at the Foundation. Someone had broken into the electronics shop next door, and the police were all over the place. The Foundation's manager was going to temporarily shut down the West London premises on the advice of the police, who feared a greater civil disturbance. There was even vague talk of a curfew. None of the desperate would receive aid this Christmas Sunday evening.

Tanner stepped to the window to draw the curtains tighter around the brightly lit tree. Snow was now falling heavily again, and the street outside was entirely still. A Christmas carol came unbidden to his thoughts: 'Silent night… all is calm, all is bright.' Would the street, the capital, remain so overnight, or would it be lit by something altogether different, by flames?

141

JOEN HAD ALWAYS KNOWN THIS WOULD BE THE HARDEST PART. The waiting game. Her life, for the past eight years, had been consumed by activity. She was either working towards her goal or she was sleeping. Now she was within touching distance of achieving everything she'd wanted, and there was nothing more she could do. She was so close, she could almost feel it, an agonising proximity.

Joen suspected LJ was one of the sensible, decent ones, but even the prime minister's chief of staff was likely to be hamstrung by the intransigence of the establishment. Inefficiency, corruption and waste were deeply entrenched, and the great ship of state had a slow turning circle. Still, logic dictated that Allen would come to the negotiating table eventually. What was Thatcher's famous line? *There is no alternative.* Allen would probably waste another day assuming the police or security services would find her, but she held all the cards. All she had to do was wait. But doing nothing went against every instinct she had.

She killed time by devouring the only book in the flat, an enormous hardcover art book: the complete works of Caravaggio. She had always loved his paintings, their realism and the lighting and the sensual immediacy he conjured. This huge book reproduced all his major works in sumptuous detail and provided a chronology of his tumultuous life. For an hour it was possible to lose herself in lurid tales of his gambling, brawls, and murders – and the pictures they clearly inspired. But then the real world intruded; lucidity came whipping back across her awareness, and she found herself sitting on the floor, staring at nothing, wondering when contact would come.

It was already dark by the time it did. She'd assumed the first move would be from LJ. After the way she had treated Tanner, his was the last name she'd expected to appear on her screen. But there it was. Rob Tanner. He had even signed off with a kiss.

Tanner had been the one person she'd trusted when she was Holly Brand, back at National Bank a decade ago. She had been naïve, then, to cross Kellett in his own lair, but it had never crossed her mind that the Toad's deputy would fail to sort things out. She was sure that her demonstration was so persuasive, the logic of what she was saying so irrefutable, that they'd have no choice but to forgive her any overstep and implement her suggestions. If anything, she had expected to be rewarded for her breakthrough. Her demonstration had been an opportunity, a free pass – not a threat!

But not only had Tanner failed to save her from her boss's retribution, he hadn't even bothered to call afterwards to see how she had taken her sacking. And had National Bank overhauled their legacy security in her absence? No, they had simply marched her from the building, ignored her warning and heaped on more sticking plasters, like before.

So, while Kellett had always been a primary target, what did it matter if Tanner became collateral damage? He had aided and abetted the Toad for all these years. It was a question of choices and consequences.

And ironically, he was the one who had opened the door, shown her a way back to National. Ever diligent, Joen had worked the FinTech conference circuit in the US—pressing the flesh, making connections—and Brin Eliot had been just one of many heavyweights she'd cosied up to. A future Congressman was a good card to have up your sleeve, but the revelation that he was best buddies with Rob Tanner made him a magic ace.

A firm plan had been born from this encounter: use Tanner to get at National, deliver retribution to Kellett, and change the world in the process. All along, she had intended to play Tanner, but then he'd been so honest about his own complicity, and there was something curious about his background that suggested redemption. But then he'd gone back on his word and returned to the bank. She'd been naïve again. So, she'd had no compunction in using him. He was a big boy; he even got the kudos of being on COBRA for his troubles. In light of this, she had resolved to stick to the plan and keep on playing Tanner like the fiddle he was.

But then she'd looked up the Foundation through the Charities Commission. It had been founded fifteen years before to provide support to disadvantaged young people across its west London community, with no heed to race, gender or creed. Particularly youngsters from backgrounds where there was a parent missing. Death, imprisonment, it didn't matter. Joen had worked the numbers. Most of Tanner's income went into the Foundation. Moreover, there was an impressive list of donors, whose involvement could only be down to him. The programme was a model of its kind.

Then there'd been that second dinner, the story about his brother. More pieces had fallen into place. She'd fallen willingly—and *so* satisfyingly— into his bed. And now he'd gone and spoilt it all by saying he understood what she was doing. And that he loved her. No one ever said that. She wasn't lovable. She was a loner without a heart. Ask Joan Morris. Joen had walked away from her elderly neighbour without a backward glance. No, she reminded herself, *Holly* had.

Life was simple on your own. So simple, and so lonely. But there was nothing for it. Just like how there was nothing she could do but wait for the prime minister to capitulate, and then she could finally untangle this mess, back away from the brink, and put all of this behind her, hopefully without having hurt anyone who didn't deserve it. She barely moved. She just sat and gazed out of the window, letting the weight of the last eight and a half years bear down on her. She didn't see the thickening snow, only the ghosts of all the others cast aside in that time, like tragic Caravaggio lying at her feet.

142

SIR RICHARD LINDSELL HAD PROMISED LJ an update at five-thirty. That way even the smallest morsel of hope could be spun in time for the six o'clock news. The policeman could be counted on to be punctual, but LJ realised the gravity of the situation when he called ten minutes early.

'Sir Richard?' answered the chief of staff. 'Have we…'

'Don't get your hopes up too much, LJ. But you asked for anything, and we do have *something*.' For once, there was the slightest intonation in his voice. 'Something peculiar, to be honest.'

'Really?' LJ kept her voice level, but inside she wanted to throw her phone against the wall. Why couldn't he just get on with it, just this once!? 'What have you got?' she asked.

'It's Tanner.'

'*Tanner?*'

'Seems he may not be an innocent bystander after all,' said Sir Richard. LJ heard a keyboard clacking away in the distance, on the other end of the line. 'Turns out he's got another phone hidden away.'

'Well, National Bank confiscated his work phone.'

'I know. And we took his personal mobile. But he didn't disclose that he had a back-up this morning.'

LJ was about to point out that this was hardly a hanging offence, then she remembered who she was talking to. She waited, and Sir Richard rewarded her patience.

'He used it to contact Markham, just after four o'clock.'

'And?'

'And she replied almost immediately, directing him to what turned out to be a phone box in Hammersmith. We couldn't get there in time to eavesdrop, but GCHQ have run the relevant time and place through their databanks. We may have a hit on their voices. Some coded references to numbers—possibly a phone number—but too few and obscure to give us a definite hit.'

'And even so,' offered LJ, 'Markham's end would surely be scrambled. Untraceable?'

'Indeed. But at least it's a link. As I said, it's *something*.' Lindsell's reserve of optimism was clearly in danger of running dry. 'It's the only thing, in truth. So, the question is, do you want us to pull him in?'

LJ weighed up the options. On the one hand, it would provide Zack with momentum; he could get the news networks to spin that a suspect was helping the police with their enquiries. But then she glanced at the notepad in front of her. She had been writing something earlier that day, trying to cook up a coherent strategy by feeding off the scraps they knew about Markham and her cryptic clues. Earlier, in a moment of extreme consciousness of all the lives which would come down with the financial system, LJ had double underlined three words: Don't stop negotiating. She reread her earlier note now, and with Lindsell waiting on the other end of the line, she played for time.

'Anything else?'

'No. Now, we wait. We have Tanner under full surveillance. He can't say or do anything without our knowing.'

The absolute certainty in Lindsell's answer gave LJ hers.

'In that case,' she instructed, 'let's play along. See what happens. Markham can't contact Tanner if we have him in a police cell, so leave him. Who knows? It may just give us our break.'

'Along with the weather,' ventured the policeman.

'I don't follow.'

'Haven't you looked out of your window in the last half hour?'

In truth, she hadn't, and a single glance explained Lindsell's words. The earlier snowfall was now a raging blizzard. LJ sat staring at the storm, unaware that Sir Richard was still talking.

'…and the weathermen say it's not letting up any time soon. So, I think it's safe to say the only people on the streets tonight will be police officers. Let's just hope it keeps up till noon tomorrow! It may spare us the march; *Zero Use*, and their band of anarchists, activists, and troublemakers. We were thinking there might be a couple of hundred, but if it's like this they'll struggle to raise so much as a handful.'

'Yes, of course.' LJ retuned her focus to her notes. 'Excellent. Well done. And thank you.'

'In that case,' said the policeman, 'I'll leave you to brief the PM. *Good luck.*'

143

MARTIN KELLETT WAS DAMNED if he could remember a better day than this one. From the moment he walked into National Bank's glass and chrome atrium, his mood just soared higher and higher. He'd done something he hadn't done for years and gone walkabout, meandering through the bank's floors at random. The looks of astonishment as his lumbering presence hove unexpectedly into view were priceless, every single one a palpable adrenalin boost. David Nash's face was a picture, and Mike Sorensen's expression might have defined the very word abject – his visage turning whiter than the blizzard outside at the sight of his returning overlord.

As satisfying as this exercise had been, it was nothing compared to the knowledge that he, the great Martin Kellett, was now un-sackable; he had earned himself a free pass for life. Rob Tanner had brought Ashley Markham into National, and *she* was the one behind it all. So, you could say the whole crisis was Tanner's fault. And Sir Peter's for backing him. And the prime minister's for making Tanner—and not Kellett—a member of his ridiculous COBRA committee.

Still, that was yesterday's news. Today's headline—and tomorrow's and every other day's for that matter—was that Martin Kellett was blameless.

He had been wronged, in fact, and really, he was a visionary for having seen, when no one else could, the danger Ashley Markham posed to his bank. And that was the narrative he would be spinning around his return. Which reminded him: the Glasgow witch was the one person with whom he hadn't yet had the pleasure of reconnecting.

'Get Pattie Boyle here, now!' he bellowed into the vast space of the office.

While the Toad was struggling to think of better days, Chrissie's mind was filled only with thoughts of the worst ones – days she thought she had successfully banished from memory. The taste of alcohol in her mouth; hands all over her in a filthy backstreet; the sick feeling when she had seen the pregnancy test; the bright lights and surgical tang of the clinic. She tried to console herself. Surely, after everything that had happened, now that he was back, now that he had won, Kellett wouldn't bring it up again? Her heart sank anew. Of course he would; he'd never be able to stop himself. Feeling utterly wretched, she called the head of communications as instructed.

'Tell him I'm in Glasgow.' In Pattie's brogue, the last word was a rasped 'Glerss-gah.' Chrissie wondered how much Pattie had had to drink at lunchtime. And since.

'He knows you're in from your security pass,' Chrissie said. 'He's checked on all the ExCo members.'

'Bastard.'

'If you only knew.'

'Why don't we tell him to go an' fuck himself?'

The PA wanted to do nothing more. But she couldn't afford the consequences. None of them could, in their own ways. She opted for emollience.

'Pattie, don't let him win. Not today, anyway. Suck it up, and maybe it'll all change again tomorrow. Please.'

'Fine.' Pattie sighed heavily down the line, a noise like a deflating hot-air balloon. 'Tell the wee shite I'm oan ma way.'

Having resolved to avoid face-to-face contact with Kellett wherever possible, Chrissie buzzed the intercom.

'She's on her way down,' she said.

'Good,' replied Kellett. 'Now get hold of Tommy Steele. I want him on standby to take me home at seven – snow or no snow. No excuses.'

'Yes, Martin.'

'Oh… and one last thing, Christina. No mourning weeds tomorrow. No Amy Winehouse.'

'*What?*' asked a bewildered Chrissie.

Kellett could barely contain his glee. 'Come on, *Christina*. It's a new game. That bitch Markham gave me the idea with her stupid emails. Guess the song.'

From the open door came the unmistakeable opening piano chords of *Back to Black,* followed by peals of raucous laughter. As Chrissie let the meaning settle, her eyes fell to her lap – the bright fabric of her dress. She gave it a second before standing up and heading for the toilets. She would wear whatever Kellett wanted her to, but she wouldn't give him the satisfaction of seeing her cry.

144

IT WAS THE HEAVIEST SNOWSTORM IN A GENERATION. Northern Europe was in the weather's chokehold, and across Britain, only the bravest dared to travel. Most hunkered down indoors—glued to the rolling news, refreshing their online bank accounts, scrolling social media to confirm the rumours of impending martial law—as they waited for the weather to pass. It was much the same on the continent, although the European police weren't being briefed on the prospect of riots. And James Allen's counterparts weren't kept up with contingency planning in an underground war room in case nobody could get their prescriptions or their weekly shopping. All most people could do was wait for it to pass. And if some of them were up to no good, they were mostly up to the kind of harmless misdeeds which can be accomplished without getting out of bed. All progress on the cyber crisis was frozen, as were the two investigators who had braved the storm in search of a breakthrough.

With the Eurostar delayed by the weather, Nikki and Gérard didn't reach the sanctuary of their hotel until just before 10 p.m. As in every other city in the world, it seemed Gérard not only knew the best hotel in Brussels but had stayed there previously. The hotel proved to be a warm den of soft lighting and even softer upholstery, and Nikki and Gérard thawed as soon as they stepped into the lobby. It didn't hurt that Gérard was on first-name terms with the concierge.

'It's a pleasure to see you again, Monsieur Dumont,' gushed the latest in the week's cadre of grovelers and fawners, guiding them up the lift and ultimately to the door of a spacious two-bedroom suite. 'Welcome home.'

Once the concierge had been dispatched—with a fat tip for his trouble, of course—Nikki and Gérard set down their bags and surveyed the room. Gérard seemed to have a glow about him after the concierge's gold-standard treatment. Nikki hit him playfully on the arm.

'You're incorrigible.'

The Swiss laughed, and the pair locked eyes. They were alone, and tired, and there was a perfect quiet in the suite. Gérard stepped closer, thick carpet underfoot, until there was nothing between them. After a heartbeat, he kissed her full on the mouth. She kissed him back. Neither wanted to be the first to stop, and neither would ever remember which of them did, but eventually they broke off.

Gérard spoke first, more serious than ever. 'I'm sorry, Nikki, I shouldn't have.'

'No, you're not, you liar.' Nikki laughed. 'But you will be sorry… if you don't do that again.'

He did. Many, many times. First on the lips, then her neck, her ears… it was a shower of lust, and all of it was expressed so, so lightly. He took control, undressing her layer-by-layer, covering each newly revealed piece of skin with kiss after kiss, before carrying her to a dimly lit bedroom of deep reds and russet shades. The bed had already been turned down for the night, but within moments its perfect sheets were as tangled as their bodies. Nikki found herself submitting to Gérard's gentle ministrations willingly and absolutely until she lost all notion of time. The pleasure she felt was absolute; only at Gérard's touch did she realise how hollow she had been before him, how much she needed him to fill her. He did just that.

Nikki came back from the bathroom to find their clothes laid neatly on the sofa. Gérard was resting on one arm under newly straightened bedding that, a moment ago, had been so rucked and awry. She couldn't help but smile.

'Are you always so meticulous?' she asked.

'*Méticuleux, cherie*? I'm not sure that's very flattering. Would Casanova want to be called meticulous? Valentino? Passionate, yes. Sexy, yes. But *méticuleux? Akribisch?*' The last word was uttered in harsh, guttural German. 'It must be the Swiss-Deutsch in me.'

Nikki made her way over to the bed. She crawled on top of him and kissed him again with an animal hunger.

'I could make love to you all night,' he told her, when she finally came up for air.

'Well then, what's the problem?'

'The problem, darling Nikki, is that it's nearly midnight and we must be at the train station at seven. We should get some sleep. We have a fugitive to find.'

She stared back into the serious, rugged face, the eyes cobalt in the dimmed light. So appropriate for this mountain man, she thought.

'Okay, boss,' she intoned. 'I'll be good.' She pushed her lips into a pout, a parodic image of saccharine sexuality. Then an impish smile widened across her face. 'But not *quite* yet.'

DAY EIGHT

MONDAY 30 DECEMBER 2024

145

GROUNDHOG DAY. Or more accurately, Groundhog Night.

It was gone midnight, and once again, LJ was stretched out on the sofa in her flat, surrounded by papers. The TV continued to broadcast silent images of snowfall; in true Great British fashion, the weather had become the lead story. Zack Hardy would end up claiming credit for that, no doubt.

Craig had long since retired to bed. LJ realised with a sudden pang that she'd hardly spoken to him since Christmas Day, other than to exchange the barest of practicalities. She'd have to make it up to him once this was over. She had never been one for escapism, but right now she would gladly pack her things and take him to a tropical island of his choosing – preferably a haven with no phones or internet. She asked herself when that might be. Then, more tellingly, she had to consider whether she really meant it.

She was spared having to answer by the ping of an incoming notification. It echoed in triplicate from her phone, tablet, and laptop.

> TO: Leah Oladapo
> FROM: Joen van Aken
> DATE: Monday, 30 December 2024 at 01:00
> ONE AFTER THIRTEEN
>
> Hello again, LJ.
>> I'm glad you're a music lover. All the best people are.
>> Life's a Blur sometimes. And you've been so busy lately.
>> But you're not dreaming. You don't need a Think Tank for

this decision, just the PM to make a clear public commitment. Quickly.

　Or you really will be...

　J.

P.S. Remember, we've only Lust & Pride to go. After that... now, what is it?

Weary as LJ was, she latched quickly onto JvA's message. She had loved Blur as a student and had spent countless hours lying on another sofa, in her shared rooms at college, listening to their albums. None stuck in her memory as much as *Think Tank*, which had been released just as she was doing her finals. The album cover was a Banksy stencil – a couple trying to kiss while wearing diving helmets.

Wikipedia told LJ it was Blur's seventh album, released in May 2003, some four years since the previous album, titled *13*. The one after thirteen, she realised with a wry smile. And she didn't need a search engine to appreciate the reference to being so busy lately. "*Out of Time*" was her favourite track. She found it on Spotify and pressed play. The long, familiar instrumental came through her laptop speakers, then the lyrics, which had seemed so apposite twenty years ago and yet all the more so now. The hauntingly catchy chorus about never having time.

JvA's message was clear enough: the clock was ticking on that public commitment to truth and change. The postscript needed little explanation: pride comes before a fall. If tomorrow—today—was the day for Lust and tomorrow, New Year's Eve, for Pride, then the assumption had to be that Wednesday, New Year's Day, would see the great fall.

LJ wondered whether she should wake Allen for the third night in a row. But what was the point? He'd just rant and threaten. No, she'd attack him with a clear head, first thing in the morning. Persuade him to forget about the bloodhounds and follow Markham's roadmap. To the letter.

But first she'd send a musical message of her own. It took no thought; the words just came:

TO: Joen van Aken
FROM: Leah Oladapo
DATE: Monday, 30 December 2024 at 01:19
BLURRED LINES

Hi, Joen.
 Life's a Blur sometimes, as you rightly say, but sometimes it's crystal clear, like the water in an Oasis.
 Whatever happens today, please Don't Look Back in Anger, just think of Blondie in American Gigolo.
 07469 898106
 LJ

LJ pressed send without a second thought and headed for the bedroom. Craig was fast asleep on his side, a picture of still serenity. LJ curved herself carefully around him, willing him not to wake, craving the same oblivion for herself. He didn't stir, but she was too full of adrenalin to emulate him. She couldn't get the Blur lyrics out of her head. She pulled herself closer to Craig, drawing on his warmth and tranquillity, trying to focus her thoughts solely on him, on the ever-present sunshine of his face.

But to no avail. An altogether darker refrain would not be stilled: "It's in the computer now."

146

TANNER MAY HAVE BEEN OUT OF A JOB, but his body clock hadn't got the memo. It was still pitch dark when he woke, and a glance at the bedside clock told him it was 05:29 – one minute before his alarm usually went off. There was no point trying to go back to sleep now. Creature of habit that he was, he made tea, checked the news, showered and dressed. Even at half-speed, that left him all dressed up with nowhere to go before the clock was anywhere near seven. Christ, what on earth was he going to do all day? There *was* one call he had to make, but it was too early. Far too early. And he had already taken care of the emails, for now; he had

had Chrissie forward them all to his father last night. Perhaps he'd have another look at them himself.

The trill of his landline broke Tanner's contemplation. He didn't care who was calling; anything was better than breakfast TV. His relief as he picked up the phone and stated his name was patently evident to the caller.

'You're sounding more cheerful today,' came the voice on the other end. It was accompanied by a chuckle.

'Dad?' asked Tanner. He could barely believe his ears. 'Are you okay?'

'I'm fine,' replied Harry. 'No, forget that, I'm well.' There was a pause. Then, 'Have you got *company*? Thought you might fancy breakfast. Maybe a nice walk *outside*. Don't often get snow like this – and don't worry, son; I'll be more careful today. Down by the canal would be nice. All that nature. Might see a fox or two *with no one about*.' Harry paused, seemingly to catch his breath. Or to let his dumbfounded son gather his wits. 'Be nice to catch up. *Properly*.'

It had taken the younger Tanner a couple of seconds to realise what the older one was driving at. They both knew Rob was alone. For his father to ask about that was clearly nonsensical… or the exact opposite. The mention of the canal put it beyond doubt. The waterway ran behind the park where Rob and his brother had been playing on that day which haunted him still. It had never been mentioned in the subsequent thirty years; Tanner had assumed it never would be. His father might as well have played an emergency siren down the phone.

Tanner swallowed down the rising emotion. His response, when it came, was studiously nonchalant.

'Why don't you make us a couple of bacon rolls then, if you're feeling up to it. I'll change into some outdoor gear and come over. About eight okay?'

Neither the words nor their tone gave the slightest hint of the effort its breezy affectation required. No eavesdropper was present to witness the pain the memory caused. But Harry knew. His succinct, softened, 'Okay, son,' said it all.

Three-quarters of an hour later, Tanner pulled up in front of his father's house, his own childhood home. Liz had evidently dropped him back first thing; Harry had undoubtedly insisted on it.

Tanner had barely seen another car on the road during the drive from

Hammersmith, which wasn't surprising given the hour or the weather. Even though the snow had let up, the wind was wicked, and Tanner's breath came out as a cloud at his lips. The gritting lorries had been out overnight, but their coverage was patchy, and Tanner had been forced to drive at a slow crawl. That meant it was impossible to miss the unmarked car that crawled along behind him – all the way along the A4 to Boston Manor. Harry had been right about *company*, Tanner realised. And his father must have been waiting ready at the window; he was out of the front door, bag in hand, before Tanner had a chance to gather his parka and lace up his snow boots.

The bruises on Harry's face had come up in great purple welts, but he appeared to be moving without discomfort or effort. The damage was clearly all superficial, because the old man's eyes still shone with that new-found vitality and intelligence. Tanner was impressed at his father's robustness. He felt bad as soon as he thought it, but it occurred to him that his father's fall might have knocked some life into the old boy.

'You seem full of beans today,' acknowledged the younger Tanner.

'I am,' smiled Harry. 'Better than ever, actually.' He gestured through thick gloves at his cheek, territory claimed by the worst of the bruise. 'Ignore this mess. I had far worse hidings before I met your mum and settled down.'

Harry strode down the front path, a hearty chuckle echoing behind him. Then he stopped, turning to face a dumbfounded son.

'Get a move on!' Harry chivvied warmly.

'Is there a rush?' queried Tanner.

'Course there is.' Amusement creased the older man's craggy features in return. 'The rolls will get cold if you don't get a shift on. Come on.' He held up his carrier bag and began marching towards the park.

Tanner caught him up halfway there. At exactly the point where he'd left Matt all those years ago, running for England on a glorious summer evening. Where had the years gone? He'd been ten; now he was the age his father had been then, and his father was a senior citizen. Harry's gloved hands shook, as if to illustrate that point, as he dipped into his carrier bag and produced a foil-wrapped package.

'Go on,' he said. 'Get this down.'

'I'm not sure I can,' replied Tanner, suddenly overcome. He felt his eyes begin to water and turned away, blaming his stinging tear ducts on the cold air.

Harry, too, looked away for a moment, taking his bearings. Then he did something he hadn't done in those intervening decades. He stepped forward and embraced his son. Awkwardly, it must be said, because of the bag and its contents – or maybe the history. But it was a hug all the same.

Tears streamed down Tanner's face. Thank God it was murky winter dawn and not bright midsummer, after all. He hoped Harry couldn't see how emotional he was. Embarrassed, he tried to pull away, to wipe his face.

'Sorry, Dad.'

But Harry wouldn't be pushed off so easily. He dropped the roll back into the bag, then he swung his free hand to grab the younger man's forearm. He gave it a surprisingly powerful squeeze.

'I don't know what you're apologising for. It's me that's been the fool. I can see that now.' Harry let out a long sigh. 'Still, better late than never. Eh? Bygones and all that?'

Tanner returned the gesture. 'I'd like that. And I'd also like to know what's so important that you want only the foxes to hear?'

Harry smirked. 'I bet you would. Get some breakfast down you, and I'll let you in on another secret.'

147

LJ FOUND THE PRIME MINISTER in his study, reviewing the newspapers with Zack Hardy. The cyber crisis had been relegated, at last, to the inside pages. The front pages were dominated now by pictures of snow: pristine white tumuli of buried vehicles, children tobogganing and snowballing and adults shovelling. Allen indicated for LJ to take a chair. If he was behaving without his customary warmth, at least there was none of the previous evening's froideur. Perhaps he'd forgotten? Maybe she'd completed her time on the naughty step? Or maybe not.

There was a knock on the door and in walked cabinet secretary Jonathan Morse. To an effusive welcome from the PM.

'Thought we'd all benefit from a fresh pair of eyes,' gushed Allen. 'See what we can do differently. There's no substitute for experience, after all.' He turned and fixed LJ with his best hustings smile. 'Don't you agree?'

So, she was still in the doghouse, and Allen was going out of his way to put her in her place, punishing her by turning to Morse for advice instead. LJ returned the insincerity, with interest.

'Absolutely, sir. I'm with George Bernard Shaw. There's nothing like learning from experience.' She could do saccharine too.

Morse did indeed have plenty of miles on the clock – more than enough to know when he'd been dragged into a spat. He responded by launching into a review of the night's events. There was no progress in finding Markham. A frame-by-frame review of CCTV footage hinted circumstantially towards an individual that might be her in various disguises, but there was no facial recognition or other evidence to confirm the theory. And that trail, real or false, had run out near Russell Square over twenty-four hours ago. The long and the short of it was that nothing had changed, except the weather. It struck LJ as a very British summary.

'So, she's still holed up somewhere in the West End?' prompted Allen.

'That's as good a guess as any,' replied Morse. 'There's certainly no camera evidence of anyone leaving the area that fits the profile.'

'And no signs of a network spike, unusual computer traffic? *Anything at all* from the security services?'

'I'm afraid not, sir. But they're convinced they'll pick something up when—if—another email or manipulation comes.'

LJ decided that now was not the time to bring up JvA's 1 a.m. email, which had given no such indication that the attacks were about to let up. Allen, meanwhile, shook his head. All traces of campaign-trail niceties had disappeared from his visage. His face was a mask of rage.

'Unbelievable!' he exclaimed. It was almost a shout, and his eyes were set in a withering glare, trained firmly on Morse. 'We've actually reached the stage of hoping for another intervention from Markham? And what about the demonstration in Trafalgar Square?'

'*Zero Use?* It looks very low-key at the moment, I'm glad to say.' The cabinet secretary gestured towards the newspapers. 'Let's hope for more of that.'

'Snow?' The PM's eyebrows rose. 'That's our strategy? Rely on the perpetrator herself and the weather?'

There was no response, although LJ knew there was only one course of action: negotiation. But she'd been sent to her kennel, and it would be pointless to bark now. Instead, she decided to do what Markham had clearly been doing for many years; she would bide her time, and she would wait. And when a chance arose, she would take it.

148

THE TOAD HADN'T EXPECTED FESTIVE BUNTING to be strung up for his return, but even he had a limit as to how much despondency he could bear. It was like a bloody morgue in the office today. He was in a foul mood and ruminating on it as he buzzed through to his PA.

'Christina, get ExCo together.'

'When?' she asked.

'When the fuck do you think?' Kellett spat. 'Now.'

'Yes, Martin.' Chrissie's voice, over the intercom, sounded fragile, as if she would crack under the slightest increase in pressure.

The PA, Kellett resolved, would have to be the first to go. It had been fun to have her at his beck and call over the years—her seething, silent resentment had made it all the more satisfying—and she was bloody good at her job. But he couldn't stomach this new misery. The woman looked like she was going to slit her wrists, for God's sake! He'd tell that sap Ollie Lawrence to find a replacement for the start of the new year. That gave him two days. And if the useless bastard couldn't do something as simple as that, he could fuck off too.

Thirty minutes later and the management group had taken their customary positions in the boardroom. It was six days—to the minute—since they'd gathered for that fateful meeting which had been interrupted by JvA's first email.

Kellett ran his eyes around the wretched assembly. Miserable underlings left, right and centre.

'Well, isn't this a cheerful gathering?' he began.

Nobody answered. Seven pairs of eyes found renewed interest in their fingertips. Only Pattie Boyle held his gaze.

'Something you'd like to say, Pattie?'

'Naw.' She gave a nonchalant shake of the head. 'Though I *was* wondering where Rob is.'

From her delivery, she might have been asking why the coffee was late. And it almost worked. Kellett had the hook in his mouth and was about to bite, but he stopped himself in time.

'Very droll, Pattie.' He leered a trapped-wind smile. 'But that does bring me neatly to the matters at hand. Now, it seems we need a new COO.' A few among the assembly looked up. Kellett let his eyes run round the table. 'I wondered if any of you were keen to put your names forward?' The rapid sinking of those heads provided unspoken answer.

'No, I thought not. In which case, item two: Tanner's task force. I understand that not only do we have a bunch of techies from the competition in *our* building, looking at *our* systems and data, but we also have a bunch of fucking geriatrics playing computer games on our payroll.'

'Martin…' interjected Mike Sorensen.

Kellett slammed the table with his fist. 'Did I ask for a fucking comment?'

'Martin, with respect, it's not Rob's task force – it's the prime minister's!'

The mention of James Allen served only to further antagonise Kellett.

'With respect,' he wheedled in angry parody, 'that useless toff is heading for the same door as Tanner. And so will you be if you don't fucking shut up.'

The threat stopped the Californian before he could offer another similarly rational justification for the presence of the ancient architects: *the chairman's* ancient architects. Sorensen had been brought up by peace-loving San Franciscans who had raised him to believe that there was no place in the world for antagonism and ill-feeling. The American was a dude; he'd been chilled his entire life. But not anymore. Not today.

Now Sorensen rose slowly to his feet. He walked silently around the table towards his bemused antagonist. With surprising strength, he hauled Kellett to his feet so that their noses were only inches apart.

'You know what, Martin,' he said. 'You're not a Toad. You're a fucking Klingon.' And with that—presumably ultimate—insult, he pushed Kellett forcefully back into the chair and swaggered toward the door.

'And you're easily replaced,' Kellett bellowed at Sorensen's back. But he was rattled now. Shaken and embarrassed, he tried to re-establish his authority through his signature method: intimidation. 'Who'd have thought it? One of you found a backbone.'

Pattie had been watching the exchange with unconcealed amusement; the Toad's meltdowns were better than any reality TV show would ever be. Threats were ten-a-penny, but this time he'd gone too far. You could call Pattie many things, and many did—if only behind her back—but not a coward.

She waited until Kellett's breathing had fully subsided, before asking calmly, 'Martin, did you get Mike's reference to Star Trek?'

Kellett made no response. He merely sat and seethed.

'Me neither, so see if you ken this one.' Pattie rose inelegantly from her chair before standing ramrod straight. She looked Kellett dead in the eye. Then she said, 'I am Spartacus. And *you* can fuck off.'

The Toad's jaw dropped. Every jaw dropped. And Pattie waddled from the room as happily as any actor has ever trodden the boards.

149

FATHER AND SON TRAVERSED THE WHITE MEADOW in easy silence. A pair of dogs gambolled in the distance, but no other footsteps had disturbed the path to the canal. A fragile peace seemed to be holding in the city, and this spot, less than nine miles from the centre of the capital, was as quiet as Uffington had been a week before. More importantly, no one followed in the Tanners' tracks. There were no trees, no cover for any pursuer. No one would overhear whatever Harry had to say. Not that he would start until they'd finished their *al fresco* breakfast.

And it wasn't just bacon rolls and napkins that Harry pulled from the depths of his carrier; a thermos flask also provided steaming hot coffee. The younger man couldn't remember the last time he saw a flask. He didn't remember his father drinking coffee, either.

'I suppose you're wondering about all the cloak and dagger?' asked Harry. He smiled between deep lungfuls of the cold air.

'Actually, no,' said Tanner. 'It's bloody sensible, if you ask me. But I am intrigued if you think you've got something?'

Harry took a quick look over his shoulder, for good measure, before answering.

'Well, you know I like my cryptic crosswords?'

Tanner bit his tongue and nodded. He'd let his father tell it in his own time. A second here, a minute there... it made no difference.

'Well,' explained Harry, 'every letter, capitalisation, anagram, whatever... it all counts. So, for starters, what's different in your Joen's emails?'

Tanner shrugged. There were a hundred things he might suggest, all meaningless.

'I don't know. They're...'

'Yes, gobbledygook, I know. I don't mean that. I mean between them.'

Another shrug persuaded Harry to continue.

'Look at the titles of the emails for a start. That's where I started. The very first email is titled NUMBERS, NUMBERS, NUMBERS in capital letters. I doubt Joen wastes words, so that's the biggest clue of all. Numbers are important, clearly.'

'Of course, Dad,' countered Tanner. Despite his best efforts to be patient with this wounded old bear, exasperation was rising within him. 'Everything's about numbers. Bank accounts. Zeros.'

'I'm not talking about the bloody accounts, son. It's the emails themselves.'

Tanner looked over at his father. For a moment, the only sound was the crunch of thick snow underfoot. Breath rose now in great plumes from his mouth, condensed in the cold.

'Why don't you just explain from start to finish?' suggested Tanner.

'Okay,' agreed Harry. He smiled and clapped his gloved hands together for warmth – or perhaps just for emphasis. 'Let's just assume that numbers in the emails are important. That first one, like all the deadly sin emails, contains figures: Bible references, that sort of thing. If you add them up, you get a different total each day. You have to be careful, because a couple of the numbers look like minus figures and your Joen's a crafty devil with her wording. But I think I've got it.' He pulled a slip of paper from his pocket. '50, 78, 17, 47, 6 and 4. *So far.*'

'But there have been other emails, too, Dad. What about them?'

'I know,' acknowledged Harry. 'But those six emails were the only ones guaranteed to be sent on a particular day, in a particular order. The rest were unplanned. Which leads me onto the next thing. Why are they in the order they're in?'

A shrug. 'Does it matter?'

His father pulled his crib sheet closer again. 'Well, the Catholic Church catechism orders them as: pride, greed, envy, wrath, lust, gluttony and sloth. Why doesn't Joen?'

'Emphasis?' offered Tanner half-heartedly. 'To fit her attack on banks for laziness first?'

A vigorous shake of the head from Harry suggested no such lack of conviction.

'It's deliberate. And there's the Latin too: *Acedia, Invidia, Gula, Avaricia, Ira*. They're bound to be followed by *Luxuria* or *Superbia*, although right now we don't know the order of the final two sins. Can you guess where I'm going with this?'

Yet another shrug from the younger man.

'Well, have you noticed how she only uses capitals for the first letter of those Latin words? The rest of the words are in lower case. That's completely different to her other email titles, which are all capitals.'

'So what are you saying?'

'Put those first initials together. You get AIGAILS or AIGAISL. Now, I'm pretty sure that means something. *That's* what I'm saying.' Father fixed son with his best you-youngsters-think-you-know-it-all look. 'Your prime minister and all his merry men and women may think it's nonsense, but I'll bet you a pound to a penny there are two more sins and two more numbers coming that complete the sequence and that it leads to someone, somewhere or something – all tied in with those Latin initials. She's too meticulous, too exacting in her words, for this to be a coincidence. There *has to* be a deeper meaning.'

Harry let out a long sigh, as if suddenly tired from the exertion, then held out the piece of paper to his son, followed by the carrier bag.

'Will you drop this on my doorstep, son? I think I'll go for a walk.' He indicated the downhill path to the canal. 'Before you ask again, I'm fine. The last thing I need is any more fussing. And as for you, you need to think about what you're going to do. Although I know you'll do the right thing.'

They stood looking at each other for a good thirty seconds. Then the eye-hold was released, and they set off in their opposite directions: the older man into virgin snow and the younger back down the path of their earlier footsteps. They'd both gone twenty paces when Harry's voice rang through the still cold air.

'And make sure you mind that bloody road.'

But when the son looked back, the father had disappeared from sight.

150

FOR THE FIRST TIME IN YEARS, LJ now found herself on the outside, in the wilderness. Challenging Allen was always going to be risky; in his zero-sum accounting, everyone outside of his inner circle was out to get him. Now she had been effectively ejected from that circle, LJ realised it was true what they said: a week really was a long time in politics.

LJ had been keeping one eye on the clock all morning. For the past three days, JvA's regular, scheduled emails had arrived at 11 a.m. on the dot. This time, LJ had prepared by spending a quarter of an hour looking at the Wikipedia entry for *luxuria*—lust—and familiarising herself with that section of Bosch's painting. And the demon Asmodeus, for good measure. Perhaps it would be time wasted, but it was a bet she'd happily take. And what else was there to do?

The digital clock ticked over another minute to 10:52. Eight minutes to go. Should she try to fill the time or just savour doing nothing for eight blessed minutes? The ringing of her mobile took the matter out of her hands. There was no caller ID, but fate was clearly at play, so she answered.

'I never did like Oasis,' declared the lightly accented female voice on the other end of the line. There was no spiel, no introduction. 'I thought that was the best joke in that movie, *Yesterday*. No Beatles, therefore, no Oasis. As for Blur? Well, their second album title said it all. Blondie, though, now you're talking. I could listen to "Parallel Lines" all night long… or watch Richard Gere.' The declamation let up. Then, 'LJ, are you there?'

'Sorry,' offered LJ. It took her a moment to rouse herself from slack-jawed silence. 'I wasn't expecting you to call.'

'Well, you gave me your number,' Joen laughed. 'Oh, and don't bother trying to organise a trace. It won't work.'

'I wasn't going to.'

'Oh, good! Then let's have a chat.'

LJ was taken aback. The voice at the other end of the phone sounded more like one of her uni mates calling for a catch-up than a scheming cyber-terrorist who was currently holding the country to ransom.

'How can I help?' asked LJ. But she regretted the words as soon as they slipped out. She was a natural facilitator; she couldn't stop her own impulses any more than she could stop the sun from rising.

Joen scoffed on the other end of the line. 'You can start by answering a question. Do you think my demands are unreasonable?'

LJ started to speak but caught the words just in time.

'Oh, come on, LJ!' said Joen. 'You're a smart woman. Simple question: am I being unreasonable?'

'Well, you have to admit, Ashley, destroying the UK banking system is pretty extreme.'

'You know I could restore it in a heartbeat if I wanted to. I've not done any lasting damage… yet. And by the way, I've got used to Joen. Never did like Ashley. Too American.' A chuckle echoed down the line.

It struck LJ that she might be dealing with a woman who genuinely was stark, staring bonkers. She didn't have time to dwell on it, however, as Joen continued.

'Anyway, back to the point. Would your boss have listened if I'd politely asked him to do what I've requested—even demanded with menaces—without action?'

'If I'm being honest, then no.'

'So, I'll ask again—and *please* answer the question, LJ—are my demands unreasonable? It's only you and me. Just pretend you're not the PM's adviser. No evasion or deflection.'

LJ took the bait and dived head-first into the vortex. She was by nature and nurture a decent, straightforward person who hated obfuscation and deception. She believed passionately in speaking truth to power, which was why she had gone into politics in the first place. Now, for once, she had a chance to do just that.

'No, Joen,' she said. 'I think the changes you're suggesting—*demanding*—would be for all our benefit.'

'Excellent. That's what I figured.' A gush of relief blew down the line. 'So please tell our darling PM to stop all the macho anti-terrorist nonsense, quit stalling and let's get back to normal. Then everyone can have a Happy New Year.'

'Oh, it's as simple as that?'

Joen ignored the barb. 'Yes, LJ, it really is that simple. If Allen concedes to my demands, I'll have all the accounts back to where they were on Christmas Eve before you can sing "*Auld Lang Syne*".'

It all sounded too good, too utterly reasonable, to be true. LJ tried to keep any scepticism from her tone. 'And nothing else?'

'Well, I could go further if you'd like me to? We could work together on more sweeping reforms, but your boss will probably be too busy trying to find and punish me.' Joen let out a rueful sigh. 'Oh, well. Better dash. No time to lose, eh? Ask Patrick O'Brian. Oooh, now I think of it, Russell Crowe is fab, too!'

The line went dead, and LJ found herself in an entirely unfamiliar place – between two stools. She knew she should inform Allen and the security services immediately, but had she already gone too far? Negotiating with a terrorist, with no oversight or approval from the prime minister? When you put it like that, it didn't sound great. LJ realised that what she needed—really, really needed—was a strategy to redeem herself and get back on the inside. Then she could try to convince Allen to give in to what were, in her eyes, very reasonable demands.

The clock ticked over to 10:59. She'd have to wait and see how Ashley—Joen—had manipulated everyone's accounts today. Get an update from Paul Benham at Treasury. Gather the facts. Give her brain a moment to formulate a reasoned argument. Show how indispensable she was.

In the silence, there was no need to watch the hour change; the ticking of the clock would be unmissable. Her phone, iPad and laptop were laid out neatly in front of her, competing to be first with the inevitable notification. She took a deep breath, wondering which gadget would win.

Tick, went the clock. Nothing.

Tock. LJ checked the time stamp on her desktop PC and hit refresh on the keyboard. No email appeared. She kept going, every few seconds, until 11:01, then she dialled Benham's number. He answered on the first ring.

'Anything?' asked LJ bluntly.

'Nothing.'

'Call me if that changes.'

'Of course.'

Then silence as the line went dead. A classic Benham call, if ever there was one.

LJ's brain geared into overdrive. Had she missed a clue from Joen? She ran the conversation back in her mind. She'd forgotten the order of Blur's early albums. A quick search reminded her the third was *Modern Life is Rubbish*. Not very helpful. Then there'd been the final couple of references to Patrick O'Brian and Russell Crowe. Another search, another straightforward answer: the Aussie actor had starred in *Master & Commander*, an adaptation of the former's novels which feature nearly 170 variations of the phrase, "There's not a moment to lose." Everything in the conversation could be taken at face value without obfuscation or deception. In which case, why no email or account changes?

There might not have been a moment to lose, but LJ knew that running around like a headless chicken would get her nowhere. What was the old mantra? More haste, less speed. Or, as LJ preferred to think of it: focus on the important, not the urgent. She closed her eyes. She was seeking clarity, listening for a signal among the noise. There *was* one person who might help her, she realised. The only problem was that he might need some persuading.

151

ROB TANNER WAS STUCK. He knew he was being watched, but he didn't know how closely. He needed to get online, but he had no idea what activities the security services would pick up on. Was WhatsApp safe? Did he need a VPN? Would that even help? Were there any secrets a citizen could keep in modern Britain? He had no idea. It made him wonder at all these things we do in life without the faintest notion of their consequences.

Pathetically, his mind led him to the *Jason Bourne* movies. He remembered the eponymous hero sitting in grimy, interchangeable internet cafés around the globe. Well, if it was good enough for Matt Damon, he reasoned, it would do for him.

With these images in mind, Tanner drove slowly through the backstreets of suburban West London. There was no sign of the earlier tail. Perhaps he was under satellite surveillance now. More likely, he was deluded, flattering himself. He was an ex-banker, for heaven's sake, not a rogue intelligence operative.

In a sleazy part of Acton that not even the most enthusiastic of estate agents could term "up-and-coming," he found what he was looking for: an internet-café-cum-vape-shop-cum-mobile-phone-repair outfit. With, from the look of it, not a single customer. He parked at a nearby supermarket and spent fifteen minutes walking back and forth to establish he really wasn't being followed. Then he returned to the café. As he pushed open the heavy door, he was greeted by the sound of a bell tinkling. Soon he was at an ancient PC, the sole customer among a bank of dilapidated desktops.

He'd committed Harry's numbers to memory as he drove, hoping for subconscious inspiration, but none had come. Now he was disappointed to yield no sensible results from an internet search. The missing number and pattern sequence calculators he found online were no more useful. It left him basking in the white glow of the screen with his head in his hands, trying desperately to work out what it was that he was missing. There had to be something. Harry was right; Joen was far too meticulous in everything she did to have laid this breadcrumb trail by chance.

Tanner had always thought himself a reasonable mathematician – he'd worked in a bank for nearly twenty-five years, for heaven's sake! He also thought he was good at seeing patterns, but he couldn't make head or tail of these. Drawing a line through the page of the pocket notebook in which he was writing, he began again.

50 78 17 47 6 4.

There was no discernible correlation: just six numbers adding up to 202; an average of 34. The first Google search result had been a random number table and that's all they appeared to be.

Tanner scrubbed another sheet. Harry might have found something, but it was beyond his son to work out what. Perhaps the number from the next—today's—email would make it clearer. Tanner doubted it. He checked his watch for the umpteenth time. Why did it have to move so slowly?

More to kill the time than out of any genuine hope for a breakthrough, he took a deep breath and wrote Harry's letters on a fresh page:

AIGAILS
AIGAISL

It looked like an anagram. Tanner's first thought was to try to solve it on his notepad, but that was just his ego talking. An online anagram solver would serve the purpose. Then, he remembered Harry's injunction that the order was key. When he searched the first arrangement of letters, he was confronted with a prompt asking, 'Did you mean: ABIGAIL'S?'

Well, he hadn't, but the hairs on the back of his neck told him he should have. He fed "ABIGAIL" into the search engine, feeling the excitement rising just as it did whenever he was close to decoding one of Joen's emails. The second listing informed him that the name Abigail derives from the Hebrew name Avigail, meaning "my father's joy." He navigated to Wikipedia, skimming the passages in search of details he couldn't even anticipate.

The original Abigail had been a wife of the great biblical king David. Described as both intelligent and beautiful—one of the four women of surpassing beauty in the world, no less—she was one of the Old Testament's female prophets. One of seven female prophets. The magic number. But was he seeing patterns where none existed? Had a week of Joen's emails addled his brain?

No. Tanner could picture Ashley's—Joen's—face. He remembered the throwaway line in one of the emails about Joen meaning "a gift from God." How she would have laughed when she realised the capital letters from the deadly sins provided seven of the eight letters of the name. All that was missing was a B.

He felt his heartbeat skip, a sensation as real as a blow to the chest.

All that was missing was a B. Not a, but *the* missing B: the missing Brand. Holly Brand!

Tanner wanted to call his father. He wanted to thank him, to share the thrill, to speculate on where "Abigails" might lead next. But it was a pleasure he wanted to share in person. He wanted to see his father's bruised and battered face, hear the chuckle rise from deep inside him, watch him fail to contain the urge to say, "I told you so." He didn't want any of that lost to the sterility of a phone line – and certainly not to a phone line that had almost certainly been bugged by the very people to whom he ought to be reporting this development.

Harry's words from the previous afternoon came back to him. "Have you thought what you would do if you found her?" Her – Holly, Ashley, Joen. "Your Joen," as his father had christened her.

No, Tanner hadn't seriously thought what he would do. Until now. Now he knew exactly what it was he had to do. He had to play both sides against the middle and finesse a deal with Allen which protected Joen and her invention before this whole mess escalated into a full-blown Mexican standoff. That probably meant protecting Joen from herself. This realisation came with the awareness that it was rapidly approaching 11 a.m., when she would almost certainly send her next email.

He'd need help. An intermediary he could trust. An insider. He wasn't spoilt for choice—Hobson's was the only one on offer—but that gut of his told him LJ would suffice. She had to help him. Joen's and his future depended on it.

152

NIKKI AND GÉRARD HAD A PLAN. They would split up and head to the city halls in Den Bosch and Aachen—the two cities evoked by the names Hieronymus Bosch and Joen van Aken—and work systematically through property records in the hope of turning up a lead or two. They knew they were looking for the proverbial needle, but together they had tracked down Joen's trail before – and it wasn't as if they had a better plan.

The pair had agreed a uniform set of criteria for which to search: properties acquired in the past five years, in modern buildings with more than 250m^2 of space and by an acquiror with no previous purchase history. The logic was that Joen would need to house a serious amount of computer equipment in state-of-the-art, or at least recent, premises with decent infrastructure and utilities. The downside was that there was no way to narrow down the type of unit: it could be office, warehouse, residential or even former retail space.

In order to make the search even remotely manageable, they decided to focus on corporations rather than looking through the individual records for horticultural names in three or four languages. The cities they were searching weren't exactly small. Den Bosch had a population of 150,000; Aachen was home to a quarter of a million.

All this led the investigators, having gone their separate ways, to computer terminals in the two cities' respective municipal offices. Fortified by large coffees and acutely conscious of the distance between one another, they scrolled through record after record.

For Gérard, fluent in French and German, the task was at least workable. It made no difference if the property had been acquired by Flower PLC, the *Fleur* Company or *Blume* Incorporated. But for Nikki in Holland, it was hopeless. Entities had names not just in standard Dutch but also in derivations that she guessed was the local Brabantian dialect.

Thankfully, one of the municipal clerks, a fresh-faced youngster in his first job, couldn't help but notice the attractive blonde shaking her head at the monitor. He rose from behind the information desk and made his way over to Nikki's terminal. She didn't even hear his approach.

'May I help you, Miss?' he asked in faltering but perfect English.

Nikki jumped – so perfect had been the quiet in her mind. Caught unawares, she searched for a credible response. From nowhere, a cover story sprang to mind. She planned to wash it down with lashings of feminine charm – the kind young men can seldom resist.

'That's really kind.' She turned her full pixie beam on the innocent young man. 'You see, I'm an author researching a book.'

'An author!' exclaimed the clerk. 'Really?'

'I'm right at the end, you see. The big finale. But I'm a bit stuck.' She fixed him with a look of wide-eyed desperation. 'I don't suppose there's any way you might be able to help? I'd be *so* grateful.' The accompanying fluttering of eyelashes should have been far too obvious to anyone over the age of sixteen, but the young clerk was hooked.

'Of course, Miss—?'

'Austen,' replied Nikki. 'But don't tell anyone.' She held out a hand. 'Janey.'

The boy was smitten. He sat with Nikki and went through each line of the database. She'd convinced him that her novel, involving diamond-smuggling in consignments of tulips, required a location owned by a company with an appropriately floral name, which was why she was here; looking for inspiration. If he'd stopped, or been able to think for a second, he'd have seen through the obvious flaws in Nikki's fiction, but he was blinkered by infatuation, enchanted by the peroxide fairy. By the end of the morning, Nikki had a list of a couple of dozen properties which met the agreed criteria. The clerk had even marked them on a map for her and offered to accompany her around the city as soon as he had clocked off for the day. Nikki had forgotten, after spending so much time with Gérard, just how much like boys most men were.

Eighty miles to the south, her fellow investigator had come up with a much longer, wholly un-sifted list. In contrast to Nikki's experiences, no one on the skeleton staff in the municipal office in Aachen showed the slightest inclination to help. When Gérard had more names than he could handle, he gathered up his papers, uttered sarcastic thanks to the empty counter and went in search of fresh air, fresh coffee and inspiration.

No matter how clever you are—and Gérard was undoubtedly smarter than the average bear—there are times in life when intelligence is not enough. Sometimes, you have to be lucky, instead. He knew now that he would have to hope for a bit of that luck as he started to work through the list of properties where Joen's operation might possibly be based. Otherwise, things were going to get a lot worse before they got better.

153

LJ PULLED UP TANNER'S SECURITY FILE. Along with the basic biographical data, and some surprising information about his involvement with a charitable organisation he had founded, it listed email addresses, a landline and two mobile numbers. One mobile was now in the hands of

GCHQ, the second had been dormant for years – until the morning of the 29th. Yesterday. A flag on the file suggested, without stating anything explicitly, that both the landline and second mobile were being monitored. LJ knew she would have to somehow approach Tanner without raising the eyebrows of those listening in.

She was formulating what she might say when her own mobile rang, number withheld. She answered anyway, assuming it was Benham on a treasury secure line.

'Hi LJ,' came the voice on the other end. 'It's Rob Tanner.'

LJ was taken aback. 'But I was just about to call you!'

'Yeah, right,' came back Tanner. 'I've heard that one before.'

LJ laughed, despite herself, and relaxed a little. 'What can I do for you?'

'It's more what we might do for each other,' offered Tanner.

'Really?'

'Really. I had a couple of ideas,' Tanner said. His delivery was strangely stilted, but it was something you would only notice if you knew him. 'It's probably nothing, so I wasn't sure if I should make them official. No point troubling the powers-that-be unnecessarily – not given my status. I felt sure you'd know the right thing to do. Good judgement and all that.'

LJ understood what Tanner was getting at, and she responded in kind. 'Well, it's always good to talk. See if things are worth passing on.'

'Excellent. I had a feeling you'd be the person to speak to.' There was a slight pause before he continued. 'Have you seen the time? I don't suppose you fancy a sandwich?'

'Well, I suppose I have to eat,' offered LJ, knowing she had to play along. 'Where do you suggest?'

'I'd been intending to go to my local. It's the Thatcher's Arms. I was there yesterday, although you probably already know that.'

LJ ignored the wisecrack. 'Why don't I call you when I'm finished up here?'

'Perfect. Thanks, LJ. I knew you'd know what to do.'

She reciprocated with matching blandness of tone. 'And thank you for offering your help, Rob. It's good to know we're pulling in the same direction.'

154

DESPITE KELLETT'S THREATS, news of the tumultuous management meeting—and the departures of Mike Sorensen and Pattie Boyle—raced ahead of him faster than a California wildfire. So, when the Toad returned to his desk, he found a PA transformed. The earlier pall of misery had gone. If anything, the bloody woman actually looked happy.

'What are you looking so cheerful about?' he snapped.

Chrissie shot him her best butter-wouldn't-melt smile. 'Well, you did say that I shouldn't go "Back to Black." By the way, the chairman called for an update. He was really quite insistent that you call him back. Shall I get him on the line?'

'Don't you fucking dare or I'll…'

'Yes, Martin.' The cheer dropped from her face as she cut him short. 'I know exactly what you'll do.'

Kellett, brimming with bile, vowed to get even with her – with all of them. All he needed was a little peace and quiet, some time to think and make a plan. Sir Peter could call all he liked.

Kellett slammed his office door as he realised the depth of his predicament. Not only did he have to find a replacement for his COO, now he had to find a new CTO and Head of Comms – and fast. He summoned Lawrence, the HR chief, and while he was at it, he called in the respective deputies of his departed department heads to see if any had a shred of competence about them. As far as Kellett was concerned, they did not. In a paroxysm of rage, he gave the order that the techies from the other banks should be sent packing, while the chairman's ancient architects were to be returned to whatever pasture electric sheep grazed in retirement.

Kellett had half a mind to take Sir Peter's call and tell him where to go as well. Although, on second thoughts, he supposed a little discretion might be in order. There'd be plenty of time for bombast when things were back to normal and Kellett had three more of his own people in place on ExCo. Still, throughout the morning, the chairman kept ringing. And Chrissie kept informing the chairman that Kellett wasn't at his desk. It was a charade which, in a perverse way, the CEO was rather enjoying, and his mood lifted as he imagined Sir Peter's mounting exasperation.

To make things better, there were no 11 a.m. account modifications to

411

deal with – the first respite in days. And the other good news, as Kellett saw it, was that all the banks were in the same boat now, and they knew exactly who was responsible. Even that useless hand-wringer James Allen would surely find Markham before long. Order would be restored, eventually, and the one and only Martin Kellett would still be the top dog when it was.

The intercom buzzed. Christina. That must be Wilford on the phone again.

'Yes,' answered Kellett, wondering which way he ought to yank the PA's chain. 'This had better…'

'Shut up,' said Christina, a curt, snarled instruction without a hint of subservience. 'Look at your email, right now.' Then came the sound of a phone being slammed into its cradle, loudly and violently enough that it registered through Kellett's closed door. Shocked to be on the other end of a rude imperative, Kellett did as he was told.

TO: Leah Oladapo; MAKCEO2024@NatBank.uk
FROM: Joen van Aken
DATE: Monday, 30 December 2024 at 12:00
Luxuria

Well, well. Guess who's back! No, not me: *Martin.Andrew.Kellett.* The Toad!

And how appropriate, given today's subject matter. This could be one of Martin's holiday snaps. You should see the real thing… I have!

Sorry if you were expecting this at eleven. Twelve – High Noon – is so much better. Ask Gary.

People say a picture's worth... now how many words was it? It's so easy to lose numbers. But a picture, you can enjoy it, Luxuriate in it, give it your undivided attention.

I trust I have yours, but remember Peanut Jimmy quoting Matthew 5:28... it's what's in your heart that matters.

And it's not just sex – don't forget the drugs. Ask Begbie – or Iggy – how much they're worth in prizes?

Money, money, money. Easy come, easy go. You mustn't waste it like railfan Renton: TVs, washing machines, but not "a luxurious bed" from the Upstart Crow. Geoffrey's Household cat will have nowhere to sit!

Now, everyone wants luxuries without thinking there might be Punishment. Ask OMD (they like pictures too!)

Abyssinia!

J.

Kellett couldn't believe his eyes. He didn't give a fuck about medieval imagery or pop-culture wordplay, and he didn't really care what was happening to the bank accounts, so long as all rival banks were equally screwed. But he did give a fuck about this bitch who had the nerve to make fun of him in an email to the prime minister's chief of staff. It was a message that Allen would read. And not just him, but COBRA, the whole cabinet… eventually, the entire world. Everything always leaked. He'd be a laughing stock! And the suggestion that Markham had photos of him *in flagrante*, so to speak. It couldn't be true. Could it? His head fell into his hands with an animal wail of realisation.

'Ziegler!' Markham must have paid the Swiss pimp in return for some of his clandestine kompromat; or else, the procurer had gone rogue, or been raided by the police. Kellett didn't know what exactly had happened, but he knew it couldn't be anything good.

Kellett's fellow addressee, meanwhile, read the email with less personal interest but no less dread. LJ understood many of the allusions without the need for a search engine. Begbie and Renton were from the movie *Trainspotting*. It had one of her favourite opening scenes ever, with Ewan McGregor running madcap through Edinburgh to the sound of Iggy Pop's "Lust for Life." *High*

Noon had to be the classic western with Gary Cooper. The Upstart Crow was Shakespeare. Peanut Jimmy could only refer to former US President Jimmy Carter's famous quote in an interview with *Playboy* magazine that he had committed adultery in his heart many times but had never transgressed bodily. Unlike the suggestions about Kellett's private life, clearly.

But it was what wasn't said that LJ found most interesting. Or not so much interesting as terrifying. All the numbers were missing. A picture is worth *a million* words. Iggy was worth *a million* in prizes. Joen had said herself, "It's so easy to lose numbers." The inference was obvious.

It took but a second for LJ's worst fears to be confirmed, via a call from Paul Benham at Treasury. He sounded grave, even by his cheerless standards.

'Account reductions across the board, LJ.'

'How much?' How many?' LJ huffed, annoyed at her own inexactitude. 'You know what I mean.'

'All of them. Reduced by an order of magnitude.'

'Shit.'

'You said it. I'll call back when I've got more detail.'

There was no need for further embellishment. The line went dead without either of them knowing or caring who had been the one to cut it.

Meanwhile, the third person to read the email did so with no such heaviness of heart. Chrissie had full access to Kellett's inbox. She didn't care a fig for opaque references to films, books or music. Bank accounts would be sorted in due course. The earth would still revolve on its axis. All that mattered were the first two paragraphs. The exposure of Martin Kellett for the vile pig that he was.

Chrissie took screenshots of the email then calmly forwarded them from her own to Rob Tanner and Pattie Boyle's personal accounts. That ought to be enough to scupper the Toad, she thought. Then another thought struck her, since she was in for a penny anyway. Using her access privileges, she replied from Kellett's account:

TO: Joen van Aken
FROM: MAKCEO2024@NatBank.uk
DATE: Monday, 30 December 2024 at 12:09
RE: Luxuria

I wasn't sure if you had Rob Tanner's personal email.
RSGTanner@gmail.com
Just in case x

She sent and deleted the message. Kellett would never know, and if it came back to bite anyone on the backside, it wouldn't be her. She'd be long gone. And hopefully, now, so would the Toad. The Pig.

155

THE WEATHER WAS STILL HOSTILE – like the atmosphere in the seamier parts of the capital. Considering these facts, the *Zero Use* protest march ought to have been a write-off. While demonstrations against Brexit and the conflict in Gaza had drawn hundreds of thousands of protesters, anti-capitalist demonstrations were usually a fraction of the size. And that was in good weather – not amid the wintry tail of a great storm.

Today's ragbag coalition of activists was gathering in Trafalgar Square, with plans to start marching at noon. It appeared the authorities' most optimistic wishes would be granted, with maybe five or six hundred doughty protesters more intent on keeping their feet warm than venting political spleen.

Ringleaders clad in Guy Fawkes masks milled about at the base of Nelson's column, trying to interest the assembly in their refrain, "Fiddles like Nero, he's the zero; we want Allen out!" If hardly the angriest of revolutionary slogans, it was at least catchy and kept people jolly. The watching police officers settled into the seats of their heated transit vans, and the head of the Met's public order command was able to report to Sir Richard Lindsell that the event was likely to pass off without any need for reinforcements.

Then, just after twelve o'clock, word began to filter through of further, significant changes to bank accounts. In stark contrast to the ever-escalating adjustments of the previous five days, there were now suggestions that ordinary people's balances had been reduced.

One of the organisers of the protest was a profoundly middle-class university dropout. Tim Farley by birth, but Ciro—'rhymes with Nero'—for the purpose of agitation, his revolutionary politics were strangely at odds with the family trust from which he was still happy to draw. He hurriedly checked his bank balance and immediately saw his chance for fifteen minutes of fame.

He made a beeline for the bored-looking BBC junior correspondent who he'd chatted up earlier that morning. Serendipitously, they had both studied at the same university, and they knew some of the same people. He'd even bought her a coffee from one of the international chains across the road – an act which was surely heretical for an avowed anti-capitalist even if it was very much appreciated by the cub reporter. But now his timing was perfect, his arrival coming at the same time as a message from her producer to find and interview one of the protest organisers to 'add a bit of colour' to the news bulletins. There was a limit to viewers' appetites for snowy white nothingness, after all.

The reporter saw Ciro, deeply sinister in his Vendetta mask and full-length black coat, and thanked her lucky stars. Two minutes later, they were primed for broadcast. Thirty seconds later they were live, and she began her introduction to camera.

'I'm here with Ciro, one of the organisers of today's protest.'

The rookie turned—and the camera followed her gaze—to find a bespectacled young man in smart suit and tie. While she had been speaking, Ciro had ditched the mask and coat. Clark Kent in perfect reverse.

He took advantage of the reporter's surprise and spoke into the mic, his Home Counties accent the epitome of middle-class reason.

'If anyone was in any doubt, this latest news about account reductions confirms just how dangerous this government is to the ordinary citizen. Arrogant, incompetent and *dangerous*.' Ciro angled his face to look directly at the camera lens, his school drama lessons finding an outlet at last. 'I would ask everyone to check their bank accounts. The government says that nothing new has happened, and if that's the case then, by all means, do nothing; stay at home, stay warm, and don't risk getting into trouble at an empty cash machine. But if you think they're lying to you, *as I do*, then please join us and let's march to Downing Street together. Let's show that fiddler James Allen—the Emperor Nero of our times—that we won't accept his bluster and blunders any longer. Please listen…'

Ciro gestured theatrically—and with perfect timing—towards the main body of the crowd, just as the loudest chorus yet of the anti-Allen chant filled the air, anger joining ridicule for the first time. The cameraman, inadvertently, made the mob seem like an army. The novice interviewer, meanwhile, tried to wrest back control and wrap up her segment. But she was flustered, her guard was down, and she didn't know what to say.

'Well, there you have it,' she said. 'If you think the government's lying to you, get down to Downing Street.'

Back in the studio, the producer hurriedly cut the broadcast, and viewers were presented with a momentary shot of a flabbergasted anchor. With the autocue rolling, she thanked her colleague and reminded viewers of the latest headline: a thousandfold reduction in the notional values of the nation's bank accounts.

This news, coupled with the segment from Trafalgar Square and the reporter's unintentional repetition of Ciro's message, acted as a summons to muster more effective than any recruiting sergeant's. All over the country, people were rushing to check their online bank balances. A fair few succeeded before the systems collapsed under the surge of demand. No one likes losing money – even fanciful, fabricated, theoretical sums of money which had never been earned in the first place. And news editors, television producers, journalists, commentators and bloggers are no different to anyone else. This was how the news gathered steam, and how a spark became a conflagration.

In the newsroom of MailOnline, Trish Dixon repeated her Christmas Day stratagem of asking colleagues to check their balances at nearby cash machines, all of which were besieged by long queues. She was ready to go live with a story confirming both the sharp reductions and the ensuing threat to public order within thirty minutes. There were no prizes for subtlety in online news, and having seen his own bank balance reduced, the grouchy sub-editor was in no mood to do anything but stick his boot into Allen. He made Trish's story the lead, under the banner headline: "HERO TO NERO TO ZERO: Allen Fiddles While Banks Burn."

156

THE PRIME MINISTER HAD SECLUDED HIMSELF with Zack Hardy with strict instructions that he was not to be disturbed unless absolutely necessary, so he didn't appreciate LJ's interruption. He came around soon enough, however, when he heard her triple-whammy of the latest developments: not only was there a new, hour-late email, but there had been massive account reductions *and* the BBC had inadvertently turned a march into a movement, all in the space of a few minutes. Allen was apoplectic.

'I'll scrap their bloody licence fee!' he raged, after LJ showed him a clip of the BBC's *Zero Use* coverage on her phone. 'The bastards are inciting the fucking protest!' LJ had to admit he had a point. She found herself grimacing at the naivety of the broadcast as much as the prime minister's verbal onslaught.

'Get the Director General on the phone,' ordered Allen. 'I want that demonstrator's video pulled from the rolling news NOW!'

'With respect, sir, he can't and won't do that.' LJ knew she had to stay calm at all costs. She turned to the press secretary for support. 'We need to focus on a response don't you think, Zack?'

'Absolutely, LJ. I'll start making calls.'

'And say precisely what?' asked Allen. 'That we've got no bloody idea what's going on? Get Lindsell on the phone.'

The deputy commissioner, as it turned out, had nothing new to add about Markham. Sadly, the same couldn't be said of the Trafalgar Square demonstration.

'The numbers do appear to be growing, sir,' Lindsell conceded.

'No, really? What a surprise.' No veneer of politeness could conceal the sarcasm in Allen's tone. 'And what do you propose to do about that?'

'They haven't broken any laws yet, sir,' replied Lindsell. 'Obviously we're bringing in reinforcements, regardless. And don't worry, sir, we'll have a strong security cordon in place around Whitehall.'

'Thank you, Sir Richard. A moment please.' Allen leaned forward on the conference table, arms crossed, head down, collecting his thoughts. The room filled with the heavy stillness of a minute's silence. LJ forced herself not to fidget, unable to push that metaphor from her mind. Eventually, the referee's whistle blew, or rather, Allen exhaled noisily.

'Let me sum up, Sir Richard. Just to make sure I get this right.' Allen paused for effect. 'We're halfway through the day, and the combined police, security and secret services of the world's sixth largest economy can't find a lone woman who has single-handedly brought down our biggest banks and, before long, will undoubtedly do the same for our economy?'

Allen sat, staring coldly at the conference phone, until a subdued, 'No, sir,' emerged from the handset. The PM wasn't finished yet, though.

'And I don't suppose you have any ideas, any masterstrokes up your sleeve, to save the day? So to speak.'

'No, sir.'

'Well, that's a shame.' Allen effected a laugh. 'At this rate, I'll be out of a job by New Year. And you know what?'

'Sir?'

'The only satisfaction I'll have left will be taking you down with me.'

Allen reached forward and cut the line.

LJ cringed. She was thoroughly sick of her boss and the political class he represented. She wanted nothing more than to leave them all to their self-serving devices, but then she considered her place in all this, remembered the duties bestowed upon her. She was one of very few people who could set this straight. She thought of Craig's unwavering support, of all the people who would be hurt if she abdicated responsibility. The millions she'd joined government to serve. Her grandmother. Gary Cooper in High Noon. She spoke, feigning brightness in a masque of assurance.

'Actually, sir. I *do* have an idea.'

Allen mutely nodded for her to continue.

'Why don't we see if we can use Rob Tanner as an intermediary to try to broker a deal with Markham?' LJ gave thanks for her earlier acting rehearsal with Tanner; she'd managed to make the idea sound entirely spontaneous.

'You're not serious.'

'Why not, sir? It's no different to working back channels in any normal diplomatic situation. Give me a couple of hours to see what I can come up with, while you work on comms with Zack. What have we got to lose?'

With no answer to hand, Allen gave a morose shrug of the shoulders—the most committal assent he could bring himself to sanction—and waved her out.

157

TANNER HAD EXPECTED THE SECOND HALF of the morning to match the pace of the first. After the excitement of Harry's numbers, "ABIGAIL'S," and the phone call with LJ, he'd assumed there would be an

11:00 email with more clues to chew over. Lord, how many times had he told himself: never assume anything.

Having been shut out of his National Bank email account, Tanner had to rely on second-hand information. Someone from the bank would surely call, and if not, there was always the TV news, which he left playing mutely in the background.

Eleven o'clock came. Then 11:10, 11:20 and 11:30, with no sign of Joen and no call from LJ saying she was on her way. Tanner watched the news on the half-hour, but beyond a report on the knot of hardy demonstrators who had turned out in Trafalgar Square, there was nothing. He couldn't even call Nikki or Gérard; they'd agreed to take the SIM cards out of their phones and switch them off before they boarded Eurostar to avoid being tracked via their mobiles. Just before noon, he gave up waiting and headed to the pub.

Tanner couldn't remember the last time he'd been to a pub two lunchtimes in a row. At Cambridge, after exams, possibly? Christ, he'd forgotten what it was to be alive. All those hours in meetings, site visits and virtual conferences. What a waste.

He settled himself in the same armchair as yesterday with a pint and a book for company. It made a change to read something that wasn't a risk report or a balance sheet. He'd picked the novel up in an airport, God knows when, and then forgotten about it. But now, as he opened the first page and tried to read, his mind was elsewhere, with Joen. How was he going to persuade her to meet him? Could LJ help, and was she to be trusted? Where did "Abigail's" fit in the puzzle? Questions, questions, and not an answer in sight. When he returned to the bar, he caught sight of the television in the corner. It was a news report, helicopter footage: a tide of bodies sweeping through central London. The march was no damp squib after all, the numbers having thickened considerably since the last report. The text on the ticker was even more shocking.

Well, thought Tanner, that explained why LJ hadn't called yet. Every bank balance in the country had been *reduced* – and by a number of zeros. He took an involuntary breath; Joen really did enjoy raising the stakes. He wished there was something else he could be doing, other than waiting, but no sooner had he returned to his seat than his wish was granted; his phone pinged with a notification, an email from Chrissie. And the attachment – the extraordinary, lustful attachment. Tanner offered an imaginary toast to the PA.

He read and reread Joen's noon email. Like LJ before him, he understood most of the references. Knowing the Toad, the insinuations about Kellett were undoubtedly true and unlikely to be attractive. But none of that was important. All that mattered was Joen's unambiguous indication that millions would disappear. And a new number for Harry's sequence: 56 or, possibly, 57. What the hell was 50 78 17 47 6 4 57? The urge to search for the new string was almost unbearable, but he couldn't risk it. Just then, another notification popped onto the screen: a message from LJ saying she was leaving Downing Street. At least he knew now how long he'd have to wait.

But then he realised he didn't have to sit idle. There was bound to be an internet café in Hammersmith, ten minutes' walk away. LJ wouldn't be here for at least three-quarters of an hour. Tanner explained to the puzzled publican that he'd be back shortly and asked him to keep a table free, then set off into the wintry gloom. He doubted he'd be followed—the security agencies presumably knew he'd be meeting LJ at the pub shortly—but he made a point of cutting through a quieter side street here and a rubbish-strewn back-alley there just to make sure that was the case.

As he hoped, he found an internet café at the wrong end of the High Street, next to a shabby bookmaker. Neither had a single customer, and Tanner wondered again if the miscellany of vape and phone paraphernalia was a front for something more dubious.

A fiver secured Tanner another dingy workstation and grimy screen. He knew he had to try, but nothing he could think of gave the slightest hint of how he might unlock that combination of numbers. Discouraged by the surroundings as much as his lack of progress, Tanner prepared to throw in the towel. LJ would be at the pub in fifteen minutes, which left him five before he should leave. He drummed his fingers furiously on the chipped tabletop. Come on, Rob, *think*!

Tanner opened the Wikipedia page for Hieronymus Bosch, rapidly scanning the page for numerical references. There were plenty of dates and totals, but nothing which felt like it would fit the code – for that was undoubtedly what Joen had given him. He scrolled back to the top, searching desperately for clues, inspiration, anything. He frantically clicked each hyperlink in turn, skimming the linked pages for numbers: List of Famous Dutch People, Terminology of the Low Countries, Duchy of Brabant, Early Netherlandish Painting, Hell. It was useless. There was nothing. Time to go.

Then, just as he was about to give up, Tanner spotted a link to the article on the town of s-Hertogenbosch – better known as Den Bosch. Along with Aachen, the city was one of Nikki and Gérard's targets. Tanner knew Aachen had been Charlemagne's capital, a hugely important medieval metropolis, but he knew nothing of the Dutch city. Compulsively curious, he couldn't resist this one last link. The Wikipedia page was relatively short, with statistics on population and religious denominations, a table of climate data and a list of notable residents. But nothing remotely linked to Harry's numbers. He scrolled back to the top, his eye drawn to the colourful images of the city, with its statue of Hieronymus Bosch at the centre.

And for the second time that day, his heart missed a beat. No, more than that – his entire chest went missing in a hollowing of shock. Above the pictures was another link: Coordinates: 51° 41' N 5° 18' E. Oblivious to the time now, Tanner clicked. Map coordinates can be shown in numerous different ways; one longer form for Den Bosch was shown as 51° 41' 0" N, 5° 18' 0" E. The string of numbers was evocative, he thought, as he pulled out Harry's slip of paper to compare.

His heart sank… close but no cigar. But hold on, he thought – that wasn't the point. Tanner entered "Aachen" into the search bar. The coordinates read: 50° 46' 32" N, 06° 05' 01" E. The first digit was 50, the number corresponding to the first email. It couldn't be, surely, could it?

Tanner realised he was going about it the wrong way. A quick search led him to a coordinate website which generated exact longitudes and latitudes. His mind racing, he dropped the marker on the centre of Aachen. The status bar provided a digital coordinate to six decimal places, beginning with 50.77 and 6.08 respectively. Instinctively, Tanner edited the numbers to use Harry's: 50.781747 and 6.0457. He pressed enter. No rubbing of a genie's lamp was ever more effective. The map scrolled a little to the left, a nudge westwards, and settled on a point only three kilometres from Aachen city centre. The final words of Joen's letter flashed into his brain. Was he dealing literally, he wondered, not with Joan of Arc but Joen of Aachen?

Tanner's phone buzzed – a message from LJ. She had reached the tube station. She'd be at the pub in five minutes, and she was sorry she'd taken so long.

Tapping demonically, Tanner swapped the page for its equivalent on Google Maps and located the same spot. He switched to satellite view, then zoomed in to street level. The cameras hadn't reached the exact point on the map he needed, but they came within a hundred metres or so. They showed an office block on what appeared to be a modern campus.

'*Gotcha*!'

The exhortation was loud enough to draw the proprietor's attention, if not the punters in the bookies next door. Tanner cleared the browser history, closed the search engine and surreptitiously pulled the power cable from the computer before dashing from the shop. It was all he could do not to run, but his sliding traverse was no bad substitute.

158

TANNER RETURNED TO THE PUB, apology at the ready, to find LJ already seated at his table, looking perfectly content. She was cradling a large glass of white wine, and she had evidently ordered for Tanner too, as a fresh pint waited opposite her. LJ shrugged off his apologies and thanks and, with a mimed toast, indicated he should take it.

'Look,' she began, once he had sat down and taken a sip. 'I could give you a bunch of stuff about the Official Secrets Act, state security or some other bullshit, but since I need your help, there's not really much point, is there?' Her voice had a naturally agreeable tone, bespeaking reason and honesty. 'You've heard about the reduction in accounts. It's obviously a warning—what goes up must come down—and the bottom line is that we're no closer to finding Joen, nor to solving the problem. I'll be blunt: the PM has miscalculated, as he has throughout this crisis.'

Tanner concealed his surprise at LJ's open disloyalty by taking another sip of his pint. This would have to be his last one, lest they started going to his head. He had to be doubly on his guard around a woman as sharp as LJ, but it was hard not to trust her. She was just so damn believable. He let her continue.

'Allen assumed—everyone assumed—that the police or MI5 would bring her in, or at least pinpoint the mechanism she's using to manipulate the accounts. So, he chose not to negotiate with her, despite my urgings. He wants the glory of a total victory.' The contempt in LJ's delivery made it sound anything but glorious. 'But Joen's miles ahead of us. And what's to say she won't zero every account in the country, or put them all into minus amounts? And even if we do find her, it might not be the end of it. Maybe her moves are already pre-programmed in a back-up somewhere? Or there's a self-destruct mechanism in her system? Can you imagine? No money in *any* bank account in the country!'

LJ sat back, taking first a sip then a deep pull of her wine, while Tanner contemplated exactly that eventuality.

'So, how do I come into this?' he asked. 'What can I do that you can't?'

She fixed him with a smile. 'Use your charm, obviously!'

'Nice try.' Tanner couldn't help but laugh. 'But the real answer is…?'

All trace of humour disappeared from LJ's features. 'I'm not joking, Rob. Joen called me this morning.'

'Joen? She called you?'

'Yes, *Joen* called and asked if I thought what she was doing was reasonable. It was as if she wanted… affirmation, perhaps? It got me thinking; she's been on the run for years, never settling down, never letting her guard down. No close relationships.'

'She said as much to me.' Tanner was starting to see where LJ was going.

'Her parents died when she was young. She's had no real friends. She's a genius, and it wouldn't be remotely surprising if she's somewhere out on the spectrum. Then she spends nine years seeking revenge, finding an even bigger purpose. Looking forward to sticking it to Kellett…' LJ paused to look Tanner in the eye. '*And you.* And, lo and behold, you turn out to be Mr Nice Guy. More than that, you turn out to be Prince Charming, with a social conscience and a bloody charitable foundation to boot.'

Tanner started to form a question. Then he remembered who was sitting opposite and kept his mouth shut.

'I don't just think you *could* reign her in,' went on LJ. 'I think you're the *only* person who can.' She took another decent quaff of her wine, never once taking her eyes from Tanner.

'Okay,' he replied evenly. 'Even if I could get her to talk, why should I?'

'Because I think you care about doing the right thing, and because you agree with her… as do I.' Tanner had been about to interrupt, but his surprise shut him up. LJ continued into the silence. 'What? You don't think that just because I work for Allen I don't care about climate change, sexual exploitation, criminal justice? Racism? Inequality? Poverty? Why do you think I went into government? It wasn't for party infighting or backstabbing or spin. The whole point was that I wanted to change things for the better. Sometimes I look around this country and I think we're only making things worse.' The polemic tailed into a deep sigh, her tone changing from angry to wistful. 'Did she tell you her demands?'

Tanner shook his head. 'I haven't heard them exactly. Allen never mentioned anything at COBRA.'

'She wants a truth commission,' said LJ. 'An independent body to focus on the biggest problems facing society. No party-political bullshit, just impartial experts reporting annually on the government's progress, making recommendations and maybe commitments where necessary. She wants a check on the power of parliament. An independent balance against the party politicians.'

'That's all she wants?' asked Tanner. He decided not to mention the letter—the evidence he had destroyed—where Joen had alluded to just such a commission without stating anything so explicitly. He hadn't told anyone about the letter; it had seemed right to burn it, as if that was what Joen had wanted him to do all along.

'That's all she wants,' confirmed LJ.

'And Allen said no?'

LJ answered with a nod. 'He comes from the mushroom growing school of politics: keep the people in the dark and feed 'em shit.'

'But I can't believe he would say no to something so… so sensible. Could a commission like that work?'

LJ shrugged. 'Who knows? But I've not heard a better idea to fix the mess we're in.' Her face clouded over, as if she suddenly remembered where she was and what was at stake. 'Either way, Rob, you have to convince Joen to stop. To turn the clock back. To come over from the dark side and work with us, not against us.'

'She'll never do that.'

'Why not? You can offer her immunity. A full pardon. Call it what you want. Her demands aren't impossible; tell her we can meet them. Tell her whatever she needs to hear to get us all off this ride. Be creative – just come up with *something*. It's what you're good at.' There was more than a hint of desperation in her voice now.

'Are you acting on the prime minister's authority?' asked Tanner.

'Not yet, but I will be soon enough. He has no choice now.'

'And what if he tries to backtrack? To double-cross?'

'Then we'll find a way to go round him. Beyond him. Whatever it takes.'

'You'd do that?'

'You have my word, whatever happens.'

They stared at each other—one weighing the value, the other the cost—of this commitment.

'So, will you contact her?' asked LJ.

'I already have,' answered Tanner flatly. 'The truth is that I'm already on her side, come what may.'

'I figured,' said LJ. She scoffed. 'Funny, isn't it? I'm an insider wanting out. And Joen's an outsider we need to bring in.'

LJ was cut off by the vibrations of her phone. She looked at the screen and then began gathering her belongings.

'Sorry, Rob, I'm needed back at Downing Street.' She stood, then turned so she was looking down at Tanner. 'One more thing before I go… what happened to your investigators?'

Tanner had almost forgotten about Nikki and Gérard. He was sure he could trust LJ, but Aachen was his trump card, and he suspected that was one ace best kept safely tucked away up his sleeve.

'Gérard's got a hunch that there may be more to the Joen van Aken connection than we think, so they've gone off to the continent. Museums, galleries, God knows what.'

It wasn't an outright lie—more a half-truth—and if it provided a little cover should the pair of investigators come onto GCHQ's radar, it would be worth it.

LJ shook her head wearily, unable to prevent a rueful laugh. 'It's no laughing matter, but it really does seem like one of those ridiculous disaster movies: the fate of the nation depending on clues from a sixteenth century painter. But if it is, I'm glad you've got the lead part.'

With a squeeze of his arm for emphasis, LJ turned and headed out through the doors. No sooner had she stepped outside than she was gone, swallowed in the snowy gloom. He continued to stare, replaying LJ's words in his mind. This was one role that he had never asked for. He would have given it up in an instant, but there was no understudy waiting in the wings. The part was his and his alone.

159

THE TRICKLE OF PROTESTERS HAD TURNED INTO A FLOOD. Across the country, the consequences of Joen's latest move were beginning to sink in. It was inconvenient when bank accounts were artificially inflated—not least because ATMs dried out, card purchases were limited, and online banking kept crashing—but if cyber-threats, too, were subject to the laws of gravity, then that was a very different matter. And what the hell was the government doing about it?

The mood shift in Trafalgar Square was palpable. The police, lulled into a false sense of security, struggled to cope with ever increasing numbers of demonstrators, for that's what they had become. Reinforcements were being bussed in, but the decision to establish a security cordon in Whitehall had left the officers in Trafalgar Square short-handed. The small police blockades on the Mall and Northumberland Avenue were quickly overwhelmed, and then a fresh mob of agitators appeared from nowhere in Parliament Square. Suddenly, thousands of people were heading towards Downing Street from each point of the compass as the thin, yellow lines of police officers were forced into shambling retreat, merely slowing rather than stopping the advance of the crowds.

The anti-Allen chants were now accompanied by the sounds of breaking glass and the distant wail of sirens. Small groups of masked protesters started scuffles with the police officers, but the police didn't have the manpower to arrest anyone, and each hit-and-run merely fed the energy of the crowd.

Step by step, the retreating groups of police were pushed back on Whitehall until, bolstered by reinforcements routed through the back streets of New Scotland Yard, they were able to stem the tide. Two solid shield walls, fronted by officers in full riot gear, held their lines a mere hundred metres from Downing Street, with the Monument to the Women of World War II to the north and the Cenotaph to the south.

Meanwhile, another small army of police officers managed to clear a route from Victoria in the west, reinforcing the hard-pressed contingent at the Horse Guards end of Downing Street. They were too late, however, to stop a huge crowd gathering on the parade ground itself.

Hunkered down in Number Ten, James Allen watched these scenes unfold on TV with disbelief. Cocooned in noiseless security by the reinforced, bomb-proof glass of the residence windows, it seemed inconceivable that a throng tens of thousands strong was encamped little more than a stone's throw away from his vantage point. Were Anna and the kids viewing the same pictures back home in Norfolk? Would they be worried? He'd been so wrapped up in events, he'd barely spoken with his wife since Boxing Day. Still, they were all used to it, and even the kids recognised their father's emotional and physical distance as the price of power.

For now, there were far worse things to worry about, like the awful realisation that only the trees at the bottom of his garden and a very thin line of police officers stood between him and the baying mob. He was trapped, like a fox desperately hiding in a culvert, as the hounds circled. The victim of his own bloody hunt. Had a prime minister ever felt so cornered in his own bastion? And the threat, it seemed, had come from nowhere.

Even if his security detail was able to effect an escape by road, which seemed unlikely, Allen's retreat would be captured live on television for all the world to see. The Prime Minister of the United Kingdom in ignominious flight! Alternately, he could use the network of tunnels deep underground to make his way to the Crisis Command Centre under the Ministry of Defence on Whitehall, or the Admiralty Citadel, an ivy-clad monstrosity of brutalist Second World War architecture hidden in plain sight 500 metres away on the Mall. But he'd just be exchanging a comfortable prison for a windowless bunker, and word would leak anyway that the PM had skulked from Downing Street like a rat in a sewer. Fight or flight, the most basic human response since the beginning of time. He was damned if he would run; he would just have to sit it out.

Allen called through to his PA, who informed him that LJ was stuck in Hammersmith. At least Jonathan Morse, the cabinet secretary, was at hand. Morse was with the home secretary, Sara Jafari, at the Home Office Command & Control Centre, aka HOC3. This was the secure communications centre within the main Home Office headquarters in Westminster. Upgraded significantly after the re-establishment of the UK's Border Force as a directly accountable law-enforcement command in 2012, it had been remade into a state-of-the-art comms facility, integrated seamlessly with the security and intelligence services. HOC3 provided other logistical advantages, lying only 400 metres from MI5 on Millbank and less than a mile to its sister service SIS, MI6, on the other side of the river.

Within a minute, a connection was made between the prime minister and his conjoined subordinates. Allen spoke into the unmistakeable echo chamber of a conference room speakerphone.

'Jonathan. Sara. What have you got for me?'

The noticeable pause before either volunteered a reply told Allen all he needed to know. *Nothing*. He wondered how they'd try to sweeten this particular pill.

'I'm so sorry,' said Sara. 'We didn't anticipate anything like this. Our forces were spread across the city as a show of strength to local communities. Bobbies on the beat, like you wanted.'

Allen allowed himself a wry smile at the buck-passing. Never an attractive quality, particularly in a home secretary. He effected a nonchalance he certainly didn't feel.

'Jonathan?' Allen prompted. 'Should I be worried?'

'No, Prime Minister. At least, not for your own safety. We have more than enough officers on the ground to keep order in Whitehall now. Plus, it's going to be dark soon, with the promise of more snow. People will get cold, and bored, they'll start going home and the crowds will disperse.'

'But?'

'We're getting multiple reports of serious public order disturbances up and down the country since the latest cyber-attack. Mostly theft, supermarkets being cleared out, that sort of thing. But a worrying number. *Too many*, James.' Morse and Allen had been good colleagues, near friends, for a long time. Allen picked up the genuine discomfort in Morse's voice.

'The sun going down may be a good thing for the crowds in Whitehall,' he added, 'but I'm worried about what darkness will bring elsewhere.'

Although nobody could see him, Allen raised his eyebrows. 'The cloak of night covering a multitude of sins, eh?'

'Exactly.'

Allen didn't need to hear any more. He was always happiest when he was doing something, and he'd been far too acquiescent for far too long.

'All right, Jonathan. It's time. I want you to prepare emergency powers under the 2004 Act. A curfew, a ban on assembly, troops on the streets. Whatever it takes.'

Jafari tried to interrupt. 'But Prime Minister, we've never even used those powers before.'

Allen swatted her aside. 'With respect, Sara, you're forgetting your history. There were troops on the streets after the Manchester Arena bombings, and tanks were sent to Heathrow after 9-11. How about the General Strike and Northern Ireland? Far-reaching plans were drawn up for Brexit and Covid.'

'But not under general emergency powers!'

'Semantics. This is just as great a threat as anything we've faced. Bigger, in fact. What do we need to do, legally speaking, Jonathan?'

Morse picked up the baton. 'We need formal ratification by COBRA. Then for the use of troops, we'll need a further specific approval by the Defence Council of the MoD. You should call the chief of defence staff. I'll speak to the defence secretary.'

'You might care to remind him there's a reshuffle on Wednesday, Jonathan. If we're still here, that is.'

'Yes, Prime Minister.'

'But hurry. We need to move this evening. We can't have these bastards running loose all night.'

160

A SOLID WALL OF RIOT SHIELDS blocked LJ to the front. Meanwhile, a multitude of bodies pressed into her back, a breathless crush amid a febrile atmosphere of shouts and screams. Extreme violence seemed only a spark away. And yet none of the officers, clad in helmets and balaclavas, showed the slightest interest in her proffered Number Ten security pass. Through their snow-blurred visors, it may as well have been a Tesco Clubcard. There was simply no way through. Getting the few hundred yards from Westminster station to Downing Street was proving even less pleasant than the rammed ten-stop tube journey from the west.

She crabbed her way slowly to the side of the road and clambered over the balustraded wall of the Foreign and Commonwealth Office. It was a relief to be out of the press. A pair of officers detached themselves from the large group guarding the entrance to the building. They strode towards LJ, their postures suggesting a martial state of readiness, like they were coiled springs ready to leap.

But even when threatened with arrest, LJ surprised them by standing her ground, and their language took on an altogether more deferential tone once her identity had been established. She was funnelled into the eerily quiet F&C building, and within ten minutes she was collected by one of the PM's own security detail, and whisked through back corridors into Downing Street. Where a furious James Allen was cloistered with Zack Hardy, hunched over the heavily edited draft of his next speech.

'Where the hell have you been?' spurted Allen, looking up at the sound of LJ's footsteps.

'Excuse me?' LJ had witnessed enough of Allen's tongue lashings to know what he was capable of, but it was a rare day when he spoke to her with such vitriol.

'A simple enough question, LJ.'

'I was doing what I thought we'd agreed: enlisting Rob Tanner's help to mediate with Ashley Markham.'

'And you couldn't do that here?'

'Well, there's the small matter that GCHQ have his phone. And, sir, we could hardly have got him into Downing Street with all this going on.' She tilted her head towards the window.

'No,' conceded Allen. He shook his head, defeat drawn on his face. 'I suppose not.' All the fight appeared to rush out of him, like air from a vacuum.

431

LJ tried to bolster the prime minister's spirits. 'At least the march is under control.'

'Out there's not the problem, LJ. Trouble's starting everywhere now, up and down the country.' Allen turned to face her; his expression as grim as she'd ever seen it. 'There's widespread theft and looting—mostly supermarkets—and mindless vandalism when people find the shelves have been emptied. The police are just about containing it, but they're stretched to the limit. They're worried it will spiral out of control once the sun sets.' His eyes panned back to the window, where the winter twilight was fading as quickly as it had fallen. 'Particularly once the troublemakers have had a few drinks.'

'What does the home secretary recommend?' asked LJ.

Allen laughed, but there was no humour in the sound, only scorn. 'You mean the caterpillar? You know; moves slowly, no backbone. She's still taking soundings from her advisers, apparently.'

'You're kidding? But we have to act now!'

Allen fixed with LJ with a hard look. 'Don't worry, I *am* acting. I'm calling out the army. We'll have them on the streets by ten. See, I can do some things without you.' He smiled without warmth. 'So, what about Tanner? Will he help?'

'Yes, sir, he'll try to make contact with Markham,' LJ replied, a study of counterfeit composure. 'On two conditions.' There had been no such stipulation, but then Tanner wasn't used to dealing with politicians, as LJ was.

'Conditions? What sort of conditions? Who does he think he is?'

'One, you accept Joen's demand for a Truth Commission. Two—'

It only took one to set Allen off. He leapt to his feet.

'How dare you?' he shrieked. 'How dare he!'

'Seriously?' asked LJ. She was probably even closer to her limit than her boss was. 'Does it matter if you meet her demands? Would more openness in government be so terrible? Let's face it, at this rate, in forty-eight hours you're not even going to *be* in government.' She paused to catch her breath. Allen looked on in stunned silence. 'Condition two. You grant Markham immunity from prosecution. An amnesty, or whatever you want to call it.'

'What? You must be joking!'

'Come on! Markham won't engage if you're going to stick her in jail.' LJ realised she was dangerously close to sounding disrespectful, so she forced herself to take on a less abrasive tone.

'Look at the upside, *sir*. If you bring her onside and benefit from her breakthrough, you haven't lost – you've won. Think of the prize! And if it doesn't work, you can deny it was an official approach. Fire me. Say I'd gone rogue.'

Only a fool or the truly unperceptive could have missed the glint in Allen's eye at this notion of optionality. LJ was neither. She went on, 'But I need your assurance you won't backtrack on this. If Tanner can get Markham to engage with us, I can't have you cutting me off at the knees with some covert shit.' The last word sounded all the dirtier for the fact that LJ had never once uttered an obscenity in the PM's presence before.

'Don't you trust me, LJ?' asked Allen, with a plastic show of amity.

'Of course, sir,' she lied, fixing her boss with a smile of identical sincerity. 'But I have to be able to negotiate with a clear conscience. In good faith.'

'Right, of course.' Allen's manufactured charm now showed signs of returning. 'As you say, what have we got to lose?'

'I have your word?' LJ stood and held out a hand to seal the pledge.

'You have my word.' Allen had no option but to stand and shake on his promise. Only then did LJ look away – to Zack Hardy. *The witness.*

'In that case, sir,' she said, 'I'll get straight on it. Unless there's anything else you need?'

The veneer of warmth fell from the prime minister's face. LJ realised for the first time just how much he had aged over the last four days. He glanced nervously at his watch, another realisation taking precedence over this latest spat.

'No, you deal with Tanner. I've got a speech to write.' Allen's gaze returned to the window, his own reflection. 'At six o'clock, I have to tell my people that they're subject to a military curfew for the first time in our nation's history. I need to somehow find the right words. But for the life of me, I can't think what they are.'

LJ grimaced, then smiled. 'Maybe the truth will have to do then, sir.'

Allen turned to respond, his face taut with fury, but his chief of staff was already heading for the door.

161

BACK AT HIS HOUSE, Tanner was struck by everything LJ had said. Her line of argument at the pub corroborated what he already knew in his heart. Perhaps Holly Brand had always been on the spectrum, maybe she'd had devastating bad luck with her parents' early deaths, but he—*Rob Tanner*—had been instrumental in pushing her over the edge. Another nine years of atonement to add to the thirty-five for Matt.

Still, he'd managed to turn the tide with Harry, so he had faith that redemption was possible. He'd have liked to call his father, let him in on the plan, but it would have to wait. He was waiting for another call instead – from LJ. He didn't have to wait long.

'Allen has agreed to establish the Truth Commission,' she said, as soon as Tanner picked up. 'And he's granting Joen full immunity from prosecution.'

Tanner didn't trust Allen, but he did have faith in LJ. He thanked her, laced himself into his sturdy Timberland boots for the third time that day and set off once more into the near dark. The street was deserted. His neighbours would have seen the same news reports he'd had playing mutely in the background, the evidence of mounting social disorder. Anyone living in a middle-class enclave like his would stay tucked up at home, with the door bolted, if they had an ounce of sense.

While Tanner doubted much trouble would spread to suburbia, there was no point in taking chances. He certainly wouldn't be going into any shops, and his wallet and phone could stay safe at home. All he needed was a debit card, a few well-hidden banknotes, and his trusty pocket notebook, in which he had written three numbers: one each for Joen, Tommy and Chrissie. At the last moment, he had also retrieved a large torch from the understairs cupboard and secreted it in the deep inner pocket of his Moncler trench coat. It would be hopeless as a weapon—not that he'd ever been in a real fight, anyway—but he might need the light. And besides, the weight was comforting.

Tanner began a circuitous trek towards the far side of Ravenscourt Park. An occasional jogger with a good visual memory, he had a fair idea where phone boxes were to be found. Even if the majority were out of order, he was sure he'd find three that worked. Intermittent snow flurries stung his face, but the wind had largely died down, so the effect was strangely refreshing. Stimulating, in fact. Just what he needed.

He got a dial tone with the second phone box he tried, the first having been out of order. From his vantage point among the rusted red iron, he could see clearly in every direction for at least a hundred metres. He was alone; he was sure of it. Now came the moment of truth. Reading from his notebook, even though he knew it by heart, he dialled Joen's number, bringing forth the same series of metallic clicks and bleeps as yesterday. He pictured the call being routed and re-routed through piece after piece of equipment, location after location. There was one final, harsh click, then a bright, female voice.

'Hello, you! I was hoping you would call.'

Tanner took a breath; there would be no second chance if this one failed. 'Joen, it's me.'

'I know.'

'Then listen to me. There are three things I need to tell you. It's important. *Really* important. So please hear me out.'

'Okay,' agreed Joen, after a brief pause. 'Shoot.'

'First, Allen has promised you total immunity from prosecution if you come to the negotiating table.'

'And you think…'

'Joen, listen to me,' insisted Tanner. He looked through the slats of the phone box, but the night beyond was absolute, dark and unspoilt by any living presence.

'I don't trust Allen either,' he went on, speaking quickly and in slightly hushed tones. 'But I do have LJ's word, and that's good enough for me. Between the three of us, we can sort this. Second, I know about Charles the First, and the king's clever wife.' He paused to make sure she got the allusions to Charlemagne—the king associated with Aachen. And Abigail – the clue whose significance he was yet to fully grasp.

'Henrietta?' queried Joen airily. "Well, aren't *you* clever!'

Tanner had no idea who Henrietta was, but he knew Joen, and he could smell a smokescreen. He wasn't mad, and Harry had been right; there was at least some method to Joen's cryptic emails, and he was right about the coordinates and the initials. Joen laughed. 'Sorry, I interrupted again. You said three things.'

Tanner could picture her face, that urge to tease lurking behind every smile. But he ploughed on; he had to. The first two points had been recitals of fact, now it was time to speak from the heart.

'Joen,' Tanner began again, 'I've failed two people in my life, with awful consequences. There's nothing I can do about Matt, but I can make it up to you. I'm not a religious person, so I can't make a pledge on any Bible or relic to make it sound more convincing. But I swear—*on my life*, I swear—I won't let anything bad happen to you. If you can let me help you untangle all this, I promise I'll make up for the past nine years.'

The line fell silent. Joen was mercurial by nature, but even Tanner was surprised by the eventual, tinny response.

'Have you opened your Christmas present?'

'Of course,' he replied. 'I forgot to say thank you.'

'Write this down then,' instructed Joen. 'Ready?' She waited for Tanner's confirmation that he was, then continued, '3, 7, 18, -3, 18, 7, -4, 9, 0, 16. Got it?' She gave Tanner just long enough to confirm that he had before she spoke again. 'That's good, Rob. Very good.' Then a breezy, 'Byeee,' and she hung up.

That was it. No reasoned argument, no passionate outburst – just another string of numbers in an ever-deepening mystery.

Still, Tanner supposed, that was Joen all over. There was nothing to do but follow her directions, for Tanner knew that's what they were. The only question was whether he could remember the exact wording of the slip of paper that had accompanied the Japanese carving, his Christmas present. He knew this obscure gift was about to take on enormous significance; Joen wouldn't have asked if he had opened it otherwise. He wrote the first words that came to mind:

"Masanao *netsuke*. 18th century. *Sansukumi-ken*. Snake and toad."

Tanner wasn't sure about the spelling of the finger game, but if it was wrong—if the message made no sense—he could be home in fifteen minutes to check.

The first in this latest string of numbers was a three. Tanner counted three letters along the text which had accompanied his gift: M, A, S. He supposed the S was the first character he was looking for, and he followed this approach with the other numbers, working backwards from the end for the negative digits.

3 - S
7 - O
18 - H
-3 - O
18 - H
7 - O
-4 - T
9 - E

The penultimate number was a zero, but there was no zero in the carving description. Tanner was sure of it. It had to be a letter missing from the label, and it didn't take Alan Turing to work out this missing letter was an L. So, the first nine numbers corresponded to the words: Soho Hotel, which left a single digit.

16 - 8

The Soho Hotel at eight o'clock. It was a classic book cipher. Unless you had the text, the numbers were meaningless. There was no pattern: 7 and -3 both fell on O, and minus figures were used for numbering from the end. Even if the intelligence agencies had heard every word of Tanner and Joen's conversation, they'd be clueless as to what had come out of it. They had no idea what the gift was, let alone the accompanying description.

Tanner had his answer, then. It was all he could have wished for: a meeting, in person. But at a hotel? Out in the open? It seemed unlikely—mad, even—but all he could do was make sure he wasn't followed there. Which took him neatly onto his second call: Tommy Steele.

Another ten-minute perambulation found him another working phone box a quarter of a mile away.

'Tommy,' he began, 'it's Rob. My car's broken down and I need a taxi for this evening, to pick Judith up from the airport. I thought one of your cabbie pals might fancy a run out to Heathrow?'

He half-expected a guffaw in response to this patent nonsense, but it seemed his friend was as adept at playing the straight man as his more customary wise guy.

'Of course, Rob. What time do you need to head out?'

'About seven-fifteen?' offered Tanner nonchalantly. 'It should take about half an hour if there's no traffic.'

Tommy could do blasé as well as anyone, with a touch of vaudeville worthy of his namesake.

'No problem, sir. I know just the man.'

Mission two accomplished, Tanner set off in search of a third call box. The fresh air, cold as it was, was better than any shot of adrenalin, and fifteen minutes later, he had Chrissie on the line.

162

PROPERTY-BY-PROPERTY, STREET-BY-STREET, Nikki and Gérard had covered, between them, a patchwork of neighbourhoods in the two ancient cities. Den Bosch—*the Forest*—had been founded on wooded dunes in the twelfth century and remained a charming mix of the old and new. Nikki had been content to criss-cross the city's canals and skirt its lakes, but it was all to no avail. Not one of the properties she checked housed a financial terrorist or their cyber-lair. Most of the addresses had reputable, or at least visible, occupants. The few that looked empty, at first sight, had neighbours or other tenants who could vouch for their use. By late afternoon, Nikki's list was exhausted, and there was nothing to do but find a connection back to Brussels.

Her gloom had mounted with each dead end, and the realisation that she had failed now settled ever heavier on her conscience. As a taxi driver whisked her to the station, she called Gérard. They had agreed to speak at five-thirty or to leave an anodyne message about the weather if either had made progress before then. The fact that the Swiss had left no such update indicated he, too, had failed to make a breakthrough.

'Hey you,' she tried to effect jauntiness, but to no effect.

And there was only weary resignation in Gérard's reply. 'You too?' he asked.

Nikki had so wanted to find a lead, to vindicate her partner's theory, but it seemed that on this count, he had been wrong. Secrecy didn't matter now.

'I checked all the leads I could find,' said Nikki. 'Twenty-three of them. But they're all clean. I'm sorry.'

A wry laugh came down the line. 'What on earth are you sorry for? It was my dumb idea.'

'What's the next one?'

'Dinner with a beautiful lady in Brussels. I know a place, although I may need a little luck with reservations. What time is *mam'selle* due in?'

'If I make the connection in Breda, I'll be in Brussels by eight-thirty.' Nikki's voice brightened at the prospect. 'You?'

'There's a direct service from here, so I should only be twenty minutes or so behind you. Let's meet at the station.'

'Okay.'

Gérard couldn't miss the sad lilt in the acknowledgement. He was beginning to understand what Nikki was like, and could imagine her beating herself up all the way back to Brussels.

'Hey,' he said. 'We tried. We can't save the world every day, Superwoman.'

'Superwoman?' offered Nikki with a laugh. 'No way. Give me Batwoman any day. All that cool black leather.' She blew a kiss down the line. 'And, *maybe*, if you play your cards right, you'll get lucky with her tonight, my super *monsieur*!'

Gérard pressed the now silent handset to his lips in invocation. He wasn't one to pray, but maybe, just maybe, he would get doubly lucky. The Swiss had omitted to mention that he had one last lead to follow. He didn't want to raise Nikki's hopes, and on the slim chance that their conversation was being monitored, it was better that any listener thought his race was run.

The last stop on his map of potential sites was a little way out of town, a modern mixed-use complex which appeared to be part of a university campus. He'd left it until the end because it was furthest out.

His taxi pulled up outside a new office building—the science park was full of them—on the ground floor of which stood a cheerfully lit café. The windows were strung with fairy lights, and the place was humming with festive drinkers.

The café occupied half of the frontage beneath a three-storey block. Next to it was a yoga and dance studio, closed for the evening – or maybe for the holidays. Little light, perhaps just the glow of a few forgotten desktop computers, permeated the heavy blinds at the second and third floor windows. There were more obvious signs of life on the first floor, the angle of the blinds offering glimpses of movement here and there.

Entrance to the office lobby required a keypad code or admittance by a receptionist, but no one was sitting at the security desk. Gérard checked his watch: 5.46 p.m. It was hardly surprising; there would be little need for security on a university campus in a place like this, the week after Christmas. Most students would have gone home for the holidays, and locals would be at home readying themselves for New Year's Eve tomorrow. It seemed unlikely this was the place.

A quick stroll around the block revealed nothing of interest. Gérard wished he'd kept the cab's meter running. At least he'd made a note of the taxi firm's number, but now he'd have to go into the café to wait for another car to arrive. Still, there were probably worse places to be stuck waiting than a warm bar. His train wasn't until 7:20 p.m., so there was no rush, and, by God, he felt like a cocktail.

The place, he was surprised to discover, was seriously *cool*. There was no other word for it. The furnishings were a modern take on Art Deco. A long, narrow bar ran along one side, and booth seating upholstered in deep red leather ran down the other. In between were smaller tables for two or four. Every one was full.

Mirrors behind the bar reflected glass and light. It felt like a New York speakeasy, a sensation amplified by the huge black-and-white movie prints which adorned the walls. Gérard wished he had more time now to enjoy the cosy ambience. And that Nikki was with him.

Gérard walked over to the bar. He was soon furnished with the cocktail menu, which turned out to be a thing of beauty. Not just the extensive range of cocktails, but the design of the card itself. As he waited to be served, Gérard took in again the typeface of the café's name—AbIGAIL'S—all in uppercase but for the lowercase 'b.' The logo was an old 1920s candlestick telephone. As he looked along the bar, he saw what might have been the inspiration, an original rotary dial instrument at the end of the counter.

'What can I get you?' asked the bartender.

'A Manhattan, please,' returned the Swiss. 'It seems appropriate!' He pointed at the décor, gesturing his appreciation, 'It's certainly beautifully done up in here.'

The barman nodded acknowledgment. 'We were very lucky.'

'Lucky?'

'It was already done out like this when we took it on.'

Gérard scoffed. 'What? The old occupants left it like this? But this place must be a goldmine!'

The barman shook his head. 'No, we're the first tenants. It was the owner who did this. They own the whole building and wanted a high quality café at its heart. To attract townspeople *and* students. They did a beauty parade for managers, and we won. How lucky is that? Now, let me get you that drink.'

'Wait a second.' Gérard couldn't ignore the tingle at the back of his neck.

'What? Changed your mind?'

'No… sorry.' Gérard picked up a menu to cover his embarrassment. 'It's just… why is the "b" in AbIGAIL'S lower case?'

The bartender had met plenty of nutty customers in his time. Best just to humour them and move on, was his philosophy. This guy was clearly well-off, so maybe today there'd be a decent tip in it.

'We figure it's a joke,' he said. 'On the part of the owner. Maybe something to do with the artwork?'

Gérard looked around, intrigued, but it was hard to see over the heads of his fellow drinkers. 'Why the artwork?'

'Take a look around.' The barman wafted a hand towards the back of the café. 'There are eight photos—stills—from the silent movie era. I thought maybe Abigail's was a play on the actors' names. B for Brooks, G for Garbo, L for Lloyd, that kind of thing, but I can't make the sequence work. Your Manhattan's on the house if you can break the code and tell me all eight!' He raised his eyebrows playfully and escaped to make the cocktail.

Gérard went in search of the eight movie stills. He was seized by a sudden excitement, a fever, which led the usually courteous Swiss to push past other patrons with only the barest of apologies.

The first still was at the end of the bar. It was unmistakeably Greta Garbo, in a passionate clinch with a male actor Gérard didn't recognise. He moved on to the next, in an alcove near the restrooms. The large square image showed a fat man being fed what looked like cake by a young woman perched on his knee at a table laden with food, while a napkinned dog looked on. There was something familiar about the man's piggy, baby-faced features.

The investigator turned to look for the third, then cursed his stupidity. Why on earth wasn't he taking photographs of the posters so he could work out who and what they were while he enjoyed his cocktail? He pulled out his phone and took a photo of the fat man and his dog. Then he pushed his way back to the Garbo print, apologising again, and snapped that too.

Gérard figured he knew as much about the silent movie era as the average person his age—in other words, next to nothing—but was sure this was a famous image. He hated not knowing things; it really bugged him when he couldn't find answers. Crosswords, quizzes, anything. Thank God for mobile phones.

Taking no chances, he double-checked he'd removed the SIM from his phone, then he connected first to the bar's Wi-Fi and then to a VPN. Barely able to contain his excitement, he was finally able to search "Garbo+kiss" and *voilà*, there, among many embraces, was the image. Oblivious to the jolly buzz around him, he clicked through and was taken to a whole page of different versions of the scene: close-ups and crops in landscape and portrait. But none of that mattered. All Gérard saw on the page were four words. *Flesh and the Devil*. The name of the film, clearly. But, oh my God, it was potentially so much more than that. The tingle which had started in his neck was now a throbbing pulse, coursing his entire body.

Time slowed. Lost in a world of his own, Gérard began to catalogue the other images. Oblivious to anyone or anything else in the room, he might have been in a silent movie of his own, a modern-day pilgrim following stations of the cross in search of enlightenment. He found each poster, took a photo, then Googled the image. In his heart, he'd known what was coming as soon as soon as he'd seen the title of the Garbo film, and now each search revealed why. He had soon found seven of the movie stills, but where and what was the eighth?

He saw the bartender looking at him, miming that his cocktail was ready. Gérard fumbled in his wallet for a note to pay for the drink.

'You mentioned eight stills,' the investigator queried. 'I can only find seven.'

'That's because the eighth is in the ladies' room. Go and look – if it's free!' he cautioned with a laugh. 'Oh, and if you're interested in silent movies, there's a movie poster in the men's.'

Desperate for the answer, Gérard forced himself not to run the short distance to the washrooms. He was besieged by the images; links were swirling in his mind. What could be more lustful than Garbo's kiss, and the gluttony of the fat man was unmissable. And the name, AbIGAIL'S, with each of the capitals standing for one of the sins, from Acedia to Superbia, and each sin represented by a movie still!

The mystery yielded further ground in the ladies' room. There Gérard found the final still and, a pleasant surprise, this was one he recognised immediately. It was Douglas Fairbanks, the first of many famous actors to play the dashing masked vigilante *Zorro*, in full swashbuckling glory. Gérard wondered if that was another punchline in this increasingly elaborate, intricate joke, but if it was, he didn't get it. *Zorro* obviously sounded like zero, which was precisely where all the affected bank accounts were heading, but by JvA's exacting standards it seemed a clumsy link.

Gérard dashed now to the men's room, much more familiar territory. The poster—the final clue—was in plain sight. The vintage artwork depicted a seemingly naked lady. She was kneeling, her modesty covered by an outsized book, with a block of German text beneath, *Tagebuch einer Verlorenen. Diary of a Lost Girl*. Gérard shook his head in amazement. It was the final piece of the puzzle, the final confirmation that he was on the right track… the track of the lost girl behind the cyber-attacks. In that moment, Gérard's whole world concertina'd to the size of the film poster. This discovery, the café hiding in plain sight, seemed like an impossible stroke of fortune, but he knew it wasn't chance that had brought him here.

He was still shaking his head in disbelief as he returned to the bar.

'You didn't work it out then?' asked the barman. He took Gérard's silence for an answer, then watched dumbfounded as the customer drained the untouched cocktail in one draught, added a fifty euro note to the change waiting on the counter and turned on his heels without a further word.

His first instinct had been right. Just another nutter.

163

KELLETT WAS BAFFLED by the resilience of his PA. No matter how much scorn he heaped on her, she met it at every turn with an implacable Mona Lisa smile. Yesterday, she'd looked on the verge of slitting her wrists, but from the way she was going about today, you'd think she had won the lottery. He knew she'd seen the latest Markham email, but surely that couldn't explain it?

No matter, thought Kellett. She'd be gone by the end of the week. Markham as well, with any luck. Even Allen and his merry men, useless as they were, had to catch a break at some point.

The brooding CEO chewed over these thoughts as he stood at his window. They were saying there would be more snow later. They were saying, also, that the rumours about martial law might yet turn out to be more than just idle paper talk.

It occurred to Kellett that it might be wise to get home in time for the prime minister's 6 p.m. address to the nation. He buzzed though to his PA.

'Get hold of Tommy Steele, I want him to take me home and then be on standby this evening. Do it now.'

Chrissie came back on the intercom a few minutes later. 'He's not picking up,' she said. 'I'll keep trying.'

'Make sure you fucking do.'

At least that made Kellett's decision for him. He supposed it made no real difference if he watched Allen here or in Marylebone. He spent the time coming up with a mental 'Bastards List'—all the people owed a screwing in the New Year—with his Zermatt procurer in pole position. If Ziegler had somehow acquired compromising material, and if he really had leaked it to Markham, of all people, then the pimp would be owed one hell of a comeuppance. Kellett vowed to make sure it reached him. Suitably revived by these dark thoughts, vengeance surging like adrenaline in his blood, he poured himself a whisky and settled down to see what the PM had to say.

At six on the dot, a sombre, besuited James Allen appeared on screen. He wasn't on the steps of Downing Street today. This time, he was speaking directly from a lectern in front of a fireplace inside Number Ten. The grey and white backdrop of the Carrara marble served only to highlight the darkness of Allen's suit and tie; if they weren't a funereal black, they might as well have been.

There was no preface. Allen simply took a long, deep breath and began to speak.

'Good evening.

'We live in extraordinary times. In recent years, we have learned what it means to have our very way of life threatened. The coronavirus pandemic upended normal life and had us wondering whether we would ever reclaim what we had lost. We now face a different threat of a potentially even greater magnitude.

'The cyber-attacks of the past few days are an assault on every member of our society. They pose a more serious risk to this country's economy than anything we've seen in any of our lifetimes. We know the identity of the lead perpetrator. The full resources of our intelligence and law enforcement services are currently engaged in their capture. They will not escape justice; they can expect to face the full weight of the law.

'The pandemic was a direct threat to our physical wellbeing. These cyber-attacks, desperate as they are, pose no such inherent, certain danger. We must not let them frighten us into chaos and disorder. The overwhelming majority of you recognise that and have gone about your daily business as normal. I thank you for that.

'However, a small but sizeable minority have chosen to use this situation as a pretext for anti-social behaviour, for lawlessness. For criminal activity. There is no excuse for vandalism, theft or thuggery. Let me repeat: the minority engaged in those acts will be held accountable. We will identify everyone who has broken the law, and they can expect neither sympathy nor lenience.

'I cannot, however, let the actions of the few undermine the safety and security of the many. When the activities of an irresponsible few begin to hurt millions of law-abiding people, I must act. Therefore, I have this afternoon taken action under the Emergency Powers legislation to ban all gatherings, and all but essential movement, across the country from eight o'clock this evening. Only those moving to and from work may leave their homes until eight o'clock tomorrow morning.

'I will make no bones about this: it is a curfew. The actions of a trouble-making minority have forced me to introduce this measure, and I do so with the greatest regret. Anyone leaving their home during the hours of curfew must carry with them both a means of formal identification and an attestation document giving the reason for travel. Any person breaking curfew without this document and without good reason will be subject to an immediate fine of two hundred pounds. These fines will double with each subsequent offence. Anyone gathering in groups of two or more will be liable to immediate arrest.

'I have instructed the relevant ministers to take all necessary steps to ensure the curfew is applied and enforced throughout the land. To that end, I have today given orders for members of the armed forces to be sworn in as special constables in order to support our police services wherever the need arises. I do this with the heaviest of hearts. To introduce troops to the streets of this great country is a step beyond any of our worst imaginings, but our brave soldiers have been drafted in for one purpose: to protect you. We will not be cowed by criminals and hooligans.

'My greatest predecessor, Winston Churchill, in the darkest hour when our nation's very existence was threatened, urged his countrymen to do their duty and to conduct themselves in a way that would make future generations proud. I now ask each one of you, in this dark moment, to emulate those forebears who rose to the challenge in difficult times—our parents, grandparents and great-grandparents—and to behave in a way that would make them proud.

'I also would like to use this address to remind you that it often appears darkest just before dawn. Wrongdoers will fail and the forces of good will prevail, as surely as thaw follows snow. Together we will come through stronger as individuals and as a nation.

'Thank you, and good evening.'

The camera panned slowly to a close-up of the PM's face before the screen faded to black. With the fade, Kellett let out the breath that had been building inexorably within him. Around the country, most of his fellow viewers did the same.

A military curfew. Troops on the streets. In the UK! Was Allen declaring martial law, after all? Whatever it was, Kellett wanted to get home before any trouble started. He bellowed through to Chrissie.

'Christina! Get Steele; I'm going home.'

'I'm sorry, Martin, but he's still not picking up.' She didn't let it show in her voice, but she took absurd satisfaction from this small denial.

'Well, get me a cab, then find out where the fuck he is. That's what the tracking software is for, so use it!'

Kellett, convinced that Steele was favouring the chairman, or other colleagues, or skiving—he didn't care which—had recently insisted Tommy's car be fitted with a tracking device. Tommy had bridled at the imposition, but it wasn't a choice. He'd rather enjoyed the fact that Kellett had never been able to catch him out, no matter how often he tried.

Now, Chrissie hoped that Kellett would find something new to distract him; she dared to imagine he might forget about Tommy by the time he was heading out of the building and making a dash for home. She kept her eyes resolutely glued to her desk, exchanging neither word nor glance as the Toad waddled towards the lift. She heard the lift bell ring, but just as the doors opened, his voice barked bitterly into the silence.

'Find out what Steele's up to, Christina, or you'll regret it. You've got an hour.'

164

JOEN WENT THROUGH ONE FINAL CHECK. The main entrance to her flat was on Dean Street, at the corner of Richmond Buildings. It was a cul-de-sac which you'd only enter if you were going to the Soho Hotel at its mid-point, where the street name mutated effortlessly into a Mews with the same prefix – as so many of London's ancient backstreets do. Unknown to anyone but the builder who had made the final inter-connection, there was also a second access point. Twenty metres down Richmond Buildings stood an incongruous single-storey building currently housing an arts and crafts shop. Next to its brightly coloured entrance was a drab second doorway that appeared to go nowhere and was certainly never used. Which was strange, given that the whole surrounding area was covered by a dusty but very much state-of-the-art surveillance camera high above the two doors.

Joen had bought the freehold to the shop and the small warehouse it abutted four years ago and, from an external perspective, had left it untouched. But internally she had made a significant change, carving out a corridor to the small yard behind the Dean Street building. Hence the second door. But even if you managed to get though that entrance—past the hidden, electronic locks—there was nothing to see; the ground space at the rear was empty.

Not so the airspace above. On the back of the main building, Joen had added an American-style fire escape with pull-down ladders. A particularly observant viewer might have noticed that the ladders did not actually serve any access points on the first or second floors, but in the jumbled mix of structures and extensions, all of which had varying roof heights, there was no clear sightline to confirm it. Not that anyone was interested in this shabby exterior amongst the plush renovations and colourful roof furniture of Soho's private members' clubs.

The security consultants who had installed the locks and CCTV had no link to the builder who had created the corridor, who in turn had no knowledge of the fire escape. And so on, up to the final contractor who had crafted an escape hatch onto the dirty-grey ladders. Joen had tested them in the middle of the heaviest recent snowstorm. All was as it should be.

Thus, when Joen wanted to enter or leave the flat she had two options: front and rear. From the back door, it was a distance of some ten car lengths to the Soho Hotel. From the front, only six or seven more. Fifty-three or eighty-eight metres. She had counted.

Joen knew there was no chance that her communications with Tanner could be traced to this location. She had put in place too many re-routes and cut-outs, and the messages were too short. The security cameras trained on Dean Street and Richmond Buildings gave her a clear view of all movement on those roads, and she'd be able to spot any unusual activity immediately.

Which just left Tanner. Would he give away the whereabouts of their meeting? She doubted it. More than that, she desperately wanted to believe that he wouldn't. That his promise was good. But she had to assume their meeting would be compromised somehow.

She glanced around the flat for probably the last time, a wry smile pulling at the worry lines on her face. Even if—more likely *when*—the police found this flat, there was nothing that would lead them to her other properties. They would find a single book, a TV, a monitor for the CCTV cameras and a satellite dish at the end of a long line of encrypted circuit breakers. Joen would carry her laptop—which had its own very special security measures—but it was only a portal, many times removed from her main system. Even if they found that, it was only the first entry point into a digital labyrinth of which she was the sole architect.

Joen guessed they'd be able to crack her system in a couple of days once they were in her bunker, maybe twenty-four hours, if they were lucky. But it was irrelevant. If she didn't log in regularly, fail-safe measures would kick in automatically, pre-programmed commands would be initiated and, well, that would be that. If she was apprehended, the same rules applied. She figured she held most, if not all, the cards, but her lifelong motto was still ringing in her memory. Hope for the best and prepare for the worst – a mantra which had served her well, thus far.

Joen looked at the clock on the CCTV monitor: 19:07. It was time for another, final, costume change, and then she would be reunited with Tanner.

165

TOMMY STEELE COLLECTED TANNER at 7:15 p.m. Snow continued to fall, but the wind had relented, so it was a gentle confetti of flakes that filled the night air. The city was draped, once again, in white, and the bootprints of earlier demonstrators, looters, and panic-buyers were slowly filling in. Nothing stirred in the still, pristine coldness. The streets were empty as Londoners surrendered to the orders of the prime minister and the whims of the weather gods. It was as if the world had been put to sleep under a spell of snow.

To Tommy's surprise, Tanner chose to sit in the front passenger seat rather than in the back of the limousine, offering the reason before the question was asked.

'Need your eyes on the road in these conditions, Thrup,' the passenger explained. 'Not looking at me in the rear-view mirror.'

Tommy would have taken umbrage were it not for the broad grin creasing Tanner's face.

'Cheeky sod,' Tommy laughed, relieved to see the spark in his old friend's features. 'I've been driving since you were in nappies, and I haven't had an accident yet.'

'I know, Tommy.'

'So, what's the plan?'

Tanner leaned in close to the driver, his voice barely a whisper. 'I take it you've guessed who I'm meeting?'

A stage wink from Tommy answered succinctly. He'd known something was up from Tanner's phone call, and it didn't take a genius to work out what.

'I have the prime minister's permission to offer her a deal,' continued Tanner. His voice was grave, betraying his reservations.

'What's the problem?'

'I don't trust him.'

'So what? You need a getaway driver?' Tommy affected a stage mockney accent. 'A transporter.'

'You might say that.' Tanner laughed. 'I couldn't possibly comment.'

'What's the plan, then?'

'I haven't got that far yet.' Tanner pulled the notebook from his pocket and passed it underhand to Tommy. 'All I do know is that I have to be at the Café Royal at eight.'

Tanner's knowledge of government surveillance ran to whichever espionage movie he'd last seen. He had no idea, therefore, if spy satellites were recording their conversation as he spoke, but why take the chance? It was at least worth a try, throwing off any potential listeners with some nonsense about the Café Royal. He babbled on about Regent Street and Piccadilly Circus while Tommy read the directions Tanner had written on the pad:

- Meeting Ashley Markham at the Soho Hotel
- Need to get her away from there ASAP
- You wait on Dean Street
- We'll be gone in a couple of minutes
- Then > the bank's flat @ St Katharine Dock

Tanner watched the driver's reaction as he read, following the downward trace of his finger. None of it fazed Tommy until the last entry.

He turned to Tanner and mouthed, 'You're kidding?'

In response, Tanner flipped the page. On the next he'd written:

- Think about it
- It's the last place anyone would look
- No one's using it. It's empty
- I checked with Chrissie!

Tommy offered him a look of pure admiration. Then, instructions received, the driver turned to more prosaic matters.

'And what if we get stopped on the way? There's a curfew, remember.'

Tanner pulled a piece of paper from his inside pocket with a theatrical flourish. 'An authority to travel from the prime minister's office, no less.'

'How on earth…'

Tanner cut him short by tapping the clock in the centre of the walnut fascia. 'Let's get going, and I'll explain.'

The idea had come to him as he was sitting at home that afternoon, watching the relentless ticking of minutes on his kitchen clock. He had no idea if he could persuade Joen to row back from the course on which she was engaged, but he was damn sure he'd need time to try. Possibly a lot of time. And a safe location. That was when he remembered the bank's executive apartment on the edge of St Katharine Dock, the marina development beside Tower Bridge, in the heart of London. The flat was kept for the use of directors or visiting clients and dignitaries, and with its panoramic views over the Thames, it was usually booked for months ahead. But not, as a matter of policy, over Christmas and New Year. Unless the chairman or CEO wanted it, of course. The cherry on top was that Chrissie managed the bookings.

Tanner had called her from the park, expecting that she'd be full of questions and chat, anticipating having to shut her up, but instead she was monosyllabic, clearly preoccupied. Maybe Kellett was watching over her. He gave her the number of a fourth phone box he'd checked *en route* and asked her to call him from an outside line, but when she did return the call ten minutes later, she was no more engaged. He'd prepared an alibi, a pretext for needing to use the flat, involving getting away from fictional journalists camped outside his house, but she'd shown not the slightest interest. She'd merely confirmed the apartment was vacant but had seemed so incurious that his swearing her to secrecy over his plans to use it had seemed wholly unnecessary.

Then, back in the warmth of his kitchen, he'd used his old phone to send LJ a five-word text:

✉ Contact made. Send travel authorisation.

Within minutes, he received a pdf file and the words, 'Good luck.'

The message also had full contact details for the prime minister's personal security detail in case of emergency. Tanner prayed they wouldn't be needed this evening, but the authorisation was required almost immediately. As the Merc reached the end of the Westway, at the start of the Marylebone Road, Tanner saw that the two outer lanes were coned off, funnelling traffic into a police checkpoint. Moreover, he was shocked to see an army truck a further twenty metres down the road, cigarette butts glowing from an obviously full contingent of troops sheltering inside.

'Never thought I'd see that in this country,' offered Tommy.

'Me neither,' sighed Tanner. 'Strange world.'

There were only two cars ahead of them in the queue, and both were only allowed to proceed after prolonged discussions and demands for documentation. Then it was their turn. Tommy inched the car forward and lowered his window, which was soon filled by a burly police sergeant. The copper was clearly not enjoying this spell of wintry traffic duty.

'May I ask your business, sir?' he asked, with officious, feigned deference. 'You do know there's a curfew from eight?'

Forewarned by the checks on the preceding vehicles, Tanner was ready. He'd always harboured a particular dislike for jobsworths, and he was sorely tempted to have a little fun at the officer's expense. Instead, he leaned across Tommy and looked up into the policeman's face with a plastic imitation of a smile.

'Yes, thank you, Sergeant. We're on government business, you'll be glad to know.' He thrust the form forward. 'I believe you'll find this documentation will provide all necessary confirmation.'

Clearly peeved, the policeman began a slow, line-by-line appraisal of the form under the beam of a high-intensity flashlight.

'If there's a problem, Sergeant, please feel free to call Number Ten.' Tanner emphasised the next two words, '*Downing Street*, that is. Or perhaps you'd like me to?'

Bluff called; the officer gave the car a final blinding sweep of illumination before fixing his gaze on Tanner.

'No, sir,' he said. 'That won't be necessary. Have a safe journey.'

The car was waved off, but in the rear-view mirror Tommy saw the policeman making an entry in his notebook.

They drove the rest of the way in silence, neither wanting to intrude on the other's thoughts. That there was little other traffic and hardly a living soul on Harley Street wasn't a huge surprise—it was often deserted in the evening—but the emptiness of Regent Street was astonishing. Even in the dead of the quietest night there would normally be a solitary bus or taxi winding its way home. But tonight, there were no vehicles at all, and not even a handful of pedestrians. It was quieter, even, than it had been at the height of the pandemic. The scene was all the more extraordinary because Christmas lights still shone the entire length of the street, a grand, sweeping canopy of luminescence reflecting in the windows and dappling the white thoroughfare. A festive stage hushed in anticipation, waiting for guests who might never arrive.

Perhaps it was a subliminal stimulus—perhaps that first memory of Joen framed by the lights of the Lanesborough tree—or more conscious awareness of their location, but Tanner realised with a start that they were nearly at their rendezvous.

'How long, Tommy?'

The driver held up five fingers, adding, 'Depends where there is to park… and if we get stopped again.'

They were.

After the tranquillity of Regent Street, Piccadilly Circus was a hive of olive-clad activity. Teams of soldiers were unloading portable barriers and crates of equipment from a convoy of trucks parked all the way down to the Mall. Again, Tommy was flagged down, but this time it was by a rather more cheerful young policeman who seemed pleased to have something to do amidst the bustle.

Pleasantries were exchanged and papers checked, and the youngster was about to wave them on their way when he dipped his head back into the car.

'Just a word of advice, sir. Once it gets to eight o'clock, we've strict instructions to stop and search every person, every vehicle. "*To send a message,*" we were told. You should expect delays up ahead.'

Tanner brushed aside the young man's embarrassment with cheerful good humour. 'Thanks, Constable, I'll ensure the PM gets the message.'

But his guts were churning. As soon as they were out of sight, he asked Tommy to pull over.

'Hell, Tommy, what are we going do we do?' he half-mouthed, half-whispered. 'We're bound to be stopped on the way to the docks. Someone is sure to recognise Joen; her face has been all over the news for days.'

Tommy gave himself a moment to think, tapping the steering wheel in silent metronomy, weighing up the options. Then a smile began to spread over his craggy features. He leaned forward to turn the radio to deafening full volume, simultaneously indicating for Tanner to step out of the vehicle and follow. Only when they were a good ten metres away did Tommy huddle close enough to whisper in his ear.

'The way I see it, Six, it's just like my old days as a cabbie. It's why we did the Knowledge. When the main roads were blocked with traffic, you had to duck and dive round the backstreets.'

Tanner doubted anyone knew London's streets better than his friend. 'So?'

'So, I know I can get from Dean Street to the Embankment beyond Temple using only side roads. From there, it's a straight run through to Tower Bridge. My guess is that's where there'll be a major roadblock. As you say, we're bound to be stopped. If we're unlucky, we may get stopped once before that, but with your pass we'll get them to call ahead and say you've been checked already.' Tommy paused, evidently pleased with himself.

'And that solves our problem, how?'

'Because it means less time for your lady friend to be in the boot.'

'What?'

'You heard the copper, Six. We *will* get pulled over. Your travel pass can't stop that. It isn't going to prevent any officious plod from checking you. They'll check me too – and anyone else in the vehicle.' Tommy turned to eyeball Tanner. 'Now, I've no idea how Miss Markham's ID documents stack up, but I don't think we want to take that risk, do we?'

'No,' Tanner had to agree. 'You're right.'

'Now,' the driver went on, 'We may well get a twat like that first copper, but he'd have to be fucking ballsy to insist on checking our boot, given we're an aide to the prime minister and his driver on their way home from Downing Street.'

'We are?'

'Of course we are!'

Tanner could only marvel at his friend's audacity. 'Brave call, Thrup.'

'Just playing the odds, Six, like my old man taught me. And anyway, I've got the easy job… you've got the hard bit.'

'I have?' asked Tanner, mystified.

'You have!' Tommy laughed, despite the gravity of the situation. 'You're the one who's got to persuade the lovely Miss Markham to do as she's told, for once.'

166

NIKKI KNEW, JUST FROM LOOKING AT HIM, that Gérard hadn't told her everything.

He had found her on the Brussels station concourse, calmly studying a tourist map of the city with a bulging shopping bag in her hand, seemingly without a care in the world. He was struck by how a woman could look so beautiful and so mischievous all at once. And she, in turn, was struck by how easily she could read him, how this once-inscrutable character had opened himself up to her so completely that she could tell he was harbouring a secret before he had even opened his mouth.

'Kiss me,' she said, pulling him close, before whispering, 'And then perhaps you'll tell me what the hell's going on.'

Gérard carried out the first of her instructions with the greatest of pleasure, then persuaded her by dumb show to hand over her mobile phone. Which she did unquestioningly, regarding him silently as he extricated the SIM card, before shooting him a wink of exquisite self-satisfaction.

They did not exchange a single word as he led her to the Eurostar terminal or through the whole process of boarding. Only when they were seated in an almost empty first-class compartment, and they had been served complimentary glasses of Champagne was the silence broken. And finally, the Cheshire cat smile dropped from Nikki's face.

'Am I that obvious?' Gérard asked. 'Was it so clear that I had something up my sleeve?'

Nikki leant forward and kissed him softly, a long, slow, featherweight meeting of lips in which every pulse in their bodies willingly converged. Then, with her small features alight, she sat back.

'Luckily, only to me. Now, spill the beans.'

They ate a surprisingly good dinner, washed down with a delightfully smooth Pinot Noir, while he did exactly that. He'd done some research during the journey from Aachen, utilising the train's predictably efficient Wi-Fi and the VPN. He'd found each of the films represented by the stills, discovering the names of the actors he didn't know and the storylines behind the movies. He had also organised his photos, the blown-up stills amid the sparkling interior of AbIGAIL'S, into the correct order, and now he held his phone to Nikki, offering a running commentary as he presented each one in turn: Harold Lloyd hanging from a clockface high on a skyscraper; a man staring enviously at a New York skyline; Fatty Arbuckle with the mountain of food; Buster Keaton in an early heist movie; a sultry Valentino in *The Four Horsemen of the Apocalypse*; Garbo and Gilbert in the passionate clinch; and, finally, Gloria Swanson captivated by her younger self in *Sunset Boulevard*.

'So, you see,' gushed Gérard. 'AbIGAILS is the name of the establishment, and we've got Acedia, Invidia, Gula, Avaricia, Ira, Luxuria and Superbia. The initials of the seven sins almost spell out the name, and each is represented in one of these movie stills!'

Clever as it was, Nikki couldn't help but be slightly disappointed at the pay-off.

'But where's the B?' she asked.

Gérard said nothing but simply gestured towards the phone, indicating that Nikki should swipe right. One of the most famous images of the entire silent era slid into view: a masked Douglas Fairbanks in his most iconic, most swashbuckling role. The first movie superhero.

'*The Mask of Zorro!*' Nikki exclaimed happily, then frowned, disappointed. 'I don't get it?'

In contrast, Gérard looked even more pleased with himself.

'That's what I thought,' he answered. 'But actually, the early versions were called The *Mark* of Zorro. Or maybe we should say *zero*?'

Nikki was lost for words, but Gérard had one more surprise for her.

'There's more. That was in the ladies' room. *This* was in the men's.' He swiped to his shot of the stylised movie poster.

Nikki would have recognised Louise Brooks' ultra-cool Jazz Age bob anywhere; she'd once tried one herself. Once. And the star's name was on the poster, but the rest of the text was German. Gérard provided the explanation.

'It's the second of her collaborations with Pabst after *Pandora's Box*.' He waited until she lifted her eyes from the display, wanting her full attention. '*Diary of a Lost Girl*. And who are we dealing with here if not a lost girl?'

'You're kidding?'

A vigorous shake of the head told her he most definitely wasn't.

'So, is the missing B for Brooks?' asked Nikki. 'Or B for Brand?'

'Who knows?' replied Gérard. 'Does it matter?' His eyes took on a faraway look. 'Nikki, finding them was so surreal. It was as if the world stopped around me. I so wanted you to be there, to share it.' Embarrassment creased his face. 'I know we're doing something important here, and I know it's the premises we're looking for. The offices above AbIGAIL'S are clearly what matters, where Brand's been hiding herself all this time, but it's *such* a lovely bar. In that moment, when I was tearing around, taking photos of those stills, I just wanted to make time stand still, have a few drinks, enjoy the artwork and forget all the madness. Promise you'll go with me one day?'

She reached forward and kissed him again. 'I promise.' She gave his wrist a gentle squeeze. 'Don't worry, you old romantic, there will be lots of time for that. But first, what's the plan? I know you've got one.'

167

MARTIN KELLETT WAS AN AWFUL DRIVER. He figured cars were like dogs in that they somehow knew if you didn't like them and always misbehaved accordingly. He'd never understood what deficiency prompted people to love cars so much and to fetishize, of all things, a means of getting from A to B. Still, Kellett had always kept a car—an electric vehicle scarcely big enough for him—'just in case.' And this was that case. He'd tried to get an Uber, a black cab, even a limo, but no one was picking up passengers this late after the prime minister's warning. And he had to get to St Katharine Docks in a hurry. A real hurry. Which was how he came to be behind the wheel himself, traversing the five snowy miles to Docklands with as much confidence as he would have exhibited on the slopes of Zermatt. That is to say: none.

As soon as he had got home and poured himself a drink, he'd logged in to National Bank's new vehicle tracking software. He could see that Tommy Steele was driving into the centre of London from the west and had tried to call him, but the bastard's phone was off. Kellett left an expletive-ridden message demanding an immediate response, but none came. Kellett swore Steele would be sorry, but he'd had to make do with taking it out on the PA.

'Why the fuck haven't you called me back?' Kellett had asked.

'I'm sorry, Martin, but I haven't got hold of Tommy yet.' There was an unmistakeable edge of desperation to Chrissie's voice. 'His phone's off. What would you like me to do?'

'I want you to find out where he's going, of course.'

Chrissie erupted with a mix of anguish and frustration. 'I'm not a mind-reader, Martin!'

'Well then…' Momentarily thrown off balance, Kellett groped for the upper hand. 'Where the fuck has he *been*? Look at the bloody tracker and tell me what you know about this.'

'Oh, for heaven's sake,' she huffed, not bothering to hide her exasperation. Kellett heard the faint noise of a keyboard being tapped and silence as the software loaded. Then a scarcely audible, 'Oh, shit.'

'Care to share, Christina?' Kellett prompted lightly.

'What?'

'Stop fucking about and tell me what's going on.'

Christina took a deep breath, weighing her decision, her loyalties. The debt—the threat—to her parents took precedence over anything else in her life. Whatever Rob or Tommy had got themselves into was of their own volition. As her father had always drummed into her: choices and consequences. So now she made hers; she *chose* to tell, her voice bereft of emotion.

'The tracker shows Tommy stopped at Rob Tanner's house.'

Kellett's excitement was palpable, like a hound catching the first faint whiff of the fox.

'So I saw. And why might he have stopped at Tanner's?'

'Maybe he's taking him somewhere?'

'What do you know, Christina?'

'Me, Martin? What could *I* possibly know?'

There was no pretence at artifice or subtlety; Chrissie's challenge was clear. Kellett took the bait as she had expected.

'Don't mess with me, Christina. Remember what *I* know.'

'Yes, Martin,' she replied, 'I'm fully aware of what *you* know. But *you* don't know what *I* know. So, the question is, how much is that knowledge worth?'

'I'm warning you, Christina.'

'Yes, yes, Martin.' Chrissie sighed. 'I get it. You'll spill the beans about my *abortion*.' There, it was said. The horrid, hateful word that had cowed and tormented her for so long. But now Christina confronted it, giving it real form in the shape of Martin Kellett. She faced down the two horrors as one, willing herself to stay strong, as she revealed her hand.

'I'm sure you'll get a hard-on sticking it to me. But not as much as you'd like to stick it to Tommy and Rob and—well—who knows *who else*?' She poured every scrap of meaning into those last two words, picturing the bloodhound beginning to slobber at the other end of the phone.

'Who?' asked Kellett.

Chrissie remained silent.

Then the revelation struck, and Kellett's tone changed to one of pure ecstasy.

'Oh my God! Not Markham?'

Chrissie knew now that she held all the cards. Dare she raise the stakes? She chose her words carefully.

'I can't promise *who*, Martin, but I can absolutely guarantee *where*.'

She need not have worried. Kellett was transported by desire. 'Where?' he moaned pathetically. 'I need to know.'

'Yes, Martin, I know. But there's something I need first. A release. From you. From the bank. From your threats. A full and final release.'

'Okay, fine. Whatever. I told you already. We're done.'

Chrissie's guffaw must have been heard the length and breadth of the City. 'You really think I'm going to take you at your word, Martin?'

'But…'

'No. I'm going to send you a couple of documents to sign. And when you've returned them—like the good secretary I am—I'm going to send you the travel attestation form, all nicely filled in, for the journey you'll soon be making. It's not far.'

'Where, though?'

Chrissie tutted, as if chastising a small child. 'All in good time, Martin. All in good time.'

She composed herself and quickly typed not one but two documents. The first was a letter from Kellett to Head of HR Ollie Lawrence, confirming that Chrissie would be leaving the bank's employment on 31st December and that she was to be paid a year's salary in lieu of notice. The second was a personal letter from Kellett, addressed to her, acknowledging that he had paid for Christina's termination on 17 June 2008—she knew the date by heart—and that he agreed never to mention the matter again. It had no real legal value, but she very much doubted he would want her releasing it to one of Pattie's media chums. Two could play at blackmail. Finally, she downloaded a blank travel permit and filled in the required information.

Only when the first two letters had been signed and returned did Christina send Kellett the travel form. She pictured his expression when he learned that Tanner was heading for the bank's own apartment in St Katharine Docks: an ecstasy of elation and expectation inflamed with indignation. She forced herself to cast such fancies aside and turned to the more prosaic matter of warning Tommy that she had had no choice but to betray his intentions, but his phone remained resolutely switched off.

It was unheard of for the driver to be out of contact, but all she could do was leave voice and text messages, stressing the urgency of calling her back, and keep trying. But what if he didn't switch back on? Well, she had good legs and suitably fine boots, for heaven's sake. She hurriedly forwarded the first letter to Lawrence and the second to her home email. She filled in a travel attestation in her own name. Then, suitably dressed, she headed for the destination on the form without a single backwards glance.

To St Katharine Docks.

168

AFTER HIS SPEECH TO THE NATION, James Allen sped with his security detail through the maze of underground tunnels to the principal secure COBRA conference room under 70 Whitehall. This was the UK's equivalent of the White House Situation Room. No one could recall its original name, nor was it certain who had coined the sobriquet "Room 68," by which it was now known. Regardless, the label had stuck for the subterranean chamber two levels below number seventy.

Twelve 98" television monitors lined the far wall, while each of the side walls held two even larger screens. The conference table at the centre seated sixteen, with space behind for myriad advisers and minions. Filtration units kept the air pure at a constant 23 degrees, and the latest security-proofing prevented any sound entering or leaving.

The facility was manned by a permanent staff hand-picked from the intelligence services, operating round-the-clock in six-hour shifts. There were dedicated liaison officers for all the main agencies of state, a team of analysts to handle secure communications and data feeds, and a group of technicians to operate the panoply of audio-visual devices. Refined over two decades, this was the command hub for the rapid, coordinated response to any major crisis.

As he entered, Allen recognised the duty commanding officer: Vivienne Claydon. A major from Army intelligence, Claydon was a lean, hard-faced woman who you'd be well advised to avoid in a fight. She was the walking, minimally talking, embodiment of 'calm in a crisis,' and the briefest handshake was enough to imbue Allen with renewed confidence. He was glad she would be joining him at the helm.

'What have we got, Major?' he inquired, gesturing to the silent black-and-white video feeds playing across the bank of TV screens.

'CCTV of the major city centres, sir.'

Allen hardly dared ask the question but ask he did. 'Trouble?'

'There's been plenty, sir, I'm afraid.' The gloomy look on Allen's face would have stopped many in their tracks, but the Major continued in the same even tone.

'Yorkshire and Humberside were particularly… troublesome. Then the North-West and the West Midlands. Cardiff. Glasgow, Bristol.'

Allen pointed at the images of deserted streets. 'But they're all quiet?'

'Exactly, Prime Minister. I did say they *were* troublesome. The arrival of units from the Catterick garrison soon had Yorkshire and the North East quiet. Ditto the Marines in the west. A couple of squadrons of Gurkhas happened to be at Stafford, so we soon got those into Birmingham, Coventry and Stoke.' There was the faintest hint of a rise at the corners of the major's usually tight lips, quickly suppressed. 'I don't think your average opportunistic troublemaker wants to mess with them – particularly in this weather. A bit of snow doesn't mean much to a Gurkha, sir.'

Allen scoffed. 'Quite.' He looked up to the bank of monitors, his personal panopticon of all the nation's major cities. 'Nothing imprudent, I hope?'

'Absolutely not, sir. Necessity. Humanity. Proportionality.' Claydon reeled off the mantra of military engagement Allen had heard many times before.

LJ, meanwhile, had been listening dutifully to this exchange. Now she spoke up for the first time.

'I don't want to labour the point, Major, but you're sure there haven't been any public relations "*incidents*" we need to deal with?' She inverted the word "incidents" with her fingers to cover any number of sins, real or imagined, that could become a kiss of death on social media.

'All officers in charge have been given very strict orders to proceed with extreme caution,' replied Claydon. She indicated the team of head-phoned analysts secreted behind a glass partition. 'So far, there's nothing at all on any of the social media sites.'

'So, the show of force is working?' Allen's stomach eased a notch, and the tightness in his chest dissipated, just a fraction.

'So far, sir,' agreed Claydon.

'Well done, Major, well done.'

The tiniest flicker in Claydon's eyes betrayed her satisfaction. Now she turned back to the bank of technicians and clicked her fingers. At her signal, the picture on the screens changed. Now all ten screens combined to form a single display of what appeared to be a roadblock and security check.

'This was the Marylebone Road twenty minutes ago, sir.'

The left half of the wall of monitors changed again, revealing a map of West and Central London, with a dotted red line indicating a trail from Hammersmith to a point in the heart of the West End. LJ's mouth hung open, but a sharp look from Allen forestalled any comment. He motioned for the major to continue.

Claydon indicated the left-hand portion of the wall. 'We've been monitoring

Robert Tanner, as per your orders. As you can see, sir, Tanner was picked up from his home address by National Bank's driver, Tommy Steele, at nineteen-fifteen. They drove eastwards on the Westway and were stopped at a first checkpoint fifteen minutes later, as you see here.' She raised her hand again, and a staccato slideshow of CCTV images began as she resumed her commentary. 'From Marylebone Road, they cut south down Harley and then Regent Street.'

The video scroll on the right paused, revealing the car at another checkpoint. The statue of Eros stood in the foreground.

'This was them eight minutes ago, sir, being stopped at another blockade in Piccadilly Circus.' No questions followed, so an unseen hand moved the feed forward another scene. 'Then they stopped for a couple of minutes. Here.' Claydon pointed at the left-hand monitors, which now depicted a large-scale map of Shaftesbury Avenue.

'Were they waiting for someone?' asked Allen.

'No, sir. They got out of the car for two minutes but then moved on. Perhaps they were early for something, or maybe they were just talking. Making a plan.'

'Go on.' Allen was hooked, impatient for the denouement.

Claydon recommenced her narration, CCTV video feeds giving life to the linear progress outlined on the maps. 'They turned left into Greek Street and then doubled back around Soho Square.' She clicked her fingers, but with more force. 'Now you're seeing a *live* feed.' The twelve screens merged into one again.

'Do we have someone following?' asked LJ. Inside she was seething, but she was careful not to let it show. Allen's plan was obvious; he was hoping Tanner would lead the security services straight to Joen, at which point his attack dogs could pounce. Any talk of compromise, of negotiation, had been just that: talk. Allen had wanted to snare Joen all along; his word had been worth nothing.

'Only at a distance, ma'am,' said Claydon. It took LJ a moment to remember what she had asked. 'With the streets so empty, any tail would be spotted a mile off. However, they're only a block away, and we have every security camera in the vicinity trained on them. They can't escape.'

They watched in silence as the car slowly negotiated a left-turn onto

Dean Street. It began to crawl up the snow-covered road. Then, abruptly, it disappeared from view. The screen split into two, a camera on the left panning south from where the car had last been seen, another—presumably from further along the road—searching northwards.

'Fuck!' Allen was not one for swearing, so it meant something when he let loose an obscenity. 'Where did it go?'

Perhaps Major Claydon was human after all. Because now, for the first time in either Allen's or LJ's experience, she began to look nervous.

169

JOEN WATCHED TANNER'S ARRIVAL on her own security feed. She'd guessed he would lean on Tommy Steele and was relieved to see the bank's limousine heave into view. Using a remote control, she panned her cameras up and down the street, but no one and nothing else moved. She wondered if Steele's car was being followed or traced; she had to assume it was. Hoping for the best and preparing for the worst had never failed her yet.

Her clock read 19:54. Somehow, she'd known Tanner would be early, and she was ready to go. It wasn't as if she had much to prepare, after all; to say she'd be travelling light was an understatement. She carried as little sentiment as she could, and in terms of physical baggage, she had even less. In the pockets of her Fjällräven goose down parka she had a credit card, a passport and a phone. An alternate set, in a different name, was tucked away in the laptop bag. Two more identities sat, unused, in safety deposit boxes at local branches of one of the new challenger banks.

Outside, the Mercedes glided forward at little more than walking pace. Joen imagined Steele checking his rear-view mirror for signs of a tail. Then he pulled into the kerb directly in front of her building. She angled the CCTV camera down. Despite the wintry conditions and reflected glare on the dark windscreen, it was still possible to make out two figures in the front seats, heads together in deliberation. Steele and Tanner.

Whatever they'd been debating, a decision was clearly reached. Steele eased the car slowly away from the pavement but stopped a matter of metres later – just past the entrance to Richmond Buildings. Next, he executed the first two elements of a perfect three-point turn, so that he reversed rather than drove into the cul-de-sac. Then he inched the car forward again, so that only its bonnet and the front windows protruded into the main street. 'Clever, Tommy, *clever*,' Joen thought. Now the driver had a perfect line of sight up and down Dean Street and was ready for a quick getaway if necessary.

Joen swept the apartment for a final time. She'd left so many places over the past eight years that there was no more room for attachment, but she couldn't help taking some pride in this one. With the laptop bag slung tightly over her shoulder, she climbed carefully out and down the fire escape. The temperature had dropped; she could feel it on the metal handrails, despite her gloves, and the snow in the small yard was unmistakeably crisp underfoot.

At the end of the short passage to the rear exit, she stopped. There was a touch-screen video panel showing the feed from the security camera above the doorway, which she used to survey the scene outside. She panned to the right. The back of Steele's car was no more than ten metres from where she was standing. Then she arced the feed to the opposite end of the lane. The entrance to the Soho Hotel was quiet; even the doorman had sought shelter inside. She swept the camera back a final time and, confident there had been no change, eased the door ajar. Just as Tanner got out of the passenger side of the parked car.

Joen had made three different plans for what would happen after her rendezvous with Tanner. Which of them she followed depended on his answer to a very simple question. This coming encounter, she realised, was her best chance at untangling the mess with the bank accounts—her own mess, admittedly—and escaping the cycle which had trapped her for so many years. Hell is other people, as the saying goes, but now she found herself wondering whether salvation might be other people as well. Or to be more specific, the man with the Mercedes.

Tanner had taken only half a dozen paces when a door to his left swung open and a figure in a hooded parka stepped into his path. The person's head was lowered, Tanner presumed, to protect themselves from the worst of the weather, and he had to pull up short to avoid crashing into them. Instinctively, he began to apologise, but then from the depths of the hood came the instantly recognisable, honeyed voice.

'Now, what's a nice boy like you doing in a place like this?'
'Joen?'

Before Tanner could draw any more attention to himself, she lifted a finger to her lips in the time-honoured signal for silence and pulled him back through the doorway into the corridor.

She fixed her eyes on his as she slowly mouthed the all-important question.

'Are you on their side?' A question of the heart.

Tanner's gaze remained fixed on hers. There was no ambivalence or equivocation, nor any gesture of emphasis. He simply mouthed the word, 'No.'

Joen smiled in explicit acceptance and indicated the small video panel on the wall. She pressed it twice and the display switched to a view of Dean Street. On it, they saw a car coming up the one-way street from the south. As it approached, it became obvious that the driver and passenger were looking for something. Then, as they reached the junction with Richmond Buildings, they found it. It was like watching the over-exaggerated body language and facial expressions of early silent movies. Tommy had spotted the bonnet of their car nose into Dean Street before they could see him and, unseen in return, had pulled back a couple of metres. No part of the car jutted from the narrow side street.

The pursuers had no forewarning of Tommy's location until they were literally in front of him. The shock on the passenger's face was worthy of any Chaplin villain. The driver, too, gave the game away. The car slowed for the merest second before carrying on up the road and turning right.

Neither Joen nor Tanner needed the other's confirmation of what they had just witnessed. Joen now had the answer to not one but two questions. Tanner hadn't agreed to be a stooge for the prime minister, but that hadn't stopped Allen trying to use him unwittingly. In a fraction of a second, all this information coalesced in her mind, making it clear which of her plans she had to implement. The decision, ultimately, was easy.

Joen made a final check of the streets outside. Satisfied at the renewed stillness, she turned to give Tanner his initial instructions, the route she wanted him to follow. Instead, she found herself being directed to look at a sheaf of paper that he now held towards her. She read the contents, her eyes unable to hide the surprise at the travel authorisation from the PM's office, signed personally by LJ. This certainly hadn't been factored into her thinking. Suddenly, the calculation changed.

The now-familiar look of boyish mischief was back on Tanner's face as he turned the tables. He met her eyes and slowly mouthed a question: 'Do. *You*. Trust. *Me*?' A pointed index finger accentuated the second and fourth words.

None of this had been in Joen's script, and every brain cell she possessed screamed the answer, 'No!' But she had already made her decision. She was tired of being alone: *Joen contra mundum*. She desperately wanted the world to be a better place, to do her bit, to be on the side of the angels. But more than that, more than anything, she wanted to be loved. By this man standing in front of her, no less. She pulled back the hood of her anorak and stepped close to Tanner.

'Yes,' she whispered. 'Completely.' Before planting a slow, gentle kiss on his unsuspecting lips.

Tanner was shocked. Not by the kiss, but by the revelation of Joen's new look. The lustrous chestnut locks had been sheared off and close-clipped into an army buzz cut of polished platinum. The transformation was startling. Rather than make her features appear harder, the stark contrast gave more definition to the softness of her beauty.

The moment of lightness was short-lived. Joen tapped Tanner's wrist, a reminder that time was ticking. In response, he held up a single finger and pointed to the door.

'One minute,' he mouthed.

Joen let him out and watched through a crack in the door as he walked to Tommy's car and opened the boot. It took her but a second to realise what Tanner was suggesting. Once more, her thoughts were overrun by alarm bells. But again, she followed her heart. She trusted him, as hard as it was to admit it. As much as she hadn't wanted to let anyone in, she had to concede that her old way of doing things wasn't working any more. Einstein said it best: madness is doing the same thing over and over again, and expecting something to change. Which was why Joen allowed herself to be picked up at the rear of the Mercedes and lowered—with almost excessive care—into its cavernous trunk. She watched as Tanner pulled the rear entrance door to her building closed. He retraced his steps and gave her a last, bright smile of reassurance. And then her world went dark.

170

BACK IN ROOM 68, James Allen was struggling to maintain his composure. Claydon, for her part, had one hand pressed to her ear. She was straining to hear the audio feed in her tiny earpiece, which had gone unnoticed until now. Her face turned tight with worry, concentration – perhaps both. But then the lines at her mouth eased. She pointed to the screens.

The left-hand side now showed a street level photo, a vantage point down Richmond Buildings towards the Soho Hotel, clearly taken in very different weather conditions. The right displayed the updated positions of Steele's vehicle and its tail on a detailed scale map. Using a red laser pen, Claydon indicated the exact spot where Steele had parked.

'The car is here, Prime Minister. Steele is definitely still in the car, but Tanner may not be.'

'*May* not be?' Allen tried to keep irritation out of his question.

'The shadow detail only had a split second to react, sir. They had no way of knowing where it was. As I said—'

'Yes, I know, they didn't want to reveal themselves.' Allen made a show of studying the displays, mainly to still his frustration. Then, 'Major, why haven't we got CCTV or satellite footage?'

At a nod from Claydon, unseen hands changed the display again. Now the left showed security camera footage of the Mercedes passing in front of a restaurant's outdoor terrace, its snow-furled umbrellas standing isolated sentry duty.

'This footage was taken two minutes ago, *here*.' She pointed to a location on Dean Street to the south. 'It's the nearest camera. Eighty-five metres away. And this,' Claydon said, waiting for the screen to change, 'is the current satellite feed.' The feed was suddenly snuffed out by indistinct fuzz, a dark nothingness randomly interspersed with streaks of foggy, orange light. 'With the low cloud and snow, this is all we have, I'm afraid. We're repositioning one of our new military satellites which will give us a better picture, but it will take a few minutes.' She glanced at her watch. 'Hopefully less than ten.'

'Well done, Major.' Allen had to admit that he was impressed by Claydon's restored command of the situation, 'Any thoughts on what's going on?'

The street-view shot returned, the road leading to the Soho Hotel. Claydon trained the red beam on the hotel entrance as she replied.

'The most obvious inference is that Tanner is meeting someone at the hotel, but then why have Steele wait here?' She brought the focus of the beam to the front of the image. 'It's not as if there isn't parking space next to the hotel.'

'What's on either side of the street opening?' asked LJ. She couldn't help herself; puzzles were there to be solved.

As if by magic, the right side of the screen changed to show floor plans of the adjoining buildings. Presumably receiving the information in her earpiece, Claydon began to run through the list, using the pointer to identify each property in turn: first the image and then the corresponding floorplate.

'On the right, as you can see, there's a noodle restaurant. Above that, there are—' she paused, hand to her ear again, before gesturing at the display. 'This is *live*, sir.'

The entire wall of monitors merged to form a single projection of dashcam footage: an empty side street with what appeared to be a Tudor-style hut in the middle distance, framed through a windscreen. The bare, landscape image was filled then with the movement of a passing luxury sedan, a silver Mercedes emblem unmistakeable on the boot's dark paintwork. Claydon provided a staccato commentary.

'That's Soho Square, sir. Tanner and Steele. No other passengers.'

Allen was excited now, the thrill of the chase giving an immediate adrenalin rush. 'Is your car going to follow?'

'No sir, we have to assume that vehicle is compromised. But don't worry, we have other vehicles ahead. And other aces up our sleeve.'

'We do?' echoed Allen and LJ in stereo surprise.

The major gestured airily and the screen flipped into a large-scale map of central London. A ring of red dots formed a rough circle at the outer edges intersected by two straight lines, upright and diagonal, with Waterloo Bridge at their vertex.

'We have roadblocks at every major artery. It isn't possible to drive out of the centre without being stopped. Depending on which route they take, they might encounter three, even four, checks. At each one they'll be asked specifically where they're heading.'

'You'll ask? Your plan is to stop them and *ask* where they're going?' Disbelief and derision dripped from the PM's question, but Claydon was not so easily cowed.

'Yes, sir, and while we're doing that, we'll attach a tracking device to the vehicle. We're rushing trackers to each location as we speak.'

'Right,' said Allen, duly chastened. 'Of course.'

As logical as the major's reasoning was, she'd failed to take account of two crucial factors. Firstly, she'd made no allowance for Tommy's knowledge of London's highways and byways, gained over three painstaking years preparing for the Knowledge. And secondly, she'd assumed he'd obey the law. But with no other traffic on the roads, and most signs and markings covered in a whitewash of snow, the invitation to ignore traffic instructions was too great to resist. Or as Tommy put it to Tanner as they sailed blithely past the first of many stop signs: 'I hardly think they're going to do us for offences against the Road Traffic Act if we get nicked tonight.'

From Soho Square, Tommy began a slow, convoluted meander through backstreets that even Tanner, a Londoner, had never known existed: Bucknall Street, Short's Gardens, Serle Street, Dorset Rise – the list was endless as Tommy circumvented the major thoroughfares in a labyrinthine zigzag. Eventually, they came to rest at the side of a large, white-faced, neo-classical building just north of Blackfriars Bridge. Tommy stopped and fixed his gaze on Tanner.

'We've got two choices: try to wriggle through the City or drop down on to Upper Thames Street and hope there's no check until Tower Hill. Your call.'

Tanner's face broke into a grin. 'I was warned a long time ago never to tell a London cabbie which route to take, Tommy. I'm not going to start now.'

In acknowledgement, Tommy made an illegal right turn onto the pristine chalk-white carpet leading to the bridge. The foreground was utterly deserted, but fifty yards beyond the approaching traffic lights, the road was blocked by a cordon of army trucks. In front of which stood half a dozen soldiers and a couple of policemen.

'Shit!' exclaimed Tanner.

No left turn was permitted at the junction, and the pavement jutted sharply to prevent one. Tanner glanced at Tommy, expecting to see concern, but he was rewarded with a casual wink instead.

'Don't worry, Six. Low pavement.'

Steele swung the Mercedes to his left in a perfect arc. There was a slight jar as it mounted the shallow kerb edge, and then they were gliding over a wide footpath under the watchful gaze of a black friar standing guard over an art nouveau pub. Further illegal turns took them into a service tunnel next to the underpass that bordered the river.

Tanner let out the breath he'd been unintentionally holding through the entire sequence. 'Nice manoeuvre, Tommy.'

'Let's just hope they're not local cops. At that distance they wouldn't have known we'd gone off-road, but let's not hang about, just in case.'

True to his word, the car shot forward, the sudden acceleration exhilarating after the slow crawl from Soho. With any other driver at the wheel, Tanner would have found the speed alarming on a snow-covered road, but he had complete confidence in his friend – even as they ran three sets of red lights without so much as a feathering of the breaks. The tempo only slowed once they were climbing the long, gentle hill towards the Tower of London.

The next traffic signal, by the Hung, Drawn and Quartered pub, was in their favour, but Tommy took it at little more than walking pace. He glanced towards the magnificent fortress, its single flag a tiny spec of colour under fluorescent illumination, then at his passenger. For the first time all evening, Tanner saw real concern.

'This is where the checkpoint will be, Six. I'll bet you a pound to a penny. Ready to perform?'

Whether it was intuition, premonition or plain common sense, Tommy was bang on the money. No sooner had they crested the rise, than the unmistakeable glow of arc lamps filled the horizon. It might have been an enormous outdoor movie set, or else the scene of a very modern public execution.

171

JOEN HAD WEDGED HERSELF FOETALLY into the rear luggage well of the cavernous boot; it was the only way to brace herself against the interminable succession of bumps and turns. Tommy was usually the smoothest of drivers, but not today. Joen guessed he was slaloming through back streets to avoid the main thoroughfares or, more worryingly, to throw off pursuers. Whichever it was, there was nothing she could do about it now. She'd made her decision.

And she was happy with it. More than that, she realised, she was happy, full stop. The world's most-wanted fugitive, trapped in a pitch-black boot in the middle of the biggest manhunt (now, wasn't that a term that needed updating?) in UK history. And yet, she was happy.

Perhaps it was the darkness, but for the first time in years she dared to imagine a life beyond revenge – beyond the crusade to which she had committed herself without regard for personal consequences. She thought she had planned for everything, as a woman like her was wont to do, but none of her plans had involved falling in love. The realisation that Tanner was committed to helping her, despite everything… well, if that wasn't love in reciprocation, what was?

She tried to picture him now, conjuring his image from the tumultuous darkness of her moving cocoon. The stone-chiselled cheekbones, the eyes shaded with melancholy, the reverse metamorphosis brought on by sudden laughter, transforming him into the happy little boy after the rather sad man. He had been a loner, by his own admission. Until he met Ashley, chose Joen.

The car went over a series of bumps, executed a sharp chicane turn and then accelerated rapidly. Joen felt suddenly nauseous and prayed she wouldn't vomit, but soon the movement slowed, and her stomach settled.

Then came a complete halt. She imagined she heard a low buzzing sound outside the vehicle, but it was hard to tell. The sound of voices, however, was unmistakable. The noises were heavily muffled, but she knew Tommy had driven into a checkpoint – and perhaps a trap. Instinct made her hold her breath, but her left-brain told her not to be so stupid. No one outside could hear her if she stayed still. All she could do was wait and hope. She was in the hands of fate.

Unbidden, a line from Romeo and Juliet came to her in the blackness.

'Some consequence yet hanging in the stars.' A foreshadowing of disaster. Dear God, let it not be fate but Tanner and Tommy steering her a safe course this night.

172

EMOTIONS IN ROOM 68 HAD FISHTAILED as wildly as Tommy's manoeuvres. Claydon had confidence in her security personnel – those detailed to track the Mercedes, at least. But in practice, her people were on the back foot from the very start. The instruction to stay out of sight meant the pursuers had to leave an ever-increasing gap as Steele zigzagged through a warren of London's unlikeliest thoroughfares. Not knowing the streets, the pursuers had to keep one eye on their sat-nav, and while they could follow the Mercedes' tracks in the snow, Claydon's bloodhounds kept stopping at one-way and no entry signs before deciding to ignore them – as Steele appeared to have done. Each check, each stop, added only a second or two to the pursuit, but it was enough to widen the gap.

Allen and LJ followed the procession on the big screens. Each confirmed sighting on a surveillance camera brought a new red dot on the projection of central London, and soon the map was a wild patchwork of red. James Allen, for his part, was struggling to stay calm.

'I thought you said he'd have to stop at a security checkpoint?' he spat.

By means of reply, Claydon pointed at the screen, the right of which merged to show a camera feed looking down a major thoroughfare. Hand clasped to her ear, she relayed the details, renewed confidence in her voice.

'That's the approach to Blackfriars Bridge, sir. He *has* to stop there.'

Allen was mollified, content to watch the unfolding drama as the Mercedes sped towards the waiting cordon. But then the vehicle went off-script and off-road. The car swung abruptly to the left, narrowly avoiding the entrance to a subway and almost clipping a set of railings.

'That's not allowed!' gasped Claydon, dumbstruck. She was thrown at the very idea of disobeying an order, even one written upon a street sign.

'Well fucking tell *him* that!'

The exchange hung in the air as red dots continued to mount. One screen showed the pursuit vehicle stop and, after two failed efforts, mount the pavement to continue the chase. The other screens showed stills of the Mercedes, clearly now some distance ahead, passing through shadowy tunnels before emerging onto a busier road.

Claydon clicked her fingers furiously, barking orders into her microphone. The screen panned to reveal a line of vehicles blocking a major intersection. Allen recognised the Tower of London.

'He absolutely *has* to stop here, sir,' stated Claydon with assurance.

The PM caught a caustic reply on his tongue. This time, Claydon was correct. Silence duly fell in Room 68.

All eyes were on the Mercedes as it finally slowed down and stopped at the security barrier. The screen tracked a police officer as she approached the passenger side door. A second officer made his way around to the back of the car. LJ felt the hairs on the back of her neck rise in anticipation.

'Sound!' barked Claydon.

Static crackled through the audio system, then the room filled with a female voice: metallic and computer-enhanced but clearly audible.

'May I ask where you're going, sir?'

'To Canary Wharf, officer.' That was Tanner. 'My bank has a security centre there.'

'And is your visit essential, sir?'

'Yes, officer, I fear it is. Another computer problem.'

Tanner's answers were less distinct, presumably a function of his distance from the policewoman's collar mike, not helped by the weather. From the video feed, it was clear that snow was now falling more heavily again. The splenetic ups and downs of the weather seemed to Allen like a meteorological reflection of the turbulence in which his nation—and his premiership—now found itself.

'May I see your travel attestation, please?' asked the officer.

'Of course, but you might care to look at this first?' On screen, the policewoman could clearly be seen leaning into the passenger window. A sheet of paper appeared to have been brandished from within. 'I'm acting on the specific orders of the prime minister.'

Along with every other set in the room, LJ's eyes swung to look at the PM. It was the most wondrous sight. His face had turned an extraordinary shade of puce, all wind and fury. LJ wanted to prick him to see if he would explode. And best of all, he had to suck it up for the moment, so as not to miss the conversation on screen.

Tanner, meanwhile, doubled down on his gambit. 'Perhaps you'd like to call his office to check. The number is on the paper. We're in rather a hurry, you see.'

The police officer was young, and her orders were to ascertain the passengers' destination and ensure the vehicle was bugged; nothing more. Thrown off guard by Tanner's sangfroid—his personal authority even more convincing than the credentials he carried—the officer meekly stepped back and wished them on their way.

'Fuck!' Allen had long stopped caring about his image in the room; retribution over the travel attestation in his name could come later. 'Why didn't she hold him up?'

'It doesn't matter, sir,' replied Claydon. 'The bug's in place.' She pointed at the map on the left of the screen. Whereas before there had been intermittent marks delineating Tanner's route, there was now a flowing live movement. A blood-red line pulsed, an abstract vein, as the Mercedes slowly wound its way around the Tower Hill one-way system.

Now, Major Claydon was in her element. The conductor of an unseen orchestra, she controlled her soloists with quiet, absolute authority. An instruction here, a request for clarification there, totally confident in her preparation, looking forward to the performance. Then, without warning, she raised a hand for silence, simultaneously cupping the other to her ear. The hint of a smile appeared at Claydon's mouth. She directed their gaze to the screen, on which a moving satellite image was beginning to crystallise.

'The satellite will be directly overhead in two minutes,' she said. 'Then we'll have them.'

173

TOMMY SLOWED THE CAR the moment they were out of sight of the Tower Hill checkpoint, heading towards Canary Wharf. He had less than a minute to warn Tanner what he planned to do.

'Rob, shut up and listen.'

Tanner did as he was told. Tommy had never spoken to him like that in all the years they'd known each other; no second bidding was needed. Tommy spoke quickly, and Tanner took in every word.

'While you were giving your Oscar performance back there, Miss Plod's mate was trying to look inconspicuous at the back of the car. I thought he was going to open the boot, but he just seemed to be having a look. A long look. *Underneath.*'

'So?'

'He wasn't looking. He was attaching something. Presumably a bug. No wonder it was so easy to talk our way through. They think they've got us in a web and can gobble us up whenever they like.'

Tanner knew intuitively where Tommy was leading. 'Time to fly?'

'You got it Six. I'll stop opposite the entrance to the docks, then you and Miss Markham need to be on your toes. *Pronto.*' Steele's irrepressible cheerfulness returned. 'While I put my foot down to the Wharf.'

Less than a minute later, Tommy was at their drop-off point, and the two friends were on their respective ways.

Tanner made ready to haul Joen from the boot and carry her bodily across the road. She was in his arms before she even had a chance to question what was happening – not that she made any effort to resist as he swooped down to pick her up.

'One pair of footprints,' he explained, and amusement replaced concern on the lovely face within the hood. His strength, she realised, wasn't just of the mental kind.

Safely under cover at the entrance to the docks, Tanner relayed the change of plan. Joen listened intently, nodding silent concurrence, and had but a single question when he'd finished.

'Who knows where we're heading, Rob?'

'Just Tommy and Chrissie.'

'Tommy I understand. But do you trust Chrissie?'

'Yes,' replied Tanner instinctively. An image of the PA flashed through his mind, a reminder of Chrissie's recent mood swings. The colourful clothing after years of monochrome; the bright, luminescent presence of the past week and the austere, business-first manner which had resurfaced today. It was odd, for sure, but there had to be a genuine reason.

As Tanner offered the words, he realised the truth of them. 'I trust her with my life.'

'*Our* lives,' Joen corrected him with a smile. 'But I'm glad.' She took his hand, looking for all the world like an ingénue about to set out for an evening's promenade with her beau. 'Come on then. What are you waiting for?'

The direct route to the bank's flat, through the heart of the marina, was less than five hundred metres. The dock was private property, so there was little chance of running into a police patrol. But still, they took no chances, skirting the well-lit centre, scouting each few metres ahead for security cameras and keeping deep in the shadows like soldiers on patrol in bandit country. Finally, they reached a barrier marking the perimeter of the development. They hadn't seen a living soul, and Tanner was sure they weren't being followed.

He gave Joen's hand a gentle squeeze: half encouragement, half stress release. 'The flat's just a hundred metres on the right,' he said. 'We're safe now.'

174

KELLETT HAD JUST ABOUT MANAGED to keep his car on the road. With poor visibility, deteriorating road conditions and no natural aptitude for driving, every metre of the journey was a hazard in waiting. Even in his corpulent state, he could probably have walked about as quickly as he drove. Fortunately, there were only a handful of other cars around, and they gave him an extremely wide berth.

Kellett was stopped at three different roadblocks, each security check taking longer than the last, but, for once, he managed to rein in his mounting irritation. His eyes were on the bigger prize—sticking it to Tanner—so he could bear a little self-restraint. Just.

At 8.44 p.m., Kellett turned, or rather slid, off the main highway to negotiate the last third of a mile to the bank's apartment. He grimaced. The major roads had been gritted, at least to a degree, whereas the narrow street ahead was a plane of fresh, deep snow. He was tempted to stop and walk the last stretch, but the thought of trudging through the worsening weather was enough to make him persevere. Oh well, two minutes, and he'd be there. And he'd be leaving this fucking car there, that's for sure. Tommy could drive him home. Then he'd fire the bastard. Kellett's mood brightened just thinking about it.

Meanwhile, the atmosphere in Room 68 had taken on a distinct chill. The first sign of trouble was Claydon's tell-tale pressing of index finger to earpiece. Neither Allen nor LJ missed the brief tautening at the major's mouth.

'What is it?' asked the PM.

'It's probably nothing sir,' said Claydon, 'but Steele stopped not long after the checkpoint, then took off at speed towards Canary Wharf.'

Allen saw no reason for concern. 'I know. That's where he said he's going. We've been watching on the map.' He pointed to the line of red heading eastwards on screen. 'What's the problem?'

'It's the telemetrics, sir. They appear to show the car stopped fifty metres *after* a set of traffic lights. And Steele hasn't bothered to stop at any signal before now. It's just not consistent.'

'What exactly are you saying, Major?'

Claydon did well not to shrug, but the uncertainty was plain in her voice. 'We need to check, in case someone got out.'

'I thought you said the satellite was due overhead?'

'It is, sir. Directly overhead.' She gloomily indicated the screen to her right, which was now filled with the unmistakeable outline of dozens of boats and barges at mooring. 'But Steele has just entered the Limehouse Link Tunnel. The car's underground.'

'Get a patrol to intercept!' screeched Allen.

LJ stepped between the pair, so she was directly in front of her boss. She inclined her head towards him, her face barely an air kiss from his, but there was no warmth in her expression.

'With respect, sir, I think this has gone on long enough. You authorised Tanner to act on our behalf. Shouldn't we leave him to do what we've asked?'

'Sod that!' spat back Allen. 'He's clearly up to something. And imagine how sweet it will be when he leads us to Markham. It saves us having to negotiate, LJ! Why give anything away when we can settle this for free?'

LJ stood her ground, her voice still low. She didn't know what Tanner was up to exactly, but she trusted him to talk Joen back from the brink. And she had shaken hands on terms which seemed favourable to everyone.

'You gave your word,' she insisted, eyes fixed on Allen's.

'Well, things change.' Allen shook his head and turned away.

Claydon cleared her throat. 'If anyone did get out of the vehicle, I think we know their intended destination,' she said. She drew their attention to the right-hand corner of the screen, where a video clip of a vehicle at a police checkpoint began to play. 'This is National Bank CEO Martin Kellett at the Tower Hill security barrier just minutes ago.' She paused while a large-scale diagram of a building, overlaid on an aerial map, filled the left-hand monitors. 'And this is the property where he says he's heading: National Bank's apartment on the river by St Katharine Docks.' Claydon was enjoying herself now, a conjurer toying with her audience, sure of her timing. 'And here… is the live satellite feed.'

Allen and LJ were transfixed as the entire wall merged to form a single satellite image, a vast aerial display of a triangular space in front of riverside wharves. It was grainy but clear enough to make out a large tree and, further along the road, a number of parked cars. One more vehicle was moving into shot, at painstaking speed.

'That, I'm sure you've guessed, is the River Thames. And this…' Claydon used the infrared pointer to highlight a building. 'This is the bank apartment.' At the major's instruction, the screen took on a dark hue, akin to a photographic negative. A heat camera. Two orange splotches flared at the top of the screen, near the southern exit from the marina.

If the major was tempted to shout, 'Voilà!' she settled for a low-key, 'Two heat signatures. Two *people*.' Then to ram home the point. 'Due south of Steele's stopping point.'

'Don't wait!' barked Allen. He clapped his hands together, glee unrefined. 'Take them!'

175

JOEN SENSED THE DANGER before she heard it. Years of living on edge had given her a sixth sense – or at least sharpened the five she definitely possessed. Her hand stiffened and dropped from Tanner's.

'Something's not right.'

The eerie silence was broken by the deep hum of an engine—no, *engines*—heading in their direction.

'Motorbikes. Behind us.' Joen turned to look down the small lane from which they'd just come. A narrow, residential access route for the houses bordering the marina, the road was blocked at each end by security barriers. But there was more than enough room for a motorbike to pass. In the distance, the reflected beam of headlights indicated they'd done exactly that. Betrayal flashed through her mind.

'Come on!' implored Tanner. He tried to pull Joen into movement, pointing to the converted wharf where the bank had its penthouse flat. 'We're there!' The entrance was only fifty metres away.

'No.' Joen planted her feet in the snow, looking anxiously around for a line of escape. Like a cornered animal, her eyes flared wide as her primeval brain took over. Which would it be today: fight or flight?

'Joen, listen,' pleaded Tanner. 'I have the prime minister's word that no harm will come to you. It's okay.'

Joen snapped back to the moment. She met Tanner's eyes and shook her head sadly.

'Oh, Rob, you're so naïve. So decent, but so naïve. It's why I love you.' She hadn't meant to say it, it just came out.

'You do?' Tanner pulled her towards him, his face exultant. For a moment, the growing whine of engines didn't matter – nor the cold, nor politics, nor the nation's imminent collapse. He wanted to kiss her, to never stop kissing her, to never let go, but she was determined to break from his embrace. He was naturally stronger, but she was running on pure adrenaline.

'We don't have time for this, Rob. I have to go. *Please.*' She gave an almighty tug and wrenched herself free. She staggered, almost fell, backwards into the road. Straight into the path of the electric Fiat 500 that was approaching unheard and unnoticed from the opposite direction as they focused on the noisier motorcycles.

There was a sickening thud and the screech of brakes… but too late. Thrown forward by the impact, Joen lay spread-eagled, unmoving, on the ground. A fragile form inert on virgin snow. Her hood had been thrown back by the impact, and for the first time, Tanner saw just how short her hair had been cut, the peroxide crop tinted orange in the reflected streetlight. She was lying on her side, her head resting on one extended arm, the other limp beside her, fingers still curled where the strap of her laptop bag had been.

Tanner rushed to her. As he dropped to the ground he was blinded by the beam of headlights. He tried to shield his eyes as he screamed into the glare.

'Turn the fucking lights off!'

Whether by direction or coincidence, the lights dimmed. Joen's face was unmarked, still and beautiful, but her eyes, usually so full of life and mischief, were fixed in a glassy stare. Dread clawed at Tanner's stomach, his chest tightened, pain tore through his heart. The sound of approaching steps registered somewhere in his brain, then he was pulled forcefully away. It was one of the motorcyclists – a policeman in a fluorescent jacket.

Numb, Tanner watched the other policeman take off his helmet, kneel, and check Joen's pulse. The officer looked at him and demanded his overcoat. Released from the first rider's grip, Tanner scrambled out of the coat and knelt to lay it gently over Joen's prone form.

'She's alive,' affirmed the policeman. 'Her pulse is weak, but at least there is one. She may have internal injuries, so we can't move her. All we can do is keep her warm. An ambulance won't be long. Understand?'

Whether he'd taken this in or not, Tanner nodded the agreement the officer was looking for. She was alive! Relief surged for a second. It was like a drug: filling him, changing the textures of the world around him before the realisation dawned that Joen's fate was very much in the balance. At least he had hope. Perhaps that was all he had.

'Now, please step back. We know what we're doing.'

Tanner did as he was told and backed off, his conscious brain beginning to reboot after the shock of the accident. For the first time, he registered a bulky presence behind him. He turned, and a second shockwave ripped through him. It was Martin Kellett, the Toad's mouth agape as he stared at the small figure on the ground – the small figure he had hit with his car.

Tanner's senses took flight once again. With them went any self-control he might have possessed. He lurched towards his former colleague with a scream of primal rage.

'YOU!'

Kellett made for the safety of his car, but he had no chance against the berserker at his back. He'd barely begun to open the door before Tanner was on him.

'You bastard!' Tanner had Kellett by the neck and, from the savage wildness in his eyes, had every intention of throttling him. Kellett was frantically trying to prise away his fingers, to put some distance between him and Tanner, to croak an explanation – anything to stop the onslaught.

'It was an accident!' Kellett gasped. His face was red, stinging with cold and fear and exertion. 'She slipped!'

Before he could even respond, an arm was thrust around Tanner's neck, and he was dragged away a second time. Panting heavily, Kellett forced himself into the car and locked the door.

Now it was the erstwhile attacker who was struggling to break free, but the policeman had the benefit of surprise, training, and brute strength. Trapped in an unbreakable headlock of heavy yellow PVC, the fight drained from Tanner. He stopped resisting. His arms dropped to his side. The officer took no chance, maintaining his hold, but instead of censure he spoke to his captive with unexpected softness.

'It's not going to help the young lady if you go off on one, is it, sir?'

The truth of the comment shamed Tanner into immediate passivity. Thoroughly embarrassed, he felt the animal madness seeping out of him, leaving only fear. It was the worst fear he had ever known, the kind of fear which descends only in those situations when you find yourself completely and utterly helpless.

176

FOR LJ AND THE PRIME MINISTER, the entire scene had unfolded in the ghostly monochrome of security camera footage. The two figures at the side of the road, the motorbikes approaching from the north, a single slow-moving car from the east… a ghastly convergence overlaid with commentary from the senior officer's helmet mike. They listened in shocked silence as he radioed for an ambulance, and then came the sounds of an altercation followed by a bizarre peace, broken only by static.

Claydon was in her element. In seconds, she had dismantled the chain of command and taken full direct control of the officers at the wharf. After no more than a minute, she turned to Allen.

'A woman. White. Thirty, or thereabouts. She's alive, but her pulse is weak. I'm sending in more units now.'

'Very good,' said Allen. This wasn't how it had played out in his imagination, but at least they had Markham. There was hope for the country, yet.

'One more thing,' offered Claydon. 'We've recovered a laptop bag which was thrown clear in the collision. The snow must have cushioned the fall.'

Allen was suddenly ecstatic. In contrast to the sober faces all around, his was animated, unable to contain his excitement. That laptop was surely the key to all this! Even without Markham's cooperation, given time and the right people, her laptop could surely be cracked open like a golden egg. Her technological secrets would be laid bare, Britain would wake from the nightmare of impending financial collapse, and Allen's legacy would be forever secure! Churchill, Thatcher, Allen. He liked the sound of that.

'We've *got* her!' the PM shouted. 'We've bloody got her!'

'Sir,' answered LJ. 'With respect, *she* may be fighting for her life.'

'So what?' asked Allen, with a snort of derision. 'Think of all the misery she's put people through. The woman's a terrorist; she deserves it. All that matters is that we have her computer.'

'And your word? Does that matter?' LJ was oblivious, now, to the astonished looks around the room.

Allen's demeanour changed instantly. His eyes narrowed, merriment replaced by cold fury. He'd suspected it earlier, and now he was sure. LJ was not with him; therefore, she was against him. His voice took on a low, threatening tone.

'Perhaps you should go home, LJ. You're obviously overtired.'

'Don't worry, sir, I'm going.' LJ ripped the lanyard from her neck and threw it at the prime minister. 'And yes, I am tired. Tired of you… and your lies.' She strode out of the room, head held high. Not a single person would meet her gaze as she went by.

177

THE DAY BELONGED TO ORDER, TO JUSTICE. The day should also have belonged to a certain James Allen, the way he saw it.

He had remained in Room 68 for another hour, watching developments on screen, with rising confidence. Ashley Markham was taken—under police escort, of course—to hospital. And her laptop—the real prize—was duly delivered to the National Cyber Security Centre in Victoria. Tanner, Kellett and Steele were taken into custody. The hidden entrances to Markham's apartment in Soho were discovered and bypassed. Public order, too, was under control, thanks to the presence of the army on the streets. It looked set to be a quiet night throughout the land, and by the time everyone woke up, the nightmare would be over. With a smile of satisfaction at an evening's work well done, and an election-night wave for Claydon's subterranean subordinates, the PM headed back to Number Eleven. It seemed he had won.

Allen poured himself a stiff rum and settled into his favourite armchair to await news of the expected breakthrough. He wasn't surprised when his phone rang, but he was surprised when he saw who was calling: LJ.

He'd intended to deal with her in the morning, once all this nonsense was sorted, but the silly woman obviously wanted to beg forgiveness, so he answered.

'Good evening, Prime Minister,' she said. 'Might I take a couple of minutes?'

'Yes, LJ, of course.' He affected nonchalance. 'What can I do for you?'

'Two things, please, sir,' LJ replied. 'Firstly, in case there was any doubt earlier, I resign.' LJ waited long enough for that to sink in, but not for any reply. 'And, secondly, I want Tanner and Steele released, immediately.'

Allen was knocked back by LJ's words, but he was far from knocked out. In fact, he laughed.

'I hardly think you're in a position to demand anything, LJ,' he huffed.

'*Demand*, sir? I'm not sure what you mean. I'm simply expecting you to honour your word. To let Tanner engage with Markham unimpeded.'

'Yes, but that was then. Needs must...'

'Your *word*, in front of a witness, recorded on my phone.' LJ didn't know what made her add the embellishment, but it had the desired effect.

'You were recording me? And now you're threatening me? How dare you?'

The question was ignored. 'Let me be clear,' LJ went on. 'If you don't release them right now, the recording and a copy of *your* travel authorisation will be in the hands of Trish Dixon at the *Mail* before you can say "Prime Minister Lied To Parliament." Now, wouldn't that make an interesting exclusive?'

Allen coughed down the response forming in his throat. His eventual reply came as a threatening whisper.

'You'll regret this, LJ.'

'Possibly, sir, but not as much as you will if you don't do as I ask. I'll give you till midnight.' The line went dead.

Unpleasant though the blow to his ego was, Allen consoled himself with the thought that Tanner and the driver weren't who he was after. Freeing them made not the slightest difference. LJ's departure, meanwhile, could easily be spun, and ultimately buried, in the furore of the forthcoming reshuffle. Another tot of rum helped him swallow the indignity.

Allen called Claydon to give the necessary instructions, thankful for the major's disposition to accept orders unconditionally, without comment or curiosity. Her update on progress was much less welcome.

'I'm afraid Markham's laptop is proving difficult, sir.'

'*Difficult?*' asked Allen. This was one of the very few things about power that he didn't enjoy: the way those beneath him so often suffered from bouts of euphemism in their dealings with him. Particularly during the delivery of unpleasant truths.

'As you might expect, sir,' explained Claydon, 'Markham has protected her computer with multiple security features. Passwords, biometrics—fingerprints, iris and voice recognition—encryption.'

'Yes, yes, major, but surely that's why we have GCHQ, to unlock this sh… stuff.'

Claydon maintained the level of her voice. 'Of course, sir. But getting the biometrics takes time. And the security features are incremental, like unlocking the challenges in a computer game. You can only attempt the next level when you've mastered the previous one, and each failure takes you back to the start.'

'How long?'

From what the technicians at GCHQ had told her—or rather, hadn't—this was one hostage to fortune the major was not going to give. No matter how much Allen pushed. She opted for deflection with the blandest of blandishments.

'The team at GCHQ are the best, sir. There's no one who can do it quicker.'

Claydon seemed to have judged this one well, as always. Whether the fight had gone out of the PM or the alcohol had settled in, it didn't matter. All that did was that he'd had enough for one day.

'Well, I'm going to bed. Wake me as soon as there's news.'

Claydon put the phone down with relief. According to the boffins at GCHQ, the laptop's file structure was completely novel. The technicians' best guess was that there was a blockchain element to the more sophisticated encryption features. But that was only speculation; they'd never seen the like before. That meant there was a chance that possession of the laptop might be immaterial: they'd need access to all Markham's databases to join the blocks of data together to form an entry-chain. And even then, who knew?

Worse still, there was nothing in Markham's Soho apartment to help the investigation. Luckily, the prime minister hadn't asked about that, and Claydon certainly wasn't about to volunteer that kind of information off the cuff. All she could do was hope that there would be a breakthrough before morning so that she could wake her boss with good news. If not, she'd have her work cut out dodging his ire – the wrath and pride of a premier's bruised ego.

178

FOR ROB TANNER, HOURS PASSED IN A BLUR. Years later, long after the events of that evening had lost their power to shock, the memories would come back only as a series of dislocated images, clips from a silent movie. Someone else's movie. An out-of-body experience through which he floated, wraithlike, unable to influence the physical world and barely subject to its laws or processes.

He vaguely remembered the sound of an ambulance. Blue lights fluorescent against white snow. Concern on the faces of the paramedics turning to something much worse, as they examined Ashley. No, not Ashley: Joen, his Joen.

Then the ambulance leaving and him crying out for her even as he was bundled into a windowless van. Demanding his right to speak to a lawyer and being told that such fundamental entitlements were negated by this being a matter of national security. Brandishing his letter of authorisation from LJ—from the prime minister—and being told that the chief of staff was unavailable for confirmation. Having to repeat his account twice, in excruciating detail; first to a police officer and then to a nameless individual he assumed was from the security services. Worst of all, his repeated requests for news of Joen's condition—or even her whereabouts—being met with indifference and insult. And then, just as suddenly, finding himself released on the steps of New Scotland Yard. With Tommy Steele waiting outside, car at the ready. And LJ Oladapo, the architect of his release, in one of the back seats.

Tanner thought he'd lost the capacity to be surprised, but this, after all that had gone before, was truly mind-numbing. Fortunately, Tommy and LJ were prepared. While Tommy pulled a hip flask from the glove compartment and insisted he take a drink, LJ tucked a heavy travel rug over his knees. Life and colour returned to Tanner's face, but with them came distress.

'How's Joen?' he asked, the only question that mattered.

LJ leaned across and took his wrist. 'Didn't they tell you? She's in intensive care. She's had emergency surgery, but she's fighting. We're taking you there now.'

Relief and hope gave Tanner renewed strength. He took a deep breath, and then a second swig of brandy, before offering the container to LJ.

'I'm guessing you deserve this more than me,' he offered. 'What on earth's been going on, LJ?'

A sad smile appeared on her lips as she took the flask. Now wasn't that a question? She took a nip, then a second deeper draught, savouring the hit to the back of her throat.

'It's a long story and not a very pleasant one. I'll tell you on the way. Joen's at the National Hospital in Queen Square, by the way. It's a dedicated neurological facility.' The words had been intended to reassure. Instead,

487

she saw them fall like further blows upon a bruise. LJ squeezed his arm again. 'Rob, she'll be okay. She's in the best hands.'

'I know,' he replied. He didn't, of course. He doubted he knew a single useful thing at this time, other than that he had to be strong. He sat up straighter, shaking off the self-pity. He caught Tommy's eye in the rear-view mirror and realised, only then, that they still weren't moving. 'Thanks, Thrup.'

His friend gave the briefest nod of acknowledgement. 'No probs, Six. Now, let's get going, shall we?'

Gloom dispelled, or at least deferred, they pulled on to the empty Embankment, and LJ began her account of the night's proceedings.

'So, just to be clear,' said Tanner. 'You quit? In front of a room full of witnesses?'

'In rather more colourful terms.'

'And threatened to go to the press with the whole story?'

'That's about it.'

'So where does that leave you? Us? Are you on our side?'

LJ let out a deep sigh of reflection. 'I guess you'd call it a Mexican stand-off. Allen can't afford more bad publicity right now, but at the end of the day, he's got Joen's computer. Assuming he unlocks her software and gets the banks back to normal, no one will care how he did it.' She gave a wry laugh. 'In fact, he'll spin it so that he comes out as the tough guy, the hero. Churchill not Chamberlain.'

'But what if they can't break her systems?'

'Then he's toast, anyway.' The humour went out of her. 'We all are. But let's be optimistic – they have her laptop and her apartment in Soho.'

Doubt creased Tanner's brow. 'I wouldn't be so convinced Joen's systems are that easy to break.'

LJ shrugged. 'Not my problem, now.' She looked to the window; the streets of London still quiet beyond the glass. The absence of pedestrians, of life and laughter, served as a reminder that the crisis was far from over. Martial law, effectively, still applied. The curfew was going nowhere.

Tanner had one last question. 'Are we in trouble?'

'Probably not,' said LJ, turning to face him once more. 'I have a witness who saw Allen authorising me to negotiate with Joen through you. You have the document to prove it. They can tie us up with the Official Secrets Act, but *no*, I think we're safe, legally speaking. Although, all three of us are out of a job.' A broad grin played across her face. 'And Tommy's facing a few points on his licence.'

For once, there was no comeback. Instead, the car slowed to a halt in front of a large Victorian building, its red brick façade and pink stonework a colourful contrast to the white all around. The National Hospital for Neurology and Neurosurgery. And inside: his Joen.

DAY NINE

NEW YEAR'S EVE
TUESDAY 31 DECEMBER 2024

179

IT WAS SNOWING AGAIN. Tanner watched the flakes falling from his vantage point in the hospital waiting room. He looked through his own reflection in the window and out to the pure, white vista beyond, to a garden draped in white. No vehicle had passed for an hour, so even the road was perfect in its evenness. The Inuit may have fifty words for snow, but the Japanese actually have a word for the sound of it falling. *Shin shin.* Now that's attention to detail.

LJ's soon-to-be-obsolete Downing Street credentials had gained them access to the hospital and a brief audience with a junior doctor, who had assisted in Joen's emergency surgery, but Tanner was none the wiser for it. He'd heard phrases you'd find trotted out in any medical soap on TV: "She has swelling on the brain; she's sedated; she's stable… the next twenty-four hours are crucial." And no, he wasn't allowed to see her. They'd notify him as soon as there was any change. Please would he stay in the waiting room?

'And might I ask what your relationship is with Miss Markham?'

'Yes, of course,' answered Tanner. He couldn't even bring himself to take offence at the stiff indelicacy of the question as he bluffed an answer which felt right, even though he knew it was wrong. 'I'm her fiancé.' This information made the young registrar a bit more solicitous, but no more informative. So, Tanner stood and watched the snow fall, wondering if it would be inimically hypocritical to pray, in this moment, to a God he'd given up on half a lifetime ago.

He was alone. No other families, friends or loved ones kept night-time vigil in the stark waiting room. LJ and Tommy had both wanted to stay with him, but he sent them home. Nikki and Gérard, meanwhile, were apparently back in London, but there was nothing they could do – or say. Knowing the location of Joen's continental hideout changed nothing. The plan was to regroup in the morning, by which time Tanner hoped there would be an update. Or maybe there would be no news, which, in Joen's case, really might be good news. Tanner had no idea.

There was a television in the corner, but Tanner soon switched it off; he supposed he should care about what was happening beyond the square, but it could wait. Instead, he pulled a chair to the window. He tried to stay awake, but fatigue overcame his head-bobbing resistance and he slumped into sleep.

Deep into the night, something woke him. His first reaction was that he'd been prodded, but no one else was there and no movement had triggered a change in the automatic lighting; the room was still cloaked in its weak nightlight. Tanner pulled out his phone to check the time. He was unable to believe his eyes; the banner on the screen told him he had received a mail message from Joen van Aken "one minute ago." A single touch took him to the body of text.

TO: Robert Tanner
CC: Leah Oladapo
FROM: Joen van Aken
DATE: Tuesday, 31 December 2024 at 02:50
Superbia

Hello Rob (and LJ).

If you're reading this then I guess it's all gone Pete Tong and there's no sanctuary for this Esmerelda, no Disney finale. I always suspected our PM had a touch of the Claude Frollo. Not that the story ended well for him, either. I did warn that Pride comes before a fall.

There won't be much need for numbers today, but I'll give you $_{15}$P for good measure (although the Proverbial 16:18 might help). Vesper's brother really isn't very good in the morning; in fact, he really can be rather cast down.

Sophocles knew his stuff: "All men make mistakes, but…"

Why the strange timing you may ask? It just seemed appropriate

    And Certainty? and Quiet kind?

    Deep meadows yet, for to forget

    The lies, and truths, and pain?… oh! yet

Allen certainly won't like it when the clock strikes three this morning. Ask Hemingway!

Anyway, that's it from me. But you never know? What's that old saying… "more comebacks than Sinatra?" Well, Frankie knew one thing: if a man – or woman – hasn't got themselves, then they've got what?

Sorry, I just had to do it My Way.

J.

Tanner recognised the image: Bosch's representation of the seventh deadly sin, *Superbia,* or Pride, but his weary brain struggled to make much sense of the rest. He reread the message slowly, line by line, searching for meaning, but his eyes kept returning to the melancholic opening sentence. There would be no fairy-tale ending. Where Quasimodo had saved Esmeralda from execution with his cry of "sanctuary," Tanner had failed Joen.

Tanner tried to put the thought to one side, to focus on the words, but deciphering such a cryptic message required all his critical faculties at full strength. He was tired and emotional; he hadn't eaten anything for twelve hours, and he was probably dehydrated. Still, there was a coffee machine in the corner; that would perk him up. Maybe then he'd see the wood for the trees. Not that the view outside the window offered much encouragement. There wasn't a tree to be seen. Snow continued to fall, blanketing the world in white.

Snow continued to fall! Christ, how could he be so stupid? That was the whole point! The world still turned, and neither the wood nor the trees nor the meaning mattered.

Joen—confined, unconscious Joen—continued to send messages. Well, of course *she* didn't – not in real time, anyway. The delivery had clearly been pre-arranged. The realisation cut deep; she had envisaged this exact outcome – she anticipated that he would fail her. There was nothing he could do about that now, he'd just have to make it up to her somehow, one day – if she made it through. Tanner rubbed his forehead. What was he thinking, "Make it up to her?" There was nothing he could do, other than follow her clues.

He read the message again, focusing on the concrete, not the abstract. "Allen certainly won't like it when the clock strikes three this morning." Three o'clock: two minutes from now… pride before a fall. Energy came rushing back to Tanner; he needed no external stimulation now. Oh, Joen, what have you done?

And then he knew, exactly. The tune had planted itself in his brain as soon as he'd read the words. Sinatra, *"My Way."* The last verse. The big finale. Frankie's answer to Joen's question. If you're not true to yourself, you have *"naught."*

Naught. Nought. Nothing. Nil. *Zero.*

'Oh, fuck!' Tanner reached for his phone; he had to warn LJ.

180

MAJOR CLAYDON HAD A COPY of Joen's email to Tanner and LJ within seconds of it dropping into the former chief of staff's inbox. The major didn't need all her prodigious IQ to work out the tone of the message. It was unrelentingly grim.

Claydon knew that Frollo was the principal antagonist in Victor Hugo's *The Hunchback of Notre-Dame* and that he came to a sticky end, pushed off the Cathedral roof by an enraged Quasimodo. Esmerelda also dies in the novel, but not in the Disney film. The thought of the hunchback inevitably gave rise to images of bells ringing, leading the major to Hemingway's *For Whom The Bell Tolls*. The first number looked like a chemical element from the periodic table, but she couldn't remember that particular entry. Sinatra's "*My Way*" was self-evident, but the two lines quoted in the email bore no obvious relevance.

Claydon's team of analysts had divided the text between them before she even finished reading the first line. By the time she was done with the last, they were queuing in her earpiece with answers and explanations.

'Pete Tong. An English DJ and music producer. Rhyming slang for wrong.'

'$_{15}$P. The chemical element Phosphorus. The name is taken from Greek mythology, literally "light-bearer." Its Latin equivalent is Lucifer, the demon of pride on Binsfeld's list. Sometimes characterised as a fallen angel. The Romans used the name for the planet Venus in its morning appearances, before it fell and reappeared in the evening as Vesper. In ancient mythology, the pair were brothers.'

'Clever!' replied Claydon, despite herself. Markham had crammed all those references into little more than a sentence.

'The Bible quotation—Proverbs 16:18—is, "Pride goes before destruction, And a haughty spirit before a fall."'

'The complete line from Sophocles' *Antigone* reads: "All men make mistakes, but a good man yields when he knows his course is wrong and repairs the evil. The only crime is pride."'

'The three lines of poetry are the penultimate lines from Rupert Brooke's poem, "*The Old Vicarage, Grantchester*." It ends, "Stands the Church clock at ten to three? And is there honey still for tea?"'

Claydon couldn't help but smile at the time reference, but then she remembered that Brooke had died on the way to Gallipoli, an early casualty of the Great War described in his famous sonnets. She motioned silently for the stream to continue.

'Hemingway's 1940 novel, *For Whom the Bell Tolls*.' As she'd known. But not the further explication that followed: 'Talk of the clock striking three and the toll of bells probably refers to the ancient custom of ringing bells at the time of death. First when the person was dying, then a death knell upon their passing, and finally the lych bell, or funeral toll, as the burial procession approached the church.'

Claydon nodded her head in mute appreciation of the detail. 'Which just leaves Sinatra, I believe. Any ideas?'

'It's a lyrical reference, ma'am,' replied a metallic voice in her ear. 'What you've got, I'm afraid, is *naught*.'

It took Claydon no longer to spot the significance than it had taken Rob Tanner. And now she knew she had the unenviable job of breaking the news to the prime minister. But first, she called her liaison at GCHQ. She had been praying for something positive with which to soften the blow, but she knew from the tone on the other end of the line that there was no good news to be found there.

'The bottom line is that we can't access part of the software because it requires external blocks of data to form an entry circuit. An interdependent two-way protocol. Similar to blockchain, but different.'

'And we have no way of knowing where this other data is stored?' Claydon could guess the answer, but she asked anyway.

'Correct.'

'Anything else?'

There was a moment's hesitation. 'We can't prove it yet, but I'll have a small wager that possession of the laptop is of little benefit to us even if we could open it. It's hard to explain, but the nearest comparison I can think of is a TV remote control. The laptop is just a command module, sending instructions to the mothership.'

The major blew out her cheeks. 'So, it's like a remote control that only works if the TV allows itself to be switched on? An interdependent one-way remote?'

'Yes, just like that. And if you want some encouragement for the PM, which I assume is why you called, then tell him that finding Markham's base is now the most important thing he'll ever do. Whoever secures this technology will revolutionise computing. He just has to get to it first.'

181

LJ WAS WOKEN FROM THE WEIRDEST DREAM by the insistent buzzing of her mobile phone. It was just gone three, and Rob Tanner's name flashed on the screen.

'I'm guessing there's news?' she asked, dreading the answer before she had even heard it.

But Tanner's answer was entirely matter of fact. 'Nothing on Joen, no. But there has been a development. You need to check your bank balance.'

She opened her banking app, and the fog of sleep began to lift. Being woken in the middle of the night wasn't exactly an unusual occurrence for LJ, and it was one aspect of her life in politics that she wouldn't miss. She let face ID work its magic, unlocking the screen where her balance was displayed. She did a double take, then tapped the statement to make sure.

Tanner came back on the line. 'From the silence, I'm guessing you've just seen your new balance.'

'Zero.' She was too shocked to say more.

Tanner had ten minutes and a cup of coffee's advantage over her. 'Put the kettle on, read your email and call me back. Five minutes won't matter.'

LJ did just that, and the conversation resumed. Tanner spoke as she sipped scalding tea.

'You've got to assume that every account in the country is the same, LJ. The email from Joen promises a fall—the final line from Sinatra should be "then he has *naught*"—and that's what she's given us. *Nought*. Nada. Zero.' Tanner's commentary carried no hint of emotion; he might have been talking about the actions of a complete stranger. 'She must have pre-programmed her system so that if she didn't log in by 3 a.m., all balances would be wiped automatically.'

'So?'

'So,' Tanner continued, 'Allen has failed to crack her system. They've got access to her apartment, her laptop, presumably the ID she's been using, but nearly six hours later they're no further forward.'

LJ tried to take in what Tanner was suggesting. 'But surely it's just a matter of time?'

'Maybe, but if every account in the country has been zeroed, how much time does Allen have?' There was a catch in Tanner's voice as he added. 'And what if she… Joen…?' He couldn't finish the sentence. LJ stepped in.

'When everyone wakes up today with nothing in the bank, all hell will break loose,' she said. 'Things have been getting hairy already, but this will be orders of magnitude worse. Theft, violence, vandalism… you name it.

Allen will have to keep the army on the streets 24/7. Martial law will be in place until they find her control centre.'

'And do you want Allen to be the one in charge when they do?' Tanner's question was so casual and so entirely unexpected that it took a moment for his meaning to register. Or maybe she'd misunderstood.

'What are you suggesting, Rob?'

Tanner's anger erupted in a burst of pent-up feeling. 'I'll tell you what I'm suggesting, LJ. I'm suggesting that it's time to stop treating people like those mushrooms of yours. Stop feeding them shit. I'm suggesting we should call Trish Dixon at the *Mail* and give her the scoop of her life. I'm suggesting we do our little bit for truth.'

'You're serious, aren't you?'

'Never more so.'

LJ knew that was the end of sleep for this night. She understood where Tanner was coming from, but acting on raw emotion was never a wise strategy.

'Let me think it through, Rob. As you said, a few minutes—a few hours, even—won't matter in the grand scheme of things. My gut tells me it's going to be a long day, so try to get a little rest if you can.' She resorted to the lowest of arguments. 'Save your strength for Joen.'

182

GÉRARD WOKE BEFORE HIS ALARM. He eased his arm from under Nikki's sleeping form and found his watch. Five-forty. He guessed they'd finally fallen asleep in the early hours, passion spent, and sated beyond imagination, so he'd only had four hours sleep. And yet he felt wonderfully alive. The power of lovemaking, he thought. No, it was more than that. Wonderful as the physical intimacy had been, the woman lying so beautifully still next to him had opened the door to a much deeper happiness.

Now, without waking her, he crept to the adjoining sitting room and found his phone. And a waiting email from Tanner, updating him on the night's events. Sent over two hours ago!

It took a second reading for the enormity to sink in. He quietly ordered tea and coffee, then tiptoed back into the bedroom and knelt by Nikki's side of the bed. Allowing himself one last moment to enjoy her blissful repose, Gérard began to stroke her hair. Her eyes flickered open, and she rewarded him with a smile of undiluted warmth.

'Hello, you.' Nikki leant forward and kissed him gently. 'Is it six already?'

Gérard shook his head. 'Not even, but a lot's been happening. It's going to be a busy day.'

Nikki sat up, waiting a moment before drawing the duvet slowly to her shoulders with a modesty wholly at odds with the come-hither look in her eyes. She knew exactly what she was doing, and she knew the effect it had on him. Gérard forced himself to resist.

'Nikki,' he said, 'there is nothing I want to do more in the world than make love to you, I promise. But you need to see this. Honestly.'

He found the TV remote and the BBC News channel. The sound was muted, but the chyron scrolling across the bottom of the screen spoke for itself: "HACKER WIPES OUT ALL UK BANK ACCOUNTS. Suspect in custody. PM to make statement after COBRA meeting at 8 a.m."

'Bloody hell.' Nikki shuffled forwards; duvet pulled to her chin. 'What's going on? Turn the sound up.'

Gérard handed her his phone, displaying the email from Tanner. He watched her expression change, incredulity building with each successive revelation.

A discreet knock at the door pre-empted Nikki's questions. By the time Gérard returned with a tray of tea and coffee, she was robed in a dressing gown and listening intently to the news.

Gérard reached for the remote, and the TV snapped off. The screen was suddenly black, a mirror of the room. Nikki turned to him with an expression of accusation, but the Swiss was already pushing digits on the bedside phone.

'I think, my darling Nikki, that we'd do better to hear the story from, as you say, the horse's mouth. *Non?*' He blew a smiled kiss in his partner's direction.

Tanner answered on the second ring. He was sombre, but there was a steely edge to his voice as he described the night's events and shared his plan to leak what he knew to the press.

'You're sure that's a good idea?' asked Nikki.

'Nope,' replied Tanner, 'but I have to do something. Anyway, how are you two getting on?'

Tanner would have been intrigued, had he been able to see the look his unknowing *double entendre* occasioned between the pair of investigators.

Eyes fixed on the carpet; Gérard managed to stumble out a precis of the investigators' activities the previous day – leaving out only the climactic denouement at AbIGAIL'S. They were almost certainly being listened to, and now was not the time to reveal this crucial piece of information.

'So, you didn't find what you were looking for?' queried Tanner. Gérard noticed how he refrained from stating exactly what they sought, the European base of the criminal who had emptied every account in the country. 'Oh, well,' Tanner's voice trailed off, 'I thought I had a lead, too, not that it matters now.'

The Swiss deflected before the conversation turned maudlin. 'Rob, a very dear friend of mine once said, "Gérard, genius is one per cent inspiration, and ninety-nine per cent perspiration, so stop standing there with your head in the clouds and get your ass moving." Which is advice I must take literally, I'm afraid; there's something I need to attend to back on the continent. A family matter. I may be out of contact for a few hours, but don't worry, Nikki will be here if you need her.'

Tanner laughed. 'Thank you, both. I don't know where I'd be without you.'

Thirty minutes later, the two investigators were saying their goodbyes before heading their separate ways – Gérard to the airport and Nikki to Highgate. They turned their backs on one another reluctantly, and only after a final, lingering, spine-tinglingly prolonged kiss on the hotel steps.

Gérard had to force himself to relegate Nikki in his mind; he had a plan to execute, and he could afford no distractions – not even one as beautiful and alluring as his partner. He couldn't help but feel he was leaving her behind, and he couldn't help but feel sad that he was doing so. Clearly, his solo days were over. But before they could be together again, there was one more ace that he alone could play.

183

ALLEN SURVEYED THE GLUM FACES around the Downing Street table. All the usual suspects, with one obvious exception: there was no LJ.

The place to his left was filled by the dependable bulk of the Chief of the Defence Staff, General Sir Simon Moore. Allen had also requested the presence of the home and foreign secretaries, the commissioner of the Metropolitan Police, and the heads of MI5 and MI6 for this particular COBRA meeting. And he'd asked Major Claydon to attend in LJ's place as note-taker, sounding board and factotum. Whichever it was, he knew he could rely on her.

He counted heads around the table. There were too many, he knew, but he wanted no buck-passing today. Eleven, the *First XI*. He cast a final glance at the portrait dominating the opposite wall.

Right, Winston, who shall we ask to open the batting today? Churchill's eye fell upon the commissioner of police, Dame Juliet Thompson. Sir Richard, the deputy commissioner, had been cut out. Allen insisted on dealing with the organ grinder, as he had put it.

'Commissioner,' commenced Allen, 'perhaps you'd be so good as to kick us off?'

The nation's most senior police officer shuffled slightly in her seat. Not a good start, thought Allen.

'Thank you, Prime Minister,' she deferred in the moderated tones familiar to compulsive news viewers. 'The property in Soho was empty. It was acquired five years ago by a shell company, which is owned by a series of other offshore entities in countries, which refuse to co-operate on corporate disclosure.' Allen dug his nails into the palms of his hands as she continued. 'Their ultimate ownership is untraceable, and no other properties in the UK are owned in those names.'

'A dead end,' summarised Allen.

The commissioner nodded and resumed her recital. 'The CCTV cameras at the location are no help, and there was nothing of note in the building itself, other than some extremely sophisticated gadgetry. All of which is lawfully available in the UK, at a price… a very high price. The apartment itself had a hidden entrance, which does contravene building regulations. All the contractors involved in the work and all tenants on the other floors are legitimate, but none has been able to tell us anything new. Markham was as invisible as the companies through which all contact was funnelled.'

'Any good news?' prompted Allen, expecting none. But he was wrong.

'Actually, yes, sir,' chirped the commissioner, at last showing some sign of vitality, 'One of the passports she was carrying had been used.'

The prime minister sat up in his chair.

'She was carrying two IDs. An unused British passport in the name of Heather Scarman and a German one in the name of Erika Welt.' The commissioner glanced around the table, letting the words sink in. 'You'll note the continuation of the naming convention, the flower and the mark – Erica being the Latin word for heather, as it happens. More importantly, the German document was used three times this year to enter the UK. In January from Toronto, in July from Dublin and in November from Beijing.'

'Beijing!' exclaimed Allen. The others shifted in their seats.

'Yes, sir.' The commissioner waited for the dust to settle then pressed on. 'We're liaising with the Foreign Office and security services on this, so I'll hand over to the foreign secretary.'

The foreign secretary loved being the centre of attention. And as only the third woman in history to hold the post, she deserved enormous credit for her advancement. But sadly, no one held Andrea Cooper in higher esteem than the lady herself. She was, as the saying went, a self-made woman who worshipped her creator.

Now, immaculately coiffed as ever, Cooper puffed herself up and began to opine in the stentorian voice that she believed befitted her position.

'I've spoken with my opposite number in Berlin. It appears the passport was issued at their consulate in New York in December last year, but they have no other record of her. The identity must have been counterfeit. I am assured this is highly unusual. Exceptional, in fact.'

Allen could take no more. He waved her to a stop with a gesture that might have conveyed thanks and might have alluded to something entirely less respectful.

'Thank you, Andrea.' Allen turned to the head of MI6. 'Tim, anything you'd like to add at this point?'

'Yes, Prime Minister.' Tim Miles was the opposite of Cooper, never using two words where one would do. 'The Germans are impressed at how Markham circumvented their security checks. Ditto the Chinese. The latter's visa application requires deep background information, which they check, carefully. Not easy to outwit. And dangerous if you get caught.'

'But obviously it's possible?'

'To fool both parties? With actual applications, not forgeries?' Miles considered the question for a moment before replying. 'Until today, I'd have said no, but clearly Markham proves the answer is yes. The Canadians, meanwhile, have no entry record for "Erika Welt." She'd obviously entered the country using different credentials. Ditto Dublin. The Chinese have indicated she was in Beijing for a couple of days. She entered the country through Hong Kong.'

'Does this help with facial recognition, or anything like that?'

'No, sir. Bottle-top spectacles. Heavyset features, possibly augmented. Dark hair. Headwear. Not subtle, but effective. And easy to discard.'

'And the Chinese connection?'

'Helen and I have been comparing notes.' His eyes moved reflexively towards the Head of MI5, Helen Ingram. 'There isn't a single piece of intel to tie them in. And it's too obvious, sir. We find one live passport and it has a Chinese connection? Her laptop might as well have a shot of The Forbidden City as its screensaver.'

Allen looked to Moore and Ingram for a response, receiving two nods in the affirmative. Moore explained his thinking.

'I agree, sir. If this were the Chinese, they'd be doing everything possible to hide their involvement. I'd assume this is a false trail, unless proven otherwise.'

'Okay,' sighed Allen. 'But in that case, a trail laid by whom?'

In the absence of any answer, the PM turned to the Head of GCHQ. 'Saeed, on the subject of laptops, what's the latest?'

'I'm sorry, sir, but the laptop's not going to provide the answer. We think we have a work-around to confirm what it *does*, even if we can't access the full data or system, but essentially, it's a communications device. A remote control. It can forward a message or confirm an order, but only if they've been pre-programmed somewhere else. The laptop simply chooses a command from a menu.'

'So, we need access to her control centre? We're looking for a physical place where all this can be traced to?'

'Correct.'

'And we have no more idea of where that might be?'

Akhtar's embarrassed shake of the head was matched three times over as Allen made deliberate eye contact with the heads of the police, MI5 and MI6. He spoke to all and none of them, throwing out his words like a callous dealer tossing cards across the table.

'You're effectively telling me that one woman has outfoxed the entire security resources of the sixth most prosperous country in the world?' The pain of the accusation registered on all three faces, and Allen was forced to check himself. 'I'm sorry, everyone. Just letting off steam.'

Silence settled for a moment or two, and then Moore shuffled in his seat and cleared his throat.

'If it's a remote control,' he suggested, 'can we not use it too? Presumably one of the "menu" items is to return everything to normal. We just have to "press the right button," so to speak.'

'Yes,' said Akhtar. 'In principle. But doing that… it would be rather like trying to decipher hieroglyphics without the Rosetta Stone.' The GCHQ man took in the prime minister's look of confusion. 'What I'm saying is that we're trying to recreate an instruction manual, but we don't know how it works or what language it's written in. I've no doubt we can decode it, just as hieroglyphics were eventually deciphered. But that took hundreds of years.'

'I take it that's your worst-case scenario, Saeed,' offered Allen. 'Care to hazard your best?'

'With access to her full system, probably just a few hours. Without it, many days—perhaps weeks—of trial and error. With who knows what consequences.'

'You're talking about time we certainly don't have.' Allen cradled his fingers in a pyramid of contemplation, his brain free-associating the shapes of Ancient Egypt. 'The riddle of the Sphinx?' he mused airily. 'Speaking of which, or whom… what's the latest on Markham's condition?'

The commissioner answered. 'No change, sir. Heavily sedated.'

'Can we wake her?' Allen knew the answer full well but wanted the question on record.

'I'm afraid not, sir. It might well kill her and there'd be little likelihood of a coherent response.'

'No chance, or a slim one?'

Consternation spread across the commissioner's face.

'Don't worry, Juliet,' said Allen. 'I'm not that callous.' Looking around the table, however, he wondered if he ought to be. He certainly needed to do something to change the mood.

'Let me see if I've got this right.' Allen searched for balance. 'The good news is that we're within touching distance of the greatest technological advance in decades. A holy grail, powerful enough to fool all of us. Who knows what advantage such a technology could offer?' Faces lifted at the PM's newly optimistic tone. 'The not-so-fantastic news is that we're broke. Think about it. You, me, everyone out there.' He pointed randomly at members of the committee as he made his point. 'Broke. On paper at least. So, the rather more than sixty-four thousand dollar question is, how the hell do we get through the latter to exploit the former? Governor, would you give us your thoughts, please?'

'Of course, Prime Minister.' There was no shuffling or fidgeting from Anthony Fleming. Nothing appeared to faze him, an attribute of inestimable value in a central banker. From his manner, you'd think he'd been asked for his opinion on an entry at the Chelsea Flower Show.

'Let's consider the three key elements here,' he began. 'Reality, perception and time. The last is the most straightforward. We are where we are. From what I'm hearing, there's only a small chance of the issue being resolved before markets open on Thursday after the New Year break tomorrow, so we must assume that we are *out* of time and behave accordingly. That takes us on to the reality.' Fleming paused. 'Which is a figment of our imagination.'

Quiet settled on the room. Allen took a breath. 'Perhaps you'd care to explain, Anthony?'

'Well, would anyone here care to tell me if accounts being zeroed is good or bad for the balance of payments? Or the two trillion of government debt?' Blank faces stared back at him. 'How about corporate borrowing?' Still, no one moved to answer. 'And finally, what proportion of the population will be better or worse off?' Silence reigned while Fleming looked around the room, deliberately catching eyes. 'Then, with respect, ladies and gentlemen, if a dozen of the finest minds in the country can't answer those questions, what hope for the average man and woman in the street?'

Allen played the role of magician's assistant. 'So?'

'So, there will be a natural *perception* that this is terrible and that is the only "*reality*" that matters.' He added air quotes with his right hand, before shifting his gaze to the prime minister. 'And there are three things that we must do about it. First, we must ensure people have access to essentials: food, medicine, etc. Through a daily allowance if the banks can somehow add funds to customer accounts, or a voucher system… or free, if they can't.'

'For free? There will be mayhem!'

There was a very different composure to Fleming now, cool imperturbability replaced by cold resolution. 'Sir, make no mistake, this is a human crisis now, not a financial one. Which leads me on to my second recommendation. We must assume every bank account is compromised and begin migrating them—or rather, copying their original balances—to new accounts with new entities. The existing accounts and providers are worthless.'

Hugh Westwood, the Chancellor of the Exchequer, was usually the most sober of souls. But now he erupted into life.

'Oh, come on, Anthony, we have Markham in custody!' Westwood scoffed. 'Surely we just reset those balances to where they were on Christmas Eve, and all's fine?'

'I'm sorry, Hugh, but what's to say that Markham hasn't pre-programmed her system to reset all accounts to zero every day? I'm afraid we must assume that's the case until proven otherwise.'

'And lastly, Anthony?' pressed Allen, already dreading the response.

Hesitation flickered in Fleming's eyes for the briefest moment. 'You're not going to like this, sir. But you must call the president and get him to underwrite whatever we have to do. For as long as it takes. *Whatever* the cost.'

Allen grimaced. 'Whatever he demands?'

'I'm afraid so, sir. The Europeans aren't big enough individually, and it would take them weeks to agree to anything. It's the same with the World Bank or IMF. And I don't think anyone would suggest getting into bed with the Chinese.' Fleming looked pointedly at the head of MI6. 'Which leaves our American friends. Their economy's seven times the size of ours. We're little larger than California to them. If they guarantee us, we can get through.'

'But at what cost?' asked Allen. 'You know he'll want a damn sight more than a pound of flesh.'

Fleming's shrug of the shoulders was answer enough. 'I'm sorry, sir, but we have no alternative. Think about it. The next adjustment by Markham could be *negative*. You have to be able to stand in front of the British people and say that they will have new accounts, fully guaranteed by an unassailable power, to the value of their old. I can't see any alternative.'

'Anyone else?' Allen sought desperately for ideas and alternatives, for succour, but found no takers. But then one head did raise itself above the parapet. Simon Moore indicated a desire to speak. The former soldier was always a reassuring presence, physical solidity twinned with ready humour. A hint of the latter played at his mouth as he spoke.

'If you'll excuse the mixed metaphor, it strikes me that whilst we're in a bit of a jam, we still have a weapon up our sleeves. A rather powerful one.' Moore ignored the prime minister's surprised reaction and pressed on. 'Everyone believes we'll have control of Markham's technology eventually, no?'

Saeed Akhtar and the other security heads all nodded in agreement.

'Well then, we have a pretty tasty carrot to offer the president. And a pretty large stick with which to threaten him.'

'Go on, Simon,' said Allen. 'I can see you're on a roll.'

'I'm afraid that takes me on to the security situation, sir.' The devilish mischief dropped now from Moore's ruddy complexion. It was replaced by the steel of a soldier preparing for battle. 'Prime Minister,' he repeated formally. 'It's important that everyone here recognises that the armed forces will not be able to keep peace on the streets if there's a major escalation in disorder. Servicemen and women are a deterrent—a bloody powerful deterrent—but there are limits to what they can do. They can support the police, they can urge restraint, but they, we, cannot use force against our own citizens. If the people rise up against the military in large numbers, there's very little we can do but retreat.'

Here, Sara Jafari spotted her moment for the limelight.

'But Sam, we have the necessary legal powers,' she interjected. 'I don't see the problem?'

'With respect, Sara,' replied Moore, that time-honoured phrase denoting exactly the opposite, 'it's not a legal matter, now. It's simple human practicalities.'

Jafari's face went blank. 'I don't follow,' she said.

'Sara, there are nearly a hundred cities in the UK with populations of over one hundred thousand. Even with reservists, we've only got a hundred thousand soldiers. How many police officers do you have? A hundred and fifty thousand? So even with every single serviceman and woman, we're not even doubling police numbers. And the moment a single soldier is filmed causing harm to a civilian, no matter how out of context, then centuries of respect for our armed forces will be lost. *Forever*.'

'You're right, of course.' The cabinet secretary, Jonathan Morse, relished the chance to put the boot into Jafari. 'It's a confidence trick. And it depends on that very respect to succeed.'

Allen had been watching Moore, scrutinising the defence chief carefully. 'Do I sense you have an idea, Simon?'

Moore's mischievous grin returned. 'I'm afraid the chancellor's not going to like it, but it's back to the carrot and stick. What did the Americans do when the pandemic first started to bite? They posted everyone a cheque for twelve hundred bucks. It was so popular, they did it twice more. Well, why don't we do the same? As Jonathan said, it's all about *confidence*. So, what better way to show that than to tell people they're getting a nice windfall? Say, a thousand pounds? But only if they're good and law-abiding for the next few days while everything's sorted.'

The prime minister turned to the two finance experts. 'Hugh? Anthony?'

'That would cost about forty billion if it went to every adult,' answered the governor. 'It's obviously a huge number in isolation, but in the context of everything else over the past few years…' He didn't bother to end the sentence, merely shrugged.

The chancellor seemed content to go along too, declining a second invitation to speak up with a facial contortion that might have easily been an attack of the gripe. Allen knew Westwood was hoping to avoid having his response committed to the official note of the meeting. Deniability! Well, he could think again.

'In that case,' declared Allen, 'given the seriousness of the matter at hand, I believe it right we have a formal vote. For the record. All in favour?'

Teeth have been drawn more easily and less painfully, but eventually the eleven, *the first XI*, had no alternative but to comply. Even Westwood's vote was recorded for posterity.

There had been much talk about confidence, and now Allen tried to force some into his expression. He'd need the practice for the press conference to follow and, just as importantly, for a discussion with the president. The first he knew he could manage. The second would take some work.

184

THE APPEARANCE OF TWO POLICEMEN on Sir Peter's doorstep the previous morning had been an unwelcome surprise. Finding Tommy Steele there at the same hour a day later was no less shocking. And judging from the driver's grimace, this intrusion was to be no more enjoyable.

Sir Peter did a double take. 'Unless I'm losing my marbles—which, after the events of the last week, is entirely possible—I don't remember asking you to pick me up this morning, Tommy.' The chairman stepped to one side and gestured toward the sitting room. 'In which case, I think you'd better come in.'

Once the pair were settled with a cup of tea, Sir Peter got down to business.

'I was waiting to see what the prime minister has to say…' a tilt of the chairman's head indicated the darkened TV screen, 'but I'm guessing you've saved us the trouble.'

'Yes, sir,' replied Tommy, in a tone uncharacteristically stiff and formal. It took him a few minutes to regain his powers of storytelling, but soon Tommy was in full flow. The chairman, for his part, listened in spellbound disbelief as the chauffeur ran through the evening's events: the snowy circumnavigation of the City, the bug-planting at the Tower and Tanner's attempt at flight through St Katharine Docks. Then Steele's own high-speed getaway to Canary Wharf, his arrest and—to the grandee's astonishment—LJ's part in his, and Tanner's, release. But that wasn't the half of it. Next came Steele's account—gleaned from Tanner and LJ—of the accident in front of the Bank's apartment by the river, the revelation of the guilty party's identity, Markham's emergency surgery at the neurological hospital, Tanner's night-time vigil, and his burning desire for revenge on Allen.

And still there was more.

On being released, Tommy had turned on his phone for the first time that evening to find a raft of increasingly anxious messages from Chrissie, urging the driver to return her call at the earliest opportunity.

'She was in a terrible state, sir,' said Tommy. 'Sobbing, beside herself, repeating, "It's my fault, it's my fault!" over and over again. I've known her for the best part of twenty years and never heard anything like it. Naturally, I had to go to find her.'

'Of course. Good man.' Sir Peter paused, searching, perhaps, for something in Tommy's eyes. 'Where was she?'

'At the bank's apartment, sir. In St Katharine Docks.'

'What?'

'Turns out she'd witnessed the whole bloody saga. It was her who'd told Kellett where Rob and Miss Markham were headed.' He held up a hand to stay the chairman's attempt to interrupt. 'I'll come back to it, sir. Anyway, she sees the accident, the police—everything—from the doorway of the apartment block. There was nothing she could do, no point getting her collar felt, so she went into the flat to try to reach one of us. And of course, we were all banged up. Well, I went and fetched her, managed to calm her down a bit and took her home.'

'How extraordinary!'

'She told me the whole story: how she wanted to help Rob by letting him use the apartment to be with Miss Markham, how Kellett forced her to reveal what was going on. How she decided to warn them by getting there first. And how she'd been too late.'

Sir Peter exhaled loudly. He picked up his mug of tea, which was still steaming. 'Lord, Tommy, it's like one of those TV thrillers.'

'Yes, sir. And with a proper villain.'

Sir Peter's grey eyebrows lifted. 'Kellett, I take it?'

'More than you know.' The ebullience drained from Tommy's face. 'Seems he's more of a wrong 'un than any of us thought. And I didn't think that was possible. It goes back to when Chrissie first started working for him.' Tommy relayed the full story of Chrissie's abortion, revealing how Kellett had held it over her all this time and how she had finally prised herself free of the Toad's grasp.

Sir Peter found himself staring at his fingertips as Tommy finished the story. 'The bastard! So, let me get this straight. Rob's at the hospital?'

A nod from Tommy. 'And there's one other thing you should know. Well two, actually. Mike Sorensen and Pattie Boyle…'

'Yes?'

'Kellett fired them yesterday. Or accepted their *resignations*.'

'You're not serious? Why wasn't I informed?'

Tommy said nothing. This was just the latest in a long list of questions that should have been asked, about a whole range of things, but that was water under the bridge now. Recognising the implied rebuke, the chairman fixed Tommy with the purposeful into-battle look he'd mastered at Sandhurst.

'I'd like you to tell Rob and Christina they have my—and the Bank's—full support. As, of course, do you. So, you do that, and leave me to deal with Mike and Pattie and, more importantly, that *Toad*, Martin Kellett.'

This time it was the driver who raised a quizzical eyebrow.

'Don't you worry, Tommy,' said Sir Peter. 'I'm going to do what I should have done years ago. No mealy-mouthed words, just a simple statement that he has been fired. Hopefully the bastard will rot in jail, but I can assure you he's never setting foot in my bank again.'

The chairman rose and offered a hand to the chauffeur, helping the slightly younger man to his feet. There was no release of grip. Instead, Sir Peter firmed the hold into the warmest of handshakes. A matching smile played across his face.

'And he's certainly never getting into your car again.' He gave a final squeeze. 'Thank you, Tommy. You're a true friend to the bank, and you're a true friend to me.'

185

TANNER HAD BEEN LEFT LARGELY TO HIMSELF. He'd been told the surgeon usually did his rounds about 10 a.m., so he resigned himself to his quiet vigil until then, at the earliest.

He exchanged messages with LJ, Nikki and Tommy, suggesting they meet up at noon. He let Allen's address to the nation play soundlessly in the background; he couldn't bear to hear the PM's voice, and the fact that

Allen had to appear on the nation's screens at all told its own story. Joen's code, her systems, had outwitted all attempts to break and enter. The country was in a stand-off, with the clock ticking louder by the minute. LJ had even suggested Allen would have to go cap-in-hand to the Americans for a bailout before the day was out. Happy New Year, James. Or not.

Tanner had tried calling his father, but the phone rang through to voicemail. He wanted to make sure the old boy was okay after his fall, after the mugging. More than that, he wanted to let the older man know about the coordinates – although that wasn't something that could be done over the phone. There had been no chance to add the last number—52—to the sequence. Tanner had to assume he was being monitored and couldn't risk anything to do with clues or locations – not right now. The numbers only added detail, anyway: a fifth and sixth decimal point. Enough to pinpoint a precise location, hopefully. If luck and time didn't run out.

A voice cut suddenly across these thoughts – the chiding voice of a parent.

'Why are you sitting there staring into space like a great lummox? Isn't there something useful you can be doing?'

Tanner leapt to his feet and was enveloped immediately in a hug. He'd never in his life been hugged by the older man, his father. Even in the early days they weren't that sort of family, and Harry wasn't that kind of dad. He was the strong and silent kind, not the demonstrative type. But now he held his son as if it was the most natural thing in the world. Nor was there any awkwardness to his words.

'I'm so sorry, son. So sorry.' Harry stepped back so he could look properly at Tanner's face, and his son stared back. The swelling around the older man's eyes had come down, but the bruise hung over his face still, like a shadow. Intensity burned in Harry's gaze as he fixed his son with a fortifying smile. 'Don't give up,' he encouraged. 'It will be all right.'

As if on cue, a white-coated physician appeared. Confirmation or disavowal of Harry's thesis was imminent. There had been no change in condition—which was good—and, if Tanner liked, he could see her. Which was better. So much better.

The surgeon, to whom Tanner was warming rapidly, had no objection so long as the visit was limited to just a few minutes, so it was the Tanners junior *and* senior who were led into the sterile critical facility. A police officer sat mutely outside the door as they passed, affecting disinterest. But Tanner caught movement from the corner of his eye as soon as he and Harry were through, the policeman presumably rushing to report the visit to his superiors. They were still being watched closely then, Tanner thought. He and his associates. Not that it mattered.

Joen was propped up at an angle, surrounded by equipment. She was the only patient in the critical care ward. The only other person in the room was the nurse, and yet the space seemed impossibly cluttered. There was just so much equipment, all of it in that curious medical shade merging cream, off-white and grey. And banks and banks of monitors, all displaying their own readings, their own numbers. Tanner was struck by the irony.

How could a body give out so many? How many vital signs could one human being have? And how many tubes were there, pumping heaven-knows-what into and out of her arms? Her head, meanwhile, was swathed in bandages, and a ventilator covered much of her face.

The two men stood either side of the bed, each trying to peer closer, both afraid to get too close, barely daring to breathe. It was Harry who spoke first.

'So, this is your Joen, then. You did say she was beautiful.'

Tanner didn't try to speak. He knew the words wouldn't come. But Harry was not one to be put off.

'You know what this reminds me of?' he went on. 'It reminds me of the end of *Snow White*. The film.'

Tanner nodded. He was holding himself together through sheer force of will alone, listening as Harry continued.

'Snow White lying there—to all intents and purposes, dead to the world— waiting for her prince to come. And, you know what he does? He gives her a right smacker. Then she wakes up, and they live happily ever after. Don't you forget that. Now… you'll want a minute alone.' He turned on his heel. 'I'll see you back in the waiting room.'

A chaste kiss on the cheek, let alone a smacker, was barely possible. But it would have to do. Tanner wasn't going to tempt fate by not following his father's instructions.

Then he whispered three words, knowing they would go unheard, and went off in search of Harry. Joen had to rest, and that meant Tanner could only wait.

186

TANNER RE-ENTERED THE WAITING ROOM to find Harry introducing himself to three new visitors: LJ, Nikki and Tommy.

'We thought you might need some support,' explained Nikki. 'So, we agreed to come a little earlier.'

'And we knew you'd need sustenance,' LJ held up a small paper carrier which held the steaming promise of coffee. 'And probably some fresh air.'

'I could do with a break,' agreed Tanner flatly. 'Let me just tell the receptionist where we'll be.'

'I'll be off then,' said Harry. 'Leave you all to it.'

But the younger Tanner was having none of it. He cut his father off at the door. 'And where do you think you're going?' he whispered. 'Don't think I haven't got your *number*, old man… and hand over your phone!'

The look on Harry's face was priceless. He did as he was told, then mutely followed as the party made its way into the centre of the gardens, still an expanse of pristine whiteness. Frozen snow crunched underfoot; a stillness only broken by the wail of a siren in the near distance. Tanner didn't have to think too hard to imagine what that might be in response to; the London Riots would be nothing compared to the current situation with the zeroed accounts, a veritable tinderbox. When he closed his eyes, he saw the Foundation's premises: windows smashed and fires raging down the road. The year dying in screams and a hail of broken glass. It was all imminent, if Joen's manipulations weren't reversed.

Once the group was far enough from the doors, Tanner pulled his father's phone from his pocket and ostentatiously removed its SIM card. He regarded the three new visitors in turn.

'You lot don't fool me you know,' he scoffed. 'That talk of support. *Fresh air*, indeed. So, why the cloak and dagger?'

It was Nikki who answered, her face a picture of animated mischief. 'It's Gérard. He only went and found the…' she soundlessly mouthed the words, '*you know*.' A stage wink completed the performance.

'I know, alright!' whispered Tanner, a picture of schoolboy self-satisfaction. 'Joen's base is in Aachen.'

'Wait, what?' Nikki couldn't hide her confusion. 'How do you already know? Did she tell you?'

Tanner tilted his head towards his father. 'No. *He* told me. The numbers in Joen's emails provide a set of coordinates, corresponding to a science park in Aachen. My clever old father worked it out.' He offered Harry a smile of acknowledgement, then turned his gaze to the investigator. 'And I'm assuming Aachen is where your clever boyfriend is now?'

For once, Nikki was silenced. She managed a single nod before Tanner continued.

'So, LJ, what's the move?'

The former chief of staff was ready with the playbook. 'I've still got friends on the inside at Number Ten. They tell me there's been no real progress. They can't crack Joen's code, and without access to her data centre, they're really no better off. Without a breakthrough, Allen's screwed.' LJ took a breath and continued. 'The PM has a one o'clock call with the president to beg for help. The expectation is that it will only come at a price: the highest price. So, the only question is: can they find Joen's HQ before they have to pay it?'

'And, even if they do find the location, will there be anything there?' asked Nikki. No Delphic utterance was ever breathed with greater inscrutability.

'I'm guessing this has something to do with Gérard's sudden trip to the continent,' suggested Tanner, looking directly at the investigator. 'Care to share?'

'Well,' smiled Nikki. 'The scion of a Swiss banking family has to know a thing or two about vaults. And a man from that kind of lineage would surely have some idea about how one might break into them – or, at least, how to get hold of the people who do. Moreover, it seems that *Monsieur* Dumont has relatives who own a trucking company, alongside their financial concerns. Given our predicament, I'd say that's a useful combination.'

Tanner laughed, but Nikki wasn't quite finished yet.

'And there's one more thing you should know,' she went on. 'AbIGAILS. It's the name of the café at the entrance to the complex where Joen stashed all her equipment. Gérard had a drink there and put two and two together. We know beyond any doubt that it's the place we're looking for.'

Tanner understood now exactly why Gérard had gone back to Aachen. Clearly, his connections offered a means of breaking into Joen's hideout and moving all her equipment out of the firing line before the PM's merry men stumbled on the location. Nikki's eyes had twinkled as she recounted her partner's plan, but now the humour disappeared from her face, replaced by anxiety.

'But he needs *time*,' she stressed. 'Ten, twelve hours.'

'That's perfect, Nikki,' LJ assured her. 'Allen will be at his wits' end by then. He'll agree to anything. And I doubt he'll find the location that quickly.'

'I just worry about what he'll do in the meantime,' said Nikki. 'Allen, that is. I have enough friends and family still in Hong Kong to know what can happen when a power-crazed leader feels the need to lash out.'

'It's okay,' replied LJ. She placed a reassuring hand on the investigator's arm. 'I know Allen better than anyone. He'll be furious, but he won't do anything too rash in the meantime. The president might even keep him in check. We've just got to trust that Gérard can get everything sorted at his end.'

Tommy spoke for the first time. 'What do *we* do in the meantime?'

'We wait, Tommy,' volunteered Tanner quietly. 'We wait and hope.'

187

WHENEVER JAMES ALLEN HAD TO SPEAK with the President of the United States, he thought of his mother.

'James,' she had said, one day after school when he came home and threw a histrionic fit about one classmate or another. 'We never, ever, say we hate people. There's good in everyone. There's nothing good about hate.'

Throughout his life, Allen had tried his best to heed her words. With hand on heart, there were only a couple of people he truly, deeply disliked, and many he didn't like but forced himself to tolerate. But the President of the United States? The PM hated him with a visceral passion. There was no single cause; the tumour grew remorselessly from exposure to the president's toxic mix of holier-than-thou smugness, folksy insincerity and his tendency to confuse cliché and sagacity. Not to mention the small matter of the president's inclination to distrust anything—and anyone— British. To cap it all, the vice president, on whom the detailed workload of state appeared to be delegated, was even worse. The pair were known to all within Number Ten as Omission and Commission. The Special

Relationship, under the harsh glow of this new reality, wasn't looking so special these days.

The digital wall clock ticked over to 12:58. Allen could feel his heart beating faster already. His secretary put her head round the door.

'Two minutes, sir. Jonathan and Major Claydon are here.'

In LJ's absence, Allen had retained the services of Vivienne Claydon as an ADC. He liked her unfussy, actions-speak-louder approach. And whilst the cabinet secretary could be dour at times, he was a quintessential calming influence wherever the president was concerned.

Morse flashed Allen a reassuring smile, as if he had been reading his mind.

'Chin up, sir. It'll soon be over. Just think, the boot will be on the other foot once we have Markham's technology.'

Allen nodded thanks through gritted teeth. He did so without pausing the deep-breathing exercises he'd been encouraged to practice at times like this. The speakerphone on his desk buzzed, and they all took their seats. A series of metallic bleeps were followed by silence, then the east-coast drawl of the president's secretary came on the line.

'Good morning, Prime Minister. I have the president for you.'

Allen fought back the urge to tell the bitch it was afternoon in the UK. But before he could muster a sufficiently polite response, the president's reedy tenor echoed across the waves.

'Morning, Jim. I hear you're still having a few problems over there.'

No one, ever, had called James Allen "Jim." The president's advisors had been told as much, which, of course, was a big mistake.

'Temporary problems, Mr President,' said Allen. 'Temporary.'

'Oh, I see.' The president affected surprise. 'Then you don't need my help? My people must have been under a misunderstanding. In that case…'

'Mr President,' interjected Allen. He made sure to coat his words with an extra dollop of honey, hoping future students of history, but not the receiver, would note their ambiguity. 'You follow in a long line of great presidents who have been steadfast supporters of our country.'

'Yada, yada. What's the deal?'

Allen did his best to sound confident. 'We have the perpetrator of the attacks in custody. We…'

'No, you don't. She's in a coma. You've got diddly squat. All you've got is a bust banking system, a bankrupt economy and peace on the streets being kept by an army outmatched by the Texas National Guard.' The prime minister was lost for words, but the president seemed keen to offer more. 'Hey Jim, you mentioned those great presidents.'

'Yes, Mr President.'

'Well, who was the greatest of them all?'

Too late, Allen realised where the conversation was leading. He tried to deflect the question. 'Present company excepted?'

A brief pause on the line suggested the egomaniac at the other end might actually be considering his place in the pantheon, but then the rasping resumed.

'No, Jim, not me. Not yet. But I'll tell you who Americans think of as their greatest president. George W – that's who. And I don't mean Bush.' Again, hush invited a response. Allen refused to give him that satisfaction, so the president growled on.

'George Washington. And you know why? Because he stuck it to you Brits, Jim. We're always bailing you out, and does it get us anything? No. You're the past, Jim. History. And so's the "Special Relationship." Now, don't worry. I know exactly what you're after. You need the good ol' US of A to back up your currency. Your economy. The whole nine yards. You need Uncle Sam and the mighty Greenback. Correct?'

'As I said, Mr President, we would value your support.' Allen was floundering. He'd known this would be a brutal contest, but he was used to fighting by the rules. The president, on the other hand, probably thought the Marquess of Queensberry was a pub.

'Support?' The president's mocking laughter echoed down the line. 'Good choice of words, Jim. You do need support. Life support. Without us, you're dead. Like your empire.' The tone changed abruptly, the bully replaced by the snake-oil salesman. 'Well, Jimbo, nothing comes for nothing anymore. Everything has its price. And this, my friend, is gonna cost you.' He didn't bother to wait for a reply, eager to lay out his terms. 'Number one. Your pound is history.'

'But—'

'No buts, Jim, so zip it. I'll tell you when I'm finished.' The president returned to the list from which he was obviously reading. 'Number two. Your banks get acquired by ours. Same with pharmaceuticals; that's about all you're good for. Number three, the governor of the Bank of England gets replaced by my appointee.'

'But it's an independent…'

'Jim, next time you interrupt, the phone goes down. Got it? Four, your GCHQ guys pass all their little secrets on to my guys. They say it's the only other thing you Brits can still do. Although from what I've seen the last few days, I have my doubts.' Allen bit his tongue, trying to process the information. The president droned on. 'Five, we're gonna privatise that NHS of yours. Make some money out of it for God's sake. Same with the BBC and your fancy universities. Oxford, Cambridge, and the rest.'

'You're kidding?'

'Hey, Jim, I don't joke when it comes to money. Six – or is it seven? Anyways, lastly, the King invites me to Buckingham Palace for a nice visit to sign this all off.' Allen was too dumbstruck to reply. 'Oh, and I nearly forgot. It goes without saying that you'll hand over Miss Markham to us. We'll take over her little *system*. We're gonna have some fun with that.'

Mention of Markham was the jolt Allen needed, the charge to the prime minister's fighting spirit.

'Thank you for your—what shall I call them?—*terms*, Mr President. I'll consider them.'

'You'll consider them?' The response came out as a comical, high-pitched squeal. The president took a second to regain his composure, and then there was nothing funny about his next sentence. 'I don't think you're in any position to *consider* anything, Jim. You're pretty much out of time.' The sneering bully was back in control now. 'But I'm feeling generous today, so I'll give you the rest of the day. Let's say eleven tonight your time, in time for New Years. Oh, and Jim, no negotiations. A simple yes or no. Final answer. Like in that lousy *Who Wants to Be a Millionaire?* show you gave us. Appropriate huh?'

There was no sign-off, just a loud chortle and more metallic clicks. Then silence.

188

TOMMY PERSUADED TANNER to take a short break from his vigil. There was no change in Joen's condition, and none was expected in the very short term. A shower, a change of clothes and something to eat would set him up for the rest of the day. Meanwhile, Nikki, LJ and Harry had gone their separate ways, with an agreement that—in the absence of major developments—the group would reconvene at the hospital before curfew fell at 8 p.m.

Nikki was sure Gérard would be back from Aachen by then, hopefully bearing good news. Tanner wasn't convinced that any safe-breaker or bank-vault-designer could defeat Joen's security systems, but Nikki had made the sound argument that they were hardly likely to be wired to the local police station, so what was there to lose? They all just had to pray that the intelligence services failed to find the location and didn't manage to hack into Joen's computers. Tanner didn't know about the first supposition—Harry had decoded the coordinates, after all—but he'd place a sizeable bet against the second. Such was his faith in Joen's intelligence and foresight.

LJ, meanwhile, had clandestine discussions with former colleagues to arrange, and Harry claimed to need a nap. But from the way he'd skipped off into the snowy distance, Tanner doubted the older man would be able to rest—nor, despite his injuries—did he seem to need it. Knowledge of his part in the success had taken years off his father. More likely, he'd go and terrorise his grandchildren to while away the time.

Tanner accepted Tommy's offer of a ride home to Hammersmith. He knew the driver had more to tell him than he'd wanted to share in front of the other conspirators, but waited until they reached the main westward artery before broaching the subject.

'Something you want to tell me, Thrup?'

'Is it that obvious?'

'Well, we've only known each other twenty years.'

'That we have.' Tommy laughed, but it was without humour. His eyes flashed to the mirror, where they met Tanner's. 'Long enough for me to know you're not going to like this, one bit.'

Tanner listened in disbelieving silence as Tommy described first Chrissie's part in leading Kellett to National Bank's flat and then her reason for doing so. By the end, Tanner was seething.

'I'll kill him, Tommy.'

'You'll have to join a long queue, Six.' As ever, the driver's dry humour was the best antidote to anger.

'But why didn't she tell me, us... anyone?'

'Fear, of course. And shame. Not wanting to let her parents down.' Tommy shook his head. 'All sorts of stuff probably. Anyway, you can ask her yourself.'

'What?'

'She's coming to see you. To apologise. She's desperate to make amends somehow. She wants to help.'

'I don't know, Tommy,' Tanner exhaled heavily. 'With Joen... I mean, I know it's not Chrissie's fault, but...'

Tommy didn't let him finish. Again, he took his eyes deliberately from the road to catch his passenger's.

'Rob, you of all people understand guilt.' There was no traffic, but Tommy still paced his sentences with checks ahead. 'You know better than anyone how destructive it is. The personal cost. Don't add more to Chrissie's load, eh?'

Tanner had spent a lifetime trying to get over Matt's death. The guilt had poisoned everything he'd touched until Joen offered him a way out. And yet his first thought had still been to blame Chrissie. Tommy allowed him to wallow in it for all of five seconds.

'Right,' he said. 'If you're quite done being maudlin, let's work out how we're going to shaft that nice prime minister of ours.'

They pulled up outside Tanner's front door just as Chrissie was walking through the front gate. The sight of her cut short their conversation, in which Tanner had been brainstorming aloud all the ways they could get Allen out of the picture. But Chrissie was a real shock. Funereal black had returned, and nothing could have been more appropriate. She looked utterly disconsolate, dark-eyed and haggard. Desolate, even.

Shocked at her appearance, Tanner ushered Chrissie inside. Tommy made a hasty exit under cover of a suddenly remembered errand, and soon Tanner and Chrissie were alone, seated with cups of tea. Tanner searched for the words.

A chance glance in the mirror brought Harry to mind, and the memory of his father's embrace at the hospital that morning stirred within him.

Pulling the unexpecting but unresisting Chrissie to her feet, he did what he should have done first. And wrapped her in a tight hug.

Snuffles begat tears, which turned to sobs. Tanner had no idea how long it took, but only when he could feel the physicality draining from her gale of misery did he release her. The tea tray was duly ditched in favour of stronger substitutes, and not until Chrissie had joined him in a measure of cognac decidedly larger than a nip would he allow her to speak.

'Has Tommy told you everything?' she asked.

'The bare details, but I'd like to hear the full story from you… if you want to share it?'

Chrissie gave the merest nod and, haltingly, began to retell the tale of Spring 2008. Slowly and quietly at first, nervously dabbing at her eyes, unable to look into Tanner's. Then, more forcefully, anger building as she described the rape and Kellett's role in its aftermath.

Tanner had told himself not to interrupt, but he was unable to prevent the obvious question, 'Why didn't you say something?'

'Come on, Rob,' replied Chrissie, with a weary shake of the head. 'This was sixteen years ago. You remember the City then. Boozy lunches, wandering hands. The only "MeToo" was the second bloke wanting to grope you.'

'But…'

'No buts. It's history, Rob. I can't change it. Same as I can't change what happened last night.' Her eyes fell to the floor. 'I am sorry, though. Desperately sorry. I tried to warn you and Tommy, but your phones were off.'

'I know.'

'Can you forgive me?'

It took a moment for Tanner to respond. He surprised her, and himself, by answering with a recounting of Matt's death. If her story had built over two decades, the weight of his had accumulated over three.

'You see, Chrissie,' he went on, 'no one understands the tragedy of accidents better than me. That's the whole point. You don't intend an accident or expect it. Usually they're mishaps, or difficulties – not disasters. You *get away* with them. That's life. Or not.' He shrugged wistfulness into another wan smile.

'I know, but…'

'You said no buts.' A raised palm brooked no argument, and Tanner deliberately stood and refilled their glasses. He wouldn't let introspection settle. 'There's just one thing I've never understood. Why is Martin so bitter? Surely, he has everything he's always wanted?'

Chrissie took another small sip of her drink. 'You're not going to believe this. After the last week.' The emphasis on recent events was evidently important. And completely over Tanner's head.

'The last week?' he asked, intrigued.

'Names,' laughed Chrissie humourlessly. 'Image. Background.' She sighed heavily, as if delivered at last of a burden, then saw the bafflement on Tanner's face and realised she'd revealed nothing.

'He's not Martin Kellett at all.' She corrected herself, 'Well, he is *now*. Officially. But he was born Andrea Martino. His parents were Italian immigrants, like mine. Peasants from the south who came to England after the war. Whole villages of them came over to work at a huge brickworks south of Bedford, in a new model village like those Victorian ones. You know? Like Bourneville. The brickworks is long gone, but apparently the Italian connection's still there. There's even an honorary consulate. Anyway.' She took another small sip. 'Martin—Andrea—was one of two kids; the only son. A smart kid. Grammar school material. But his dad was a working man. A horny-handed son of toil. He thought young Andrea should be the same. Shovels and overalls, not protractors and fancy uniforms.'

'How do you know all this?' asked Tanner.

'Martin got a letter from a former pupil in Stewartby—that was the village—asking if he'd ever heard of Andrea Martino. Kellett went berserk—even by his standards—and said if I ever mentioned it again, he'd...'

'I get it. Go on.'

'Anyway, this was back in the days of Friends Reunited. Remember it?'

'Vaguely. Forerunner of Facebook? Back in the early 2000s?'

'Exactly. Well, there was a message board of former pupils wanting to make contact with lost classmates. A number of them wanted to know if anyone had ever heard what happened to young Andrea. So, to cut a long story short, my dad knew someone who knew someone who worked for London Brick. We're talking the post-war Italian immigrant community, remember. Three degrees of separation got you to the Pope.' A little of the colour was coming back into Chrissie's face with the telling of the tale.

'It turned out that *Papa* Martino was a bad lot. Too much of this,' she indicated the alcohol on the coffee table in front of them, 'and too ready with these.' She held up her fists. 'Saturday nights weren't a lot of fun for *Signora* Martino. Sex and beatings, in either order, and the fact that the couplings failed to provide another son or three only made it worse.' She let out a sigh, 'Anyway, Andrea was a promising young boxer and big for his age. One night, Dad decided to take out his aggression on Mum, as usual, and this time, Andrea tried to protect her. The police were called, and the authorities had no choice but to take Martin into care – for his protection.'

'Poor Martin.' Tanner couldn't help himself.

'No,' Chrissie shook her head firmly. 'It wasn't for the son's protection, but the father's. Martin nearly killed him.'

'How old was he?'

'Fourteen.'

Tanner blew out a stream of air. 'And?'

'As I said, the son went into care. Went to a different school. As soon as he was old enough, he anglicised his mother's maiden name—Galletti—to Kellett, and never looked back. Actually, that's not strictly true. It seems he went back once to see his mother. To persuade her to leave. Offered to buy her a house, anything, to get her away from the father. But she said she couldn't leave the husband; marriage is a sacred sacrament, for richer, for poorer, for beatings or worse. You know the drill.'

'Are they still alive?'

'Well, they were last summer. In their eighties, living in a bungalow. I drive out there once a year to check – to see for myself.'

'But he's always said they died years ago?'

Chrissie rejected the notion with a sad shake of the head.

'Christ!' exhaled Tanner. 'Who'd have thought?' A half-smile crossed Tanner's face. 'I wonder if Joen…' The name stopped Tanner in his tracks. He took a moment to gather himself, forcing strength back into his voice. There would be plenty of time for Kellett, but there was a bigger fish to fry first. And who better than a chef's daughter to help?

'Come on, let's go for a walk. We need to talk about "*Martin.*" You can leave your phone here.'

189

THE EIGHT O'CLOCK CURFEW found the conspirators back at the Neurological Hospital as agreed. They had hoped there would be six in the evening's group, and that was the case – but it was Chrissie who made up the number now, not Gérard. Nobody had heard from the Swiss investigator all day.

The hospital basement provided perfect cover for the team huddle. Tanner had scouted the building earlier and had been delighted to find a humming power room unlocked. On New Year's Eve, with a strict curfew, there was little risk of company unless there was an emergency, and the noisy backdrop was perfect. There was no chance the electrical supply room was bugged, and no surveillance satellite in the world would be able to hear their conversation, were it even listening.

'There's still been no breakthrough,' began LJ. She had been in contact with her friends at Number Ten all day. 'They can't crack Joen's code, and without access to her data centre, they're really no better off. The president's terms are extreme. It's total surrender; essentially, Britain becomes a fifty-first state, but without the powers or benefits. Forget "No Taxation Without Representation." This is just no representation.' Anguish eddied at the corner of her eyes.

It took a moment for the former chief of staff's composure to return. Former she might be, but she still cared deeply about her country, and she knew good people in government who shared her sentiments.

'Sorry,' she said. 'Back to our immediate predicament. One of the president's specific demands is that Joen be handed over to the US authorities.' Every head swivelled naturally toward Tanner, but before he could say anything, LJ pressed on. 'Which is bad enough in itself. The worse news is that the PM only has until eleven o'clock to accept the terms.' She looked at her watch. 'Which gives us less than three hours. I'm starting to worry that we haven't heard from Gérard yet.'

'Don't worry,' replied Nikki. Who, to everyone's surprise, appeared radiantly unconcerned. 'He'll do it. I know it.'

Unease at eight spawned nervousness at nine and trepidation at ten. Nikki remained resolutely confident, but by quarter past that hour, a twitch at the corner of her mouth was threatening to break ranks and render her face scrutable.

And then, with no forewarning, their wait ended. Fittingly, snow had begun falling again. No mountain rescuer had ever shown better timing or displayed greater sangfroid. Granite-faced at the best of times, Gérard entered the waiting room that night without a word. Once all eyes were on him, he raised an index finger, waited a moment and then let a grin wash any trace of stone from his face.

'I rather think there's someone you need to call,' he suggested, looking directly at LJ, before allowing himself to be enveloped by in the joyous embrace of his beaming partner.

190

THEY HEARD THE SIRENS TEN MINUTES LATER. LJ had called Major Claydon as soon as she had the gist of Gérard's news, and within a moment, the prime minister was on the line.

'What can I do for you, LJ?' demanded Allen. His voice was acid. 'I'm rather busy, you know.'

LJ couldn't resist the obvious retort. 'It's not what you can do for me, sir. It's what I can do for you.' She channelled JFK. 'And my country.'

'Well?'

'I thought you might be interested to know the location of Markham's HQ.'

'Are you serious?' asked Allen. She could hear movement on the other end of the line, a miscellany of action. 'Where?'

'I don't want to talk over the phone.'

'Yes, of course. Where are you?'

'At the Neurological Hospital in Russell Square with Rob Tanner. As I'm sure you know.'

'Well, stay there. I'll send a car for you.'

It wasn't just a car that arrived, but a full security detail with two police outriders and two other support vehicles. LJ and Tanner were ushered into the middle vehicle, and the cavalcade set off. They were relieved to see that none of the reinforcements stayed behind at the hospital.

As for the others: Harry would return to the waiting room in his son's stead; Tommy and Chrissie would wait in the Mercedes, in case a fast getaway was needed; and Gérard and Nikki? Well, they had done all they could and would shortly return to their hotel.

Another ten minutes and the government vehicles were sweeping into Downing Street, leaving sprays of newly fallen snow in their wake. Tanner and LJ were shown straight into the Cabinet Room, where Allen was seated in his customary position at the centre of the table, flanked by Sir Simon Moore and Vivienne Claydon on his left, and the heads of MI5 and MI6 on his right. The prime minister pointed wordlessly to the two empty seats opposite. All other chairs had been withdrawn to the room's perimeter. Had the lighting been subtly altered, too? The attempt at psychology was blatant on so many levels: the might of the state versus the individual. It meant nothing, Tanner realised. A favourite phrase of Kellett's sprang to mind: "I've got your balls in a vice."

LJ had anticipated this set-up. She had warned him that Allen would ooze charm – at first. The prime minister's gilded tongue dutifully obliged.

'Well done, Rob, LJ. You've really saved the day. Your country owes you a great debt.'

They'd agreed to lap up the soft soap until Allen's mask slipped and then hit him just once, *hard*. The only question was how long it would take for threats to replace flattery.

'We all appreciate everything you've done,' added Allen. 'And, of course, the nation will show it's appreciation.' Silence. 'But time is ticking.'

Tick. Tock. Was that a tic at the corner of Allen's mouth, Tanner wondered? He and LJ resolutely held their stations.

'So, I—we—really *do* need you to expedite things,' Allen continued, speaking gamely into the wall of silence. 'You'll understand, this is a matter of state security.'

There it was – the first slip. The smile was still there, but Allen's eyes were as hard as the menacing undertone in the last two words.

Tanner focused on the stillness. What was the comparative for greater silence? Deeper silence? Colder?

'Now, look.' Allen leant forward on the table, all pretence at civility gone. 'I don't know what game you're playing but I must warn you…'

Tanner calmly raised his palm towards the prime minister and uttered a single word. 'Stop.'

The effect in the room was electric, as if a current had passed between the two men. Tanner ignored the open mouths and wide eyes to each side and looked straight at, *into*, the premier. Then he spoke.

'You have one chance to listen, Prime Minister. Interrupt me and neither of us…' he shared a look with LJ, 'will say another word until we're well into the New Year. Do you understand, *sir*? You hear me out, in full, without interruption. As you said, time is ticking.'

If nods could kill, Tanner would have been on his way to the otherworld. Instead, the former banker, former everything, took a moment to appreciate that moment, the surroundings. To savour his life. In the corner of his vision, he saw Claydon, pen raised, ready to take a note of his offer. Then, he quietly presented the terms they'd agreed back at the hospital.

'*One*: All charges against Ashley Markham will be dropped. She will have full immunity from prosecution for life. *Two*: Ms Markham will be transferred immediately to our care with no barrier to travel. *Three*: You will agree to share Ms Markham's technology with all other countries by the end of twenty twenty-five.' Tanner saw the disappointment in the three advisors' faces. 'Don't look so glum. That still gives you a year's headstart.' He took a breath and continued. '*Four*: Ms Markham's demands for a Truth Commission will be met in full. Immediately. And lastly…'

Tanner turned away from Allen to look at LJ. She masked her surprise well, but an unspoken question drew the faintest of lines on her smooth brow. They'd agreed four demands, not five. He met the unspoken question by intensifying his stare.

'*Lastly*,' he emphasised. 'You will create a new position—Commissioner of State—as a formal deputy to the prime minister. To ensure the new Commission is effective. The appointment will be for the full length of the Government's term of office, so it's not a political perk to be offered and withdrawn. And the first appointee will be LJ Oladapo.'

Tanner hadn't planned the extra stipulation; it had just come to him in the moment. It was the right thing to do, to have someone at the heart of power committed to bringing to fruition Joen's desire for open, honest government.

Allen looked as if he would spontaneously combust. LJ, too, appeared ready to blow. Tanner spiked both by standing and turning his attention to first Moore, then the others in turn. He dipped his head politely at each, speaking to all and none of them.

'You'll want to confer, I'm sure. But let me be clear on two things.' Now Tanner spoke directly to Allen. 'Firstly, this is a take-it-or-leave-it offer. No negotiations, no changes. Secondly, we will reveal the location of Miss Markham's headquarters exactly three hours after you withdraw all police presence from her hospital. So, the sooner that's done, the sooner this is all over.' He fixed his eyes on the prime minister one last time. 'We'll wait in LJ's office.'

191

LJ MANAGED TO KEEP HER PEACE until they reached the privacy of her former office, but only just. She slammed the door and spun on her heel to face Tanner.

'How dare you?'

'LJ, I'm sorry.' Tanner looked at her, imploring. 'It wasn't planned. I know I shouldn't have done it without asking you, but it was… it was… it was a divine revelation!'

That his suggestion was given without a hint of humour or abashment made it all the more ludicrous.

'You are kidding me?' asked LJ. 'Right?'

Tanner shrugged hopelessly. 'I don't know, LJ. Of course not. I mean, I… *I don't know*! But at the end of the day, someone has to do it, and who better than you? Why not you?'

'Because Allen will do everything to kill it. It's a hiding to nothing. No one's ever tried it before. What if I fail?' At each objection she raised, she heard a voice inside her head reproaching her timidity. There had been various times in her life when, full of doubt, she'd lacked the certainty that she could do something difficult. Every time, as her grandmother had assured her she would, she had overcome. Now she shook her head, not believing her own stupidity. 'All right. Fine. I'll do it.'

192

IN A ROOM DOWN THE HALL, the prime minister, too, was coming to accept his fate. He had no choice but to acquiesce, to take Tanner and

LJ's deal, he realised. And when he took the emotion out of the equation, put aside the blow to his ego, what wasn't to like? The cyber-threat was nullified, public order could be restored immediately, and Britain would have an untold technological advantage, at least for a little while. Who knew what could be achieved in a year?

The Truth Commission sounded all fine and dandy in theory, but it would soon descend into inertia. He'd pad it out, so it became a meaningless talking shop. What did people care about truth as long as the economy was ticking over and they had strong leadership? And who was stronger than him, James Allen, the nation's saviour? Particularly after he'd seen off that playground-bully president.

Allen forced himself through the excruciating humiliation of a face-to-face accession to LJ and Tanner's terms. He gritted his teeth through bitter handshakes of agreement. Then, as soon as he was able, he excused himself with the very real justification that he had a call scheduled with the President of the United States. Moore was delegated to deal with Tanner and LJ, while the PM and Claydon decamped to his study.

There they heard the same sequence of bleeps and pings as ten hours before, and then they were put through. The president, evidently in very good humour, boomed across the waves.

'Hey, Jim. Good evening to you. It sure is a beautiful one here.'

'And a very good evening to you too, Mr President.'

A less self-obsessed man might have wondered why someone in Allen's position would sound so equable – carefree, even. But the president bulldozed on, enthralled by his own magnificence.

'I guess you've seen the right path,' he boomed.

'Indeed, I have, Mr President.' The prime minister's reply did nothing to disabuse the American. Had it been a video conference, Allen's expression most certainly would have. Few Cheshire cats have appeared more content. A satisfied grunt from Washington was Allen's cue to press on.

'You were keen to speak of history earlier, and you were absolutely right, Mr President. This is, indeed, an historic moment between our two countries.'

A chortle echoed down the line. 'You better believe it, Jim.'

Allen permitted himself a small laugh too before continuing. 'I know you like your little *vignettes*, so perhaps you'd allow me to add another anecdote to your repertoire.' He coughed down the emotion forming in his throat. 'Over eighty years ago, when it looked as though Britain would fall to Hitler, long before you Americans—how did you put it—"bailed us out," Marshal Pétain warned that we would have our neck wrung like a chicken's if we tried to fight on alone.'

'I don't…'

'No, you wouldn't understand, so let me explain. We don't like bullies trying to grab us by the neck, Mr President. It's really not… *cricket*.' He enjoyed the stunned silence for a moment before winding up. 'So, thank you, but no, we won't be accepting your offer, Mr President. Perhaps I might leave you with some words from Winston Churchill, *our* greatest leader. "Some chicken, some neck." Good night,' he waited a stage pause, 'and Happy New Year!'

193

TANNER LEFT LJ TO DEAL WITH THE PRACTICALITIES of framing an agreement with Moore and the prime minister's advisers. She was used to the machinations of Downing Street and Whitehall; if anyone could ensure their terms were met, it was her.

Tanner was in no state to help, anyway. He was dog-tired. He hadn't slept for God knows how long, and the encounter with Allen had drained his remaining energy. More than anything, he really did need fresh air.

Fortunately, the snow had paused for wintry breath, so with a new travel authorisation safely tucked in his overcoat pocket, he set off into the darkness, heading for Holborn by foot. He figured it would take him half an hour or so, more if he was stopped by a security patrol, but he'd be at the hospital by midnight. Another day. No, he realised, another year! What a ridiculous thought.

In the event, he was stopped and questioned at two roadblocks, but his Downing Street credentials saw him through. No other pedestrians challenged the weather or the curfew, and so the West End was his personal fiefdom, a kingdom of frozen enchantment. For a few minutes, Tanner lost himself in the sights of the soundless city, forgetting all about bankers, politicians and their schemes. Then his phone buzzed inside his jacket.

He had already reached Holborn, so he was near the hospital, but what if it was important? He stood under the bright lights of the locked tube station entrance and opened his screen.

The breath caught in his throat. It was a new email. From Joen.

TO: Robert Tanner
FROM: Joen van Aken
DATE: Tuesday, 31 December 2024 at 23:45
THE LAST ONE

Dearest Rob,
   Don't worry, this really is The Last One. No ciphers or codes.
   We had The One with All the Kissing and The One Where Everyone Finds Out, but so many others we didn't get to do... no Vegas, no Thanksgiving. That's a shame.
   There's so much I'd like to explain, but time is short and I'm assuming this will be read by others, so I'll just keep it to one message, from my heart.
   I hope one day you'll be able to forgive me. I did all this for the best of reasons: to try to bring the bad guys to heel – or at least make them more accountable. But I hurt you, and for that, and only that, I'm sorry. I wish I could make it up to you. I wish we had a second, or would it be a third, chance? But wishes are for fairy tales and beyond my power.
   It's not beyond me to ensure a happier New Year for other people, though. So, when the clock strikes twelve...
   Me, I'd just settle for another kiss.
   Love
   Jx

   p.s. Never forget what "Wise men say"... it's not gold, frankincense or myrrh that matters, especially at Christmas. Ask Elvis x

The catch in Tanner's throat turned to a lump, an unbearable swelling that threatened suffocation. He began to run, somehow keeping his balance on the treacherous surface. The email had surely been pre-prepared for one set of eventualities but, for once, Joen was wrong. There could still be a fairy-tale ending. She could wake up. She *would* wake up. She had to! They could still do all those wonderful things together in the future. For now, all that mattered was that he was there, with his Snow White, his sleeping beauty, at midnight.

194

THE MOMENT THE EMAIL ARRIVED, Major Claydon's team of analysts was on it. Within seconds, the message was forwarded to Claydon, who was still with the prime minister, and within a minute they, too, had devoured the contents.

'What do you make of it?' asked Allen.

'On the face of it,' said Claydon, 'it sounds like good news is coming at midnight. Unless there's a hidden code, it's as simple as that. I'm guessing the references in the first couple of sentences are a play on episodes of Friends, but I think that's just one last nod to pop culture, nothing more. The postscript refers to Elvis's *Can't Help Falling in Love*. I think we can safely assume that's personal. My team are running security checks just in case—word and sentence composition versus earlier emails, that kind of thing—but nothing's flagged up.'

'That's how I read it, too,' agreed Allen. Suddenly agitated, he began to drum his fingers on his desk – a gambler dealt a good hand at last after a run of bad luck, wondering if he should bet large to recoup his losses. He went all in. 'In which case, put the guard back on Markham. Don't let *anyone* in or out of that hospital. And tell Moore to stall with LJ. The deal's off.'

'But, sir?' Claydon couldn't hide her surprise. 'You gave your word.'

'I didn't ask for your opinion, Major, I gave you an order. You of all people should understand that concept.'

Claydon reverted to military subservience. 'Yes, sir.'

Even as Allen was altering the terms of their deal, Tanner was tearing towards the hospital. He could see the outline of trees in the garden square now, only a hundred metres ahead. Still nothing moved. He half-ran, half-glided through the snow like a musher behind an invisible sled.

But then came the first faint notes of sirens. Police, not far behind him. No doubt they would slow him down by demanding to see his papers, and no doubt running only made him look more suspicious, but Tanner had to get to Joen's bedside before it was too late. He tried to go faster and nearly fell. The wails grew louder, more insistent, drawing ever closer. He glanced over his shoulder. They were hard on his heels, probably two hundred metres away. He was halfway between them and the hospital.

He turned right, into the square, sprinting now, slaloming between trees and rises of white that barely registered as park benches. A *No Entry* sign blazed at the start of the finishing straight. No more than the length of a football pitch now, but the headlights were directly on his back. There were at least three police vehicles chasing him, sirens and rooflights blaring, and they had no intention of stopping for the road sign. Or for him.

Eighty metres, seventy. He urged himself on. A horn blasted a warning. The entrance was only forty, thirty, twenty metres away now. He spun off the end of a parked trailer, presumably a mobile testing unit but now an unidentifiable hummock of snow. Ten metres. His left foot slid forward, but his right hit the concrete of a hidden kerb and sent him spinning to the ground. He didn't feel the pain; the cold didn't register. His every thought was centred on Joen.

The first police car pulled onto the pavement in front of the entrance, completely blocking all access, and a burly officer jumped out. His exaggerated grin was strikingly at odds with the situation, with Tanner sprawled on the floor.

'Sorry, sir,' said the copper. 'Visiting hours are over.'

Great, thought Tanner, a comedian. Chest heaving, he dragged himself to his feet, via his knees. He pulled the travel attestation from his pocket, determined to keep his cool.

'I have the prime minister's personal authorisation to be here.'

The policeman crossed his arms, adopting the tone and posture of jobsworths the world over.

'Sorry, sir, that's above my pay grade. I'm afraid you'd have to speak to him about that. *My* orders are no visitors. *None.*' The smirk disappeared, and the officer stepped forward, jutting his face directly into Tanner's. 'So, be a good boy and go home, *sir*, or I'll have to arrest you for breaking curfew.'

DAY TEN

NEW YEAR'S DAY
WEDNESDAY 1 JANUARY 2025

195

THERE WAS NO FROIDEUR in the prime minister's study as Allen and Major Claydon waited for Big Ben to ring in the new year, only nervous anticipation. As the hands of the famous old clock signalled the last minute of the old year, Allen poured them both generous shots and raised a glass to his new right-hand woman. The sonorous tolling began.

At the twelfth strike, Claydon downed her drink and wished the prime minister a Happy New Year.

'May I?' she asked, indicating the phone she had fished from her pocket.

'Of course. And a Happy New Year to you too… I hope.'

Claydon logged into her bank account. Was it taking longer than usual to go through the security rigmarole, or was it just her eagerness? The balance eventually flashed up on screen.

'Yes!' The major's cheeks flushed with colour, either due to excitement or alcohol or both. 'Sir, would you be so kind?' She pointed at the computer on the PM's desk. 'Perhaps you'd check your account while I call the team.'

Asking Allen to log into his account was entirely unnecessary when she'd have reports from the entire security network in seconds, but the diversion would give her a moment or two to think. Claydon suspected she'd need it.

Within a minute she had confirmation; it seemed all accounts had been restored to their pre-Christmas levels, or thereabouts. Social media picked up the news almost instantly. The chyron on BBC News, playing on the television, flashed breaking-news red in acknowledgement.

Press Secretary Zack Hardy was summoned. Now he sat ready, constantly checking three different handsets, while Claydon relayed updates from

Room 68. Fifteen minutes into the year, direct contact had been made with all the major banks, their data checked and re-checked.

'Sir,' said Claydon. 'I'm confident we have the information we need.'

'You're sure?' asked Allen.

A faint smile crossed Claydon's lips. 'Sir, we've made it quite clear to the bank CEOs that you'll hold them personally responsible if they get this wrong. I think you can be sure they double-checked. If not treble.'

'In that case,' replied Allen, turning to Hardy. 'We need to make a statement.' He began to pace, words spewing faster than his steps. 'Delighted to resolve this. Perpetrators in custody. Understand it's been a worrying time. Security measures repealed. Curfew lifted. Thanks to police and armed forces and, above all, to the people. Cheques in post. Go and celebrate. Happy New Year. What have I missed?'

Claydon's poker-face had returned. 'Sir, I don't…'

'Don't worry, Major,' he interrupted. 'I know what you're going to say. But we have to take control of the narrative here.'

'But…'

'But me no buts, Major. Who was it that said that? Shakespeare?'

Claydon guessed Allen was having a joke at her expense. It wasn't the first time a cocksure superior had lorded it over her, and she doubted it would be the last. She'd long ago taught herself to name it and forget it: SCS. Small Cock Syndrome. The thought gave her renewed strength.

'In that case, sir, I should get back to the control room and leave you to Zack. They don't teach us PR in the army.'

'No, no, of course not. Well done, Major. Keep me updated.'

Allen's attention had already crystalised on the screen of Hardy's iPad, where the press secretary was frantically typing a draft statement. Claydon headed for the door, wondering whether to take the subterranean paths back to Room 68 or brave the elements. The fresh air would do her good, she supposed. Then her phone rang – a call from the control room. Allen and Hardy stopped what they were doing as she took the call. Neither could hear the words on the other end of the line, but they couldn't miss the expression on the major's face.

'What kind of situation?' she asked into the handset. Then, 'Hang on; I'm with the prime minister and his press sec. I'm going to put you on speaker.'

Claydon set the phone on the desk as the voice of her deputy came rushing into the room.

'We've just had the police security detail call in from the hospital. It's Markham, sir. She's dead.'

'*Dead*?!' The chorus came from all three listeners, each in entirely different tones.

'Yes, sir. Complications arising from an acute subdural haemorrhage, which is to say a blood clot on the brain. There was no time to operate.'

'And, you're sure?' pressed Allen.

'Yes, sir. The officer on security detail—a PC Melwood—has been on duty outside the ICU all evening. He went for a coffee at twenty-three forty when he received the instruction to stand down but didn't leave the hospital building and went straight back when your order changed. He was only off station for ten minutes or so. Otherwise, he was literally outside the door all shift. It seems that complications arose at zero-oh-five. One of the surgeons on standby tried to resuscitate, but there was no chance.'

'There's no room for doubt? He's seen the body? He's sure?'

'Yes, sir. PC Melwood was admitted to the ICU seconds after the unsuccessful attempts to resuscitate. He saw the flat line on the monitors. He witnessed the equipment being turned off and the body being covered. He questioned the doctor immediately and took a statement. There's absolutely no doubt, sir. Markham is dead.'

Nobody spoke. Eventually, a nod from Claydon reminded the prime minister that he was still on a call.

'Thank you,' offered the PM. 'Good work. Obviously, we need to keep this under wraps. No leaks. Understood?'

'Understood, sir.'

Allen ended the call. He exhaled, a long and loud deflation. 'Okay,' he said. 'Zack, where does this leave us?'

'I'm sorry for the choice of words, Prime Minister,' began the press secretary, although he clearly wasn't. 'But we should bury the news in the announcement. It's the perfect opportunity. Something along the lines of "One of the perpetrators was in a road accident while trying to escape and has sadly died." It has the benefit of being true. The driver wasn't one of our people, so we can't be blamed. It's Tanner and Kellett's fault, not ours. You're dealing with Tanner, and Kellett's still in custody. Not that anyone's going to care anyway, now everyone has their money back. Frankly, with Markham out of the picture we can be a little more creative with the narrative.'

Allen turned to Claydon. 'Major?'

'Well, sir. Our only concern is finding the location of Markham's HQ. With Markham out of the picture, there are four people who know that for sure: Tanner, LJ, and their two investigators. And one of those is a Swiss national. Markham's death means one fewer lead, I'm afraid, and you might argue that the others no longer have any incentive to tell us. Markham was a bargaining chip for us, sir.'

'Bugger.'

'In fact, they might now have every incentive to sell the information to another party.'

'The highest bidder?'

'Exactly.'

Allen contemplated the bleak news. 'We can't threaten them?'

'I don't see how.' Claydon's brain was ticking faster now. 'But we do have some negotiating chips still in our back pocket. We could offer them a modified version of Markham's demand – you could water down the commission, or something like that. Remember, sir, we don't *have* to give them anything. They must know we'll find Markham's HQ eventually. In the meantime, we can monitor every single step they all take: every conversation, every communication. That won't be much fun for them.' She paused, as if weighing up an idea, the sternness lifting from her features as it took shape. 'Actually, sir, there *is* something. There's a personal angle with Tanner.'

Allen shrugged incomprehension. 'There was, but she's dead now.'

'Exactly, sir. That's the angle. *The body.*'

Allen's brow creased. 'Sorry Major, I'm not following.'

'With regard to Miss Markham's body, Tanner has no official standing. He's not kin. Nothing official at all. Therefore, he has no claim.'

A look of pure admiration filled the prime minister's face. 'Oh, that is genius, Major. Cold, hard genius. No info, no body.' He shook his head disbelievingly. 'We'll tell him that we're sending Miss Markham for cremation *immediately* unless he spills the beans. Forget about post-mortems or inquests. There's no way he'll hold out!' Malevolence supplanted marvel. 'And you know what? I think we'll let LJ give him the good news.'

196

TANNER TRIED TO CALL LJ, without success. Presumably she was still squirrelled away inside Number Ten. Nikki and Gérard's phones, too, both rang straight to voicemail. That meant they were turned off, possibly SIM-less. Tanner had lingered at a discreet distance from the hospital, but within minutes, more police cars had arrived. A security cordon was soon established at the entrance to the square. Tanner couldn't stand out in the snow all night, so he began to retrace his steps towards Westminster.

In contrast to the lockdown in Queen Square, the rest of London was noisily breaking free from its binds. Revellers appeared at doorways, windows were thrown open and cars began to appear on the streets, horns a-honking as merrily as any goose delivered from its Christmas fate. Celebrations were starting everywhere. So, Tanner reasoned, Joen had been good to her word. Accounts had been restored, and the end was in sight. But if that was the case, why the increased security at the hospital? The agreement with Allen clearly stipulated that Joen would be freed.

The realisation hit him like a blast of the icy wind still blowing powdery tumbleweed down the street. Allen had reneged on his promise. The prime minister obviously believed the resetting of accounts would give him cover to steal Joen's technology without releasing her. He could have his Christmas cake and eat it! Tanner prayed LJ hadn't already revealed the location of Joen's HQ; they'd need the bargaining chip now, more than ever. As if in answer, his phone rang. But it wasn't LJ. It was Tommy Steele.

'Where are you, Rob?' asked the driver bluntly. Clearly there was no time for preamble. 'LJ needs to speak to you. She asked me to find you and take you to her.'

'Why, what's going on?'

'Where are you? I'm coming to pick you up.'

'Tommy,' Tanner persisted. 'Whatever it is, you can tell me. It can't be that bad.'

Except that it was. In an instant, he understood. The light disappeared from his world. It was so much worse than bad. 'Oh, Christ. *No!*'

In his heart, Tommy had known this would happen. He'd warned LJ that Tanner could read him like a book. He had tried to prepare something to say, but it was impossible.

'I have to see her,' demanded Tanner. 'I have to get back to the hospital.'

'They won't let you,' replied Tommy. 'Allen's up to something. You need to speak with LJ; I'll take you to her. Where are you?'

'What?' The question jolted Tanner back into some semblance of consciousness. He had no idea. He looked up to find himself staring at the imposing edifice of the Royal Opera House, a winter palace of brilliant illumination. He'd walked this way without thinking, instinct bringing him to this spot at this moment. The playbill for the current season stared back at him from an ornate wooden presentation case. *The Nutcracker.* He forced out the words, fighting desperately to hold back the tears, the sobs, the wracking misery, but it was an impossible fight. He slumped to his haunches and howled. And didn't stop until Tommy found him, covered in snow, half an hour later.

197

TANNER REMEMBERED NOTHING OF THE NEXT HOUR. Much later, Tommy told him that he'd forced brandy into him and then blanketed him, soaked through, on the back seat of the Merc, shaking with cold and wretchedness, choking with anger at Allen and Kellett and the world – and sick with guilt at his failure to protect Joen from it all. Tommy had taken him home, forced another brandy into him and manhandled him into the shower. Gradually, the steaming jets had begun to wash away the madness. By the time Tanner reappeared downstairs, a modicum of composure had returned. As had the rest of the gang of seven.

With them came more tears. These were different tears, though – a shared outpouring of grief between friends. Tommy stayed on, a reassuring presence and the perfect gentleman's gentleman.

Tanner had allowed himself to lose touch with reality for a while, but now he was able to face it head on. He listened attentively, but without emotion, as LJ described the events at Number Ten, how the situation had changed in the run-up to midnight.

'It must have been Joen's email,' interjected Tanner. A fact for the record, nothing more.

LJ nodded. 'Negotiations stopped as soon as it arrived. There was a hell of a kerfuffle. Moore clearly didn't like what he was being ordered to do, so I was left alone to twiddle my thumbs. Then at twenty past twelve, Major Claydon came back. She told me…' LJ's composure and eye contact gave way. She took a deep breath, cleared her throat and forced herself on. 'She told me Joen had died. Apparently, the doctor we met earlier had tried everything: CPR, defibrillation, but…' The word hung in the air. 'Major Claydon also had a message from the prime minister. There'll be no commissioner for truth, no focus on Joen's specific issues. There will still be an independent commission of some sort, but it'll be watered down to worthlessness.'

'That's it?' asked Tanner. Somehow, he sensed there was more to come.

'There's one more thing.' LJ looked nervously around the group before continuing. 'It's Joen. Allen's offering a trade.'

'I don't understand,' replied Tanner. He felt the sympathy in LJ's gaze as one second passed, another. But then, of course, he did understand, after all. 'The bastard. Allen won't release Joen's body unless we give him what he wants?'

Gérard had sat quietly through the conversation until this point. In stark contrast to those around him, he now appeared surprisingly relaxed.

'Rob,' he said, 'please forgive my unforgivable lack of delicacy, but I believe that's a trade we should make.'

'What?' Tanner was genuinely surprised. 'You'd give up Joen's technology to that man? After everything he's done.' Of all of them, Tanner had expected the investigator to be the most resolute. The last one to give in to emotion.

Gérard's expression was unreadable. 'I didn't say that.'

'Gérard, stop being so inscrutably Swiss,' snapped Nikki. 'And tell us what you *are* saying.'

'Rob, I have made certain… arrangements.' The Swiss's cheekbones twitched, a hint of mystery beyond the blank wall of inscrutability. 'We can give your Churchill wannabe the location of what he wants, without actually giving him anything. As I believe Nikki has alluded to, my wider family happens to have transport and *logistics* interests in Germany. I have, also, a sum of private wealth I can draw on to help in times like these. And, well, the rest I don't think any of you need bother with now. What you don't know, you can't tell. Or be accused of hiding.' He checked his watch. 'Just give me another couple of hours.'

Stunned silence settled over the gathering.

A moment later. Gérard broke it, all hint of playfulness gone. 'I have done this for you, Rob, but also for Joen. Because, despite my privileged upbringing, and much as I disagree with her methods, I do agree with what she was trying to achieve. A world with fewer social ills, more truth and greater accountability can only be a better world for the majority, and it is the majority that suffers under the current system.' Gérard paused, perhaps in acknowledgement of his own status as a member of the enriched minority.

'Once this has all settled down—once you have had time to come to terms with your loss—then we will all get together and discuss what to do with Joen's legacy, but that's a matter for another day. And, my friend, I should like to do one more thing for *you*, personally.' Receiving no rebuttal, Gérard kept going. 'I know what it's like to deal with the practicalities of death. I've just buried my father. It's not a pleasant experience. Let me make the arrangements for you. You've done all you can.'

'But I want to see her, Gérard.' Tanner's voice trailed off miserably. 'Just one last time.'

It was Harry who intervened. He knelt forward and took Tanner's hands in his own. Eyes brimming with tears, the father pleaded with the son.

'Rob, it's not her. It's a shell. I saw your brother's body after he died, on a mortuary slab in a hospital, and I shall always regret it. I didn't make that mistake with your mum. Remember your Joen in life. Whatever else you want, we'll try to do it, but please trust me on that.'

Tanner slumped forward, devastated by the terrible logic – all the more dreadful for his knowledge that it was true. Arms were drawn around his shoulders, the kettle clicked once more into life, and the tears rolled again.

198

THE PRIME MINISTER WAS TOO EXCITED TO SLEEP. He had Tanner and LJ where it hurt, and he wanted to enjoy every single moment of it. Major Claydon brought Allen the news of his adversaries' capitulation just before 2 a.m.

'They accept your terms in full, sir. LJ will chair the commission, and Tanner will retire from National Bank.'

'Yes, yes,' interrupted Allen irritably. 'But what about the location of Markham's HQ?'

Claydon kept her tone neutral. 'They say we can have it at 4 a.m., sir.'

Allen exploded. 'At four? What the hell are they waiting for?'

The major had known the PM would want everything wrapped up in minutes, but that just wasn't realistic. She spoke calmly to the premier.

'Sir, they need time to make arrangements for Markham's body.'

'Why? If we agree to hand it over, then we'll do it. Don't they trust us?'

Claydon would have liked nothing more than to give Allen LJ's verbatim answer to that question, but she doubted it would do much for the PM's blood pressure – nor her career prospects.

'Sir, it's going to take us until then to get our security personnel in place. Markham's HQ is on foreign soil. LJ will reveal the country at two-thirty, the city an hour later and the precise location at three forty-five. We'll have it secure at four.'

'Even so.'

'It works perfectly for us, actually, sir. We'll probably have to fly personnel in, get them in place and secure the location. We'll need every minute of that time.'

'And they can't double-cross us?'

Claydon shook her head, though whether in response to the question or the hypocrisy only she knew. 'No sir, we'll have the exact location at three forty-five. We can run full checks on ownership, utility usage, everything. Maybe it will unlock clues from the emails. From what we know of Markham, it will be very clear if the property fits the profile we're looking for. Any red flags and we'll have time to pull out.'

Allen waved his assent, allowing Claydon to get back to her planning. So now it was just a matter of time. And for the first time in a week, time was his friend, not an enemy.

The PM allowed himself another drink. It had better be the last; he'd have to be on television at sparrow-fart to announce the capture of Markham's technology. And what an announcement! He, James Allen, was responsible for securing the nation's greatest technological advance in fifty years. The prize would be Britain's and no one else's. The country would be great again. That LJ should be the one to deliver his victory made his triumph all the sweeter. That would teach the bitch to turn on him. And just in case she was under any illusions, he'd scupper her bloody commission too, make no mistake.

199

TANNER AND LJ WERE TRUE TO THEIR WORD. At precisely 2.30 a.m. they notified Major Claydon that Joen's data centre was located in Germany. Within two minutes, an unliveried BAe 146 with a full complement of technologists from GCHQ and other security personnel was in the air from RAF Northolt, heading for the German border. They would not arrive in time for the handover—securing the location would be the job of local forces already on the ground—but with luck, they would be in place within two hours. By breakfast time, the riddle of Markham's technology would be solved.

Allen swapped Number Ten for Room 68. He'd never been one for sport, but this was one show he was not going to miss. He wanted every movement on the big screen, close-up in glorious HD. And in Germany too! The irony was just too perfect. Just as Churchill's cryptologists at Bletchley Park had cracked the Nazi's Enigma codes, now he was to enjoy his own triumph over the Teutons. *Vorsprung durch Technik*, indeed! It was going to be the New Year's celebration to end all celebrations – with him at the centre. All he needed was a name. The technology couldn't be named after Markham, it needed something portentous like Enigma. Something reflecting his own role, perhaps?

Claydon broke into his reverie.

'Aachen, sir,' the major revealed. 'In western Germany.'

Allen glanced instinctively at his watch. 03:31. Twenty-nine minutes to kick-off. He could hardly contain himself. 'How long until the tech team is in place, Major?'

'They'll land at Maastricht, just across the border, in twenty-five minutes, sir. ETA oh-four-fifty-five local time. Aachen is thirty kilometres from there. If all goes to plan, they'll be in situ by oh-six-hundred latest. 5 a.m. here.'

Maastricht! There was another connection to British history, and another of the titanic political figures he so idolised. Maastricht immediately evoked the hated Treaty and Maggie's fight against European integration. Allen's grin widened yet further before his joy burst like a balloon.

'Wait,' he said. 'What about getting the equipment out? Is Germany a problem?'

'Actually, it's a stroke of luck, sir.'

'But I thought we'd pulled the army out of there?'

'All combat units *were* withdrawn, sir, but we keep various bases open. Just in case.' She didn't bother to say in case of what. 'The good news is that we have a huge facility at Mönchengladbach, less than forty miles away. We store hundreds of armoured and support vehicles there in climate-controlled warehouses. It's the perfect place to hide things away.'

'Well done, Major,' drawled Allen with real admiration. '*Well done!*'

'Thank you, sir. Now, if you'll excuse me, I'll go and make the final checks.'

The prime minister kicked his heels while he waited. Nothing was happening on the television monitors, and Claydon's team was glued to their computer terminals. Allen scrolled through the news feeds on his phone. Unbounded joy appeared to be the order of the day. The New Year had dawned, and with it, the nightmare after Christmas had ended.

At last, one by one, the screens sprang to life. A large-scale map of Aachen occupied one third, with electronic dots of various colours converging on a central point. Dash-cam and head-cam feeds showed deserted streets, blanketed in snow. It was an unmistakeably European scene: wide boulevards, ancient stone and modern concrete. Allen was so engrossed in the collage, he hadn't noticed Claydon coming back in.

'We have the address, sir. We're checking it now. It's a large, modern office block in an area with lots of technology companies. There's a restaurant or bar on the ground floor – AbIGAIL'S, it's called. We're running that name against all known data on Markham.'

'A plant name?'

'No sir, it's from the Hebrew. It means, "my father's joy."'

Allen shrugged. 'I guess a name link would be too obvious. What about the chain of ownership?'

A list of names and countries appeared on the fourth monitor. The last of these was Abigail's Speakeasy GmbH, incorporated in Aachen. The previous half a dozen were corporate-sounding entities with impersonal names. More importantly, they were domiciled in a Who's Who and Where's Where of international tax havens.

'The trail runs out in Belize, sir. It's exactly the same pattern as Markham's property in Soho.'

'Excellent!' Allen had already worked out the significance, but it was good to have it confirmed.

Claydon stopped to listen to something in her ear. She responded with an instruction: 'Hospital left; target right.' The screen duly separated into two moving black and white images. The left-hand display showed a CCTV feed of a hearse waiting in front of a balustraded Victorian building, a police car blocking its path. The right, presumably fed from a hand-held camera, displayed the frontage of a modern six-storey building with what appeared to be five floors of offices above a bar. Even in the shadowy nightlight, the *AbIGAIL'S* signage was clear. Claydon checked her watch then spoke directly to Allen 'Three fifty-nine, sir. Are we good to go?'

The prime minister's face creased in contemplation. He pointed at the left screen. 'What's to prevent us taking them into custody? The whole bloody lot. LJ, Tanner, their investigators, even the bloody undertakers?'

Claydon had hoped it wouldn't come to this, but she'd known in her heart that it probably would. She had the measure of Allen. And so, clearly had "the whole bloody lot" in question.

'It's straightforward, sir. If we don't give permission for the hearse to leave, Gérard Dumont, the Swiss investigator, will reveal our operation in Aachen to the head of German Military Intelligence. It seems they have a number of mutual acquaintances from Dumont's time in the Swiss equivalent.' The major didn't see the need to spell out what sort of diplomatic meltdown that would lead to.

Allen gave an airy wave at the screen, as if it was of no account anyway. 'Let them go.' Then, unable to disguise his pique at being outmanoeuvred, he spat an angry coda. 'And get into that damned building.'

200

THE REST OF THE GROUP HAVING DEPARTED to facilitate Gérard's plan for the extraction of Joen's body, Tanner and LJ were left to organise a very different removal – that of James Allen from political office. The first step was to wake Pattie Boyle.

Tanner guessed the PR guru would have had a few drinks to see in the new year. And a 'few drinks' for Pattie would be enough to anaesthetise the average reveller long beyond Hogmanay. Tanner called and called, and finally the line was answered with an almost animal sound of discomfort. Then came a nicotine-heavy croak.

'Christ, Rob, do you not know what time it is?'

'I'm sorry Pattie, but I need your help.'

'Are you back in charge again?' Pattie laughed, then descended into a coughing fit. 'I can't keep up.'

'No, it's much better than that,' said Tanner. 'I'm offering you the chance to scupper Martin Kellett for good.'

Pattie's mumbled response was unintelligible but left Tanner in no doubt that she was wholly unimpressed. The Toad wasn't worth an hour of her precious sleep on any night, let alone tonight. Like a gambler holding back an unexpected ace, Tanner played his trump card.

'And James Allen.'

Pattie was a lifelong socialist. Quite how she squared that with working for the nation's second-largest bank was not a debate into which anyone with a care for their personal wellbeing was advised to enter. But to her, any Conservative prime minister was the spawn of the devil. James Allen, an ardent devotee of She-Who-Must-Not-Be-Named, was the Antichrist incarnate.

'Did I just hear you right?' All muzziness disappeared from Pattie's voice. 'The chance to stick it to James Allen? *The* James Allen?'

'Not just to stick it to him, but to scupper him completely. Nuke, destroy, annihilate. Terminate!'

'Awright, pal,' said Pattie. 'Count me in. What's the plan?'

'I'm at my house with LJ Oladapo,' replied Tanner. 'It would be great if you'd join us. Tommy is on his way to collect you. He'll be outside your flat in fifteen minutes.'

Two enormous coffees (and two accompanying cigarette breaks) later, Pattie was fully briefed. She tried to express her condolences, but Tanner waved them away. There was a hardness to him now, a focus on revenge that brooked no sentimentality. That belonged to another day. For now, he had only one thing on his mind.

Tanner began calmly to lay out the issue at hand. 'It's very simple, Pattie. We have the scoop of the decade: conclusive proof that our prime minister is a liar and a snake.' He smiled at LJ. 'The only question is, how do we target it most effectively to ensure Allen can't wriggle out?'

Pattie sucked air through her teeth. 'I've got two words for you: *Sunday, Times*. I know the *Mail* have led on this so far, but they're too Tory. The story wouldn't be safe with them and their kid gloves. If we give it to the *Sunday Times* lot, it'll get the *Full Monty*.'

'You're sure?'

'I'm always sure! And the timing's perfect. They go to print on Saturday afternoon, so it gives them three days to nail every detail… and to trail how big an exclusive it is. In the first edition of the year too!' A low whistle emphasised just how enormous an exclusive it was. Pattie had the bit between her teeth now. 'I'll go to the head of their *Insight* investigative team. They exposed Cash for Questions, the FIFA bribery scandal, you name it. They're not afraid of politicians. Putting a stick into hornets' nests is what they do.'

'And you trust them?' asked Tanner.

'Trust a pack of journalists?' Pattie guffawed. 'Rob, I thought you had more brains than that. But yes, more than most. It's in their interest.'

LJ sat forward, eager to get started. 'So, what do we do first?'

Pattie too leaned forward, giving the younger woman her total, undivided attention.

'First, LJ? First, I'm going for a fag.'

201

JAMES ALLEN WATCHED EVENTS UNFOLD on the split screen, still peeved at having been outmanoeuvred by LJ and Tanner. He knew the advance party in Aachen couldn't just walk into a tightly secured office block, but it was galling all the same to watch the hearse with Markham's body disappear from the left-hand screen before his team gained access to her HQ on the right.

'Are we tailing the hearse?' he asked Claydon.

The major wondered for a second if Allen was joking, but the PM's sour face offered no hint of amusement. Words failed her.

'Well?' prompted Allen.

Options flashed through Claydon's mind. She had worked too hard to throw it all away. It wasn't worth it. *He* wasn't worth it. For the first time in her career, she lied, outright, to a superior. It must be catching, she thought bitterly. She'd just have to pray that her team bailed her out.

'Of course, sir. A police motorcycle should be following at a discreet distance.'

She was spared from having to provide further details by movement on the right-hand screen, in Aachen. Until now, there had been nothing to see on the feed but a couple of people standing on the pavement outside the café. But now the few dim lights in the building turned off. The screen turned to night vision. From nowhere, ghostly figures poured into the building's main reception. Commentary, too, flooded Room 68's audio system. It was a deep male voice, clear despite the static.

'We're in. We had to take out primary power and a secondary back-up; we couldn't risk motion sensors.'

At Claydon's command, the wall rearranged itself into five separate displays. The central block was dark for the moment, but the four displays on either side carried live feeds from different cameras.

'The group is divided into five units,' explained Claydon. 'Four are active and one is back-up. Alpha and Bravo will provide security cover at the front and rear of the building. They'll keep out of sight for as long as everything stays quiet at street level.' Claydon pointed to the two smaller displays on the left, which were now clear of all movement. 'That's those two monitors. And if they stay like that, we'll all be happy.'

The major turned her attention to the two right hand monitors. 'The team you just saw enter the ground floor reception area is Charlie. That's them, top right. Delta will be in place on the roof in thirty seconds. They're bottom right.' She paused for questions, but none came. 'The first and second floors are occupied by legitimate businesses, the top three by shell companies, presumably Markham's. Depending on what security systems they find in the building, Charlie Unit will either try to enter the third floor directly or will go in from underneath. Delta will access the top floor from above. Worst case, we'll have a camera into both pretty quickly. We'll switch the main screen to wherever the progress is fastest.'

Allen gave an animated nod of understanding, his mood seemingly buoyed by expectation. But then the seconds started to tick by. The main screen stayed resolutely dark, but there was plenty to watch on the monitors to the side. Members of Charlie Unit had emerged from a lift and were examining a security control panel to one side of a nondescript pair of doors. A metallic voice filled the audio system.

'Major, this is Charlie Leader. Do you read?'

'Go ahead, Charlie Leader. Reading you loud and clear.'

'The lift only serves the first three floors, Major. Access to the third floor is via multiple security checks. We're looking to bypass them, but it's ultra-sophisticated. Fingerprint, retina and then some. It won't be quick. My guess is that without blowing the doors out, we'll need the boffins.' There was a slight break in the transmission. 'That's the bad news.'

'I take it there's some good news as well, then.'

'Yes, ma'am. The second floor is a piece of cake. We'll be in there in a flash and put a camera up through the ceiling. At least you'll be able to compare the third with what Delta shows you from the fifth.'

The feed from Delta came online first. There was an initial burst of bright light as the microscopic inspection camera was switched on, and then came an indistinct blur as the telescopic head was fed down through the roof, past joists and ceiling tiles, into the floor below. Auto-focus kicked in, and the picture began to clear. In daytime, or with reasonable background illumination, the image would be full colour, but in the dead of night, with all power cut off, it was distorted in the spectral glow cast by the camera head itself, like an old colour negative lit by torchlight. It was enough, though, to offer the PM a glance into Markham's hidden lair, the light at the end of the tunnel, his personal Holy Grail. The camera head swivelled, revealing the clear outlines of a large open-plan office.

An entirely empty office.

'What the f…' began Allen, but his startled outburst was cut short by the coming to life of the second bank of screens, as Charlie's camera was fed up through the second level's ceiling and then through the floor above. A mirror of the Delta feed's top-down perspective from ceiling height, the new images gave a ground-up view from floor-level of an identical open space.

An identically empty open space.

Expletives rang through the loudspeakers, but none louder than Allen's. He bawled at Claydon; his face contorted with anger.

'They've tricked us! They've led us to an empty bloody office!' He jabbed a finger, wasting no time in attributing blame. 'I told you they'd double-cross us. So bloody well stop them!'

Claydon didn't reply. She was no coward, but one look at the PM's eyes told her a wrong move would be career-destroying. She'd probably gone too far already. Choosing her words precisely, she gave instructions into the mic.

'The *prime minister* has ordered that the vehicle with Dumont and Markham's body be taken into custody.'

202

THE ATMOSPHERE IN ROOM 68 reflected the wintry footage which was being beamed live from Aachen. Four of the five video feeds had been shut down as the units withdrew from the building, whose upper floors had been confirmed to be completely and humiliatingly empty. This was Ashley Markham's lair alright, but her technology was nowhere to be found. Allen had been outsmarted.

A cadre of soldiers would maintain a small security presence to watch the front and rear entrances, but unlike the snow on the pavement outside AbIGAIL'S, the main body of operatives had melted away. The jet carrying the technology personnel, meanwhile, had landed at Maastricht. For now, the tech experts were on standby, awaiting further orders.

At Claydon's command, the display changed again. The view from Aachen shifted to the top left corner, and an illuminated map appeared on the right. The whole of the central console was now filled by a new panorama of wintry streets – this time, here in London. The source of the pictures was a motorbike policeman's helmet camera. A siren whined in the audio feed, and blue light flared at intervals. The road slipped by beneath the motorbike's wheels.

'The hearse is 200 metres ahead, sir,' said Claydon. She had discreetly scrambled every officer who happened to be nearby, and as far as Allen was concerned, these units had been tailing the hearse all along. 'Heading west on the Marylebone Road. We have two unmarked cars following less than a mile behind. What would you like to do?'

'Pull it over.'

Claydon bit her tongue, took a deep breath and issued the instruction. The motorcycle began to reel in the hearse ahead. For a few seconds, the bike followed the hearse in unhurried single-file, but then the hearse's passenger-side indicators came on and it glided to a halt at the side of the deserted road. The motorcycle officer stepped off his bike and walked to the driver's door. At his signal, the window slid down and he leaned into the opening.

'Would you please step out of the vehicle, sir.' Despite the grammar of the sentence, this was no question.

The undertaker didn't move but replied in a clear, rich baritone. 'With respect, officer, you're stopping a funeral vehicle which has express permission to make this journey. Here, see this.' He pushed a piece of paper through the window. 'We are acting lawfully. We have committed no offence. And we have specific authorisation from Ten Downing Street. So no, I won't step out, and we *will* be on our way.' The driver's finger moved to the window control.

'I'm sorry, sir. You can't do that.'

'Why ever not?' asked the undertaker forcefully.

Panicked, the officer blurted out the first thing that sprang to mind: the truth. 'I'm sorry, sir, express orders from the prime minister.'

'The prime minister has personally ordered you to stop a hearse conveying a dead body?' The driver's tone was incredulous, bordering on theatrical. 'On what charge?'

'If you'd step out of the vehicle, please, sir, my colleagues will be here in a moment to explain.'

'Of course, of course. Anything you say,' agreed the funeral director evenly.

Relieved at the sudden agreeableness, the officer stepped back, allowing the driver's door to open and his own attention to lapse. The undertaker eased his large frame out of the driver's seat. Simultaneously, the passenger door opened, and a tall man appeared – of the suave yet rugged type. Meanwhile, from the rear passenger door stepped a headscarved female figure dressed in funereal black. She was brandishing a phone, whose camera was brazenly pointed in the officer's direction. The officer reached out to seize the phone, but the woman was already turning and running for Baker Street, carrying on her person the kind of footage that can bring down a government.

The entire scene had been witnessed by the hushed gathering in Room 68. Claydon knew she should have stepped in and told the motorcycle policeman to back-off, but the orders were Allen's to give. This had turned into a night where every move had to be played by the book. The PM, for his part, had about him a look of volcanic befuddlement.

'What the fuck is going on?' he raged. His expression was as pyrotechnic as any display seen so far this night.

Claydon bit the inside of her mouth. 'I'm not sure, sir,' she managed, when she was sure she had regained her composure. 'There appeared to be a third person in the car.'

'What the hell are you doing about it?' asked Allen.

Claydon fixed him with wide, butter-wouldn't-melt eyes. 'Sir?'

'ARREST THEM!'

'For what, sir?' she asked.

And at that, the prime minister duly exploded.

203

IT TOOK NEARLY THREE HOURS and a call from the Swiss Ambassador before Gérard, having been arrested with the undertaker, was released from custody. His and the ambassador's families had known each other for generations, and they were distant cousins through marriage (as were 99.9% of the country's ruling elite, but that was beside the point when a favour was required). Gérard had committed no crime in the hearse, and the police had neither the grounds nor inclination to hold him in the face of extreme diplomatic pressure. As for the woman who had been filming in the back, Gérard gave nothing away as to who she was or what she had been doing there.

He emerged from New Scotland Yard into a thin, wintry dawn to find Tommy and the Mercedes waiting kerbside. The Londoner's trademark grin was etched firmly in place, despite the early hour and a night without sleep.

'You're looking very chipper, Tommy,' offered Gérard.

'I try my best, Mr Dumont, I try my best. And anyway, it's going to be a beautiful day.'

Gérard cast a disbelieving skywards glance skywards. 'It is?'

'Oh, yes. I can feel it in my bones. Well, that and a bit of inside knowledge. Get in and I'll spill the beans.' Tommy opened the passenger door for the Swiss.

For the second time in as many days, Tommy pulled away from the Met Police headquarters and onto the Victoria Embankment. He looked over and caught Gérard's eye.

'Pattie sent the *Sunday Times* a copy of the video. Chrissie did a lovely job. The copper's face is priceless.'

Tommy's enthusiasm was infectious. Gérard, for all his tiredness, couldn't help but laugh. 'They took the bait?'

'Hook, line and sinker,' said Tommy. 'Rob, LJ and Pattie are meeting with the *Insight* team at eight-thirty.' He glanced at his watch. 'They'll be on their way now.'

'And Chrissie?'

'She's safe and sound at home in Dulwich. I took her there after your little escapade and collected Miss Cheung from Stockwell on my way back. *She's* safely tucked up in Claridge's, you'll be pleased to know.'

'I don't know where you get the energy, Tommy,' said Gérard. He shook his head in astonishment. 'You're a marvel, you know that? And you didn't have any problems with the police?'

'None at all, thanks to your phone's location sharing feature. I was less than half a mile away when you and the hearse were stopped. I picked up

Chrissie within a couple of minutes and had her home by five. The wonders of modern technology, eh?'

'And your knowledge of London's streets, Tommy.'

Tommy shrugged off the compliment with an abrupt change of subject. 'There's no traffic, so we'll be at Claridge's in no time. I should think you and Miss Cheung will want a rest after all your jet-setting, won't you? Put your feet up, have a nice meal?'

Gérard nodded but was then struck by an altogether less cheerful thought. 'What about Rob?'

'Don't you worry about him.' Tommy sounded surprisingly unperturbed. 'I've known Rob for more than twenty years. He's the most decent man you'd ever wish to meet and, on the face of it, a sociable one too. But he's actually a very private person. He'll not want any fuss. He'll bottle everything up and throw himself into hard work.'

'But that's terrible.'

'Is it? We're all different, aren't we? I don't know all the ins-and-outs of what Miss Markham was up to, but I do know Rob. He'll move heaven and earth to make sure something good comes out of her death. Only then will he be ready to talk about it. As long as he knows we'll be there when he does eventually want to, that'll be enough. And he's got his dad back now.' Tommy looked over at Gérard, and the men shared a look. 'Usually pays to listen to your old man, in my experience.'

Gérard reflected on the wise words. For a chauffeur, Tommy had an uncanny knack for putting his finger on things. It made Gérard think of his own father and of Félix. He wondered if Tommy knew about that side of him, whether he'd gleaned that most personal morsel of information from Nikki or another of the group. He found out soon enough.

'Any other words of wisdom?' he queried.

'I don't know about wisdom, Mr Dumont.' Tommy made sure Gérard was paying attention. 'But you certainly do pick up interesting little snippets driving around all night.'

'Anything you'd care to share?'

'Well, a little bird did whisper something in my ear.' He waited a cruel second before coming clean. 'Seems Miss Cheung has always wanted to go on a safari but has never had the opportunity.' He added a knowing wink. 'Downright sad, that.'

Tommy really was a marvel, Gérard realised. And he was still laughing as the car pulled up outside Claridge's.

204

A COUPLE OF HOURS' SLEEP settled the prime minister's nerves; a decent breakfast did the same for his stomach. And a sense of perspective descended in the meantime. The night's events had come too late for the morning papers, but the news channels were reporting a success for the government – and for him. Bank accounts had been restored, the economy was safe, and Markham's death was an unfortunate and blameless footnote, nothing more.

It wasn't the glorious triumph that James Allen had envisaged. Sure, he wouldn't have to stand before the nation and admit he had sold the country's soul to the Americans. But nor would there be a Downing Street press conference trumpeting a technological breakthrough for the ages. Of course, Markham's technology was obviously still out there somewhere. From a brighter vantage point, Allen might say that the opportunity was delayed, rather than lost. And the real good news was that there was nothing on social media about that incident with the hearse. Everything was calm.

Shops, restaurants and pubs would soon be filled with punters desperate to spend their newly restored cash and their £1000 bounty, a stimulus package from the gods. Football fans were heading to the handful of fixtures that had survived the weather. The country was thawing in the pale morning sun as if nothing had happened. Another day, another year. On the face of it, nothing really changes.

Allen turned off the television and headed for his office. Number Ten was strangely quiet. The skeleton staff paid him polite obeisance, but they took care to keep a safe distance. Were they being more stand-offish than usual? Had word of his meltdown last night spread? Allen comforted himself with the knowledge that everyone lost their temper occasionally. Prime ministers were only human.

It was blissfully quiet in his office and, from the look of things beyond the window, just as quiet outside. Without meaning to, Allen caught his own reflection in the glass. The last time he'd looked into his own eyes had been when the demonstrations were at their height, when he'd given LJ his word that he wouldn't double-cross Ashley Markham. The thought made him wince, but only for a second. Oh, well. What was that about him being only human?

And LJ? Would she come back? No, of course she wouldn't. What would she do, he wondered? Pursue the figment of a truth commission? He permitted himself a small chuckle. No, of course she wouldn't, she'd make a ton of money in the private sector if she had any sense. Lord, he'd miss her. At least she'd have time to spend with her poor husband now.

The thought of family struck Allen from nowhere. He hadn't seen Anna and the kids for a week. Everyone else was going to enjoy a day of normality, so why shouldn't he? He called the head of his security detail and told him they were heading for Norfolk. The car was ready in minutes.

Allen was accompanied on the journey by his red box, but he was content to pass most of the time looking out of the window. Mile after mile of nothing but white. Pristine and unspoilt. The beauty of nature covering humanity's mess.

His mind turned to Ashley Markham. What an extraordinary woman. To have achieved everything she'd done, seemingly on her own. She had wanted a cleaner world, too. A more truthful world. Allen shook the thought away. What a hopelessly naïve idea. That was when the phone rang. It was Zack Hardy. Apparently, there was a 'situation' with the *Sunday Times*.

'What kind of situation?' asked Allen. He was tired of these calls from the blue, of crises and complications.

For once, the press secretary made no effort to sugar the pill. 'It's a complete and utter disaster. They have the whole story. Everything. Corroborated by people on the inside.'

'What? *Who?*'

'The *Insight* Team, sir.'

'No, Zack, who on the inside? What story?'

'Sorry, sir.' Hardy gathered his thoughts, 'Obviously they won't reveal their sources, but I'm guessing they've been speaking to LJ, Tanner, the home secretary, the chancellor. Maybe others.'

'You're joking?'

Silence told him that Hardy wasn't.

'Bastards,' spat Allen angrily. He forced himself to count: *one, two.* 'We can reshuffle the troublemakers.' *Three, four.* 'But that's for later.' *Five, six.* 'So, what do the *Insight* people want? An exclusive interview?'

'Nothing.'

'For heaven's sake, Zack! Pull yourself together! There's always something. No story is too big to be buried.'

'I'm serious, sir. They don't want an interview, a comment, a rebuttal… anything. They say they're one hundred per cent confident of their sources. They're going to run a special edition devoted just to this.'

'What? Then why are they telling us?'

'So you can consider your position, sir.'

'You're fucking kidding me.' Fury consumed the PM. 'Well, hit them with a DSMA-Notice, Official Secrets Act, *the works.*' Allen knew he mustn't direct his anger at the press secretary, but he had to steel Hardy's backbone. 'Come on Zack! Step up, man.'

'I've tried, sir. I've spoken to the editor. I've suggested the proprietors would want to speak with you directly. But the line is that the owners are fully aware of everything and, I quote, "would never dream of compromising editorial independence."' He answered the follow-up question before Allen could ask it. 'And in any event, they're unavailable, due to travel commitments.'

'Bastards!' repeated Allen, but with little strength. His voice trailed into a pained whisper. 'What happens next?'

'They'll brief the news media mid-evening so that it's flagged on the ten o'clock news that they're sitting on something colossal. And they'll begin to drip elements of the story onto the web at the same time, for the benefit of their online subscribers.' Hardy's response was purely factual. 'Apparently they have an incrim…' he stopped himself, 'an embarrassing video with a hearse.'

'And what am I meant to do?' Allen's question carried an appropriately elegiac tone.

'It rather depends on whether you believe your actions will stand up to scrutiny, sir. On whether a reasonable man and woman will think what you did was justifiable?'

205

TANNER HAD EXPECTED A DETAILED INTERVIEW, but this was a forensic interrogation, with every statement questioned, every sentence cynically picked apart. After that, he and LJ were left to kick their heels while the journalists conferred and cross-referenced the information they'd been given. Towards the end, Tanner was asked was if he had any idea just how incendiary this story would be. His answer was simple and from the heart.

'I just know it's the truth… and the one thing people deserve is truth. Leadership would be great. Statesmanship even better. All those lofty ideals we look for in politicians. But if you don't start by telling the truth, keeping your word, the basic things, how on earth is anything ever going to get better?'

The follow up question was more personal.

'You do realise you're going to be at the heart of the storm? You'll be in the public eye for days. Weeks, probably. LJ has had media training – she knows the drill. But this is all new for you. Are you ready for the maelstrom?'

Tanner shrugged. 'Who knows? Maybe I'll disappear for a while. I haven't given it any thought, to be honest.' His face clouded. 'I guess I'll issue a statement saying that I'm not making any further comment. I can only ask people to respect my privacy. At least until after the funeral.'

Eventually, the grilling was over. LJ and Tanner emerged from the *Sunday Times* offices to find they had missed the entire day. Tanner was relieved to see the bright yellow light of a waiting taxi. He was keen to make a quick getaway and didn't doubt LJ was too, not that she showed any sign of flagging.

'You're sure you don't want company?' she asked.

'No, LJ, that's really kind, but I just want to get home and try to put this out of my mind for a couple of hours. I'll call Nikki, Gérard and Tommy to tell them what's happening, and then I'm turning my phone off. We'll start again tomorrow. Pattie will know what to do.'

Tanner understood now how Garbo must have felt: he just wanted to be alone. Fortunately, the cabbie was of the same mindset. He accepted the destination—Ravenscourt Park—then pulled the panel closed between them and resumed the hands-free conversation in which he'd been engrossed, leaving Tanner to his thoughts. Dark thoughts of loss and guilt. Ghosts from the past. Darker ghosts of Christmas present.

What was it about him and death? On one level, he knew he hadn't caused Joen's death any more than he had caused Matt's all those years ago, but he had been negligent in both. He could have been more careful. Should have been. Coulda, woulda, shoulda: the three most worthless words in the English language.

After Matt died, he'd nearly been broken on the wheel of compassion, crushed by the sorrowing weight of pitying looks, sympathetic gestures and words of consolation – some to his face and far more behind his back. He'd dealt with Matt's accident by hiding the memory of it away and never ever talking about it. Pretending it hadn't happened. He wouldn't make the same mistake with Joen's.

He called Nikki's number and gave her a brief summary of the day spent with journalists. She listened without a word until she was certain he had finished.

'Why not come out to Switzerland?' she suggested. 'Get away from it all? Gérard's got a chalet high in the mountains. No one will disturb you. If you want company, we'll join you; if not, he says it's yours for as long as you want it.'

Tanner couldn't help shaking his head. Not at the offer itself but at the kindness that underpinned it. He'd known these people for a week, and already they were friends for life. He wanted desperately to express his gratitude, but he didn't have the words. Not yet. There would be a better time, and he looked forward to it.

'That's incredibly kind of you both, but it would feel like running away. I'll stick it out here. I've got the funeral to take care of. When they eventually release Joen's body, that is.'

'Of course,' said Nikki. 'We'll be there, obviously.'

'No. Please don't.' The words came out more firmly than he'd intended: an order, not a request. 'It's just going to be a simple, private cremation, not a funeral as such. No one really knew her—not even me—so it doesn't seem right to have a ceremony full of mourners. Whatever, *whoever* Joen was, she was a free spirit… she wasn't tied to one place in life, so it doesn't seem right to tie her now. I'm sure an idea will come in time.' The line went quiet. He hadn't meant to cause offence. 'Maybe we'll learn more about her in time or be able to reflect—maybe even celebrate—but that's for the future. For now, all I can do is try to make sure something good comes out of this.' He let out a wistful sigh. 'Sorry. I'm just a bit tired, all of a sudden.'

'It's okay, Rob, I get it. *We* get it. You promise you'll call if we can help in any way?'

'I will.' The facile response was automatic. An instinctive lie shaped by thirty years in which he had shouldered all his burdens alone. He had been afraid to let people get close to him for too long. Not anymore. 'Nikki, *I mean it*. Honestly. And I appreciate you both more than I can say. Now go and give that mountain man a hug from me.'

Next, he called Tommy. From the background noise, it seemed his old friend was in a bar.

'Hang on Rob, I'm just in the pub. Give me a minute. I'll call you back.'

Tanner pictured Tommy, pint in hand, at the centre of a happy throng.

'No, don't do that,' he insisted. 'Everything's fine. I just wanted you to know everything's on track. Just one thing though…'

'Anything. You know that.'

'I *do* know that. That's why I just wanted to say thank you. For *everything*.'

'Oh, don't start getting all soppy on me, Six. My bloody beer will spoil if I start blubbing in it.'

Sill smiling, Tanner hung up and made his final call.

'Dad, it's Rob.'

'I do know my own son, you know.' A week ago, the mockery would have been caustic, now it was comforting. There was only warmth and support in Harry's voice. 'What's up?'

'I wondered if I might cadge a bed for the night?' volunteered Tanner meekly. 'Maybe grab a pint first? In a pub. The two of us.' There was no immediate response. Perhaps he'd pushed things. Too much, too soon.

'A pint? No, I don't think so.' His father's deadpan reply was like a blow. But only for a second. 'No, with all we've got to catch up on, I'm thinking a quart… If not a gallon.' A chuckle echoed in his ears. 'Get your skates on. It's time we got started.'

Tanner gave the cabbie his new destination. He was about to switch his phone off when an email pinged into view. It was short and to the point, a preview of tomorrow's *Times* front-page. Tanner opened the attached pdf, the banner headline screaming the entire width of the page.

ALLEN'S FATAL DOUBLE-CROSS

Seven days of duplicity and disaster at Number Ten

PM told: quit or be forced out

He didn't need to read more. The final act of the tragedy had begun. Or was it the first act of an entirely new production? Whichever it was, it could wait until tomorrow. Beers, a lot of beers—and, if he knew his father, whisky too—would do very well for tonight.

—

THE END

ACKNOWLEDGEMENTS

If you've got this far, thank you! I wrote *Zero Ri$k* with one overriding purpose, to entertain, and I really hope I have managed to do that over the preceding pages.

The idea for *Zero Ri$k* first occurred to me ten years or so ago. In the intervening decade, the relentless march of technology has only quickened, and our dependence on tech has become more deep-rooted. Whilst there is much that's good, there's an awful lot that's not, or worse, that just gets taken for granted. My second hope, therefore, is that *Zero Ri$k* has provoked a few thoughts and raised a few questions along the way.

Zero Ri$k is my first novel. I don't come from a literary family (more of them anon). I don't know any novelists. So, being an analyst at heart, I read various "How to be an author" books in the hope of inspiration. The best of them all said the same thing: treat it as a full-time job, not a hobby, and just write.

It was the James Bond books that first got me hooked on thrillers as a youngster, and I'd read somewhere that Ian Fleming had a set daily writing routine in Jamaica: up early, swim, good breakfast, visualise what he was going to write that morning and, at 9.a.m., hit the typewriter keys. As a former journalist he was a quick writer, so by noon he'd cranked out two thousand words. Then, another swim, a good lunch, a snooze and maybe a little editing in the afternoon before a damn fine dinner.

A great friend of mine, James Allen, is a keen sailor who particularly loves a small Caribbean island off Grenada named Carriacou. He has acquaintances there who rent out an eco-shack at the top of a hill looking out over the ocean. So, I put two and two together and, in May 2019, headed off to Carriacou and set up my laptop on a veranda overlooking the distant sea. There were a few smaller problems—the ocean was too far away for a swim, for example—but one major one: whereas Fleming could crank out two thousand Bond words in three hours it often took me eight. Still, at the end of four weeks

I'd managed to put fifty-six thousand words on paper. More than the entire length of Casino Royale. But only a quarter of the story I envisaged.

The perceived wisdom is that thrillers, particularly debut novels, should be 90,000-110,000 words long, so I spent the summer of 2019 thinking about how to cut the book I wanted to write, but I just couldn't come up with a plan. So in the autumn of that year I took myself off to stay at the wonderful farm outside Cork of another friend, Canice Sharkey, and banged out another forty thousand words. Then Covid came and, with it, lockdowns. By the end of summer 2020, the first draft was finished. And it was twice the length of anything that a commercial publisher would ever take on!

As a novice, naïve, writer, you think that conceiving and writing the book is the journey; the be all and end all. In fact, the writing is the easy part and finishing the first draft really is just the beginning. Identifying, and finding a way to work with, the editors and other professionals who combine to get that first manuscript into a publishable final edition is the real journey.

I've been lucky to work with some wonderful people on that journey. Troon Harrison was the first professional to read the book and was immediately encouraging and constructively critical. Becky Sweeney, Roland Alexander, Nathaniel Zetter and Rebecca Millar all made invaluable contributions to the rewrites that followed. Then, lastly and most importantly, George Harrison helped me shape the final version.

Editing completed, my biggest stroke of luck was finding the fantastic Helen Lewis and her wonderful team at Literally PR: Becky Smith, Diana Ashlee, Hollie McDevitt, Kay Kett, Lisa Goll, Maleeha Mir and Rachel Knight. Independent publishing is a tough gig, and it would be far harder and much less fun without the LitPR team. Ditto my sales distributor Rupert Harbour, the proofreading team at Ink! Publishing Services, typesetter Rebecca Elphick at Easypress, Amelia Douglas at hard copy printers TJBooks, and Matt Horner at eBookPartnership.

And a special shout out to Tom Weaver who published a great debut novel *Artificial Wisdom* seven months before *Zero Ri$k*, and generously shared his own genuine wisdom around all aspects of the publication process in the run-up to my own launch day.

Brett Gascoigne was as fantastic to work with on the early graphics for *Zero Ri$k* as he has been on other projects, and Mark Terry brought the final cover and marketing material to life.

My early readers—Clive Bannister, Chris Blackhurst, Stefan Ciecerski, Sarah Eastabrook, Mark Hall, Ian Hawkins, Jonathan Klein, John Minshull Beech, Desmond O'Hara, Nigel Parker and Freddie Preston—all provided constructive comments and that invaluable commodity, encouragement.

I started *Zero Ri$k* because I didn't want to get to the end of my life and regret something I hadn't done. We all do things in life we later regret, but to not try to do something important would have been soul-destroying. Thanks to the collective efforts of all of those mentioned, *Zero Ri$k* has come to life and saved me that regret.

The one sadness I do have is that my parents aren't here to see *Zero Ri$k*'s publication. I'd love more than anything to have given them each a copy to say thank you for everything they did for me over so many years. My father was born into unfathomable poverty in a Nottinghamshire mining village in the 1920s. His mother died when he was only seven years old, and my grandfather moved to London shortly afterwards to find work, bringing three young sons, but leaving their elder sister in Nottingham. After the minimum secondary education, my father served in the RAF throughout WWII, learning a trade and, even more fortunately, meeting my mother on an RAF base where her own father was serving and where she was working in the laundry. The rest, as they say, is history. They were happily married for fifty years and gave my older bothers David and Noel and me, everything a child could want: a loving home, an unambiguous work ethic and a fantastic education (in the broadest sense). Both my brothers have always looked out for their little brother and it's nice to be able to tell them here how much I appreciate it.

I've been blessed with some amazing friends in life. Unbelievably, three of them date back to those early schooldays in West London and we're still muckers to be found talking nonsense in random London hostelries on a regular basis. Thanks, Des, Barry and Stevie, you are princes all. Just so you know.

Our school was a rugby-playing one, but it was the round-shaped ball that I always craved. It was dad's fault or, rather, grandad's. Arriving in West London in the early Thirties, the team "on the up" was their local one, Brentford FC. Grandad took dad to Griffin Park on Saturday afternoons and, eventually, dad took me… by which time Brentford were in the fourth division. Now, you can change your car, your house, your job, your religion, even your spouse, but you can't change your football club. So I was saddled with half a lifetime of watching the Bees in the lower reaches of the Football League until Matthew Benham came along and launched a revolution that has over the last decade taken Brentford to the PL (Premier League or Promised Land as you prefer). And the best part of that journey is that I've shared it with Tony Smith and my cousin Steve. We only found out, by chance, after they had died, that whilst the two brothers—our fathers—hadn't spoken for some thirty years, they had each taken their sons to Brentford regularly. Priorities, eh? Happily, their sons do speak (yet more nonsense) on weekly trips home and away watching the Bees. Thanks Matthew, and thanks Cuz.

I hope my daughter India and son Ivo will be proud to have a copy of *Zero Ri$k* on their bookshelves in years to come. I'm certainly proud of them. Great credit for that goes to their mother, Iona, for which my gratitude is endless. And to Diana and Fred, their peerless grandparents. Thank you to Philly, too, for being such a great stepmother to them, and support to me, often when times weren't easy. And to Lolly and Lucy for their welcome and warmth.

The last thank you is the most important one. The smartest lady I've ever met assures me that the best Russian fairy tales are long and convoluted, with multiple, often bizarre, twists and turns along the way—dragons to be slain, ogres and witches to be outwitted, foes vanquished and stolen possessions returned, and frequently much more besides—before the hero wins the day and, hopefully, the princess. I don't know if *Zero Ri$k* passes muster in this regard, but I do know that it is your unstinting, unconditional support, Tanya, that has enabled me to reach the end of this particular tale, and I will be eternally grateful. *Spasiba*.

PICTURE ACKNOWLEDGEMENTS

Representations of four wonderful artworks are shown in the text:

1. The Seven Deadly Sins and the Four Last Things
   Hieronymus Bosch; Museo del Prado, Madrid, Spain
   Art Heritage / Alamy Stock Photo

2. The Haywain Triptych
   Hieronymus Bosch; Museo del Prado, Madrid, Spain
   Giorgio Morara / Alamy Stock Photo

3. Time Saving Truth from Falsehood and Envy
   François Lemoyne; The Wallace Collection, Marylebone, London, UK
   The Picture Art Collection / Alamy Stock Photo

4. The Lovers II (1928)
   René Magritte; MoMA, New York, USA
   Artepics / Alamy Stock Photo

MUSIC ACKNOWLEDGEMENTS

A number of fantastic songs are mentioned, or alluded to, in the text:

1. Back To Black – Amy Winehouse
   Written by Amy Winehouse; Mark Ronson
   From the album Back To Black (Island Records; 2006)

2. Battle Hymn Of The Republic - Traditional
   Written by Julia Ward Howe; William Steffe
   Traditional (1861)

3. Big Time – Peter Gabriel
   Written by Peter Gabriel
   From the album So (Charisma Records and Virgin Records; 1986)

4. Bohemian Rhapsody – Queen
   Written by Freddie Mercury
   From the album A Night At The Opera (EMI Records; 1975)

5. Call Me – Blondie
   Written by Debbie Harry; Giorgio Moroder
   From the soundtrack album American Gigolo (Polydor Records; 1980)

6. Can't Help Falling In Love – Elvis Presley
   Written by Hugo Peretti; Luigi Creatore; George David Weiss
   From the soundtrack album Blue Hawaii (RCA Victor Records; 1961)

7. Don't Give Up – Peter Gabriel and Kate Bush
   Written by Peter Gabriel
   From the album So (Charisma Records and Virgin Records; 1986)

8. Don't Look Back In Anger – Oasis
   Written by Noel Gallagher
   From the album (What's the Story) Morning Glory? (Creation Records; 1995)

9. Half A Sixpence – Tommy Steele
   Written by David Heneker
   From the soundtrack album Half A Sixpence (RCA Victor Records; 1967)

10. Hallelujah – Leonard Cohen
    Written by Leonard Cohen
    From the album Various Positions (CBS Records; 1984)

11. Jealousy – Pet Shop Boys
    Written by Chris Lowe; Neil Tennant
    From the album Behaviour (Parlophone Records; 1990)

12. Lust For Life – Iggy Pop
    Written by Iggy Pop; David Bowie
    From the album Lust For Life (RCA Records; 1977)

13. My Way – Frank Sinatra
    Written by Paul Anka; Claude François; Jacques Revaux; Gilles Thibaut
    From the album My Way (Reprise Records; 1969)

14. Nessun Dorma – Luciano Pavarotti
    Written by Giacomo Puccini
    From the album The Essential Pavarotti (Decca Records; 1990)

15. Out Of Time – Blur
    Written by Damon Albarn; Alex James; Dave Rowntree
    From the album Think Tank (Parlophone Records; 2003)

16. Secret Love – Doris Day
    Written by Sammy Fain; Paul Francis Webster
    From the soundtrack of Calamity Jane (Columbia Records; 1953)

17. The Harder They Come – Jimmy Cliff
    Written by Jimmy Cliff
    From the soundtrack album The Harder They Come (Island Records; 1972)

18. The Nutcracker – Valery Gergiev, Kirov Orchestra
    Written by Pyotr Ilyich Tchaikovsky
    The complete ballet (Philips Classics; 1998)

19. The Punishment Of Luxury – Orchestral Manoeuvres In The Dark
    Written by Paul Humphreys; Andy McCluskey
    From the album The Punishment Of Luxury (100% Records; 2017)

20. Two Out Of Three Ain't Bad – Meat Loaf
    Written by Jim Steinman
    From the album Bat Out Of Hell (Epic; 1977)

21. Who Wants To Be A Millionaire – Frank Sinatra and Celeste Holm
    Written by Cole Porter
    From the soundtrack album High Society (Capital Records; 1956)

22. You Can Get It If You Really Want – Jimmy Cliff
    Written by Jimmy Cliff
    From the soundtrack album The Harder They Come (Island Records; 1972)